A VINTAGE AFFAIR

A Vintage Affair

A Novel

ISABEL WOLFF

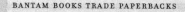

BANTAM BOOKS TRADE PAPERBACKS

NEW YORK

2011 Bantam Books Trade Paperback Edition

Copyright © 2009 by Isabel Wolff
Reading group guide copyright © 2011 by Random House, Inc.

Published in the United States by Bantam Books,
an imprint of The Random House Publishing Group,
a division of Random House, Inc., New York.

BANTAM BOOKS and the rooster colophon are registered
trademarks of Random House, Inc.
RANDOM HOUSE READER'S CIRCLE and colophon is a
trademark of Random House, Inc.

Originally published in Great Britain in paperback by Harper, an imprint of
HarperCollins Publishers, London, in 2009, and subsequently in hardcover
in the United States by Bantam Books, an imprint of The Random House
Publishing Group, a division of Random House, Inc., in 2010.

LIBRARY OF CONGRESS CATALOGING-IN-PUBLICATION DATA
Wolff, Isabel.
A vintage affair : a novel / Isabel Wolff.
p. cm.
Includes bibliographical references.
ISBN 978-0-553-38662-2
eBook ISBN 978-0-553-90770-4
1. Women dressmakers—Fiction.   2. Vintage clothing—Fiction.
3. Blackheath (London, England)—Fiction.   4. World War,
1939–1945—France—Fiction.   I. Title.
PR6073.O355V56 2010
823'.914—dc22   2010001830

Printed in the United States of America

www.bantamdell.com
www.randomhousereaderscircle.com

2 4 6 8 9 7 5 3 1

Book design by Dana Leigh Blanchette

In memory of my father

What a strange power there is in clothing.

ISAAC BASHEVIS SINGER

A VINTAGE AFFAIR

Prologue

Blackheath, 1983

"...*seven*-teen, *eight*-teen...*nine*-teen...*twenty!* Com-ing!" I yell. "Ready or *not*..."

I uncover my eyes and begin the search. I start downstairs, half expecting to find Emma huddled behind the sofa in the sitting room or wrapped, like a sweet, in the crimson curtains, or crouched under the baby grand. I already think of her as my best friend, although we've only known each other six weeks. "You have a new classmate," Miss Grey had announced on the first day of term. She'd smiled at the girl in the too-stiff blazer standing next to her. "Her name is Emma Kitts, and her family have recently moved to London from South Africa." Then Miss Grey had led the newcomer to the desk next to mine. The girl was short for nine, and slightly plump, with large green eyes, a scattering of freckles, and uneven bangs above shiny brown braids. "Will you look after Emma, Phoebe?" Miss Grey had asked. I'd nodded. Emma had flashed me a grateful smile...

Now I cross the hall into the dining room and peer under the scratched mahogany table, but Emma's not there; nor is she in the kitchen, with its old-fashioned cabinet stacked with mismatched blue-and-white plates. I would have asked her mother which way she'd gone, but Mrs. Kitts has just "popped out to play tennis," leaving Emma and me on our own.

I walk into the big, cool pantry and slide open a low cupboard that looks promisingly large but contains only some old Thermos flasks; then I go down the step into the utility room, where the washing machine spasms in its final spin. I even lift the lid of the freezer in case Emma is lying among the frozen peas and ice cream. Now I return to the hall, which is oak-panelled and warm, smelling of dust and beeswax. To one side is a huge, ornately carved chair—a throne from Swaziland, Emma said—the wood so dark that it's black. I sit on it for a moment, wondering where precisely Swaziland is, and whether it has anything to do with Switzerland. Then my eyes stray to the hats on the wall opposite—a dozen or so, each hanging from a curving brass peg. There's an African headdress in a pink-and-blue fabric and a Cossack hat that could be made of real fur; there's a Panama, a trilby, a turban, a top hat, a riding hat, a cap, a fez, two battered boaters, and an emerald-green tweed hat with a pheasant feather stuck through it.

I climb the staircase with its wide, shallow treads. At the top is a square landing with four doors leading off it. Emma's bedroom is the first on the left. I turn the handle, then hover in the doorway to see if I can hear stifled giggles or telltale breathing. I hear nothing, but then Emma's good at holding her breath—she can swim a width and a half underwater. I flip back her shiny blue duvet, but she's not in the bed—or under it; all I can see there is her secret box in which I know she keeps her lucky Krugerrand and her diary. I open the big white-painted corner cupboard with its safari stencils, but she's not in there either. Perhaps she's in the room next door. As I enter it I realise, with an uncomfortable feeling, that this is her parents' room. I look for Emma under the wrought-iron bed and behind the dressing table, the mirror of which is cracked in one corner; then I open the wardrobe and catch a scent of orange peel and cloves, which makes me think of Christmas. As I stare at Mrs. Kitts's brightly printed summer dresses, imagining them under the African sun, I suddenly realise that I am not so much seeking as snooping. I retreat, feeling a vague sense of shame. And now I want to stop playing hide-and-seek. I want to play rummy, or just watch TV.

"Bet you can't find me, Phoebe! You'll never, ever find me!"

Sighing, I cross the landing and step into the bathroom, where I check behind the thick white plastic shower curtain and lift the lid of the hamper, which contains nothing but a faded-looking purple towel. Now I go to the window and part the semi-closed slats of the Venetian blind. As I peer down into the sun-filled garden a tiny jolt runs the length of my spine. *There's* Emma—behind the huge plane tree at the end of the lawn. She thinks I can't see her, but I can because she's crouching down and one of her feet is sticking out. I dash down the stairs, through the kitchen, and into the utility room, then I fling open the back door.

"Found you!" I shout as I run toward the tree. "*Found* you," I repeat happily, surprised by my euphoria. "Okay," I say, panting, "my turn to hide! Emma?" I peer at her. She's not crouching down but lying down, on her left side, perfectly still, eyes closed. "Get up, will you, Em?" She doesn't reply. And now I notice that one leg is folded beneath her at an awkward angle. With a sudden *thud* in my rib cage I understand. Emma was hiding not behind the tree but *in* it. I glance up through its branches, glimpsing shreds of blue through the green. She was hiding in the tree, but then she fell.

"Em," I murmur, stooping to touch her shoulder. I'm trembling now. I gently shake her, but she doesn't respond, and now I notice that her mouth is slightly agape, a thread of saliva glistening on her lower lip. "Emma!" I shout. "Wake *up*!" But she doesn't. I put my hand to her ribs but can't feel them rise and fall. "*Say* something," I plead, my heart pounding. "*Please,* Emma!" I try to lift her up, but I can't. I clap my hands by her ears. "*Emma!*" My throat is aching and tears prick my eyes. I glance back at the house, desperate for Emma's mother to come running over the grass, ready to make everything all right; but Mrs. Kitts is still not back from her tennis, which makes me angry because we're too young to have been left on our own. Resentment at Mrs. Kitts gives way to terror at the thought of what she's likely to say—that Emma's accident was *my* fault because it was my suggestion that we play hide-and-seek. From inside my head I hear Miss Grey asking me to "look after" Emma, then her disappointed *tut-tutting*.

"Wake *up*, Em," I implore her. *"Please."* But she just lies there looking... crumpled, like a flung-down rag doll. I know I have to run and get help. But first I must cover her, as it's turning chilly. I pull off my cardigan and lay it across Emma's upper body, quickly smoothing it over her chest and tucking it under her shoulders.

"I'll be back soon. Don't worry." I try not to cry.

Suddenly Emma sits bolt upright, grinning like a lunatic, her eyes popping with mischievous delight.

"*Fooled* you!" she sings, clapping her hands together, then throwing back her head in glee. "I *really* fooled you there, didn't I?" She scrambles to her feet. "You were worried, weren't you, Phoebes? Admit it! You thought I was *dead*! I held my breath for *ages*!" She gasps as she brushes down her skirt. "I'm *right* out of puff ..." She blows out her cheeks and her bangs lift a little in the gust, then she smiles at me. "Okay, Heebee-Phoebee—your turn." She holds out my cardigan. "I'll start counting—up to twenty-five, if you like. Here, Phoebes, take your cardi, will you." Emma stares at me. "What's up?"

My fists are balled by my sides. My face feels hot. "Don't *ever* do that again!"

Emma blinks with surprise. "It was only a joke."

"It was a *horrible* one!" Tears sting my eyes.

"I'm ... sorry."

"Don't *ever* do that again! If you do, I won't talk to you anymore—not ever!"

"It was only a *game*," she protests. "You don't have to be all"—she throws up her hands—"silly . . . about it. I was only . . . playing." She shrugs. "But . . . I won't do it again—if it upsets you. Honestly."

I snatch my cardigan. "Promise." I glare at her. "You've got to *promise.*"

"O-kay," she murmurs, then she takes a deep breath. "I, Emma Mandisa Kitts, promise that I won't play that trick on you, Phoebe Jane Swift, ever again. I *promise,*" she repeats, then she makes an extravagant slashing gesture. "*Cross* my heart." Then, with this funny little smile that I have remembered all these years, she adds, "and hope . . . to . . . *die!*"

One

September is at least a good time for a new start, I reflected as I left the house early this morning. I've always felt a greater sense of renewal at the beginning of September than I ever have in January. Perhaps, I thought as I crossed Tranquil Vale, it's because September so often feels fresh and clear after the dankness of August. Or perhaps, I wondered as I passed Blackheath Books, its windows emblazoned with Back to School promotions, it's simply the association with the new academic year.

As I walked up the hill towards the Heath, the freshly painted fascia of Village Vintage came into view and I allowed myself a brief burst of optimism. I unlocked the door, picked the mail up off the mat, and began preparing the shop for its official launch.

I worked nonstop until four, selecting the clothes from the stockroom upstairs and putting them out on the racks. As I draped a 1920s tea dress over my arm I ran my hand over its heavy silk satin, then fingered its intricate beading and its perfect hand stitching. This, I told myself, is what I love about vintage clothes. I love their beautiful fabric and their fine finish. I love knowing that so much skill and artistry have gone into their making.

I glanced at my watch. Only two hours to go until the party. I remembered that I'd forgotten to chill the champagne. As I dashed into the little kitchen and ripped open the cases I wondered how many people would come. I'd invited a hundred, so I'd need at least seventy glasses at the ready. I stacked the bottles in the fridge, turned it up to Frost, then made myself a quick cup of tea. Sipping my Earl Grey, I looked around the shop, allowing myself to savour for a moment the transition from pipe dream to reality.

The interior of Village Vintage looked modern and light. I'd had the wooden floors stripped and limed, the walls painted a dove grey and hung with large silver-framed mirrors; there were glossy potted plants on chrome stands, a spangling of downlights on the white-painted ceiling, and next to the fitting room, a large cream-upholstered bergère sofa. Through the windows, Blackheath stretched into the far distance, the sky a giddying vault of blue patched with towering white clouds. Beyond the church, two yellow kites danced in the breeze while on the horizon the glass towers of Canary Wharf glinted and flashed in the late-afternoon sunlight.

I suddenly realised that the journalist who was supposed to be interviewing me was over an hour late. I didn't even know which paper he was from. All I could remember from yesterday's brief phone conversation with him was that his name was Dan and that he'd said he'd be here at three-thirty. My irritation turned to panic. What if he didn't come at all? I needed the publicity. My insides lurched at the thought of my huge loan. As I tied the price tag on an embroidered evening bag, I remembered trying to convince the bank that its cash would be safe.

"So you were at Sotheby's?" the lending manager had said as she went through my business plan in a small office, every square inch of which, including the ceiling and even the back of the door, seemed to be covered in thick, grey baize.

"I worked in the textiles department," I'd explained, "evaluating vintage clothes and conducting auctions."

"So you must know a lot about it."

"I do."

She scribbled something on the form, the nib of her pen squeaking across the glossy paper. "But it's not as though you've ever worked in retail, is it?"

"No," I said, my heart sinking. "That's true. But I've found attractive, accessible premises in a pleasant, busy area where there are no other vintage dress shops." I handed her the real estate agent's brochure for Montpelier Vale.

"It's a nice site," she said as she studied it. My spirits rose. "And being on the corner gives it good visibility." I imagined the windows aglow with glorious dresses. "But the lease is expensive." The woman put the brochure down on the grey tabletop and looked at me grimly. "What makes you think you'll be able to generate enough sales to cover your overhead, let alone make a profit?"

"Because . . ." I suppressed a frustrated sigh. "I know that the demand is there. Vintage has now become so fashionable that it's almost mainstream. These days you can even buy vintage clothing in High Street stores like Miss Selfridge and Topshop."

There was silence while she scribbled again. "I know you can." She looked up again, but this time she was smiling. "I got the most wonderful Biba fake fur in Jigsaw the other day—mint condition and original buttons." She pushed the form towards me, then passed me her pen. "Could you sign at the bottom there, please?" . . .

Now I arranged the evening gowns on the formal-wear rack and put out the bags, belts, and shoes. I positioned the gloves in their basket, the costume jewellery in its velvet trays, then, on a corner shelf, high up, I carefully placed the hat that Emma had given me for my thirtieth birthday.

I stepped back and gazed at the extraordinary sculpture of bronze straw, its crown seeming to sweep upwards into infinity.

"I miss you, Em," I murmured. "Wherever you are now . . ." I faltered as I felt the familiar piercing sensation, as though there was a skewer in my heart.

I heard a sharp rapping sound behind me. On the other side of the glass door stood a man of about my age, maybe a little younger. He was tall and well built with large grey eyes and a mop of dark blond curls. He reminded me of someone famous, but I couldn't think who.

"Dan Robinson," he said with a broad smile as I let him in. "Sorry to be a bit late." I resisted the urge to tell him that he was *very* late. He took a notebook out of his battered-looking bag. "My previous interview ran overtime, then I got caught in traffic, but this should only take twenty minutes or so." He shoved his hand into the pocket of his crumpled linen jacket and produced a pencil. "I just need to get down the basic facts about the business and a bit of your background." He glanced at the hydra of silk scarves spilling over the counter and the half-dressed mannequin. "But you're obviously busy, so if you haven't got time, I'd quite—"

"Oh, I've got time," I interrupted. "Really—as long as you don't mind me working while we chat." I slipped a sea-green chiffon cocktail dress onto its velvet hanger. "Which paper did you say you were from?" Out of the corner of my eye I registered the fact that his mauve striped shirt didn't go with the sage of his chinos.

"It's a new twice-weekly free paper called the *Black & Green*—the *Blackheath and Greenwich Express*. It's only been going a couple of months, so we're building our circulation."

"I'm grateful for any coverage," I said as I put the dress at the front of the day-wear rack.

"The piece should run on Friday." Dan glanced round the shop. "The interior's nice and bright. You wouldn't think it was old stuff that was being sold here—I mean, vintage," he corrected himself.

"Thank you," I said wryly, though I was grateful for his observation.

As I quickly scissored the cellophane off some white agapanthus, Dan peered out the window. "It's a great location."

I nodded. "I love being able to look out over the Heath. Plus the shop's very visible from the road, so I hope to get passing trade as well as dedicated vintage buyers."

"That's how I found you," said Dan as I put the flowers into a tall glass vase. "I was walking past yesterday, and your sign said"—he reached into the pocket of his trousers and took out a pencil sharpener—"that you were about to open, and I thought it would make a good feature for Friday's paper." As he sat on the sofa I noticed that he was wearing mismatched socks—one green and one brown. "Not that fashion's really my thing."

"Isn't it?" I said politely as he gave the pencil a few vigorous turns. "Don't you use a tape recorder?" I couldn't help asking.

He inspected the newly pointed tip, then blew on it. "I prefer speed writing. Okay now." He pocketed the sharpener. "Let's start. So . . ." He bounced the pencil against his lower lip. "What should I ask you first?" I tried not to show my dismay at his lack of preparation. "I know," he said. "Are you local?"

"Yes." I folded a pale blue cashmere cardigan. "I grew up in Eliot Hill, closer to Greenwich, but for the past five years I've been living in the centre of Blackheath, near the station." I thought of my snug railwayman's cottage with its tiny front garden.

"Station," Dan repeated slowly. "Next question . . ." This interview was going to take ages—it was the last thing I needed. "Do you have a fashion background?" he asked. "Won't the readers want to know that?"

"Er . . . possibly." I told him about my fashion-history degree from Saint Martin's and my career at Sotheby's.

"So how long were you at Sotheby's?"

"Twelve years." I folded an Yves Saint Laurent silk scarf and laid it in a tray. "In fact I'd recently been made head of the costumes and textiles department. But then . . . I decided to leave."

Dan looked up. "Even though you'd just been promoted?"

"Yes..." My heart ached. I'd said too much. "I'd been there al-most from the day I'd graduated, you see, and I needed..." I glanced out the window, struggling to quell the surge of emotion breaking over me. "I felt I needed..."

"A career break?" he suggested.

"A...change. So I went on a sort of sabbatical in early March." I draped a string of Chanel paste pearls round the neck of a silver mannequin. "Sotheby's said they'd keep my job open until June, but in mid-May I saw that the lease here had come up, so I decided to take the plunge and sell vintage myself. I'd been toying with the idea for some time," I added.

"Some...time," Dan repeated quietly. This was hardly "speed writing." I stole a glance at his odd squiggles and abbreviations. "Next question..." He chewed the end of his pencil. The man was useless. "I know: Where do you find your stock?" He looked at me. "Or is that a trade secret?"

"Not really." I fastened the hooks on a café au lait–coloured silk blouse by Georges Rech. "I bought quite a bit from some of the smaller auction houses outside London, as well as from specialist dealers and private individuals who I already knew through Sotheby's. I also got things at vintage fairs, on eBay, and I made two or three trips to France."

"Why France?"

"You can find lovely vintage garments in provincial markets there—like these embroidered nightdresses." I held one up. "I bought them in Avignon. They weren't too expensive because French women are less keen on vintage than we are in this country."

"Vintage clothing's become rather desirable here, hasn't it?"

"Very desirable." I quickly fanned some 1950s copies of *Vogue* onto the glass table by the sofa. "Women want individuality, not mass production, and that's what vintage clothing gives them. Wearing vintage suggests originality and flair. I mean, a woman can buy an evening dress on High Street for two hundred pounds," I went on, warming to the interview now, "and the next day it's worth almost nothing. But for the same money she could have bought something made of gorgeous fabric, that no one else would have been wearing and that will, if she doesn't wreck it, actually *increase* in value. Like this." I pulled out a Hardy Amies petrol-blue silk taffeta dinner gown, from 1957, admiring its elegant halter neck, slim bodice, and gored skirt.

"It's lovely," said Dan. He cocked his head. "You'd think it was new."

"Everything I sell is in perfect condition."

"Condition . . ." he muttered as he scribbled again.

"Every garment is washed or dry-cleaned," I went on as I returned the dress to the rack. "I have a wonderful seamstress who does the big repairs and alterations. The smaller ones I can do here myself—I have a little den in the back with a sewing machine."

"And what do these things sell for?"

"They range from fifteen pounds for a hand-rolled silk scarf, to seventy-five for a cotton day dress, to two or three hundred pounds for an evening dress. A couture piece can cost up to fifteen hundred pounds." I pulled out a Pierre Balmain gold faille evening gown from the early 1960s, embroidered with bugle beads and silver sequins, and lifted its protective cover. "This is an important dress, made by a major designer at the height of his career. Or there's this." I took out a pair of silk velvet palazzo pants in a psychedelic pattern of sherbety pinks and greens. "This outfit's by Emilio Pucci. It'll almost certainly be bought as an investment piece rather than to wear, because Pucci, like Ossie Clark, Biba, and Jean Muir, is very collectable."

"Marilyn Monroe loved Pucci," Dan said. "She was buried in her favourite green silk Pucci dress." I nodded, surprised and not liking to admit that I hadn't known that. "Those are fun." He glanced at the wall behind me. Hanging on it, like paintings, were four strapless, ballerina-length evening dresses—one lemon yellow, one candy pink, one turquoise, and one lime—each with a satin bodice beneath which foamed a mass of net petticoats, sparkling with crystals.

"I've hung those there because I love them. They're fifties prom dresses, but I call them cupcake dresses," I added with a smile, "because they're so glamorous and frothy. Just looking at them makes me feel happy." *Or as happy as I can be now,* I thought bleakly.

Dan stood up. "And what's that you're putting out there?"

"This is a Vivienne Westwood bustle skirt." I held it up for him. "And this"—I pulled out a terra-cotta silk kaftan—"is by Thea Porter, and this little suede shift is by Mary Quant."

"What about this?" Dan had pulled out an oyster-pink satin evening dress with a cowl neckline, fine pleating at the sides, and a sweeping fishtail hem. "It's wonderful—it's like something Katharine Hepburn would have worn, or Greta Garbo—or Veronica Lake," he added thoughtfully, "in *The Glass Key.*"

"Oh. I don't know that film."

"It's very underrated. It was adapted from a novel by Dashiell Hammett in 1942. Howard Hawks borrowed from it for *The Big Sleep.*"

"Did he?"

"But you know what?" He held the dress against me and looked at me appraisingly. "It would suit you. You have that sort of film noir languor."

"Do I?" Again he'd surprised me. "Actually, this dress *was* mine."

"Really? Don't you want it?" he asked almost indignantly. "It's rather beautiful."

"It is, but... I just... went off it." I returned it to the rack. I didn't have to tell him the truth. That Guy had given it to me a little less than a year ago. We'd been seeing each other for a month and he'd taken me to Bath one weekend. I'd spotted the dress in a shop window and had gone in to look at it, mostly out of professional interest. At £500, it was too expensive for me. But later, while I'd been reading in our hotel room, Guy had slipped out and returned with the dress, gift-wrapped in pink tissue. Now I'd decided to sell it because it belonged to a part of my life that I was desperate to forget. I'd give the money to charity.

"And what, for you, is the main appeal of vintage clothing?" I heard Dan ask as I rearranged the shoes inside the illuminated glass cubes that lined the left-hand wall. "Is it that the things are such good quality compared with clothes made today?"

"That's a big part of it," I replied. I placed one 1960s green suede pump at an elegant angle to its partner. "Wearing vintage is a protest against mass production. But the thing I love most about vintage clothes . . ." I looked at him. "Don't laugh, will you?"

"Of course not."

I stroked the gossamer chiffon of a 1950s peignoir. "What I really love about them . . . is the fact that they contain someone's personal history." I ran the marabou trim across the back of my hand. "I find myself wondering about the women who wore them."

"Really?"

"I find myself wondering about their lives. I can never look at a garment—like this suit"—I went over to the day-wear rack and pulled out a 1940s fitted jacket and skirt in a dark blue tweed— "without thinking about the woman who owned it. How old was she? Did she work? Was she married? Was she happy?" Dan shrugged. "The suit has a British label from the early forties," I went on, "so I wonder what happened to this woman during the war. Did her husband survive? Did *she* survive?"

I went to the shoe display and took out a pair of 1930s silk brocade slippers embroidered with dainty yellow roses. "I look at these exquisite shoes, and I imagine the woman who owned them walking along in them, or dancing in them, or kissing someone." I went over to a pink velvet pillbox hat on its stand. "I look at a little hat like this"—I lifted up the veil—"and I try to imagine the face beneath it. Because when you buy a piece of vintage clothing you're not just buying fabric and thread—you're buying a piece of someone's *past.*"

Dan nodded thoughtfully. "Which you're bringing into the present."

"Exactly. I'm giving these clothes a new lease on life. And I love the fact that I'm able to restore them. Where there are so many things in life that can't be restored." I felt the sudden familiar pit in my stomach.

"I'd never have thought of vintage clothes like that," said Dan after a moment. "I love your passion for what you do." He peered at his notepad. "You've given me some great quotes."

"Good," I replied quietly. "I've enjoyed talking to you." *After a hopeless start,* I was tempted to add.

Dan smiled. "Well . . . I'd better let you get on—and I ought to go and write this up, but . . ." His voice trailed away as his eyes strayed to the corner shelf. "What an amazing hat. What period's that from?"

"It's contemporary. It was made four years ago."

"It's very original."

"Yes, it's one of a kind."

"How much is it?"

"It's not for sale. It was given to me by the designer, a close friend of mine. I just wanted to have it here because . . ." My throat tightened.

"Because it's beautiful?" Dan suggested gently. I nodded. He flipped shut his notebook. "And will your friend be coming to the launch?"

I shook my head. "No."

"One last thing," he said, taking a camera out of his bag. "My editor asked me to get a photo of you to go with the article."

I glanced at my watch. "As long as it won't take long. I've still got to tie balloons to the front, I have to change, and I haven't poured the champagne. That's going to take time, and people will be arriving in twenty minutes."

"Let me do that," Dan said. "To make up for being late." He tucked his pencil behind his ear and grinned at me. "Where are the glasses?"

"Oh. There are three boxes of them behind the counter, and there are twelve bottles of champagne in the fridge in the little kitchen there. Thanks," I added, anxiously wondering if he'd manage to spill it everywhere. But he deftly filled the flutes with the Veuve Clicquot—vintage, of course, because it had to be—while I washed and changed into my outfit, a thirties dove-grey satin cocktail dress with silver Ferragamo sling-backs. Then I put on a little makeup and ran a brush through my hair. Finally I untied the cluster of pale gold helium balloons that floated from the back of a chair and attached them in twos and threes to the front of the shop, where they bobbed and danced in the stiffening breeze. Then as the church clock struck six I stood in the doorway, with a glass in my hand, while Dan took his photos.

After a minute he lowered the camera and looked at me, clearly puzzled.

"Sorry, Phoebe—could you manage a smile?"

My mother arrived just as Dan was leaving.

"Who was that?" she asked as she headed straight for the fitting room.

"A journalist named Dan," I replied. "He's just interviewed me for a local paper. He's a bit chaotic."

"He looked rather nice," she murmured as she stood in front of the mirror scrutinising her appearance. "He was hideously dressed, but I like curly hair on a man. It's unusual." Her reflected face looked at me with anxious disappointment. "I *wish* you could find someone again, Phoebe. I hate you being on your own. Being on your own is no fun. As I can testify," she added bitterly.

"I rather enjoy it. I intend to be on my own for a long time, quite possibly forever."

Mum snapped open her bag. "That's very likely to be my fate, darling, but I don't want it to be yours." She took out one of her expensive new lipsticks. The tube resembled a gold bullet. "I know you've had a hard year, darling."

"Yes," I murmured.

"And I know"—she glanced at Emma's hat—"that you've been . . .

suffering." My mother could have no idea quite how much. "But," she continued as she twisted up the lipstick, "I still don't understand"—I knew what was coming—"*why* you had to end things with Guy. I know I only met him three times, but I thought he was charming, handsome, and nice."

"He was all those things," I agreed. "He was lovely. In fact, he was perfect."

In the mirror Mum's eyes met mine. "Then what *happened* between you?"

"Nothing," I lied. "My feelings just . . . changed. I told you that."

"Yes. But you've never said *why.*" Mum drew the lipstick—a slightly garish coral—across her upper lip. "The whole thing seemed quite perverse, if you don't mind my saying so, dear. Of course, you were very unhappy at the time." She lowered her voice. "But then what happened to Emma . . ." I closed my eyes to try and shut out the images that will haunt me forever. "Well . . . it was terrible." She sighed. "I don't know how she could *do* that . . . And to think what she had going for her . . . so *much.*"

"So much," I echoed bitterly.

Mum blotted her lower lip with a tissue. "But what I don't understand is why it *then* followed, sad though you were, that you had to end what appeared to be a happy relationship with a *very* nice man. *I* think you had a sort of nervous breakdown," she went on. "It wouldn't be surprising." She smacked her lips together. "I don't think you knew what you were doing."

"I knew exactly," I retorted calmly. "But you know what, Mum, I don't want to talk ab—"

"How did you meet him?" she suddenly asked. "You never told me that."

I felt my face heat up. "Through Emma."

"Really?" Mum looked at me. "How typically sweet of her," she said as she turned back to the mirror. "Introducing you to a nice man like that."

"Yes," I said uneasily . . .

. . .

"I've met someone!" Emma had said excitedly over the phone a year ago. "My head's in a spin, Phoebe. He's . . . wonderful." My heart had sunk, not just because Emma was always saying that she'd met someone "wonderful," but because these men were usually anything but. Emma would be in raptures about them, then a month later she'd be avoiding them, saying they were "dreadful." "I met him at a fund-raiser," she'd explained. "He runs an investment fund, but the *good* thing," she'd added with her usual endearing artlessness, "is that it's an ethical one."

"That sounds interesting. So he must be smart then."

"He graduated near the top of his class. London School of Economics. Not that *he* told me that," she added hastily. "I Googled him. We've been on a few dates, but things are moving pretty quickly, so I'd like you to check him out."

"Emma," I said with a sigh. "You are thirty-three years old. You are becoming *very* successful. You now design hats for some of the most famous women in the U.K. Why do you need *my* approval?"

"Well . . . ," I heard her clicking her tongue. "Because I guess old habits die hard. I've always asked your opinion about men, haven't I, Phoebes?" she mused. "Right from when we were teenagers."

"Yes, but we're not teenagers now. You've got to have confidence in your *own* judgement, Em."

"I hear what you say. But I still want you to meet Guy. I'll have a little dinner party next week and sit you next to him, okay?"

"Okay." I sighed.

I wish I didn't have to be involved, I thought as I helped Emma in the kitchen of her tall narrow house in Marylebone the following Thursday evening. From the sitting room came the sound of people laughing and talking. Emma's idea of a "little" dinner party was a five-course meal for twelve. As I got down the plates I thought of the men Emma had been "madly in love with" over the past couple of years: Arnie, the fashion photographer who'd two-timed her with a hand model; Finian, the garden designer who spent every weekend with his six-year-old daughter—and her mum. Then there'd been Julian, a bespectacled stockbroker with an interest in philosophy but precious little else. Emma's latest attachment had been to Peter, a violinist with the London Philharmonic. That had looked promising—he was very nice and she could talk to him about music; but then he'd gone on a three-month world tour with the orchestra and had come back engaged to the second flute.

Maybe this chap Guy would be a better bet, I thought as I rummaged in a drawer for Emma's napkins.

"Guy is *perfect!*" she exclaimed as she opened the oven, releasing a burst of steam and an aroma of roasting lamb. "He's the one, Phoebe," she told me happily.

"That's what you always say." I began folding the napkins.

"Well, *this* time it's true. I'm going to kill myself if it doesn't work out," she threatened gaily.

I stopped mid-fold. "Don't be so *silly,* Em. It's not even as though you've known him that long."

"True—though I know what I feel. But he's *late,*" she wailed as she slid the lamb out of the oven. She thumped the Le Creuset meat dish down onto the table, her face a mask of anxiety. "Do you think he's going to turn up?"

"Of course he is," I answered. "It's only eight forty-five—he's probably just been held up at work."

Emma kicked the oven door shut. "Then why didn't he phone?"

"Maybe he's stuck on the subway." Anxiety contorted her features again. "Em, don't *worry.*"

She began basting the meat. "I can't help it. I'd love to be calm and collected like you usually are, but I've never had your poise." She straightened. "How do I look?"

"Beautiful."

She smiled with relief, and suddenly her pretty girl-next-door features *did* look beautiful. "Thanks, Phoebes—not that I believe you, as you always say that."

"Because it's always true," I retorted firmly.

Emma was dressed in her characteristically eclectic way, in a Betsey Johnson floral silk dress, with canary-yellow fishnets and black ankle boots. Her wavy auburn hair was held off her face by a silver band.

"And does this dress *definitely* suit me?" she asked.

"Definitely. I like the sweetheart neckline, and the silhouette's flattering," I added, then instantly regretted it.

"Are you saying I'm fat?" Emma's face fell. "Please don't say that, Phoebe—not today of all days. I know I really should lose a few pounds, but—"

"No, *no*—I didn't mean that. Of course you're not fat, Em, you're lovely, I just meant—"

"Oh God!" She clapped her hand to her mouth. "I haven't done the blinis!"

"*I'll* do them." I opened the fridge and got out the smoked salmon and the tub of crème fraîche.

"You're a fabulous friend, Phoebe. What would I do without you." she added as she began sticking bits of rosemary into the lamb. "Do you know"—she waved a sprig at me—"we've now known each other for a quarter of a century."

"Is it that long?" I murmured as I began to chop the smoked salmon.

"It is. And we'll probably know each other for, what, another fifty years?"

"If we drink the right brand of coffee."

"We'll have to go into the same old people's home!" Emma giggled.

"Where you'll *still* be getting me to check out your boyfriends. 'Oh, Phoebe,'" I said in a crotchety voice, "'he's ninety-three—do you think he's a bit *old* for me?'"

Emma snorted with laughter, then chucked the bunch of rosemary at me.

I began grilling the blinis, trying not to burn my fingers as I quickly turned them over. Emma's friends were talking so loudly—and someone was playing the piano—that I'd only dimly registered the ring of the doorbell, but the sound electrified Emma.

"He's here!" She checked her appearance in a small mirror, adjusting her hair band; then she ran down the narrow staircase. "Hi! Oh, thanks!" I heard her squeal. "They're *gorgeous*. Come on up—you know the way." I'd registered the fact that Guy had been to the house before—that was a good sign. "Everyone's here," I heard Emma say. "Were you stuck on the tube?" By now I'd assembled the first batch of blinis. Next I reached for the pepper mill and vigorously turned the top. Nothing. Damn. Where did Em keep the peppercorns? I began to look, opening a couple of cupboards before spotting a new jar of them on top of her spice rack.

"Let me get you a drink, Guy," I heard Emma say. "Phoebe." I had taken the seal off the peppercorns and was trying to prise off the lid, but it was stuck. "Phoebe," Emma repeated. I turned round. She was standing in the kitchen, smiling radiantly, clutching a bouquet of white roses; just behind her, framed in the doorway, was Guy.

I looked at him in dismay. Emma had said that he was "gorgeous," but it had meant nothing to me—she always said that, even if the man was hideous. But Guy was heart-stoppingly handsome. He was tall and broad-shouldered, with an open face, dark brown hair that was cut endearingly short, and dark blue eyes that had an amused expression.

"Phoebe," Emma said, "this is Guy." He smiled at me and I felt a little *thud* in my rib cage. "Guy, this is my best friend, Phoebe."

"Hi!" I was smiling at him like a lunatic as I wrestled with the peppercorn jar. *Why* did he have to be so attractive? *"God!"* The lid suddenly came off, and the peppercorns shot out in a black arc, scattering like rifle shot across the countertop and floor. "Sorry, Em," I breathed. I grabbed a broom and began vigorously sweeping, desperate to disguise my turmoil. "I'm sorry!" I laughed. "What a klutz!"

"It doesn't matter," Emma said. She thrust the roses into a jug, then grabbed the plate of blinis. "I'll take these in. Thanks, Phoebes, they look lovely."

I'd expected Guy to follow her; instead, he went to the sink, opened the cupboard underneath, and pulled out the dustpan and brush. I registered with a pang the fact that he knew his way round Emma's kitchen.

"Don't worry," I protested.

"It's okay—let me help you." He hitched up the knees of his trousers, then stooped down and began to sweep up the peppercorns.

"They get everywhere," I twittered. "So clumsy of me."

"Do you know where pepper comes from?" he asked abruptly.

"No idea," I replied as I dropped to my knees to scoop up a few in my fingertips. "South America?"

"Kerala. Until the fifteenth century, pepper was so valuable that it could be used in lieu of money, hence 'peppercorn rent.'"

"Really?" I said politely. Then I pondered the weirdness of finding myself crouched on the floor with a man I'd met a minute earlier, discussing the finer points of black pepper.

"Anyway." Guy straightened, then emptied the dustpan into the garbage pail. "I guess I'd better go join the others."

"Yes . . ." I smiled. "Emma will be wondering what's keeping you. But . . . thanks."

The rest of the dinner party passed in a blur. As promised, Emma had put me next to Guy, and I struggled to control my emotions as I politely chatted to him. I kept praying that he'd say something offputting—that he'd just come out of rehab, for example, or that he had two ex-wives and five kids. I'd hoped that I'd find his conversation dull, but he only said things that increased his appeal. He talked interestingly about his work, and of his responsibility to invest his clients' money in ways that not only were not injurious but that could even have a positive effect on the environment and on human health and welfare. He spoke of his association with a charity that was working to end child labour. He talked affectionately about his parents and his brother, whom he played squash with at the Chelsea Harbour Club once a week. *Lucky Emma,* I thought. Guy seemed to be everything she'd claimed he was. As the meal progressed she frequently glanced his way or made passing references to him.

"We went to the opening of the Goya exhibition the other night, didn't we, Guy?" Guy nodded. "And we're trying to get tickets for *Tosca* at the Opera House next week, aren't we?"

"Yes . . . that's right."

"It's been sold out for months," she explained, "but I'm hoping to get hold of tickets online."

Emma's friends were gradually picking up on the connection. "So how long have you two known each other?" Charlie asked Guy with a sly smile. The words "you two," which had produced in me a stab of envy, made Emma blush with pleasure.

"Oh, not that long," Guy replied quietly, his reticence seeming only to confirm his interest in her . . .

"So what did you *think*?" Emma asked me over the phone the next morning.

I fiddled with my Rotadex. "What did I think of what?"

"Of *Guy,* of course! Don't you think he's gorgeous?"

"Oh . . . yes. He is . . . gorgeous."

"Beautiful blue eyes—especially with his dark hair. It's a devastating combination."

I glanced out the window onto New Bond Street. "Devastating."

"And he's a great conversationalist. Don't you agree?"

I could hear the hum of the traffic. "I . . . do."

"Plus he's got such a terrific sense of humour."

"Hmm."

"He's so nice and *normal* compared with the other men I've dated."

"That's certainly true."

"He's a *good* person. Best of all," she concluded, "he's really keen on me!"

I couldn't bring myself to tell her that Guy had phoned me an hour earlier to ask me out to dinner.

I hadn't known what to do. Guy had tracked me down easily enough through the Sotheby's switchboard. At first I was elated, then horrified. I'd thanked him but said that I wouldn't be able to come. He phoned me another three times that day, but I was frantically preparing for an auction of twentieth-century fashion and accessories and didn't take the calls. The fourth time Guy had phoned I'd spoken to him briefly. "You're very persistent, Guy."

"I am, but that's because I . . . I *like* you, Phoebe, and I think—if I don't flatter myself—that you like *me.*" I'd tied the lot number to a Pierre Cardin flecked green wool trouser suit from the mid-seventies, my heart thudding with confusion. "Why don't you say yes?" he pleaded.

"Well . . . because . . . it's a bit tricky, isn't it?"

There was an awkward silence. "Look, Phoebe . . . Emma and I are just friends."

"Really?" I inspected what looked suspiciously like a moth hole on one leg. "You seem to have seen quite a bit of her."

"Well . . . that's largely because Emma rings me and gets tickets for things, like the Goya opening. We've hung out together and had a few laughs, but I've *never* given her the impression that I'm . . ." His voice trailed away.

"But it was clear that you'd been to her flat before. You knew *exactly* where she kept her dustpan and brush," I whispered accusingly.

"Yes—because last week she asked me to mend a leak under her sink and I had to take everything out of the cupboard."

"Oh." Relief swept through me. "I see. But . . ."

Guy sighed. "Look, Phoebe, I like Emma—she's extremely talented and she's fun."

"Oh, she is—she's lovely."

"I find her a bit intense, though," he went on. "If not slightly bonkers," he confided with a nervous laugh. "But she and I aren't . . . *dating.* She can't really think that." I didn't reply. "So will you *please* have dinner with me? How about next Tuesday? At the Wolseley? I'll book a table for seven-thirty. Will you come, Phoebe?"

If I'd had any idea then where it would lead, I'd have said, "No. I won't. Absolutely not. Never."

"Yes," I heard myself say . . .

I considered not telling Emma. But we were friends—I *couldn't* keep it from her, not least because it would be awful if she somehow found out. So I told her on that Saturday when we met at Amici's, our favourite coffee shop on Marylebone High Street.

"Guy's asked you out?" she repeated faintly. "*Oh.*" Her hand trembled as she lowered her cup.

"I haven't . . . encouraged him," I explained gently. "I didn't . . . flirt with him at your dinner party, and if you'd rather I didn't go, then I won't, but I couldn't *not* tell you. Em?" I reached for her hand, noticing how red her fingertips were from all the stitching and gluing and straw stretching that she did. "Emma—are you okay with this?" She stirred her cappuccino, then stared out the window. "Because I wouldn't see him, not even once, if you didn't want me to."

Emma didn't reply at first. Her large green eyes strayed to a young couple walking hand in hand on the street. "It's okay," she said, after a moment. "After all . . . I haven't known him that long, as you pointed out—although he *didn't* discourage me from thinking . . ." Her voice suddenly trembled. "And those roses he brought me. I thought . . ." She pressed a paper napkin to her eyes. It had AMICI's printed on it. "Well," she croaked. "It doesn't look as though I'll be going to *Tosca* with him after all. Maybe *you* could take him, Phoebe. He said he was really looking forward to it . . ."

I sighed with frustration. "Look, Em, I'm going to say no. If it's going to make you miserable, then I'm not the least bit interested. Your friendship means too much to me—"

"No," Emma interrupted. She shook her head. "You should go, Phoebes—if you like him, which I assume you do, otherwise we'd hardly be having this conversation. Anyway . . ." She reached for her bag. "I'd better be off. I've got a bonnet to be getting on with—for

Princess Eugenie, no less." She gave me a cheery wave. "I'll speak to you soon. I promise."

But she didn't return my calls for six weeks . . .

"I wish you'd ring Guy," I heard Mum say. "I think you meant a lot to him. In fact, Phoebe, there's something I need to tell you . . ."

I looked at her, surprised at the sudden seriousness of her tone. "What?"

"Well . . . Guy phoned me last week." I felt a falling sensation, as though I was sliding down a steep incline. "He said he'd like to see you, just to talk to you—now *don't* shake your head, darling. He feels you've been 'unfair'—that was the word he used, though he wouldn't say why. But I suspect you *have* been unfair, darling—unfair and, quite frankly, idiotic." Mum took a comb out of her bag. "It's not as though it's easy, finding a terrific man. I think you're lucky that he still holds a candle for you after the way you threw him over."

"I want nothing to do with him," I insisted. "I just don't . . . feel the same about him." Guy knew why.

Mum ran the comb through her wavy blond hair. "I just hope you won't come to regret it. And I hope you won't also come to regret leaving Sotheby's. I still think it's a shame. You had prestige there, and stability—the excitement of conducting auctions—"

"The stress of it, you mean."

"You had the company of your colleagues," she persisted, ignoring me.

"And now I'll have the company of my customers—and of my part-time assistant. When I can find myself one." This was something I really needed to pursue—there was a fashion auction coming up at Christie's that I wanted to go to.

"You had a regular income," Mum went on, swapping her comb for a powder compact. "And now here you are, opening this . . . *shop*." She managed to make the word sound like *bordello*. "What if it doesn't work out? You've borrowed a small fortune, darling—"

"Thanks for reminding me."

She dabbed powder on her nose. "And it's going to be *such* hard work."

"Hard work will suit me just fine," I replied evenly. *Because then I'll have less time to think.*

"Anyway, I've said my piece," she concluded unctuously. She snapped shut her compact and returned it to her bag.

"And how's work going?"

Mum grimaced. "Not well. There've been problems with that huge house on Ladbroke Grove—John's going insane, which makes it hard for me." Mum works as a personal assistant to a successful architect, John Cranfield, a job she's been doing for twenty-two years. "It's not easy," she said, "but then I'm very lucky to have a job at my age." She peered at herself in the mirror. "Just look at my face." She moaned.

"It's a lovely face, Mum."

She sighed. "More furrows than Gordon Ramsay in a fury. None of those new creams seem to have made the slightest difference."

I thought of Mum's dressing table. It used to have a single bottle of Oil of Olay on it; now it resembled the cosmetics counter of a department store with its tubes of Retin-A and vitamin E, its pots of Derma Genesis and Moisture Boost, its pseudoscientific capsules of slow-release ceramides and hyaluronic acid with cellular-nurturing, epoxy-restoring this, that, and the other.

"Just dreams in a jar, Mum."

She prodded her cheeks. "Perhaps a little Botox might help . . . I've been toying with the idea." She stretched up her brow with the index and middle fingers of her left hand. "With my luck, it would go wrong and I'd end up with my eyelids round my nostrils. But I do so loathe all these lines."

"Then learn to love them. It's normal to have lines when you're fifty-nine."

Mum flinched, as though I'd slapped her. "*Don't*. I'm dreading getting the free bus pass. Why can't they give us a taxi pass when we hit sixty? Then I wouldn't mind so much."

"Anyway, lines don't make beautiful women less beautiful," I reminded her as I put a stack of Village Vintage shopping bags behind the cash register. "Just more interesting."

"Not to your father." I didn't reply. "Mind you, I thought he liked old ruins," Mum added dryly. "He is an archaeologist, after all. But now here he is with a girl barely older than you are. It's *grotesque,*" she muttered.

"It was certainly surprising."

Mum brushed an imaginary speck off her skirt. "You didn't invite him tonight? *Did* you?" In her hazel eyes I saw a heartrending combination of panic and hope.

"No, I didn't," I replied softly. Not least because *she* might have come. I wouldn't have put it past Ruth. Or rather Ruthless.

"Thirty-*six,*" Mum said bitterly, as though it was the "six" that offended her.

"She must be thirty-eight now," I pointed out.

"Yes—and he's sixty-two! I wish he'd never *done* that wretched TV series," she wailed.

I took a forest-green Hermès Kelly out of its dust bag and put it in a glass display case. "You couldn't have known what would happen, Mum."

"And to think I persuaded him—at *her* behest!" She picked up a glass of champagne, and her wedding ring, which she continued to wear in defiance of my father's desertion, gleamed in a beam of sunlight. "I thought it would help his career," she went on miserably. She sipped her fizz. "I thought that it would raise his profile and that he'd make more money, which would come in handy in our retirement. Then off he goes to film *The Big Dig,* but the main thing he seems to have been digging"—Mum grimaced—"was *her.*" She sipped her champagne again. "It was just . . . ghastly."

I had to agree. It was one thing for my father to have his first affair in thirty-eight years of marriage; it was quite another for my mother to find out about it in the gossip pages of the *Daily Express*. I shuddered as I remembered reading the caption beneath the photo of my father, looking uncharacteristically shifty, with Ruth, outside her Notting Hill flat:

TELLY PROF DUMPS WIFE AMIDST BABY RUMOURS.

"Do you see much of him, darling?" Mum asked with forced casualness. "Of course, I can't stop you," she went on. "And I wouldn't want to—he's your father; but to be honest, the thought of you spending time with him, and *her*... and... and..." Mum can't bring herself to mention the baby.

"I haven't seen Dad for ages," I answered truthfully.

Mum knocked back her champagne, then carried the glass out to the kitchen. "I'd better not drink any more. It'll only make me cry. So," she said briskly as she came back, "let's change the subject."

"Okay. Tell me what you think of the shop. You haven't seen it for weeks."

Mum walked round, her elegant little heels tapping on the wooden floor. "I like it. It's not remotely like being in a secondhand shop. It's more like being somewhere *nice*, like Phase Eight."

"That's good to hear." I lined up the flutes of gently fizzing champagne on the counter.

"I like the stylish silver mannequins, and there's a pleasantly uncluttered feel."

"That's because vintage shops can be chaotic—the racks so crammed that you give yourself an upper-body workout just going through them. Here there's enough light and air between the garments so that browsing will be a pleasure. If an item doesn't sell, I'll simply bring out something else. But aren't the clothes lovely?"

"Ye-es," Mum replied. "In a way." She nodded at the cupcakes. "Those are fun."

"I know—I adore them." I tried to imagine who would buy them, and if the dresses would give them as much pleasure as they did me, just to look at them. "And what about this kimono? It's from 1912. Have you seen the embroidery?"

"Very pretty."

"*Pretty?* It's a work of art! And this Balenciaga opera coat. Look at the cut—it's made in just two pieces, including the sleeves. The construction is amazing."

"Hmm . . ."

"And this coatdress—it's by Jacques Fath. Look at the brocade with its pattern of little palm trees. Where could you find something like that today?"

"That's all very well, but—"

"And this Givenchy suit. Now, this would be great on *you,* Mum. You can wear a knee-length skirt because you've got great legs."

She shook her head. "I'd never *wear* vintage clothes."

"Why not?"

She shrugged. "I've always preferred *new* things."

"I don't know why."

"I've told you before, darling—it's because I grew up in the era of *rationing.* I had nothing but hideous hand-me-downs—scratchy Shetland sweaters and grey serge skirts and coarse woollen pinafores that smelled like a damp dog when it rained. I used to long for things that *no one else* had owned, Phoebe. I still do—I can't help it. I can't bear to wear things other people have worn."

"But everything's been washed and dry-cleaned. This isn't a charity shop, Mum." I gave the counter a quick wipe. "These clothes are in pristine condition."

"I know. And it all smells delightfully fresh—I detect no mustiness whatsoever." She sniffed the air. "Not the faintest whiff of a mothball."

I plumped up the cushions on the sofa where Dan had been sitting. "Then what's the problem?"

"It's the thought of wearing something that belonged to someone who's probably"—she gave a little shudder—"*died.* I have a thing about it. I always have had. You and I are different in that way. You're like your father. You both like old things . . . piecing them together. I suppose what you're doing is a kind of archaeology, too," she went on. "*Sartorial* archaeology. Ooh, look, someone's arriving."

I picked up two glasses of champagne, then, with adrenaline racing through my veins and a welcoming smile on my face, I stepped forward to greet the people walking through the door. Village Vintage was open for business.

Two

I always wake early. I don't need to look at the clock to know what time it is—it's ten to four. I've been waking at ten to four every night for six months. My doctor said it's stress-induced insomnia, but I know it's not stress. It's guilt.

I avoid sleeping pills, so sometimes I'll try to make the time pass by getting up and working. I might put in a wash—the machine's always on the go; I might iron a few things, or do a repair. But I know it's better to try and sleep, so I usually lie there, attempting to lull myself back to oblivion with the BBC World Service radio or some late-night phone-in show. But last night I didn't do that—I just lay there thinking about Emma. Whenever I'm not busy she goes round and round my brain, on a loop.

I see her at our little primary school in her stripy green summer dress; I see her diving into the swimming pool like a seal; I see her kissing her lucky Krugerrand before every tennis match. I see her at the Royal College of Art with her milliner's blocks. I see her at Ascot, photographed in *Vogue*, beaming beneath one of her fantastic hats.

Then, as my bedroom began to fill with the grey light of dawn, I saw Emma as I saw her for the very last time.

"Sorry," I whispered.

You're a fabulous friend.

"I'm sorry, Em."

What would I do without you?

As I stood under the shower I forced my thoughts back to work and to last night's party. About eighty people had come, including three former colleagues from Sotheby's as well as one or two of my neighbours from here on Bennett Street and a few local shop owners. Ted from the real estate firm up the street had popped in—he'd bought a silk waistcoat from the menswear rack; then Rupert, who owns the florist's, had turned up, and Pippa, who runs the Moon Daisy Café, dropped by with her sister.

One or two of the fashion journalists I'd invited were there. I hoped that they'd become good contacts, borrowing my clothes for photo shoots in return for free publicity.

"It's very elegant," Mimi Long from *Woman & Home* said to me as I circulated with the champagne. She tipped her glass towards me for a refill. "I adore vintage. It's like being in Aladdin's cave—one has this wonderful sense of *discovery*. Will you be running the place on your own?"

"No, I'll need someone to help me a couple of days a week so that I can be out and about buying stock, and taking things to be cleaned and repaired. So if you hear of anyone . . . They'll need to have an interest in vintage," I added.

"I'll keep my ear to the ground," Mimi promised. "Ooh—is that real Fortuny I can see over there?"

I'll have to advertise for an assistant, I decided now as I dried myself and combed my wet hair. I could place an ad in a local paper—perhaps the one Dan worked for, whatever it was called.

As I dressed—in wide linen trousers and a short-sleeved fitted shirt with a Peter Pan collar—I realised that Dan had correctly identified my style. I do like the bias-cut dresses and wide-leg trousers of the late thirties and early forties; I like my hair shoulder length and falling over one eye. I like swing coats, clutch bags, peep toes, and seamed stockings. I like fabric that drapes like oil.

I heard the clatter of the letter box and went downstairs, where there were three envelopes on the mat. Recognising Guy's handwriting on the first, I tore it in half and dropped the pieces in the trash bin. I knew from his others what this one would say.

Next was a card from Dad. *Good luck with your new venture,* he'd written. *I'll be thinking of you, Phoebe. But please come and see me soon. It's been too long.*

That was true. I'd been so preoccupied that I hadn't seen him since early February. We'd met at a café in Notting Hill for a conciliatory lunch. I hadn't been prepared for him bringing the baby. The sight of my sixty-two-year-old father with a two-month-old clamped to his chest was—to put it mildly—a shock.

"This is . . . Louis," he'd said awkwardly as he fumbled with the baby sling. "How *do* you undo this thing?" he muttered. "These damn clips . . . I can never . . . ah, *got* it." He sighed with relief, then lifted the baby out and cradled him with a tender but puzzled expression. "Ruth's away filming so I had to bring him. Oh . . ." Dad peered down at the small puckered face anxiously. "Do you think he's hungry?"

I looked at Dad, appalled. "How on earth should *I* know?"

As Dad rummaged in the changing bag for a bottle I stared at Louis, his chin shining with dribble, not knowing what to think, let alone say. He was my baby brother. How could I not love him? At the same time, how *could* I love him, I wondered, when his conception was the cause of my mother's distress?

Meanwhile Louis, unfazed by the complexities of the situation, had grasped my finger in his tiny hand and was smiling at me gummily.

"Pleased to meet you," I'd said . . .

The third letter was from Emma's mother. I recognised her writing. My thumb trembled as I ran it under the flap.

I just wanted to wish you every success with your new venture, she'd written. *Emma would have been so thrilled. I hope you're all right, Phoebe,* she'd gone on. *Derek and I are still taking things one day at a time. For us the hardest part remains the fact that we were away when it happened—you can't imagine how this torments us.* "Oh yes, I can," I murmured. *We still haven't gone through Emma's things . . .* I felt my insides coil. Emma had kept a diary. *But when we do, we'd like to give you some small thing of hers as a keepsake. I also wanted to let you know that there'll be a little ceremony for Emma on the first anniversary—February 15.* I needed no reminder—the date would remain seared in my memory for the rest of my life. *I'll be in touch nearer the time, but until then, God bless you, Phoebe. Daphne.*

She wouldn't be blessing me if she knew the truth, I thought bleakly, fighting back tears.

I collected myself, took some French embroidered nightdresses out of the washing machine, hung them to dry, then locked the house and walked to the shop.

There was still some clearing up to be done, and as I opened the door I detected the sour scent of last night's champagne. I returned the glasses to Oddbins in a cab, put the empty bottles out for recycling, swept the floor, and squished spot remover on the sofa. Then as the church clock struck nine I turned over the CLOSED sign.

"This is it," I said aloud. "Day one."

I sat behind the counter for a while repairing the lining of a Jean Muir jacket. By ten o'clock I was dismally wondering whether my mother might not be right. Perhaps I *had* made a huge mistake, I thought as I saw people pass by with no more than a glance at my beautiful window displays. Perhaps I'd find sitting in a shop dull after the busyness of Sotheby's. But then I reminded myself that I wouldn't simply be sitting in a shop—I'd be going to auctions and seeing dealers and visiting private individuals to evaluate their clothes. I'd be talking to Hollywood stylists about sourcing dresses for their famous clients, and I'd be making trips to France. I'd also be running the Village Vintage website, as I'd be selling clothes directly from that. There'd be more than enough to do, I told myself as I rethreaded my needle. Then I reminded myself of how stressful and hectic my previous life had been.

At Sotheby's I'd constantly been under the gun. There was the continual pressure to put on successful auctions, and to conduct them competently; there was the fear of not having enough for the next sale. If I did manage to get enough, then there was always the worry that the clothes wouldn't sell, or wouldn't sell for a high enough price, or that the buyers wouldn't pay their bills. There was the ever-present anxiety that things would get stolen or damaged. Worst of all was the perpetually gnawing fear that an important collection would go to a rival auction house—my bosses would always want to know why.

Then February 15 happened and I couldn't cope. I knew I had to get out.

Suddenly I heard the *click* of the door. I looked up expecting to see my first customer; instead it was Dan Robinson, in salmon-coloured cords and a lavender checked shirt. The man had zero colour sense. But there was something about him that was attractive. Perhaps it was his build—he was comfortingly solid, like a bear, I realised. Or perhaps Mum was right and it was his curly hair.

"I don't suppose I left my pencil sharpener here yesterday, did I?"

"Er, no. I haven't seen it."

"Damn," he muttered.

"Is it . . . a special one?"

"Yes. It's silver. Solid," he added.

"Really? Well . . . I'll keep a look out for it."

"If you would. And how was your party?"

"Good, thanks."

"Anyway . . ." He held up a newspaper. "I just wanted to bring you this." It was the *Black & Green*. On the front page was Dan's photo of me, captioned PASSION FOR VINTAGE FASHION.

I looked at him. "I thought you said the article was for Friday's paper."

"It was to have been, but then today's lead feature had to be held back for various reasons, so Matt, my editor, put yours in instead. Luckily we go to press late." He handed the paper to me. "I think it's come out quite well."

I glanced quickly through the piece. "It's . . . great," I said, trying to keep the surprise out of my voice. "Thanks for putting the website at the end and—*oh.*" I felt my jaw slacken. "*Why* does it say that there's a five percent discount on everything for the first week?"

A red stain had crept up Dan's neck. "I just thought an introductory offer might be . . . you know . . . good for business."

"I see. Well, that's a bit of a . . . cheek, to put it mildly."

He grimaced. "I know . . . but I was busy writing it up and I suddenly thought of it, and I knew your party was going on, so I didn't want to phone you, and then Matt said he wanted to run the piece right away and so . . . well . . ." He shrugged. "I'm sorry."

"It's okay," I said grudgingly. "I must say, you took me by surprise, but five percent is . . . fine." In fact it *would* be good for business, I reflected, not that I was prepared to concede that. "Anyway," I said and sighed, "I was a little distracted when we were talking yesterday. Who did you say gets this paper?"

"It's handed out at all the stations in this area on Tuesday and Friday mornings. It also goes through the doors of selected businesses and homes, so potentially it reaches a wide local audience."

"That's wonderful." I smiled at Dan, genuinely appreciative now. "And have you worked for it long?"

He seemed to hesitate. "Two months."

"From the start then? You said it was a new paper."

"More or less from the start, yes."

"And are you from round here?"

"Just down the road in Hither Green." There was another odd little pause, and I was just waiting for him to say that he ought to be on his way when he said, "You must come Hither."

I looked at him. "I'm sorry?"

He smiled. "All I mean is you must come round sometime."

"Oh."

"For a drink. I'd love you to see my . . ." *What?* I wondered. *Etchings?*

"Shed."

"Your *shed*?"

"Yes. I've got a fantastic shed," he said evenly.

"Really?" I imagined a jumble of rusty gardening tools, cobwebbed bicycles, and broken flowerpots.

"Or it will be when I've finished."

"Thanks," I said. "I'll bear that in mind."

"Well . . ." Dan tucked the pencil behind his ear. "I guess I'd better find my sharpener."

"Good luck." I smiled. "See you around." He left the shop, then gave me a little wave through the window. I waved back. "What an oddball," I said under my breath.

Within ten minutes of Dan's departure, as if he'd been a harbinger of good luck, a trickle of people began to arrive, at least two of them holding copies of the *Black & Green*. I tried not to annoy them with offers of help or to watch them too obviously. The Hermès bags and the more expensive jewellery were in lockable glass cases, but I hadn't put electronic tags on the clothes for fear of damaging the fabric.

By twelve, I'd had about ten people through the door. I'd also made my first sale—a 1950s seersucker sundress with a pattern of violets. I felt like framing the receipt.

At a quarter past one a petite red-haired girl in her early twenties came in with a well-dressed man in his mid- to late thirties. While she looked through the clothes he sat on the sofa, one silk-socked ankle resting on his knee, thumbing his BlackBerry. The girl went through the evening-wear rack, finding nothing; then her eye was drawn to the cupcake dresses hanging on the wall. She pointed to the lime-green one, the smallest of the four.

"How much is that?" she asked me.

"It's two hundred seventy-five pounds." She nodded thoughtfully. "It's silk," I explained, "with hand-sewn crystals. Would you like to try it on? It's a size six."

"Well . . ." She glanced anxiously at her boyfriend. "What do you think, Keith?" He looked up from his BlackBerry and the girl nodded at the dress, which I was now taking off the wall.

"That won't do," he said bluntly.

"Why not?"

"Too colourful."

"I like bright colours," the girl protested meekly.

He turned back to his BlackBerry. "It's not appropriate for the occasion."

"But it's a *dance.*"

"It's too colourful," he insisted. "Plus it's not smart enough." My dislike of the man turned to detestation.

"Let me try it." She smiled pleadingly. "Please."

He looked at her. "*O-kay.*" He sighed extravagantly. "*If* you must . . ."

I showed the girl into the changing room and drew the curtain round. A minute later she emerged. The dress fitted her perfectly. It showed off her small waist, lovely shoulders, and slim arms. The vibrant lime complimented her red-blond hair and creamy skin, while the corseting flattered her bust. The green tulle petticoats floated in layers around her, the crystals winking in the sunlight.

"It's . . . gorgeous," I murmured. I couldn't imagine any woman looking more beautiful in it. "Would you like to try a pair of shoes on with it?" I added. "Just to see how it would look with heels?"

"Oh, I won't need to," she said as she stared at herself, on tiptoe, in a side mirror. She shook her head. "It's . . . fantastic." She seemed overwhelmed, as though she'd just discovered some wonderful secret about herself.

Behind her another customer had come in, a slim, dark-haired woman of about thirty in a leopard-print shirtdress with a gold chain belt worn low on the hips and gladiator sandals. She stopped in her tracks, gazing at the girl. "You look *glorious!*" she exclaimed. "Like a young Julianne Moore."

The girl smiled delightedly. "Thanks." She stared at herself in the mirror. "This dress makes me feel . . . as though I'm in . . ." She hesitated. "A fairy tale." She glanced nervously at her boyfriend. "What do you think, Keith?"

He looked at her, shook his head, then returned to his Black-Berry. "Like I say—much too bright. Plus it makes you look like you're going to hop about in a ballet, not go to a sophisticated dinner dance at the Dorchester. Here." He stood up, went over to the evening-wear rack, and pulled out a Norman Hartnell black crêpe cocktail dress and held it up to her. "Try this."

The girl's face fell, but she retreated into the fitting room, emerging in the dress a minute later. The style was far too old for her, and the colour drained her complexion. She looked as though she was going to a funeral. I saw the woman in the leopard-print dress glance at her, then discreetly shake her head before turning back to the racks.

"*That's* more like it," Keith said. He made a circulating gesture with his index finger, and with a sigh the girl slowly spun round, her eyes upturned. At that I saw the other customer purse her lips. "Perfect," said Keith. He thrust his hand into his jacket. "How much?" I glanced at the girl. Her lips were quivering. "How much?" he repeated as he opened his wallet.

"But it's the green one I like," she murmured.

"How *much*?" he repeated.

I felt my face flush. "It's one-fifty."

"I don't *want* it," the girl pleaded. "I like the *green* one, Keith. It makes me feel . . . happy."

"Then you'll just have to buy it yourself. If you can afford it," he added pleasantly. He looked at me again. "So that's £150?" He tapped the newspaper. "And it says here that there's a five percent discount, which makes it £142.50, by my reckoning."

"That's right," I said, impressed by the speed of his calculation and wishing that I could charge him twice the amount and *give* the girl the cupcake dress.

"Keith. Please," she moaned. Her eyes were shining with tears.

"C'mon, Kelly," he groaned. "Give me a break. That little black number's just the ticket, and I've got some important clients coming, so I don't want you looking like bloody Tinker Bell, do I?" He glanced at his expensive-looking watch. "We've got to get back—I've got that conference call about the Kilburn site at two-thirty, remember. Now—am I buying the black dress or not? Because if I'm not, then you won't be coming to the Dorchester on Saturday, I can tell you."

She looked out the window. Then she nodded mutely.

As I tore the receipt off the register the man held his hand out for the bag, then slipped his credit card back into his wallet. "Thanks," he said briskly. Then, with the girl trailing disconsolately behind him, he left.

As the door clicked shut, the woman in the leopard-print dress caught my eye.

"I wish she'd had the fairy-tale gown," she said. "With a prince like that, she needs it." Not sure that I should be seen to be knocking my customers, I smiled a rueful smile of agreement, then put the green cupcake dress back on the wall. "She isn't just his girlfriend—she works for him," the woman went on as she inspected a Thierry Mugler hot-pink leather jacket from the mid-eighties.

I looked at her. "How do you know?"

"Because he's so much older than her, because of his power over her and her fear of offending him . . . her knowledge of his calendar. I like people watching," she told me.

"Are you a writer?"

"No. I love writing, but I'm an actor."

"Are you in anything at the moment?"

She shook her head. "I'm 'resting,' as they say—in fact, I've had more rest than Sleeping Beauty lately, *but*"—she heaved a theatrical sigh—"I refuse to give up." She looked at the prom dresses again. "They really *are* lovely. I don't have the curves for them, sadly, even if I had the cash. They're American, aren't they?"

I nodded. "Early fifties. They're a bit too frothy for postwar Britain."

"Gorgeous fabric," the woman said, squinting at them. "Dresses like that are usually made of acetate with nylon petticoats, but these ones are all silk." So she had knowledge and a good eye.

"Do you buy much vintage?" I asked as I refolded a lavender cashmere cardigan and put it on the knitwear stand.

"I buy as much as I can afford, and if I get bored with anything, I can always sell—not that I do, because I've always bought well. I've never forgotten the thrill of my first find," she went on as she put the Thierry Mugler back on the rack. "It was a Ted Lapidus leather coat bought in Oxfam in '92. It still looks good."

I thought about *my* first vintage find. A Nina Ricci guipure lace shirt bought in Greenwich Market when I was fourteen. Emma had pounced on it for me on one of our Saturday foraging trips.

"Your dress is Cerutti, isn't it?" I asked her. "But it's been altered. It should be ankle length."

The woman smiled. "Spot on. I got it at a jumble sale ten years ago, but the hem was ripped, so I shortened it." She brushed an imaginary speck off the front. "Best fifty pence I ever spent." She went over to the day-wear rack and picked out a turquoise crêpe de Chine tiered dress from the early seventies. "This is Alice Pollock, isn't it?"

I nodded. "For Quorum."

"I thought so." She glanced at the price. "Out of my reach, but I can never resist looking, and when I read in the local paper that you'd opened I just had to come and see what you had. Oh well." She sighed. "I can dream." She gave me a friendly smile. "I'm Annie, by the way."

"I'm Phoebe. Phoebe Swift." Impulsively, I asked, "I'm just wondering . . . are you working at the moment?"

"I'm temping," she replied. "Just doing whatever comes along."

"Do you live nearby?"

"Yes." Annie was looking at me curiously. "I live in Dartmouth Hill."

"The reason I'm asking . . . Look, I don't suppose you'd be interested in working for me, would you?" I blurted. "I need a part-time assistant." I explained why.

"Two days a week?" Annie echoed. "That might suit me very well—I could use some regular work—as long as I could go to auditions. Not that I have many to go to," she added ruefully.

"I'd be flexible about the hours, and there'd be some weeks when I'd need you for more than two days. And did you say you can sew?"

"I'm fairly nifty with a needle."

"Because it would be helpful if you could do a few small repairs in the quiet times, or a bit of ironing. And if you could help me dress the windows—I'm not much good with mannequins."

"I'd enjoy all that."

"And you wouldn't have to worry about whether or not you and I would get on, because when you were here I'd mostly be out, which would be the whole point of it. But here's my number." I handed Annie a Village Vintage postcard. "Think about it."

"Well . . . actually . . ." She laughed. "I don't have to. It would be perfect for me. But you ought to check my references," she added, "if only to make sure I'm not going to run off with the stock, because it would be *extremely* tempting." Her smile widened mischievously. "But apart from that, when can I start?"

So this morning, Monday, Annie began work, having provided letters from two previous employers extolling her honesty and indus-

try. I'd asked her to come early so that I could show her how everything worked before I left for Christie's.

"Spend some time familiarising yourself with the clothes," I advised her. "Evening wear is here. This is lingerie. There's some
menswear here . . . shoes and bags are on this stand. Knitwear on
this table. Let me open the till." I fiddled with the electronic key to
the register. "And if you could do a little mending . . ."

"Sure." I went into the den to pick up a Murray Arbeid skirt that
needed a small repair. "That's an Emma Kitts, isn't it?" I heard
Annie say. I came back into the shop. She was gazing up at the hat.
"That was so sad. I read about it in the papers." She turned to me.
"But why do you have it here? It's not vintage and it says it's not for
sale?"

For a split second I fantasised about confessing to Annie that
looking at the hat every day was a form of penance.

"I knew her," I explained as I put the skirt on the counter with the
sewing box. "We were friends."

"That's hard," said Annie softly. "You must miss her."

"Yes . . ." I coughed to cover the sob that I could feel rising in my
throat. "Anyway, this seam here—there's a little split." I breathed
deeply. "I'd better get going."

Annie took the lid off the sewing box and selected a reel of
thread. "What time does the auction start?"

"At ten." I picked up the catalogue. "The lots I'm interested in
won't come up until after eleven, but I want to get there early so that
I can see what's selling well."

"What are you going to bid for?"

"A Balenciaga evening gown." I turned to the photo of Lot 110.
Annie peered at it. "How *elegant.*"

The long sleeveless indigo silk dress was cut very simply, its
scooped neckline and gently raised hem encrusted in a wide band of
fringed silver glass beading.

"I want to buy it for a private client," I explained. "She's a Beverly
Hills stylist. I know exactly what her customers want, so I'm sure

she'll take it. Then there's this dress by Madame Grès that I'm dying
to get for my own collection." I turned to the photo of Lot 112. A neo-
classical sheath of cream silk jersey fell in dozens of fine pleats from
an empire-line bust with crossover straps, and a chiffon train
floated from each shoulder. I sighed wistfully.

"It's magnificent," Annie murmured. "It would make a fabulous
wedding dress," she teased.

I smiled. "That's *not* why I want it. I simply love the incompara-
ble draping of Madame Grès's gowns." I picked up my bag. "Now I
really *must* go—oh, one other thing—" I was just about to tell Annie
what to do if anyone brought clothes in to sell when the phone rang.

I picked up. "Village Vintage." The novelty of saying it still gave
me a thrill.

"Good morning," said a female voice. "My name is Mrs. Bell."
The woman was clearly elderly. Her accent was French, though almost imperceptibly so. "I saw from the local newspaper that you
have just opened your shop."

"That's right." So Dan's article was still having an effect. I felt a
rush of goodwill towards him.

"Well, I have a selection of clothes I no longer want—some quite
lovely things that I am never going to wear again. There are also
some bags and shoes. But I am elderly. I cannot bring them—"

"No, of course not," I interjected. "I'd be happy to come to you, if
you'd like to give me your address." I reached for my calendar. "The
Paragon?" I repeated. "That's very near. I could walk up. When shall
I come?"

"Is there any chance that you could come today? I am in the mood
to dispose of my things sooner rather than later. I have an appointment this morning, but would three o'clock be possible?"

I'd be back from the auction by then, and I had Annie to mind the
shop. "Three o'clock would be fine," I said as I scribbled down the
house number.

As I walked down the hill to Blackheath Station I reflected on the art of evaluating a collection of clothes in someone's home. The usual scenario is that a woman has died and you're dealing with her relatives. They can be very emotional, so you have to be tactful. They're often offended if you leave some garments out; then they can be upset if you offer less than they'd hoped for those things you do choose. "Only forty pounds?" they'll say. "But it's by Hardy Amies." And I'll gently point out that the lining's ripped, that three buttons are missing, and that it'll have to go to the specialist dry cleaners for the stains on the cuff.

Sometimes the family can find it hard to part with the garments at all and resent your presence, especially if the estate is being sold to pay debts or taxes. In those cases, I reflected as I waited on the station platform, you're made to feel like an intruder. Quite often, when I've gone to do a valuation in a grand country house, I've had the maid or valet standing there weeping, or telling me—and this is very annoying—not to touch the clothes. If I'm with a widower, he'll often go into excruciating detail about everything that his wife wore, and how much he paid for it in Dickins & Jones in 1965 and how beautiful she looked in it on the *QE2*.

The easiest scenario by far, I thought as the train pulled in, is where a woman is getting divorced and wants to be rid of everything that her husband ever bought her. In those cases I can justifiably be brisk. But when it comes to seeing elderly women who are selling their entire wardrobe, it can be emotionally draining. As I say, these are more than clothes—they're the fabric, almost literally, of someone's life. But however much I like to hear the stories, I have to remind myself that my time is limited. I try to keep my visits to no more than an hour, which is what I resolved to do with Mrs. Bell.

As I came out of the underground at South Kensington I called Annie. She sounded upbeat, having already sold a Vivienne Westwood bustier and two French nightdresses. She also told me that Mimi Long from *Woman & Home* had asked if she could borrow some clothes for one of her shoots. Cheered by this, I walked down the

Old Brompton Road to Christie's, then turned into the crowded foyer. I queued to register, then picked up my bidding paddle.

The fashion auctions are popular, and the Long Gallery was already two-thirds full. I sat at the end of an empty row halfway down on the right, then looked around for my competitors, which is always the first thing I do when I go to an auction. I saw a couple of dealers I know and a woman who runs a vintage dress shop in Islington. I recognised the fashion editor of *Elle* sitting in the fourth row, and to my right I spotted Nicole Farhi. The air seemed clogged with expensive scent.

"Lot number 102," announced the auctioneer. I sat bolt upright. Lot 102? But it was only ten-thirty. When I was conducting auctions I never dawdled, but this man had *torn* through the list. Pulse racing, I looked at the Balenciaga gown in the catalogue, then flicked forward to the Madame Grès. It had a reserve of £1,000 but was likely to go for more. I knew I shouldn't be buying anything I wasn't planning to sell, but told myself that this was an important piece. It would only appreciate in value. If I could get it for £1,500 or less, I would.

"Lot 105 now," said the auctioneer. "An Elsa Schiaparelli 'shocking pink' silk jacket from her Circus collection of 1938. Note the original metallic buttons in the shape of acrobats. Bidding for this item starts at £300. Thank you. And £320, and £340 . . . £360, thank you, madam . . . Do I hear £380?" The auctioneer peered over his glasses, then nodded at a blond woman in the front row. "So, for £360 . . ." The gavel came down with a *crack*. "*Sold*. To?" The woman held up her bidding paddle. "Buyer number 24. Thank you, madam. On now to Lot 106 . . ."

Despite my years as an auctioneer my heart was pounding as "my" first lot approached. I glanced anxiously round the room, wondering who my rivals for it might be. Most of the buyers were women, but at the very end of my row was a distinguished-looking man in his mid-forties. He was flicking through the catalogue, marking it here and there with a gold fountain pen. I idly wondered what he was going to bid for.

The next three lots were each despatched in less than a minute with telephone bids. It was time for the Balenciaga. I felt my fingers tighten around my bidding paddle.

"Lot number 110," announced the auctioneer. "An elegant Cristóbal Balenciaga evening gown of dark blue silk, made in 1960." An image of the dress was projected onto the two huge flat screens on either side of the podium. "Note the typical simplicity of the cut and the slightly raised hem, to reveal shoes. I'm going to start the bidding at £500." The auctioneer looked around the room. "Do I hear £500?" As there were no bids, I waited. "Who'll offer me £450?" He scrutinized us all over his glasses. To my surprise, there were no raised hands. "Do I hear £400 then?" A woman in the front row nodded, so I nodded too. "I have £420 ... £440 ... £460. Do I hear £480?" The auctioneer looked at me. "Thank you, madam—the bid is yours, at £480. Any advance above £480?" He turned to the other bidder, but she was shaking her head. "Then £480 it is." Down came the gavel. "*Sold* for £480 to buyer number"—he peered at me and I held up my paddle—"220. Thank you, madam."

My euphoria at having gotten the Balenciaga at such a good price was swiftly replaced by stomach-churning anxiety as bidding for the Madame Grès approached. I shifted on my seat.

"Lot number 112," the auctioneer said. "An evening gown, circa 1936, by the great Madame Grès, famed for her masterful pleating and draping." An aproned porter carried the dress, which had been put onto a mannequin, up to the podium. I cast a nervous glance around the room. "I'm going to start at £1,000," the auctioneer announced. "Do I hear £1,000?" To my relief, only one other hand went up with my own. "And £1,100. And £1,150." I bid again. "And £1,200. Thank you—and £1,250?" The auctioneer looked at us in turn—the other bidder was shaking her head—then landed his gaze on me. "Still at £1,250. The bid is with you, madam." I held my breath—£1,250 would be a fabulous price. "Last call. Last call then," the auctioneer repeated. *Thank you, God,* I closed my eyes with relief. "*Thank* you, sir."

Confounded, I looked to my left. To my irritation, the man at the end of my row was now bidding. "Do I hear £1,300?" enquired the auctioneer. He glanced at me and I nodded. "And £1,350? Thank you, sir." I felt my pulse race. "And £1,400? Thank you, madam. Do I hear £1,500 now?" The man nodded. *Damn.* "And £1,600?" I raised my hand. "And will you give me £1,700, sir? Thank you."

I threw another glance at my rival, noting his calm expression as he drove up the price. "Do I hear £1,750?" This suave-looking creep wasn't going to stop me from getting the dress. I raised my hand again. "At £1,750—still with the lady at the end of the row there. *Thank* you, sir—with you now at £1,800. And £1,900? Are you still in, madam?" I nodded, but beneath my excitement I was seething. "And £2,000? Will you bid, sir?" The man nodded again. "Who'll give me £2,100?" I raised my hand. "And £2,200? *Thank* you, sir. Still with you, sir, at £2,200 now . . ." The man gave me a sideways glance. I raised my hand again. "I have £2,300 now," said the auctioneer happily. "Thank you, madam. And £2,400?" The auctioneer stared fixedly at me, while extending his right hand to my rival as though to keep us locked in competition—a familiar trick. I'd used it myself. "£2,400?" he repeated. "It's the gentleman against you, madam." I nodded now, adrenaline scorching my veins. "£2,600?" said the auctioneer.

I could hear people shift their seats as the tension mounted. "Thank you, sir. Do I hear £2,800? Madam—will you bid £2,800?" I nodded, as if in a dream. "And £2,900, sir? Thank you." There were whispers from behind. "Do I hear £3,000 . . . £3,000?" The auctioneer peered at me as I raised my hand. "Thank you very much, madam—£3,000 then." What was I *doing*? "At £3,000 . . ." I didn't *have* £3,000—I'd have to let the dress go. "Any advance on £3,000?" It was sad, but there it was. "£3,100?" I heard the auctioneer repeat. "No, sir? You're out?"

I looked at my rival. To my horror he was shaking his head. Now the auctioneer turned to me. "So the bid is still with you then,

madam, at three *thousand* pounds . . ." Oh my God. "Going *once* . . ."
The auctioneer raised his gavel. *"Twice . . ."* He flicked his wrist, and
with a strange mix of euphoria and dismay I watched the gavel come
down. "Sold then for three thousand pounds to buyer—what was the
number again, please?" I held up my paddle with a shaking hand
"220. *Thank* you, everyone. Terrific bidding there. Now on to Lot
113."

I stood up, feeling sick. With the buyer's premium, the total cost
of the dress would be £3,600. How, with all my experience, not to
mention my supposed sangfroid, could I have gotten so carried
away?

As I looked at the man who'd bid against me, an irrational hatred
overwhelmed me. He was a City slicker financial type, polished in
his Savile Row pinstripe and his handmade shoes. No doubt he'd
wanted the dress for his wife—his trophy wife, in all probability. I
conjured her, a vision of blond perfection in this season's Chanel.

I left the saleroom, my heart still thudding. I couldn't possibly
keep the dress. I could offer it to Cindi, my Hollywood stylist—it
would be a perfect red-carpet gown for one of her clients. For a moment I imagined Cate Blanchett wearing it to the Oscars—she'd do it
justice. But I didn't *want* to sell it, I told myself as I headed downstairs to the cashier. It was sublimely beautiful and I had battled to
get it.

Queuing to pay, I wondered nervously whether my MasterCard
would combust on contact with the machine. I calculated that there
was just enough credit on it to make the transaction possible.

As I waited my turn, I looked up. Mr. Pinstripe was coming down
the stairs, his phone pressed to his ear.

"No, I didn't," I heard him say. He had a very pleasant voice, I noticed, with a slight huskiness to it. "I just didn't," he repeated
wearily. "I'm sorry about that, darling." Trophy Wife—or possibly
Mistress—was clearly furious with him for not getting the Madame
Grès. "Bidding was intense," I heard him explain. He glanced at me.

"I had stiff competition." At that, to my astonishment, he winked at me. "Yes, I know it's disappointing, but there'll be lots of other lovely dresses, sweetie." Trophy Wife was obviously *not* happy. "But I did get the Prada bag that you liked. Yes, of course, darling. Look, I have to go and pay now. I'll call you later, okay?"

He snapped his phone shut with a slightly conspicuous air of relief, then came and stood behind me. I pretended not to know he was there.

"Congratulations," I heard him say.

I turned around. "I'm sorry?"

"Congratulations," he repeated. "You've got the lot," he added jovially. "The wonderful white dress by . . . who was it again?" He opened the catalogue. "Madame Grès—whoever she was." I was outraged. The jerk didn't even know what it was that he'd been bidding for. "You must be pleased," he added.

"Yes." I resisted the temptation to tell him that I was far from pleased with the price.

He tucked the catalogue under his arm. "To be honest, I could have gone on bidding."

I stared at him. "Really?"

"But then I looked at your face, and when I saw how *intensely* you seemed to want it, I decided to let you have it."

"Oh." I nodded politely. Was the wretch expecting me to *thank* him? If he'd quit the race earlier, he'd have saved me two grand.

"Are you going to wear it to some special occasion?" he asked.

"No," I replied frigidly. "I just . . . adore Madame Grès. I collect her gowns."

"Then I'm delighted that you got this one." He adjusted the knot of his Hermès silk tie. "Well, I'm through for the day." He glanced at his watch, and I caught a glint of antique Rolex. "Will you be bidding for anything else?"

"Good God, no—I've blown my budget."

"Oh dear—so it was a case of sticker shock, was it?"

"It was rather."

"Well . . . I guess that's my fault." He gave me an apologetic smile, and I noticed that his eyes were large and deep brown with hooded lids that gave him a slightly sleepy expression.

"Of course it's not your fault." I shrugged. "That's how auctions work." As I knew only too well.

"Yes please, madam?" I heard the cashier say.

I turned and handed her my credit card. As I did so I asked her to make out the invoice to Village Vintage, then I sat on the blue leather bench and waited for my lots to be brought out.

Mr. Pinstripe completed his payment, then came and sat next to me while he waited for his purchases. As we sat there, side by side, not talking now because he was reading his BlackBerry—with a slightly intense air, I couldn't help noticing—I found myself wondering how old he was. I stole a glance at his profile. His face was quite lined. Whatever his age, he was undeniably attractive with his iron-filings hair and aquiline nose. Forty-three-ish, I decided as a porter handed us our respective garment bags. I felt a thrill of ownership as mine was handed to me. I quickly checked the contents, then gave Mr. Pinstripe a farewell smile.

He stood up. "Do you know"—he glanced at his watch—"all that bidding has made me hungry. I'm going to pop into the café across the street. I don't suppose you'd feel like joining me, would you? After bidding so vigorously against you, the least I can do is to buy you a sandwich." He extended his hand. "My name's Miles, by the way. Miles Archant."

"Oh. I'm Phoebe. Swift. Hi," I added impotently as I shook his hand.

"So?" He was looking at me enquiringly. "Can I interest you in an early lunch?"

I was amazed at the man's audacity. He (a) didn't know me from Eve, and (b) clearly had a wife or girlfriend—a fact he knew that *I* knew because I'd overheard him on his mobile.

"Or just a cup of coffee?"

"No, thank you," I replied firmly. He probably made a habit of picking up women in auction houses. "I have to . . . get back now."

"To . . . work?" he asked pleasantly.

"Yes." I didn't have to say where.

"Well, enjoy the dress. You'll look stunning in it," he added as I turned to leave.

Unsure whether to be indignant or delighted, I gave him an uncertain smile. "Thanks."

Three

On my return I showed Annie the two dresses. I told her that I'd had to fight for the Madame Grès, though I didn't go into details about Mr. Pinstripe.

"I wouldn't worry about the cost," she said as she gazed at the gown. "Something as magnificent as this should transcend such petty considerations."

"If only," I said wistfully. *Three thousand pounds,* I thought. *For a dress I could have bought for twelve fifty!* "I still can't believe how much I spent."

"Couldn't you say it's part of your pension?" Annie suggested as she restitched the hem of a Bill Blass skirt. She shifted on her stool. "Perhaps the Inland Revenue would knock the cost of it off your tax bill."

"I doubt it, as I'm not selling it, although I rather like the idea of a *pension-à-porter.* Oh," I added. "You've put those up there." While I'd been out, Annie had hung six hand-embroidered evening bags on a bare patch of wall by the door.

"I hope you don't mind," she said. "I thought they'd look good in a little group there."

"They do. And you can see the detail on them so much better." I zipped the two dresses I'd bought into new protective covers. "I'd better put these in the stockroom."

"Can I ask you something?" Annie said as I turned to go upstairs. I looked at her. "Yes?"

"You collect Madame Grès?"

"That's right."

"But you have a lovely gown by Madame Grès right here." She went over to the evening-wear rack and pulled out the dress that Guy had given me. "Someone tried it on this morning, and I saw the label. The woman was too short for it—but it would look great on you. Don't you want it for your own collection?"

I shook my head. "I'm . . . not mad about that particular gown."

"Oh." Annie looked at it, her brow furrowing. "I see. But—"

To my relief the bell above the door began to tinkle. A couple in their late twenties walked in. I asked Annie to look after them while I went up to the stockroom. Then I nipped back down to the office to check the Village Vintage website for any new online orders.

"I need an evening dress," I heard the girl say as I opened the e-mail enquiries. "It's for our engagement party," she added with a giggle.

"Carla thought she'd get something a bit more original in a shop like this," her boyfriend explained.

"You will," I heard Annie reply. "The evening wear is over here—you're a size ten, aren't you?"

"Gosh no." The girl snorted. "I'm a fourteen. I should go on a diet."

"*Don't,*" said her boyfriend. "You're lovely as you are."

"You're a lucky woman," I heard Annie chuckle. "You've got the perfect husband-to-be there."

"I know I have," the girl said fondly. "What are you looking at there, Pete? Ooh, what lovely cuff links."

Feeling a sting of envy at the couple's evident happiness together, I turned to the orders. Someone wanted to buy five of my French nightdresses. Another customer was interested in a Dior long-sleeved dress with a bamboo pattern and was asking about the sizing.

When I say that the garment is a U.K. 12, I e-mailed back, *that really means it's a 10 because women today are bigger than the women of fifty years ago. Here are the dimensions that you requested, including the circumference of the sleeve at the wrist. Please let me know if you'd like me to set it aside for you.*

"When is your party?" I heard Annie ask.

"It's this Saturday," the girl replied. "So I haven't given myself much time to find something. These aren't quite what I'm looking for," I heard her add after a few moments.

"You could always accessorise a dress you already have with something vintage," Annie suggested. "You might add a silk jacket—we've got some lovely ones over there—or a pretty shrug. If you brought something in, I could help you give it a new look."

"*Those* are wonderful," the girl suddenly said. "They're so... *joyous.*" I smiled, knowing that she could only be talking about the cupcake dresses.

"Which colour do you like best?" I heard her boyfriend say.

"The . . . turquoise one, I think."

"It'd go with your eyes," I heard him add.

"Would you like me to get it down for you?" Annie asked.

I glanced at my watch. It was time to go and meet Mrs. Bell.

"How much is it?" the girl asked. Annie told her. "*Ah.* I see. Well, in that case . . ."

"At least try it on," her boyfriend urged.

"Well . . . okay," she replied. "But it's way too expensive for me."

As I went out into the shop a minute later the girl emerged from the dressing room in the turquoise cupcake. She wasn't in the least bit fat, she just had a lovely voluptuousness. Her fiancé had been right about the blue-green complementing her eyes.

"You look wonderful in it," Annie told her. "You need an hour-glass figure for these dresses, and you've got one."

"Thank you." She tucked a hank of glossy brown hair behind one ear. She really did look wonderful in the dress; it might have been designed just for her. "I must say, it really is"—she sighed with a mixture of happiness and frustration—"*gorgeous.* I love the tutu skirts and the sequins. It makes me feel ... happy," she said wonderingly. "Not that I'm not happy," she added with a warm smile at her fiancé. She looked at Annie. "And it's two hundred seventy-five pounds?"

"That's right. It's all silk," Annie added, "including the lace banding round the bodice."

"And there's five percent off everything at the moment," I said as I picked up my bag. Why not continue the special sale? "And we can put things on hold for up to a week."

The girl sighed again. She gazed at herself in the mirror, the tulle petticoats whispering as she moved. "It's lovely," she said, "but ... I don't know ... Perhaps ... it's not really ... quite *me.*" She retreated into the changing room and drew the curtain. "I'll just ... keep looking," I heard her say as I left for the Paragon.

I know the Paragon well—I used to go there for piano lessons. My teacher was named Mr. Long, which used to make my mother laugh, as Mr. Long was *very* short. He was also blind, and his brown eyes, magnified behind the thick lenses of his metal-framed specs, used to roll incessantly from side to side. When I was playing he would pace behind me in his worn Hush Puppies. If I fumbled something, he'd smack the fingers of my right hand with a ruler. I wasn't so much offended as impressed by his aim.

I went to Mr. Long every Tuesday after school for five years until one June day his wife phoned my mother to say that Mr. Long had collapsed and died while walking in the Lake District. Despite the hand smacking, I was very upset; I'd grown to like him.

I haven't set foot in the Paragon since then, although I've often passed by it. There's something about the imposing Georgian crescent, with its seven massive houses, each linked by a low colonnade, that still makes me catch my breath. In the Paragon's heyday each house had its own stable, carriage room, fish pond, and dairy, but during the war the terrace had been bombed. When it was restored in the late 1950s it was carved into flats.

Now I walked up Morden Road past the Clarendon Hotel, skirting the Heath with its swirl of traffic trundling around the perimeter; then I passed the Princess of Wales pub, and the nearby pond, its surface rippling in the breeze, then I turned into the Paragon. As I walked down the terrace I admired the horse chestnut trees on the huge front lawn, their leaves already flecked with gold. I climbed the stone steps of number 8 and pressed the buzzer for flat 6. I looked at my watch. It was five to three. I'd aim to be out by four.

I heard the intercom crackle, then Mrs. Bell's voice. "I am just coming down. Kindly wait a little moment."

It was a good five minutes until she appeared.

"Excuse me." She lifted her hand to her chest as she caught her breath. "It always takes me some time . . ."

"Please don't worry," I said as I held the heavy black door open for her. "But couldn't you have let me in from upstairs?"

"The automatic catch is broken—somewhat to my regret," she added with elegant understatement. "Anyway, thank you so much for coming, Miss Swift—"

"Please, call me Phoebe."

As I stepped over the threshold Mrs. Bell extended a thin hand, the skin of which was translucent with age, the veins standing out like blue wires. As she smiled at me, her face folded into myriad creases, which here and there had trapped particles of pink powder. Her periwinkle eyes were patched with pale grey.

"You must wish there was a lift," I said as we began to climb the wide stone staircase to the third floor. My voice echoed up the stairwell.

"A lift would be extremely desirable," agreed Mrs. Bell as she gripped the iron handrail. She paused for a moment to hitch up the waist of her caramel wool skirt. "But it's only lately that the stairs have bothered me." We stopped again on the first landing so that she could rest. "However, I may be going elsewhere quite soon, so I will no longer have to climb this mountain, which would be a distinct advantage," she added as we carried on upwards.

"Will you be going far?" Mrs. Bell didn't seem to hear. I decided that in addition to her general frailty she must be hard of hearing.

She pushed on her door. *"Et voilà."*

The interior of her flat, like its owner, was attractive but faded. There were pretty pictures on the walls, including a luminous little oil painting of a lavender field; there were Aubusson rugs on the parquet floor and fringed silk lampshades hanging from the ceiling of the corridor along which I now followed Mrs. Bell. She stopped halfway and stepped down into the kitchen. It was small, square, and time-warped, with its red Formica-topped table and its hooded gas stove upon which stood an aluminium kettle and a single white-enamelled saucepan. On the laminate counter was a tea tray set out with a blue china teapot, two matching cups and saucers, and a little white milk pitcher over which she'd put a dainty white muslin cover fringed with blue beads.

"Can I offer you a cup of tea, Phoebe?"

"No, thank you—really."

"But I have everything ready, and though I may be French, I know how to make a nice cup of English Darjeeling," Mrs. Bell added wryly.

"Well . . . ," I said, smiling, "if it's no trouble."

"None at all. I have only to reheat the water." She took a box of matches off the shelf, struck one, then held it to the gas ring with a shaky hand. As she did so I noticed that the waistband of her skirt was secured with a large safety pin. "Please, take a seat in the sitting room," she told me. "It's just there—on the left."

The sitting room was large, with a big bow window, and was papered in a light green slubbed silk, which was curling at the seams in places. A small gas fire was alight despite the warmth of the day. On the mantel above it, a silver carriage clock was flanked by a pair of snooty-looking Staffordshire spaniels.

As I heard the kettle begin to whistle I went over to the window and looked down at the yard. The lawn swept the entire length of the crescent, like a river of grass, fringed by a screen of magnificent trees. There was a huge cedar that cascaded to the ground in tiers, like a green crinoline, and two or three enormous oaks. There were three copper beeches and a sweet chestnut in the throes of a half-hearted second flowering. To the right, two young girls were running through the skirts of a weeping willow, shrieking and laughing. I stood there for a few moments, watching them.

"Here we are," I heard Mrs. Bell say. I went to help her with the tray.

"No, thank you," she said, almost fiercely, as I tried to take it from her. "I may be somewhat *antique,* but I can still manage quite well. Now, how do you take your tea?"

"Black with no sugar," I told her.

She picked up the silver tea strainer. "That's easy then." She handed me my tea, then lowered herself onto a little brocade chair by the fire. I sat on the sofa opposite her.

"Have you lived here long, Mrs. Bell?"

"Long enough." She sighed. "Eighteen years."

"So are you hoping to move to ground-floor accommodation?" It had crossed my mind that she might be moving to one of the flats for the elderly just down the road.

"I'm not sure where I'm going," she replied. "I will have a clearer idea next week. But whatever happens, I am . . . how can I put it . . ."

"Downsizing?" I suggested after a moment.

"Downsizing?" She smiled ruefully. "Yes." There was an odd little silence, which I filled by telling Mrs. Bell about my piano lessons, though I decided not to mention the ruler.

"And were you a good pianist?"

I shook my head. "I was pretty bad. I didn't practise enough, and then after Mr. Long died I just didn't want to continue with it. My mother wanted me to, but I guess I wasn't that interested." From outside came the silvery laughter of the two girls. "Unlike my best friend, Emma," I heard myself say. "She was brilliant at the piano." I picked up my teaspoon. "She passed grade eight when she was only fourteen—with Distinction. It was announced in school at assembly."

"Really?"

I began stirring my tea. "The headmistress asked Emma to come up onstage and play something, so she played this lovely piece from Schumann's *Scenes from Childhood*. It was called 'Träumerei'—Dreaming..."

"What a gifted girl," said Mrs. Bell. Her expression was faintly puzzled. "And are you still friends with this...paragon?"

"No." I studied a solitary tea leaf at the bottom of my cup. "She's dead. She died earlier this year, on the fifteenth of February, at about ten to four in the morning. At least, that's when they think it happened, although they couldn't be sure; but I suppose they have to put something down, don't they..."

"How terrible," Mrs. Bell murmured. "What age was she?"

"Thirty-three." I continued to stir my tea, gazing into its topaz depths. "She would have been thirty-four today." The spoon gently chinked against the cup. I looked at Mrs. Bell. "Emma was really talented in other ways, too. She was a wonderful tennis player—although..." I felt myself smile. "She had this peculiar serve. She looked as though she was tossing pancakes. It worked, mind you—her serves were unreturnable."

"Really."

"She was a terrific swimmer—and a brilliant artist."

"What an accomplished young woman."

"Oh yes. But she wasn't in the least bit conceited—quite the opposite, actually. She was full of self-doubt."

I suddenly realised that my tea, being black and sugarless, didn't need stirring. I laid my spoon in the saucer.

"And she was your best friend?"

I nodded. "She was. But I wasn't really a best friend to her or even a good friend, come to that. In fact, when the chips were down, I was a terrible friend." Without warning, there were tears in my eyes. What was I doing? I hardly knew this woman, and here I was, weeping in her sitting room. I was aware of the steady sound of the gas fire, like an unending exhalation. "I'm sorry," I said quietly. I put down my cup. "I came here to look at your clothes. I think I'll get on with that now. But thank you for the tea—it was just what I needed."

Mrs. Bell hesitated for a moment, then she stood and I followed her across the corridor into the bedroom.

Like the rest of the flat, it seemed not to have been touched for years. It was decorated in yellow and white, with a pale yellow duvet on the small double bed, and yellow Provençal curtains and matching panels set into the doors of the white cupboards that lined the far wall. There was a cream alabaster lamp on the bedside table and next to it a black-and-white photo of a handsome, dark-haired man. On the dressing table was a studio portrait of Mrs. Bell as a young woman. She had been striking rather than beautiful, with her high forehead, Roman nose, and wide mouth.

Lined up against the nearest wall were four cardboard boxes, all spilling over with gloves, bags, and scarves. Mrs. Bell asked me to start with these. So, while she sat on the bed, I knelt on the floor and quickly went through them.

"These are all lovely," I said. "Especially these silk squares here— I adore this Liberty one with the fuchsia pattern. This is smart . . ." I pulled out a boxy little Gucci handbag with bamboo handles. "And I like these two hats. What a pretty hatbox," I added, looking at the hexagonal box the hats were stored in, with its pattern of spring flowers on a black background. "What I'll do today," I went on as Mrs. Bell walked, with visible effort, towards the wardrobe, "is offer you a price for those clothes I'd like to buy. If you're happy with it, I'll write you a check now, but I won't take anything until the check's cleared. Does that sound all right?"

"It sounds *fine,*" Mrs. Bell replied. "So..." She opened the wardrobe and I caught the scent of Ma Griffe. "Please go ahead. The clothes for consideration are in the left-hand section here, but please don't touch anything beyond this yellow evening dress."

I nodded, then began to pull out the clothes on their pretty satin hangers, laying them in "yes" and "no" piles on the bed. For the most part, the things were in very good condition. There were nipped-in suits from the fifties, geometric coats and shifts from the sixties—including a Thea Porter orange velvet tunic and a wonderful candy-pink raw-silk Guy Laroche "cocoon" coat with elbow-length sleeves. There were romantic smocked dresses from the seventies and a number of shoulder-padded suits from the 1980s. There were some labels—Norman Hartnell, Jean Muir, Pierre Cardin, Missoni, and Hardy Amies Boutique.

"You have some lovely evening wear," I remarked as I looked at a Chanel sapphire-blue silk-faille evening coat from the mid-sixties. "This is wonderful."

"I wore that to the premiere of *You Only Live Twice,*" said Mrs. Bell. "Alastair's agency had done some of the advertising for the film."

"Did you meet Sean Connery?"

Mrs. Bell's face lit up. "Not only did I meet him—I *danced* with him at the after-film party."

"Wow...And this is gorgeous." I pulled out an Ossie Clark chiffon maxidress with a pattern of cream-and-pink florets.

"I adore that dress," she said dreamily. "I have many happy memories of it."

I felt in the left-hand seam. "And here's the tiny trademark pocket that Ossie Clark put in each one. Just big enough for a five-pound note—"

"And a key," Mrs. Bell concluded. "A charming idea."

There was also quite a bit of Jaeger, which I told her I wouldn't be taking.

"I've hardly worn it."

"It's not that—it's because it's not old enough to qualify as vintage. I don't have anything in the shop that's later than the early eighties."

Mrs. Bell fingered the sleeve of an aquamarine wool suit. "I don't know what I'll do with it, then."

"They're lovely things—surely you could still wear them?"

She gave a little shrug. "I rather doubt it."

I looked at the labels—size 12—and realised that Mrs. Bell was at least two sizes smaller than when she'd bought these clothes, but then people do shrink in old age.

"If you'd like any of them altered, I could take them to my seamstress for you," I suggested. "She's very good, and her charges are fair. In fact, I have to go there tomorrow, so—"

"Thank you," Mrs. Bell interjected, shaking her head, "but I have enough to wear. I no longer need very much. They can go to the charity shop."

Now I pulled out a chocolate-brown crêpe de Chine evening dress with shoestring straps, edged in copper sequins. "This is by Ted Lapidus, isn't it?"

"That's right. My husband bought it for me in Paris."

"Is that where you're from?"

She shook her head. "I grew up in Avignon." So that explained the lavender-field painting and the Provençal curtains. "It said in that newspaper interview that you go to Avignon sometimes."

"I do. I buy things from the weekend markets in the area."

"I think that's why I decided to phone you," she said. "I was somehow drawn to that connection. What sort of things do you buy?"

"Old French linen, cotton dresses and nightgowns, broderie anglaise vests. They're popular with young women here. I love going to Avignon—in fact, I'll need to go again soon." I pulled out a black-

and-gold silk-moiré evening gown by Janice Wainwright. "And how long have you lived in London?"

"Almost sixty-one years."

I looked at Mrs. Bell. "You must have been so young when you came here."

She nodded wistfully. "I was nineteen. And now I am seventy-nine. *How* did that happen?" She looked at me as though she genuinely thought I might know, then shook her head and sighed.

"And what brought you to the U.K.?" I asked as I began looking through a box of shoes. She had neat little feet, and the shoes, mostly by Rayne and Gina Fratini, were in excellent condition.

"What brought me to the U.K.?" Mrs. Bell smiled. "A man—or more precisely, an Englishman."

"And how did you meet him?"

"In Avignon—not quite '*sur le pont,*' but close by. I had just left school and was working as a waitress in a smart café on the place Crillon. And this attractive man called me over to his table and said, in atrocious French, that he was *desperate* for a *proper* cup of English tea and could I *please* make him one? So I did—to his satisfaction, evidently, because three months later we were engaged." She nodded at the photo on the bedside table. "That's Alastair. He was a lovely man."

"He was very good-looking."

"Thank you." She smiled. "He was *un bel homme.*"

"But didn't you mind leaving your home?"

There was a little pause. "Not really," Mrs. Bell replied. "Nothing felt the same after the war. Avignon had suffered occupation and bombing. I had lost . . ." She fiddled with her gold watch. "Friends. I was in need of a new start, and then I met Alastair . . ." She ran her hand over the skirt of a damson plum-coloured gabardine two-piece. "I adore this suit," she murmured. "It reminds me so much of my early life with him."

"How long were you married?"

"Forty-two years. But that is why I moved to this flat. We'd had a very nice house on the other side of the Heath, but I couldn't bear to stay there after he . . ." She paused for a moment to collect herself.

"And what did he do?"

"Alastair started his own advertising agency—one of the first. It was an exciting time; he did a lot of business entertaining, so I had to look . . . presentable."

"You must have looked fantastic." She smiled. "And did you—do you—have a family?"

"Children?" Mrs. Bell fiddled with her wedding ring, which was loose on her finger. "We were rather unfortunate," she said softly.

As the subject was clearly painful, I steered the conversation back to her clothes, indicating the ones I wished to buy. "But you must only sell them if you're truly happy to do so," I added. "I don't want you to have any regrets."

"Regrets?" Mrs. Bell echoed. "I have many. But I will *not* regret parting with these garments. I would like them to go on and—how did you put it in that newspaper article—have a new life."

Now I began to go through my suggested prices for each piece.

"Excuse me." I looked up at Mrs. Bell. From her hesitant demeanour I thought she was about to query one of my valuations. "Please forgive me for asking," she said, "but . . . your friend . . . Emma. I hope you don't mind . . ."

"No," I murmured, aware that, for some reason, I didn't mind.

"What happened to her? Why did she . . ." Her voice trailed away.

I lowered the dress I was holding, my heart thudding, as it always does when I recall the events of that night. "She'd become ill," I replied carefully. "No one realised quite how ill she was, and by the time any of us did realise, it was too late. . . . So I spend a large part of each day wishing that I could turn back the clock." Mrs. Bell was shaking her head with an expression of intense sympathy, as though she was somehow entangled in my sadness. "As I can't do that," I went on, clearing my throat, "I have to find a way of living with what happened. But it's hard." I stood up. "I've seen all the clothes now, Mrs. Bell. There's just that one last dress there."

From down the corridor I could hear the telephone ringing. "Please excuse me," she said.

As I heard her retreating footsteps I went to the wardrobe and took out the final garment—the yellow evening dress. The sleeveless bodice was of a lemon-coloured raw silk. The skirt was of knife-pleated chiffon. But as I pulled the dress out I found my eye drawn to the garment hanging alongside it—a blue woollen coat. I peered at it through its protective cover and saw that it wasn't an adult's coat but a child's.

"Thank you for letting me know," I heard Mrs. Bell say as she concluded her phone call. "I wasn't expecting to hear from you until next week . . . I saw Mr. Tate this morning . . . Yes, that remains my decision . . . I do understand, perfectly . . . Thank you for calling . . ."

As Mrs. Bell's voice carried down the hall, I wondered why she would have a girl's coat hanging in her wardrobe. The garment had clearly been cherished. A tragic explanation flashed into my mind. Mrs. Bell *had* had a child—a girl—and this coat had been hers; something awful had happened to her and of course Mrs. Bell couldn't bear to part with it. She hadn't said that she hadn't *had* any children—only that she and her husband had been "rather unfortunate"—very likely an understatement. I felt a wave of sympathy for Mrs. Bell. But then, as I furtively unzipped the clear plastic cover to look at the coat more closely, I realised that it was much too old to fit my scenario. As I lifted it off the rail I saw that it was from the 1940s and was of woollen worsted with a reused silk lining. It had been hand-made with considerable skill.

Hearing footsteps, I quickly zipped up the cover, but too late: Mrs. Bell saw me holding the coat and flinched.

"I am not disposing of that particular garment. Kindly put it back, Miss Swift." Surprised by her icy tone, I did. "I did ask you not to look at anything beyond the yellow evening dress," she added as she stood in the doorway.

"I'm sorry." My face went hot with shame. "Was the coat yours?" I added quietly.

Mrs. Bell hesitated, then came back into the room. I heard her sigh. "My mother made it for me. It was in February 1943. I was thirteen. She stood in line for five hours to buy the fabric, and it took her three weeks to make. She was rather proud of it," she added as she sat on the bed again.

"I'm not surprised—it's beautifully sewn. But you've kept it for . . . sixty-five years?" What had motivated her to do so? I wondered—pure sentimentality, because it had been made by her mother?

"I have kept it for sixty-five years," Mrs. Bell reiterated quietly. "And I will keep it until I die."

I glanced at it again. "It's in amazing condition. It looks almost unworn."

"That's because it *is* almost unworn. I told my mother that I had lost it. But I hadn't—I had only hidden it."

"You hid your winter coat? During the war? But . . . why?"

Mrs. Bell looked out the window. Then she said, "Because there was someone who needed it far more than I did. I kept it for that person, and I have been keeping it for her ever since." She heaved another profound sigh; it seemed to come from her very depths. "It's a story I have never told anyone—not even my husband." She glanced at me. "But lately I *have* felt the need to tell it . . . just to one person. If just *one* person in this world could hear my story, and tell me that they understand, then I would feel . . . But now . . ." She lifted her hand to her temple, then closed her eyes. "I am tired now."

"Of course. I'm sorry. I'll go." I heard the carriage clock in the sitting room chime five-thirty. "I didn't mean to stay for so long. I've really enjoyed talking to you. I'll just put everything back in the wardrobe."

I hung up on the left side the clothes that I intended to buy, then I wrote a check for £800. As I gave it to her, Mrs. Bell shrugged as though it was of no interest.

"Thank you for letting me see your things, Mrs. Bell. They're lovely. I'll phone you next Monday, to arrange a time for me to collect everything, if that's okay?" She nodded. "Can I do anything for you before I go?"

"No. Thank you, my dear. But I would be grateful if you could let yourself out."

"Of course. So"—I held out my hand—"I'll see you next week then, Mrs. Bell."

"Next week," she echoed. She looked at me, then suddenly clasped my hand in hers. "I look forward to it—*very* much."

Four

This morning as I drove to see my seamstress, Val, in an unexpected drizzle my mind kept returning to the little blue coat. It was sky-blue—the blue of freedom—yet it had been hidden away. Crawling up Shooter's Hill Road in nose-to-tail traffic, I tried to imagine what the reason might be. Sometimes—and now I remembered my mother's remark about sartorial archaeology—I can work out a garment's history from the way it's been worn. When I was at Sotheby's, for example, someone brought me three dresses by Mary Quant. They were all in good condition, except that each had a threadbare patch on the right sleeve. The woman who'd brought them in told me that they had belonged to her aunt, a novelist, who wrote all her books in long-hand. A pair of Margaret Howell linen trousers with a worn left hip had been owned by a model who'd had three babies in the space of four years. But now, as I flicked on the windscreen wipers, I could come up with no theory for Mrs. Bell's coat. Who, in the winter of 1943, had needed it more than she did? And why had Mrs. Bell never told the story to anyone—not even her adored husband?

I hadn't mentioned the coat to Annie when she'd arrived for work this morning. I'd simply said that I'd be buying quite a few things from Mrs. Bell.

"Is that why you're going to your seamstress?" she asked as she refolded the knitwear. "To have some of them altered?"

"No. I've got some repairs to collect. Val phoned me last night." I picked up my car keys. "She doesn't like things hanging around once they're done."

Val, who'd been recommended to me by Pippa at the Moon Daisy Café, is extremely quick and very reasonable. She is also a dressmaking genius. She can restore even a wrecked garment to its former glory.

By the time I parked outside her house on Granby Road the drizzle had become pelting rain. I peered through the misted windscreen and watched the raindrops bounce off the hood like ball bearings. I'd need my umbrella just to get to Val's porch.

She opened the door with a tape measure slung round her neck and her pointy little face folded into a smile. Then she noticed my umbrella and looked at it suspiciously. "You won't put that up in here, will you?"

"Of course not," I replied as I lowered it. Standing on the steps, I gave it a good shake, then stepped inside. "I know you think it would be—"

"Unlucky." Val shook her head. "It *would* be—especially as it's black."

"Is black worse?"

"Much worse. And you won't drop it on the floor, will you?" she added anxiously.

"No, but why not?"

"Because if you drop a brolly, it means there'll be a murder in the house in the near future, and I'd rather avoid it, especially as my husband's been driving me up the wall lately. I don't want to—"

"Push your luck?" I teased as I placed the umbrella in her stand.

"Exactly."

Val is short, sharp, and thin—like a pin. She is also superstitious to the point of obsession. It isn't just that she—by her own admission—salutes solitary magpies left, right, and centre, bows to the full moon, and strenuously avoids greeting black cats. She has an encyclopaedic knowledge of superstition and folklore. In the four months that I've known her I have discovered that it's unlucky to eat a fish from the tail towards the head, to try and count the stars, or to wear pearls on your wedding day. It's unlucky to drop your comb while doing your hair—it portends disappointment—or to stick knitting needles through balls of yarn.

On the other hand it's *lucky* to find a nail, to eat an apple on Christmas Eve, and to accidentally put a garment on inside out.

"Right then," Val said as we went into her sewing room, every surface of which was stacked with shoe boxes brimming with cotton reels and zippers, sewing patterns, cards of ribbon, swatches of fabric, and spools of bias binding. She reached under the table and produced a large shopping bag. "I think these have come up quite nicely," she said as she handed it to me.

I pulled out the garments. They had. A maxi-length Halston coat with a ripped hemline had been shortened to midcalf; a fifties cocktail dress with perspiration stains had had the arms cut out so that it was now elegantly sleeveless; and an Yves Saint Laurent silk jacket, which had been sprayed with what looked like champagne, was now speckled with bright sequins to cover the stains. I'd have to point out these alterations to prospective buyers, but at least the clothes had been saved. They were much too beautiful to be thrown away.

"They've come up brilliantly, Val," I said as I reached for my purse to pay her. "You're amazing."

"Well, my gran taught me to sew; and she always said that if there's a fault on a garment, then don't just mend it—make a *virtue* of it. I can still hear her saying it to me now: 'Make a *virtue* of it, Valerie.' *Oh.*" She'd knocked her scissors off the table and was staring at them with a look of insane happiness. "*That's* great."

"What is?"

"They've landed with both points sticking into the floor." She stooped to pick them up. "That's *really* good luck," she explained, waving them at me. "It means that more work's coming into the household."

"It is." I told her that I was buying a collection of clothes and that at least eight of the garments would need minor repairs.

"Bring them in," Val said as I handed her the money I owed her. "Thanking you. Ooh . . ." She peered at my jacket. "That bottom button's a bit loose—let me fix it for you before you go."

Suddenly the doorbell rang three times in quick succession.

"Val?" called a gravelly voice. "You there?"

"That's my neighbour Maggie," Val explained as I took off my jacket and handed it to her. She threaded a needle. "She always rings three times to let me know it's her. I leave the door on the latch as we're forever popping in and out of each other's houses. We're in the sewing room, Mags!"

"Thought you would be! Hiya!" A woman was standing in the doorway, almost filling it. She was the physical opposite of Val—big, blond, and spready. She wore tight black leather trousers, gold stilettos, the sides of which struggled to contain her plump feet, and a low-cut red top, which displayed a massive, if somewhat crêpey, cleavage. She was also wearing tawny-toned foundation, bright blue eyeliner, and false lashes. As for her age, she could have been anywhere between thirty-eight and fifty. She exuded the scent of Magie Noire mingled with cigarettes.

"Hi, Mags," said Val. "This is Hoebe," she added through gritted teeth as she bit the end of the cotton thread. "Phoebe's just opened a vintage dress shop over in Blackheath, haven't you, Phoebe. By the way," she added to me, "I hope you put salt on the doorstep like I told you to. It helps protect against misfortune."

I'd had so much misfortune it would have made no difference, I reflected. "I can't say I did do that, no."

Val shrugged as she put a rubber thimble on her middle finger. "Don't say I didn't warn you." She began to restitch the button. "So how's it going then, Mags?"

Mags sank into a chair, evidently exhausted. "I've just had *the* most difficult client. For ages he refused to get started—he just wanted to talk; then he took forever about it, and afterwards he was tricky about paying because he wanted to write a check and I said it's cash or nothing, as I had made *quite* clear beforehand." She rearranged her breasts indignantly. "When I said I'd call the cops he produced the money quick enough. I couldn't half do with a cup of something though, Val—I'm beat and it's only half eleven."

"Put the kettle on then," said Val.

Mags disappeared into the kitchen, her nicotine rasp carrying down the passageway. "Then I had this other customer. He had this weird thing about his mother, he'd even brought one of her dresses with him. *Super* demanding, he was. I did what I could for him, but he then had the cheek to say that he was 'dissatisfied' with my 'services.' Imagine!"

The probable nature of Maggie's business was by now clear.

"You poor sweetheart," said Val warmly as Mags reappeared with a box of cookies. "Those punters of yours don't half take it out of you."

Mags heaved a long-suffering sigh. "You can say that again." She took out a cookie and bit into it. "Then to cap it all, I had that woman at number twenty-nine—Sheila Whatsit. She was a real nuisance. Wanted to get in touch with her ex-husband. He'd dropped dead on the golf course last month. She said she felt so bad about how she'd treated him when they were married that she couldn't sleep. So I get through to him, right"—Mags sprawled in the chair—"and I begin passing on his messages to her, but within two minutes she's furious with him about something and starts screaming and shrieking at him like a bagful of cats—"

"I think I heard her through the wall," Val remarked evenly as she pulled the thread taut. "Sounded like a real banshee."

"You're telling me," agreed Mags as she flicked crumbs off her lap. "So I said, 'Look, sweetheart, you really shouldn't *talk* to dead people like that. It's disrespectful.'"

"So . . . you're a medium?" I asked bewildered.

"A medium?" Maggie looked at me so seriously that I thought I'd offended her. "No, I'm *not* a medium," she said. "I'm a *large!*" At that, she and Val hooted with laughter. "Sorry," Maggie said with a snort. "I can never resist that one." She wiped away a tear with a scarlet talon. "But to answer your question"—she patted her banana-yellow hair— "I *am* a medium, or clairvoyant, *yes.*"

"I've never met a medium before."

"Never?"

"No. But—"

"*There* you are, Phoebe—all done!" Val snipped the end of the thread, deftly wound it round the shank five or six times, and handed the jacket back to me. "So when do you want to bring the other garments over?"

"Well, probably a week from today, as I have help in the shop on Mondays and Tuesdays." I put the jacket back on. "Will you be here if I come at the same time?"

"I'm always here," Val replied wearily. "No rest for the wicked."

I looked at Maggie. "So . . . I'm . . . just wondering . . ." My pulse was racing. "Someone very close to me died recently. I was very fond of . . . this person. I miss them . . ." Maggie nodded sympathetically. "And . . . I've never ever done this before and in fact I've always been sceptical—but if I could just talk to them, if only for a few seconds, or *hear* something from them," I went on anxiously. "I've even looked up a few psychics in the Yellow Pages—there's this thing called 'Dial-a-Medium'; and I actually selected one and even called the number but then I couldn't bring myself to speak because I felt so embarrassed, but now that I've met *you* I feel I—"

"Do you want a reading?" Maggie interjected patiently. "Is that what you're trying to tell me, sweetheart?"

I sighed with relief. "It is."

She reached into her cleavage and pulled out first a pack of cigarettes, then a little black diary. She slid the tiny pen out of its spine, licked her index finger, and flicked over its pages. "So when shall I put you in for?"

"Well . . . after I've dropped off the things I'm bringing Val?"

"This time next week then?" I nodded. "My terms are fifty quid cash, no refunds for a bad connection—and *no* dissing the deceased," Mags added as she scribbled away. "That's my new rule. So"—she tucked the diary back into her bosom, then opened the pack of cigarettes—"that's a private sitting at eleven A.M. next Tuesday. See you then, sweetheart," she said as I left.

Driving back to Blackheath, I tried to analyse my motives for going to a medium. I'd always regarded such activities with distaste. My grandparents had all died, but I'd never felt the slightest urge to try and contact any of them on "the other side." But since Emma's death I'd increasingly been aware of the desire, somehow, to reach her. Meeting Mags had made me feel that I could at least try.

But what did I hope to get out of the experience? I wondered as I approached Montpelier Vale. A message from Emma, presumably. Saying what? That she was . . . okay? How *could* she be? I reflected as I pulled up outside the shop. She's probably floating around in the ether, bitterly pondering the fact that thanks to her so-called "best friend" she was now never going to get married, have children, go to Peru like she'd always wanted to do, let alone get the Order of the British Empire for services to the fashion industry as we'd often drunkenly predicted. She would now never get to enjoy the prime of her life, or the peaceful retirement that should have followed it, surrounded by her adoring children and grandchildren. That Emma had been deprived of all this was, I reflected bleakly, thanks to me—and to Guy. If only Emma had never *met* Guy, I wished as I parked . . .

"It's been an amazing morning." Annie exclaimed as I stepped into the shop.

"Has it?"

"The Pierre Balmain evening gown has sold—subject to the check clearing, but I doubt there'll be a problem."

"Fabulous," I said. That would help the cash flow.

"And I've sold two of those fifties circle skirts. Plus you know the pale pink Madame Grès—the one you don't want?"

"Yes."

"Well, that woman who tried it on yesterday came back—"

"And?"

"Bought it."

"Great." I clapped my hand to my chest in relief.

Annie looked at me with puzzlement. "Well, yes, it means you've taken in over two thousand pounds and it's still only lunchtime." I couldn't tell Annie that my reaction to the sale of the dress had nothing to do with the money. "The woman's completely the wrong shape for it," she went on as I went through to the office, "but she said she *had* to have it."

For a split second I wrestled with my conscience—the £500 from the sale of the gown would be so useful. But I had vowed to give the money to charity, and that's what I'd do.

Suddenly the bell over the door tinkled. In came the girl who'd tried on the turquoise cupcake dress.

"I'm back," she announced happily.

Annie's face lit up. "I'm delighted," she said with a smile. "The prom dress looked lovely on you." She turned to get it down.

"Oh, I haven't come for that," the girl explained, although she threw the dress a glance that was clearly tinged with regret. "I've come to buy something for my fiancé." She went over to the jewellery display and pointed to the eighteen-carat-gold art deco octagonal cuff links with abalone insets. "I saw Pete looking at these when we were here the other day and thought they'd make a perfect wedding present for him. How much are they?"

"They're a hundred pounds," I replied, "but with the five percent discount that's ninety-five, and there's an additional five percent off as I'm having a good day, so that makes them ninety pounds."

The girl smiled. "Perfect," she said. "Thank you!"

I manned the shop alone for the rest of the week. In between helping customers I assessed clothes that people brought in, photographed stock for the website, processed online orders, did small repairs, talked to dealers, and tried to keep on top of my accounting. I posted the check for Guy's dress to UNICEF, relieved to have no more reminders of our few months together. Gone were the photos, the letters, the e-mails—all deleted—the books, and the most hated reminder of all, the engagement ring. Now, with the dress sold, I breathed a sigh of relief. Guy was finally out of my life.

On Friday morning my father phoned, imploring me to visit him.

"It's been such a long time, Phoebe," he said sadly.

"I'm sorry, Dad. I *should* have come; you see, I've had so much on my mind."

"I know you have, darling, but I'd love to see you; and I'd love you to see Louis again. He's so sweet, Phoebe. He's just . . ." I heard Dad's voice catch. He gets a bit emotional sometimes, but then he's been through a lot, even if it is of his own making. "How about Sunday?" he tried again. "After lunch."

I drew in my breath. "I *could* come then, Dad—but I'd rather not see Ruth—if you'll forgive my honesty."

"I understand," he replied softly. "I know the situation has been hard for you, Phoebe. It's been hard for me, too."

I felt a spark of anger. "I hope you're not appealing for sympathy, Dad."

I heard him sigh. "I don't really deserve it, do I?" I didn't reply. "Anyway," he went on, "Ruth's flying to Libya on Sunday morning for a week's filming, so I thought that might be a good time for you to come over."

"In that case, yes, I will."

. . .

On Friday afternoon, Mimi Long's fashion editor came in and chose some clothes for the *Woman & Home* shoot—a seventies-style spread for the January issue to be called "Ring in the Old." I had just given her the receipt for the things she'd chosen when I looked up and saw Pete the fiancé tearing over the road towards Village Vintage, his tie flapping over his shoulder.

He hurried inside. "I've just dashed here from work," he said, panting. He nodded at the turquoise cupcake dress. "I'll take that." He reached for his wallet. "Carla still hasn't found anything to wear for the party tomorrow and she's in a panic about it and I know that the reason *why* she still hasn't found anything is because she really liked *this* dress and okay, it is a bit pricey, but I want her to have it and to hell with the money." He put six £50 notes on the counter.

"My assistant was right," I said as I folded the dress into a large shopping bag. "You *are* the perfect husband-to-be."

As Pete waited for his change I saw him idly looking at the tray of cuff links. "Those gold-and-abalone cuff links," he said, "the ones you had the other day—I don't suppose—"

"Oh, I'm sorry," I said. "But they've sold."

As Pete left, I looked at the other cupcake dresses arrayed on the wall and wondered who would buy them. I thought of the sad girl who'd looked so lovely in the lime one. I'd seen her standing outside the shop once or twice, looking preoccupied, but she hadn't come in. I'd also seen a photo of her boyfriend in the *South London Times.* He'd been the guest speaker at a Business Network dinner at Blackheath Golf Club. It seemed he owned a successful real estate company, Phoenix Land.

Saturday started badly and only got worse. First, the shop was very busy, and although I was happy about this, it was as much as I could do to keep an eye on the stock. Then someone came in eating a sandwich so I had to ask her to leave, which I disliked doing, especially in front of other customers. Then Mum phoned, clearly needing a bit of a cheer-up.

"I've decided not to have Botox," she declared.

"That's great, Mum. You don't need it."

"That's not the point. The clinic I went to said I've left it too late for Botox to make any difference."

"Then . . . Never mind."

"So I'm going to have gold threads in my face instead."

"You're what?"

"Basically they insert these gold threads under your skin, and on the ends of them are these tiny hooks, which they catch up so that the thread pulls taut—and up comes your face with it! The trouble is, it costs four thousand pounds. But then it is twenty-four-carat . . . ," she mused.

"Don't even *think* about it," I said. "You're still very attractive, Mum."

"Am I?" She said it mournfully. "Ever since your father left me, I've felt like a gargoyle."

"Nothing could be further from the truth." In fact, like many dumped wives, Mum had never looked better. She'd lost weight, bought some new clothes, and was now far better groomed than when she was with Dad.

Then at lunchtime the woman who'd bought Guy's dress came back with it.

At first I didn't know who she was.

"I'm *so* sorry," she began as she lifted a Village Vintage bag onto the counter. I looked inside it and my spirits sank. "I don't think the dress is right after all." How could she ever have thought that it was? As Annie had said, the woman was completely the wrong shape, being short and broad, like a loaf of bread. "I'm *so* sorry," she repeated as I took the dress out of the bag.

"Don't worry, it's not a problem," I lied. As I refunded her the money, I wished I hadn't been quite so quick in sending the £500 to UNICEF. It was now a donation that I couldn't afford.

"I guess I got carried away with the romance of it," she explained. "But this morning I put on the dress, looked at myself in the mirror, and realised that I'd been, well . . ." She turned up her palms as if to say, *I'm not exactly Keira Knightley, am I!* "I don't have the height," she went on. "But do you know what?" She cocked her head. "I can't help thinking that it would suit *you.*"

After the woman had left, a succession of customers came in, including one fifty-something man who showed an unhealthy interest in the corsets; he even wanted to try one on, but I wouldn't let him. Then a woman phoned offering me some furs that had belonged to her aunt, including—and this was meant to be the clincher—a hat made out of a leopard cub. I explained that I don't sell fur, but the woman insisted that as these particular furs were *vintage* there shouldn't be a problem. So I told her that I can't bring myself to touch let alone deal in bits of dead baby leopard, however long it might have been since the poor creature had been murdered. Next my patience was tested again when a woman came in with a Dior coat that she wanted to sell me. I could see at a glance that it was fake.

"It *is* by Dior," she protested after I'd pointed this out to her. "And I'd call one hundred pounds a *very* reasonable price for a genuine Christian Dior coat of this quality."

"I'm sorry," I said. "But I've worked in vintage fashion for twelve years, and I can assure you that this coat is not by Dior."

"But the label—"

"The label *is* original. But it's been sewn into a non-Dior garment. The interior construction of the coat is all wrong, the seams aren't finished properly, and the lining, if you look a little more closely, is by Burberry." I pointed to the logo.

The woman flushed the colour of a Victoria plum. "*I* know what you're trying to do," she sniffed. "You're trying to get it at a bargain-basement price, so that you can sell it for five hundred pounds like that one you've got over there." She nodded at a mannequin on which I'd put a Dior emerald-green New Look winter coat from 1955 in pristine condition.

"I'm not trying to 'get' it at all," I explained pleasantly. "I don't want it."

The woman, bristling with affected indignation, stuffed the coat back into the bag. "Then I shall have to take it elsewhere."

"That's a good idea," I replied calmly, resisting the temptation to suggest Oxfam.

The woman turned on her heel, and as she stomped out, another customer, on his way in, politely held the door open for her. He was elegantly dressed in pale chinos and a navy blazer. I felt my heart lurch.

"Good God!" Mr. Pinstripe's face had lit up. "If it isn't my bidding rival—Phoebe!" So he'd remembered my name. "Don't tell me—is this *your* shop?"

"Yes." The euphoria I'd felt on seeing him instantly evaporated as the door opened again and in came Mrs. Pinstripe on a cloud of perfume. As I'd imagined, she was tall and blond—but so young that I had to fight the urge to call the police. She *couldn't* be his wife, I decided as she pushed her sunglasses on top of her head. She was his twenty-five-year-old mistress, and he was her sugar daddy—the man was brazen. Her scent—J'adore—made me feel queasy.

"I'm Miles," he reminded me. "Miles Archant."

"I remember." I forced a pleasant tone. "And what brings you here?" I added, trying not to look askance at his companion, who was now riffling through the evening wear. He nodded at the girl. "Roxy . . ." Of course. A suitably sexy name for a mistress. Foxy Roxy. "My daughter."

"Ah." The wave of relief I felt astonished me.

"Roxanne's looking for a special dress to wear for a teenagers' charity ball at the National History Museum, aren't you, Rox?" She nodded. "This is Phoebe," he added. As the girl gave me a tepid smile I could now see how young she was. "We met at Christie's," her father explained. "Phoebe bought that white dress you liked."

"Oh," she said resentfully.

I looked at Miles. "You were bidding for the Madame Grès for . . . ?" I indicated Roxy.

"Yes. She saw it on the Christie's website and fell in love with it—

didn't you, darling? She couldn't come to the auction because she
was at school."

"What a shame."

"Yeah," said Roxy. "It clashed with English class."

So it was *Roxy* who'd been giving Miles such a hard time at the
auction. Why would anyone be prepared to spend nearly £4,000 on
a dress for a teenager?

"Roxanne wants to work in fashion," Miles explained. "She's extremely interested in vintage clothing—aren't you, darling?"

Roxanne nodded again, looking bored. As she browsed through
the items on the racks I wondered where her mother was and what
she looked like. The same, I imagined, only in her mid-forties.

"Anyway, we're still looking," Miles told me. "That's why we've
come here. The ball isn't until November, but we happened to be in
Blackheath, and we saw this shop had opened . . ." I saw Roxy give
her father a quizzical glance. "So we thought we'd take a look and we
find—*you*! An unexpected bonus," he added.

"Thank you," I said, wondering what his wife would think if she
could see him chatting to me in such a blatantly friendly fashion.

"An amazing coincidence," he concluded.

I turned to Roxanne. "So what sort of things do you like?" I asked,
trying to keep things professional.

"Well . . ." She pushed her Ray-Bans a little higher on her head. "I
thought something a bit *Atonementy* or—what was that other film?—
Gosford Parky."

"I see . . . So that's mid- to late thirties then. Bias cut. In the style
of Madeleine Vionnet . . . ," I mused as I went up to the evening-wear
rack.

Roxy shrugged. "S'pose . . ." It cynically occurred to me that there
might be an opportunity here to get rid of Guy's dress. Then I realised that Roxy was too slim for it—it would hang off her.

"See anything you like, darling?" her father asked.

She shook her head, and her hair, a hank of blond silk, swished
around her slender shoulders. Suddenly her mobile phone rang—

what was that ring tone? Oh yes. It was "The Most Beautiful Girl in the World."

"Hi there," Roxy drawled. "No. With my dad. In some vintage dress shop...Last night? Yeah...Mahiki's. It was cool. Yeah. Cool...Then it got hot...*Really* hot. Yeah. Cool..." I felt like checking the thermostat.

"Do take that call outside, darling," her father said. Roxy shouldered her Prada bag and pushed open the door, then she stood outside, leaning against the glass, one coltish leg crossed in front of the other. Her "conversation" was clearly not going to be brief.

Miles rolled his eyes in mock despair. "Teenagers..." He smiled indulgently, then began to look round the shop. "What lovely things you have here."

"Thanks." I noticed again how attractive his voice was—it had this slight break in it that I found somehow touching. "Do you know, I might buy a pair of those suspenders."

I opened the counter and took out the tray. "They're from the 1950s," I explained. "They're unsold stock, so they've never been worn. They're by Albert Thurston, who made top-quality English suspenders." I pointed to the straps. "You can see that the leather is hand-stitched."

Miles peered at them. "I'll have these," he said, picking out a green-and-white striped pair. "How much are they?"

"Fifteen pounds."

He looked at me. "I'll give you twenty."

"I'm sorry?"

"Twenty-five then."

I laughed. "You *what*?"

"Okay, I'm prepared to go up to thirty pounds, if you're going to be hard-nosed about it, but that's *it*."

I smiled. "It's not an auction—I'm afraid you'll just have to pay the asking price."

"You drive a hard bargain," Miles muttered. "In that case, I'll have the navy pair too." As I put them both in a bag I was aware that

Miles was scrutinising me and I felt my face go warm. I was surprised to find myself wishing that he wasn't married. "I enjoyed bidding against you the other day," I heard him say as I opened the register. "I don't suppose you felt the same, though."

"No, I didn't," I replied pleasantly. "In fact, I was rather furious with you. But as you were prepared to pay so much for the dress I assumed that you were trying to get it for your wife."

Miles shook his head. "I don't have one." Ah. So he lived with someone—or maybe he was an unmarried father or a divorced dad. "My wife died."

"Oh." My euphoria returned, to my shame. "I'm sorry."

Miles shrugged. "It's all right—in the sense that it happened ten years ago," he added. "So I've had plenty of time to get used to it."

"Ten years?" I echoed wonderingly. Here was a man who hadn't married again in a whole *decade*? Let alone the week after his wife's funeral, as so many widowers do. I felt my frostiness thaw.

"At home it's just Roxy and me. She's just started at Bellingham College." I'd heard of it—an upmarket crammer. "Can I ask you something?"

I handed him his receipt. "Of course."

"I just wondered . . ." He cast an anxious glance at Roxanne, but she was still chatting away, twirling a white-blond tendril around her finger. "I just wondered whether you'd . . . have dinner with me sometime . . ."

"Oh . . ."

"I'm sure you think I'm too old," he went on quickly. "But I'd love to see you again, Phoebe. In fact—can I confess something?"

"What?" I admit it: I was intrigued.

"It isn't *entirely* due to coincidence that I'm here. In fact, to be perfectly honest, coincidence has *nothing* to do with it."

I stared at him. "But . . . how did you know where I was?"

"Because as you were paying for the dress at Christie's I heard you say 'Village Vintage.' So I Googled you there and then, and up came your website." So *that's* what he was looking at so intently on his

BlackBerry as he sat next to me! "As I don't live far away—in Camberwell—I thought I'd just drop in and say . . . hi." So his honesty had triumphed over his cunning. I smiled to myself. "Now . . ." He shrugged in a good-natured way. "You didn't want to have lunch with me the other day—or even a coffee. You probably thought I was married."

"I did think that. Yes."

"But now that you know that I'm not, I wonder whether you might like to have dinner with me?"

"I . . . don't know." I felt the flush on my face deepen.

Miles glanced at his daughter, still talking on her cell phone. "You don't have to say now. Here . . ." He opened his wallet and took out his business card. I glanced at it. *Miles Archant LLB, Senior Partner, Archant, Brewer & Clark, Solicitors.* "Just let me know if you're tempted."

I suddenly realised that I *was.* Miles was very attractive, and he had this lovely husky voice—and he was a real grown-up, I reflected, unlike so many men of my own age. *Like Dan,* I suddenly found myself thinking, with his unruly hair and his ill-matching clothes, and his pencil sharpener and his . . . *shed.* Why would I want to go and see Dan's *shed*? I looked at Miles. He was a man, not an overgrown boy. But on the other hand, I now reflected as reality took hold, he was a virtual stranger, and, yes, he was much older than me— forty-three or -four.

"I'm forty-eight," he said, as if he'd read my mind. "Don't look so shocked!"

"Oh, sorry, I'm not, it's just that . . . you don't look that . . ."

"Old?" he finished wryly.

"That's not what I meant. It's really nice of you to ask me, but to be honest I *am* pretty busy at the moment." I began rearranging the scarves. "And I have to focus on my business," I floundered on. *Forty-eight.* Nearly *fifty* . . . "And the thing is—oh." The phone was ringing. "Excuse me." I picked up the handset, grateful for the interruption. "Village Vintage."

"Phoebe?" At the sound of the voice, my heart was suddenly pounding in my chest. "Please speak to me, Phoebe," said Guy. "I must speak to you. You've ignored all my letters and—"

"That's . . . right," I interrupted quietly, struggling to control my emotions in front of Miles, who was now sitting on the sofa, gazing out at the Blackheath cloudscape. I closed my eyes and took a deep breath.

"I need to *talk* to you," Guy insisted. "I refuse to let things be left like this, and I'm not going to give up until I've got you to—"

"I'm sorry, I can't help you," I said with a calmness I did not feel. "But thank you for calling." I put down the phone without a scintilla of guilt. Guy knew what he'd done.

You know how Emma exaggerates, Phoebe.

I switched the phone over to silent mode. "I'm sorry," I said to Miles. "What were you saying?"

"Well . . ." He stood up. "I was just telling you that I'm . . . forty-eight, and that if you were prepared to overlook that handicap, I'd be delighted if you'd have dinner with me sometime. But it doesn't sound as though you'd want to." He gave me an anxious smile.

"Actually, Miles . . . I *would*."

Five

On Sunday afternoon I made my way over to Dad's—or, more accurately, to Ruth's. Although I'd met her—once—for about ten seconds—this would be the first time I'd set foot in her flat. I'd asked Dad if we could meet on neutral territory, but he said that because of Louis it would be easier if I could come and see him "at home."

"At home..." I reflected as I walked down Portobello. All my life "home" had been the Edwardian villa in which I'd grown up and in which my mother, for the time being, still lives. The idea that home, for Dad, was now a smart duplex in Notting Hill with the hatchet-faced Ruth and their baby son was still impossible to grasp. Going there would make it all depressingly real.

Dad simply wasn't a Notting Hill kind of person, I thought as I passed the fashionable boutiques of Westbourne Grove. What did L. K. Bennett or Ralph Lauren mean to my father? He belonged in friendly, old-fashioned Blackheath.

Ever since the separation, Dad had had this slightly stunned expression on his face, as though he's just been slapped by a stranger.

That was how he looked now, as he opened the door of number 88 Lancaster Road.

"Phoebe!" Dad bent to hug me, but it was hard to do with Louis in his arms. The baby got squished between us and squawked. "It's so lovely to see you." He ushered me inside. "Oh, would you mind taking your shoes off—it's the rule here." No doubt one of many, I thought as I removed my sling-backs and tucked them under a chair. "I've missed you, Phoebe," he said as I followed him down the limestone-tiled hallway into the kitchen.

"I've missed you too, Dad." I stroked Louis's blond head as he sat in Dad's arms at the brushed stainless-steel table. "*You've* changed, sweetie."

Louis had morphed from a wrinkled, liver-coloured scrap of flesh into the sweet-faced infant who was waving his bendy little limbs at me like a baby octopus.

I glanced at all the gleaming metal surfaces. Ruth's kitchen struck me as far too hygienic an environment for a man who'd spent most of his professional life grubbing around in the dirt. It didn't even look like a kitchen—it resembled a morgue. I thought of the old scrubbed-pine table at *real* home, and the stacks of Portmeirion Botanic Garden crockery. What the hell was my dad doing *here*?

I smiled at him. "Louis looks like you."

"Do you think so?" said Dad happily.

I didn't, but I didn't want Louis to look like Ruth. I opened the Hamley's bag I'd been carrying and handed Dad a big white bear with a blue ribbon round its neck.

"*Thank* you." He jiggled the teddy in front of Louis. "Isn't this lovely, sweetie? Oh look, Phoebe, he's smiling at it."

I stroked the baby's plump little legs. "Don't you think Louis should be wearing more than just a diaper, Dad?"

"Oh yes," he replied vaguely. "I was just changing him when you arrived. Now *where* did I put his clothes? Ah. Here we go." I watched, appalled, as Dad clamped a surprised-looking Louis to his chest with his left arm, then somehow slotted his pat little limbs into a stripy blue sleep suit. Having done that, he wrestled him into his stainless-steel high chair, getting two legs jammed down one hole so that Louis was stuck, rigid, in a bobsledding position. Dad then went to the gleaming American fridge and took out an assortment of small jars.

"Let's see," he said, unscrewing the first. "I'm getting him onto solids," he explained over his shoulder. "We'll try this one, shall we, Louis?" Louis opened his mouth wide, like a baby bird, and Dad began to spoon the contents of the jar into it. "*What* a good boy. Well *done,* my little boy. *Oh . . .*" Louis spat a mouthful of beige mush at Dad.

"I don't think he likes it," I remarked as Dad wiped what I now knew to be organic chicken-and-lentil casserole off his glasses.

"Sometimes he does." Dad grabbed a washcloth and wiped Louis's chin. "He's in a funny mood today—probably because his mum's away again. We'll try this one now, shall we, Louis?"

"Aren't you supposed to heat it up first, Dad?"

"Oh, he doesn't mind it straight from the fridge." Dad opened the second jar. "Moroccan lamb with apricots and couscous—yum." Louis opened his tiny mouth again, and Dad ladled a few teaspoons into it. "Oh, he likes *this,*" he said triumphantly. "Definitely."

Suddenly Louis extruded his tongue, expelling the Moroccan lamb in an orange dribble that now flowed down his front like lava.

"You should have put a bib on him," I pointed out as Dad scraped the ejecta off Louis's chest. "No, Dad. Don't put it back in his mouth!" On the table was a leaflet called "You Can Wean Your Child!"

"I'm not much good at this," Dad said miserably. He tossed the rejected jar into the gleaming chrome trash bin. "It was so much easier when I could just give him a bottle."

"I'd help you, Dad, but I'm clueless myself—for obvious reasons. But why do *you* have to do so much child care?"

"Well . . . because Ruth's away again," he answered wearily. "She's very busy at the moment, and the thing is, I *want* to do it. There's no point paying a nanny now that"—Dad winced—"I'm not working. Plus, when *you* were a baby I was away so much that I missed out on fatherhood."

"You *were* away a lot," I agreed. "All those field trips and excavations. I always seemed to be waving good-bye to you," I added ruefully.

"I know, darling." He sighed. "And I'm very sorry for it. So now, with this little chap"—he stroked Louis's head—"I feel I've been given the chance to be more of a hands-on father." Louis scrunched up his wet face as though he'd prefer Dad to be hands-off.

Suddenly the phone rang. "Sorry, darling. That'll be Radio Lincoln. I'm doing a telephone interview with them. They called me half an hour ago."

"Radio Lincoln?"

Dad shrugged. "It's better than Radio Silence."

As Dad did the interview, the phone clamped to his ear with his right hand while he dropped more goo into Louis's mouth with his left, I reflected on his calamitous professional fall. Only a year ago Dad was still a widely respected professor of comparative archaeology at Queen Mary's College, London. Then came the Big Dig, and in the wake of the humiliating media coverage—the *Daily Mail* had dubbed him "the Big Pig"—Dad was asked to take early retirement. He'd had five years lopped off his career, had taken a huge cut in his pension, and, despite six weeks of prime-time exposure on Sunday night, his burgeoning TV career had ground to a halt.

"Well, when we ask what archaeology *is,*" Dad said as he shovelled mango-and-lychee purée into Louis, "we might say that it's the study of artefacts and habitation—the discovery of 'lost' civilisations even, using the increasingly sophisticated means that we now have of interpreting past societies, the most important of which is of course carbon dating. *However,* when we say 'civilisation' we should be aware that that is of course a modern definition imposed upon the past from a Western intellectual perspective . . ." He grabbed the grubby washcloth. "Sorry, should I try that again? You did say it's prerecorded, didn't you? Oh, I'm so sorry . . ."

On TV, Dad had come across very well, largely because he'd had a scriptwriter to render his more erudite phrases into homely ones. If it hadn't been for the media uproar about Ruth's pregnancy, perhaps he'd have gotten more TV work, but all he'd been offered since his series ended was *Ready, Steady, Cook!* Ruth's career, on the other hand, had flourished. She'd been promoted to executive producer and was producing a major profile of Colonel Qaddafi, for which she was even now flying to Tripoli.

The front door banged open.

"Can you *believe* it?" I heard Ruth yell. "Effing terrorists closing down Heathrow *again*! Except that it *wasn't* terrorists, was it? No! Of *course* not." She sounded almost disappointed. "Just some loony trying to thumb a lift to Tenerife on the tarmac. Terminal three's been shut down—it took two hours for me and the crew to get out. I'm going to try and get us all on a flight tomorrow. Christ, what a mess you've made in here, darling. And *don't* put shopping bags on the table"—she removed the Hamley's bag—"they carry bacteria. And *no* toys in here, please—it's a kitchen, not a playroom—and do *please* keep the cupboard doors shut as I can't *stand* seeing them open like that— Oh." She'd suddenly noticed me.

"Hello, Ruth," I said calmly. "I've come to see my father." I looked at Dad, who had quickly finished the radio interview and was now frantically tidying up. "I hope you don't mind."

"Not in the least," she replied airily. "Make yourself at home." *That would be hard here,* I was tempted to retort.

"Phoebe brought Louis that lovely teddy bear," Dad said.

"Thank you," said Ruth. "That's very kind." She kissed Louis on the head, ignoring his outstretched arms, then swept upstairs. Louis threw back his head and started to wail.

"Sorry, Phoebe." Dad gave me a baleful smile. "Could we make another date soon?"

. . .

The next morning, as I walked to Village Vintage, I thought about Dad and about how he seemed to have stumbled into an affair with no idea of the turmoil that might follow. It was Mum's belief that he'd never strayed before, despite the opportunities he must have had over the years with attractive archaeology students hanging on his every word as they huddled over the dust together, delightedly scraping up bits of the Phoenicians or the Mesopotamians or the Mayans or whoever it was. The ineptitude with which Dad had handled his relationship with Ruth certainly suggested that he was hardly an experienced adulterer.

After he'd left Mum, Dad had written to me. In his letter he'd said that he still loved Mum, but that once Ruth was pregnant he'd felt he had to stay with her. Then he'd added that he was genuinely fond of Ruth and that I needed to understand that. I couldn't understand it. I still can't.

I could perfectly well see why Ruth would be attracted to my father, despite the twenty-four-year age gap. Dad was one of those tall, handsome, craggy-looking men who'd somehow grown into their faces, added to which he was intelligent, easygoing, and kind. But what did he see in Ruth? She wasn't soft or pretty like my mother had been. She was as hard as a plank—with about as much sensitivity. The trauma of seeing Dad move his things out of the marital home had been made infinitely worse for Mum by the sight of a heavily pregnant Ruth waiting for him, outside, in her car.

Mum and I had sat there that night, trying not to look at the yawning spaces on the shelves where Dad's books and treasures had stood. His most prized artefact, a small bronze of an Aztec woman giving birth—presented to him by the Mexican government—was no longer on the kitchen mantelpiece. Given the circumstances, Mum said she wouldn't miss it.

"If only it wasn't for the *baby*," she'd wept. "I don't want to be mean about a poor little baby that hasn't even been born yet, but I can't help wishing that this *particular* baby had never happened, because if it *hadn't*, then I could have forgiven and forgotten—instead of which I'm now going to be spending the rest of my life on my *own!*"

With a sinking heart I'd realised that I was going to be spending the rest of her life cheering her up.

I'd tried to persuade Dad not to leave Mum. I'd pointed out that at her age it wasn't fair.

"I feel awful about it," he'd said over the phone. "But I've got myself into this . . . situation, Phoebe, and I feel I have to do the right thing."

"Why is leaving your wife of thirty-eight years the right thing?"

"Why is not being there for my child the right thing?"

"You weren't there for me, Dad."

"I know—and that has a bearing on my decision now." He sighed. "Perhaps it's because I've spent my whole life poring over the distant past, and now, with this baby, I'm being offered a piece of the *future*. At my age, that's the most amazing thing. Plus I do *want* to be with Ruth. I know that's hard for you to hear, Phoebe, but it's true. Your mother will get the house and half my pension. She has her job and her bridge circle and her friends. *I'd* like to stay friends with her," he'd added. "How can we *not* be friends after such a long marriage?"

"How *can* we be, when he's deserted me?" Mum had wailed when I'd repeated this to her. I could perfectly well see her point.

I made my way up Tranquil Vale wishing that I could feel more tranquil myself. Annie wouldn't be coming until midmorning; she'd gone to an audition. As I unlocked the door I found myself guiltily hoping that she wouldn't get the job, as it was for a two-month regional tour. I liked having Annie around. She was always smiling and punctual, she was terrific with customers, and she took initiative in rearranging the stock to keep the displays looking fresh. She'd become a real asset to Village Vintage.

I'd started the day with a sale, I realised happily as I read my

e-mails. Cindi had messaged me from Beverly Hills to say that she
definitely wanted the Balenciaga gown for one of her A-listers to
wear to the Emmys and that she'd phone me with payment at the end
of the day.

At nine I turned the sign to OPEN, then I phoned Mrs. Bell to ask
her when I could come and collect the clothes I was buying.

"Can you come this morning?" she asked. "Say at eleven?"

"Could we make it eleven-thirty? My assistant will be here by
then. I'll bring my car."

"Very well, I'll expect you then."

Suddenly the doorbell jangled and a slim blond woman in her
mid-thirties walked in. She spent a few moments sifting through
the racks with a slightly intense, distracted air.

"Are you looking for anything in particular?" I asked after a
minute.

"Yes," she replied. "I'm looking for something... *happy*. A happy
dress."

"Right. And is that for day or evening?"

She shrugged. "Doesn't matter. It just has to be very bright and
cheerful."

I showed her a Horrocks polished-cotton sundress from the
mid-fifties with a pattern of luminous cornflowers alternating with
little gold bows. She fingered the skirt. "It's lovely."

"Horrocks made gorgeous cotton dresses—they used to cost a
week's wages. And have you seen those?" I nodded at the cupcakes.

"*Oh.*" The woman's eyes widened. "Those are *fabulous*. Can I try
on the pink one?" she asked, like a child, almost. "I'd love to try the
pink one!"

"Of course." I took it down. "It's a ten."

"It's wonderful," she enthused as I hung it in the changing room.
She went inside and pulled the linen curtain shut. I heard her un-
zipping her skirt, then the soft rustle of the net petticoats as she
stepped into the dress. "It looks so... joyful," she said. "I adore the
tutu skirts—I feel like a flower fairy." She poked her head through

the curtain. "Could you pull up the zip for me? I can't quite manage . . . Thanks!"

"You look gorgeous," I said. "It's a perfect fit."

"It really is." She gazed at herself in the mirror. "It's just what I
had in mind—a lovely, *happy* dress."

"Are you celebrating something?"

"Well . . ." She fluffed up the mille-feuille of stiffened tulle. "I've
been trying for a baby." I nodded politely, unsure what to say. "And I
wasn't getting pregnant naturally, so after two and a half years we
went for IVF—a ghastly business," she added over her shoulder.

"You don't have to tell me this," I protested. "Really . . ."

The woman stepped back and appraised her reflection. "Anyway,
I took my temperature ten times a day, and I sniffed all these chemicals, and I injected myself until my hip was like a pincushion. And
I went through this hell *five times*—bankrupting myself in the
process, by the way—and then a fortnight ago it came to the sixth
cycle, which was to be the last-ever attempt because my husband
had told me that he wasn't prepared to go through it again." She
paused for breath. "So it was the very last throw of the dice . . ." She
stepped out of the cubicle and gazed at herself in the side mirror.
"And I got the results this morning. My gynaecologist phoned me to
tell me that"—she patted her tummy—"it hadn't worked."

"*Oh,*" I murmured. "I'm so sorry." Of course. Why would she be
buying a prom dress if she was pregnant?

"So just for today I've called in sick and I'm looking for ways to
cheer myself up." She smiled at her reflection. "And this dress is the
perfect start. It's *wonderful,*" she enthused as she turned to face me.
"I mean, how could anyone feel sad in a dress like this? It would be
impossible, wouldn't it?" Her eyes were shimmering. "Quite impossible . . ." Dissolving into tears, she sank onto the changing-
room chair.

I ran to the door and turned over the sign.

"I'm sorry . . . ," she said, weeping, "I shouldn't have come in. I'm
feeling . . . fragile."

"It's totally understandable," I said quietly.

She looked up at me. "I'm thirty-seven." A fat tear rolled down her cheek. "Women a lot older than me have babies, don't they? So why can't *I* have one? Just one," She sobbed. "Is that *too* greedy?"

Impulsively, I gave her a hug, then handed her some tissues and pulled the curtain round her so that she could change.

A couple of minutes later the woman brought the dress to the counter. She was calm now, though her eyes were red.

"You don't have to buy it," I told her.

"I want to," she protested gently. "Then whenever I'm feeling down, I'll just put it on. Or I could hang it on the wall like you've done here, and just looking at it will make me feel positive again."

"Well, I hope it has the desired effect, but if you change your mind, just bring it back. You need to be sure."

"I *am* sure," she protested. "But thanks."

"Well . . ." I smiled at her, feeling helpless to diminish her misery. "I wish you the very best." Then I handed her the happy dress in its bag.

Annie came back from her audition at eleven. "The director was *vile*," she raged. "The jerk actually asked me to turn round—like I was a piece of meat!"

I remembered the ghastly Keith making his girlfriend turn round for him. "I hope you didn't."

"Of course I didn't—I walked out! I should report him to Equity," she muttered as she took off her jacket. "Anyway, after that experience it's very nice to be back in your shop."

Feeling guiltily happy that Annie's audition hadn't been a success, I told her about the girl who'd bought the pink cupcake.

"Poor kid," she murmured, calm again now. "Do *you* want children?" she added as she quickly glossed her lips.

"No," I replied firmly. "Babies are not on my radar." *Except for my father's baby*, I thought wryly.

"Do you have a boyfriend?" Annie asked as she zipped up her bag. "Not that it's any of my business."

"No. I'm single—except for an occasional date." I thought of my forthcoming dinner with Miles. "My priority now is my work. How about you?"

"I've been seeing this chap Tim for a few months," Annie replied. "He's a painter—he lives down in Brighton. But I'm still too focused on my career to want to settle down, plus I'm only thirty-two. I've got time." She shrugged. "You've got time."

I looked at my watch and laughed. "No, I haven't—I'm going to be late. I'm collecting the clothes I've bought from Mrs. Bell." Leaving Annie in charge, I walked home, got two suitcases, and drove up to the Paragon.

In the week since I'd last been there the catch on the front door of number 8 had been mended, so Mrs. Bell didn't have to come down, which was just as well, I thought when she opened her own door, since she seemed a little frailer even than when I'd last seen her.

She greeted me warmly as I stepped inside, laying her thin, freckled hand on my arm. "Go and collect the clothes—and then I do hope you'll stay and have a cup of coffee with me?"

"Thank you, I'd love to."

I went into the bedroom with the cases and put the bags, shoes, and gloves in one of them, then I opened the wardrobe to take out the garments. As I did so, I caught a glimpse of the little blue coat. Again I wondered about its history.

I heard Mrs. Bell's soft footsteps behind me and turned. "Are you all done now, Phoebe?" She was fiddling with the waistband of her green-and-red plaid skirt, which was slipping a little.

"Almost," I replied, glad to hear her address me by my first name again. I put the two hats into the lovely old hatbox that Mrs. Bell was including; then I folded the Ossie Clark maxidress into the second suitcase.

"The Jaeger," she said as I snapped shut the clasps. "I would like to give it all to a charity shop. I want to get rid of as much as I can while I'm in the mood to do so. I would ask my home help, Paola, but she is away. Is there any chance that *you* might do it for me?"

"Of course." I put the clothes into a large plastic bag. "There's the Oxfam shop—shall I take them there?"

"Please," said Mrs. Bell, smiling faintly. "Thank you. Now, go and make yourself comfortable while I make our coffee."

In the sitting room, the gas fire emitted its low hiss. The sun shone through the small square panes of the bow window, casting a grid of shadows across the room like the bars of a cage.

Mrs. Bell came in with the tray and with a trembling hand poured us cups of coffee from the silver pot. As we drank them she asked me about my shop, and about how I'd started it. I told her about myself and my background. I discovered that she had a nephew by marriage who lived in Dorset who sometimes visited her, and a niece in Lyon who didn't.

"It's difficult for her, as she has to look after her two young grandchildren, but she phones me from time to time. She is my closest relative—the daughter of my late brother, Marcel."

We chatted for a few more minutes, then the carriage clock chimed half past twelve.

I put down my cup. "I really ought to get going. But thank you for the coffee, Mrs. Bell. It's been lovely to see you again."

A look of regret shadowed her face. "I have so enjoyed seeing you, Phoebe. I am rather hoping you will stay in touch. But you are a very busy young woman. Why ever would you want to bother?"

"I'd love to stay in touch," I interjected. "But for now I don't want to tire you."

"I am not tired," Mrs. Bell protested. "For once I have a strange kind of energy."

"That's good to hear. Is there anything I can do for you before I go?"

"No," she replied. "But thank you."

"I'll say good-bye then—for now," I promised and stood up.

Mrs. Bell was staring at me, as though weighing something in her mind. "Stay a little longer," she said abruptly. "Please."

My heart filled with pity. The poor woman was lonely and needed company. I was about to tell her that I could stay for another twenty minutes or so when Mrs. Bell disappeared, crossing the corridor into the bedroom. When she returned, she was holding the blue coat.

She looked at me, her eyes shining with a strange intensity. "You wanted to know about this . . ."

"No." I shook my head. "It's . . . none of my business."

"But you were curious."

"A . . . little," I conceded uncomfortably. "But it's not my concern, Mrs. Bell. I shouldn't have touched it."

"But I *want* to tell you about it," she said. "I *want* to tell you about this little coat, and why I hid it. More than anything else, Phoebe, I want to tell you why I have kept it for so long."

"You don't have to tell me anything," I protested weakly. "You barely know me."

She sighed. "That's true. But, lately, I have felt a great need to tell someone the story—the story that I have kept inside all these years— here—right *here*." She jabbed at her chest, hard, with the fingers of her left hand. "And for some reason, I feel that if I were to tell anyone, it would be *you.*"

I stared at her bewildered. "Why?"

"I'm not sure," she replied carefully. "I only know that I feel some . . . affinity with you, Phoebe—some connection that I can't explain."

"Oh. But . . . in any case, why would you want to talk about it *now*?" I asked. "After so long?"

"Because . . ." Mrs. Bell sank onto the sofa. Anxiety etched her face. "Last week—in fact, while you were here—I received the results of some medical tests. They do not exactly augur well for my future," she went on calmly. "I had already guessed that the news would not be positive from the way my weight has been falling lately." Now I understood Mrs. Bell's odd reaction when I'd suggested that she was "downsizing." "I have been offered treatment, but I have declined. It would be very unpleasant, it would buy me only a little extra time, and at my age . . ." She held up her hands, as if in surrender. "I am almost eighty years old, Phoebe. That is a longer life than many—as you know only too well." But now, with this acute sense I have of life retreating . . ." She looked imploringly at me. "I *need* to tell just one person about this coat, now, while I am still clear in my mind. I need that one person just to listen, and perhaps to understand what I did, and why." She looked towards the yard, the shadows from the window bisecting her face. "I suppose the truth is that I need to confess. If I believed in God, I would go to a priest." She turned her gaze back to me. "Could I tell *you*, Phoebe? Please? It will not take long, I promise—no more than a few minutes."

Mrs. Bell leaned forward on her chair, fingering the coat, which was laid across her lap, lifeless. She took a deep breath, her eyes narrowing as she now looked past me, through the window, as though it was a portal to the past.

"I come from Avignon," she began. "You know that." I nodded. "I grew up in a large village about three miles from the city centre. It was a sleepy sort of place, with narrow streets leading to a large square that was shaded by plane trees, with a few shops and a pleasant bar. On the north side of the square was the church, over the door of which was carved, in huge Roman letters, LIBERTÉ, ÉGALITÉ ET FRATERNITÉ." At that a sardonic smile flickered across Mrs. Bell's face. "The village bordered open countryside," she went on, "and was skirted by a railway line. My father managed a hardware store in Avignon. He also had a little vineyard not far from the house. My mother was *maîtresse de maison*, looking after my father, me, and my younger brother, Marcel. To make a little extra money she took in sewing."

Mrs. Bell tucked a stray wisp of white hair behind her ear. "Marcel and I went to the local school. It was very small—there were no more than a hundred children, many of them descended from families who had lived in the village for generations—the same names would come up again and again: Caron, Paget, Marigny . . . and Aumage. . . ." Mrs. Bell shifted a little on her seat. "In September 1940, when I was eleven, a new girl joined my class. I had seen her once or twice over the summer, but I hadn't known who she was. My mother said that she'd heard that the girl and her family had moved to our village from Paris. My mother had added that, after the occupation, many such families had fled to the south." Mrs. Bell looked at me. "I could not know it at the time, but that little word *such* was to prove of immense significance. Anyway, this girl's name was . . ." Mrs. Bell's voice caught. "Monique," she whispered after a moment. "Her name was Monique . . . Richelieu, and I was assigned to look after her." At this, Mrs. Bell began to stroke the coat, then she looked through the window again.

"Monique was a sweet, friendly girl, clever and hardworking; she was also exceptionally pretty with a quick expression in her dark eyes, lovely cheekbones, and hair so black that in certain lights it looked blue. And however much she tried to disguise it, she had a foreign inflexion to her voice that stood out all the more among the Provençal accents that were spoken around her." Mrs. Bell looked at me. "Whenever Monique was teased about this at school, she would say that her accent was Parisian. But my parents said that it wasn't Parisian—it was German."

She clasped her hands together, the enamelled bangle she was wearing clinking gently against her gold watch. "Monique started coming over to my house to play, and we would roam the fields and hillsides together, picking wildflowers, chatting about girlish things. I sometimes asked her about Paris, which I had only ever seen in photographs. Monique told me about her life in the city, although she was always vague about where her family had lived. But she often talked about her best friend, Miriam. Miriam"— Mrs. Bell's face suddenly lit up—"*Lipietzka*. The name has *just* come back to me—after all these years!" She looked at me, shaking her head in wonderment. "This is what happens, Phoebe, when you are old. Things *long* buried suddenly surface with startling clarity. Lipietzka," she murmured. "Of course . . . I think she said that her family was originally from the Ukraine. But Monique told me that she very much missed Miriam, of whom she was terribly proud, not least because Miriam was a wonderful violinist. I remember feeling quite a pang as Monique talked so lovingly about Miriam, and I secretly hoped that in time *I* might become Monique's best friend— even though I had no musical ability at all. I remember I enjoyed going to Monique's house, which was some way away, on the other side of the village, near the railway line. It had a pretty front garden with lots of flowers, and a well, and above the front door was a plaque with the head of a lion carved on it."

Mrs. Bell put down her cup. "Monique's father was a dreamy, rather impractical sort of man. Each day he cycled into Avignon, where he worked as a bookkeeper for a firm of accountants. Her mother stayed at home looking after Monique's twin brothers, Olivier and Christophe, who were then about three. Once when I was there, Monique cooked the entire evening meal, despite being only ten at the time. She told me that she'd had to learn how to cook because her mother had been bedridden for two months after the twins were born. Monique was a very good cook, though I remember not liking the bread very much.

"Anyway . . . on went the war. We children were aware of it, but we knew little about it because of course there were no televisions, few radios, and the adults sheltered us from it as much as they could. In fact, they hardly spoke of it in our hearing, except to complain about rationing—my father's main complaint was that it was hard to get beer." Mrs. Bell paused again, her lips pursing slightly. "One day, in the summer of 1941, by which time we had become close friends, Monique and I went for a walk. After about two miles or so along one of the little back roads that crisscross the area we came upon a ramshackle old barn. As we went inside it to explore we happened to be talking about names. I said that I didn't like my name—Thérèse. I felt it was too ordinary. I wished that my parents had called me Chantal. Then I asked Monique if she liked hers. To my surprise she went very red, then she suddenly blurted out that Monique wasn't her real name. Her real name was Monika—Monika Richter. I was . . ." Mrs. Bell shook her head in wonderment. "*Amazed.* Then Monique said that her family had moved to Paris from Mannheim, five years earlier, and that her father had changed their name to make them fit in. He'd decided on Richelieu, she told me, because of the famous cardinal."

Mrs. Bell looked out the window again. "When I asked Monique why they'd left Germany, she replied that it was because they didn't feel safe. At first she refused to say why. But when I pressed her, she told me that it was because her family was Jewish. She told me that they never spoke of this to anyone, and that they hid all outward signs of it. Then she made me swear never to reveal what she had said to a living soul, otherwise we could no longer be friends. I agreed immediately, of course, although I couldn't understand why being Jewish had to be a secret—I knew that Jewish people had lived in Avignon for hundreds of years; there was an old synagogue in the city centre. But if that was how Monique felt, I would respect it."

Mrs. Bell began to finger the coat again, stroking the sleeves. "I felt I should offer Monique a secret of my own in return for hers. So I confided that I had recently fallen in love with a boy in our school—Jean-Luc Aumage." Her lips pressed into a thin line. "I remember, when I told Monique about Jean-Luc, that she looked a little uncomfortable. Then she said that he did seem to be a nice boy and that he was certainly good-looking."

Mrs. Bell's eyes strayed to the window again. "Time went by, and we did our best to ignore the war, thankful to be living in the southern 'free' zone. But one morning—it was in late June '42—I could see that Monique was very upset. She told me that she had just received a letter from Miriam in which Miriam had told her that she was now required, as were all Jewish people in the occupied zone, to wear a yellow star. This six-pointed star, which had to be sewn onto the left side of her jacket, had in the centre one word—*Juive*."

Mrs. Bell rearranged the coat on her lap, repeatedly smoothing the blue fabric. "From that time on I opened my ears to the war. At night I would sit on the landing, outside my parents' room, straining to hear the broadcasts from BBC London, which they covertly tuned in to; like many people, my father had bought our first wireless just for that purpose. I remember that when they were listening to these bulletins I would hear my father exclaim in disgust or despair. From one of these programmes I learned that there were now special laws for Jewish people in both zones. Jews were not allowed to join the army, or to hold important jobs in government or to buy property. They had to observe a curfew, and in Paris they were obliged to travel in the last carriage on the Metro.

"The next day I asked my mother why these things were happening, but she would say only that we were living in difficult times and that it was best for me not to think about this dreadful war, which would soon be over—*grâce à Dieu.*

"So we tried to carry on with our lives as 'normal.' But in November 1942 that pretence of normality came to an abrupt end. On November 12 my father came home early, all out of breath, to say that he had seen two German soldiers, with machine guns attached to the sidecars of their motorbikes, stationed at the main road leading from our village to the city centre.

"The next morning, along with many others, my parents, my brother, and I walked into Avignon. We were horrified to see German soldiers standing beside their official, shiny black Citroëns, which were parked outside the Palais des Papes. Other German troops were stationed outside the town hall, or riding down our streets in armoured vehicles, wearing helmets and goggles. To us children, they looked funny, like aliens, and I remember my parents being angry with Marcel and me for pointing at them and laughing. They told us to look through them as though they weren't there. They said that if all the people of Avignon did that, then the Germans' presence wouldn't affect us. But Marcel and I knew that this was just bravado—we understood perfectly well that the 'free zone' no longer existed and that now we were *all 'sous la botte'*—under the boot."

Mrs. Bell paused and tucked another wisp of hair behind her ear.

"From that morning on, Monique became distant and watchful. At the end of school each day she would go straight home. She was no longer free to play on Sundays, and I was no longer invited to her house. I was terribly hurt by this, but when I tried to talk to her about it, she just said that she had less time now because her mother needed her to help at home more.

"A month later, I was queuing to buy flour when I overheard the man in front of me complaining that from now on all Jewish people in our area had to have their identity and ration cards stamped with the word *Jew.* The man, who I realize now must himself have been Jewish, said it was a dreadful affront. His family had lived in France for three generations—had he not fought for France during the Great War?" Mrs. Bell narrowed her pale blue eyes. "I remember he shook his fist at the church and said where now was the notion of *liberté, égalité, et fraternité*? I just thought to myself, naïvely, "At least he's not being made to wear the star, like Miriam has to—that would be ... awful." She shook her head. "Little did I know that wearing the yellow star would have been *infinitely* preferable to the stamping of official papers."

For a moment, Mrs. Bell closed her eyes, as if exhausted by her memories. Then she opened them again. "In early 1943, around the middle of February, I saw Monique standing by the school gate, deep in conversation with Jean-Luc, who by now was a very handsome young man of fifteen. I could see from the way he wrapped her scarf a little closer round her neck—it was bitterly cold—that he was very attracted to Monique. I could also see that she liked *him,* because of the way she was smiling up at him, not encouragingly exactly, but sweetly and ... a little anxiously, I suppose." Mrs. Bell sighed, then shook her head. "I was still infatuated with Jean-Luc, even though he'd never so much as looked at me. What a fool I was," she added bleakly. "What a *fool*." She tapped her chest again, as though striking herself. Then she went on, her voice shaking: "The next day I asked Monique if she liked Jean-Luc. She just looked at me very intently, almost sadly, and said, 'Thérèse, you don't understand,' which only seemed to confirm that she *did* like him. Then I remembered how she'd reacted when I'd first told her about my crush. She'd seemed uncomfortable, and now I knew why. But Monique was right—I *didn't* understand. If only I had," she whispered. "If only I *had* . . ."

Mrs. Bell paused to collect herself, then said, "After school that day, I ran home in tears. My mother asked me why I was crying, but I was too embarrassed to tell her. Then she put her arms round me and told me to dry my eyes because she had a surprise for me. She went to her sewing corner and brought out a bag. Inside was a lovely little coat of wool as blue as the sky on a clear June morning. As I tried it on, she told me that she had waited in line for five hours to buy the material and that she had sewn it for me at night, while I was asleep. I hugged her and cried and said that I loved the coat *so* much that I would keep it forever. My mother laughed and said, 'No you won't, silly.'" Mrs. Bell gave me a wan smile. "But I *have*."

She stroked the lapels again, the lines on her brow scored a little deeper now. "Then, one day in April, Monique didn't come to school. She didn't come the next day either, or the day after that. When I asked our teacher where Monique was, she told me that she didn't know but that she was sure she'd be back before long. Then the Easter holidays started, and still I didn't see Monique. I kept asking my parents where she might be, but they told me that it would be better to forget her—I would make new friends, they said. I said I didn't *want* new friends—I wanted Monique. So the next morning I ran to her house. I knocked on the door, but no one answered. I peered through a gap in the shutters and saw the remains of a meal on the table. There was a broken plate on the floor. Seeing that they'd left in a dreadful rush, I resolved to write to Monique at once. I sat down by the well, and I'd started to compose a letter to her in my head when I realised that of course I *couldn't* write to her because I hadn't the faintest idea where she was. I felt just terrible..."

She squeezed her eyes shut, then continued, "At that time, the weather was still cold." She shivered. "Although it was late spring I was still wearing my blue coat. I was obsessed with finding out where Monique could have gone, and why she and her family had left so suddenly. But my parents refused to discuss it with me. Then, in my selfish child's way, I realised that there was a silver lining to the situation. No doubt Monique would return, if not now, then when the war was over—but in her absence maybe Jean-Luc might notice *me.* I decided to do whatever I could to try and make him. I had just turned fourteen, and I began to steal a little of my mother's lipstick; I put curling papers in my hair at night, like she did, and I darkened my pale lashes with a little boot polish—sometimes with comical results; I pinched my cheeks to make them rosy. Marcel, who was two years younger than me, began to notice these things and teased me mercilessly.

"Then one warm Saturday morning I had a row with Marcel—he was goading me so much, I couldn't stand it. I ran out of our house, slamming the door. I'd walked for perhaps an hour or so when I came to the old broken-down barn, the place where Monique had first told me about her family fleeing Germany for Paris. I went inside and sat down on the floor in a patch of sunlight with my back to a hay bale, listening to the swifts chattering in the eaves and the distant rumble of trains. Suddenly I felt overwhelmed with sadness. I started crying and couldn't stop. And as I sat there, my face bathed in tears, I heard a faint rustling sound. I thought it might be a rat; I was scared. But then curiosity overwhelmed me. I got up and went to the back of the barn, and there, behind a stack of hay bales, lying beneath a coarse grey blanket, was... *Monique.*" Mrs. Bell looked at me, bewildered, despite all the years that had passed since that discovery. "I was *astounded.* She was sleeping. I couldn't understand *why* she was there. I gently called her name, but she didn't respond. I began to panic. I clapped my hands by her ear, then I knelt down and shook her..."

"Did she wake up?" I asked. My heart was pounding. "Did she wake *up*?"

"She did wake up—thank God. But I will never forget her expression when she did so. Because even as she recognised me, her eyes were straying over my shoulder; her look of terror then changed to one of *relief* mingled with anxiety. Then she told me, in a tiny whisper, that she had not heard me come in because she had been asleep, because she found it so hard to sleep at night and was exhausted. Then she put her arms round me and clung to me, gripping me so tightly while I tried to comfort her..." Mrs. Bell's eyes shimmered with tears.

"We sat together on a bale of hay. Monique told me that she had been in that barn for eight days. In fact, it was ten days. I knew this because she said that on April nineteenth the gestapo had come to her house while she was out getting bread, and that they had taken her parents and her brothers, but that their neighbours, the Antignacs, had seen her returning and had headed her off. They'd hidden her in their attic, then at nightfall they'd brought her here to this barn that they no longer used. She said that Monsieur Antignac had told her to stay there until it was safe. He'd said that he had no idea how long that would be and that she would have to be patient and brave. He'd told her not to make a sound, and never to leave the barn, except to creep to the stream when it was dark to collect water in the pitcher that he'd given her.

"My heart broke for Monique—she was all alone, separated from her family, with no idea where they were, and with the terrible thought of their abduction tormenting her every waking moment." Mrs. Bell's mouth was quivering. "I tried to imagine how I would cope in such a horrible situation. That was when I *truly* understood the dreadfulness of this war." Mrs. Bell's eyes blazed. "How *could* it be that people guilty of *no* crime, men and women—and children," she added vehemently. "*Children* . . . How could it *be* that they could just be taken from their homes like *that* and bundled onto trains bound for . . . 'new horizons,' " she spat. "That was the euphemism we learned afterwards—and 'work camps in the east.' " Her voice had caught. " 'Destinations unknown.' That was another . . ." Her eyes shimmered with tears, and her hands sprang to cover them.

I listened to her soft sobs, hearing nothing but her grief and the slow, relentless ticking of the clock. "Are you sure you want to go on?" I asked her gently.

Mrs. Bell nodded. "I do want to." She reached into the sleeve of her blouse and pulled out a hanky. "I *need* to . . ." She pressed the hanky to her eyes, then continued, her voice fracturing again with effort and emotion. "Monique already looked so gaunt and thin. Her hair was matted and her clothes and face were dirty. But round her neck was a beautiful Venetian glass necklace that her mother had given her for her thirteenth birthday. The beads were large and rectangular, with a swirling pattern of pink and bronze. Monique fingered it constantly as she spoke, as though it consoled her just to touch it. She told me that she was desperate to find her family but she understood that for now she had to stay hidden where she was. She said that the Antignacs were very kind, but that they weren't able to bring her food every day.

"So then I said that *I* would. Monique protested that I mustn't, because I would be putting myself in danger. 'No one will see me," I assured her. 'I'll pretend that I'm picking wild strawberries—who's going to care what *I* do?" For the second time in that place, Monique swore me to secrecy. She made me promise to tell *no one* that I had seen her—not even my parents or my brother. I vowed to say nothing, then I ran home, my head spinning. I went into the kitchen and took some bread from my ration and put a little butter on it, then I cut a piece of cheese from my meagre allowance. I found an apple and put all this into a basket. Then I told my mother that I was going out again because I wanted to pick some irises that grew wild at that time of year. She made some comment about my having lots of energy and told me not to go too far. Then I ran back to the barn, slipped in very quietly, and gave Monique the food. She ate half of it, ravenously, saying that she would have to make the other half last for the next two days. She said that she was worried about rats, so she put the rest of the provisions under an old pot. I told her that I would come again, soon, with more. I asked her if there was anything else that she needed. She replied that although she was warm enough during the day, she was wretchedly cold at night—so cold she couldn't sleep. All she had was the cotton dress and the cardigan she was wearing, and that thin grey blanket. "You need a coat," I told her. "A really warm coat. You need . . ." And all at once I knew. "I will bring you mine," I promised, "tomorrow, in the late afternoon. But I'd better go now or my parents will miss me." I kissed her on the cheek and left.

"That night I could hardly sleep. I was tortured by thoughts of Monique, all alone in the barn, trembling at the scrabbling of rats and mice and the hooting of owls, and having to endure cold so biting that she would wake in the morning aching from shivering. Then I thought about the coat, and how warm it would make her, and I felt elated at the thought of giving it to her. Monique was my best friend"—her voice quivered—"and I was going to look after her."

I looked away, almost unable to bear this story, with its painful echoes of my own.

Mrs. Bell was stroking the coat again now. "I planned all the wonderful things I would take to Monique—this coat, some pencils and paper to pass the time, a few books, a bar of soap, and some toothpaste. And of course food—lots of it . . ." From somewhere far away I thought I could hear ringing. "I went to sleep dreaming of the feast that I would lay before Monique." She tapped her chest again. "But I didn't do that. Instead, I let her down—terribly. In fact, catastrophically—"

Drrrrrrring.

Mrs. Bell looked up, startled, as she registered the sound of the front doorbell. Then she got to her feet, carefully laid the coat over the back of her chair, and left the room, smoothing down her hair as she went. I heard her steps in the hallway, then a woman's voice.

"Mrs. Bell? . . . district nurse . . . sorry, didn't your doctor tell you? . . . about half an hour . . . sure it's convenient?"

"No, it's *not*," I whispered. As Mrs. Bell came back into the sitting room, followed by a fair-haired woman in her fifties, she quickly swept up the coat and took it back into the bedroom.

The nurse smiled at me. "I hope I'm not interrupting." I fought the urge to tell her that she was. "Are you a friend of Mrs. Bell's?" she asked.

"Yes. We were just having a . . . chat." I stood and looked at Mrs. Bell, who had now returned. The emotion of her story was still etched on her face, which was very pale and drawn. "I'll go now, Mrs. Bell, but I'll ring you very soon, I promise."

She laid her hand on my arm, gazing at me intently. "Yes, Phoebe," she said quietly. "Please do."

I descended the stairs feeling weighed down, though not by the two suitcases, which I barely noticed. As I drove the short distance back home, I thought about Mrs. Bell's story. My heart ached for her, that she was still so distressed about events that had happened such a long time ago.

At home I separated those clothes of hers that would go to Val —I thought with a shiver of my private sitting—then I put the others aside to be washed or dry-cleaned.

On the way back to the shop I stopped at Oxfam. I handed the bag of Mrs. Bell's things to the volunteer, a woman in her early seventies whom I'd often seen in there. She can be a bit grumpy. "These are all Jaeger and in excellent condition," I explained. Out of the corner of my eye I noticed the calico curtain that was pulled across the changing cubicle twitch. I took out the aquamarine suit. "This would have cost two hundred fifty pounds new—it's only two years old."

"It's quite a nice colour," said the volunteer, grudgingly.

"Yes, it's lovely, isn't it?"

Now the curtain was drawn back and there stood Dan, in a bright turquoise corduroy jacket and crimson trousers. I felt like reaching for my sunglasses.

"Hi, Phoebe. I thought it was you." He studied himself in the mirror. "What do you think of the jacket?"

"What do I think of the jacket?" What could I say? "The cut's okay, but the colour's . . . ghastly." His face fell. "Sorry, but you did ask."

"I like this colour," he protested. "It's . . . well . . . How would *you* describe it?"

"Peacock blue," I suggested. "No—cyan."

"Oh." He squinted at himself. "As in *cyanide*?"

"Exactly. And it is a bit . . . *toxic*." I grimaced at the volunteer. "Sorry."

She shrugged. "Don't worry, I think it's vile, too. Mind you, he can *almost* carry it off." She nodded at him. "He's got a lovely face under all that hair." I looked at Dan, who was smiling gratefully at the woman. He did have a lovely face, I realised—a strong straight nose, nice lips that dimpled slightly at the corners; a clear, grey-eyed gaze. Who *was* it he reminded me of? "But what will that jacket *go* with?" the volunteer demanded. "You've got to think about that. As you're a valued customer, I feel I should give you that advice."

"Ooh, it'll go with lots of things," Dan replied amiably. "These trousers, for a start."

"I'm not sure that they *do* go," I felt compelled to say. Dan's approach to clothes seemed to be mix 'n' don't match.

He took the jacket off. "I'll take it," he announced happily. "And the books." He nodded at the pile of hardcovers on the counter. The top one was a biography of Greta Garbo. "Did you know that Louis B. Mayer wanted her to drop the name Garbo because he thought it sounded too much like *garbage*?"

"Erm . . . no, I didn't." I gazed at the beautiful face on the cover. "I love Garbo's films. Not that I've seen one for ages," I confessed as Dan handed the volunteer the cash.

He looked at me. "Then you're in luck. The Greenwich Picturehouse is doing a 'Mother Russia' season later this month, and they're showing *Anna Karenina.*" He accepted his change. "We'll go."

I stared at him. "I'm not . . . sure. I—"

"Why not?" He dropped the coins into the collection tin by the register and turned to me. "Don't tell me—you *vont* to be alone."

"No, it's just that . . . I'd like to think about it."

"I don't know *why,*" the volunteer said as she tore off Dan's receipt. "It sounds marvellous to me—going to see a Greta Garbo film with a nice young man."

"Yes, but . . ." I didn't want to say that, apart from objecting to the presumptuous way in which I'd been invited, I'd only ever met Dan twice. "I don't know whether I . . . can," I finished lamely.

"Don't worry." Dan had opened his bag. "I've got the Picture-house leaflet right here." He took it out. "The screening's on . . . Wednesday the twenty-fourth at seven-thirty. Is that okay for you?" He was looking at me expectantly.

"Well . . ."

The volunteer heaved a sigh. "If you don't go with him, *I* will. I haven't been to the pictures for five years. Not since my husband died. We used to go *every* Friday; there's no one to go with now; I'd give anything for an invitation like that." She shook her head as if disbelieving of my churlishness, then handed Dan his bags with a consoling smile. "Here you go, sweetheart. See you again soon."

"You will," said Dan, smiling. Then he and I left the shop together. "Where are you going?" he asked as we strolled down Tranquil Vale.

"I've got to go up to the bank—I meant to do it earlier."

"I'm going that way, too. I'll walk with you. So how's Village Vintage doing?"

"It's . . . good," I replied. "Thanks, largely, to your article," I added, feeling a little guilty now at my irritability. But as usual Dan had thrown me off balance with his . . . spontaneity. "And what about the paper?"

"It's going okay," he replied judiciously. "The circulation's gone up to eleven thousand, from ten thousand at launch, which is good. But we could use more advertising—a lot of the local advertisers still aren't aware of us."

We went down the hill, then crossed over at the junction. Suddenly Dan stopped outside the Age Exchange Reminiscence Centre. "Well, I'm going in here."

I looked at the maroon-painted shop front. "Why?"

"I'm planning a feature on it, so I need to do a recce."

"I haven't been in here for years," I mused as I gazed at the window.

"Come in with me now then," Dan said.

"Well . . . I'm not sure I've got time, so I don't think I will, Dan. I'll just . . ." Why was I refusing, I wondered? Annie was minding the shop—there was no particular time pressure on me. "All right, then. But just for a minute."

Going into the Age Exchange was like stepping back in time. The interior was decorated in the style of an old-fashioned general store, the shelves stocked with prewar packaging for Sunlight soap, Brown & Polson's custard, Eggo dried egg, and Player's and Navy Cut cigarettes. There was an ornate brass cash register like an old typewriter, a Bakelite wireless radio, and some Brownie box cameras; there was also a wooden chest, the little drawers of which had been left open to reveal an assortment of old medals, crochet hooks, knitted dolls, and spools of thread—the bric-a-brac of times gone by.

Dan and I walked through to the gallery at the back of the centre. Here there were black-and-white photos forming part of an exhibition about life in the East End in the 1930s and '40s. One of the figures, a little girl playing on a bombed-out street, was circled because, now in her eighties, she lived here in Blackheath.

"So this place is a kind of museum," I said.

"It's more of a community centre," Dan replied, "where the elderly can reminisce about their lives. There's a theatre at the back and a café. In fact, I'm dying for some coffee—will you have one?" I said I would.

As we sat at a table, Dan got out his pad and pencil, which he began to sharpen.

"So you found it." I nodded at the sharpener.

"Yes, thank goodness."

"Is it special?"

"My grandmother left it to me. She died three years ago."

"She left you a pencil sharpener?" He nodded. "Is that all she left you?" I couldn't help asking.

"No." He blew on the sharpened pencil tip. "She also left me a rather hideous painting. I did feel a tad . . . disappointed," he concluded delicately. "But I like the sharpener."

As Dan began to scribble a few notes in his odd shorthand, I asked him how long he'd been a journalist.

"Only a few months," he replied. "I'm a rookie." So that explained his inept interviewing technique.

"What did you do before?"

"I worked for a marketing agency, designing product promotions—mostly voucher giveaways, cash-back incentives, buy-one-get-one-free offers—"

"Five percent off everything for the first week?" I teased.

"Yes." Dan blushed. "That sort of thing."

"So why did you give it up?"

He hesitated. "I'd been doing the same thing for ten years; I was looking for a change. And my old school friend Matt had just left the *Guardian,* where he'd been business editor, to set up his own paper—a long-held dream—and he said he needed . . . help," Dan went on. "So I decided to go for it."

"He asked you to come and write for his newspaper?"

"No. He'd already hired two full-time reporters; I do the marketing, but I have carte blanche to write about anything that interests me."

"So I should feel flattered then."

Dan was staring at me with a very odd expression on his face. "I saw you," he said. "The day before you opened—I was walking past on the other side of the road, and you were in the window, dressing a dummy—"

"Mannequin, please," I corrected with a laugh.

"—and you were having trouble—one of its arms kept falling off."

I rolled my eyes. "I hate wrestling with those things."

"And you were *so* determined to remain composed, and I thought, *I'd love to talk to that woman,* so I did. That's the good thing about journalism," he added with a smile.

"Two coffees!" said the volunteer, putting them on the counter. I went and got them, then held them out to Dan. "Which do you want? The red or the green?"

"The . . ." He hesitated. "Red." He put out his hand.

"But that's the green one you've taken."

He squinted at it. "So it is."

The penny dropped with a clatter. "Dan, are you colour-blind?" He pursed his lips, then nodded. How slow I'd been. "Is that . . . tricky?"

"Not really." He gave a philosophical shrug. "It just means that I was unable to become an electrician."

"Oh, all those coloured wires."

"Or an air-traffic controller—or a pilot, for that matter. Being colour-'deficient' as they say, also means that tabby cats have green stripes, that I'm useless at picking strawberries, and that I often mismatch my clothes—as you've clearly noticed."

I felt my cheeks heat up. "If I'd known there was a reason for it, I'd have been more tactful."

"People do sometimes make rude remarks about what I'm wearing. I never explain unless I have to."

"And when did you find out?"

"On my first day at school. We were asked to paint a tree. Mine had bright red leaves and a green trunk. My teacher advised my parents to get my vision tested."

"So your trousers don't look crimson to you, do they?"

Dan looked down at them. "I don't know what crimson is—to me it's an abstract concept, like the sound of a bell to a deaf person. But these trousers look olive green."

I sipped my coffee. "What colours can you see well?"

"Pastels—pale blue, mauve—and of course black and white. I do like looking at things in black and white," he added, with a nod at the exhibition. "There's something about monochrome that just—"

From somewhere I could hear "As Time Goes By"; for a moment I thought it was coming over a sound system, then I realised that it was Dan's ring tone.

He threw me an apologetic glance then took the call. "Hi, Matt," he said quietly. "I'm round the corner at the Age Exchange . . . Yes, I can talk—just for a minute. *Sorry*," he mouthed at me. "Oh . . . right . . ." He stood up, his expression serious now. "Well, if she'll stand by the story," he added as he walked away. "Hard evidence," I heard him say as he stepped into the courtyard garden; ". . . have to be libel-proof . . . I'll be there in two minutes."

"Sorry about that," he said to me as he returned to the table. He looked distracted. "Matt needs to discuss something with me. I'd better go."

"And I've got things to do." I picked up my bag. "But I'm glad I came in here. Thanks for the coffee."

We left the centre, then stood on the pavement for a moment. "Well, I'm going this way." Dan nodded to the right. "The *Black & Green* is just up there, next to the post office, and you're going that way. But . . . we'll go and see *Anna Karenina*."

"Well, why don't you let me think about it?"

Dan shrugged. "Why don't you just say yes, Phoebe?" Then, as if it was perfectly normal for him to do so, he kissed me on the cheek and left.

As I pushed on the door of Village Vintage five minutes later, I saw Annie putting down the phone. "That was Mrs. Bell," she told me. "Apparently you forgot the hatbox when you left this morning."

"I forgot the hatbox?" I'd been so affected by her story that I hadn't even noticed.

"She suggested that you collect it tomorrow at four. She said to call her back only if you can't make it. But I could run up and get it for you—"

"No, no, I'll do it myself. Thanks, Annie. Tomorrow at four would be good. Very good . . ."

Annie gave me a puzzled glance. "So how *was* Mrs. Bell?" she asked as she picked up a satin evening dress that had slipped off its hanger.

"She's . . . lovely, an interesting person."

"I imagine some of the older people chat to you sometimes."

"They do."

"I bet some of them have incredible stories to tell. I'd find that part of the job fascinating. I love hearing the elderly talk about their lives. I think we should listen to old people more."

I was just telling Annie about the Age Exchange, which she said she'd never been to, when the phone rang again. This time, it was a producer from Radio London saying that he'd seen the interview with me in the *Black & Green,* and would I come in on the following Monday to talk about vintage clothing. Delighted, I said I'd be happy to. Next, Miles texted me to say that he'd booked a table at the OXO Tower for Thursday at eight. Then I had a number of website orders to deal with, five of which were for French nightdresses. Seeing how low my stock was getting, I booked a Eurostar ticket to Avignon for the last weekend in September. The rest of the afternoon was taken up with talking to people who'd brought in clothes for me to buy.

"I won't be in until lunchtime tomorrow," I said to Annie as I closed the shop for the day. "I'm going to see Val, my seamstress." I didn't add that I was also going to see a medium—a thought I suddenly found terrifying.

Six

The next morning I mailed the Balenciaga gown to Cindi in Beverly Hills, idly wondering which of her A-listers it was destined for. Then, with butterflies in my stomach, I drove to Kidbrooke for my reading. In my handbag I'd put three photos of Emma and me. The first was taken when we were ten—on the beach in Lyme Regis, where Dad had taken us for a day's fossil hunting. In the photo Emma was holding up a large ammonite that she'd found and which I knew she'd always kept. Both of us had flatly refused to believe my dad when he said that it was about two hundred million years old. The second photo was taken at Emma's graduation at the Royal College of Art. The third was a picture of us together on what was to be her last birthday. On her head was a hat she'd made for herself, unusually—a green straw cloche with a starched silk pink rose "growing" out of it. "I *like* this," she'd said with mock surprise as she'd looked at herself in a hand mirror. "*This* is the hat I'm going to be buried in!"

Now I lifted my hand to Val's doorbell. When she appeared she announced, without saying hello, that she was upset because she'd just spilled a jar of peppercorns.

"What a nuisance," I said, recalling, with a sharp pang, Emma's dinner party. "They get everywhere, don't they?"

"Oh, I'm not upset because it's a nuisance," Val replied. "I'm upset because spilling peppercorns is terribly unlucky."

I stared at her. "Why?"

"Because it usually portends the end of a close friendship." I felt a shiver run the length of my spine. "So I'll have to mind my p's and q's with Mags for a while, won't I?" she added. "Now"—Val nodded at my suitcase—"what have you brought me?" Feeling shaken from what she'd just said and the memory it sparked, I showed Val Mrs. Bell's six dresses and three suits. "Just small repairs," she commented as she appraised them. "Ooh, I love this Ossie Clark dress. I can just imagine it strolling down the Kings Road in '65." She turned it inside out. "Torn lining? Leave it to me, Phoebe. I'll call you when they're done."

"Thanks. Okay then," I added with false brightness. "I'll just... pop next door."

Val gave me an encouraging smile. "Good luck."

As I rang Maggie's bell I realised that my heart was pounding like a tom-tom.

"Come in, sweetheart," Mags yelled. "I'm in the living room." I followed the trail of Magie Noire mingled with stale cigarette smoke down the corridor and found Mags sitting behind a small square table. She nodded for me to sit in the chair opposite her. As I did so I glanced around. There were no fringed lampshades or crystal balls. No decks of tarot cards. There was simply a huge plasma TV, a carved oak sideboard, and an inglenook shelf on which sat an enormous china doll with glossy brown ringlets and a vacant expression.

"If you were expecting a Ouija board, you're going to be disappointed," Mags said flatly. It was as though she'd read my mind—pathetically, I found this encouraging. "I don't go in for that holding-hands-and-waiting-for-the-lights-to-go-out nonsense. No. All I'll be doing is linking you to your loved one. Just think of me as your switchboard operator, putting you through."

"Mags . . ." I was suddenly filled with apprehension. "Now that I'm here, I'm feeling a little . . . worried. I mean, don't you think it's a bit profane to, well . . . call up the dead?" Especially in the "living" room, it suddenly occurred to me.

"No, it's not," she replied. "Because the point *is* they're not really dead, are they? They've just gone somewhere else, *but*"—she held up her finger—"they can be contacted." She was looking at me expectantly. "Let's start then." She nodded at my handbag.

"Oh. Sorry." I reached for my purse.

"Business before pleasure," Mags chuckled. "Thanking you." She took the £50 from my fingers, then tucked it into her cleavage. I imagined the notes becoming warm. Then I wondered what else she kept down there. A hole punch? Her address book? A small dog?

Now that Mags was ready, she placed her hands, palms down, on the table, pressing her fingers against the tabletop as if to steady herself for the psychic journey. Her vermillion nails were so long that they curved at the ends, like little scimitars. "So . . . you lost someone," she began.

"Yes." I'd already decided that I wasn't going to show Mags the photos or give her any clues about Emma.

"You lost someone," she repeated. "Someone you loved."

"Yes." I could feel the familiar constriction in my throat.

"Very much."

"Yes," I repeated.

"A close friend. Someone who meant the world to you." I nodded, struggling not to cry.

Mags closed her eyes, then breathed in deeply through her nose. "And what would you like to say to this friend?"

I was taken aback: I hadn't expected to be asked to say anything. I closed my eyes. I thought that most of all I wanted to tell Emma that

I was sorry; then wanted to tell her how much I missed her—it was like a constant ache at the heart. Lastly I wanted to tell Emma that I was furious with her for doing what she did.

I opened my eyes, looked at Mags, and realized I was shivering with panic. "I . . . can't think of anything right now."

"All right, sweetheart, but—she paused theatrically—"your friend wants to say something to *you.*"

"What?" I said weakly.

"It's very important."

"Tell me what it *is.*" My heart was beating wildly. "Please."

"Well . . ."

"*Tell* me."

She took a deep breath. "He *says*—"

I blinked. "It isn't a *he.*"

Mags opened her eyes and looked at me, dumbfounded. "Not a *he*?"

"No."

"Are you sure?"

"Of course I'm sure."

"That's odd—because I'm getting the name Robert." She peered at me. "It's coming through very strongly."

"But I don't know anyone named Robert."

"How about Rob?" I shook my head. Mags cocked her head to one side. "Bob?"

"*No.*"

"Does David ring any bells?"

"Maggie, my friend was a *woman.*"

She narrowed her eyes, squinting at me through her false lashes. "Of course she was," she said reasonably. "I *thought* so . . ." She closed her eyes again, inhaling noisily. "Okay. I've got her. She's coming through . . . I'll be connecting you in just a moment now." I half expected to hear a call-waiting beep, or a tinny recording of the *Four Seasons.*

"So what name are you getting?" I asked.

Mags pressed her forefingers to her temples. "I can't answer that yet, but I *can* tell you that I'm getting a strong connection with overseas."

"Overseas?" I said happily. "That's *right*. And what *is* the connection?"

"Well, that your friend enjoyed . . . going overseas. Didn't she?"

"Ye-es." *Along with nearly everyone else.* "Mags, just to make sure that you're getting the right person, can you tell me which country my friend had a particular connection with—a country that in fact she'd visited just three weeks before she—"

"Passed over? I *can* tell you that." Mags closed her eyes again. Her lids were rimmed with electric-blue eyeliner that flicked up at the corners. "I'm getting it now—loud and clear." She clapped her hands to her ears, then looked crossly at the ceiling. "I *heard* you, sweetie! No need to shout!" Calmly, she turned her gaze back to me. "The country your friend had a particular connection with *is* . . . South . . ." I held my breath. ". . . America."

I groaned. "No. She'd never even *been* there. She'd always wanted to go," I added.

Mags stared at me blankly. "Well . . . that's . . . *why* I'm getting it. Because your friend wanted to go there, and she never did . . . and now it's bugging her." She scratched the side of her nose. "Now, this friend of yours . . . whose name was . . ." She squeezed her eyes shut. "Nadine." She opened one eye and peered at me. "Lisa?"

"Emma," I supplied wearily.

"*Emma.*" Mags tutted. "Of course. Now . . . Emma was a very sensible, no-nonsense sort of person, wasn't she?"

"No," I replied. This was hopeless. "Emma wasn't like that at all. She was intense and slightly naïve—a bit . . . neurotic, even. Although she could be a lot of fun, she was prone to black moods. She was also unpredictable; she could do . . . reckless things." I thought bitterly of the final reckless thing that Emma had done. "But could you tell me about her career? Just to make sure you get the right Emma?"

Mags closed her eyes again, then opened them wide. "I'm seeing a hat..." I felt a burst of euphoria mingled with terror. "It's a black hat," Maggie went on. At that my excitement increased. Emma had made lots of black hats, including a really spectacular one she'd designed for Gwyneth Paltrow in the shape of a shell.

"What shape is it?" I asked, my heart beating wildly.

"It's flat, and... it's got four corners and... a long black tassel."

My spirits plummeted. "You're describing a mortarboard."

Mags smiled. "That's right—because Emma was a teacher, wasn't she?"

"*No.*"

"Well... did she wear a mortarboard for her graduation? Maybe *that's* what I'm seeing." Mags narrowed her eyes, lifting her head slightly, as though trying to focus on something that was just disappearing over the horizon.

"No." I sighed with exasperation. "Emma went to the Royal College of Art."

"I *thought* she was artistic," Mags said happily. "Got that right then." She wriggled her shoulders, then closed her eyes again as if in prayer. From somewhere I could hear a ring tone. What was the tune? Oh yes—"Spirit in the Sky." I realised that it was coming from Mags's chest. "Do excuse me," she said as she pulled out of her cleavage first a packet of cigarettes, then her cell phone. "Hi there," she said into it. "I see... You can't... That's quite all right. Thanks for letting me know." She snapped the phone shut and tucked it back into her bosom, daintily pushing it down with her middle finger. "You're in luck," she told me. "My twelve o'clock's just cancelled. Now we've got plenty of time."

I stood up. "Thanks, Mags, but no."

Serves me right for doing something so dodgy, I fumed as I drove back to Blackheath. I was insane even to have contemplated it. What if Mags *had* made a connection with Emma? The shock might have given me a nervous breakdown. I was *glad* that Mags was a charlatan. My indignation subsided and was replaced by relief.

I parked in my usual place outside the house, went inside just to empty the washing machine and put in another load, then I walked to the shop. Realising that I was hungry, I stopped at the Moon Daisy Café for a quick lunch. As I sat at a table outside, Pippa, who runs the café and who'd first told me about Val, brought me a copy of *The Times*. I idly looked at the home news, then the foreign pages, and then I read a piece about London Fashion Week, which had just started. Then, as I turned to the business pages, I found myself staring, shocked, at a photo of Guy. It was captioned GOOD GUY FLIES HIGH. As I read the article beneath it, my mouth dried to the texture of felt. *Guy Harrap...36...Friends Provident...went on to found Ethix...investing in companies that have no negative environmental impact...clean-tech...that do not use child labour...animal welfare...companies committed to enhancing human health and safety.*

I felt sick. Guy hadn't exactly enhanced Emma's human health or safety, had he! *You know how she exaggerates everything, Phoebe. She's probably just looking for attention.* He wasn't such a "good Guy" as he liked to think.

I surveyed the omelette Pippa had brought me with a sudden lack of interest. My cell phone rang. It was Mum.

"How are you, Phoebe?"

"I'm fine," I lied. With a trembling hand I closed the newspaper so that I didn't have to look at Guy. "What about you?"

"I'm fine too," she replied airily. "I'm fine, fine, I'm absolutely...miserable, actually, darling." I could hear her struggling not to cry.

"What's happened, Mum?"

"Well, I'm on site today, at Ladbroke Grove. I had to bring John some drawings that he needed, and..." I heard her gulp. "It's upset me, knowing that I'm so close to where your father lives now with...*her*...and...*and...*"

"Poor Mum. Just . . . try not to think about it. Look to the future."

"Yes, you're right, of course, darling." She sniffed. "I will. And actually to that end I've just found a wonderful new"—*man,* I was hoping she'd say—"treatment." My heart sank. "It's called fractional resurfacing or Fraxel. It's done with this laser thingy—it's very scientific. It actually *reverses* the ageing process."

"Really?"

"What it does—I've got the leaflet here"—I heard the squeak of glossy paper—"is to 'eliminate old epidermal pigmented cells. It restores the patient's face one piece at a time, just as a fine painting is restored one piece at a time.' The only downside," she added, "is that it causes 'vigorous exfoliation.'"

"Then keep the Hoover handy."

"And you need a minimum of six sessions."

"At a cost of?"

I heard her draw in her breath. "Three thousand pounds. But the difference between the before and after photos is amazing."

"That's because in the after photos the women are smiling and wearing makeup."

"Wait until *you're* sixty." Mum groaned. "You'll be having all these things plus whatever else they'll have thought of by then."

"I won't be having anything," I protested. "I don't hide from the past, Mum—I value it. That's why I do what I do."

"No need to be all pious about it," she retorted huffily. "Now do tell me, what's been happening with you?"

I decided not to tell her that I'd just been to a medium. Instead, I told her that I'd be going to France at the end of the month; then, on an impulse, I mentioned Miles. I hadn't meant to, but I thought it might cheer her up a little.

"That sounds promising," she said as I began to describe him. "A daughter of sixteen?" she interjected. "Well, you'd make a lovely stepmother, and you can still have a few of your own. So he's divorced is he? . . . A widower? Oh, *perfect* . . . And how old is Miles? . . . Ah. I *see.* On the *other* hand"—her tone brightened as she seemed to glimpse the possibilities of the situation—"that means he's not young and broke. Oh gosh, John's waving at me. I'd better go, darling."

"Chin up, Mum. No—on second thought, leave your chin where it is."

I spent the two hours after lunch taking inventory, phoning dealers, and looking at the auction-house websites, noting any upcoming sales that I'd want to go to. Then at ten to four I slipped on my jacket and headed for the Paragon.

Mrs. Bell let me in from upstairs and I climbed the three flights, my heels ringing against the stone steps.

"Ah, Phoebe. I'm so glad to see you again. Come in."

"I'm sorry I forgot the hats, Mrs. Bell." On the hall table I saw a booklet about home-care cancer nurses.

"It doesn't matter a bit. I'll make some tea. Go and sit down."

I went into the sitting room and stood at the window, looking down into the garden, which was deserted, except for a small boy in grey shorts and shirt, kicking through the leaves, looking for horse chestnuts.

Mrs. Bell appeared with the tray, but this time, when I offered to carry it, she let me. "My arms are not as strong as they were. My body is going over to the enemy. I will feel reasonably well this first month, apparently, and then . . . not so good."

"I'm . . . sorry," I said feeling impotent.

She shrugged. "Nothing to be done—except to appreciate every moment of the time I have left while I am still able to do so." She lifted the teapot, though she had to use both hands.

"And how was the nurse?"

Mrs. Bell sighed. "As pleasant and well organised as one would expect. She said I may be able to stay here until . . ." Her voice faltered. "I wish to avoid the hospital."

"Of course."

We sat in silence, drinking our tea. By now it was clear that Mrs. Bell was not going to resume her story. For whatever reason, she'd decided against it. Perhaps she regretted telling me what she *had* told me. She put down her cup, then straightened her shoulders. "The hatbox is still in the bedroom, Phoebe. Do go in and get it." I did so, and as I picked the box up I heard her call, "And would you be very kind and bring the blue coat?"

My pulse began to race as I went to the wardrobe. I took the coat out of its cover, then carried it into the sitting room, where I handed it to Mrs. Bell.

She smoothed it across her knee, her hand stroking the lapel. "So," she said quietly as I sat down again. "Where was I?"

"Well..." I put the hatbox by my feet. "You...told me that you had found your friend, Monique, in the barn, and that she'd been there for ten days." Mrs. Bell nodded slowly. "You took her some food..."

"Yes," she murmured. "I took her some food, didn't I—then I promised to take her this coat."

"That's right." I held my breath, fearful she'd decide not to continue her story.

She gazed into the distance again as her memories flooded back. "I remember how happy I was to think that I was going to help Monique. But I didn't help her," she added quietly. "I..." She pressed her lips together for a moment. "I was due to go back to Monique in the late afternoon. I kept thinking of all that I would do for my friend..." She paused.

"After lunch I went to the *boulangerie* to get my ration of bread. I had to queue for an hour, enduring the mutterings of my fellow customers about this person or that, supposedly buying things on the *marché noir.* The black market," she explained. "At last I got the half-baguette I was entitled to, and then, as I was walking back across the square, I saw Jean-Luc sitting outside the Bar Mistral, on his own. To my astonishment, he didn't look past me as he usually did—he looked *at* me. Then, to my further amazement, he beckoned to me to join him. I was so thrilled I could barely speak. He bought me a glass of apple juice, which I sipped while he had his beer. I felt intoxicated

with joy and excitement, suddenly finding myself sitting there in
the April sunshine with this divinely handsome boy who I had han-
kered after for so long.

"On the bar radio I could hear Frank Sinatra, singing "Night and
Day," which was a popular song at that time. I suddenly thought of
Monique in that barn night and day, and I realised that I had to
leave—that very minute. But then the waiter brought another beer
for Jean-Luc, and Jean-Luc asked me if I'd ever tried beer, so I said
no, of course not, I was only fourteen. He laughed and said that it
was high time I did. He offered me a taste of his Kronenbourg, and
again this felt so romantic to me, not least because beer was strictly
rationed. So I had a little sip, then another, and another—even
though I didn't like it at all—but I wanted Jean-Luc to think that I
did. Daylight was fading. I knew I *had* to go—*now*. But by then my
head was whirling, and it was almost dark, and I realised, to my
shame, that there was no way that I'd be walking to the barn that
night. So I resolved to go at dawn. I told myself that it would be a
delay of only a few hours."

Mrs. Bell was still stroking the coat, as if to comfort it. "Jean-Luc
said that he would take me home. It felt so romantic to be walking
across the square in the dusk, past the church, with the first stars
shining in the evening sky. I realised that it was going to be a clear
night—and a cold one." Her thin fingers absently sought the coat's
buttons. "I felt racked with guilt now about Monique—and my head
felt light and strange. And it suddenly occurred to me that maybe
Jean-Luc could help her. His father was a gendarme, after all—the
authorities surely must have made some mistake in allowing her
family to be taken away. And so, just before we reached my
house . . ." Mrs. Bell's hands clutched at the coat. Her knuckles were
white. "I told Jean-Luc about Monique . . . I told him that I had found
her in the old barn. I explained that I was only telling him this in
case he could possibly help her. Jean-Luc looked very concerned, so
much so that I remember even feeling a little stab of jealousy, and
then I recalled that affectionate gesture of his with Monique's scarf.

Anyway . . ." She swallowed. "He asked me where the barn was, so I told him." She shook her head. "For a moment Jean-Luc didn't speak, then he said that he'd heard of other children hiding in similar places, and even being hidden in people's homes. He added that it was a tough situation for all concerned. Then we came to my house, so we said good-bye.

"My parents were listening to a music programme on the radio, so they didn't hear me creep in and go up the stairs. I drank a lot of water because I felt thirsty, then I got into bed. On my chair, visible in the moonlight, was the blue coat . . ." Mrs. Bell lifted it now, hugging it to her. She sighed. "The next morning I awoke—not at first light, as I'd intended, but two hours later. I felt terrible that I'd failed to keep my word to Monique. But I consoled myself with the thought that I would soon be at the barn and that I would be giving her my lovely coat—a significant sacrifice, I reminded myself. Monique would be warm and she'd be able to sleep at night and everything would be okay—and maybe Jean-Luc might really be able to help her." At that Mrs. Bell smiled grimly.

"Because I felt so guilty about not meeting her the night before, I packed as much food into the basket as I could without my mother missing it, then set off for the barn. When I got there I crept inside. 'Monique,' I whispered as I took off the coat. There was no answer. Then I saw her blanket in a heap in the corner. I called her name again, but there was no reply—just the sound of the swifts darting about in the eaves. By now I had this pit in my stomach—except that it was like having a pit in my whole body. I walked round to the back of the barn, behind the hay bales, and on the patch of floor where Monique had been sleeping I saw her glass beads scattered among the straw."

Mrs. Bell gripped one of the blue wool sleeves. "I could not imagine where Monique had gone. I went out to the stream, but she wasn't there. I kept hoping that she would suddenly come back so that I could give her the coat—she *needed* it." Involuntarily, Mrs. Bell offered the coat to *me*, then, realising what she'd done, she let it fall back onto her lap. "I waited there for hours, then I guessed that it must be lunchtime and that my parents would be worried about me, so I ran all the way home. When I got there they saw that I was distressed and asked why. I lied. I said that it was because there was this boy I liked—Jean-Luc Aumage—but that I didn't think he liked me. "Jean-Luc Aumage!" my father exclaimed. "René Aumage's boy? That no-good chip off a nasty old block. Don't waste your time, my girl—there'll be better men for you than that!"

"Well . . ." Mrs. Bell's eyes were shining with indignation. "I wanted to slap my father for his nasty remarks. He didn't know what *I* knew—that Jean-Luc had agreed to help Monique. Then I wondered whether he had *already* helped her. Perhaps *that* was why she wasn't in the barn, because even now Jean-Luc was taking her to find her parents and brothers. I felt confident that he would do everything he could. So with hope in my heart I ran to his house; but Jean-Luc's mother said that he had gone to Marseille and would not be back until the following afternoon.

"That evening I went to the barn again, but Monique still wasn't there. Even though it was quite cold I couldn't bring myself to put on the coat, because by now I saw it as *hers.* So when I got home I went up to my room. Under my bed was a loose floorboard beneath which I kept a few of my secret things. I decided to hide the coat there until I could give it to Monique. But first I needed to wrap it in newspaper to protect it. So I found the copy of the *Gazette Provençal* that my father had been reading, but as I separated the pages an article caught my eye. It was all about the 'successful' arrest' of 'aliens' and other 'stateless persons' in Avignon, Carpentras, Orange, and Nîmes on April 19 and 20. The 'success' of this roundup, it went on, had been directly due to the policy of stamping the ration cards of Jewish people with their ethnic identity." Mrs. Bell looked at me. "*Now* I knew what had happened to Monique's family. The article talked of trains heading north, 'loaded' with 'foreign Jews' and 'other aliens.' I hid the coat and went downstairs, my head reeling.

"The next afternoon I went back to Jean-Luc's house and

knocked on the door. To my joy he opened it and, my heart pounding, I asked him, in a whisper, if he had been able to help Monique. He laughed. He said he'd 'helped her, all right.' With a sick feeling, I asked him what he meant. He didn't reply, so I told him that Monique needed to be looked after. Jean-Luc replied that she *would* be looked after—along with 'others of her kind.' I demanded to know where she was, and he replied that he had helped his father take her to Saint Pierre Prison in Marseille, from where she would be put on a train to Drancy as soon as possible. I knew what Drancy was—an internment camp on the outskirts of Paris. What I didn't know," Mrs. Bell added softly, "was that Drancy was the place from which Jewish people were being sent farther east—to Auschwitz, Buchenwald, and Dachau." Her eyes shone with tears. "Then, as Jean-Luc shut the door, the enormity of the situation hit me.

"I sank to the ground and whispered to myself, 'What have I *done*?' I had tried to help my friend. But, instead, my utter naïveté and *stupidity* had led to her being discovered, and sent to . . ." Mrs. Bell's mouth quivered, and I saw two tears fall onto the coat, darkening the fabric. "I heard the whistle of a train in the distance, and I thought Monique could be on *that* train, *now.* I wanted to run down to the track and make it *stop . . .*" She reached for the tissue that I held out to her and pressed it to her eyes. "Then, after the war, when we all learned what the true fate of the Jews had been, then I was . . . *distraught.* Every day, without cease, I imagined the ordeal that my friend Monique Richelieu—born Monika Richter—must have suffered. I was in torment, knowing that she had certainly died, in God knows what hellish place—and in what terror—because of *me.*" Her voice was raw with contempt. "I have never forgiven myself, and I never will." My throat was aching, as much for myself now as for Mrs. Bell. "As for the coat . . . I kept it hidden under the floor, despite my mother's angry protestations that I must find it. But I didn't care—it was Monique's. I longed to be able to give it to her. I longed to be able to help her into it, and to do up the buttons." She fingered one of the buttons now. "I also longed to give Monique this." She slipped her hand into the coat pocket. The pink and bronze glass of the necklace shimmered in the sunlight. Mrs. Bell laced the beads through her fingers, then held the necklace to her cheek. "It was my fantasy that I would one day give Monique the coat and this necklace, and, can you believe?" She looked at me. "It still *is.*" She gave me a wan smile. "You probably find that very strange, Phoebe."

I shook my head. "No."

"But I kept the coat in its hiding place until 1948, when, as I told you, I left Avignon for a new life here—a life far from where these terrible events had happened, a life in which I would not be bumping into Jean-Luc Aumage or his father in the street, or passing the house where Monique and her family had lived. I could not bear to see it again, knowing that they had never returned to it. And I never did see it again." Mrs. Bell heaved a deep sigh. "But even then, when I moved to London, I took the coat with me, still hoping to have the chance someday to keep my promise to my friend—which, yes, really *was* insane, because by then I had learned that the last known sighting of Monique was on August 5, 1943, the day she arrived at Auschwitz." She blinked. "But I have kept the coat, nonetheless, all these years. It is my . . . my . . ." She looked at me. "What is the word I am searching for?"

"It's *penance,*" I replied quietly.

"Penance." She nodded. "Of course." Then she slipped the necklace back into the pocket from which she'd taken it. "And that," she concluded, "is the story of this small blue coat." She stood up. "Thank you for listening, Phoebe. You have no idea what you have just done for me. All these years I have longed for just one person to hear my story, and if not to condemn me then at least to . . . understand. *Do* you understand, Phoebe?" she asked bleakly. "Do you understand why I did what I did? Why I still feel what I feel?"

"Yes, I do, Mrs. Bell," I answered softly. "More than you know."

. . .

Mrs. Bell went into the bedroom, and I heard the wardrobe door being shut. Then she came back and sat down across from me. Her face was drained of emotion.

"But . . ." I shifted on my seat. "Why didn't you tell your husband? From all you've said about him, you obviously loved him."

Mrs. Bell nodded. "Very much. But it's *because* I loved him that I didn't dare tell him. I was terrified that if he knew what I'd done, he might regard me differently. Or even condemn me."

"For what? For being a very young girl who tried to do the right thing but ended up doing . . ." I faltered.

"The wrong thing," Mrs. Bell concluded. "The worst thing I *could* have done. Of course it wasn't a deliberate betrayal," she went on. "As Monique had said, I didn't understand. I *was* very young, and I've often tried to console myself with the thought that Monique might have been discovered anyway. Who knows?"

"Yes," I said quickly. "She might. She might have died anyway, and it might have had nothing to do with you, Mrs. Bell—nothing at all, absolutely nothing." Mrs. Bell was staring at me curiously. "What you did was just an error of judgement," I added, more calmly.

"But that's made it no easier to live with, because it was an error of judgement that led to the death of my friend." She drew in her breath, then softly released it. "And that's been *so* hard to bear."

"I do . . . understand that—only too well," I said impulsively. "It's as though you're staggering around with this huge rock in your arms, and no one but you can carry it, and you can't see anywhere to put it down . . ." A sudden silence enveloped us. I was aware of the soft gasp of the fire. I picked up the hatbox and held it on my lap.

"Phoebe," Mrs. Bell murmured. "What really happened to your friend? To Emma?" I stared at the little bouquets of flowers on the box; the design was semiabstract, but I could see tulips and blue-bells.

"You said she was ill . . ."

I nodded, aware now of the light *tick* of the carriage clock. "It started almost a year ago, in early October."

"Emma's illness?"

I shook my head. "The events that led up to it—that, in a way, caused it." I told Mrs. Bell about Guy.

"So Emma must have been hurt by that."

"Yes," I answered quietly. "I didn't realise quite how much. She insisted that she'd be okay about Guy and me seeing each other, but it became clear that she wasn't okay—she was suffering."

"And you feel you're to blame?"

My mouth felt full of ashes. "Yes. Emma and I had been best friends for almost twenty-five years. But after I started seeing Guy, her almost daily phone calls just . . . stopped. When I phoned her she either didn't call me back or was distant with me. She simply withdrew from my life."

"But your relationship with Guy went on?"

"Yes, you see, we couldn't help it—we'd fallen in love. Guy's view was that we'd done nothing wrong. It wasn't our fault, he said, if Emma had read too much into his friendship with her. He said that she'd come round in time. He added that if she was a real friend, she'd have accepted the situation and tried to be happy for me."

Mrs. Bell folded her hands. "Do you think there's some truth in that?"

"Yes, of course. But it's easier said than done, when your feelings have been hurt. And I knew, from what Emma did next, how badly hers had been."

"What did she do?"

"After Christmas, Guy and I went skiing. On New Year's Eve we went out to dinner, and to start with we had a glass of champagne. And as Guy handed my glass to me I could see that there was something in it."

"*Ah,*" said Mrs. Bell. "A ring."

I nodded. "A beautiful solitaire. I was elated—and also amazed.

We'd only known each other three months. But even as I accepted, and we kissed, I was already in knots about how Emma would take it. I was to find out soon enough, because the next morning, to my surprise, she phoned to wish me a Happy New Year. We chatted for a while, and she asked me where I was. So I told her that I was in Val d'Isère. She asked me if I was there with Guy, so I said yes. Then I blurted out that we'd just gotten engaged. There was this... stunned silence."

"*La pauvre fille,*" Mrs. Bell murmured.

"Then, in this thin, shaky voice Emma said she hoped we'd be very happy. I told her that I'd love to see her soon and that I'd phone her right away on my return."

"So you were trying to keep your relationship with her going?"

"Yes. I thought that if she could just get used to seeing Guy with me, then she'd come to view him in a different way. I also believed that she'd soon fall in love with someone else and that our friendship would return to normal."

"But that's not what happened."

"No." I threaded the string of the hatbox through my fingers. "She'd clearly had very intense feelings for Guy and had convinced herself that their friendship would have developed into something more, if only... he..."

"Hadn't fallen for you."

Tears stung my eyes. "Anyway, when I got back to London on January sixth I phoned Emma first thing, but she didn't pick up. I rang her cell phone, but she didn't answer. I sent her texts and e-mails, but she didn't reply. Her assistant, Sian, was away, so I couldn't find out from her where Emma was, so then I rang Emma's mother, Daphne. She told me that Emma had decided quite suddenly, just three days before, to go to South Africa to visit old friends and that's where she was, in Transvaal. The phone signal was poor, Daphne said; that's probably why I hadn't gotten through to her. Then she asked me... if I thought that Emma was okay, because she'd seemed upset lately but had refused to say why. I pretended not to know what the problem might be. Daphne added that Emma could be moody at times and one just had to let it pass. Feeling an utter hypocrite, I agreed."

"Did you hear from Emma while she was in South Africa?"

"No. But by the third week of January I knew she was back because I got her written RSVP to the engagement party that Guy and I were having on the following Saturday. She sent her regrets."

"That must have hurt you."

"Yes," I murmured. "I can't tell you how much. Then came Valentine's Day . . ." I hesitated. "Guy had booked a table at the Bluebird Café in Chelsea, not far from his flat. And we were just getting ready to leave when, to my surprise, Emma phoned me—it was the first time she'd called me since New Year's Day. I thought her voice sounded a bit strange—as though she was short of breath—so I asked her if she was okay. She said that she was feeling 'rotten.' She sounded weak and shivery, as though she had the flu. I asked her if she'd taken anything for it, and she said she'd had some pain killers. She added that she felt 'so bad' that she 'wanted to die.' That set alarm bells ringing, so I said that I was coming right over. And I heard Emma whisper, '*Will* you? Will you come, Phoebe? Please come.' So I promised I'd be there in half an hour.

"As I shut my phone I could see that Guy was very upset. He reminded me that he'd booked a nice Valentine's Day dinner for just the two of us and that he wanted us to enjoy it—plus he didn't believe that Emma *was* in such a bad way. 'You know how she exaggerates things,' he said. 'She's probably just looking for attention.' I insisted that Emma had really sounded ill, and pointed out that a lot of people had the flu. Guy said that, knowing Emma, it was probably just a bad cold. He added that I was overreacting out of misplaced guilt, when it was Emma who should feel guilty. She'd sulked for three months and had even shunned our engagement party. Now here I was getting ready to rush round the second she deigned to call. I told Guy that Emma was a slightly fragile person; we needed to understand how sensitive she was. He said he'd had enough of the 'mad milliner,' as he'd taken to calling her. We were going to have dinner. He stood up and put on his coat.

"Every instinct told me that I should go and see Emma, but I couldn't bear the thought of arguing with Guy. I remember standing there, twisting my engagement ring around, saying, 'I just don't know what to *do*...' Then...as a compromise...Guy suggested that we have dinner and that I ring Emma when we got back. Reluctantly, I agreed. So we went to the Bluebird. I remember we discussed our wedding, which was to have been this month. It's weird to think of it now," I added bleakly.

Mrs. Bell was shaking her head in sympathy.

"Anyway...when we got back to Guy's flat at ten-thirty, I phoned Emma. To my horror, at the sound of my voice she started crying. She said she was sorry that she hadn't been nicer about Guy and me. She said she'd been a terrible friend. I told her that it didn't matter and she didn't need to worry about anything because I was going to look after her." I felt tears tickle my lashes. "Then I heard her mumble, 'Tonight, Phoebe?' 'Tonight,' I repeated. I looked at Guy, but he whispered that I'd had too much to drink at dinner to drive and I realised that I probably had, so I told her..." I tried to swallow but it was as though my throat was crammed with rags. "I told her...that I'd be there in the morning." I paused. "At first Emma didn't respond. Then I heard her whisper, '...sleep now.' So I said, 'Yes, you go to sleep now. I'll see you first thing. Have a lovely sleep, Em.'" I looked down at the hatbox. I couldn't see the tulips and bluebells through my tears.

"I woke at dawn with a churning feeling in my stomach. I thought about phoning Emma but decided it was too early; I didn't want to wake her. So I drove to Marylebone and parked close to the house she rented on Nottingham Street. I knew where she kept her spare key, so I fished it out of its hiding place and let myself in. The house looked unusually untidy. There was a pile of mail on the mat. The kitchen sink was full of unwashed plates.

"It was the first time I'd been to Emma's house since the fateful dinner party. As I stood there I remembered the dismay I'd felt when Emma had first introduced me to Guy, then my euphoria when he'd phoned me. Our friendship had been tested to destruction, I reflected, but now everything was going to be all right. Then I went into the sitting room and that was a mess too, with towels on the sofa and the wastepaper basket overflowing with used tissues and empty water bottles. Emma had obviously been in a bad way. I went up the narrow stairs, past photos of models wearing her lovely hats, and stood outside her bedroom door. There was silence from the other side, and I remember feeling so relieved, because it meant that Emma was in a deep sleep, which would be the best thing for her.

"I pushed on the door and crept in. As I moved closer to the bed I realised that Emma was sleeping so deeply that I couldn't hear her breathing. Then I remembered that she'd always been good at holding her breath. When we were children she used to scare me by swimming underwater and holding it for ages. Then I thought, But why would Emma be doing that *now*, when we're both thirty-three?

" 'Emma,' I said gently. 'It's me.' There was no movement. 'Emma,' I whispered, 'wake up.' She didn't stir. 'Wake *up*, Emma,' I said, my heart pounding. 'Please. I need to see how you are. Come on, Em.' She didn't reply. 'Emma, would you please wake *up*,' I said, panicking now. I clapped my hands, twice, by her head. And suddenly I remembered how once, when we were playing hide-and-seek, she'd played dead so convincingly that I'd thought she *was* dead and I'd been distraught; but then she'd suddenly jumped to her feet, roaring with laughter. I'd been so upset and angry with her that I'd cried.

"I half expected Emma to jump up now, laughing and shouting, '*Fooled you, Phoebe! You thought I was dead, didn't you!*' until I remembered that she'd sworn never to do that again. But still she wasn't moving. 'Don't *do* this to me, Em,' I pleaded. '*Please.*' I put out my hand and touched her . . ." I stared at the hatbox in my lap, and now I could see lupins—or were they foxgloves? "I pulled back the duvet. Emma was lying on her side, in jeans and a T-shirt, her eyes half open, just staring ahead. Her skin was grey. Her fingers were curled round the phone.

"I remember letting out a cry, then fumbling for my cell phone. My hand was shaking so much that I kept missing the nine button. I saw a bottle of pain killers on the floor and picked it up—it was empty. Now I could hear the 999 woman asking me what emergency service I required. I was gasping with shock and could hardly speak, but I managed to stutter that my friend needed an ambulance immediately, this very minute, so would they please send one *now*, right now... *please*..." I tried to swallow. "But even as I said it, I knew that it was... that Em... that Emma had..."

A tear fell onto the hatbox with a tiny *splash*.

"Oh, Phoebe," I heard Mrs. Bell whisper.

"They told me afterwards that she'd died about three hours before I got there."

I sat in silence, still cradling the hatbox, running the pale green string back and forth through my fingers.

"But how terrible to do that," said Mrs. Bell quietly after a few moments. "Whatever her sadness... to commit..."

I raised my head and looked at her. "But that's not what it was— although that's how it seemed at first. For a while there was confusion about what had actually happened to Emma... about what had caused her... what had..."

"I'm sorry, Phoebe." Mrs. Bell sighed. "It's too upsetting for you to talk about."

"Yes, it is. Because I'm to blame."

She shook her head. "But it wasn't your fault that Guy fell in love with you, rather than Emma."

"But I *knew* how much she liked him. I shouldn't have pursued the relationship, knowing that. Not if I cared for Emma."

"But it might have been your one chance in life at love."

"That's what I told myself. I told myself that I might never feel this way about anyone ever again. And I consoled myself that Emma would get over Guy, and fall in love with someone else, because that's what she'd always done before with men. But this time she didn't," I said wretchedly. "And I can understand her *hating* the thought of having to see him with me when she'd so hoped to be with him herself."

"You can't blame *your*self that that hope of hers was misguided, Phoebe."

"No. But I can and do blame myself for not going to see her that night, when every instinct told me I should."

"Well . . ." Mrs. Bell shook her head again. "Perhaps it might have made no difference."

"That's what my doctor said. She said that by then Emma would have been slipping into the coma from which she would never . . ." I drew in my breath in a juddery gasp. "I'll never know. But I believe that if I had gone when she'd first called me, rather than twelve hours later, Emma would still be alive."

I put down the hatbox, then went to the window. I gazed down at the deserted garden.

"So that's why you've felt an affinity with me, Mrs. Bell," I said softly. "Because we both had friends who waited for us to come."

Seven

There are some people who say they're able to "compartmentalise" things, as though it's possible to put negative or distressing thoughts into neat mental drawers to be taken out only at a psychologically convenient time. It's a beguiling idea, but I've never bought it. In my experience, sadness and regret seep into one's consciousness willy-nilly, or they suddenly leap out at you with a snarl. The only real remedy is time, though even the best part of a lifetime, as Mrs. Bell's story proved, may still not be time enough. Work is also an antidote to unhappiness, of course, as is distraction. Miles was a welcome distraction, I decided as I went to meet him on Thursday for dinner.

I'd dressed up a little, in a sixties cocktail dress in pale pink sari silk. Over it I'd draped an antique gold pashmina.

"Mr. Archant is already here," the maître d' of the OXO Tower restaurant informed me. As I followed him across the floor, I saw Miles sitting at a table by the vast window, studying the menu. With a sinking heart I registered his grey hair and his half-moon reading glasses. Then as he looked up and saw me, his face lit up with a delighted but anxious smile that dispelled my disappointment. He got to his feet, tucking his spectacles back into his top pocket and holding his yellow silk tie to stop it from flapping. It was endearing to see such a sophisticated man behaving so awkwardly.

"Phoebe." He kissed me on both cheeks, placing his hand on my shoulder, as though to draw me towards him. Seeing now how attractive Miles was, I felt a sudden surge of interest in him that surprised me.

"Would you like a glass of champagne?" he asked.

"That would be lovely."

"Is Dom Pérignon okay?"

"If there's nothing better," I teased.

"They're out of vintage Krug—I did ask." I laughed, then realised that Miles hadn't been joking.

As we chatted, enjoying the views across the sunlit river to the temple and Saint Paul's, I was touched by how much Miles was trying to impress me, and by how happy he seemed to be in my company. I asked him about his work, and he explained that he was a founding partner of the law firm that he now consulted for three days a week.

"I'm semiretired now." He sipped his champagne. "But I like to keep my hand in, and I help bring in new business by entertaining clients. Now tell me about your shop, Phoebe. What made you decide to open it?" I briefly told Miles about my time at Sotheby's. His eyes widened. "So I was bidding against a professional that day."

"You were," I said as he handed the wine list back to the waiter. "But I behaved like a rank amateur. I let my emotions get the better of me."

"I must say, you *were* rather intense. But what's so wonderful about—sorry, what was the name of that designer again?"

"Madame Grès," I said patiently. "She was the greatest couturiere in the world. She draped and pleated vast amounts of cloth, pinning it directly onto the body to form an amazing gown that turned the woman into a beautiful statue almost. She was also very brave."

Miles folded his hands. "In what way?"

"When she opened the House of Grès in Paris in 1942 she hung a huge French flag out of her window in defiance of the occupation. Each time the Germans ripped it down, she'd put out another one. They knew she was Jewish, but left her alone because they hoped she'd dress their officers' wives. When she refused to do so, they shut her down. Tragically, she died in obscurity and poverty. But she was a genius."

"And what will you do with the dress?"

I gave a little shrug. "I don't know."

He smiled. "Keep it for your wedding."

"That *has* been suggested to me, but I doubt it will ever be worn for that purpose."

"*Have* you been married?" I shook my head. "Ever come close?" I nodded. "Were you engaged?" I nodded again.

"Am I allowed to ask you about it?"

"Sorry—I'd rather not talk about it." I pushed Guy from my thoughts. "What about you?" I asked as our appetizers arrived. "You've been on your own for ten years. Why haven't you . . . ?"

"Married again?" Miles shrugged. "There've been a few girl-friends." He picked up his soup spoon. "They were all very nice, but . . . it just hasn't happened." Now the conversation naturally turned to his wife. "Ellen was a lovely person. In fact I adored her," he added. "She was American—a successful portrait painter, of chil-dren mostly. She died ten years ago, in June." He drew in his breath, then held it, as though he was considering a difficult question. "She just collapsed one afternoon."

"Why?"

He lowered his spoon. "It was a brain haemorrhage. She'd had a terrible headache all that day, but as she often got migraines, it didn't even occur to her that it was anything different." Miles shook his head. "You can imagine the shock . . ."

"Yes," I said quietly.

"But I could at least console myself that it was no one's fault." I felt a stab of envy. "It was simply one of those dreadful, unavoidable things—the finger of God, or however one wants to put it."

"And how terrible for Roxanne."

He nodded. "She was only six. I sat her on my lap and tried to explain that Mummy . . ." His voice faltered. "I'll never forget the expression on her face as she struggled to understand the incomprehensible—that half her universe had simply . . . *vanished*." Miles sighed. "I know that it's always there with Roxy—just beneath the surface. She has this acute sense of not *having* . . . a sense of . . . of . . ."

"Deprivation?" I suggested gently.

Miles looked at me. "Deprivation. Yes. That's it."

Suddenly his BlackBerry rang. He took his glasses out of his top pocket and placed them on the end of his nose as he peered at the screen. "That's Roxy now. Oh dear—would you excuse me, Phoebe?" He removed his glasses, then went out of the restaurant onto a corner of the terrace. I watched him leaning against the railing, his tie flapping a little in the breeze, evidently having a serious chat with Roxanne. Then I saw him pocket the phone.

"I'm sorry about that," he said as he returned to the table. "It must have seemed rude, but when it's your child . . ."

"I understand," I said.

"She's stuck on her ancient-history essay," he explained as the waiter brought our main courses. "It's on Boadicea."

"Isn't she called Boudica these days?"

Miles nodded. "I always forget. I still have to remind myself that Bombay has become Mumbai."

"And how about the Dome being 'O2'?

"*Is* it?" he said, then smiled. "Anyway, Roxy has to hand this essay in tomorrow and she's hardly started. She's a bit disorganised about her work sometimes." He gave an exasperated sigh.

I picked up my fork. "And does she like her school?"

"She seems to, though it's very early days—she's only been there two weeks."

"Where was she before?"

"At Saint Mary's, a girls' school in Dorking. But..." I looked at him. "It didn't really work out."

"Didn't she like boarding school?"

"She didn't mind it, but there was..." He hesitated "...a misunderstanding—a few weeks before her final exams. It was all... cleared up," he went on. "But after that I felt it would be better for her to have a fresh start. So now she's at Bellingham. She seems to like it there, so my fingers are crossed that she'll get good grades." He sipped his wine.

"Then go to university?"

Miles shook his head. "Roxy says it's a waste of time."

"Really?" I put down my fork. "Well, it *isn't*. Didn't you say she wants to work in the fashion business?"

"Yes, though doing what I don't know. She talks about working for a glossy magazine, like *Vogue* or *Tatler.*"

"But it's an extremely competitive world. If she's serious, she'd be much better off with a degree."

"I've told her that," Miles replied wearily. "But she's quite headstrong."

The waiter came to take our plates, so I seized the opportunity to change the subject. "Your surname's unusual," I pointed out. "I once met a Sebastian Archant who owns Fenley Castle. I had to go there to evaluate a collection of eighteenth-century textiles." I remembered a velvet tailcoat and breeches from the 1780s, beautifully embroidered with anemones and forget-me-nots. "Most of them went to museums."

"Sebby's my second cousin," Miles explained, slightly wearily. "Now, don't tell me: he tried to ravish you behind the gazebo?"

"Not exactly." I rolled my eyes. "But I had to stay at the castle for three nights because it was a very big job and there were no hotels nearby and..." I cringed at the memory. "He tried to come into my room. I had to push a trunk against the door—it was ghastly."

"That's Sebby all over, I'm afraid—not that I blame him for trying." Miles held his gaze in mine for a moment. "You're lovely, Phoebe." The directness of his compliment made me catch my breath. I felt an unexpected wave of desire ripple through me. "I'm closer to the French side of the family," I heard Miles say. "They're wine growers."

"Where?"

"In Châteauneuf-du-Pape, a few miles to the north of—"

"Avignon," I interjected.

He looked at me. "Do you know it?"

"I go to Avignon from time to time to buy stock; in fact, I'll be there next weekend."

Miles lowered his glass of red wine. "Where are you staying?"

"At the Hôtel d'Europe."

He was shaking his head in delighted wonderment. "Well, Miss Swift, if you're agreeable to a second date with me, I'll take you out to dinner again. I'm going to be in the area, too."

"You are?" Miles nodded happily. "Why?"

"Because this other cousin of mine, Pascal, owns the vineyard. We've always been close, Pascal and I, and I go down every September to help with the harvest. It's just started and I'll be there for the last three days. When will you be arriving?" I told him. "So we'll overlap then," he said with a delight that tugged at my heartstrings. "You know," he added as our coffee arrived, "I can't help feeling that this must be Fate." He suddenly winced, then reached for his phone. "Not again—I'm so sorry, Phoebe." He put on his glasses and stared at the screen, a frown wrinkling his brow. "Roxy's still in a state about her essay. She says she's 'desperate'—in capitals with several exclamation marks." He sighed. "I'd better get back. Plus I did promise her I wouldn't be home too late. Will you forgive me?"

"Of course." We'd almost come to the end of the evening, and I found his attachment to his child touching.

Miles signalled to the waiter, then looked at me. "I've enjoyed this evening so much."

"So have I," I said truthfully.

He smiled at me. "Good."

Miles paid the bill, then we went downstairs in the lift. As we stepped onto the pavement I started to say good-bye before walking the five minutes to London Bridge Station, but a taxi was pulling up beside us.

The driver lowered the window. "Mr. Archant?"

Miles nodded, then turned to me. "I booked the cab to take me to Camberwell. Then he'll go on to Blackheath to drop you."

"Oh. I was going to get the train—"

"I wouldn't hear of it."

I glanced at my watch. "It's only ten-fifteen," I protested. "It's fine."

"But if I give you a lift, then I get to spend a bit more time with you."

"In that case . . ." I smiled at him. "Thanks."

As we drove through South London, Miles and I tried to remember what we knew about Boudica. We could remember only that she was an Iron Age queen who rebelled against the Romans. Dad would know, I thought, but it was too late to ring him. He got little enough sleep these days, as he has to get up in the night to care for Louis.

"Didn't she raze Ipswich?" I asked as we drove down Walworth Road.

Miles was surfing the net on his BlackBerry. "It was Colchester," he said, peering at the screen through his half-moon glasses. "It's all here on Britannica dot-com. When I get back I'll just lift chunks straight off it and rewrite it." It occurred to me that at sixteen Roxy could surely have done this for herself.

We were crossing Camberwell Green, then we turned into Camberwell Grove and stopped halfway down on the left. So this was where Miles lived. As I looked at his elegant Georgian house set back from the road, I saw a downstairs curtain twitch, and there was Roxy's pale, oval face.

Miles turned to me. "It's been lovely to see you, Phoebe." He leaned forward and kissed me, holding his cheek against mine for a moment. "So . . . see you in France." His anxious expression told me that that had been a question, not a statement.

I smiled at him. "I'll see you in France."

I was delighted to have been asked to take part in Radio London's discussion about vintage clothes—until I remembered that their studio was in Marylebone High Street. I braced myself for the walk down Marylebone Lane on Monday morning. As I passed the ribbon shop where Emma used to buy trimmings for her hats, I tried not to imagine her house, just a few streets away, no doubt with other occupants now. I tried not to imagine her things, all packed into trunks in her parents' garage. Then I thought with dismay of her diary, which Emma wrote in every day. Her mother would surely read it before long.

As I approached Amici's, the cafe where Emma and I always went, I suddenly fancied that I could see her, sitting in the window, looking out at me with a hurt, puzzled expression. But of course it wasn't Emma—just someone who looked a little like her.

I pushed through the glass doors of Radio London. The security guard wrote out a name badge for me, then asked me to wait. As I sat in the reception area I listened to the chatter of the broadcast. *Travel news now . . . South Circular . . . incident at Highbury Corner . . . 94.9 FM . . . And the weather for London . . . highs of twenty-two . . . with me, Ginny Jones . . . and in a few minutes I'll be talking old hat—or rather old clothes—with vintage dress shop owner Phoebe Swift.* I felt a cloud of butterflies take flight in my stomach. The producer, Mike, appeared, clipboard in hand.

"It's just a friendly five-minute chat," he explained, as he led me down the brightly lit corridor. He put his shoulder to the heavy studio door and it opened with a muffled *swish*. "We've got a prerecord on, so it's okay to talk," he explained as we went in. "Ginny, meet Phoebe."

"Hi, Phoebe," said Ginny as I sat down. She nodded at the headphones lying in front of me. I slipped them on and heard the prerecord finishing. Then there was a bit of banter with the sports reporter—something to do with the London Olympics—and an ad. "Now," Ginny said, smiling at me. "From rags to riches, that's what Phoebe Swift is hoping for. She's just opened a vintage dress shop down in Blackheath—Village Vintage—and she joins me now. Phoebe, London Fashion Week has just finished; this year vintage was quite a huge theme, wasn't it?"

"It was. Several of the major houses had a vintage feel to their new collections. It's very current."

"Why *does* vintage seem to be the flavour *de nos jours*?"

"I think the fact that a style icon like Kate Moss chooses to wear it has had a big impact on the market."

"She wore that gold satin thirties dress that got ripped to shreds, didn't she?"

"She did, but that was a case of riches to *rags*, because it was said to have cost two thousand pounds. There are lots of Hollywood stars wearing vintage now on the red carpet—Julia Roberts at the Oscars in vintage Valentino, or Renée Zellweger in that 1950s canary-yellow gown by Jean Dessès. All this has changed the perception of vintage, which used to be seen as something Bohemian and quirky, rather than the highly sophisticated choice that it's become."

Ginny scribbled on her script. "So what does vintage *do* for a girl?"

"The fact that you know you're wearing something that is both highly individual and beautifully made is itself uplifting. And you're aware that the garment has a history—a heritage, if you like—which gives it a kind of backbone. No contemporary piece of clothing can offer this dimension."

"So what tips do you have when buying vintage?"

"Be prepared to spend time looking, and know what *suits* you. If you're curvy, then don't go for the twenties or sixties, as the boxy style won't flatter you; choose the more fitted silhouette of the forties and fifties. If you like the thirties, be aware that those figure-skimming designs are unforgiving on a round tummy or large bust. I'd also say be realistic. Don't go into a vintage shop and ask to be turned into, say, Audrey Hepburn in *Breakfast at Tiffany's*, because that style may well not do anything for you and you might miss something that would."

"What are *you* wearing today, Phoebe?"

I glanced at my dress. "A non-label floral chiffon tea dress from the late 1930s—*my* favourite era—with a vintage cashmere cardigan."

"Very nice too. You strike me as quite a cool lady." I smiled. "And do you always wear vintage?"

"I do—if not a whole outfit, then vintage accessories; the days when I wear nothing that's vintage are rare."

"But"—Ginny grimaced—"I don't think I'd want to wear anyone else's old clothes."

"Some people do feel like that." I thought of Mum. "But we vintage lovers are born, not made, so we're not squeamish about it. We feel that a tiny stain or mark is a small price to pay for owning something that's not just original, it may even bear an iconic name."

Ginny held up her pen. "So what are the main things to be concerned about with vintage? The prices?"

"No, for the quality, the prices remain reasonable—another plus point in these credit-crunched times. You need to be aware of the sizing; vintage clothes tend to run small. Waists were fashionably tiny from the forties through to the sixties, dresses and jackets were very fitted; and women wore corsets and girdles to be able to squeeze into them. Added to which, women today are simply bigger. My advice when buying vintage is simply to ignore the number on the label and try it on."

"What about the care of these old clothes?" Ginny asked. "Could you tell us how to keep our vintage mintage?"

I smiled. "There are some basic rules. Hand-wash knitwear using baby shampoo, and don't soak it, as that could stretch the fibres; then dry it inside out and flat."

"What about mothballs?" asked Ginny, holding her nose.

"They do smell foul, and the more fragrant alternatives don't seem to work. The best thing is to keep anything moth-prone in polythene bags; and a squish of perfume in your closet can work wonders—anything strong and sweet like Fendi will deter moths."

"It certainly deters me." Ginny laughed.

"With silk," I went on, "store it on padded hangers, away from direct sunlight, as it fades easily. When it comes to satin, *don't* let water near it—it'll wrinkle—and never buy satin that's brittle or frayed, as it won't stand up to wear."

"As Kate Moss discovered."

"Indeed. I'd also advise your listeners to avoid anything that desperately needs cleaning, as it may prove impossible. Gelatine sequins melt under modern cleaning techniques. Bakelite or glass beads can crack."

"Now there's a vintage word—Bakelite," said Ginny with an amused expression. "But where do we buy vintage clothes? Apart from at shops like yours, obviously."

"At auctions," I replied, "and at vintage fairs. They take place a few times a year in the bigger cities. Then there's eBay, of course, though make sure you always ask the seller for every single measurement."

"What about charity shops?"

"You will find vintage in them, but not at bargain prices, as the charities have become more savvy about its worth."

"Presumably you have a steady stream of people bringing in clothes they want to sell? Or asking you to look through their wardrobes and attics?"

"I do, and I love it, because I never know what I'll find; and when I see something I like, I get this wonderful feeling—*here.*" I laid my hand on my chest. "It's like . . . falling in love."

"So it's a vintage *affair.*"

I laughed. "Yes! You could put it like that."

"Do you have any other advice?"

"If you're selling, check the pockets."

"Do things get left in them?"

I nodded. "All sorts—keys, pens and pencils."

"Ever found hard cash?" Ginny joked.

"Sadly not, though I did find a postal order once—for two shillings and sixpence."

"So check your pockets then, everyone," said Ginny, "and check out Phoebe Swift's shop, Village Vintage, in Blackheath, if you want to know"—she leaned into the mike—"the way we *wore*." Ginny gave me a warm smile. "Phoebe Swift, thanks."

Mum phoned me as I was walking towards the tube. She'd been listening at work. "You were terrific," she enthused. "I was fascinated. So how did it come about?"

"Through that newspaper interview. The one that chap Dan did on the day of the party. Do you remember him? He was leaving just as you arrived."

"I know—the badly dressed man with the curly hair. I like curly hair on a man," Mum added. "It's unusual."

"Yes, Mum; anyway, the radio producer happened to read it, and as he was planning to do something on vintage for Fashion Week he phoned me."

I suddenly realised that nearly all of the helpful things that had happened lately had come about through Dan's article. It had brought Annie into the shop, and it had led me to Mrs. Bell, and now to this radio opportunity, quite apart from all the customers who'd come in because they'd read it. I felt a sudden rush of warmth towards him.

"I'm not going to have Fraxel," Mum said.

"Thank goodness."

"I'm going to have radio-frequency rejuvenation instead."

"What's that?"

"They heat up the deeper layer of your skin with lasers, and that shrinks everything so that it doesn't sag so much. Basically, they cook your face. Betty from my bridge circle's had it. She's thrilled—except that she said it was like having cigarettes stubbed out on her cheeks for an hour and a half."

"What torture! And how does Betty look now?"

"To be honest, exactly the same; but *she's* convinced she looks younger, so it was obviously worth it." I considered the bewildering logic of this. "Oh, I'd better go, Phoebe—John's waving at me..."

I stepped into the shop. Annie looked up from her repair.

"I only heard half the programme, I'm afraid, because I had a brush with a shoplifter."

My heart skipped a beat. "What happened?"

"As I was fiddling with the radio a man tried to slip one of the crocodile-skin wallets into his pocket." Annie nodded at the basket of wallets and purses I keep on the counter. "Luckily I glanced into the mirror at the critical moment, so at least I didn't have to chase after him down the street."

"Did you call the police?"

She shook her head. "He begged me not to, but I told him that if I ever saw him in here again, I would. Then I had this woman..." Annie rolled her eyes. "She picked up the Bill Gibb silver lace minidress, slapped it on the counter, and said she'd give me twenty quid for it."

"Damn cheek!"

"So I explained that at eighty pounds the dress was already very reasonable, and that if she wanted to haggle, she should go to the souk." I snorted with laughter. "Then I had a bit of a thrill—Chloë Sevigny came in. She's filming in South London. We had a nice chat about acting."

"She wears a lot of vintage, doesn't she? And did she buy anything?"

"One of the Jean Paul Gaultier Body Map tops. Now I've got some messages for you." Annie picked up a piece of paper. "Dan phoned. He's got the tickets for *Anna Karenina* this Wednesday and says he'll meet you outside the Greenwich Picturehouse at seven."

"*Will* he now?"

Annie glanced at me. "Aren't you going?"

"I wasn't sure . . . but . . . well, it seems I am, doesn't it?" I added irritably.

She gave me a puzzled look. "Then Val rang. She's finished your repairs and says please can you collect them. And there was a message on the answering machine from a Rick Diaz in New York."

"He's my American dealer."

"He's got some more prom dresses for you."

"Great. We need them for the party season."

"We do. He added that he's got some bags he'd like you to take."

I groaned. "I've got *hundreds* of bags."

"I know, but he says please can you e-mail him. Then, last but not least, *these* arrived." Annie disappeared into the kitchen. She came out carrying a bouquet of red roses so huge it obscured her face.

I stared at them.

"Three dozen," I heard her say from behind the flowers. "Are they from this chap Dan?" she asked as I unpinned the envelope and took out the card. "Not that your personal life is any of my business," she added as she put the roses on the counter.

Love Miles. Was that a salutation or a command? I wondered.

"They're from someone I've met quite recently," I said to Annie. "In fact, I met him at the Christie's auction."

"Really?"

"His name is Miles."

"Is he nice?"

"Seems to be."

"And what does he do?"

"He's a *lawyer.*"

"A successful one, judging by the flowers he sends. And how old is he?"

"Forty-eight."

"*Ah.*" Annie raised an eyebrow. "So he's vintage, too."

I nodded. "Circa 1960. A bit of wear and tear . . . a few creases . . ."

"But plenty of character?"

"I think so . . . I've only met him three times."

"Well, he's clearly smitten, so I hope you're going to see him again."

"Perhaps." I didn't want to admit that I'd be seeing Miles this very weekend, in Provence.

"Would you like me to put them in a vase for you?"

"Yes, please."

She cut the ribbon. "In fact, I'll need two vases."

I took off my coat. "By the way, you're still okay to work on Friday and Saturday, aren't you?"

"I am," Annie replied as she removed the cellophane. "But you will definitely be back by Tuesday?"

"I'm returning on Monday evening. Why?"

Annie was stripping off the lower leaves with a pair of scissors. "I've got another audition on Tuesday morning, so I won't be able to get here until after lunch. I'll make up the time on the Friday, if that's okay?"

"That would be fine. What's the audition for?" I asked with a sinking heart.

"Regional rep," she replied wearily. "Three months in Stoke-on-Trent."

"Well, fingers crossed," I said disingenuously, then felt guilty about hoping that Annie would fail. But it would only be a matter of time before she did get a job, and then . . .

My train of thought was interrupted by the bell. And I was just going to leave Annie to it when I saw who the customer was.

"Hi," said the red-haired girl who'd tried on the lime-green cupcake dress nearly three weeks earlier.

"Hi," Annie replied warmly as she put half the roses in a vase. The girl stood staring at the green cupcake dress. "Thank God," she breathed. "It's still here."

"It's still here," Annie echoed cheerfully as she put the first vase on the centre table.

"I was convinced it wouldn't be," the girl said, turning to me now. "I almost couldn't bear to come in, in case it had sold."

"We have sold two of those prom dresses recently, but not yours— I mean that one," I corrected myself. "The green one."

"I'll take it," she said happily.

"Really?" As I unhooked it from the wall I noticed how much more self-confident the girl seemed than when she'd come in with ... what was his name?

"Keith didn't like it." She opened her bag. "But I loved it." She looked at me. "And he knew that. Oh, I don't need to try it on again," she added as I hung the dress in the changing room. "It's perfect."

"It is perfect," I agreed. "On you. I'm thrilled you've come back for it," I confided as I took it to the register. "When a garment suits a customer as well as this suited you, then I really want her to have it. Have you got some glamorous party to wear it to?" I thought of her looking dismal in black at the Dorchester with the vile Keith and his "important clients."

"I've no idea when I'm going to wear it," the girl replied calmly. "I only knew that I *had* to have it. Once I'd tried it on, well ..." She shrugged. "The dress *claimed* me."

I folded it, pressing down its voluminous underskirts so that it wouldn't burst out of the shopping bag.

The girl took a pink envelope out of her purse and handed it to me. It was a Disney Princess one, with a picture of Cinderella in the corner. I opened it. Inside was £275 in cash.

"I'm happy to give you the five percent discount," I said.

For a second, she hesitated. "No. Thank you."

"I really don't mind ..."

"It's two hundred seventy-five," she insisted. "That was the price," she added firmly, almost aggressively. "Let's stick to it."

"Well, okay." I shrugged, slightly taken aback. As I handed her the dress, she emitted a little sigh, of ecstasy almost. Then, her head held high, she left the shop.

"So she got her fairy-tale dress after all," Annie murmured as I watched the girl cross the road. "I just wish she had a fairy-tale man. But she seemed quite different today, didn't she?" Annie added as she put the second vase of roses on the counter. She went to the window and looked out. "She's even walking taller—look." Her eyes narrowed as they tracked her down the street. "Vintage clothes can do that," she remarked after a moment. "They can be subtly . . . transforming."

"That's true. But how weird that she refused the discount."

"I bet it's important to her that she paid for the dress herself, every penny. But I wonder what's happened that she was able to buy it," Annie mused.

I shrugged. "Maybe Keith relented and gave her the cash."

Annie shook her head. "He'd never have done that. Perhaps she stole the money from him," she suggested. I had a sudden vision of the girl wearing the dress behind prison bars. "Perhaps a friend lent it to her."

"Who knows?" I said as I went back to the counter. "I'm just glad she's got it, even if we'll never know how she came by it."

I told Dan about the incident when I met him at the cinema on Wednesday.

"She was buying one of those fifties prom dresses," I explained as we sat in the bar before the movie started.

"I know the ones—you called them 'cupcake' dresses."

"That's right. And I offered her the five percent discount, but she said she didn't want it."

Dan sipped his Peroni. "Strange."

"It was more than strange—it was insane. How many women would turn down the chance to have fifteen pounds knocked off the price of something? But this girl insisted on paying the full two seventy-five."

"Did you say two seventy-five?" Dan echoed. As I told him about the girl's first visit to the shop with the awful Keith, something seemed to be puzzling Dan.

"Are you okay?" I asked him.

"What? Oh yes, sorry . . . I'm just a bit distracted at the moment—I've got a lot going on at work. Anyway." He stood up. "The film's about to begin. Would you like another drink? We can take them in."

"Another glass of red wine would be great."

As Dan went up to the bar I reflected on the start to the evening. As I'd arrived at the cinema at seven, Dan had phoned to say that he'd be a bit late, so I'd sat upstairs on one of the sofas enjoying the view of Greenwich through the panoramic windows. Then I'd glanced at a newspaper that someone had left behind. At the back was a full-page ad for World of Sheds. As I'd looked at it, I'd idly wondered what Dan's fabled shed was like. Was it a Tiger Shiplap Apex, I wondered, or a Walton's Premium Overlap with double doors, or a Norfolk Apex Xtra or a Tiger Mini-barn? I was just wondering if it might be a Titanium Wonder metal-sided shed offering "excellent functionality" when Dan had arrived, at a run.

He'd sunk down next to me, then picked up my left hand and swiftly lifted it to his lips before returning it to my lap.

I stared at him. "Do you usually do that to women you've only met twice?"

"No," he replied. "Just to you. Sorry I'm a bit late. But I was busy on a story."

"The one about the Age Exchange?"

"No, that's all done. This was a . . . business piece," he explained, slightly evasively. "Matt's writing it, but I'm . . . involved. There were a few difficulties that we had to get sorted out—and now we have. Right." He clapped his hands. "Let me get you a drink. What's it going to be? Don't tell me—'Gimme a visky,' " he said huskily. " 'Ginger ale on the side—and don't be stinchy, baby.' "

"Sorry?"

"Garbo's first ever on-screen words. Until then all her films had been silent. Luckily her voice matched her face. But what would you like?"

"Definitely *not* 'visky'—but a glass of red wine would be nice."

Dan picked up the bar menu. "The choice is Merlot—the Le Carredon from the Pays d'Oc, which is apparently 'soft, rounded, and easy drinking with a full body'—or the Châteauneuf-du-Pape, Chante le Merle, which has a 'terrific nose of red berries and a seductive bouquet...' So what's it to be?"

I thought of my upcoming trip to Provence. "The Châteauneuf-du-Pape, please. I like the name."

Half an hour later—the conversation having flowed—Dan was buying me another glass of the Chante le Merle. Then we went downstairs to the screen, sank into the black leather chairs, and gave ourselves up to *Anna Karenina* and to Garbo's luminous beauty.

"With Garbo it's all about the face," Dan said afterwards as we walked out of the cinema. "Her body's irrelevant—so is her acting, even though she was a great actress. People only talk about Garbo's face—that alabaster perfection."

"Her beauty's almost a mask," I said. "She's a sphinx."

"She is. She projects this remote, rather melancholy self-containment. You do that, too," he added casually. Once again Dan had surprised me, but perhaps because of the wine, or the fact that I'd been enjoying his company and didn't want to spoil the evening, I decided to let the remark go. "Let's get something to eat," he said. Without waiting for a reply he tucked his arm through mine. I didn't mind his physical warmth. In fact I liked it, I realised. It made things... easy. "Is Café Rouge okay?" he asked. "I'm afraid it's not quite the Rivington Grill, but it's still nice."

"Café Rouge is *perfect.*" We went inside and found a corner table. "Why did Garbo retire so young?" I asked him now as we waited for the waiter to take our order.

"The story is that she was so upset by a bad review of her film *Two-Faced Woman,* that she threw in the towel on the spot. The likelier explanation is that she knew that her beauty was at its peak and she didn't want her image to be tarnished by time. Marilyn Monroe died at thirty-six," Dan went on. "Would we feel the same about her if she'd died at seventy-six? Garbo wanted to live—but not in public."

"You're very knowledgeable."

Dan unfurled his napkin. "I love film—especially black-and-white film."

"Is that because you have difficulty seeing colour?"

"No. It's because there's an essential mundanity to colour on-screen, since we see things in colour every day: with black-and-white there's the inherent suggestion that it's 'art.'"

"You've got paint on your hands," I said. "Have you been DIY-ing?"

Dan examined his fingers. "I did a bit more to the shed late last night—it's just finishing touches now."

"But what's *in* this mysterious shed of yours?"

"You'll see on October eleventh when I have the official gala opening—invitations to follow shortly. You will come, won't you?"

I'd enjoyed the evening. "Yes, I will. And what will the dress code be? Gardening clothes? Wellies?"

Dan looked affronted. "Smart casual."

"Not black tie?"

"That would be a *bit* OTT. But you can wear one of your grand vintage frocks if you like—in fact, you should wear that pale pink dress—the one that you said had belonged to you."

I shook my head. "I definitely won't be wearing that."

"Why not?"

"I just . . . don't like it."

"You know, *you're* a bit of a sphinx," Dan mused. "An enigma, at least. And I think you're struggling with something." He'd taken me by surprise again.

"Yes," I said quietly. "I am. I'm struggling with the fact that you're so . . . cheeky."

"Cheeky?"

I nodded. "You make very direct, if not downright personal remarks. You keep saying and doing things that completely . . . throw me. You're always . . . what's the word I'm looking for here?"

"Spontaneous? I'm always spontaneous?"

"No. You're always discomfiting me . . . disconcerting me . . . Discombobulating me! *That's* it—you're always discombobulating me, Dan."

He grinned. "I love the way you say *discombobulated*—could you say it again? It's rather a wonderful word," he went on. "We don't hear it often enough. Dis-com-bob-u-late," he added happily.

I rolled my eyes. "Now you're trying to . . . annoy me."

"Sorry. Perhaps it's because you're so cool and restrained. I really like you, Phoebe, but occasionally I get the urge to . . . I don't know . . . wreck your poise a little."

"Oh. I see. Well, you haven't wrecked it. I'm still *very* . . . poised, thank you! So, what about you, Dan?" I demanded, determined to wrest control of the conversation. "You know quite a bit about me— you've interviewed me, after all. But I know very little about you—"

"Except that I'm cheeky."

"Extremely." I smiled and felt myself relax again. "So why don't you tell me something about yourself."

Dan shrugged. "Okay. Well, I grew up in Kent, near Ashford. My father was a doctor; my mother was a teacher—now both retired. I think the most interesting thing about us as a family was that we had a Jack Russell, Percy, who lived to eighteen, which in human years was one hundred and twenty-six. I went to the local boys' grammar school, then to York to study history. Then followed my glorious decade in direct marketing, and now my work with the *Black & Green*. No marriages, no children, a few relationships, the last of which ended three months ago without acrimony. Bingo—my history in a nutshell."

"And are you enjoying working for the paper?" I asked him.

"It's an adventure, but it's not what I want to do long-term." And before I could ask Dan what he did want to do long-term, he suddenly changed the subject. "Okay, so we've just seen *Anna Karenina*. On Friday, as part of the same season, they're showing a new print of *Doctor Zhivago*. Would you like to come?"

I looked at Dan. "I would actually—but I can't."

"Oh," he said. "Why not?"

"Why not?" I repeated. "Dan, you're doing it again."

"Discombobulating you?"

"Yes. Because...Look...I don't have to tell you *why* I can't come."

"No, you don't," he agreed cheerfully. "I've already guessed. It's because you've got some boyfriend who, if he saw us now, would tear me limb from limb. Is that the reason?"

"No," I said wearily. Dan smiled. "It's because I'm going to France—to buy stock."

"Ah." He nodded. "I remember. You go to Provence. In that case, we'll see something when you get back. No, sorry, you need six weeks to think about it, don't you? Shall I phone you in mid-November? Don't worry, I'll e-mail you first to say that I'm going to phone—and perhaps I should write to you the week before that to let you know that I'll be e-mailing so that you don't think I'm being cheeky."

I smiled at Dan. "Wouldn't it be a lot easier if I just said yes now?"

Eight

Early yesterday morning I boarded the Eurostar at St. Pancras for my trip to Avignon. I'd decided to give myself up to the pleasure of the journey, which would take about six hours with a change in Lille. As the train waited to depart I skimmed through my *Guardian*. In the City section I was surprised to see a photo of Keith. The piece that accompanied it was about his property company, Phoenix Land, which apparently specialised in buying up suburban sites for redevelopment. It had recently been valued at £20 million and was about to be floated on the Alternative Investment Market. The piece explained that Keith had started out selling do-it-yourself kitchens by mail order, but in 2002 his warehouse had been destroyed in an arson attack by a disgruntled employee. There was a quote from Keith: *That was the worst night of my life. But as I watched the building burn I vowed to make something worthwhile rise out of the ashes.* Hence the name of his new company, I thought, as the train pulled away from the platform.

I turned to the copy of the *Black & Green* that I'd picked up at Blackheath Station. I'd been too tired to read it before. There were the usual local news stories about spiralling commercial rents, the threat to independent shops from the High Street chains, and problems with parking and traffic. There was a Social Whirl section, with snaps of well-known visitors to the area, including a shot of Chloë Sevigny looking in the window of Village Vintage. There were also photos of famous residents out and about—one of Jools Holland buying flowers and another of Glenda Jackson at a fund-raising concert at Blackheath Halls.

Filling the centre pages was Dan's piece about the Age Exchange, which was headed À LA RECHERCHE DU TEMPS: *The Age Exchange is a place where the past is treasured,* he'd written. *It's a place where the elderly can come to share their memories with one another and with younger generations . . . the importance of storytelling,* he'd gone on. *Oral history . . . Carefully selected memorabilia help to trigger recollection . . . The centre improves the quality of life for older people by emphasising the value of their reminiscences to old and young . . .*

It was a sympathetic, well-written piece.

As the train gathered speed, I closed the paper and gazed out at the Kent countryside. The harvest was recently over, the pale fields blackened here and there from stubble burning, the still-smouldering ground wafting drifts of alabaster smoke into the late-summer air. As we went through Ashford I suddenly imagined Dan, standing on the platform in his mismatched clothes, waving at me as I sped by. Then the train soon plunged under the Channel, emerging into the flatness of northern France, the featureless fields bestridden by gigantic pylons.

At Lille I changed trains, boarding the TGV, which would take me to Avignon. Leaning my head against the window, I fell asleep almost instantly and dreamed of Miles and Annie and the girl who came back for the green cupcake dress and the woman who couldn't have a baby who'd bought the pink one. I dreamed of Mrs. Bell as a young girl, walking through the fields with her blue coat, desperately searching for the friend she would never find. Then I opened my eyes, and to my surprise the Provençal countryside was already flashing past, with its terra-cotta houses, and its silvery soil, and its green-black cypress trees standing up against the landscape like exclamation marks.

In all directions were vines, planted in such straight lines that it looked as though the fields had been combed. Agricultural workers in bright colours were following grape-picking machines as they trundled down the rows, kicking up the dust. The *vendange* was clearly still in full swing.

Avignon TGV, I heard over the loudspeaker. *Descendez ici pour Avignon—Gare TGV.*

I made my way out of the station, blinking in the sharp sunlight. I picked up my rental car and drove into the city, following the road around its medieval walls, then negotiating the narrow streets to my hotel.

Once I'd checked in, I washed and changed, then strolled down Avignon's main drag, the rue de la République, where the shops and cafés hummed with early-evening trade. I stopped for a few minutes in the place de l'Horloge. There, in front of the imposing town hall, a fairground carousel whirled gently around. As I watched the children rising and falling on the gold-and-cream-painted horses, I imagined Avignon in a less innocent time. I imagined German soldiers standing where I now stood, their machine guns cradled in their arms. I imagined Mrs. Bell and her brother laughing and pointing at them, and being hushed by their anxious parents. Then I walked on to the Palais des Papes and sat at a café in front of the medieval fortress as the sun sank in an almost turquoise sky. Mrs. Bell had told me that towards the end of the war the palace cellars had been used as air-raid shelters. As I looked at the huge building, I imagined the crowds running towards it as the sirens sounded.

Then I turned my thoughts resolutely back to the present and planned the trips I'd need to make over the next couple of days. As I was looking at the map, my phone rang. I peered at the screen, then pressed Answer.

"Miles," I said happily.

"Phoebe—are you in Avignon yet?"

"I'm sitting in front of the Palais des Papes. Where are you?"

"We've just gotten to my cousin's." I registered the fact that Miles had said *we*—Roxy must be with him. Although I could hardly be surprised, my heart sank a little. "What are you doing tomorrow?" Miles asked.

"In the morning I'll go to the market at Villeneuve-lez-Avignon, then after that to the one at Pujaut."

"Well, Pujaut's halfway to Châteauneuf-du-Pape. Why don't you just come on here after you've finished, and I'll take you out to dinner?"

"I'd like that, Miles" I said. "But where's 'here'?"

"It's called Château de Bosquet. It's easy to find. You drive straight through Châteauneuf-du-Pape, then as you leave the village, take the road to Orange. It's a large square house about a mile on the right. Come as early as you can."

"Okay, I will."

So this morning I drove across the Rhône to Villeneuve-lez-Avignon. I parked at the top of the village, then walked back down the narrow main street to the marketplace, where traders had laid out their *antiquités* on cloths spread on the ground. There were old bicycles and faded deck chairs, chipped porcelain and scratched-looking cut glass; there were antique birdcages, rusty old tools, and balding teddy bears with creased leather paws. There were stalls selling old oil paintings and faded Provençal quilts, and strung between the plane trees were washing lines hung with old clothes that flapped and twisted in the light wind.

"*Ce sont que des* vrais *antiquités, madame*," said one vendor reassuringly as I looked through her garments. "*Tous en* très *bon état.*"

There was so much to look through. I spent a couple of hours selecting simple printed dresses from the forties and fifties and white nightgowns from the twenties and thirties. Some of these were made of chambray, a coarse rustic linen; others of metisse, a linen-and-cotton mix; and some of gossamer-light voile that floated in the breeze. Many of the nightgowns were beautifully embroidered. I wondered whose hands had stitched the exquisite little flowers and leaves that I now touched, and if it had given them pleasure to do such fine work, and if it had ever occurred to them that later generations would appreciate it and wonder about them.

When I'd bought all I wanted, I sat at a café, having an early lunch. Now I allowed myself to think about what day it was. I'd thought I'd feel upset, but I didn't, though I was glad to be away. Briefly I wondered what Guy was doing, and how he would be feeling. Then I phoned Annie.

"The shop's been very busy," she reported cheerfully. "I've already sold the Vivienne Westwood bustle skirt and the emerald-green Dior coat."

"That's terrific."

"But you know what you were saying on the radio about Audrey Hepburn?"

"Yes."

"Well, I had a woman in here this morning who asked me to turn her into Grace Kelly. It was rather tricky."

"Not attractive enough?"

"Oh, she was gorgeous. It's just that it would have been easier to turn her into Grace Jones."

"Ah."

"And your mother dropped in to see if you wanted to have lunch with her—she'd forgotten that you were in France."

"I'll call her." So I did, straight away, but she began going on about some new treatment she'd just been to see someone about—plasma regeneration. "I took yesterday morning off to go to this clinic about it," she said as I sipped my coffee. "It's good for deep wrinkles. They use nitrogen plasma to stimulate the skin's natural regenerative processes—they inject it under your skin, and that gets the fibroblasts going. The result, believe it or not, is a brand-new epidermis." I rolled my eyes. "Phoebe? Are you still there?"

"Yes, but I've got to go now."

"If I don't have the plasma regeneration," Mum prattled on, "I may try one of the fillers—they said there's Restylane, Perlane, or Sculptra—and they talked about autologous fat transfer, where they extract the fat from your behind and stick it in your face—cheek to cheek, as it were, but the thing about *that* is—"

"Sorry, Mum, I'm going *now*." I felt sick.

I got back into the car, forcing from my mind thoughts of the grotesque procedures my mother had just described, then set off for Pujaut.

As I saw the sign for Châteauneuf-du-Pape I felt a tingle of anticipation at seeing Miles again.

The market at Pujaut was small, but I bought six more nightgowns and some broderie anglaise vests with scalloped necks, as girls like to wear them with jeans. By now it was half past three. I found a café and changed into the dress I'd brought, a navy-and-white striped Saint Michael cotton pinafore from the early sixties.

As I left Pujaut I could see workers toiling in the vineyards that stretched away in all directions. Signs along the roadside invited me to stop at this *domaine* or that château for wine tasting.

Ahead of me now, perched on a hill, rose Châteauneuf-du-Pape, its cream-coloured buildings huddled together beneath a medieval tower. I drove through the village, then turned right towards Orange. About a mile or so on I saw the sign for Château de Bosquet.

I turned off the road onto the cypress-lined drive. At the end of it, I could see a large, square castellated house. In the vineyards on either side of the drive men and women were stooped over the vines, their faces obscured by hats. At the sound of my wheels, a grey-haired figure straightened up, shielded his eyes against the sun, then waved. I waved back.

Miles strode through the vines towards me while I parked. His smiling face was so streaked with dust that the lines round his eyes stood out like little spokes.

"Phoebe!" He opened my car door. "Welcome to Château de

Bosquet." As I stood up, he kissed me. "You'll meet Pascal and Cecile a bit later—for now everyone's working flat out." He nodded at the vineyard. "Tomorrow's our last day, so we're pushed for time."

"Can I help?"

"Would you? It's dusty work though."

I shrugged. "It doesn't matter. It would be fun." I gazed at the workers, with their black buckets and pruning shears. "Don't you use a grape-cutting machine?"

He shook his head. "In Châteauneuf-du-Pape the grapes have to be hand-picked to conform to the laws of appellation—that's why we need this small army." He glanced at my lace-up pumps. "Your footwear's fine, but you'll need an apron. Wait here." As Miles walked towards the house I suddenly noticed Roxy. She sat on a bench by a huge fig tree reading a magazine and drinking a bottle of Coke.

"Hi, Roxy," I called out. I took a few steps towards her. "Hi there, Roxy!" Roxanne looked up. Without lifting her sunglasses, she gave me a thin smile, then returned to her reading. I felt rebuffed, until I remembered that most sixteen-year-olds have poor social skills, added to which she'd only met me once, so why should she be friendly?

Miles came out of the house holding a blue sun hat. "You'll need this." He plonked it on my head. "You'll also need this." He handed me a bottle of water. "And this apron will protect your dress. It belonged to Pascal's mother. She was a sweet lady—wasn't she, Roxy?— but somewhat on the *large* side."

Roxy sipped her Coke. "You mean *fat*."

Miles unfolded the voluminous apron and put it over my head, then reached behind me to pass back the ties, brushing my ear with his breath as he did so. Then he pulled the ties around to the front. "There," he said, fastening them in a bow. He took a step back and appraised me. "You look lovely." I was suddenly uncomfortably aware of Roxy watching me from behind her Ray-Bans. Miles picked up two empty buckets and walked towards the vineyard, swinging them from either hand. "Come on then, Phoebe."

"Is much skill needed?" I asked when I caught up with him.

"Practically none," he replied as we stepped in among the gnarled vines. Here and there a sparrow flew up as we walked down the rows, or a grasshopper glided away at our approach. Miles picked a small bunch of grapes, then passed it to me.

I picked a grape and burst it against my tongue. "Delicious. What sort are they?"

"These are Grenache. The vines are quite old. They were planted in 1960, like me. But they're still fairly vigorous," he added slyly. He squinted at the sky, shielding his eyes with his hand. "Thank God the weather's been good. In '02 we had catastrophic floods and the grapes rotted—we produced five thousand bottles that year instead of a hundred thousand—it was a disaster. The village priest always blesses the harvest; he seems to have done a good job this year, because it's a bumper crop."

Scattered all around us were huge round pebbles: inside the cracked ones I glimpsed the occasional sparkle of white quartz. "These big stones are a nuisance," I said as I picked my way through them.

"They are a pain," Miles agreed. "They were deposited here by the Rhône aeons ago. But we need them because the heat they store during the day is released at night, which is one of the reasons why this is such good wine-growing country. Now, could you start here?" He stooped to a vine and pulled back the red-gold foliage to reveal a huge cluster of black grapes. "Hold them underneath." They felt warm in my hand. "Now cut the stem—no leaves, please—then place it in the first pail, with the minimum of handling."

"What goes in the second pail?"

"The ones we reject. We discard twenty percent of what we pick, and they go to make table wine."

Around us a party atmosphere prevailed—the dozen or so workers were laughing and talking: some were listening to Walkmans and iPods. One girl was singing—it was an aria from *The Magic Flute*, the one about husbands and wives. Her clear, sweet soprano rang across the vineyard.

Mann und Weib, und Weib und Mann . . .

How strange to be hearing that today of all days, I thought.

. . . reichen an die Gottheit an.

"Who are the grape pickers?" I asked Miles.

"Local people who help us every year, plus some students and a few foreign workers. On this estate the *vendange* takes about ten days, then Pascal throws a big party to thank everyone."

I put the shears to the stem. "Should I cut here?"

Miles bent down and put his hand over mine. "It's better there," he instructed. "Like that." I felt a current of desire crackle through me. "Now snip—but they're heavy, so don't let them fall." I placed the bunch carefully in the first pail. "I'll be over here," Miles said as he went back to his own pails a few yards away.

It was hot, hard work. I was glad of the water—and I was especially glad of the apron, which was already floured with pale dust. I straightened up to relieve my back. As I did so, I glanced at Roxy, sitting in the shade with her copy of *Heat* and her cold drink.

"I ought to make Roxy help," I heard Miles say, as though he'd read my mind. "But with teenagers it's counterproductive to push things."

I felt a bead of sweat trickle between my shoulder blades. "And how did her ancient-history project go?"

"In the end it was fine. I'm hoping to get an A," he added dryly. "I deserve one, as I was up all night writing it."

"Then you're an A-grade dad. My bucket's full. Now what?" Miles came and sorted the lesser-quality grapes into the second bucket, then he picked up both pails. "We'll take these to the pressing machine." He nodded at the big concrete sheds to the right of the house.

As we entered the first shed, the sweet yeasty scent was overpowering. So was the noise from the huge white cylinder juddering in front of us. Beside it was a tall stepladder from the top of which a thickset man in blue overalls was tipping in the grapes that were being passed up to him by a petite blond woman in a sunflower yellow dress.

"That's Pascal," Miles said, "and that's Cecile." He waved at them both. "Pascal! Cecile! This is Phoebe!"

Pascal gave me a friendly nod, then he grabbed the pail that Cecile passed up to him and tumbled the grapes into the cylinder. She turned and gave me a warm smile.

Miles indicated the four vast red tanks that lined the far wall. "Those are the fermentation vats. The grape juice is pumped straight into them from the cylinder with that hose there. Now we go through here..." I followed him into the next shed, which was cooler, and where there were a number of steel containers with dates chalked on them. "This is where the fermented grape juice is aged. We also age it in these oak casks over here. Then, after a year or so, it's ready to be bottled."

"And when can it be drunk?"

"The table wine after eighteen months, the decent stuff after two to three years, and the vintage wines are kept for up to fifteen years. Most of what's produced here is red."

To one side was a table with some half-empty bottles, sealed with grey stoppers; there were also glasses, a couple of corkscrews, and a number of wine reference books. The walls were studded with various framed *diplômes d'honneur* that Château de Bosquet wines had garnered at international wine festivals.

I noticed that one bottle had a pretty label, with a blackbird on it holding a bunch of grapes in its beak. I looked at it more closely. "Chante le Merle," I said. I turned to Miles. "I had this wine only last week—at the Greenwich Picturehouse."

"The Picturehouse chain does buy our wines. Did you like it?"

"It was delicious. It had a . . . seductive bouquet, I seem to re-member."

"And what film were you seeing?"

"Anna Karenina."

"With?"

"Greta Garbo."

"No, I mean . . . who did you see the film with? I . . . was just won-dering," he added diffidently.

I found Miles's insecurity touching—especially since he'd seemed so self-assured and confident when I'd first met him. "I went with this friend of mine, Dan. He's a bit of a film buff."

Miles nodded. "Well . . ." He glanced at his watch. "It's almost six. We'd better get ready. We'll have dinner in the village. Roxy will probably stay with Pascal and Cecile. She can practise her French," he added. "Now, I imagine you'd like to wash . . ."

I held up my purple-stained hands and laughingly agreed.

As we walked round to the house I saw that Roxy had vacated her seat, leaving her empty Coke bottle, the neck of which was being probed by wasps. Miles opened the enormous front door, and we stepped into the cool interior. The hall was huge, with vaulted ceil-ings, exposed beams, and a cavernous fireplace with a stack of logs to one side. Against one wall was a long settle made of old casks. At the foot of the staircase a stuffed bear stood guard, its teeth and claws bared.

"Don't worry about him," Miles said as we passed it. "He's never bitten anyone. Up we go. Now . . ." We crossed the landing and Miles pushed on a panelled door revealing a vast limestone bath, shaped like a sarcophagus. He took a towel from the rail. "I'm going to have a soak."

"Elsewhere presumably," I joked, wondering if Miles was going to strip off in front of me. I suddenly realised that I wouldn't mind if he did.

"I've got an en-suite," he explained as he left the room. "I'm at the end of the landing there. I'll see you downstairs in, what . . . twenty minutes? Roxy!" he called as he went out, shutting the door. "*Ro-xy,* I need to *speak* to you . . ."

I untied the apron, which had protected my dress perfectly, and wiped the dust off my shoes. I showered with the ancient-looking brass attachment, then twisted my wet hair into a knot. I dressed quickly and put on a little makeup.

As I stepped out onto the landing I could hear Miles's whispering voice floating up, then Roxy's plaintive tones.

—"I won't be out for long, sweetie . . ."

—"*Why's* she *here*?"

—"She has work to do in the area . . ."

—". . . *don't* want *you* to go out . . ."

—"Then come with us."

—"*Don't* feel *like it* . . ."

The top step creaked beneath my feet.

Miles seemed slightly startled as he looked up. "There you are, Phoebe," he said. "So you're ready to go?" I nodded. "I was just see-ing if Roxy wanted to come," he added as I came down the stairs.

"I hope you will," I said to Roxy, determined to try and charm her. "We could talk about clothes. Your dad says you're interested in a ca-reer in fashion."

She gave me a sullen glance. "That's what I'm going to do, yeah."

"Why *don't* you join us then?" her dad asked warmly.

"I don't *want* to go out."

"In that case, have supper with the grape pickers."

She gave a moue of distaste. "No *thanks.* "

Miles shook his head. "Roxy, there are some lovely young people here. That Polish girl Beata is training to be an opera singer. She speaks wonderful English; you could chat with her." Roxy shrugged her slim shoulders. "Then eat with Pascal and Cecile." The girl groaned. "Don't be difficult," said her father. "Please, Roxanne, I'd just like you to—" But she was already halfway across the hall.

Miles turned to me. "I'm sorry, Phoebe." He sighed. "Roxy's at that awkward age." I nodded politely, then suddenly remembered the French expression for the teenage years—*l'âge ingrat.* "She'll be fine here for a couple of hours. Now"—he jingled his car keys—"let's go. I'm starving."

Miles drove down to the village, then parked his hired Renault on the main street. As we got out, he nodded at a restaurant with tables outside, the white cloths flapping in the breeze. We crossed over to it, then Miles pushed open the door.

"Ah ... Monsieur Archant," said an unctuous-looking maître d' as he held open the door. *"C'est un plaisir de vous revoir. Un* grand *plaisir."* Suddenly the man's face cracked into a smile, and the two men slapped each other on the back, laughing uproariously.

"Good to see you, Pierre," said Miles. "I'd like to introduce you to the fair Phoebe."

Pierre lifted my hand to his lips. *"Enchanté."*

"Pierre and Pascal were at school together," Miles explained as Pierre showed us to a corner table. "We all used to hang out together over the summer holidays, what, thirty-five years ago, Pierre?"

Pierre blew out his lips. *"Oui—il y a trente cinq ans.* Before you were born," he added to me with a chuckle. I had a sudden vision of a fifteen-year-old Miles holding me, as a baby.

"Would you like a glass of wine?" Miles asked me as he opened the *carte des vin.*

"I would," I replied carefully. "But I probably shouldn't. I'll be driving back to Avignon."

"It's up to you," Miles said as he put on his reading glasses. He peered at the list. "You're having dinner, after all."

"I'll just have one then, but no more."

"And if you decide to get hammered, you can always stay at the house," he added casually. "There's a spare room—with a big trunk!"

"Oh, I won't be needing that—I mean the room," I corrected myself, blushing. "I mean, I won't be staying, thanks." Miles was smiling at my embarrassment. "So . . . you said you help with the harvest every year?"

He nodded. "It's a family obligation—the estate was founded by my great-grandfather, Philippe, who was also Pascal's great-grandfather. And I come because I was left a small share in the business, so I like to feel involved."

"So Château de Bosquet is *your* 'village vintage.' "

"I suppose it is." Miles smiled. "But I love the whole wine-making process. I love the machinery and the noise and the scent of the grapes and the connection with the land. I love the fact that viti-culture involves so many things—geography, chemistry, meteorol-ogy—and history. I love the fact that wine is one of those few things that time improves."

"Like you?" I suggested playfully.

He smiled. "Now, what are you going to drink?" I chose the Châteauneuf-du-Pape Fines Roches. "And I'll have a glass of the Cuvée Reine," Miles said to Pierre. "I drink non-Bosquet wines when I'm out," he told me as I picked up the menu. "It's good to know what the competition's like."

Pierre placed our glasses of wine in front of us with a plate of fat green olives. Miles raised his glass. "How lovely to see you again, Phoebe. When I was having dinner with you last week I hoped to see you again, but I *never* imagined that we'd be . . . oh." He reached into his pocket for his BlackBerry. "Look, Roxy," he whispered as I stud-ied the menu, "I did tell you where I was going . . . I did. We're at the Mirabelle." He stood. "You *were* invited." He sighed as he headed for the door. "You *know* you were, darling. What's the point of saying that *now*?"

Five minutes passed before he returned, looking exasperated. "Sorry about that." He sighed as he pocketed his phone. "Now she's cross because she *didn't* come! I have to say, Roxy can be rather try-ing sometimes—but at heart she's a very good girl."

"Of course," I murmured.

"She would never do anything . . . wrong." Pierre came to the table again and we placed our orders. "But I'd like to talk about you, Phoebe," Miles went on. "When we had dinner last week you avoided all my questions. I'd love to know a bit more."

I shrugged. "About what?"

"Well, personal things. Tell me about your family." So I told Miles about my parents, and about Louis.

Miles shook his head. "That's a tough one. It can't be easy for you," he said as Pierre brought our appetizers.

I spread my napkin on my lap. "It isn't. I'd like to see more of Louis, but it's all so awkward. I've decided I'm going to visit him more often and just say nothing to my mother about it. Usually, she adores babies," I added, "but how could she ever adore this one?"

"Well . . ." Miles shook his head. "I don't know."

"She feels very vulnerable now," I went on as I broke a roll in half. "She says she never thought my father would leave her; but if I think about it, they didn't really *do* anything together—or hadn't done for years—not that I can remember, anyway."

"It must still be hard for her, though."

"It is. But at least she has her work." I told Miles about Mum's job.

"So she's worked for this chap for a long time?"

I nodded. "Twenty-two years. It's like a professional marriage. When John retires, she will too. But since he says he wants to work until he's seventy, that's some way off, thankfully. She needs the distraction of work, and the money's useful, especially as my dad's having a . . . career break," I concluded carefully.

"And there's no chance that your mum and her boss . . ."

"Oh no." I laughed. "John adores her, but he's not really into women."

"I see."

I sipped my wine. "Did your parents stay together?"

"For fifty-three years—till death did them part. They died within a few months of each other. Has what happened to your parents shaken your belief in marriage?"

I lowered my fork. "You're assuming that I had one."

"As you told me that you'd been engaged, I am." Miles sipped his wine, then nodded at my right hand. "Was that your engagement ring?"

"Oh. No." I glanced at the lozenge-cut emerald flanked by two little diamonds. "This belonged to my grandmother. I'm very fond it, not least because I have so many memories of her wearing it."

"So was your engagement long ago?"

I shook my head. "It was earlier this year." Surprise flickered across Miles's face. "In fact . . ." I looked out of the window. "I was supposed to get married today."

"Today?" Miles lowered his glass.

"Yes. I was supposed to get married today at Greenwich Register Office at 3 P.M. followed by a sit-down dinner and dance for eighty people at the Clarendon Hotel in Blackheath. Instead of which I've been grape picking in Provence with a man I hardly know."

"You don't seem . . . too upset about it." Miles looked bemused.

I shrugged. "It's odd, but I'm not."

"Which means that you must have been the one to end it."

"Yes."

"But . . . why did you?"

"Because . . . I had to. That had become clear."

"Didn't you love him?"

I sipped my wine. "I did. Or rather I *had* loved him—very much. But then something happened that profoundly changed the way I felt about him, so I called it off." I looked up at Miles. "Does that make me seem callous?"

He hesitated. "A little." He frowned slightly. "But without knowing anything about it I'm not going to judge. I'm assuming that he was unfaithful to you, or that there was a betrayal of that kind."

"No. He just did something that I couldn't forgive." I looked at Miles's puzzled face. "I'll tell you, if you like. Or we could change the subject."

Miles hesitated. "Okay," he said after a moment. "I can't deny that I'm curious now." So I told him briefly about Emma, and about

Guy and me falling in love. Miles studied my face. "That must have been awkward."

"It was." I sipped my wine again. "I wish I'd *never* met Guy."

"But . . . what did the poor man *do*?"

I drained my glass, and as I felt the warmth of the wine race through my veins I told Miles about my engagement, then about Valentine's Day and Emma's phone call. Then I told him about going to her house.

Miles was shaking his head. "What a trauma, Phoebe."

"Trauma?" I echoed. *Träumerei.* "Yes. It comes back to me all the time. I often dream that I'm in Emma's room, pulling back the duvet . . ."

"So she'd taken all the painkillers?"

"She had, but according to the pathologist she'd only had four—the last four evidently, because the bottle was empty."

"Then why did she . . ." Miles looked bewildered.

"We didn't at first realise what had happened to Emma. It looked like an overdose." I clenched my napkin. "But ironically it was an *under*dose that caused her to . . ."

Miles was staring at me. "You said that you thought she had the flu."

"Yes, that's what it seemed to be when she first phoned me."

"And she'd recently been to South Africa?"

I nodded. "She'd only been back a few weeks."

"Was it malaria?" he asked gently. "Undiagnosed malaria?"

I felt the familiar sliding sensation, as though I was hurtling downhill. "Yes," I murmured. "It was." I closed my eyes. "If only I'd been as smart as you've just been."

"My sister Trish got malaria some years ago," Miles said quietly. "After a trip to Ghana. She was lucky to survive, because it was the deadly kind—"

"*Plasmodium falciparum,*" I interjected. "Transmitted by an infected anopheles mosquito—but only the female. I'm an expert on it now," I added bitterly.

"Trish hadn't finished her antimalarial pills. Is that what happened with Emma? I assume that's what you meant when you used the word *underdose*?"

I nodded. "A few days after she'd died, her mother found the antimalarial medication in Emma's luggage. From the blister packs, she could see that Emma had taken them for only ten days instead of eight weeks. Plus she started the course too late—she should have been taking them from a week before she travelled."

"Had she been to South Africa before?"

"Many times. She used to live there."

"So she'd have known the score."

"Oh yes." I paused as Pierre took away our plates. "Even though the risk of malaria is low there, Emma always gave me the impression that she'd been careful to take the pills. But this time she seems to have been reckless."

"Why do you think that was?"

I fiddled with the stem of my wineglass. "There's a part of me that thinks it could have been deliberate . . ."

"You mean, self-inflicted?"

"Perhaps. She was depressed—I think that's why she'd decided to go there so suddenly. Or perhaps she simply forgot to take the pills, or was happy to play Russian roulette with her health. I only know that I should have gone to see her the moment she phoned me." I looked away, my heart breaking.

"Phoebe—you had no idea how ill she was."

"No," I said bleakly. "It simply didn't occur to me that she might have . . ." I shook my head. "Emma's parents would have realised, but they were on a walking holiday in Spain and couldn't be reached. She'd tried to call her mother twice that night, apparently."

"So that's a regret *they* have to live with."

"Yes. Plus the way it happened . . . the fact that Emma was alone . . . It's very hard for them. I had to tell them . . ." I felt my eyes fill. "I had to tell them . . ."

Miles reached for my hand. "What an ordeal."

"Yes. But her parents still don't know that Emma was upset with me in the weeks before she died. And if she hadn't been so upset, then perhaps she wouldn't have gone to South Africa and wouldn't have fallen ill." My throat ached with a suppressed sob. Then I thought of Emma's diary. "I hope they never find out . . . Miles, could I have another glass of wine?"

"Of course." He waved at Pierre. "But if you have any more, I think it might be better if you stayed at the house tonight—okay?"

"Yes, but that won't happen."

Miles looked at me. "I *still* don't understand why you felt you had to end your engagement."

"Guy persuaded me not to go and see Emma that night. He said that she was only seeking attention." I felt a sudden rush of anger at the memory. "He said that it was probably only a bad cold."

"But . . . do you actually blame him for her death?"

"I blame myself, first and foremost, because I was the one person who might have prevented it. I blame Emma, for not taking her pills. But yes, I blame Guy too, because if it weren't for him . . . I'd have gone round to her house right away . . . if it weren't for *him,* I would have *seen* how ill she was, and I'd have called the ambulance and she might be alive today. Instead, Guy persuaded me to wait, so I didn't go until the next morning, by which time . . ." I squeezed my eyes shut.

"Did you tell Guy this?"

I shook my head. "Not at first. I was still in shock, trying to take it all in. But on the morning of Emma's funeral . . ." I paused as I remembered her coffin, on top of it her favourite green hat in a sea of pink roses. "I took off my engagement ring. When Guy drove me home afterwards he asked me where it was, so I said that I'd felt unable to wear it in front of Emma's parents. We had an awful argument. Guy insisted that I had nothing to feel guilty about. He said that it was Emma's own fault that she'd died, and that her neglect of her health had not only cost her her life, it had brought misery to her parents and friends. I told him that I did feel guilty and always would. I told him that I was tormented by the thought that while he and I were sitting in the Bluebird, eating and drinking, Emma was dying. Then I said what I'd been burning to say for weeks—that if he hadn't intervened, she might be alive.

"Guy looked at me as though I'd hit him. He was outraged at the accusation, but I said it was true. Then I went upstairs, got the ring, and gave it back to him—and that was the last time I saw him. So that's why I didn't get married today," I concluded quietly.

I heaved a sigh. "You said you didn't know anything personal about me—and now you do. But that was probably more personal than you would have liked."

"Well..." Miles reached for my hand again. "I'm sorry that you've been through something so...harrowing. But I'm glad you told me."

"I'm surprised I have. I hardly know you."

"No, you don't know me. At least not yet," he added gently. He stroked my fingers, and I felt a sudden charge go through me, like static.

"Miles..." I looked at him. "I think I *would* like that third glass of wine."

We didn't stay at the restaurant very much longer, not least because Roxy began phoning again. Miles told her he'd be back by ten. Then as our desserts arrived she called once more. I had to bite my tongue. Roxy had refused to come out with her father, but she seemed determined that he shouldn't enjoy himself.

"Couldn't she read a book?" I suggested to Miles. Or perhaps a few more issues of *Heat,* I thought dismissively.

"Roxy's an intelligent girl, but she's not as...resourceful as I'd like. No doubt because I've danced too much attendance on her over the years. But when you're a lone parent to an only child, it's almost inevitable—plus I'm trying to compensate her for what happened, I'm aware of that."

"But ten years is a long time. You're a very attractive man, Miles. I'm amazed you've never found anyone to be a mother figure to Roxy, as well as to fulfil your own needs and emotions."

Miles sighed. "Nothing would have made me happier—*would* make me happier. There *was* someone a few years ago whom I was very fond of, but it didn't work out. But maybe, now, things will come right . . ." He smiled briefly and the delta of lines beneath his eyes deepened. "Anyway . . ." He pushed back his chair. "We'd better get back."

At the house Pascal told Miles that Roxy had just gone to bed. *Having made her father come back from the restaurant early,* I reflected. Miles explained to his cousin that I needed to stay the night.

"Mais bien sûr," said Pascal, clasping his hands together. He smiled at me. *"Vous êtes bienvenue."*

"Thank you."

"I'll make up the spare bed," said Miles. "Will you give me a hand, Phoebe?"

"Sure." I followed him, a little unsteady from the wine, up the stairs. At the top he opened a huge airing cupboard that smelt deliciously of warm cotton, then he took some bedding off the slatted shelves.

"My room's at the end," he explained as I followed him down the long landing. "Roxy's is opposite. You'll be in here." We went into the large bedroom, the walls of which were hung with dark pink toile de Jouy depicting a pastoral scene of boys and girls apple picking.

It felt strange to be making up the bed with Miles; as we wrestled with the plump duvet I found the intimacy of it both discomfiting and exciting. When we smoothed the sheet our fingertips collided and I felt a sudden voltage race through me. Miles dragged the linen case over the pillow. "There." He gave me a diffident smile. "Can I lend you a shirt to sleep in?" I nodded. "Stripy or plain?"

"Tee, please."

He headed for the door. "Tee for one, coming up."

Miles quickly returned with a grey Calvin Klein T-shirt and handed it to me. "Well . . . I suppose I ought to get to bed." He bent and kissed me on the cheek. "I've got another long day in the vines tomorrow." He kissed me on the other cheek, then held me for a few seconds. "Good night, sweet Phoebe," he murmured. I closed my eyes, enjoying the feeling of being encircled by his arms. "I'm so glad you're here," he whispered. His breath was warm in my ear. "But how strange to think that this would have been your wedding night."

"It is strange."

"And now here you are, in a bedroom in Provence with a virtual stranger. But . . . I've got a problem." I opened my eyes and looked at Miles; his face was suddenly filled with anxiety.

"What?"

"I want to kiss you."

"Oh."

"I mean, *really* kiss you."

"I see." His finger stroked my cheek. "Well . . ." I murmured. "You can."

"Kiss you?" he whispered.

"Kiss me," I whispered back.

Miles cupped my face in his hands, then he leaned down and touched his upper lip to mine—it felt cool and dry—and we stood like that for a few moments. Then we kissed more intensely, then with a gathering urgency, and I felt Miles reach to the back of my dress to unzip it; but he couldn't.

"Sorry," he said with a laugh. "I haven't done this for a while." He fumbled with it a bit more. "Ah . . . there." Then he was pushing the straps down over my shoulders and the dress was falling to the floor and I was stepping out of it, and Miles was leading me towards the bed. As he unbuttoned his shirt I unzipped his jeans, releasing his erection, then I lay back on the bed and looked at him as he undressed. He might have been nearly fifty, but his body was slim and hard, and he was indeed, like the vines planted in the year of his birth, still vigorous.

"Do you want this, Phoebe?" he whispered as he lay next to me, stroking my face. "Because that trunk I told you about is just over there." He kissed me. "You just have to push it against the door."

"To keep you out?"

"Yes." He kissed me again. "To keep me out."

"But I don't want to." I kissed him back, more urgently now, and then, with a shudder of desire I pulled him to me. "I want you in."

Nine

Mann und Weib, und Weib und Mann . . .

I awoke to the sound of the Polish girl singing in the vineyard below me.

Reichen an die Gottheit an . . .

Miles had gone, leaving only an indentation on the pillow and his masculine scent on the sheets. I sat up, then hooped my arms round my knees, pondering the surprising turn my life had taken. The room was still in darkness except for some slivers of light on the floor where the sun sliced through the shutters. I could hear the cooing of doves outside, and from farther away the rumble and *whirr* of the pressing machine.

I opened the windows and looked out at the pale red landscape with its viridian cypresses and billowy pines. In the distance I could see Miles loading some pails onto a trailer. I stood there for a few moments, watching him, thinking of the intense, almost reverential way he'd made love to me, the delight he'd taken in my body. Below my window was the fig tree, in which two white doves were pecking at the overripe purple-brown fruit.

I washed and dressed, stripped the bed, and went downstairs. In the morning light, the stuffed bear seemed to be grinning, not growling.

I crossed the hall to the kitchen. At one end of an enormously long table Roxy was having breakfast with Cecile.

"*Bonjour,* Phoebe," Cecile said warmly.

"*Bonjour,* Cecile. Hi, Roxanne."

Roxy raised a salon-plucked eyebrow. "You're still here?"

"Yes," I replied evenly. "I decided I didn't want to drive back to Avignon in the dark."

"*Et vous avez bien dormi?*" Cecile asked with the faintest hint of a knowing smile.

"*Très bien. Merci.*"

She indicated the pile of croissants and *biscottes,* then passed me a plate. "And you would like a cup of coffee?"

"Please." As Cecile poured me a cup from the percolator gasping away on the range I glanced round the huge kitchen with its terracotta floor tiles, its garlands of garlic and chillies, and its old copper pans aglow on their racks. "This is lovely. It's a wonderful house, Cecile."

"Thank you." She offered me a piece of brioche. "I hope that you visit us again."

"So are you going now?" Roxanne asked as she spread butter thickly on her bread. Her tone was neutral, but her hostility was clear.

"I'll be leaving after breakfast." I turned to Cecile. "I have to go to L'Isle-sur-la-Sorgue."

"*C'est pas trop loin,*" she said as I sipped my coffee. "Perhaps one hour only."

I nodded. I'd been to L'Isle-sur-la-Sorgue before, but not from this direction. I'd need to work out the route.

As Cecile and I chatted in franglais, a pretty little black cat sauntered in, its tail at ninety degrees. I made kissing noises at it, and to my surprise it jumped up and curled itself into my lap, purring happily.

"That is Minou," said Cecile as I stroked its head. "I think she like you. *Quelle jolie bague,*" she said admiringly. "Your ring—it is beautiful."

"Thank you." I glanced at it. "I'm very fond of it. It was my grandmother's."

Suddenly Roxanne pushed back her chair and stood up. She took a peach from the bowl of fruit. She threw it up with her right hand, then deftly caught it.

"Have you had enough *petit déjeuner,* Roxanne?" Cecile asked her.

"Yes," Roxy replied casually. "I'll see you later."

"You won't see me," I told her. "But I hope to meet you again, Roxy."

She didn't answer, and after she left the room an awkward silence descended as Cecile registered the slight.

"*Roxanne est très belle,*" she remarked as she cleared away Roxy's breakfast things.

"She is beautiful, yes."

"*Miles l'adore.*"

"Of course," I agreed. I shrugged. "*Elle est sa fille.*"

"*Oui.*" Cecile sighed. "*Mais elle est aussi . . . comment dire? Son talon d'Achille*—his Achilles heel."

I feigned a renewed interest in the cat, which had twisted itself onto its back to have its tummy stroked. I drank my coffee, then glanced at my watch. "I ought to get going now, Cecile. *Mais merci bien pour votre hospitalité.*" I tipped the cat off my lap gently, then reached for my breakfast plate and cup, but Cecile took them from me, *tut-tut*ting. She walked with me to the front door.

"*Au revoir, Phoebe,*" she said as we stepped outside into the perfumed sunshine. "I wish you a nice stay in Provence." She kissed me on each cheek. "And I wish you"—she glanced at Roxanne sitting in the sunshine—"good luck."

As I walked to the car I wished Cecile hadn't said what she had. Roxy might be selfish and demanding, but weren't lots of teenagers like that? In any case I'd only just met Miles, so good luck didn't come into it. But I did like him, I realised . . . I liked him very much.

Shielding my eyes against the sunlight, I scanned the vineyard for Miles and saw him walking towards me with that slightly anxious air he always had, as though he was worried that I was going to run off. I found his blend of polish and vulnerability endearing.

"You're not going, are you?" he asked as he drew close.

"I am, yes. But, well . . . thank you for . . . everything."

Miles smiled, then lifted my hand to his lips in a way that made my heart turn over. He nodded at my travel guide. "And do you know how to get to L'Isle-sur-la-Sorgue?"

I quickly turned to the relevant map. "Yes, it looks fairly straightforward. So . . ." I got behind the wheel. As I did so I heard the silvery arpeggios of a blackbird. "Chante le Merle," I said.

"That's right." Miles bent down and kissed me through the open window. "I'll see you in London. At least, I hope I will."

I laid my hand on his, then kissed him again. "You'll see me in London," I said.

I enjoyed the drive to L'Isle-sur-la-Sorgue, along pristine roads in the bright sunshine, past neat cherry orchards and newly harvested vineyards, the golden fields splashed crimson with late poppies. I thought about Miles and about how attractive I found him. My lips felt bruised from his mouth.

I parked at one end of the pretty riverside town and strolled among the milling crowds through the first part of the market. Here were stalls selling lavender soap, flagons of olive oil, piles of pungent salamis, Provençal quilts, and straw baskets in earthy shades of terra-cotta, yellow, and green. The atmosphere in this part of the market was commercial and noisy.

"Vingt euros!"

"Merci, monsieur."

"Les prix sont bas, non?"

"Je vous en prie."

Then I walked over the little wooden bridge that spanned the narrow river. Here, in the upper part of the town, the atmosphere was calm, as shoppers quietly contemplated the *antiquités* and bric-a-brac stalls. I paused at one on which was an old saddle, a pair of red boxing gloves, a large ship in a bottle, several stamp albums, and a pile of *L'illustration* news magazines from the 1940s. I glanced through them: there were covers variously featuring photos of the Normandy landings, Resistance fighters alongside Allied troops, and the celebrations in Provence when the occupation ended. L'ENTRÉE DES TROUPES ALLIÉES, the headline read. LA PROVENCE LIBÉRÉE DU JOUG ALLEMAND.

Now I did what I'd come to do and looked through the vintage clothing, selecting white percale shirts, printed dresses and shifts, and broderie anglaise vests, all in pristine condition. Then I heard the church clock strike three. It was time to head back. I imagined Miles, helping to gather the last of the harvest; this evening, I remembered, there'd be the party for the grape pickers.

I put the bags in the trunk and got into the car, opening all the windows to let out the heat. The route to Avignon seemed straightforward, but as I got closer to it I realised that I'd missed a sign: I wasn't heading south as I should have been but due north. The frustration of knowing that I was going 180 degrees in the wrong direction was compounded by the fact that there was nowhere to turn. Worse, a long queue of cars had built up behind me. Now I was driving into a place called Rochemare.

I glanced in my mirror. The car behind me was so close that I could practically see the driver's eyeballs. I flinched at his irritable beeps. Desperate to rid myself of him, I turned abruptly up a narrow street. I followed it for about half a mile until it suddenly came out onto a large, pleasant square. On one side were a few small shops and a bar with tables outside, shaded by gnarled plane trees, where an old man was having a beer. On the opposite side of the square was an impressive-looking church. Driving by it, I glanced at the door; a jolt ran through me.

From somewhere I could hear Mrs. Bell's voice.

I grew up in a large village about three miles from the city centre. It was a sleepy sort of place, with a few narrow little streets leading onto a large square, which was shaded by plane trees with a few shops and a pleasant bar . . .

I pulled into the nearest space, outside a *boulangerie,* then I got out and walked back to the church. Mrs. Bell's voice still sounded in my ears.

On the north side of the square was the church, over the door of which was carved, in huge letters, LIBERTÉ, ÉGALITÉ, FRATERNITÉ . . .

My heart pounding, I studied the famous inscription, cut so deeply into the stone. Then I turned and looked at the square. This was where Mrs. Bell had grown up, I was certain of it. This was the church. There was the bar. Bar Mistral—I could see the name now— where she'd sat that night. It suddenly occurred to me that that old man sitting there now could even be Jean-Luc Aumage. The man was probably in his mid-eighties, so it was possible. As I stood there he drained his glass, got up, pulled down his beret, and walked slowly through the square, leaning heavily on a stick.

I went back to the car and drove on. Already the houses were thinning, and I could see pockety vineyards and little orchards and, in the distance, a railway crossing.

The village bordered open countryside and was skirted by a railway line. My father had a small vineyard not far from the house . . .

I pulled into a turnout, and as I sat in the car I imagined Thérèse and Monique walking across these fields, through these vineyards and orchards. I imagined Monique hiding to survive, in the barn. Now the dark cypress trees seemed to me like accusing fingers, pointing skywards. I reached for the ignition and drove on again.

Here, at the farthest edge of the village, were a number of newish houses; but there was a row of four that were much older. I drew up just beyond the last of these and got out.

In front was a pretty garden, with pots of pink-and-white pelargoniums. There was also an old well and, above the door, an oval plaque on which was carved the head of a lion. As I stood there I imagined the house seven decades earlier, heard the protesting, terrified voices.

Suddenly I saw a movement behind the shutters—just a fleeting shadow, nothing more—but for some reason I felt the hairs on my neck rise. I hesitated for a moment, then returned to the car, my pulse racing.

I sat in the driver's seat, looking back at the house in the rearview mirror; then, hands trembling, I drove away.

Now, as I found the village centre again, I felt my heartbeat slow. I was glad that chance had brought me to Rochemare, but it was time to leave. As I tried to find the road out I turned left down a narrow little street. At the end of it I stopped, then lowered the window. Placed there with an almost casual lack of ceremony was a war memorial. AUX MORTS GLORIEUX, it affirmed in black lettering on the slender column of white marble. There were names carved on it from the First and Second World Wars, names I'd heard before— CARON, DIDIER, MARIGNY, and PAGET. Then with a jolt, as though I'd known him myself, I saw: 1954. INDOCHINE. J-L AUMAGE.

Mrs. Bell would presumably know that, I reflected on Tuesday as I put some of her clothes out in the shop. She must have been back to Rochemare at least a few times, I thought as I hung up her Pierre Cardin houndstooth suit. As I gave it a brush I wondered what she'd felt when she'd found out.

Next I wanted to put out Mrs. Bell's evening wear, but then I remembered that most of it was still at Val's. I was just wondering

when I could go and collect it when the bell over the door rang and
two schoolgirls walked in for a lunchtime browse. While they looked
through the racks I put a Jean Muir green suede coat of Mrs. Bell's on
a mannequin. As I buttoned it I glanced up at the last cupcake dress
hanging on the wall. I wondered who would buy it.

"Excuse me."

I turned round. The two girls were standing at the counter. They
were Roxy's age, perhaps a little younger.

"Can I help you?"

"Well . . ." The first girl, who had shoulder-length dark hair and
an almost Mediterranean complexion, was holding up a snakeskin
wallet that had been in the basket with the other wallets and purses.
"I've just been looking at this."

"It's from the late sixties," I explained. "I think it's eight
pounds."

"Yes. That's what the ticket says. But the thing is . . ." She's going
to start haggling, I thought wearily. "It's got this secret compart-
ment." I looked at her. "Here." She pulled back a flap of leather to
reveal a concealed zipper. "I don't think you knew that, did you?"

"No, I didn't," I said quietly. I'd bought the wallets at auction and
had just given them a quick wipe before putting them in the basket.

The girl unzipped it. "Look." Inside was a wad of bills. She
handed the wallet to me.

"Eighty pounds," I said wonderingly. Into my mind flashed
Ginny Jones at Radio London asking me if I'd ever found cash in any
of the things I sold. I felt like ringing her to say that I had.

"I thought I should tell you," the girl said.

I looked at her. "That's incredibly honest of you." I separated two
of the twenty-pound notes and handed them to her. "Here."

The girl blushed. "I didn't mean—"

"I know you didn't, but please, it's the least I can do."

"Well, thanks," the girl said happily. She took it. "Here, Sarah."
She offered one of the notes to her friend, a girl of similar height but
with short fair hair.

Sarah shook her head. "You found it, Katie, not me. Anyway, we'd better hurry. We don't have long."

"Are you looking for anything in particular?" I asked them.

They explained that they were looking for special dresses to wear for a ball in aid of the Teenage Leukaemia Trust.

"It's at the Natural History Museum," said Katie. So it was the same event that Roxy was going to. "There'll be a thousand of us there, so we'll all be desperately trying to stand out from the crowd. I'm afraid we don't have a huge budget," she added apologetically.

"Well, just have a good browse. There are some very eye-catching fifties dresses—like this one." I unhooked a sleeveless glazed-cotton dress with a vibrant, abstract print of cubes and circles. "That's eighty pounds."

"It's very unusual," Sarah said.

"It's by Horrocks. They made wonderful cotton dresses in the late forties and fifties. This print was designed by Eduardo Paolozzi." The girls nodded, then I saw Katie's eyes stray to the yellow cupcake dress.

"How much is that one?" I told her the price. "Oh, too expensive. For me, I mean," she added hastily. "But I'm sure someone will pay that because it's just . . ." She sighed. "Fantastic."

"You'll have to win the lottery," Sarah told her, looking at it. "Or get yourself a Saturday job that pays better."

"I wish," said Katie. "I only make forty-five pounds a day at Cost-cutter, so I'd need to work for, what . . . two months to buy that dress, by which time the ball would be long over."

"Well, you've got forty pounds there," said Sarah, "so you've only got to find another two thirty-five." Katie rolled her eyes. "Try it on," her friend urged her.

Katie shook her head. "What's the point?"

"The point is that I think it will suit you."

"I can't afford it, even if it does."

"Do try it on," I urged. "Just for fun. Plus I love seeing the clothes on my customers."

Katie looked at the dress again. "Okay."

I got it down and hung it in the changing room. Katie went in and emerged minutes later.

"You look like . . . a sunflower," said Sarah, smiling.

"It is lovely on you," I agreed as Katie gazed at herself in the mirror. "Yellow's hard to carry off, but you've got the warm complexion for it."

"But you'll need to stuff your bra," said Sarah judiciously as Katie adjusted the bodice. "You could get some of those chicken-fillet things."

Katie turned to her wearily. "You're talking as though I'm going to be buying this dress. I'm not."

"Can't your mum help?" Sarah asked.

Katie shook her head. "She's a bit credit-crunched. Maybe I could get an evening job," she mused as she put her hands on her waist, then turned this way and that, the petticoats rustling.

"You could babysit," Sarah suggested. "I get five quid an hour to sit my neighbours' kids. Once I've got them into bed, I do my homework."

"That's not a bad idea." Katie stood on tiptoe looking at herself sideways. "I could put a card up in the toy shop—or in Costcutters' window, maybe. Anyway, it's been great just seeing the dress on." She gazed at her reflection for a few moments, as if trying to fix in her mind the image of herself looking so lovely. Then, with a regretful sigh, she drew the curtain.

"Where there's a will, there's a way," Sarah called out cheerfully.

"Yes," Katie replied. "But by the time I'd have saved up enough, someone else will have bought it." A minute later she came out of the changing room. "I feel like Cinderella"—she looked down mournfully at her drab school blazer and skirt—"after the ball."

"I'll keep my eyes peeled for a fairy godmother," said Sarah. "How long can you hold things for?" she asked me.

"Usually not more than a week. I'd love to keep it for longer, but—"

"Oh, you can't," said Katie as she picked up her backpack. "For all you know, I might never come back for it." She glanced at her watch. "It's a quarter to two. We'd better scoot. Miss Doyle goes berserk if we're late, doesn't she, Sarah? Anyway"—she smiled at me—"thanks."

As the girls left, Annie returned. "They looked like good kids," she said.

"They were lovely." I told Annie about Katie's honesty over the wallet.

"I'm *impressed*."

"She's fallen for the yellow cupcake," I explained. "I'd like to keep it for her in case she saves enough to buy it, but . . ."

"That's a risk," Annie said judiciously. "You could lose a sale."

"True . . . But how did your audition go?" I asked.

She took off her jacket. "Hopeless. There had to be a hundred people trying out for the role."

"Well, fingers crossed," I said disingenuously. "But can't your agent get you more work?"

Annie ran her fingers through her short blond hair. "I don't have one. My last agent was useless, so I sacked him, and I can't get a new one because I'm not in anything for them to see. So I just keep sending off my résumé, and occasionally I get an audition." She began wiping the counter. "What I hate about acting is the lack of control. I can't stand the idea that at my age I'm sitting around waiting for a director to phone me. What I really need is to write my own material."

"You said you like writing."

"I do. I'd like to find a story that I could turn into a one-woman show. Then I could write it, act in it, and set up the performances—*I'd* be in charge." Into my mind flashed Mrs. Bell's story, but even if I could tell it to Annie, the problem was that the ending was too sad.

I heard my phone bleep and looked at the screen. I felt my face flush with pleasure—it was Miles, asking me to the theatre on Saturday. I texted him back, then told Annie I was going up to the Paragon.

"Are you seeing Mrs. Bell again?"

"I'm just going to have a quick cup of tea with her."

"She's your new best friend," said Annie genially. "I hope I'll have some nice young woman to visit me when I'm old."

"I hope you don't mind me inviting myself over," I said to Mrs. Bell twenty minutes later.

"Mind?" she repeated as she ushered me inside. "I'm delighted to see you."

"Are you feeling okay, Mrs. Bell?" She looked thinner than when I'd seen her the week before, her face a little more shrunken.

"I'm . . . fine, thank you. Well, not really fine, of course . . ." Her voice trailed away. "But I like to sit and read or just look out the window. I have one or two friends who come. My help, Paola, is here two mornings a week, and my niece arrives on Thursday—she is staying with me for three days. How I wish I'd had children," she said as I followed her to the kitchen. "But I was very unfortunate—the stork refused to visit me. Women today can get help." She sighed as she opened a cupboard. They can, I reflected, but it doesn't always work. I thought of the woman who'd bought the pink prom dress. "Sadly, the only thing my ovaries have ever given me is cancer," Mrs. Bell added as she got down the milk jug. "Awfully mean of them. Now, if you could carry the tray . . ."

"I've just returned from Avignon," I told her as I poured the tea a few minutes later.

Mrs. Bell nodded thoughtfully. "And was it a successful trip?"

"In the sense that I bought some lovely stock, yes." I handed her her cup. "I also went to Châteauneuf-du-Pape." I told her about Miles.

She sipped her tea, supporting the cup with both hands. "That sounds very romantic."

"Well, not in every way." I mentioned Roxanne's behaviour.

"So you were in Châteauneuf-du-*Papa*."

I smiled. "It did feel like that. Roxanne's very demanding, to put it mildly."

"That will be tricky," said Mrs. Bell.

"I think it will be. But Miles seems to . . . like me."

"He would be quite insane if he didn't."

"Thanks. But the reason why I'm telling you this is that on the way back to Avignon I got lost, and found myself in Rochemare."

Mrs. Bell shifted on her seat. *"Ah."*

"You didn't tell me the name of your village."

"No. I preferred not to—and there was no need for you to know."

"I understand. But I recognised it immediately from your description. And I saw this old man sitting at the bar in the square, and I even got it into my head that he could be Jean-Luc Aumage—"

"No," Mrs. Bell interjected sharply. She set down her cup. "No, no." She was shaking her head. "Jean-Luc died in Indochina."

"Then I saw the war memorial."

"He was killed at the battle of Dien Bien Phu. Apparently while trying to help a Vietnamese woman to safety." I stared at Mrs. Bell. "It's strange to think of it," she observed quietly. "And I have sometimes wondered whether that gallant action of his might perhaps have been prompted by guilt over what he had done a decade before." She held up her hands. "Who knows?" she sighed. "Who knows?" Suddenly she pushed herself out of her chair, grimacing as she straightened up. "Excuse me, Phoebe. There is something I'd like to show you."

She crossed the corridor into her bedroom, where I heard a drawer being opened. In a minute or two she returned with a large brown envelope, the edges of which were faded to ochre. She sat down, opened it, and slid out a large photo, which she looked at, searchingly, for a few seconds before beckoning me to her. I pulled up a chair by her side.

In the black-and-white image were a hundred or so girls and boys, eagerly standing to attention in their rows, or looking bored with their heads cocked to one side, or with their eyes half-closed against the sunlight. The older children stood stiffly at the back, the youngest sat cross-legged in front; the boys' hair was rigidly parted, the girls' hair tamed with ribbons and combs.

"This was taken in May 1942," said Mrs. Bell. "There were around a hundred and twenty of us in the school at that time."

I scanned the sea of faces. "And where are you?"

Mrs. Bell pointed to the left-hand side of the third row, to a girl with a high forehead and a wide mouth and shoulder-length hair that framed her face in soft waves. Then her finger moved to the girl standing on her immediate left—a girl with shiny black hair cut in a bob, high cheekbones, and dark eyes that stared out with a friendly, yet somehow watchful gaze. "And that is Monique."

"There's a wariness in her expression."

"Yes. You can see her anxiety—her fear of exposure." Mrs. Bell sighed. "Poor child."

"And where is he? Jean-Luc?" I asked.

Mrs. Bell pointed to the boy in the middle of the back row whose head formed the apex of the photo's composition. As I stared at his fine features and wheat-blond hair, it was easy to understand her teenage infatuation with him.

"It's funny," she murmured, "but whenever I thought about Jean-Luc after the war, I used to think, bitterly, of how he would no doubt live to a ripe old age and die peacefully in his sleep, surrounded by his children and grandchildren. In fact, Jean-Luc was twenty-six when he was killed, far from home, in the chaos of battle, bravely helping a stranger. The citation—Marcel sent me the newspaper clipping—said that he had gone back to help the Vietnamese woman, who survived, and who described him as 'a hero.' Which to her, at least, he was."

Mrs. Bell lowered the photo. "I have often wondered why Jean-Luc did what he did to Monique. He was very young, of course, though that is no excuse. He hero-worshipped his father—though unfortunately René Aumage was no hero. And he may have been partly motivated by a sense of personal rejection—Monique had kept her distance from him, with good reason."

"But Jean-Luc could have had no idea what Monique's true fate was likely to be," I pointed out.

"No, he could not have known, because no one knew, until afterwards. And those who *did* know and were in a position to tell were simply not believed—people said they must be *mad*. If only . . . ," Mrs. Bell murmured, shaking her head. "But the fact remains that Jean-Luc behaved horribly, as so many people did at that time, and many behaved heroically," she added. "Like the Antignac family, who it turned out had been sheltering in their home four other children, who all survived the war." She looked at me. "There were many brave people like the Antignacs. These are the people I think about, Phoebe." She slid the photo back into the envelope.

"Mrs. Bell," I said gently, "I also found Monique's house." At that she flinched. "I'm sorry," I rushed on. "I didn't mean to upset you. But I recognised it because of the well—and the lion's head over the front door."

"It is sixty-five years since I last saw that house," she said quietly. "I have been back to Rochemare, of course, but I never once returned to Monique's home—I could not bear to. And after my parents died in the 1970s Marcel moved to Lyon and my association with the village ended."

I stirred my tea. "It was strange for me, Mrs. Bell, because when I was standing there, I saw a movement behind the shutters; it was just a shadow, but somehow it gave me a . . . shock. It made me feel . . ."

Mrs. Bell bristled. "Feel what?"

I stared at her. "I'm not quite sure—it was something that I can't explain, except to say that it was as much as I could do not to go up to the front door and knock on it and ask . . ."

"Ask what?" said Mrs. Bell brusquely. Her tone surprised me. "What could you ask?" she demanded.

"Well . . ."

"What could you possibly find out, Phoebe, that I do not know myself?" Mrs. Bell's pale blue eyes were blazing. "Monique and her family perished in 1943."

I returned her gaze, struggling to remain calm. "But do you know that for sure?"

Mrs. Bell lowered her cup. It rattled slightly in the saucer. "When the war ended, I searched for information about them, dreading what I might find out. I looked for them under both their French and German names through the tracing service of the International Red Cross. The records that the authorities uncovered—and this took more than two years—showed that Monique's mother and brothers were sent to Dachau in June 1943; their names were on the transportation lists. But there is no record of them after that because those who did not survive selection were not registered—and women with young children did not survive that process." Mrs. Bell's voice faltered. "But the Red Cross did find a record for Monique's father. He was selected for forced labour but died there six months later. As for Monique . . . the Red Cross could find no trace of her after the war. They knew that she had spent three months in Drancy before being sent to Auschwitz. Her camp record—the Nazis kept meticulous files—showed that she had arrived there on August 5, 1943. The fact that she had a record means that she survived selection. But she is believed to have been killed there, or to have died there at some date unknown."

I felt my pulse quicken. "But you don't know for *sure* what happened to her."

"No. I don't, but—"

"And you haven't searched again since?"

Mrs. Bell shook her head. "I spent three years looking for Monique, and what I found convinced me that she had not survived. It would have been futile and upsetting to seek for her further. I was getting married, and moving to England; I had been given the rare chance of a fresh start. I decided, ruthlessly perhaps, to draw a line under what had happened: I could not drag it through my life forever, punish myself *forever...*" Her voice caught again. "Nor did I dare mention it to my husband—I was terrified that I'd see in his eyes a look of disillusionment with me that would have...spoilt everything. So I buried the story of Monique—for decades, Phoebe—telling no one in the world about it. Not a soul. Until I met you."

"But you don't *know* that Monique died in Auschwitz," I insisted. My heart was thudding in my rib cage.

Mrs. Bell stared at me. "All right. That's true. But if she didn't die there, the chances are that she died in another concentration camp or in the chaos of January '45 as the Allies closed in and the Nazis forced those inmates who could still stand to march to other camps—less than half of them survived. *So* many people were displaced or killed in those months that thousands upon thousands of deaths went unrecorded, and Monique's could well have been one of them."

"But you don't *know.*" I tried to swallow but my mouth had gone dry. "And without that certain knowledge you must *surely* sometimes have wondered whether—"

"Phoebe," said Mrs. Bell, her pale blue eyes glimmering with tears, "Monique has been *dead* for sixty-five years. And her house, like the clothes you sell, went on to have a new life, with new owners. Whatever you felt when you stood outside her home was...irrational. Because all you had seen was a glimpse of some person who lives there *now,* not some...I don't know...'presence'—if that's what you're suggesting—compelling you to—I know not what! Now..." Her hand flew to her chest and fluttered there like an injured bird. "I am very tired."

"Of course." I stood up. "And I should get back." I took the tea tray into the kitchen, then returned. "I'm sorry if I've upset you, Mrs. Bell. I didn't mean to."

"And I am sorry to have become...agitated. I know you mean well, Phoebe, but it is painful for me—especially now, as I face up to the fact that my life will soon end and I will die knowing that I was never able to put right the wrong that I did."

"You mean the mistake that you made," I corrected her gently.

"Yes. The mistake—the awful mistake." Mrs. Bell put out her hand to me, and I held it. It felt so small and light. "But I appreciate the fact that you think about my story." I felt her fingers close around mine.

"I do. I think about it a lot, Mrs. Bell."

She nodded. "As I think about yours."

Ten

On Thursday Val phoned me again about collecting the repairs, so I drove over to Kidbrooke straight after work. As I parked outside her house I desperately hoped that Mags wouldn't be there. I felt embarrassed and ashamed about the psychic reading now. It had all been so stupid and . . . *absurd*.

As I put my hand to Val's bell I gasped. A fat-bodied spider, of the kind that emerges in the autumn, had spun its web across it. I knocked loudly instead, then, when Val opened the door, I pointed it out to her.

She stared at it. "Oh, that's *good*. Spiders are lucky—do you know why?"

"No." I shuddered.

"Because a spider hid the baby Jesus from Herod's soldiers by weaving a web over him. Isn't that incredible? That's why you should never kill a spider," she added.

"I wouldn't dream of it."

"Ah . . . *that's* interesting." Val was still peering at it. "It's running *up* its web, which means that you've been on a journey, Phoebe."

I looked at her in surprise. "I have actually. I've just been to France."

"If it had been running *down* its web, then that would have meant you were about to *go* on one."

"Really? You're a mine of information," I said as I went inside.

"Well, I think it's important to know these things."

Following Val down the hall, I detected the scent of Magie Noire with bass notes of nicotine. *Maggie Noire,* I thought dismally.

"Hi, Mags," I said with a forced smile.

"Hi, sweetheart," Mags rasped as she sat, filling the armchair in Val's sewing room. She was eating a cracker. "Shame about the other day. But you should have let me keep trying." She scraped at the corner of her mouth with a crimson fingernail. "I think Emma was just about to come through."

I stared at Mags, suddenly outraged at hearing my best friend referred to in this crass way. "I don't think so," I said, struggling to keep calm. "In fact, as long as you've brought it up, I have to tell you that I thought the sitting was a complete waste of time."

Mags looked at me as though I'd slapped her. Then she pulled a packet of tissues out of her cleavage and removed one. "The problem is you're not *really* a believer."

"That's not true. I *don't* disbelieve the idea that the human soul may continue or that we can even detect the presence of someone who's died. But as you got every single thing about my friend wrong—including her gender—I can't help feeling a bit cynical about your particular abilities."

Mags blew her nose. "I was having an off day," she sniffed. "Plus the ether's often a bit murky on Tuesday mornings."

"Mags really *is* very good, Phoebe," Val said loyally. "She put me in touch with my granny the other night—didn't you?" Mags nodded. "I'd lost her lemon curd recipe, so I got her to give it to me again."

"Eight eggs," said Mags. "Not six."

"That's what I couldn't remember," said Val. "Anyway, thanks to Mags, Gran and I had a nice little chat." I suppressed a cutting remark. "In fact, Mags is *so* good that she's been invited to be a guest medium on the *In Spirit* show on ITV 2, haven't you, Mags?" Mags nodded. "I'm sure she'll bring comfort to lots of viewers. You should watch it, Phoebe," Val added amiably. "Every Sunday at two-thirty."

I picked up the case. "I'll make a note of it," I told them.

"These will look *wonderful,*" Annie enthused the next morning as I showed her the garments that Val had mended—Mrs. Bell's yellow knife-pleated evening dress, the glorious pink Guy Laroche silk co-coon coat, the Ossie Clark maxidress, and the damson-plum gabar-dine suit. I showed her the Missoni rainbow-striped knitted dress that had had moth damage at the hem. "What a clever repair," Annie said as she examined it. Val had knitted a piece to cover the hole. "She must have used tiny needles to match the stitches, and the colour is perfect." Annie held up the Chanel Boutique sapphire-blue silk faille evening coat with elbow-length sleeves. "This is gor-geous. It should go in the window, don't you think? Maybe instead of the Norma Kamali trouser suit," she mused.

Annie had come in early to help me rearrange the stock before the shop opened. We'd put away at least half the clothes, replacing them with garments in the key shades for autumn—midnight blue, tomato red, sea green, deep purple, and gold—jewel tones redolent of the colours seen in Renaissance paintings. Then we'd found clothes that reflected the season's silhouettes—sculpted A-line coats and dresses with stand-away collars and full skirts; architec-tural leather jackets with exaggerated shoulders and curved sleeves. We'd chosen fabrics that tied in with the seductive fabrics of the mo-ment—brocade, lace, satin, and damask, crushed velvet, tartan, and tweed.

"Just because we're selling vintage doesn't mean that we can ig-nore trends in shape and colour," I'd said as I came down from the stockroom again clutching several outfits.

"In fact it's probably even more important," Annie had pointed out. "There's a 'statement' feel to this season," she'd added as I'd handed her a Balmain cherry-red dress with a flaring tulip skirt, an Azzedine Alaia Couture chocolate-brown leather suit with a nipped-in waist and huge lapels, and a Courrèges futurist orange crêpe dress from the mid-sixties. "Everything's big and opulent," Annie had gone on. "Hot, bold colours, structured shapes, stiff fabrics that stand away from the body. You've got all of that here, Phoebe; all we have to do is put it together."

Annie had put out most of Mrs. Bell's evening wear and was now looking at her gabardine two-piece. "This is lovely, but I think we should update it with a soft, wide belt and a fake-fur collar. Shall I find some?"

"Yes. Please."

As I hung the suit on a rack I imagined Mrs. Bell wearing it in the late forties. I thought of the conversation I'd had with her three days before and of how hard it must have been for her, in the aftermath of war, trying to find out what had happened to Monique. If, God forbid, there was some comparable situation today, she'd be able to launch an appeal on radio and TV; she could scatter e-mails around the globe or post requests for information on Internet message boards, on Facebook, MySpace, or YouTube. She could simply put Monique's name into a search engine and see what came out of the ether.

"Here," said Annie as she came downstairs with an "ocelot" collar. "I think this will work—and this belt should tone in." She held it against the jacket. "It does."

"Could you put them on the suit?" I asked Annie as I went into the office. "I just need to . . . check the website."

"Sure."

Ever since Mrs. Bell had told me her story I'd wondered about searching the net for any possible references to Monique, however unlikely. But what would I do if I did find something? How could I keep that from Mrs. Bell? Given that it would almost certainly be negative, if not devastating, I'd resisted the urge to do it. But since going to Monique's house I'd felt differently. I'd been gripped by the desire to *know*. And so, prompted by some inner compulsion that I couldn't explain, I sat at the computer and typed Monique's name into Google.

Nothing of any significance came up, just some references to an avenue Richelieu in Quebec, and to the Lycée Richelieu in Paris. I put in the name without the first *e*. Then I typed in "Monika Richter," and up came a Californian psychoanalyst, a German pediatrician, and an Australian conservationist, none of whom would be likely to have any connection with their older namesake. I then did the same search spelling Monika with a *c*. Then I added "Auschwitz," thinking that there just might be some eyewitness account that mentioned her, out of all the billions of words that had been written about the camp. Now I added "Mannheim," because I remembered that that was where she had originally come from. But nothing that seemed to relate to Monique/Monika or her family came up—just a few references to an exhibition there by Gerhard Richter.

I stared at the screen. So that was that. As Mrs. Bell had said, all I'd seen in Rochemare was the fleeting movement of a living person in a house that had long since shrugged off the memory of its wartime occupants. And I was about to close Internet Explorer when I decided to look at the Red Cross website.

On the home page it explained that its tracing service had been started at the end of the war and that its archive in northern Germany now contained nearly fifty million Nazi documents that related to the camps. Any member of the public could request a search, which would be carried out by the IRC archivists; on average each search took between one and four hours. Given the volume of requests, the enquirer could expect to wait three months "maximum" for a report.

I clicked on the Download Form box. I was surprised at how brief the form was; it simply asked for the personal details of the person being sought, and the place where the person was last known to have been seen. Enquirers had to provide their own personal details and to explain their connection to the person they were seeking. They then had to give the reason for their search. There were two choices for this—"Documentation for reparations" or "Desire to know what happened."

"Desire to know what happened," I murmured.

I printed off the form, then put it in an envelope. I'd take it to Mrs. Bell when her niece had left and we'd fill it in together, then I'd e-mail it to the Red Cross. If in their vast repository of information they could find any references to Monique, then, I reasoned, there'd at least be the slim chance that Mrs. Bell might finally gain closure on the issue. Three months "maximum" implied that the report might well come back in less—perhaps in only one month, I reflected, or even a fortnight. I wondered about enclosing a note, explaining that, due to illness, time was short. But then that would be the case with so many enquirers of Mrs. Bell's generation, I realized, the youngest of whom would now be well into their seventies.

"So have you got many Internet orders?" I heard Annie call.

"Oh . . ." I forced my thoughts back to the shop and quickly navigated to the Village Vintage website, then opened the mailbox. "There are . . . three. Someone wants to buy the forest-green Kelly bag, there's interest in the Pucci palazzo pants and . . . hurrah!— someone's buying the Madame Grès."

"That dress you don't want."

"That's right." The one that Guy had given me. I came back into the shop and removed it from the rack to pack up and send. "This woman asked me for the measurements last week," I said as I slipped it off its hanger. "And now she's come back with the money— thank goodness."

"You're dying to get rid of it, aren't you?"

"I suppose I am."

"Is that because it was from a boyfriend?"

I looked at Annie. "Yes."

"I did guess, but as I didn't know you I wasn't going to ask. Now that I *do* know you, I feel I can be a bit nosey . . ." I smiled. Annie and

I did know each other now. I liked her friendly, easy company and her enthusiasm for the shop. "So, was it a bit acrimonious?"

"Well, you could say that."

"Then selling that dress is totally understandable. If Tim dumped me, I'd probably chuck everything he'd ever given me—except the paintings," she added, "just in case they turned out to be worth anything one day." She put a pair of Bruno Magli scarlet stilettos in the shoe display. "And how's the sender of the red roses? If you don't mind my asking."

"He's . . . fine. In fact, I saw him in France." I explained why.

"That sounds good. And he's obviously nuts about you. Those roses must have cost a fortune."

I smiled. Then as I did up the buttons on a pink cashmere cardigan I told Annie a bit more about Miles.

"So what's his daughter like?"

I draped several heavy gold-plated chains around the neck of a wooden display head. "She's sixteen, very pretty—and terribly spoilt."

"Like so many teenagers," Annie observed. "But she won't always be a teenager."

"True," I said happily.

"But teenagers *can* be vile."

Suddenly we heard a tap on the glass and there was Katie, in her uniform, waving at us. *And teenagers can be lovely,* I thought.

I unlocked the door and Katie came in. "Hi," she said. Then she glanced anxiously at the yellow prom dress. "Thank God." She smiled. "It's still here."

"It is," I said. I wasn't going to tell her that someone had tried it on only the day before. It had made the woman look like a grapefruit. "Annie, this is Katie."

"I remember seeing you here a few days ago," said Annie warmly.

"Katie's interested in the yellow prom dress."

"I adore it," she said longingly. "I'm trying to save up for it."

"Dare I ask how it's going?" I said.

"Well, I did a babysit last night, so I've now got seventy pounds in the fund. But as the ball's on November first, I've got my work cut out."

"Well, keep at it. I wish *I* had children. Then you could babysit them."

"I was just passing on my way to school and couldn't resist having another peek. Can I take a photo of it?"

"Of course."

Katie held her phone up to the dress and I heard a click. "There," she said, looking at it, "that'll keep me motivated. Anyway, I'd better rush—it's a quarter to nine." She shouldered her school bag and turned to go, then stooped to pick up the newspaper that had just landed on the mat. She handed it to Annie.

"Thanks, sweetheart," Annie told her.

I waved to Katie, then began rearranging the evening-wear rack.

"Good God!" I heard Annie exclaim.

She was staring, goggle-eyed, at the front page of the paper. Then she held it up for me to see.

Covering the top half of the *Black & Green* was a photo of Keith. Above his drawn-looking face was the headline LOCAL PROPERTY BOSS IN FRAUD PROBE—EXCLUSIVE!

Annie read the article out to me. " 'Prominent local property developer Keith Brown, chairman of Phoenix Land, today faces the possibility of a criminal investigation after this newspaper's discovery of evidence implicating him in a massive insurance fraud.' " I thought, with a sympathetic pang, of Keith's girlfriend; this would be awful for her. " 'Brown started Phoenix Land,' " Annie read on, " 'with the proceeds from a huge insurance payout after his kitchen business had been destroyed by fire two years earlier. Brown's insurers, Star Alliance, disputed his claim that his warehouse had been torched by a disgruntled employee who had subsequently disappeared and could not be traced . . . Refused to pay out,' " I heard her say as I rearranged the dresses. " 'Brown started proceedings . . . Star Alliance eventually settled . . . Two million pounds . . .' " I heard

Annie gasp and looked at her. " 'Now the *Black & Green* has been handed compelling evidence that the blaze was started by Keith Brown *himself . . .* ' " Annie stared at me, her eyes like saucers, then returned her gaze to the paper. " 'Mr. Brown declined to answer the questions we put to him last night, but his attempt to get an injunction against the *Black & Green* failed . . .' Well!" she exclaimed with censorious satisfaction. "It's good to know we weren't too hard on him." She handed me the paper.

I quickly read through the piece myself, then I remembered Keith's quotes in the *Guardian* about how "devastated" he'd been as he watched his warehouse burn, and how he had "vowed to build something worthwhile out of the ashes." It had all felt a bit phoney; now I knew why.

"I wonder how the *Black & Green* got the story," I said to Annie.

"Presumably because the insurers, having been suspicious all along, have just come up with this 'compelling evidence,' whatever it is."

"But why would they take it to a local newspaper? Surely they'd go straight to the police."

"Ah." Annie clicked her tongue. "Good point."

So this must have been the "difficult" business story that Dan had been working on—the one that Matt had phoned him about when Dan and I were sitting in the Age Exchange.

"I hope the girlfriend isn't going to stand by him," I heard Annie say. "Mind you, she can always visit him in prison in her green prom dress, looking like 'bloody Tinker Bell.' " She giggled. "And on that subject, have you e-mailed your American dealer yet? That guy Rick? He left a message about some prom dresses, remember?"

I'd been so preoccupied with Monique that I'd forgotten. "I need to do that, don't I?"

"You do need to," Annie said. "The party season's coming up—plus prom dresses are 'in' this season according to *Vogue*—the more petticoats the better."

"I'll e-mail Rick right now. Thanks for reminding me."

I went back to the computer and opened Outlook Express to contact Rick, only to find that he'd gotten there first. I clicked on his e-mail.

Hi Phoebe—I left a message on your phone the other day to say that I've got six more prom dresses to offer you, all top quality and in perfect condition. I clicked on the photos. They were lovely cupcakes in vibrant shades that would be perfect for the autumn—indigo, vermillion, tangerine, emerald green, deep purple, and kingfisher blue. I zoomed in on the images to check whether the net looked faded anywhere, then I clicked back on the text. *Also attached is the jpeg of the purses—sorry, "bags"—that I mentioned and which I want to include with the dresses, as a job lot . . . .*

"Damn," I murmured. I didn't want them, especially with the pound having fallen so much against the dollar lately; with a sinking heart, I realised I might have to buy them in case Rick stopped sending me the things that I did like. "Let's have a look then," I said wearily.

The bags had been photographed together on a white sheet and were mostly from the eighties and nineties. They were fairly ordinary, except for a very handsome leather Gladstone bag probably from the 1940s and an elegant white ostrich-skin envelope clutch from the early seventies.

"How much does he want?" I murmured. *The deal is $750 US, inclusive of shipping.*

I clicked on reply. *Okay, Rick,* I typed. *It's a deal. I'll pay you by PayPal when I get your invoice. Please send everything asap. Cheers, Phoebe.*

"I've just bought six more prom dresses," I told Annie as I went back into the shop.

She was changing one of the mannequins. "That's good news. They should be easy to sell."

"I've also bought twelve bags; most of which I don't want—but I have to have them as they're the quid pro quo."

"There's not much space up there in the stockroom," she remarked as she repositioned the mannequin's arms.

"I know; so when they arrive I'll just give the non-vintage ones to Oxfam. But now I'm going to post the Madame Grès."

I went into the office and quickly wrapped the dress up in tissue paper with a white ribbon, then put it in a padded envelope. Then I turned the CLOSED sign on the door to OPEN. "See you later, Annie."

As I left the shop my mother called me on my cell phone. "I've decided," she whispered.

"Decided what?" I asked as I turned down Montpelier Vale.

"To forget about all these silly treatments I've been looking into—all this plasma regeneration and fractional resurfacing and radio-frequency rejuvenation nonsense."

I glanced into the window of the beauty salon. "That is such good news, Mum."

"I don't think they're going to make the slightest difference."

"I'm sure that's right," I agreed as I crossed the road.

"And they cost *so* much."

"They do. It would be a complete waste of money."

"Exactly. So I've decided I may as well go straight for a facelift."

I stopped dead. "Mum . . . *Don't.*"

"I'm going to have a facelift," she repeated quietly. "I'm terribly low and it'll give me a boost. It'll be my sixtieth birthday gift to myself, Phoebe. I've worked all these years," she added as I walked on. "So why shouldn't I have a little cosmetic 'refreshment' if I want to?"

"No reason, Mum. It's your life. But what if you're not happy with it?" I had visions of my mother's pretty face looking grotesquely stretched or oddly lumpy and bumpy.

"I've done my research," I heard her say as I passed the toy shop. "Yesterday I took the day off and had consultations with three plastic surgeons. I've decided that Freddie Church is going to wield the scalpel, at his clinic in Maida Vale. It's all booked for November twenty-fourth." I wondered whether Mum had remembered that that was Louis's first birthday. "And don't try to talk me out of it, darling, because my mind's made up. I've paid my deposit, and I'm going ahead with it."

"Okay." I sighed as I crossed the road. There was no point in protesting. Once Mum had decided on something she stuck to it; plus I had a lot on my mind and lacked the energy for a fight. "I only hope you don't come to regret it."

"I *won't*. But, tell me, how's your new boyfriend? Is that still going on?"

"I'm seeing him tomorrow. We're going to the theatre."

"Well, you seem to like him, so please don't do anything silly. I mean, you're *thirty-four* now," Mum added as I turned into Black-heath Grove. "Before you know where you are, you'll be forty-three—"

"Sorry, Mum, I have to go now." I snapped the phone shut. The post office was nearly empty, so it only took two minutes to post my parcel. As I walked out again I saw Dan coming towards me, smiling. But then today he had something to smile about.

"I was just looking out the window and saw you." He nodded up at his office, above the children's library.

I followed his gaze. "So that's where you are—very central. Congratulations, by the way. I've just read your scoop."

"It's not my scoop," Dan replied. "It's Matt's—I just sat in on the talks with the lawyers. But it's a fantastic story for a local paper like ours. We're all a bit cock-a-hoop about it."

"I'm dying to know who you got it from," I said. "Not that you can reveal your sources . . . Can you?" I added hopefully.

Dan grinned, then shook his head. "'Fraid not."

"I feel sorry for his girlfriend though. Plus she'll probably lose her job."

Dan shrugged. "She'll get another one. She's very young. I've seen photos of her." Then he asked me about France, reminding me that I'd said I'd go to the cinema with him again. "I don't suppose

you're free tomorrow night, are you, Phoebe? I know it's short notice, but I've been very preoccupied with the Brown story. We could
go and see the new Coen brothers film—or just have dinner somewhere."

"Well..." I looked at him. "That would have been great. But
I'm...doing something."

"Oh." Dan smiled at me ruefully. "But then, why wouldn't a girl
like you be busy on a Saturday night?" He sighed. "I'm an idiot. I
should have asked you before. So...are you seeing someone,
Phoebe?"

"Well...I...*Dan*," I said, "you're discombobulating me again."

"Oh. Sorry. I don't seem to be able to help it. But, look, did you
get the invitation for the eleventh? I sent it to the shop."

"Yes, I got it yesterday."

"Well, you said you'd be there, so I hope you'll come."

I looked at Dan. "Yes. I will."

This morning I found it hard to concentrate on work because I kept
thinking about Miles and about how much I was looking forward to
seeing him at the theatre. We were going to the Almeida to see *Waste*
by Harley Granville-Barker. In between customers I read a couple of
reviews of it online, partly to remind myself of the plot—I'd seen it
years ago—and partly so that I'd be able to impress Miles with my
trenchant remarks. But then the shop became very busy, as it always
is on Saturdays. I sold Mrs. Bell's Guy Laroche cocoon coat—I was
almost sorry to see it go—and a Zandra Rhodes apricot silk organza
tunic with gold beading at the hem. Then someone asked to try on
the yellow prom dress; it would be the third time it had been tried
on in a week. As the woman went into the fitting room I glanced
anxiously at her figure and realised that it would probably fit her. I
drew the curtain round, praying that she wouldn't like it. I heard the
rustle of the tulle, then the sound of the zipper being pulled up, followed by a little grunt.

"I *love* it!" I heard her exclaim. The woman opened the curtain and gazed at herself in the mirror, turning this way and that. "It's fabulous," she decided as she stood on tiptoe. "I adore the froth and sparkle of it." She beamed at me. "I'll take it!"

My heart sank as I imagined Katie's disappointment. I thought of her taking the photo of the dress, and now I remembered how lovely she had looked in it—ten times more attractive than this woman, who was too old for it, and not slim enough, with her fleshy white shoulders and plump arms.

The woman turned to her friend. "Don't you think it's fab, Sue?"

Sue, who was tall and angular—a Modigliani to her friend's fleshy Rubens—was chewing on her lower lip. "Well . . . to be honest, Jill, sweetheart, I don't. Your skin tone's too pale for it, plus the bodice is tight—look—which makes you bulge at the back, here." She turned her friend round. Jill could now see that a good half-inch of fat spilled over the stiffened panels, like dough.

Sue cocked her head. "You know those puddings you can get—a frozen lemon that's been stuffed with sorbet that's sort of squishing out of the top of it?"

"Yes?" said Jill.

"Well, you look like one of those."

I held my breath to see how Jill reacted. She stared at herself, then nodded reluctantly. "You're right, Sue. Cruel—but right."

"What are best friends for?" replied Sue amiably. She flashed me a guilty smile. "Sorry—I just lost you a sale."

"That's okay," I said delightedly. "It's got to be perfect, hasn't it? Anyway, I'll be getting some more prom dresses soon, so one of those might be a better fit—they should be here next week."

"We'll be back."

Once the two women had gone I put the yellow dress on the "reserved" rack with "Katie" on it—my nerves wouldn't take any more fittings. Then I brought down a Lanvin-Castillo raspberry-pink silk evening gown from the mid-1950s and hung it on the wall in its place.

I closed the shop at five-thirty on the dot, then sped home to shower and change before rushing up to Islington to meet Miles. As I half-ran down Almeida Street, I saw him standing outside the theatre. When he saw me, he lifted his hand.

"Sorry I'm late," I said breathlessly. The bell was ringing. "Is that the five-minute bell?"

"It's the one-minute." He kissed me. "I was worried that you weren't going to come."

I slipped my arm through his. "Of course I was." I found Miles's anxiety touching, and as we went inside I wondered whether it was prompted by the fourteen years between us, or whether he always felt a little insecure when he liked someone, whatever her age.

"It's a good play," he said an hour or so later as the house lights went up for the intermission. We stood up. "I've seen it before—years ago, at the National. I think it was in '91."

"It *was*, because I also saw that production—with my school." With a pang, I remembered Emma coming back for the second half in fits of giggles and reeking of gin.

Miles laughed. "So you would have been Roxy's age; and I'd have been thirty-one—a young man. I'd have fallen in love with you then too."

I smiled. We made our way into the foyer, then drifted towards the bar with everyone else.

"I'll get our drinks," I told him. "What would you like?"

"A glass of Côtes du Rhône, if they have one."

I looked at the board. "They do. I think I'll have the Sancerre." As I stood at the bar, Miles waited a little way behind me. "Phoebe..." I heard him whisper after a few moments. I turned round. His face had reddened and he was suddenly looking uncomfortable. "I'll see you outside," he murmured.

"Fine," I replied, bemused.

"Are you okay?" I asked when I found him a few minutes later standing by the entrance. I handed him his glass of wine. "I was worried that you might be unwell."

He shook his head. "I'm okay. But . . . as you were waiting to be served I spotted some people I wanted to avoid."

"Really?" My curiosity was aroused. "Who?" Miles discreetly nodded towards the far end of the foyer at a blond forty-something woman in a turquoise wrap and a sandy-haired man in a dark coat. "Who are they?" I asked him quietly.

"Their name's Wycliffe. Their daughter's at Roxy's old school." Miles pursed his mouth. "It's just not a great . . . connection."

"I see," I said, remembering now that Miles had said that there'd been some 'misunderstanding' at Saint Mary's. Whatever it was, it still had the power to upset him. Hearing the bell for the second half, we went back to our seats.

Afterwards, while we were waiting to cross the road to the restaurant opposite the theatre, I saw Mrs. Wycliffe give Miles a sideways glance, then discreetly tug at her husband's sleeve. As we started dinner I asked Miles what the Wycliffes had done that had so offended him.

"They were awful to Roxy. In fact it was very . . . unpleasant." As he lifted his glass of water, I saw that his hand was shaking.

"Why?" I asked, without thinking. Miles hesitated. "Didn't the girls get on?"

"Oh, they did." Miles lowered his glass. "In fact, Roxy and Clara had been best friends. Then, at the start of the summer term, there was . . . a falling-out." I looked at Miles, wondering why this would have upset him quite so much. "Something of Clara's went missing," he explained. "A . . . gold bracelet. Clara accused Roxy of having taken it." He pursed his lips again, the muscles at the side of his mouth flexing.

"Oh . . ."

"But I knew that it couldn't be true. I know Roxanne can be annoying, in the way that teenagers often are, but she would never do anything like *that*." He ran a finger under his collar. "Anyway, the school phoned me and said that Clara and her parents were insisting that Roxy had stolen this wretched bracelet. I was incensed. I said that I would not have my daughter being falsely accused. But the headmistress behaved . . . *outrageously.*" I saw a vein at his left temple jump.

"In what way?"

"In the bias she showed. She refused to accept Roxy's version of events."

"Which was . . . what?"

"As I said, Roxanne and Clara had been very good friends. They constantly borrowed each other's things, in the way that girls of that age do. I saw it when Clara stayed with us at Easter," Miles went on. "She came down to breakfast one morning dressed entirely in clothes that were Roxy's, with Roxy's jewellery—and vice versa. The girls did it the whole time—they thought it was fun."

"So . . . you mean that Roxy *had* the bracelet?"

Miles flushed. "It turned up in her drawer—but the point is, she hadn't *stolen* it. I mean, why would she need to take anything from *anyone* when she has so much of her own? She explained that Clara had *lent* her the bracelet, that Clara had some of *her* jewellery—which she did—and that they swapped their things all the time. That should have been the *end* of it. But the Wycliffes were determined to make something of it. They were vile." He heaved a bitter sigh.

"What did they do?"

Miles drew in his breath, then slowly released it. "They threatened to call the police. So I had no choice but to make a counter threat of my own that I would start libel proceedings against them if they didn't stop defaming my daughter."

"And the school?"

Miles's lips tightened. "They sided with the Wycliffes—no doubt because the man's donating half a million towards their new gym. It was . . . nauseating. So . . . I took Roxy away. The moment she'd taken her last exam, I was waiting there to drive her home. It was *my* decision for her to leave that school."

Miles reached for his water glass. And I was helplessly wondering what to say next when the waiter came to take our plates. By the

time he'd gone and then quickly come back with our main courses,
Miles seemed less agitated, the unpleasantness at Roxy's old school
receding, then seemingly almost forgotten. I chatted to him about
the play, hoping to distract him. Then Miles got the bill. "I drove
here, by the way," he said. "Which means that I can take you home."

"Thank you."

"I can take you home to your home," Miles said. "Or, if you like,
to mine." He looked into my face, seeking my reaction. "I can lend
you a T-shirt again," he added quietly, "and I can give you a toothbrush. Roxy has a hair dryer, if you need one. She's at a party tonight,
in the Cotswolds." So that explained why he hadn't had twenty calls
from her on his cell phone. "I'm going to pick her up tomorrow afternoon. So I thought that you and I could spend the morning together, then have lunch somewhere. How does that sound, Phoebe?"

I felt my face flush with pleasure. "It sounds . . . lovely."

Miles smiled at me. "Good."

As we drove through South London with Mozart's clarinet concerto on the CD player, I felt happy to be going back with Miles. He
pulled up outside his house, and I glanced at the front yard, which
was prettily landscaped with low box hedging enclosed by a
wrought-iron fence. Miles unlocked the door and we stepped into a
wide hallway with high ceilings, panelled walls, and black-and-
white marble floor tiles that had been polished to a watery shine.

As Miles took my coat I glimpsed a large dining room with
oxblood walls and a long mahogany table. I followed him down the
hall to the kitchen with its hand-painted cupboards and granite
countertops that glittered darkly under the spotlights that spangled
the ceiling. Through the French windows I could just make out an
expanse of tree-fringed lawn rolling away into the gloom.

Miles took a bottle of Evian out of the American fridge, then we
went up the wide staircase to the first floor. His bedroom was decorated in yellow, and attached to it was a big bathroom with a free-
standing iron tub and a fireplace. I got undressed there. "Could I
have that toothbrush?" I called out.

Miles came into the bathroom, gave my naked form an appreciative glance, then opened a cupboard in which I could see bottles of shampoo and bubble bath. "Now, where is it?" he murmured. "Roxy's always looking for things in here . . . Ah—got it." He handed me a new brush. "And what about a T-shirt? I can get you one." He lifted my hair and kissed the back of my neck, then my shoulder. "If you think you'll need one."

I turned to him and slid my arms round his waist. "No," I whispered. "I won't."

We woke late. As I glanced sleepily at the clock on the bedside table next to me I felt Miles's arms encircle me, cupping my breasts.

"You're lovely, Phoebe," he murmured. "I think I'm falling in love with you." He kissed me, then placed my hands above my head, and made love to me again . . .

"You could swim in this bath," I said a while later as I soaked in the tub. Miles poured in some more bubble bath, then slid in with me, leaning back behind me while I lay against his chest in a sea of foam.

After a few minutes he picked up my hand and examined it. "Your fingertips are wrinkling." He kissed each one. "Time to get dry." We both stepped out, then Miles picked up a soft white bath sheet and wrapped it round me. We cleaned our teeth, then he took the toothbrush from me and put it in the holder with his. "Keep it in there," he said.

"My hair." I touched it. "Could I borrow a dryer?"

Miles wrapped a towel round his waist. "Come with me."

We crossed the landing, the early-autumn sunshine flooding through the floor-to-ceiling sash windows. As I looked up I saw a beautiful portrait of Roxy hanging on the far wall.

"That's Ellen," Miles explained as we paused in front of it. "I commissioned it for our engagement. She was twenty-three."

"Roxy's so like her," I said. "Although . . ." I looked at Miles. "She has your nose—and your chin." I stroked it with my fingertips. "Is this where you lived with Ellen?"

"No." Miles opened a bedroom door with ROXANNE on it in pink letters. "We lived in Fulham, but after she died I wanted to move—I couldn't bear the constant reminders of her. And I'd been invited to a dinner party at this house and had loved it; so when it came up for sale not long afterwards, the owners offered me first refusal. Now . . ."

Roxy's room was immense, thickly carpeted in white; her bed was a white four-poster crowned with a pink-and-gold damask canopy. A white dressing table held an array of expensive face creams and body lotions and different-sized bottles of J'adore. In front of the pink-and-gold-curtained windows was a chaise longue in pale pink brocade, and on a low table beside it were perhaps two dozen fashion magazines, their covers gleaming icily.

I noticed a doll's house on a side table—a Georgian town house with a gleaming black front door and floor-to-ceiling sash windows. "It's just like this house!" I exclaimed.

"It *is* this house," Miles replied. "It's an exact copy of it." He opened the front and we peered inside. "Every detail is correct, right down to the chandeliers, the working shutters, and the brass doorknobs." I gazed at the replica of the claw-footed iron tub in which I'd just soaked. "I gave it to Roxy for her seventh birthday," Miles explained. "I thought it would help to make her feel more at home. She still plays with it." He straightened up. "Anyway . . . come through here." Now we were in her dressing room. "This is where she keeps her hair dryer." He nodded at a white table with an arsenal of hairdressing equipment. "I'll go and make breakfast."

"I won't be long."

I sat at Roxy's hairdressing table, with its professional hair dryer and its smoothing irons and curling tongs and carousel of heated rollers, and its paddle brushes, combs, and barrettes. As I quickly blow-dried my hair, I looked at all the clothes on the racks that ran around the three walls. There must have been a hundred dresses and suits. To my left was a brick-red Gucci suede coat that I recognised from last year's spring collection. In front of me I could see a Matthew Williamson satin trouser suit and a Hussein Chalayan cocktail dress. There were four or five skiing outfits and at least eight long dresses bagged up in muslin protectors. Ranged beneath the clothes was a chrome rack on which were at least sixty pairs of shoes and boots. Along one wall were a number of sisal baskets containing perhaps three dozen purses.

By my feet was a copy of this month's *Vogue*. I picked it up and it fell open at a fashion spread; half the garments in it had been marked with heart-shaped pink Post-its. A Ralph Lauren baby-blue silk ball gown costing £2,100 had a pink heart next to it; as did a Zac Posen one-shouldered black dress. A Robinson Brothers hot-pink silk taffeta cocktail dress at £1,700 had been similarly earmarked with *Check Sienna Fenwick's not getting this* scribbled on the heart in large, round letters. On the sticky note marking a £3,600 Christian Lacroix couture "stained glass" silk evening gown, Roxy had written, *By special order only.* I shook my head as I wondered which of these creations Roxanne was destined to possess.

I turned off the hair dryer, putting it back exactly where I'd found it. As I walked through her bedroom I paused to shut the front of the doll's house, which Miles had left ajar. I looked inside it again and noticed two dolls in the sitting room—a daddy doll in a brown suit and next to him on the sofa a little-girl doll in a pink-and-white gingham pinafore.

I went back to Miles's bedroom, got dressed and made up, retrieved my earrings from the green saucer on the bathroom mantelpiece, then followed the intoxicating scent of coffee downstairs.

Miles was standing at the breakfast bar with a tray of toast and marmalade.

"The kitchen's lovely," I said, glancing around. "But it's different from the one in the doll's house."

Miles pushed the plunger on the French press. "I had it renovated last year—not least because I wanted better wine storage." He nodded to my left and I glanced at the two large fridges and the floor-to-ceiling wooden racks for red wine. He picked up the tray. "We'll have some Chante le Merle sometime, since you like it."

On the wall by the French windows was a photo montage with a dozen or so snaps of Roxy skiing, riding, mountain biking, and playing tennis. There was a photo of her smiling in front of Table Mountain in Cape Town, and another of her standing on top of Ayers Rock in Australia.

"Roxy's incredibly lucky," I said as I looked at a photo of her fishing from the back of a yacht in what looked like the Caribbean. "For a girl of her age she's done so much—and, as you said, she *has* so much."

Miles sighed. "Probably *too* much." I didn't reply. "But Roxy's my only child, and she means the world to me—plus she's all I have of Ellen." His voice had caught. "I just want her to be as happy as possible."

"Of course," I murmured. *Elle est son talon d'Achille.* Is this what Cecile had meant? Simply that Miles spoilt Roxy?

As we stood on the terrace I gazed at the long, wide lawn fringed on both sides by lush beds of pretty plants and shrubs. Miles put the tray on the wrought-iron table. "You wouldn't get the newspaper, would you? It'll be outside the front door."

While he poured the coffee I went and picked up the *Sunday Times* and carried it back out to the garden. As we sat having our breakfast in the soft autumn sunshine Miles read the main section while I flicked through Style. Then I unfolded the Business section to take out the News Review, and as I did so I saw the heading PHOENIX FALLS. I looked at the half-page article. It had picked up on the *Black & Green* story, repeating the allegation of fraud. Except that there was a photo of Keith Brown's girlfriend, captioned WHISTLE-BLOWER. So *she* was the source?

The article alleged that Brown had once drunkenly bragged to his girlfriend, who was called Kelly Marks, about the way he had planned and carried out the fraud; he'd blamed it on a disgruntled employee who, it turned out, had false ID, and who had disappeared after the fire, presumably to evade justice. The police had circulated a PhotoFit, but the man had never been traced and was still classified as a missing person. Brown, euphoric after securing some huge property deal, had foolishly boasted to Kelly Marks that not only had the man never existed, but he himself had started the blaze. Two weeks ago she had decided "after searching her conscience" to reveal this to the *Black & Green*. The article had a quote from Matt saying that, although he couldn't comment on his sources, he stood by every word that his newspaper had printed on the matter.

"How extraordinary," I said.

"What is?" I passed Miles the article and he quickly read it. "I know about this case," he said. "A barrister friend defended the insurance company against Brown's claim. He said he never believed Brown's story, but as it wasn't possible to disprove, Star Alliance was forced to pay up. Brown obviously thought he'd gotten away with it—and then he was careless."

"It did cross my mind that it might be his girlfriend." I told Miles about their unhappy visit to Village Vintage. "But I dismissed the idea—why *would* she betray him, given that he was her employer as well as her boyfriend?"

Miles shrugged. "Revenge. Brown was probably two-timing her—that's the usual scenario—or he was trying to dump her and she found out. Or maybe he'd promised her a promotion, then given it to someone else. Her motive will come out in the wash."

I suddenly remembered what Kelly Marks had said when she'd paid for the dress:

It's two hundred seventy-five. That was the price.

Eleven

This morning I called Mrs. Bell.

"I would love to see you, Phoebe," she said, "but it will not be possible this week."

"Is your niece still staying with you?"

"No, but my husband's nephew has invited me to stay with him and his family in Dorset. He is collecting me tomorrow and bringing me back on Friday. I need to go now, while I am still well enough to travel."

"Then can I see you after that?"

"Of course. I will not be going anywhere else," Mrs. Bell answered. "So I would be particularly glad of your company, if you have a little time."

I thought of the Red Cross form still in my bag. "Could I come on Sunday afternoon?"

"I look forward to it. Come at four."

As I put the phone down I looked at Dan's invitation for his party on Saturday. It gave nothing away, being just an *At Home* card with his address and the time. It didn't even mention his shed, which was obviously something much grander, I reflected—perhaps a summer house or one of those offices in the garden. Maybe it was a games room with a massive billiards table or some slot machines—or an observatory, with a telescope and a sliding roof. Simple curiosity compelled me to go—combined with the fact that I'd come to enjoy Dan's conversation, his liveliness, and his warmth. I also hoped to be able to ask him about the Phoenix Land story. I still wondered what had made Brown's girlfriend dare to do what she'd done.

On Monday there was more about it in the press. Kelly Marks had admitted to the *Independent* that she was the source but, when quizzed about her motive, had refused to comment.

"It was the dress," Annie said as she looked at the *Black & Green*'s latest piece about it on Tuesday morning. She lowered the paper. "I told you—vintage clothes can be transforming; I bet you the dress made her do it."

"What? You mean the dress possessed her and told her to turn him in?"

"No, but I think her intense *desire* for it gave her the strength to dump the man—in spectacular fashion."

On Thursday the *Mail* ran a piece headed TOP MARKS applauding Kelly for exposing Brown, and citing other women who'd gone to the police about their "dodgy" boyfriends. The *Express* had a piece about arson-linked fraud, pegged to "Keith Brown's alleged torching of his own warehouse in 2002."

"How can the newspapers print all this?" I said to Miles that afternoon. He'd popped into Village Vintage on his way back to Camberwell; and since there were no customers, he'd stayed for a chat. "Isn't it prejudicial?" I asked him as he sat on the sofa.

"As criminal proceedings haven't started yet, no." He got out his BlackBerry, put on his spectacles, and began thumbing it. "For the time being, the papers can repeat the allegations about Brown and print anything else they can justify—like the girlfriend's role in revealing his alleged crime. Once he's been charged, they'll have to watch what they say."

"And why hasn't he been charged yet?"

Miles looked at me over his glasses. "Because the insurers and the police are probably arguing about who's going to bring the prosecution—a costly business, obviously. Now, can we please talk about more uplifting matters? On Saturday I'd like to go to the Opera House. They're doing *La Bohème,* and there are still a few seats in the front orchestra, but I'll need to book them today. In fact I could call them right now. I've just got the number." Miles began to dial it, then looked at me again, perplexed. "But you don't seem keen."

"I am—or rather I would be; it sounds wonderful. But . . . I can't."

Miles's face had fallen. "Why not?"

"I'm already doing something Saturday."

"Oh."

"I'm going to a party. It's nothing special."

"I see. And whose party is it?"

"This friend of mine, Dan."

"You've mentioned him before."

"He works for the local paper. It's a long-standing invitation."

"You'd rather go to that than to *La Bohème* at the Opera House?"

"It's not that, it's simply that I said I *would* go, and I like to keep my word."

Miles was looking at me searchingly. "I hope that he's . . . not more than a friend, is he, Phoebe? I know we haven't been together for very long, but I'd rather know if you have any other . . ."

I shook my head. "Dan's simply a friend." I smiled. "A rather eccentric one, actually."

Miles stood up. "Well . . . I'm a bit disappointed."

"I'm sorry, but it's not as though we'd planned anything for Saturday."

"That's true. But I just assumed . . . It's okay." He picked up his bag. "I'll get Roxy to come. I'm taking her to buy her ball gown in the afternoon, so accompanying me to the opera can be the quid pro quo."

I tried to grasp the notion that being taken to the Royal Opera House would be the "price" Roxanne paid for her father buying her an incredibly expensive dress.

"Perhaps we could do something early next week?" I said to Miles. "Would you like to go to the Festival Hall? Say on Tuesday? I'll get tickets."

This seemed to reassure him. "That would be lovely." He kissed me. "I'll call you tomorrow."

Saturday was, as usual, a very busy day, and although I was happy to be doing such good business, I realised that I could barely manage on my own. After lunch, Katie came in. She saw the Lanvin-Castillo dress hanging where the yellow cupcake had been, and her face fell. For a moment I feared she was going to cry.

"It's okay," I said hastily. "I've put it on the Reserved rack."

"Oh, thanks." Her eyes lit up. "I've got a hundred sixty pounds now, so I'm more than halfway there. I'm on my break from Cost-cutters, so I thought I'd dash over. I don't know why, but that dress has really *gotten* to me."

I was hoping to get away on the dot of 5:30, but at 5:25 a woman came in and tried on about eight garments, including a trouser suit that I had to get off a mannequin out of the window, before rejecting all of them. "I'm sorry," she said as she put on her coat. "I guess I'm just not in the right mood." By now, at 6:05, neither was I.

"No problem," I replied with as much geniality as I could muster. It doesn't do to be irritable if you run a shop. Then I locked up and went home to get ready for Dan's party. He'd written seven-thirty on the invitation with a request that we should be there by eight.

It was almost dark when my cab pulled up outside the house— a Victorian villa on a quiet road close to Hither Green Station. Dan had made an effort, I reflected as I paid the driver. He'd threaded fairy lights through the trees in the front garden; he'd hired caterers— an aproned waiter opened the door. As I walked inside, I could hear talking and laughing. It was quite a select gathering, I realised as I went into the sitting room, where there were a dozen or so people. There was Dan, smartly dressed for once in a dark blue silk jacket, chatting to everyone and topping up champagne glasses.

"Have some of these canapés," I heard him say. "We won't be eating until a bit later." So it was a dinner party. "*Phoebe!*" he exclaimed warmly when he saw me. He planted a kiss on my cheek. "Come and meet everyone." He quickly introduced me to his friends, one of whom was Matt, and Matt's wife, Sylvia; there was Ellie, a reporter from the paper, with her boyfriend, Mike; there were a few of Dan's neighbours, and, to my surprise, the rather grumpy woman from the Oxfam shop whose name, I now learned, was Joan.

Joan and I chatted for a bit, and I told her that I'd be getting some handbags from the States that I'd probably be bringing in to her. Then I asked her if she ever got any vintage zippers—metal ones—as I was running low.

"I did see a batch the other day," she said. "And a jar of old buttons, now that I think about it."

"Would you keep them for me?"

"Course I will." She sipped her champagne. "Did you enjoy *Anna Karenina,* by the way?"

"It was wonderful," I replied, then wondered how she knew that I'd gone.

Joan took a canapé from a passing tray. "Dan took me to see *Doctor Zhivago.* Beautiful, it was."

"Oh." I glanced at Dan. He was full of surprises—rather nice ones, I reflected. "Well, it's a fabulous film."

"Fabulous," Joan echoed. She closed her eyes, then opened them again. "It was the first time I'd been to the pictures for five years— *and* he bought me dinner afterwards."

"Really? How lovely. Did you go to Café Rouge?"

"Oh *no.*" Joan looked offended. "He took me to the Rivington."

"Ah."

I looked at Dan. Now he was chinking the side of his glass with a spoon and saying that as everyone was here it was time to get down to the main business of the evening, so would we all kindly go outside.

The backyard was a good size—sixty feet or so—and filling the end of it was a large . . . shed. That's all it was—a shed; except that there was a red carpet leading to it and across the door a red velvet rope suspended between two metal posts. On the wall was some sort of plaque, awaiting its official unveiling, judging by the pair of little gold curtains that covered it.

"I don't know what's *in* that shed," said Ellie as we walked down the carpet towards it, "but I *don't* think it's a lawn mower."

"You're right—it isn't," said Dan. He clapped his hands and cleared his throat. "Well, thanks to everyone for coming here tonight," he said as we stood outside it. "I'm now going to ask Joan to do the honours . . ."

Joan stepped forward and took hold of the curtain cord. As Dan gave her the nod, she turned to us. "It is my *great* pleasure to open Dan's shed, which I am delighted to rename . . ." She pulled on the cord.

THE ROBINSON RIO.

"The Robinson Rio," said Joan, peering at the plaque. She was clearly as mystified as the rest of us.

Dan opened the door, then pressed a lightswitch. "Come on in."

"Amazing," Sylvia murmured as she stepped inside.

"Blimey," I heard someone say.

A glittering chandelier hung from the ceiling, above twelve red velvet seats arranged in four rows of three on a swirly patterned red-and-gold carpet. A curtained screen filled the end wall; positioned in front of the near wall was a large, old-fashioned projector. On the right-hand wall was a royal-blue board with white plastic letters, announcing THIS WEEK'S PROGRAMME: CAMILLE and COMING ATTRACTIONS: A MATTER OF LIFE AND DEATH. On the left-hand wall was a framed vintage cinema poster for *The Third Man*.

"Sit wherever you like," Dan told us as he fiddled with the projector. "There's under-floor heating, so it's not cold. *Camille*'s only seventy minutes long, but if you'd rather not see it, then just go back to the house and have another drink. We'll be having dinner when the film finishes just after nine."

We took our seats. I sat with Joan and Ellie. Dan closed the door and dimmed the lights, we heard the projector whirr to life, then came the hypnotic clicking of the film as it passed over the sprockets. Suddenly the motorised curtains swished aside to reveal the MGM lion, roaring away, then music, and opening credits, and all at once we were in nineteenth-century Paris.

"That was *wonderful,*" said Joan as the lights went up again, seventy minutes later. "It was like being in the *proper* cinema. I used to love that smell of the projector lamp."

"It was just like old times," Matt said from behind us.

Joan turned in her seat and looked at him. "You're much too young to be saying that."

"I mean that at school Dan ran the film society," Matt explained. "Every Tuesday lunchtime he used to show Laurel and Hardy, Harold Lloyd, and Tom and Jerry. I'm glad to say his focusing's improved since then."

"That was on my old Universal," Dan said. "This projector's a Bell and Howell, but I've rigged up some modern amplification—and put in air-conditioning. And I had the shed soundproofed so that the neighbours don't complain."

"We're not complaining," said one of his neighbours. "We're here!"

"But what are you planning to do with the cinema?" I asked Dan as we all walked back to the house.

"I want to run it as a classic-film club," he replied as we stepped up into the big square kitchen where a long pine table had been set for twelve. "I'll do a screening every week, and people can turn up on a first-come, first-served basis, with a discussion afterwards over a drink for anyone who's interested."

"Sounds wonderful," said Mike. "And where are the films?"

"Stored upstairs in a humidity-controlled room. I've collected a couple of hundred over the years from libraries that were closing down and at auction. I've always wanted to have my own cinema. In fact, the big shed was one of the main attractions of this house when I bought it two years ago."

"Where did you get the seats?" Joan asked him as Dan pulled out her chair for her.

"I got them five years ago from an Odeon cinema that was being pulled down in Essex. I've been keeping them in storage. Now . . . Ellie, why don't you sit there? Phoebe, you come here, next to Matt and Sylvia."

As I sat, Matt poured me a glass of wine. "I recognised you, of course," he told me, "from the feature we did about you."

"That was a very helpful piece," I replied as the caterer set a plate of delicious-looking risotto in front of me. "Dan did a wonderful job."

"He seems a bit disorganized, but he's a good man. You're a good man, Dan," Matt declared with a chuckle.

"Thanks, mate!"

"He *is* a good man," Sylvia echoed. "And do you know who you look like, Dan?" she added. "I've suddenly realised—Michelangelo's David."

As Dan blew Sylvia a grateful kiss I saw that it was true. *That* was the famous person I'd been struggling to think of.

"You're a dead ringer for him," Sylvia went on. She cocked her head. "A cuddly version, anyway," she added with a laugh.

Dan slapped his rugger-player's chest. "I'd better get myself down to the gym then. Now, who needs a drink?"

I unfurled my napkin, then turned back to Matt. "The *Black & Green*'s doing . . . extremely well."

"Beyond our wildest dreams," Matt replied. "Thanks to one particular story, obviously."

I picked up my fork. "Can you talk about that?"

"As it's all been in the public domain, yes, but the interest from the national press has boosted our circulation to sixteen thousand—

which means we're starting to make money—with advertising up by thirty percent. We would have to have spent a hundred grand on PR to achieve the awareness of the paper that this one story's given us."

"And how did you get the story?" I asked, intrigued.

Matt sipped his wine. "Kelly Marks approached us directly. I knew about Brown from my time at the *Guardian*," he went on. "There'd been rumours about him for years. Anyway, there he was, just about to float his company, getting his face in the business press as much as possible, when out of the blue this woman phones me, anonymously, saying that she's got a 'good story' about Keith Brown and would I be interested?"

"So you *are* interested," Sylvia continued. She passed me the bowl of salad, then nodded at Matt. "Tell Phoebe what happened."

He put down his glass. "So—this was on a Monday, three weeks ago—I invited the woman to come in. She arrived at lunchtime the next day—I realised that she was his girlfriend, because I'd seen photos of her with Brown. When she told me the story I knew that I wanted to run it, but I told her that there was no way I'd be able to do so unless she was prepared to sign a statement saying that it was true. So she said that she would." Matt picked up his glass again. "And at that point I thought I'd better consult Dan."

I nodded. Then I wondered why he'd had to consult Dan. It wasn't as though Dan was the assistant editor, or even an experienced journalist, come to that. I glanced at Dan. He was chatting with Joan.

"You could hardly *not* consult Dan," I heard Sylvia say. "As he co-owns the paper!"

I looked at Sylvia. "I thought that Dan worked for Matt. I thought it was Matt's paper and that he'd hired Dan to do the marketing."

"Dan does do the marketing," she replied. "But Matt didn't hire him." She seemed to find the idea amusing. "He approached Dan for financial backing. They each put up fifty percent of the start-up money, which was half a million."

"I . . . see."

"So of course Matt had to have Dan's agreement about the story," Sylvia added. That was why Dan was in on the discussions with the lawyer, I realised.

"Dan was as excited about it as I was," Matt continued as he passed Sylvia the parmesan. "So then it was a question of getting Kelly's signed statement. I told her we don't pay for stories, but she insisted that she didn't want money. She seemed to be on some sort of moral crusade against Brown even though it turned out that she'd known about the fire for more than a year."

"So something must have happened to make her angry with him," Sylvia said.

"That's what I assumed," Matt agreed. "Anyway, she came in and we took her statement. But then, when it came to signing it, she suddenly lowered the pen, looked at me, and said she'd changed her mind—she *did* want money."

"Oh."

Matt shook his head. "My heart *sank*. I thought that she was about to ask us for twenty grand and that this had been her plan all along. And it was on the tip of my tongue to tell her that we were going to have to forget the whole thing when she said, 'The price is two hundred seventy-five pounds.' I was amazed. Then she said it again. 'I want two hundred seventy-five. That's the price.' I looked at Dan, and he nodded. So I opened the petty cash, got out two hundred seventy-five pounds, put it in an envelope, and handed it to her. She looked as happy as if I *had* given her twenty grand. Then she signed the statement."

"The envelope was pink," I said. "Disney Princess."

Matt looked at me in astonishment. "It was. Our accountant's little girl had come into the office with him the day before. She'd brought her writing set with her, and as that was the first envelope I saw, I used it because I was in a hurry to close the deal. But how do you *know*?"

I explained that Kelly Marks had come into the shop and bought the lime-green prom dress that Brown had refused to buy her a fort-night before. "I told you about that, didn't I, Dan?" I said. "About Kelly refusing the discount?"

"You did. I couldn't discuss it with you," he added, "but I was sit-ting there, trying to work it out. I thought, Okay, the dress cost two hundred seventy-five pounds, and she had asked Matt and me for two hundred seventy-five pounds, so there's got to be some connec-tion . . . but I didn't know what."

"I think I know," Sylvia said. "She wanted to end the relationship with Brown but found it hard to do, given that he was also her boss." She turned to me. "You said Brown refused to buy her the dress. Did she seem upset?"

"Extremely," I replied. "She was in tears."

"Well, that was probably the last straw," Sylvia said excitedly. "So she decided to blow the relationship apart by doing something from which there could be no going back. The denial of the dress trig-gered the act of revenge."

I loved it. And he knew that . . .

I looked at Sylvia. "That makes sense. I think the two hundred seventy-five pounds was symbolic. It represented the prom dress—and her freedom. *That's* why she didn't want to pay less for it."

Matt was staring at me. "Are you saying that we got this story be-cause of one of your frocks?"

Once I'd tried it on . . . the dress claimed *me.*

"I think I *am* saying that, yes."

Matt lifted his glass. "Then here's to your vintage clothes, Phoebe." He shook his head, then laughed. "My God, that dress must have *gotten* to her."

I nodded. "Those ones tend to do that," I said.

On my way to see Mrs. Bell the following afternoon in glorious au-tumn sunshine I thought about Dan. He'd had several opportuni-ties to tell me that he co-owned the *Black & Green*, but he hadn't done so. Perhaps he'd thought it might have seemed boastful. Perhaps he gave little thought to it himself. But now I remembered how he'd said that Matt had needed his "help" in setting up the paper—financial help, obviously. Yet Dan hadn't given the impression of affluence—the opposite almost, with his Oxfam-shop clothes and his slightly shambling appearance. Perhaps he'd borrowed the money, I reflected, or remortgaged. In which case it was surprising that, having invested so much in the paper, he didn't want to work for it long-term. As I turned into the Paragon I couldn't help but wonder what he did want to do long-term.

I'd stayed at the party until midnight, and as I'd picked up my bag I'd seen that I had two missed phone calls from Miles. When I'd got home there'd been another two from him on my answering machine. His voice was casual, but it was clear that he hadn't liked not being able to speak to me.

I went up the steps of number 8 and pressed Mrs. Bell's buzzer. There was a longer wait than usual, then I heard the intercom crackle.

"Hello, Phoebe." I pushed open the door and climbed the staircase.

It had been almost two weeks since I'd seen Mrs. Bell. The change in her was so marked that I instinctively put my arms round her. She had said that she would feel reasonably well for the first month and then not so well. She was clearly now "not so well." She was painfully thin, her pale eyes bigger now in her shrunken face, her hands fragile with their fan of white bones.

"What lovely flowers," she murmured as I handed her the anemones I'd brought her. "I adore their jewel colours—like stained glass."

"Shall I put them in a vase?"

"Please. And would you make the tea today?"

"Of course."

We went into the kitchen. I filled the kettle, got down the cups and saucers, and set the tray. "I hope you haven't been on your own all day," I told her as I found a crystal vase and arranged the flowers in it.

"No, the district nurse came this morning. She comes every day now."

I put three spoons of Assam into the pot. "And did you enjoy your stay in Dorset?"

"Very much. It was lovely to spend time with James and his wife. They have a view of the sea from their house, so I spent quite a bit of time just sitting by the window, gazing out at it. Would you mind putting the flowers on the hall table for me?" she added. "I don't trust myself not to drop them."

I did so, then carried the tray into the sitting room, Mrs. Bell walking in front of me, painfully, as though her back ached. When she sat down in her usual place on the brocade chair she didn't cross her legs, as she usually did, with her hands clasped on her knee. She crossed them at the ankles, leaning back, in a posture of fatigue.

"Please excuse the mess." She nodded at the pile of papers on the table. "I have been throwing away old letters and bills—the debris of my life," she added as I put the cup of tea into her hands. "There is so much." She nodded at the brimming wastepaper basket next to her chair. "But it will make things easier for James. By the way, when he collected me last week he drove past Montpelier Vale."

"So you saw the shop?"

"I did—and two of my outfits were in the window! You have put a fur collar on the gabardine suit. It looks very smart."

"It's not real fur. But my assistant, Annie, thought it would be a nice touch for the autumn. I hope it didn't make you sad to see your things there, on display for the world."

"On the contrary—it made me feel glad. I found myself trying to picture the women who will own them next."

I smiled. Then Mrs. Bell asked me about Miles, and I told her about my visit to his home.

"So he spoils his little princess."

"He does—to an insane degree," I confided. "Roxy is *so* indulged."

"Well, it's better than if he were neglectful." That was true. "And he seems to be very keen on you, Phoebe."

"I'm taking it slowly, Mrs. Bell. I've only known him six weeks—and he's nearly fifteen years older than me."

"I see. Well, that puts you at an advantage."

"I suppose so. Though I'm not sure I *want* to be at an advantage with anyone."

"But his age is not important—all that matters is whether you *like* him, and whether he treats you *well*."

"I do like him—very much. I find him attractive, and yes, he does treat me well. He's certainly very attentive." Then we moved the conversation on and I found myself telling her about the Robinson Rio.

"Dan sounds like a joyful sort of man."

"He is. He has joie de vivre."

"That's a lovely characteristic, in anyone. I'm trying to cultivate a little '*joie de mourir*,'" she added with a grim smile. "It's not easy. But at least I have had time to put everything in order . . ." She nodded at the pile of papers. "And to see my family and say my *adieux*."

"Perhaps they're only *au revoirs*," I suggested, not entirely flippantly.

"Who knows?" said Mrs. Bell. A sudden silence descended. Now was the moment. I picked up my bag.

Mrs. Bell looked crestfallen. "You're not going, are you, Phoebe?"

"No. I'm not, but . . . there was something I wanted to talk to you about, Mrs. Bell. Maybe it's not appropriate now, given that you're not well . . ." I opened my bag. "Or maybe that fact makes it even more important."

She put her cup back in its saucer. "Phoebe, what are you trying to say?"

I took the envelope out of my bag, removed the Red Cross form, and put it on my lap, smoothing it where it had creased. I took a deep breath. "Mrs. Bell, I've been looking at the Red Cross website recently. And I think that if you wanted to try again—to try to find out what happened to Monique, I mean, then you probably could."

"Oh," she murmured. "But . . . *how* could I? I did try."

"Yes, but that was a very long time ago. And in the meantime *so* much information has been added to the archive that the Red Cross has. On their website it tells you all about it, in particular that in 1989 the Soviet Union handed over to the charity a vast cache of Nazi files that they'd had in their possession since the end of the war." I looked at her. "When you began your search in 1945, all the Red Cross had was a card index. Now they have nearly fifty million documents relating to hundreds of thousands of people who went into concentration camps."

"I see." Her face did not betray her feelings.

"You could request a search. It's submitted on the computer."

She shook her head. "I don't *have* a computer."

"No, but I do. All you'd have to do is fill in a form—I have one here . . ." I handed it to her and she lifted it with both hands, closing one eye as she read it. "I would e-mail it back to them for you, and it would be sent to their archivists at Bad Arolsen in northern Germany. You would hear within a few weeks."

"As a few weeks are all I have, that would be just as well," she commented wryly.

"I know that time . . . is not on your side, Mrs. Bell. But I thought that if you *could* know what happened, you'd want to. Wouldn't you?" I held my breath.

Mrs. Bell lowered the form and stared at me. With a sinking heart, I realized that she was angry. "But *why* would I want to know, Phoebe? Or rather, why would I want to know *now*? Why would I want to request information about Monique only to read, in some official letter, that she had indeed met the dreadful end that I suspect she did meet? Do you think that would *help* me?" Mrs. Bell straightened up in her chair, wincing with pain; then her features relaxed. "Phoebe, I need to be calm now, to face my last days. I need to lay my regrets to rest, not torture myself about them anew." She lifted the form up, then shook her head. "This would bring me only turmoil. You *must* realise that, Phoebe."

"I do. And of course I don't *want* to expose you to turmoil, Mrs. Bell, or to any unhappiness." I felt my throat constrict. "I only want to help you."

Mrs. Bell blinked. "You want to help *me*, Phoebe? Are you sure?"

"Yes. Of course I'm sure." Why was she asking? "I think *that's* why I found myself in Rochemare. I don't believe it was purely by chance. I feel that I must have been guided there in some way by Fate, Destiny—whatever you want to call it. And ever since that day I've had this feeling about Monique that I've been unable to shake off." Mrs. Bell was staring at me. "I've had this overwhelming sense—I can't explain why—that she might have survived, that you only thought she had died because, okay, yes, that's how it looked. But perhaps by some miracle your friend actually *didn't* die, Mrs. Bell—she didn't die, she didn't, she didn't . . ." A sob escaped me.

"Phoebe," Mrs. Bell said quietly. "Phoebe, this isn't *about* Monique, is it?" I stared at my skirt. There was a tiny hole in it. "It's about Emma." Now I looked at her. Through my tears, her features were blurred. "You're trying to restore Monique to life because Emma died," she whispered.

"Maybe . . . I don't know." I inhaled with a teary gasp. "I only know that I'm just so . . . sad . . . and confused."

"Phoebe," said Mrs. Bell gently, "helping me by 'proving' that Monique survived won't change what happened to Emma."

"No," I croaked. "Nothing can change that. Nothing can ever, ever, *ever* change that." My head sank to my chest.

"My poor girl," I heard Mrs. Bell murmur. "What can I say? Only that you will simply have to try and live your life without too much regret for something that cannot be put right—something that was, in any case, probably not your fault."

I swallowed, painfully, then looked at her. "It's enough that I feel that it *was*. I'll blame myself forever; I'll always be carrying it. I'm going to have to *lug* this through my life." The very thought of it made my soul ache. I closed my eyes, aware of the soft gasp of the fire and the steady tick of the clock.

"Phoebe." I heard Mrs. Bell sigh. "You have a lot of life left to live; probably fifty years—maybe more." I opened my eyes. "You are going to have to find some way to live it happily. Or as happily as any of us can."

"It doesn't seem possible." A tear seeped into my mouth.

"Not now," she said quietly. "But it will." She handed me a tissue.

"You never got over what happened to you . . ."

"No, I didn't. But I learned to give it its place, so that it didn't overwhelm me. You still feel overwhelmed, Phoebe."

I nodded. "I go to my shop every day, and I help my customers, and I chat with my assistant; I do everything that needs to be done. In my spare time I get together with friends; I see Miles. I function—I function well, even. But underneath I'm . . . struggling . . ." My voice trailed away.

"This is not surprising, Phoebe, given that what happened to you took place only a few months ago. And I think this is why you have, yes, fixated on Monique. Out of your own sorrow you have become obsessed with her—as though you believe that by restoring Monique to life, you could somehow restore Emma to life too."

"But I can't." I pressed the tissue to my eyes. "I can't."

"So . . . no more of this now, Phoebe. Please. For both our sakes—no more." Mrs. Bell picked up the Red Cross form, tore it in half, then dropped the pieces into the wastepaper bin.

Twelve

Mrs. Bell was right. I sat in my kitchen for over an hour, just staring down at the table, unable to move. I *had* become obsessed with Monique; it was an obsession fuelled by my own grief and guilt. I felt ashamed to think that I had stirred up such painful emotions in a frail, elderly woman.

I waited a few days, then, tentatively, I went to see Mrs. Bell again. This time we didn't talk about Monique or Emma; we chatted about day-to-day things: what was in the news, local events—fireworks night was coming up—and programmes that we'd seen on TV.

"Someone bought your blue silk faille coat," I said as we began to play Scrabble.

"Really? And who was she?"

"A very pretty model, in her late twenties."

"It will go to some lovely parties then," said Mrs. Bell as she put her letters on her rack.

"I'm sure it will. I told her that it had danced with Sean Connery. She was thrilled."

"I hope that *you* will keep at least one of my outfits, Phoebe."

I hadn't thought of this. "I do love your gabardine suit. It's still in the window. Perhaps I'll keep that. I think it would fit me."

"I'd like to think of you wearing it. Oh dear," she said. "I have six consonants. What can I do? Ah . . ." She placed some letters on the board with a shaking hand. "There." She had made the word *thanks*. "And is romance still blossoming?"

I counted up her points. "With Miles?"

She looked at me. "Yes. Who did you think I meant?"

"That's thirty-nine—a good score. I see Miles two or three times a week. Here." I got out my camera and showed Mrs. Bell a photo of him that I'd taken in his yard.

She nodded approvingly. "He's a handsome man. I wonder why he has never married again," she mused.

"I wondered that too," I said as I rearranged my letters. "He said that there had been someone he'd liked, about eight years ago; then last Friday we had dinner at the Michelin, and he told me why it hadn't worked out with this woman, Eva—it was because she'd wanted to have children."

Mrs. Bell looked as puzzled as I had done. "Why would that have been a problem?"

I shrugged. "Miles wasn't sure that he wanted to have any more. He'd thought it might be too difficult for Roxy."

"It might equally have been a positive thing for her—perhaps the best thing," she said without looking up from the board.

"I sort of said that. But Miles said he'd been worried that it could affect Roxy negatively if there were other children clamouring for his attention when she needed it so much. Her mum had died only two years before."

I rearranged my letters as I recalled the conversation.

"I'd been agonising about it all," Miles had said as we'd had our coffee. "Time was getting on. Eva was thirty-five and we'd been together for over a year."

"I see," I said. "So it had come to the crunch."

"Yes. Naturally she wanted to know ... where things were going. And I simply didn't know what to tell Eva." He lowered his cup. "So I asked Roxy."

I looked at Miles, surprised. "You asked Roxy what?"

"I asked her if she'd perhaps like to have a little brother or sister one day. And she looked ... *stricken*, then she burst into tears. I felt that I was betraying her by even contemplating it, and so ..." He shrugged.

"So you broke it off with Eva?"

"I needed to protect Roxy from further stress."

I shook my head. "Poor girl."

"Yes. She'd been through so much."

"I meant *Eva*," I corrected him quietly.

Miles drew in his breath. "She was very upset. I heard that she quite quickly met someone else and did have children, but I came to feel ..." He sighed again.

"That you'd made a mistake?"

Miles hesitated. "I'd done what I'd thought was right for my child ..."

"Poor girl," Mrs. Bell said when I'd finished telling her this.

"You mean Eva?"

"I mean *Roxy*—that her father gave her so much power. It's so bad for a child's character."

Elle est son talon d'Achille ... Perhaps *that* was what Cecile had meant. That Miles had deferred to Roxy too much—allowing her to make decisions that he alone should have made.

I put my letters down. *Chance*. "That's twelve."

Mrs. Bell passed me the bag. "Of course I feel sorry for his girl-friend too. But what if *you* wanted to have children, Phoebe?" She pursed her lips. "I hope that Miles would not seek Roxy's opinion again!"

I shook my head. "He said that that was why he'd told me about it. He wanted me to know that if I *did* want to have a family, he would have no objections. As he pointed out, Roxy's almost grown up." I took some more letters. "But it's too early to be thinking about it, let alone talking about it."

Mrs. Bell looked up. "Have children, Phoebe—if you can. Not just for the happiness that children bring, but because I imagine that the busyness of family life leaves little time for dwelling on regrets from the past."

"I can imagine that's true. Well, I'm thirty-four, so there's still time . . ." *As long as I'm not unlucky,* I reflected, *like that poor woman who'd bought the pink cupcake dress.* "Your turn again, Mrs. Bell."

"I am going to make peace," she said with a smile. She stared at her letters, then put them down. "P, E, A, C, and E . . ."

"That's . . . ten points."

"And tell me, is the shop busy?"

"It's becoming very busy now because of the party season. Christmas will be here sooner than you know," I added, then blushed at my lack of tact.

Mrs. Bell smiled bleakly. "Well, I don't suppose *I'll* be pulling crackers with anyone. But then . . . who knows?" She shrugged. "Maybe I will."

The following Tuesday a woman brought in some clothes for me to see.

"It's all lingerie," she explained as we sat in my office. She opened the small leather suitcase. "It's never been worn."

Inside the case were beautiful silk satin nightdresses and peignoirs with lace edging, along with pretty corsets and garter belts. There was a regal ice-blue silk long slip with a gathered bust and netting at the hem.

"You could wear that one to a party, couldn't you?" the woman said as I held it up.

"You could. These are lovely things." I ran my hand over a salmon-pink quilted satin bed jacket. "They're from the mid- to late 1940s and are all wonderful quality." I lifted out a tea-rose bias-cut silk slip with lace insets, and two peach-coloured satin bras with matching teddies. "These are from Rigby & Peller—they hadn't been going very long then." Most of the garments still had their labels attached and were in perfect condition, except for one or two orange marks on a girdle where the metal of the garter clips had rusted against the fabric. "Was this someone's trousseau?" It was a scenario I had seen so many times—the delicate, special things a bride-to-be collects in anticipation of her honeymoon.

"Not exactly," the woman replied. "Because there wasn't a wedding. They belonged to my mother's sister, Lydia. She died this year, at eighty-six. She was a 'maiden aunt' and a very sweet person. A primary school teacher," the woman went on. "She never took any interest in fashion—she always wore plain, practical clothes. Anyway, a couple of weeks after her funeral I went down to Plymouth to sort out her house. I looked through her closet, and set aside most of her things to take to the charity shop. Then I went up into the attic, where I found this case. When I opened it, I was... *amazed.* I could hardly believe that these things had belonged to her."

"You mean because they're so pretty and... sexy?" The woman nodded. "So was your aunt ever engaged?"

"No, she wasn't, sadly." The woman's face clouded. "I knew that she'd had a disappointment," she went on. "But I'd forgotten the details, except that the man was American. So I immediately phoned my mum—she's eighty-three—and she told me that Auntie Lydia had fallen for this GI, Walter, who she'd met at a dance at the Drill Hall in Totnes in the spring of '44. There were thousands of GIs down there, training at Slapton Sands and Torcross for the Normandy landings."

"So, was he killed?"

She shook her head. "He survived. My mother said that he was a handsome man and very nice—she remembered him mending her bicycle for her and bringing them sweets and nylons. He and Lydia saw a lot of each other, and before he went back to the States he came to see her again and told her that he was going to send for her just as soon as he'd 'gotten things ready,' as he put it. So Walter went back to Michigan, and they wrote to each other, and in each of his letters he said that he was going to come and collect my aunt 'soon,' but . . ."

"He never did?"

"No. It went for three years—these newsy letters arriving with photos of himself, and his parents and his two brothers and the family dog. Then in 1948 he wrote to say that he'd gotten married."

I lifted out a white satin corselette. "And your aunt had been collecting all these beautiful things during that time?"

"Yes, for the honeymoon that she would never have. My mum said that she and my grandmother had kept urging her to forget about Walter, but Lydia clung to the belief that he would come. She was so heartbroken that she never looked at anyone else. Such a waste."

I nodded. "And it's so sad to look at these lovely things and to think that your aunt never got any . . . pleasure out of them." It was heartbreakingly easy to imagine the reveries and hopes that had fuelled their purchase. "And she spent a lot of money on them—and all her clothing coupons too, I should think."

"She must have." The woman gave a little shrug. "Anyway, it's a shame for them not to be worn; hopefully someone else will have a bit of . . . passion in them."

"Well, I'd love to buy them." I suggested a price. The woman was pleased with it, so I wrote her a check, then took the things up to the stockroom. As they'd been in the case for so long, I hung them on a rack in order to eliminate the faint mustiness that clung to them. I was putting the last peignoir on a hanger when I heard the sound of the bell, then a male voice asking Annie for a signature.

"It's a delivery, Phoebe," I heard her call out. "Two *enormous* boxes. It must be the prom dresses. It is," she added as I came down the stairs. "The sender is . . . Rick Diaz, New York."

"He's taken long enough," I said as Annie carefully scored open the first box with a pair of scissors. She lifted the flaps and pulled out the dresses, the tulle petticoats bouncing out, as though spring-loaded. "They're gorgeous," Annie breathed. "Look how dense the underskirts are—and what fantastic colours!" She held up a vermillion dress. "This one's so red it's as though it's on fire, and this indigo one is like the night sky in midsummer. These will *sell,* Phoebe. I'd order some more if I were you."

I picked up the tangerine one and shook out the creases. "We'll hang four of them on the wall, as before, and put two in the windows—the red one and the emerald green, I think." Then Annie opened the second box, which, as expected, contained the bags.

"I was right," I said as I quickly looked through them. "Most of them aren't vintage—in fact they're pretty second-rate. That Louis Vuitton Speedy bag's fake."

"How can you tell?"

"From the lining. The real deal has a brown cotton canvas lining, not grey; and the number of stitches along the base of the straps is wrong—there should be exactly five. I don't want *that,*" I said, discarding a Saks navy shoulder bag from the mid-nineties. "This black Kenneth Cole one's frumpy, and the beading's gone on this one here...So no to that, no, no—and no," I said as I opened a Birkin-style bag with a Loehmann's discount designer store label in it. "I'm annoyed I've had to buy these. But I guess I have to keep Rick happy, otherwise he might not send me the things I do want."

"This one's nice." Annie pulled out the 1940s leather Gladstone bag. "And it's in great condition."

I examined it. "It is—it's a bit scuffed, but it'll polish up and...oh—*this* is the one I liked." I pulled out the white ostrich-skin envelope clutch. "It's very elegant. I might even keep it myself." I tucked it under my arm and looked at my reflection. "Anyway, I'll put them in the stockroom for now."

"And what about the yellow cupcake?" Annie asked as she began to hang the new prom dresses on padded hangers. "It's still on the Reserved rack. What's happening with Katie?"

"I haven't seen her for ten days or so."

"When's the ball?"

"A week on Saturday, so there's still time . . ."

But another week passed and Katie still hadn't come in or phoned. By the Wednesday before the ball I decided to contact her. But as I heaved a large pumpkin into the window—my only concession to Halloween—I realised that I didn't know her phone number or her surname. I left a message on Costcutter's answering machine asking them if they'd contact her for me, but by the Friday I still hadn't heard; so after lunch, I put the dress back on the wall, alongside the tangerine, purple, and kingfisher-blue cupcakes—the indigo one had sold.

As I fluffed up its skirts I wondered whether Katie had found a cheaper dress that she liked as much; or whether she was no longer going to the ball. Then I thought of the dress that Roxy would be wearing—it was to be the Christian Lacroix "stained glass" evening gown from this season's collection, as featured in *Vogue*.

"That is a *staggering* amount of money," I'd said to Miles as we sat in my kitchen the day after he'd bought it for her. It was the first time he'd been to my house. I'd cooked a couple of filet steaks, and he'd brought a bottle of delicious Chante le Merle. I'd had two glasses and was feeling relaxed. "Three thousand six hundred pounds," I'd repeated incredulously.

Miles sipped his wine. "It *is* a lot of money. But what could I say?"

"How about, 'It's too expensive'?" I suggested gaily.

Miles shook his head. "It's not that easy."

"Isn't it?" I suddenly wondered if Roxy had ever heard the word *no*.

"Roxy had set her heart on that particular dress, and this is her first real charity ball. There's going to be a lot of press there, and she thinks she might be photographed. Plus they're having a Best-Dressed Guest prize, so she's feeling a bit competitive about the whole thing, and so . . ." He sighed. "I said she could have it."

"Doesn't she have to *do* anything in return?"

"What—like wash the car or pull up weeds?"

"Yes. That sort of thing—or maybe just work extra hard at school?"

"I don't operate like that," Miles told me. "Roxy knows how much the dress cost, and she's grateful to me for buying it—I feel that's enough. And the school fees are a lot less now that she's not boarding, so I don't actually begrudge it. And I was prepared to spend quite a lot at Christie's, remember?"

I rolled my eyes. "How could I forget?" As I filled our salad bowls I thought of the wonderful column of white silk jersey with its chiffon trains. "But don't you want Roxy to feel that she's *earned* the dress—or at least contributed something towards it?"

Miles shrugged again. "Not particularly. No. What's the point?"

"Well . . . I suppose the point is . . ." I sipped my wine and refilled my glass before continuing. "The point is you're letting everything just fall into Roxy's lap—without any effort from her. As though the things she wants are simply hers for the taking."

Miles was staring at me. "What the hell do you mean by that?"

I flinched at his tone. "I meant that . . . children need an incentive. That's all."

"Oh." His face relaxed. "Yes. Of course . . ." Then I told him about Katie and the yellow prom dress.

He sipped his wine and smiled indulgently at me. "So *that's* what's prompted this little lecture, is it?"

"It probably is. I think what Katie's doing is admirable."

"It *is*. But Roxy's in a very different situation. I don't feel guilty about spending this much on her because I . . . *can* and because I give generously to charity, so I'm not entirely selfish in how I spend my money. But it's my right to dispose of what the tax man leaves me in the way I choose. And I choose to spend it on my family—and that means Roxy."

"Well . . ." I shrugged. "She's your child."

Miles fiddled with his wineglass. "She is. And I've parented her alone for ten years, and that's no easy task, and I hate it when other people tell me that I'm getting it wrong."

So others had noticed Miles's indulgent parenting of Roxy, I reflected as I walked to the shop on Saturday morning. But then it was impossible not to notice. As I unlocked the door I wondered whether, if Miles and I ever had a baby, he'd be the same with our child. I wouldn't let him be, I decided. Then I found myself wondering what our family life would be like. Presumably Roxy's attitude towards me would soften over time, and if it didn't . . . She's sixteen, I reminded myself as I took off my coat. She'd soon be making her own way in the world.

As I turned over the CLOSED sign I wished I had someone to help me. Saturday was always my busiest day. Annie said she preferred not to work on weekends as she usually went down to Brighton to see her boyfriend. I'd dismissed the idea of asking Mum if she'd help out; she had no interest in vintage, plus she worked full-time and needed to relax.

I had eight customers in the first hour alone. The purple prom dress sold, and a Burberry trench coat from the menswear rack; then a man came in looking for a present for his wife and ended up buying a few pieces of Aunt Lydia's lingerie. After that there was a lull, so I leaned against the counter and took a moment to enjoy the view of the Heath. There were children cycling and chasing balls; there were people jogging, pushing prams, and flying kites. I gazed at the sky with its cloudscape of massive white cumulus and cushions of nimbus, with wisps of cirrus far, far above. As I craned my neck I could see planes glinting in the sun as they stitched their trails across the blue. Lower down, a vast underlit cloud with curiously smooth sides seemed to hover over the Heath like a spaceship. I imagined the fireworks that would fill this sky in a week's time for the annual Guy Fawkes night celebrations. I loved the Blackheath display, and it would be nice to be there with Miles. Suddenly I heard the tinkle of the bell.

It was Katie. She blushed as she came in, then she glanced at the wall and saw the yellow dress hanging there, flanked by the new prom dresses. "So you've put it back," she said despondently.

"Yes, I couldn't hold it any longer."

"I understand." Her eyes were stricken. "And I'm *really* sorry."

"So . . . you don't want it then?"

She sighed with frustration. "I *do*. But my cell phone was stolen last week and Mum said I'd have to pay for the new one, as I'd been careless. Then I had two babysitting jobs cancelled because the wife had forgotten that it was half-term, so they've gone away; and I've been laid off at Costcutters. So I'm afraid I can't buy the dress—I'm a hundred pounds short. I'd been putting off telling you because I kept hoping something would turn up."

"That's a shame. But what will you wear instead?"

"I don't know. There's a dress I've had for ages." She grimaced. "It's apple-green polyester moiré."

"Oh. It sounds . . ."

"Hideous? It is—it should have a matching vomit bag to go with it. I might run up to Next and get something, but I've left it all a bit late. I'm probably not going to *go* to the ball." She threw up her hands. "It's just . . . too difficult."

"Is there anything else here, a bit cheaper, that you might like?"

"Well . . . possibly." Katie riffled through the evening-wear rack, then shook her head. "I don't see anything."

"So you've earned a hundred seventy-five pounds?" I said impulsively. She nodded. I looked at the dress. "Do you *really* want it?"

Katie gazed at it. "I adore it. I dream about it. The worst thing about losing my cell phone was losing the photo I'd taken of it."

"That answers my question. Look, you can have it for one seventy-five."

"*Really?*" Happiness had lifted Katie onto her toes. "But surely you could sell it at full price—"

"I could. But I'd much rather sell it to you—as long as you genuinely want it. A hundred seventy-five pounds is still quite a bit of money—to most sixteen-year-olds at least"—I thought fleetingly of Roxy—"so you've got to be sure."

"I *am* sure!" Katie cried.

"Do you want to ring your mum first?" I nodded at the phone on the counter.

"No. She thinks it's lovely too—I showed her the photo. She said she couldn't buy it for me, but she did give me thirty pounds towards it. I know she wanted me to have it."

"And so you shall." I took it down. "It's yours."

Katie clapped her hands. *"Thanks."* Her face was alight with joy.

"What about shoes?" I asked as she took out her credit card.

"Mum's got a pair of yellow leather sling-backs, and I've a necklace made of yellow glass flowers—and I've got some sparkly barrettes."

"That sounds lovely. Have you got a wrap?"

"I haven't, no."

"Just a moment." I went and got a lemony silk organza evening stole with silver threads running through it and held it against the dress. "This is perfect."

"Oh, it's *beautiful*. And I'll give it back afterwards, I promise. Thank you!"

I folded the stole into the bag with the cupcake, then handed it to Katie. "Enjoy the dress—and the ball."

"*A scary evening last night for the dinosaurs at London's Natural History Museum,*" the Sky News presenter announced the following morning. Miles had the kitchen TV on, and we'd been half watching it over breakfast. "*A thousand teenagers descended on the museum for the Butterfly Ball, in aid of the Teenage Leukaemia Trust. The black-tie event was sponsored by Chrysalis, hosted by the ever youthful Ant and Dec, and the revellers, who included Princess Beatrice . . .*" Now we saw Princess Beatrice smiling at the camera as she swept into the museum in an orchid-pink silk gown. "... *enjoyed champagne and canapés, danced to tribute band the Bootleg Beatles, and were entertained by the cast of the stage production of* High School Musical. *iPhones, digital cameras, and designer goods were raffled, along with a trip to New York to include tickets to the U.S. premiere of* Quantum of Solace. *A total of sixty-five thousand pounds was raised for charity.*

"I wonder if we'll see Roxy," Miles said as we both stared at the screen.

She was still in bed, recovering. She'd been dropped off by a friend's mother just after 1 A.M. Miles had waited up, but I'd gone to bed.

"Did you tell Roxy that I'd be here?" I asked him as I spread marmalade on my toast. "You said you would," I added anxiously.

"I'm afraid I didn't. She was exhausted, so she just crashed."

"I hope she'll be okay about it . . ."

"Oh . . . I'm sure she will," he said, unconvincingly.

Suddenly Roxy appeared in her dove-grey cashmere dressing gown and pink bunny slippers. My knees began to tremble, so I pressed them against the underside of the table. Then I reminded myself that I was twice her age.

"Hi, sweetheart." Miles smiled at Roxy, who was looking at me with an expression of insolent, deliberate puzzlement. "You remember Phoebe, don't you, darling?"

"Hi, Roxy." My heart was thudding with apprehension. "So how was the ball?"

She went over to the fridge. "All right."

"I know some kids who went to it," I told her.

"How fascinating," she replied as she got out the orange juice.

"Were many of your friends there?" Miles asked as he passed her a glass.

"Yeah, a few." She heaved herself wearily onto a stool at the breakfast bar and poured herself some juice. "Sienna Fenwick, Lucy Coutts, Ivo Smythson, Izzy Halford, Milo Debenham, Tiggy Thornton . . . oh, and good old Caspar—von Schellenberg, that is, not von Eulenberg." She yawned cavernously. "I met Peaches Geldof in the loo. She's really cool." She took a piece of toast from the rack.

"And was Clara there?" Miles asked.

Roxy picked up her knife. "She was. I cut her dead. The bitch," she added casually as she spread butter on her toast.

Miles sighed but ignored the venom in her tone. "But apart from that, you had a wonderful time?"

"Yes. I did—until some idiot ruined my dress."

"Some idiot ruined your dress?" I repeated idiotically.

Roxy gave me a level stare. "That's what I just said."

"*Roxanne.*" My heart leapt. Miles was going to rebuke Roxy for her rudeness—it was about time. "That dress was *so* expensive. You shouldn't have let that happen, darling." I felt my spirits sink.

Roxy bristled. "It wasn't *my* fault. This stupid girl stepped on it as everyone went upstairs for the judging of Best-Dressed Guest. Having a rip in the back of my gown didn't exactly help."

"I could get that repaired for you," I offered. "If you show it to me."

She shrugged. "I'll get it sent back to Lacroix."

"That'll cost a lot. I'd be happy to take it to my seamstress for you—she's brilliant. Or I could do it myself—"

"Can we play tennis, Dad?" Roxy asked, ignoring me.

". . . if it's a straightforward matter," I added impotently.

"I really want to play tennis." She took another piece of toast from the rack and dropped it onto her plate.

"Have you done your homework?" Miles asked her.

"You know it's been half-term, Dad. I don't have any homework."

"But I thought you had a geography essay to write. That one you should have done before half-term started."

"Oh, yeah . . ." Roxy tucked a hank of sleep-tousled blond hair behind her ear. "That won't take me long. Maybe you could help me."

He sighed with an air of exaggerated tolerance. "All right, and then we'll play." He looked at me. "Why don't you join us, Phoebe?"

Roxy snapped the toast in half. "Tennis doesn't work with three." I looked at Miles, waiting for him to put her in her place, but he didn't. I bit my lip. "Plus I want to practise my serve, so I need you to hit balls to me, Dad."

"Phoebe?" said Miles. "Would you like to play?"

"It's okay," I said quietly. "I think I'll get back to the store. I've got lots to do."

"Are you sure?" he asked.

"Yes. Thanks." I got up to get my coat and bag. One step at a time, I decided. It was enough that Roxy knew I'd stayed overnight . . .

On Monday morning I asked Annie to nip up to the bank to get some cash for the register. She came back holding a copy of the *Evening Standard.* "Have you seen this, Phoebe?"

In the center pages was a big spread about the ball with a photo of the Best-Dressed Guest—a girl in a kind of futurist crinoline that she'd made herself, using overlapping circles of silver leather—it was breathtaking. There was also a group photo of two boys and two girls, one of whom was Katie. She was quoted as saying that her prom dress came from *Village Vintage, in Blackheath, where you can get glorious vintage dresses at affordable prices.*

"Thank you, Katie!" I exclaimed, delighted.

Annie was smiling. "Fantastic PR. So she *did* go to the ball."

"She nearly didn't." I told Annie what had happened.

"Well, you just got your hundred pounds back, Phoebe—with interest," she added as she put her jacket in the office. "Now, is there anything happening today that I need to know about?"

"I'm going to look at a collection of clothes in Sydenham. The woman's retiring to Spain and has decided to get rid of most of her stuff. I'll be out for about two hours."

In fact, it was nearly four hours. I couldn't get Mrs. Price—a superannuated sixty-something in animal prints—to stop talking. She gabbled away while she pulled out garment after garment, explaining in excruciating detail where her first husband had bought her this and her third husband had bought her that and why her second husband hadn't been able to *bear* seeing her in the other and what a nuisance men were when it came to clothes.

"You should have worn what *you* liked," I said teasingly.

"If only it had been that easy." She chuckled. "But now that I'm getting divorced again, I *will*."

I bought ten garments including two very pretty cocktail dresses by Oscar de la Renta, a Nina Ricci ball gown of black silk with white silk roses at the shoulder, and an ivory crêpe gown with scalloped edging made by Marc Bohan for Dior. I gave Mrs. Price a cheque and arranged to collect the clothes in a week.

As I drove back to Blackheath I worried about whether or not I'd have enough space to store them—the stockroom was jammed.

"You could get rid of those bags you bought from Rick," Annie suggested when I discussed the problem with her.

"Good idea," I agreed.

I went upstairs and found the box with Rick's bags in it and took out the ten that I didn't want, removing a mechanical pencil from the Saks bag and some crumpled Neiman Marcus receipts from the fake Louis Vuitton Speedy. I looked inside the Kenneth Cole bag and wasn't sure that I could even give it to Oxfam because the lining had been badly stained by a leaking pen. I put the bags into three large shopping bags, then looked at the two that I intended to keep.

The Gladstone bag could go in the shop immediately. The leather was a lovely cognac colour, a little scratched around the feet, but not too noticeable. I gave it a quick polish, then turned to the white ostrich-skin envelope clutch. It had an elegant simplicity and the surface was pristine—it had barely been used. I checked that the fastener worked properly, but as I lifted the flap I saw something inside—a leaflet, or rather a programme for something. I pulled it out and unfolded it. It was for a recital of chamber music, given on May 15, 1975, by the Grazioso String Quartet at the Massey Hall in Toronto. So the bag had come originally from Canada; and the reason why it was in such good condition was that it clearly hadn't been carried since that night thirty-five years ago.

The programme was printed very simply in black-and-white. On the front was an abstract design of the four instruments. On the back was a photo of the musicians—three men and one woman. I read that they had played Delius and Szymanowksi in the first half of the concert and, after the interval, Mendelssohn and Bruch. There was a paragraph about the group, saying that they'd been playing together since 1954 and that this recital was part of a national tour. I turned to the inside back cover to read the musicians' biographies. I read their names—Reuben Keller, Jim Cresswell, Hector Levine, and Miriam Lipietzka ...

It was as though the air had been squeezed out of my lungs.

Her name was Miriam. Miriam ... Lipietzka. It has just come back to me.

Now I was breathing again, fast, as I examined the face that went with this name. She was a dark-haired, slightly severe-looking woman in her mid-forties. This concert had taken place in 1975; so she would now be ... eighty. As I read the biography, the programme trembled in my hands.

Miriam Lipietzka (first violin) trained at the Conservatoire of Music in Montréal from 1946–49, where she studied under Joachim Sicotte. She spent five years with the Montréal Symphony Orchestra before co-founding the Grazioso Quartet with her husband, Hector Levine (cello). Miss Lipietzka gives regular recitals and master classes at the University of Toronto, where the Grazioso String Quartet is in residence.

I almost fell down the stairs in my haste.

"Careful," warned Annie. "Are you okay?" she added as I rushed past her to get to the computer.

"I'm ... fine. I'm going to be busy for a while." I closed the door, sat down, and typed *Miriam Lipietzka +violin* into Google.

It *must* be her, I thought as it loaded the results. "Hurry *up*!" I implored the screen. There were all the references to Miriam Lipietzka, linking her to the Grazioso String Quartet, to reviews of their concerts in Canadian newspapers, to recordings that they'd made, and to names of young violinists whom she had taught. But I needed a more detailed biography. I clicked on the link to the *Encyclopaedia of Music in Canada*. Up came her page. My eyes devoured the words.

> Miriam Lipietzka, distinguished violinist, violin teacher, and founder of the Grazioso Quartet. Lipietzka was born in the Ukraine on July 18, 1929 . . .

It *was* her. There could be no doubt.

> She moved to Paris with her family in 1933. She emigrated to Canada in October 1945, where she was discovered by Joachim Sicotte, whose protégée she became . . . scholarship to the Montréal Conservatoire . . . five years with the MSO, with whom she went on national and international tours. The performances of Miss Lipietzka's life, however, must surely have been during the war, when, as a girl of thirteen she played in the Auschwitz Women's Orchestra.

"Oh," I breathed.

> Lipietzka was one of the youngest members of that orchestra, whose forty members included Anita Lasker-Wallfisch and Fania Fénelon, playing under the baton of Gustav Mahler's niece, Alma Rosé.

So she was the same person, and she was clearly alive, because the entry didn't say otherwise and it had recently been updated. But how could I *contact* her? I looked at the Google results again. The

Grazioso Quartet had made a recording of Beethoven's late quartets with the Delos label; perhaps I could find her through that. But when I looked it up I saw that the label had long since folded. So now I clicked on the University of Toronto website, then went to its music faculty. My heart racing, I dialled the phone number given on their Contact Us page. It rang five times, then picked up.

"Good morning, Faculty of Music, Carol speaking. How may I help you?"

Almost incoherent with apprehension, I explained that I needed to get in touch with the violinist Miriam Lipietzka. I said that I knew that she'd taught at the university in the mid-seventies, but that I had no other information about her. I hoped that the university would be able to help.

"Well, I'm new here," Carol told me. "So I'm going to have to enquire about this and get back to you. May I have your number?"

I gave her the store number along with my cell phone and my home numbers. "When do you think you'll be able to call me?"

"Just as soon as I can," she promised cheerfully, before hanging up.

I felt sure that someone at the university would know Miriam. She was probably just a few phone calls away, I told myself. She and Monique were probably in Auschwitz at the same time, I reasoned. They might have been in touch with each other in the camp and afterwards—if there *had* been an afterwards for Monique.

The compulsion to find out what had happened to that young girl now returned to me with renewed force. Perhaps what I'd felt *hadn't* been an obsession. Surely Fate had led me down a wrong turning to Rochemaure for a reason? Now Fate had again brought me close to Monique, via a concert programme that had lain in a small white handbag for nearly thirty-five years. I couldn't shake off the feeling that I was somehow being guided towards her . . .

I shivered.

"Are you all right, Phoebe?" I heard Annie ask. "You seem a bit anxious today. Not your usual calm self."

"I'm fine, thanks, Annie." I longed to confide in her. "I'm . . .

fine." I tried to distract myself by answering enquiries from the website. By now it was 5 P.M.—an hour since I'd spoken to Carol.

Suddenly the bell over the door rang and there was Katie, in her school uniform.

"Great photo of you in the *Standard*!" Annie exclaimed.

"And a terrific plug for the shop," I added. "*Thank* you."

"It was the least I could do—plus what I said is true." Katie opened her rucksack and took out a plastic bag. "Anyway, I just wanted to return this." She pulled out the yellow stole, neatly folded.

"Keep it," I said, still euphoric over the events of the last hour. "Enjoy it."

"Really?" Katie looked at me in wonderment. "Well . . . thank you, again. I'm going to have to start calling you my fairy godmother," she added gaily as she put the stole back into her bag. "You are amazing, Phoebe."

"So how *was* the ball?" Annie asked.

"It was *spectacular*. Except for one thing." Katie grimaced. "I managed to wreck someone's dress."

"What happened?" I asked, imagining a jogged elbow and spattered red wine.

"It wasn't really my fault," she replied wearily. "I was going up the stairs and I was right behind this girl—she was wearing this amazing multicoloured silk gown with these chiffon trains floating off it. It was stunning." With a sinking heart I realised that she was talking about Roxy. "Anyway, she suddenly stopped *dead* to talk to someone and I must have stepped on her hem without realising it, because when she moved off again there was this loud rip."

"Oops!" said Annie.

"I was mortified, but before I could even say sorry she'd started yelling at me." I felt my face go warm with vicarious shame. "She said that her dress was this season's Christian Lacroix and that it had cost her father nearly four grand and that I was going to have to pay to have it fixed—if it *could* be fixed."

"I'm sure it could be," I said hastily. I was too embarrassed to let on that I knew the gown's owner and had in fact seen the damage—Miles had shown it to me—and that I'd been able to repair it myself. The tear had been minor, easily fixed.

Katie's face was pale, remembering. "Then she stormed off and I managed to avoid her for the rest of the night. Except for *that*, it really was a fairy tale. Thanks again, Phoebe. I couldn't have gone without you. And my dress was glorious. Do you think I could pop in again sometime? I love looking at the clothes. Maybe I could help you," she added.

"What?"

"If you ever need a hand with anything, just call me." She scribbled her number on a piece of paper and gave it to me. "I'd love to repay you."

I smiled at the eagerness in her face. "I might take you up on that."

"It's almost five-thirty," Annie reminded me. "Shall I cash up?"

"Please—and if you could turn over the sign." The phone was ringing. "I'll take that call in the office." I closed the door, then picked up. "Village Vintage," I said anxiously.

"This is Carol from the University of Toronto Music Faculty. Is that Phoebe?"

"*Yes*, it is. Thanks for calling back so quickly."

"I have some information about Ms. Lipietzka." I was so nervous that I could barely breathe. "I'm told that she hasn't worked here since the late 1980s. But there's someone in the department who's in close touch with her—a former pupil of hers, Luke Kramer. But he's on paternity leave right now."

My heart sank. "Can you give me his number?"

"No. He's asked not to be contacted." I let out an involuntary sigh of frustration. "But if he happens to phone in, I'll tell him about your enquiry. In the meantime, I'm afraid you'll just have to wait. He'll be back on Monday."

"And there's no one else who—"

"No. I'm sorry. As I say, you'll just have to wait."

Thirteen

As I walked up to Oxfam the next morning with the unwanted bags, I berated myself for not having looked through them when I first received them. Had I done so I wouldn't have missed Luke Kramer. How would I be able to wait for a week? Did Mrs. Bell have that long? It seemed hopeless.

"Hullo, Phoebe," said Joan as I stepped inside. She lowered her copy of the *Black & Green*. "Have you got some things for us there?"

"Yes, some not particularly wonderful bags."

"*Pre-loved*," she remarked as I handed them to her. "That's what we're supposed to say here now—not secondhand. *Pre-loved*." She rolled her eyes. "Still, I suppose it's better than *cast-off*, isn't it? Do you still want those zippers and buttons?"

"Please."

Joan rummaged under the counter and found them—a dozen metal zippers in various colours and a large jar of assorted buttons. At the bottom I could see little aeroplane buttons and teddy bears and ladybugs—they reminded me of the cardigans Mum used to knit for me when I was little.

"You missed a good film on Thursday," Joan said. "That's four pounds fifty." I opened my bag. "*Key Largo*—1948, Bogart and Bacall. A noirish melodrama in which a returning war veteran fights gangsters on the Florida Keys. We had a good chat about it afterwards, with reference of course to *To Have and Have Not,* with its mood of postwar despair. I think Dan was hoping you'd come along," she added as I gave her a ten-pound note.

"I will another time. I've been . . . preoccupied lately."

"Got a lot on your mind?" I nodded. "Dan, too. The paper's sponsoring the hot dog stand at the fireworks on Saturday, so he's got to find forty thousand sausages. Will you be going?"

"Yes, I'm looking forward to it."

Joan had put her *Black & Green* down on the counter. I glanced at it; on the front page was an article about the fireworks display, and beneath it a boxed announcement declared that the paper's circulation had hit twenty thousand—double what it had been at launch. I was happy to think that I'd played my part in this success, however obliquely; after all, the *Black & Green* had helped me. If it hadn't been for Dan's interview I wouldn't have met Mrs. Bell, and I was convinced that her friendship was taking me somewhere . . . that mattered. I didn't know where. I just felt this constant, inexorable tug.

On Friday evening I closed the store, then went to see her. She looked impossibly frail, and kept her hand protectively over her tummy, which was visibly swollen.

"Have you had a good week, Phoebe?" she asked. Her voice was weaker too. I gazed down into the garden where the trees were shedding their leaves in slow, diagonal drifts. The weeping willow was yellow and sere.

"It's been an interesting one," I replied, though I didn't tell her about finding the programme. As Mrs. Bell had said, she needed to be calm.

"Are you going to the fireworks?"

"Yes, with Miles. I'm looking forward to it. I hope the noise won't bother you too much," I added as I poured our tea.

"No. I love to see fireworks. I'll be watching them from my bedroom window." She fell silent and I knew what we were both thinking. *It will be the last time . . .*"

Mrs. Bell seemed suddenly to tire, so now I did most of the chatting. I found myself telling her about Annie, and about her acting, and how she hoped to write a play of her own to perform. I told her about the ball and Roxy's dress. Her eyes widened in amazement and she shook her head. Then I told her about Katie stepping on it. Mrs. Bell's face creased with horrified laughter, then she winced.

"Don't laugh if it hurts." I laid my hand on hers.

"That was worth the pain," she said quietly, with a wan smile. "I have to confess that I'm not terribly enamoured of this girl, from what I know of her."

"Well, Roxy isn't easy—in fact she's bloody difficult," I blurted out, happy to vent some of my negative emotion. "She's *so* rude to me, Mrs. Bell. I was at Miles's house again last night, and every time I spoke to her, she completely ignored me—and if I spoke to *him*, she'd start talking across me, as if I wasn't there."

"I hope that Miles rebuked her for this . . . impolite behaviour." I didn't reply. "Did he?" she persisted, narrowing her eyes at me.

"Not really. He said it would have led to a row and he hates having rows with Roxy—it upsets him for days."

"I see." Mrs. Bell folded her hands. After a moment she said gently, "Then I'm afraid it is you who will be upset, Phoebe."

I chewed on my lower lip. "It *is* a bit hard, but I'm sure things with Roxy will improve. After all, she's only sixteen, isn't she—and it's been just her and her dad all this time, so I guess it's bound to be a bit awkward to begin with. Isn't it?"

"I imagine that's just what Miles says."

"It is, actually." I heaved a sigh. "He says that I should feel compassion for Roxy."

"Well," said Mrs. Bell quietly, "given the way she's been brought up, you probably should."

. . .

On Saturday morning I phoned Miles in between customers to discuss our evening together. "The fireworks are at eight, so what time will you pick me up?" Through the shop window I could see the barriers being put up and refreshment tents being pitched; in the distance an edifice of planks and old furniture was being raised for the bonfire.

"We'll come to you at about seven-fifteen," Miles promised. So Roxy would be coming. "Is it okay if Roxy brings her friend Allegra?"

"Of course it is." In fact, it would make it easier, I decided. "You won't be able to drive," I reminded him. "The roads around the Heath will be closed off."

"I know," said Miles. "We'll take the train."

"I'll make something for us to eat, then we'll walk up to the Heath."

When I got home at the end of the day I found a message from Dad reminding me about Louis's upcoming birthday. "I thought we could play with him in Hyde Park and then have lunch somewhere. Just you, me, and Louis," Dad had added tactfully. "Ruth will be filming in Suffolk that day. Can't wait to see you, darling."

I turned on the radio for the six o'clock news. Yet another report on the banking crisis. Suddenly I heard Guy being introduced. I hit the Off button. Hearing him would be like having him in the room.

I put the canapés I'd bought into the oven while I dressed. At ten past seven Miles phoned. Allegra couldn't come after all, so Roxy didn't want to come either. "Which presents *me* with a bit of a problem," he began, then stopped.

"But why? Roxy's sixteen. If she doesn't want to come, surely she can stay at home alone for a couple of hours?"

"She says she doesn't want to *be* on her own."

"Then she has to come to Blackheath with you, because that's where you've arranged to be."

"Phoebe—she's not easy to persuade. I've been trying."

"Miles, I've been looking forward to this evening."

"I know . . . Look, I'll make her come with me. We'll see you later."

By seven-forty they still hadn't turned up. So I called Miles; he didn't pick up. I left a message that if they hadn't arrived by ten to eight, I'd walk up to Village Vintage and they could meet me there. At five to eight, still not having heard, and feeling despondent, I put on my coat and joined the latecomers hurrying towards the Heath.

As we walked up Tranquil Vale we could see the laser beams raking the sky and the apricot glow of the fire. Outside the shop, I waited with increasing impatience. There was no sign of Miles and Roxy. The music that had been ringing across the Heath from the fair was now drowned out by the sound of the vast crowd counting down.

"Four . . . three . . . two . . . *one* . . ."

WHOOSH!! BOOM!! KER-*ACK*!!

The rockets exploded against the night like gigantic, incandescent blooms. *Why* did Roxy always have to be such a pain? And why did Miles have to be so damn weak?

BANG!!! BANG-A-BANG!!! *BANG*!!! As more chrysanthemums flowered and shimmered, I thought suddenly of Mrs. Bell, watching from her window, alone.

PHUT . . . PHUT . . . PHUT . . . Up went the Roman candles, like distress flares, trailing an iridescence of pink and green.

RACK-A-TACK-A-TACK!! BOOM!!! Silvery fountains cascaded overhead, showering sparkles that turned blue, green, and gold.

Suddenly I felt my phone vibrate in my pocket. I put in my earpiece, then covered my other ear with my hand.

"I'm sorry, Phoebe," I heard Miles say.

I bit my lip against the surge of disappointment. "I assume you're not coming."

"Roxy threw a huge tantrum. I tried to get her to come, but she absolutely refused. *Now* she's saying that I can go on my own if I want to, but I guess it's too late."

ZIP!! ZIP!!! WHEEEEEEE . . . Little white rockets were spiralling in all directions, screaming and whistling. There was an acrid scent in the air.

"It *is* too late," I said coldly. "You've missed it." I shut the phone.

BOOOM!! RACK-A-TACK-A-RACK!!! BOOOOOOM!!

There was a final supernova explosion; its Technicolor embers trembled, then faded. The sky was clear except for drifts of pale smoke.

I didn't just want to turn round and go home, so I crossed the road and plunged into the heaving crowd, passing children waving light sabres and fizzing sparklers.

Seconds later, Miles phoned again. "I'm sorry about tonight, Phoebe. I didn't mean to disappoint you."

I shivered in the November cold. "Well, you *did* disappoint me."

"It was very difficult."

"Really?" I stalked on through the happy crowd, furious. There was the scent of frying onions. To my right I glimpsed the green-and-black logo of the *Black & Green* emblazoned across a floodlit food tent. "Never mind," I said. "I'm going to go and talk to my friend Dan." I ended the call, then wove through the throng. If Miles felt he was being punished, then fine.

I felt the phone vibrate again. Reluctantly, I answered. "Please don't be like this," Miles coaxed. "It wasn't my fault, Phoebe. Roxy can be very challenging at times."

"Challenging?" I fought the urge to tell him how she could more accurately be described: ruthlessly selfish—a spoiled *brat*.

"Teenagers are extremely egocentric," Miles lectured me. "They think the world revolves around them."

"They're not *all* like that, Miles." I thought of Katie. "Roxy should have done what *you* wanted tonight. God knows, you do enough for her. A week ago she was wearing a dress that had cost you a *fortune*."

"Well . . . yes." I heard him sigh. "That's true."

"A dress that I kindly mended for her!"

"Look, I know, and I'm sorry, Phoebe."

"And you gave in to her again. You *always* give in to her!" Miles didn't reply.

"Anyway, can we please drop it now?" I didn't want to be seen having a row in public. I pressed the End Call button, then put up my hood against the thickening rain.

As I drew nearer to the huge tent I could see caterers in smart *Green & Black* aprons grilling hot dogs, aided by Sylvia, Ellie, Matt, and Dan, who was squishing on the ketchup. I found myself wondering what colour it looked to him—green, presumably. He saw me and waved. He looked so big and solid and friendly and comforting that I found myself suddenly aching for one of his hugs. I stood to the side of the line so that I could talk to him.

"Are you all right, Phoebe?" Dan peered at me.

"Yes . . . I'm fine."

He squiggled some more ketchup onto a hot dog and handed it to the next customer. "You seem upset."

"Not really."

"Look, let's go for a drink?" He nodded toward the beer tent.

"You're too busy, Dan," I protested. "You don't have time."

"I do for you, Phoebe," he insisted. "Here, Ellie." He handed Ellie the ketchup bottle. "You're on squeezing duty now, sweetheart. Come on, Phoebe."

As Dan untied his apron, I felt my phone vibrate. It was Miles again, sounding despondent. "Look, I've said how sorry I am, Phoebe, so please don't punish me."

"I'm not," I whispered into the mouthpiece as Dan stepped out of the tent. "I just don't feel like talking to you at the moment, so please don't ring again." I ended the call.

Dan took me by the hand and led me through the still-heaving crowd to the beer tent. "What would you like?"

"Well . . . a Stella—but look, let *me* get them." But Dan was already standing at the bar, and now he was coming back with the bottles and by some miracle someone vacated the table nearest us and we were able to sit down.

Dan pulled out his chair and looked at me. "So...what's the problem?"

"Nothing." Dan was looking at me sceptically. "Okay...I was supposed to meet my...friend here, with his daughter. But then she refused to come so he didn't come either, even though she's sixteen and could have stayed at home by herself."

"So that's spoiled things?" I nodded. "But why wouldn't she come?"

"Because she likes ruining our dates. And because her dad gave in to her, because, well, because he always does."

"I see. So he's a bit...chick-pecked, is he?" I smiled bleakly. "How long have you been seeing this man?"

"A couple of months. I like him, but his daughter...she makes things difficult."

"Ah. Well, that's not easy."

"No. But that's the way it is." I glanced at Dan's apron. "I like the merchandise."

"Thanks. I thought this sponsorship would help boost our profile, so I ordered some corporate gear. I've had some *Black & Green* umbrellas made, too. I'll give you one."

"Dan..." I sipped my beer. "You didn't tell me that you *owned* the paper."

He shrugged. "I don't own it—just half of it. And why would I tell you?"

"I don't know. Because...well, why not? So...do you often buy newspapers?"

He shook his head. "Never done it before, and I don't suppose I'll ever do it again. It was purely because of my friendship with Matt."

"But how fantastic that you were able to," I said, wondering where he'd gotten the required quarter of a million but knowing that I could hardly ask.

Dan sipped his beer. "It was all thanks to my grandmother. She was the one who made it possible."

"Your grandmother?" I echoed. "Not the one who left you the pencil sharpener?"

"Yes. That one—Granny Robinson. If it hadn't been for her, I could never have done it; it was quite unexpected. You see what happened was—"

"Oh, I'm so sorry, Dan." My phone was vibrating again, the ring tone barely audible above the noise and chatter. I put in my earpiece, then pressed the green button, bracing myself for it being Miles yet again. But the number on the screen wasn't his. It had a North American area code.

"Could I speak to Phoebe Swift?" asked a male voice.

"Yes. Speaking."

"This is Luke Kramer from the University of Toronto. My colleague Carol says you wanted to talk to me?"

"I did," I replied, feeling my heartbeat quicken. "I do. I *do* want to talk to you." I stood. "But I'm out . . . it's very noisy, Mr. Kramer. Could you give me ten minutes to run back home and then I'll phone you?"

"Sure."

"That seemed like an important call," Dan remarked as I pocketed the phone.

"It *is* important." I was suddenly euphoric. "Maybe . . . really important. In fact it's—"

"A matter of life and death?" Dan interjected wryly.

I looked at him. "You could say that, yes. So I'm really *sorry*, Dan, but I've got to go, but thanks for cheering me up." I hugged him.

For once Dan seemed surprised. "Anytime. I'll . . . call you," he added. "Okay?"

"Yes. Do."

I raced back to the house, took the phone to the kitchen table, and dialled the number. "Luke Kramer?" I said breathlessly.

"Hi, Phoebe, yes, this is Luke."

"Congratulations on your new baby, by the way."

"Thanks. I'm still a little shell-shocked. She's our first. Anyway, I understand from Carol that you want to get in touch with Miriam Lipietzka."

"I do want to. Yes."

"Could I ask why?"

I explained, somewhat vaguely. "Do you think she'd talk to me?" I added, and held my breath.

There was a pause. "I don't know. But I'm seeing her tomorrow, so I'll pass on what you've told me. Let me write down the relevant names. Your friend is Mrs. Thérèse Bell?"

"Yes. Her maiden name was Laurent."

"Thérèse . . . Laurent," he repeated. "And the friend they had in common was Monique . . . Did you say Richelieu?"

"Yes. But she was born Monika Richter."

"Richter . . . And this all has something to do with what happened during the war?"

"Yes. Monique was in Auschwitz, too, from August '43. I'm trying to find out what happened to her; and when I found Miriam's name in that programme, I thought she might know—or at least know something."

"Well, I'll speak to her about it. But I need to warn you that I've known Miriam for thirty years and she rarely talks about her wartime experiences. The memories are painful, obviously; plus she may have no idea what happened to this friend . . . Monique."

"I hear what you say, Luke. But please ask."

"How were the fireworks?" Annie asked me when she arrived for work on Monday. "I was in Brighton, so I missed them."

"They were rather disappointing." I decided not to say why.

Annie threw me a curious glance. "That's a shame."

I drove over to Sydenham to collect the clothes that I'd bought from the garrulous Mrs. Price. As she chatted away at me I could now see that she had unnaturally "open" eyes, a jawline that was too tight, and hands that were a good ten years older than her face. The idea of Mum looking like that made my heart sink.

As I was driving back at lunchtime my cell phone rang, so I quickly turned onto a side road and parked. When I saw the Toronto code on my phone, my breath caught in my throat.

"Hi, Phoebe," said Luke. So he'd spoken to her. "I'm afraid there was a problem yesterday when I went to see Miriam."

I braced myself for bad news. "She doesn't want to talk about it?"

"I didn't ask, because when I got there I could see she wasn't well. She gets serious chest infections, especially in the fall. It's partly a legacy of what she went through. The doctor gave her antibiotics and ordered her to rest; so I'm afraid I didn't mention your phone call."

"No, of course." I felt a stab of disappointment. "Well, thanks for letting me know, Luke. Maybe when she's better . . . ?" My voice trailed away.

"Maybe, but for the time being, I feel I should leave it."

For the time being . . . That could be a week, I reflected as I looked in the driving mirror and drove off, *or it could be a month—or never.*

Back at the shop, I was surprised to see Miles, sitting on the sofa, chatting to Annie. She was smiling at him solicitously as though she'd figured out that there'd been some kind of problem between us.

"Phoebe." Miles got to his feet. "I was hoping you might have time to have a cup of tea with me?"

"Yes . . . sure . . . Let me just put these suitcases in the office, then we'll go to the Moon Daisy Café. I'll be about half an hour, Annie."

She smiled at us, but there was a question in her eyes. "Don't rush."

The café was crowded, so Miles and I sat at one of the empty tables outside—it was just warm enough in the sunshine, and it meant we had privacy.

"I'm sorry about Saturday," Miles began. "I should have put my foot down with Roxy. You're right—I *do* give in to her too much. It's not fair to you."

I looked at him. "I find things very hard with Roxy. You've seen how hostile she is towards me, and she always finds a way to wreck our dates."

Miles turned up his collar and nodded. "She regards you as a threat. She's been the centre of my universe for ten years now, so it's understandable." He paused while Pippa brought our tea. "But I had a long talk with her yesterday. I told her how angry I was about Saturday. I told her that she means the world to me and always will, but that I have to be allowed to be happy, too. I told her how important you've become to me and that I don't want to be without you." I was stunned to see that there were tears in his eyes. "So . . ." He swallowed, then reached for my hand. "I'd like to get things back on a happier footing with you, Phoebe. I explained to Roxy that you're my girlfriend, and that means you'll be at the house sometimes and that for my sake she has to be . . . *nice.*"

I felt my resentment suddenly ebb away. "Thank you for saying that, Miles. I . . . do want to get along with Roxy."

"I know you do. And yes, she can be a bit tricky, but at heart she's a good, decent girl." Miles laced his fingers firmly through mine. "So I hope that things feel better to you now, Phoebe. It's very important to me that they do."

"They do feel better," I smiled. "Much better," I added quietly.

Miles leaned forward and kissed me. "Good," he murmured in my ear.

What Miles had said to Roxy seemed to make a difference. She was no longer unpleasant to me—now she behaved as though my presence was a matter of indifference. If I spoke to her, she would answer, but otherwise she ignored me. I welcomed this neutrality. It represented progress, I decided.

In the meantime I'd heard nothing from Luke. After a week had passed, I left a message, but he didn't respond. Maybe Miriam was still unwell. Or, maybe, if she was better, she'd decided against talking to me. I didn't mention it to Mrs. Bell when I went to see her. She was clearly in more pain than before and mentioned that she was now wearing a morphine patch.

Louis's first birthday was coming up—along with my mother's facelift. I was still worried about it and told her so when she came for supper.

"You are still very attractive and you don't need it." I poured her a glass of white wine. "What if something goes wrong?"

"Freddie Church has done thousands of these . . . procedures," she said primly, "and not a *single* fatality."

"That's not the most glowing recommendation."

Mum opened her bag and got out her calendar. "I've listed you as next of kin, so you'll need to know where I am. I'll be at the Lexington Clinic in Maida Vale." She flicked through the pages. "Here's the number. The operation's at four-thirty, and I have to be there by eleven-thirty in the morning for pre-op. I'll be in for three days, so I hope you'll visit me."

"Are you telling anyone at work?"

Mum shook her head. "John thinks I'm going to France for two weeks. And I'm not telling *any* of my friends." She put her diary back in her bag and snapped it shut. "It's private."

"It won't be when they all see that you suddenly look fifteen years younger—or worse, that you look like someone *else*!"

"That's not going to happen. I'm going to look *great*." Mum pushed at her jawline with her fingers. "It's just a *tiny* lift. The trick is to have a new hairstyle to distract attention from it."

"Maybe that's all you *need*—a new hairstyle." And some new makeup, I thought. She was wearing that ghastly coral lipstick again. "Mum, I have a bad feeling about this. Will you *please* cancel it?"

"Phoebe, I've already paid a nonreturnable deposit of four thousand pounds—so I'm not cancelling anything."

. . .

I woke up on Louis's birthday with a sense of foreboding. I told Annie that I'd be out all day, then I went to get the train to meet Dad. As I trundled round the Circle Line I read the *Independent,* which, I was surprised to see, had a story about its owners, Trinity Mirror, being in negotiations to buy the *Black & Green.* Walking up the steps at the Notting Hill Gate station, I wondered whether this would be a good or bad thing for Dan and Matt.

It was gloriously sunny and surprisingly mild for late November. I'd arranged to meet Dad just before ten at the Orme Square Gate entrance to Kensington Gardens. When I got there, I saw him coming with the stroller. Instead of waving his pudgy arms at me as he usually did, Louis just gave me a shy smile.

"Hallo, birthday boy!" I bent down to stroke his apple cheek. His face felt lovely and warm. "Is he walking yet?" I asked Dad as we turned into the park.

"Not quite. But he will be soon. He's still in the 'Confident Crawlers' group at Gymboree, and I don't want to rush things."

"Of course not."

"But he's just gone up a level at Monkey Music."

"That's terrific." I held up my shopping bag. "I've gotten him a xylophone."

"Oh, he'll love bashing that."

Now we could hear the wind chimes tinkling from the Diana Memorial Playground; as we rounded the bend in the path, the pirate ship loomed into view, as though it was sailing over the grass.

"The playground looks deserted," I said.

"That's because it doesn't open until ten. I often come at this time on a Monday morning because it's nice and quiet. Nearly there, Louis," Dad crooned. "He's usually straining at his straps by this point—aren't you, sweetie?—but he's a bit tired this morning."

The superintendent unlocked the gate, then Dad took Louis out of the buggy and we put him in one of the swings. He seemed to enjoy just sitting there quietly while we pushed him. At one point he leaned his head against the chain, closing his eyes.

"He does seem tired, Dad."

"We had a bad night—he was a bit whingey for some reason— probably because Ruth is away. She's been filming in Suffolk, but she's driving back at lunchtime. Now, let's see if you'll stand, little man." Dad lifted him out of the swing and set him down, but Louis immediately looked upset and held up his arms, pleading to be lifted. So I carried him round the playground, going into the wooden cabins with him and posting him down the slide while Dad caught him. But I kept thinking about Mum. What if she reacted badly to the anaesthetic? I glanced at the clock tower—ten-forty. By now she'd be halfway there. She'd said that she was treating herself to a taxi to the clinic.

Dad caught Louis as he slithered down the slide. "He does seem sleepy today—don't you, darling? You didn't even want to get out of your crib, did you?" All at once, Louis started to cry. "Don't cry, sweetie." Dad cuddled him. "There's no need to cry, son."

"Do you think he's okay?"

Dad felt his head. "I think he's running a bit of a temperature."

"He felt warm when I kissed him."

"It's a little bit higher than it should be but I think he's fine. Let's put him in the swing again. He loves that."

So we did, and this seemed to cheer Louis for a moment. He stopped crying and sat there, but listlessly now, closing his eyes again, his legs dangling.

"I'll give him some Calpol," Dad said. "Could you lift him out, Phoebe?"

As I did so, Louis's little green jacket rode up, exposing his stomach. My heart lurched. On his tummy was a scattering of red spots.

"Dad, have you seen this rash?"

"I know. He's had a bit of eczema lately."

"I don't think this is eczema." I touched Louis's skin gently.

"These spots are flat, like little pinpricks—and his hands are like ice." Louis's cheeks were flushed, and there was a bluish tinge to his mouth. "Dad, I don't think he's very well."

Dad took the baby bag off the back of the stroller and got out the Calpol. "This will help—it's good for lowering a fever. Could you hold him, Phoebe?" So we sat at one of the picnic tables and I cradled Louis in my arms while Dad poured the pink medicine into the spoon. *"That's* a good boy," Dad said as he trickled it into his mouth. "Normally it's a struggle, but he's being really good about it today. Well *done,* little man." Suddenly, Louis grimaced, then threw it all up. As Dad wiped him clean I put my hand on Louis's brow. It was burning.

"Dad, what if this is something serious?"

He flinched. "We need a glass," he said quietly. "That's what your mother always did. Get me a glass, Phoebe."

I ran up to the café and asked for one but the woman said that glass isn't allowed in the Diana Playground. I fought down my panic and ran back to Dad and Louis. "Dad, do you have a glass jar with you?"

"There's a jar of blueberry pudding in the baby bag. Use that."

I got it out, ran to the loo, washed out the purple mush, and rinsed the glass, tearing off as much of the label as I could with my trembling fingers. When I came out I looked to see if there was anyone who might help us, but the playground was still almost deserted.

Dad held Louis while I pressed the glass to his tummy. He flinched at its coldness and started screaming, tears spurting from his eyes.

"How do I do this, Dad?"

"Don't you just press it and see if the spots fade?"

I tried again. "It's hard to tell whether they're fading or not." I looked up to see that Dad was dialling a number on his cell phone. "Who are you calling? Ruth?"

"No. Our GP. *Damn*—it's busy."

"There's an emergency help line." Louis was squeezing his eyes shut and twisting his head as though the sunlight was bothering him. I put the jar to his tummy again, but the glass on the bottom was too thick to see through it clearly.

"*Why* can't they answer?" Dad moaned into the phone. "Come *on*..."

Suddenly my cell phone rang. "*Mum,*" I breathed.

"Darling, I just thought I'd give you a call," she said quickly. "I *am* feeling quite nervous actually—"

"Mum—"

"I'll be arriving at the clinic in a few minutes, and I *do* have a bit of a pit in my stomach about it all—"

"*Mum!* I'm with Dad and Louis in the Diana Playground. Louis isn't well. He's got these spots on his tummy, and he's crying and he's got a fever and he's light-intolerant and sleepy and he's been sick and I'm trying to do that glass test, but I don't know how to do it."

"Press the *side* of the glass to his skin," she said, suddenly crisp and serious. "Are you doing that, Phoebe?"

"Yes, now I am, but I *still* can't see."

"Try again. But it *must* be the side."

"The thing is, it's a small jar and some of the label's still stuck to it, so I can't see if the spots are fading or not and Louis is really upset, Mum." He'd thrown back his head, and his cry was high and keening. "This has all just blown up in less than an hour."

"How's your father managing?" Mum asked.

"Not that well, to be honest," I answered quietly.

Dad was still trying to phone the doctor. "Why don't they pick *up*?" he muttered.

"He can't get through to the GP—"

"Stop!" Mum said suddenly. What was she talking about? "Pull in on the right—into that car park there." Now I heard the sound of the cab door being opened, then Mum's footsteps tapping quickly over the concrete path. "I'm coming, Phoebe," she told me.

"What do you mean?"

"Put the baby in the stroller, leave the playground *now,* and walk back towards Bayswater Road. I'll meet you there. Hurry, Phoebe."

So I strapped Louis into his stroller and pushed it out of the playground with Dad. We were walking quickly towards the park gate wondering what was going on and suddenly there was Mum, walking—no, running—towards us. She ignored Dad and focused on Louis. "Give me the jar, Phoebe."

She pulled up Louis's top, then pressed the glass to his tummy. "It's hard to tell," she said. "And sometimes the spots can fade and it can still be meningitis." She felt his brow. "He's *so* hot." She took off his hat and unbuttoned his coat. "Poor little thing," she crooned.

"We'll go to my doctor," Dad said. "He's in Colville Square."

"No," Mum said firmly. "We'll go straight to the emergency room. My taxi's just over there." We ran to it and lifted in the stroller. "Change of plan—to Saint Mary's, please," Mum told the driver as she climbed in. "The ER entrance, as fast as possible."

We were there within five minutes. Mum paid the driver, then we ran inside and she spoke to the receptionist and we sat in the pediatric emergency waiting room among the children with broken arms and cut fingers while Dad did his best to comfort Louis, who was crying inconsolably. Then a nurse came out and quickly examined Louis and took his temperature, then told us to go straight through; I noticed that she was walking fast. And the doctor who met us in the triage area said that we couldn't all come in, and he thought that *I* was Louis's mother, so I explained that I was his sister, and Dad asked Mum if she'd go in with him. So Mum handed me her overnight bag, and I took it back to the waiting room with Louis's stroller and the xylophone, and I waited . . .

I waited for what seemed like an eternity, sitting on my blue plastic chair listening to the *whirr* and *thump* of the vending machine, the low chatter of the other people, and the incessant babble of the wall-mounted TV. I glanced at it and saw that the one o'clock news was starting. Louis had been in there for an hour and a half. I tried to swallow, but there was a knife in my throat. I looked at his empty

stroller and felt my eyes fill. I'd been upset when he was born—
I didn't even go to see him for the first eight weeks of his life—and
now I loved him and he was going to die.

Suddenly I heard a baby screaming. Convinced that it was Louis,
I went up to the reception window and asked the nurse if she knew
what was happening. She went away, then returned saying that they
were doing further tests on Louis to see whether a spinal tap was
needed. I had visions of his little body trailing IVs and wires. I
picked up a magazine and tried to read it, but it was hopeless: the
words and photos bent and blurred. Then I looked up and there was
Mum walking towards me, looking upset. *Please, God,* I prayed.

She gave me a watery smile. "He's okay." Relief flooded through
me. "It's a viral infection. They blow up very quickly. But they're
keeping him overnight. It's okay, Phoebe." She choked up, then she
pulled a pack of tissues out of her pocket and gave me one. "I'm
going to go home now."

"Does Ruth know?"

"Yes. She'll be here as soon as she can."

I handed Mum her bag. "So you're not going to the clinic," I said
quietly.

She shook her head. "No. It's too late. But I'm glad I was here."
She gave me a hug, then walked out of the hospital.

A nurse directed me to the children's ward. I found Dad on a
chair, by the end crib. Louis was sitting up, playing with a toy car. He
seemed himself again, more or less, apart from a bandage on his
hand where they'd had to put in the IV. His colour seemed to have
returned to normal except . . .

"What's that?" I asked. "On his face?"

"What's what?" said Dad.

"On his cheek—there?" I peered at Louis, and then I realised
what it was—the perfect imprint of a coral kiss.

Fourteen

It took me a day to get over the trauma of Louis's trip to the ER. I phoned Mum to see how she was.

"I'm fine," she answered quietly. "It was rather an ... odd situation, to put it mildly. How's your dad?"

"Not happy. He's in the doghouse with Ruth."

"Why?"

"She's furious with him for not knowing that you go straight to the hospital if you suspect meningitis."

"Then she should take more responsibility for Louis herself! Your father is sixty-two," Mum went on. "He's doing his best, but how on earth could he be expected to know? Louis needs proper child care. Your father's not a nanny—he's an archaeologist!"

"True ..." *Not that he gets any work,* I thought, but decided not to say. "But what's happening about your procedure, Mum?"

I heard a painful sigh. "I've just paid the other four thousand pounds."

"You mean you've spent *eight thousand pounds* on a facelift that you didn't *have?*"

"Yes—because they'd had to hire the operating room and pay the nurses and the anaesthetist and then there was Freddie Church's fee, so there was no getting out of it. But when I explained what had happened, they said they'd give me a twenty-five percent discount when I do have it done."

"And when will that be?"

Mum hesitated. "I'm not . . . sure."

Two days later, Miles collected me straight from the shop and drove me back to his house for the evening. Feeling slightly grubby, I had a quick bath, then went downstairs and cooked dinner for the two of us. As we ate, we talked about what had happened to Louis.

"Thank God your mother was so near."

"Yes. It was . . . lucky." I hadn't told Miles where she'd been going. "Her maternal instincts came to the fore."

"But what a bizarre encounter for your parents."

"I know. It was the first time they'd seen each other since Dad left. I think it's shaken them both."

"Well, all's well that ends well." Miles poured me a glass of white wine. "You mentioned you've been very busy at the shop."

"It's been crazed—partly because I had a nice mention in the *Evening Standard.*" Better not to tell Miles that it had come from the girl who'd torn Roxy's dress. "So that's brought in customers, and I've had Americans coming in to buy things to wear for Thanksgiving."

"When's that? Tomorrow?"

"Yes. I've had a run on 'wiggle' dresses—all very retro."

"Good." Miles raised his glass. "So everything's going well?"

"It seems to be."

Except that I'd heard nothing further from Luke in Toronto. Two weeks had gone by. I assumed that Miriam Lipietzka had been told about my request and that her answer, for whatever reason, was no.

After supper Miles and I went into the sitting room to watch TV. As the ten o'clock news started we heard the front door open—Roxy had been out with a friend. Miles went into the hall to speak to her.

"I'm going to bed, Dad." I heard her yawn.

"Okay, darling, but don't forget I'm taking you in early tomorrow, because I've got a breakfast meeting. We'll be leaving at seven. Phoebe's going to lock up when she leaves a bit later."

"Sure. 'Night, Dad."

"Good night, Roxy," I called out.

"Good night."

Miles and I stayed up for another hour or so, watched half of *Newsnight*, then went to bed, wrapped in each other's arms. Now that the problems with Roxy were receding, I could imagine a life shared with him for the first time.

When I woke next morning I was vaguely aware of Miles moving about in the bedroom. I heard him talking to Roxy on the landing, then there was the tantalizing scent of toast and the distant slamming of the front door.

I showered, drying my hair with a dryer that Miles now kept in his bedroom for my use. Then I went back into the bathroom to do my teeth and makeup. Next I went to the mantelpiece to get my grandmother's emerald ring, which I'd left there the night before. I stared at the green saucer in which I'd placed it. In the saucer were three pairs of Miles's cuff links, two buttons, and a book of matches, but nothing else.

My first reaction was to wonder whether Miles had moved the ring for safekeeping. I didn't think that he would have done that without telling me, so now I looked along the mantelpiece to see if it had somehow been knocked out of the saucer. But it wasn't anywhere there, or on the floor. I could feel my breathing quicken.

I sat on the bathroom chair and went over in my mind what I'd done the previous night. I'd come back to the house with Miles. I'd had a quick bath. That's when I'd taken the ring off, and put it in the green saucer. After the bath, I'd decided not to put it back on because I was going to cook. So I'd left it in the saucer and gone downstairs.

I glanced at my watch. It was a quarter to eight—I'd have to get the train over to Blackheath soon, but now I was in a panic about my ring. I decided to phone Miles. He'd be in the car, but he had an ear-piece. "Miles?" I said the moment the phone picked up.

"It's Roxanne," said a crisp voice. "Dad asked me to answer. He forgot his earpiece."

"Could you ask him something for me, please?"

"What?"

"Could you tell him that I left my emerald ring in his bathroom last night, in a saucer on the mantelpiece, and it's not there now, so I'm wondering if perhaps he might have moved it."

"I haven't seen it," she answered.

"Could you ask your dad about it?" I pressed. My heart was pounding.

"Daddy, Phoebe can't find her emerald ring. She says she left it in your bathroom in the green saucer and thinks you may have moved it."

"No, of course I didn't," I heard him say. "I wouldn't do that with-out telling her."

"Did you hear that?" Roxy asked. "Dad didn't touch it. No one did. You must have lost it."

"No, I haven't. It was definitely there, so . . . if he could call me later . . . I . . ."

She'd ended the call.

I was so distracted about my ring that I nearly forgot to set the burglar alarm when I left. I dropped the key back through the mail slot, walked to Denmark Hill, got the train to Blackheath, then went straight to the shop.

When Miles phoned me an hour later he promised he'd help me look for the ring that night. He said it must have dropped somewhere—that was the only explanation.

At seven I drove over to Camberwell.

"So where did you leave it?" Miles asked as we stood in his bath-room.

"In this saucer, here . . ."

Then it came back to me. I'd been too upset for it to register at the time, but Roxy had told Miles that I'd left the ring in "the green saucer"—but I hadn't told her that it was the green one—I'd said "a" saucer. In fact there were three of them, all different colours. A sick seesaw feeling gripped me, and I had to put my hand to the mantel-piece to steady myself.

"I put it *here*," I reiterated. "I had a bath, then decided not to put it back on because I was making supper, and then I went downstairs. When I went to put it on this morning, it was gone."

Miles looked at the green saucer. "Are you *sure* you put it there? Because I don't remember seeing it last night when I took off my cuff links."

I felt my insides twist. "I *definitely* put it there—at about six-thirty." An awkward silence enveloped us. "Miles..." My mouth seemed to have dried to the texture of blotting paper. "Miles... I'm sorry, but... I can't help wondering..."

He was staring at me. "I know what you're wondering," he said coldly, "and the answer's *no.*"

Heat suffused my face. "But Roxy was the only other person in the house. Do you think there's any chance she might have picked it up?"

"Why would she?"

"By mistake," I said desperately. "Or perhaps just... to... look at it, and then she forgot to put it back." I stared at him, my heart pounding. "Miles, please—could you ask her?"

"No. I won't. Roxanne told you that she hadn't seen your ring, and that means she hadn't seen it and that's all there is to it." I told Miles about Roxy seeming to know that the saucer in question was green. "Well..." He threw up his hands. "She knows there's a green saucer because she comes in here sometimes."

"But there's also a blue saucer and a red one. *How* did Roxy know that I'd left it in the green saucer without my having told her?"

"Because she knows I keep my cuff links in the green one, so she must have assumed you'd left it in there—or maybe it was a simple association because emeralds are green." He shrugged. "I really don't know—I only know that Roxy did *not* take your ring."

"How can you be so sure?"

Miles looked at me as though I'd slapped him. "Because at heart she's a good, decent girl. She would never do anything . . . wrong. I've told you that, Phoebe."

"Yes, you have—in fact you often say it, Miles. I'm not quite sure why."

His face reddened. "Because it's true—and come on"—he ran his hand through his hair—"you've seen what Roxy *has*. She doesn't need anything that belongs to anyone else."

"Miles," I said, "would you please check her room? *I* can't."

"Of course you can't! And I *won't*."

Tears of frustration stung my eyes. "I just want to have my ring back. And I think Roxy came in here last night and picked it up, because there's no *other* way to explain why it isn't there. Miles, *please* would you look?"

"No." I saw the vein at his temple jump. "And I don't think it's right that you ask."

"*I* don't think it's right that you refuse! Especially as you know that Roxy went to bed an hour before we did, so she had plenty of time to come in here—and you told me that she *does* come in here—"

"Yes, to get bottles of shampoo—not to steal my girlfriend's jewellery."

"Miles, someone took my ring *out* of that saucer."

He glared at me. "You have *no* evidence that it was Roxanne. You've probably just *lost* it, so you're blaming her."

"I *haven't* lost it. I *know* what I did with it. I'm just trying to understand—"

"And *I'm* just trying to protect my child from your lies!"

I felt my jaw go slack. "I am *not* lying," I said quietly. "My ring *was* there, and by this morning it was gone. You didn't take it—and there was only one other person in this house."

"I am *not* going to have this!" Miles spat. "I'm *not* going to have my daughter accused." He was so angry that the veins on his neck stood out like wires. "I wasn't having it *before,* and I'm not having it *now*! That's what you're doing, Phoebe—just like Clara and her ghastly parents. They accused her too, with as little justification."

"Miles . . . that gold bracelet was found in Roxy's *drawer.*"

His eyes blazed. "And there was a perfectly valid explanation as to why."

"Really?"

"Yes! Really."

"Miles." I forced myself to remain calm. "We can resolve this. I accept that Roxy's a very young person, and that she may have been tempted to pick it up and then forgotten to put it back. But will you *please* look in her room." He turned and walked out of the bathroom. Good, he was going to do it. My heart sank, as instead he thundered downstairs. "I'm so upset," I said impotently as I trailed after him into the kitchen.

"So am *I*—and you know what?" He took a bottle of wine off one of the wooden racks. "Perhaps your ring isn't even lost."

"What do you mean?"

He rummaged in a drawer until he found a corkscrew. "Perhaps you've really got it and you're making this up."

"But . . . why *would I*?"

"To get back at Roxy, for being a bit difficult with you sometimes?"

I stared at Miles, outraged. "I'd have to be *insane.* And I don't want to get back *at* her—I want to get *along* with her. Miles, I believe the ring's in her room. So all you have to do is find it, then we say nothing more about it."

Miles's lips were pursed. "It *isn't* in Roxy's room, Phoebe, because she doesn't *take* things. My daughter does *not* steal things. She's *not* a thief. I told *them* that, and I'm telling *you*! Roxy is *not* a *thief*—she is not, *not*, NOT." Suddenly Miles threw down the bottle and it exploded against the limestone floor. I stared at the scattered green shards, and at the spreading crimson puddle.

"Please go now," Miles croaked. "Please would you go, Phoebe, I just can't . . ."

Feeling strangely calm, I picked my way around the broken glass, found my coat and scarf, then walked out of the house.

I sat in the car, trying to soothe my shattered nerves before daring to drive. Then, my hands trembling, I started the ignition. I noticed a little splash of red wine on my cuff.

It's always there with Roxy . . .

There was no other explanation.

Roxy has this sense of . . . not having.

Miles had given her so much, letting it all drop into her lap, yes, as though everything was hers just for the taking.

What do you mean by that?

So she felt entitled—entitled to take a friend's bracelet, to be bought dresses costing thousands of pounds, to sit and relax while others toiled, to pocket a valuable ring. Why would she hesitate to take something when she'd been denied nothing? But the way Miles had reacted . . . Nothing could have prepared me for it. *Now* I understood.

Elle est son talon d'Achille.

Miles was absolutely unable to accept that Roxy could do anything wrong.

As I unlocked my front door the waves of delayed shock began to break over me. I sat at the kitchen table and let the sobs come, drawing in my breath in teary gasps. As I pressed a tissue to my eyes, I became aware that people were arriving next door. The couple who lived there seemed to be having some sort of party. Then I remembered that they were from Boston. It must be a Thanksgiving dinner.

I realised that the phone was ringing. I let it go on ringing because I knew it was Miles. He was phoning to say that he was sorry—that he'd behaved horribly and that he'd just looked in Roxy's room and yes, he *had* found the ring, and would I please forgive him? The phone kept ringing. I wished it would *stop*—but on it went. I must have left the answering machine off.

I went into the hall and picked up the handset without speaking.

"Hello?" The voice was elderly and female.

"Yes?"

"Is this Phoebe Swift?" For a moment I thought it was Mrs. Bell. "May I speak with Phoebe Swift?"

"Yes, this is Phoebe. Sorry—who's this?"

"My name is Miriam Lipietzka."

I sank onto the hall chair. "Miss Lipietzka?" I repeated faintly.

"Luke Kramer told me . . ." I could hear now that she sounded wheezy. "Luke Kramer told me—that you wanted to talk to me."

"Yes," I murmured. "I do. I'd love to talk to you. I'd assumed by now that it wasn't going to happen. I knew you'd been unwell."

"Oh yes, but I am better now, and I'm therefore ready, to . . ." She paused. "Luke explained the nature of your call. I have to say that this is a time of my life that I rarely speak about. But when I heard those names again, *so* familiar to me, I knew that I *must* respond. So I told Luke that I would call you when I felt ready. And I do now feel ready."

"Miss Lipietzka—"

"Please, Miriam."

"Miriam, let me call you back—it's long distance."

"As I live on a musician's pension, that would be kind."

I grabbed the pad and took down the number. Then, calming myself, I quickly jotted down a few things that I wanted to ask Miriam, to make sure that I didn't forget. I blew my nose, wiped my eyes, then dialled her number.

"So, you know Thérèse Laurent?" Miriam began.

"I do. She lives near me. She's become a good friend. She moved here to London after the war."

"Ah. Well, I've never met her, but I've always felt that I knew her because I read about her in the letters that Monique wrote to me from Avignon. Monique wrote that she had made friends with a girl called Thérèse and that they had fun together. I remember feeling a little jealous, actually."

"Thérèse told me that she'd been a little jealous of you because Monique talked about *you* so much."

"Well, Monique and I had been very close. We met in 1936 when she arrived at our little school in the rue des Hospitalières in Le Marais, the Jewish quarter. She had come from Mannheim and spoke barely a word of French, so I translated everything for her."

"And you were from the Ukraine?"

"Yes. From Kiev. But my family moved to Paris to escape communism when I was four. I remember Monique's parents, Lena and Emil, very well. I can see them now, as though it was yesterday," she added wonderingly. "I remember when the twins were born—Monique's mother was ill for a long time afterwards, and I recall that Monique, who was then only eight, had to do all the cooking. Her mother used to tell her what to do from her bed." Miriam paused. "She could have had no idea then what a gift she was actually imparting to her daughter." I wondered what Miriam meant by that remark, but I didn't feel I could interrupt her. She was going to tell this difficult story in her own way; I would have to quell my impatience.

"Monique's family, like mine, lived on the rue des Rosiers, so we saw a lot of each other. I was heartbroken when they left for Provence. I remember crying bitterly, and I told my parents that we should go there too, but they seemed less anxious about the situation than Monique's parents were. My father still had his job—he was a civil servant in the Ministry of Education. By and large, we had a good life. Then things began to change." Miriam coughed softly, then continued. "In late 1941 my father was fired—they were reducing the number of Jewish people working in government. Then a curfew was imposed. Then on June 7, 1942, we were told that an edict had been passed requiring all Jews in the occupied zone to wear the yellow star. My mother sewed it to the left side of my jacket, as instructed, and I remember that we were stared at in the streets and how much I hated that. Then on July fifteenth, I was standing with my father, looking out the window, when he suddenly said, 'They're here,' and the police came in and took us away..."

Miriam described being taken to Drancy, where she spent a month before being put on a transport train with her parents and her sister, Lilianne. I asked her if she had been frightened.

"Not really," she replied. "We'd been told we were going to a work camp, and we didn't feel suspicious because we travelled there in a passenger train—not the cattle cars that they used later. We arrived in Auschwitz after two days. I remember hearing a band playing a lively march by Lehár as we stepped down into this barren land, and we comforted each other, saying how could it be such a bad place if there was music playing? Yet at the same time there was electrified barbed wire everywhere. An SS officer was in charge. He was sitting on a chair with one foot on a stool, his rifle across his lap; and as people walked past him he indicated with his thumb which way they were to go—to the left or to the right. We could not have known that in the movement of that man's thumb lay our destiny." I heard her sigh. "Lilianne was only ten, and a woman told my mother to tie a scarf round her head to make her look older. My mother was puzzled by this advice but did it anyway—and that saved Lilianne's life. Then we were made to put our valuables in large boxes. I had to put in my violin—I didn't understand why. I remember my mother weeping as she put in her wedding ring and her gold locket with the photos of her parents. Then we were separated from my father, who was taken to the men's barracks while we went to the women's barracks."

Miriam paused for a moment. "The next day we were put to work, digging ditches. I dug ditches for three months, at night crawling into my bunk—we were packed in, three across, on these pitifully thin straw mattresses. I used to console myself by 'practising' my violin fingering on an imaginary fingerboard; then one day I happened to overhear two female guards talking, and one of them mentioned Mozart's First Violin Concerto, saying how much she loved it. Before I could stop myself, I'd said, 'I play that.' The woman gave me this piercing look, and I thought she was going to beat me—or worse—for having spoken to her without permission. My heart was in my mouth. But then, to my amazement, her face broke into a delighted smile. She asked me if I could really play it. I said I'd learned it the previous year and had played it in public. So I was sent to see Alma Rosé."

"So that's when you joined the Women's Orchestra?"

"They called it the Women's Orchestra, but we were just girls, teenagers mostly. Alma Rosé found me a violin that had come out of this vast warehouse where all the valuables of everyone who had arrived at the camp were stored before being sent to Germany. The warehouse was known as 'Canada' because it was so full of riches."

"And what about Monique?" I asked.

"Well, this is how I *met* Monique—because the orchestra played at the gate when the work gangs went out in the morning and when they returned in the evening; and we played when the transports arrived, so that, hearing Chopin and Schumann, these exhausted, bewildered people would not realise that they had in fact arrived at the mouth of hell. And one day in early August 1943, I was playing at the gate when the train arrived and in the crowd of new arrivals I saw Monique."

"How did you feel?"

"Elated—then terrified that she wouldn't pass selection, but thank God, she was sent to the right—to the side of the living. Then, a few days later, I saw her again. Like everyone else, she'd had her head shaved, and she was very thin. She wasn't wearing the blue-and-white-striped garments that most inmates wore. She was wearing a long gold evening dress, which must have come out of 'Canada,' with a pair of men's shoes that were far too big for her. Perhaps there wasn't a prisoner's uniform available for her, or perhaps it was done for 'fun.' But there she was in this beautiful satin gown, dragging stones for road construction. And the orchestra was walking past, on our way back to our block, and Monique suddenly looked up and saw me."

"Were you able to speak to her?"

"No. But I managed to get a message to her and we met by her block three days later. By then she had been given the striped dress that the female prisoners wore with a head scarf and wooden clogs. We musicians got more food than the other inmates, so I gave her a piece of bread, which she hid under her arm. We talked briefly. She asked me if I had seen her parents and brothers, but I hadn't. She asked me about my family; I told her that my father had died of typhus three months after arriving and that my mother and Lilianne had been transferred to Ravensbrück to work in a munitions factory. I would not see them again until after the war. So it was an immense comfort to know that Monique was there, but at the same time I was very afraid for her, because her life was far harder than mine. The work she did was so arduous, and the food she had was so meagre and so *awful*. And everyone knew what happened to prisoners who got too weak to work." I heard Miriam's voice catch. She drew in a shaky breath. "And so . . . I started to hide things for Monique. Sometimes a carrot; sometimes a little honey. I remember once bringing her a small potato, and when she saw it she was so happy she cried. Whenever there were new arrivals, Monique would go down to the gate, if she could, because she knew that I would be playing there. She said it comforted her to be near her friend.

"Then . . . I remember in February 1944, I saw Monique standing there—we had just stopped playing—and one of the senior female guards, this . . . *creature*. We called her 'the Beast.'" Miriam paused. "She . . . went up to Monique and grabbed her by the arm, and demanded to know what she was doing there, 'slacking,' and she said that she was to come along with her—now! Monique started to cry. I saw her looking towards me, as though I might help." Miriam's voice caught again. "But I had to start playing. And as Monique was dragged away we were playing Strauss's 'Tritsch-Tratsch Polka'— such a lively, charming piece—and I have never played it or been able to listen to it since . . ."

As Miriam continued to talk, I glanced at my hand. What was the loss of a ring compared with what I was hearing? Now Miriam's voice was faltering again and I heard a suppressed sob; still, she continued her story to its conclusion, and all too soon we were saying good-bye. And as I put down the phone the sound of my neighbours drifted through the wall as they laughed and talked and gave thanks.

"Have you heard from him *since* this happened?" Mrs. Bell asked me the following Sunday afternoon. I had just finished telling her about the awful scene in Miles's house.

"I haven't," I replied. "And I don't expect to, unless it's to say that he's found my ring."

"The poor man," Mrs. Bell murmured. She smoothed the pale green mohair wrap that she always draped over her lap now. "It obviously brought back to him the truth of what had happened at his daughter's school." She looked at me. "Do you see *any* hope of reconciliation?"

I shook my head. "He was almost insane with anger. Perhaps if you've been with someone a long time you can withstand the occasional cataclysmic argument, but we've only known each other three months. Frankly, it shocked me. Plus his whole attitude towards what's happened is . . . wrong."

"Perhaps Roxy took the ring purely to cause conflict between you and Miles."

"I thought about that. But I decided that she would see driving a wedge between us as a bonus. I think she took it because she takes things."

"But you *must* have it back."

"What can I do? I have no proof that Roxy took it, and even if I did, it would still be . . . horrible. I couldn't face it."

"But Miles can't just *leave* it like that," Mrs. Bell insisted. I was touched by her indignation. "He should search for the ring."

"I don't think he will—because if he did, he'd probably find it, and that would destroy his myth about Roxy."

Mrs. Bell was shaking her head. "This is a very bitter pill for you, Phoebe."

"It is. But I'm just going to have to try and let it go. There are far more precious things to lose than a ring, however treasured."

"What makes you say that? *Phoebe*..." Mrs. Bell was staring at me. "There are tears in your eyes." She reached for my hand. "Why, my dear?"

"I'm fine." It would have been wrong for me to tell Mrs. Bell what I knew. "But I really need to go now. Is there anything I can do?"

"No." She glanced at the clock. "My nurse will be coming shortly." She clasped my hand in both hers. "I hope that you will be here again soon, Phoebe. I love seeing you."

I bent to kiss her. "I will," I promised. "I will."

On Monday Annie brought in her copy of the *Guardian* and showed me a short announcement in the Media section about the sale of the *Black & Green* to Trinity Mirror for £1.5 million. "Do you suppose that's good news for the paper?" I asked.

"It's good news for whoever *owns* it," Annie replied, "because they'll make money. But it might not be good for the staff, because the new management might sack everyone." I decided to ask Dan about it. Perhaps I'd go to his next screening. "What about Christmas decorations?" Annie asked, as she took off her jacket. "It's the first of December, after all."

I looked at her blankly. I'd been too distracted even to think about Christmas. "We do need to put some up—but vintage ones."

"Paper chains," Annie suggested as she glanced round the shop. "Silver and gold ones. And some holly—I'll get some from the florists by the station; and we'll need some lights."

"My mother's got some lovely old ones," I said. "Elegant gold-and-white angels and stars. I'll ask her if we can borrow them."

"Of course you can," Mum said immediately when I phoned her a few minutes later. "In fact I'll dig them out right now and bring them over—it's not as though I'm doing much at the moment." Mum had decided to continue with the charade that she was on vacation.

She arrived an hour later clutching a large cardboard box. Together, we ran the strings of lights along the front of the windows.

"They're lovely," Annie declared as we switched them on.

"They were *my* parents' lights," Mum explained. "They bought them when I was a child in the early fifties. They've had new plugs but have otherwise lasted. In fact, they look good for their age."

"Excuse me for being personal, Mrs. Swift," said Annie, "but so do you. I know I've only met you a couple of times, but you look amazing at the moment. Have you got a new hairstyle or something?"

"No." Mum looked happy but bewildered as she patted her blond waves. "It's exactly the same."

"Well"—Annie shrugged—"you look great." She went and got her jacket. "I'd better get going to my audition, Phoebe."

"Sure," I said. "What's it for this time?"

"Children's theatre." She rolled her eyes. *"Llamas in Pajamas."*

"I told you Annie's an actress, didn't I, Mum?"

"You did."

"I'm fed up with it, though," Annie told us. "I really want to write my own show. I'm researching some stories at the moment."

I wished I could tell her the story I knew . . .

As Annie left, Mum began to look through the racks. "These clothes *are* rather lovely. I used to dislike the idea of wearing vintage, didn't I, Phoebe? I was quite dismissive about it."

"You were. Why don't you try something on?"

Mum smiled. "All right then. I do like this." She held up the Jacques Fath 1950s coatdress with a pattern of little palm trees, and went into the dressing room with it. A minute later she pulled back the calico curtain.

"That looks exquisite, Mum!" I exclaimed. "You're slim, so you can wear that fitted look. It's very elegant."

Mum gazed at her reflection with an air of delighted surprise. "It *does* look nice." She fingered a sleeve. "And the fabric's so . . . interesting." She looked at herself again, then drew the curtain. "But I'm not buying anything at the moment. It's been a very expensive few weeks."

As the shop was quiet, Mum stayed for a chat. "You know, Phoebe," she said as she sat on the sofa. "I don't think I'll be going back to Freddie Church."

I tried not to show my relief. "That sounds like a good decision."

"Even at twenty-five percent off, it's still six thousand pounds. I *could* afford it, just, but now somehow, it seems such a waste of money."

"In your case, Mum, it would be, yes."

Mum looked at me. "I've come round more to your way of thinking on the subject, Phoebe."

"Why?" I asked, though I knew.

"It's since last week," she replied quietly. "Since meeting Louis." She shook her head wonderingly. "Some of my bitterness and sadness just . . . *disappeared.*"

I leaned against the counter. "And how did you feel, seeing Dad?"

"Well . . . I felt all right about that, too. Perhaps because I was touched by how much he loves Louis, I couldn't feel angry. Somehow everything looks so much . . . *better* now." And suddenly I saw what Annie had seen—that Mum *did* look different; her features had somehow relaxed, and she looked prettier and, yes, younger. "I'd love to see Louis again," she added softly.

"Well, why shouldn't you? Perhaps you could have lunch with Dad sometimes."

Mum nodded thoughtfully. "That's what he said, at the hospital. Or perhaps I could come along when *you* visit him, Phoebe. We could all take Louis to the park—if Ruth didn't mind."

"She's so busy with her work, I doubt she'd care. Anyway, she's really grateful to you for what you did for Louis. Think of that nice letter she sent you."

"Yes . . . but that doesn't mean she'd be happy for me to spend time with your dad."

"I don't know—something tells me it might be okay."

"Maybe . . ." Mum heaved a sigh. "We'll see. And how's Miles?" I told Mum what had happened. Her face fell. "My father gave that ring to my mother when I was born; my mother gave it to me when I turned forty, and on your twenty-first birthday, Phoebe, I gave it to you." Mum was shaking her head. "That's . . . heartbreaking. Well . . ." She pursed her lips. "What a misguided man he must be—as a father, at least."

"I agree he's not doing a great job with Roxy."

"Is there *any* way you might get the ring back?"

"No—so I'm trying not to think about it."

Mum was staring out the window again. "There's that man," she said abruptly.

"Which man?"

"The big, badly dressed one with the curly hair." I followed her gaze. Dan was crossing the road, coming towards us. "On the other hand, I like curly hair on a man. It's unusual."

"Yes." I smiled. "You've said that before." Dan opened the door of Village Vintage. "Hi, Dan," I said. "This is my mother."

"Really?" He peered at Mum with a puzzled expression. "Not your older sister?"

Mum roared with laughter and suddenly looked luminously beautiful. That was the only facelift she'd needed—a smile.

Now she was getting to her feet. "I'd better go, Phoebe. I'm meeting Betty from bridge for lunch. Lovely to see you again, Dan." She gave us a wave, scooped up her bag, and was gone.

Dan started riffling through the menswear rack.

"Looking for anything in particular?" I asked him with a smile.

"Not really. I just thought I ought to come and spend a bit of money in here, as I feel I owe my good fortune to this shop."

"That might be overstating it a bit, Dan."

"Not by much." He pulled out a jacket. "*This* is nice—great colour, I *think*." He peered at it. "It's a tasteful pale green, right?"

"No. It's bubblegum pink, Versace."

"Ah." He put it back.

"This one would suit you." I held out a Brooks Brothers cashmere jacket in a pale grey. "It matches your eyes. And it should be big enough across the chest. It's a forty-two."

Dan tried it on, then studied his reflection. "I'll take it," he said happily. "Then I was hoping you'd come and have a celebration lunch with me."

"Oh, I'd love to, Dan, but I never close at lunchtime."

"Well, for once why don't you just do something that you never do? We'll only be an hour—and we can go to Chapters wine bar so that you're nearby."

I thought for a second, then nodded. "Okay then—since it's not busy. Why not?" I turned over the OPEN sign and locked the door.

As Dan and I passed the church he talked about the sale of the *Black & Green*. "It's fantastic for us," he told me. "It's what Matt and I hoped for: we wanted the paper to be a success so that it would get bought, and then we'd get our money back, hopefully with interest."

"Which I presume you have done?"

Dan grinned. "We've doubled our stake. Neither of us imagined that it would happen so fast, but the Phoenix story put us right on the map." We went into Chapters and were given a window table. Dan ordered two glasses of champagne.

"What will happen to the paper now?" I asked him.

He picked up the menu. "Nothing much, because the new owners want to keep it as it is. Matt will remain editor—he's keeping a small shareholding; the idea is to start up similar titles in other parts of South London. Everyone's staying—except me."

"Why? You were enjoying it."

"I was. But now I'll be able to do what I've always wanted to do."

"Which is what?"

"Start my own cinema."

"But you've done that."

"I mean a real one—an independent—showing new releases, of course, but with an emphasis on classic films, including unusual ones that are hard to see, like, I don't know, *Peter Ibbetson,* a Gary Cooper film from 1935, or Fassbinder's *The Bitter Tears of Petra von Kant.* It would be like a mini British Film Institute, with lectures and discussions." The waiter brought our champagne.

"And with a modern projector, presumably?"

Dan nodded. "The Bell and Howell's just for fun. I'm going to start looking for premises after Christmas."

"Good for you, Dan." I raised my glass. "And congratulations. You risked a lot."

"I did, but I knew Matt very well and trusted him to produce a good paper; and then we had that huge stroke of luck. So here's to Village Vintage." Dan lifted his glass. "Thank you, Phoebe."

"Dan," I said, after a moment. "I'm curious about something. On Bonfire Night you were telling me about your grandmother—that it was thanks to her that you were able to invest in the paper . . ."

"That's right—then you had to leave. Well, I think I told you that in addition to the silver pencil sharpener, she left me a hideous painting."

"Yes."

"It was this horrible semiabstract thing that she'd had hanging in her downstairs loo for thirty-five years."

"You said you felt a bit disappointed."

"I did. But a few weeks later I took off the brown paper in which it had been wrapped, and taped to the back of it was a letter to me from Granny in which she'd said she knew I'd always hated the pic-ture, but that she thought it 'might be worth something.' So I took it to Christie's and discovered that it was by Erik Anselm. I hadn't even known that much, as the signature was illegible."

"I've heard of Erik Anselm," I mused as the waiter brought our plates of fish pie.

"He was a younger contemporary of Rauschenberg and Twombly. The woman at Christie's got very excited when she saw it. She said that Anselm was being rediscovered and that the painting might be worth as much as three hundred thousand pounds." So that's where the money had come from. "It sold for eight hundred thousand."

"Good God! So your grandmother was generous to you after all."

"Extremely generous."

"Did she collect art?"

"No, she was a midwife. She said the painting had been given to her in the early seventies by a grateful husband after a particularly hazardous birth."

I raised my glass again. "Well, here's to Granny Robinson."

Dan grinned. "I often drink to her—plus she was lovely. I used some of the money to buy my house," he went on as we ate our pie. "Then Matt told me that he was having trouble getting the capital he needed to start the *Black & Green*. I'd told him about my windfall, and he asked me if I'd be prepared to invest in the paper, so I decided to go for it."

I smiled. "A good decision."

Dan nodded. "It was. Anyway . . . it's so lovely to see you, Phoebe. I've hardly laid eyes on you lately."

"Well, I've been a bit preoccupied, Dan. But now I'm . . . fine." I lowered my fork and said impulsively, "Can I tell you something?" He nodded. "I like your curly hair."

"You do?"

"I do. It's unusual." I glanced at my watch. "But I must go—my hour's up. Thanks for lunch."

"It was nice to celebrate with you, Phoebe. Do you fancy a film sometime?"

"Oh yes. Anything good coming on at the Robinson Rio?"

"*A Matter of Life and Death.*"

"That sounds . . . perfect."

So on Thursday I drove to Hither Green. The shed was full, and Dan gave us a short preamble to the film, saying that it was a classic fantasy, romance, and courtroom drama all rolled into one in which a World War II fighter pilot cheats death. "Peter Carter—played by David Niven—is forced to bail out of his burning plane with no parachute and miraculously survives," Dan explained, "only to discover that this is due to a heavenly blunder, which is about to be put right. In order to stay alive, so that he can be with the woman he loves, Peter pleads his case at the celestial Court of Appeal. But will he prevail? And is what he sees real or only a hallucination caused by his injuries? You decide."

He dimmed the lights and the curtains swished open.

Afterwards some of us stayed for supper and chatted about the film, and about the way Michael Powell and Emeric Pressburger used both black and white and colour. "The fact that heaven is monochrome and the earth is Technicolor is meant to affirm the triumph of life over death," Dan told us, "something a postwar audience would have felt very keenly."

It had been a lovely evening, and I drove home feeling happier than I had for days.

The next morning Mum dropped in and said that she'd decided to buy the Jacques Fath coatdress after all. "Betty told me that she and Jim are having a Christmas drinks party on the twentieth, so I'd like a new outfit—a new *old* outfit," she corrected herself, smiling.

"Old's the new new," said Annie brightly.

Mum got out her credit card, but I couldn't bear the idea of taking money from her. "It's an early birthday present," I said.

She shook her head. "This is your livelihood, Phoebe. You've worked so hard for it; besides, my birthday's not for six weeks." She held out her Visa card. "It's two hundred fifty, isn't it?"

"Okay, but you get twenty percent off, which makes it two hundred."

"That's a bargain."

"Which reminds me," said Annie. "Are we going to have a January sale? People have been asking."

"I suppose we should," I replied as I folded Mum's coatdress into a Village Vintage bag. "Everyone else does, and it'll be good for moving stock." I handed Mum her bag.

"We could have a preview evening for it," Annie suggested. "Hype it up a bit. I do think we should find ways to promote the shop a bit more," she added as she tidied the gloves.

"*I* know what you should do," said Mum. "You should have a vintage fashion show—with Phoebe giving a short commentary about each outfit; I thought of it when I heard you on the radio. You could talk about the style of each garment, the social context of the era, a bit about the designer—you're very knowledgeable, after all, darling."

"So I should be, after twelve years at it." I looked at Mum. "But I like that idea."

"You could charge ten pounds a head, to include a glass of wine," Annie said, "with the ticket price redeemable against anything bought in the shop. It would get coverage in the local press. You could have it at Blackheath Halls."

I thought of the wooden-panelled Great Hall with its barrel-vaulted ceiling and wide stage. "That's a big space to fill."

Annie shrugged. "I'm sure you could do it. It would be an opportunity to learn a bit about the history of fashion in a fun way. People would love it."

"I'd have to hire models—that would cost."

"You could get your customers to be models," Annie suggested. "They'd probably feel flattered—and it'd be fun. They could wear the things they'd already bought from you as well as current stock."

"They could." I had a vision of the four cupcake dresses flouncing down the catwalk. "And the profits could go to charity. . . ."

"Do it, Phoebe," Mum urged. "We'll all help you." Then with a wave at Annie and me she left.

I had started to make notes about it all and had called someone at Blackheath Halls to find out how much it cost to hire the Great Hall when the phone rang.

I picked up. "Village Vintage?"

"Is that Phoebe?"

"Yes."

"Phoebe, this is Sue Rix. I'm the nurse who looks after Mrs. Bell. I'm with her this morning, and she asked me to call you—"

"Is she all right?" I said quickly.

"Well . . . that's a difficult question to answer. She's extremely agitated. She's insisting that she wants you to come, right away. I've warned her that you might not be able to—"

I glanced at Annie. "I can—I'll come right now." As I picked up my bag I felt a shiver of apprehension. "I'll be a while, Annie." She nodded. Then I left the shop and walked up to the Paragon, my heart aching with anticipation.

When I got there Sue opened the door.

"How is Mrs. Bell?" I asked her as I went in.

"Bewildered," Sue replied. "And extremely emotional. It started about an hour ago."

I made to go into the sitting room, but Sue pointed to the bedroom.

Mrs. Bell was lying in bed, her head on the pillow. Although I knew how ill she was, it shocked me to see how thin she was beneath the blankets.

"Phoebe . . . at *last.*" She smiled with relief. In her hand was a sheet of paper—a letter. "I need you to read this for me. Sue offered to do so, but it must be no one but you."

I pulled up a chair. "Can't you read it, Mrs. Bell? Is it your eyes?"

"No, no—I *can* read it, and I have already done so perhaps twenty times since it arrived a short while ago. But now *you* must read it, Phoebe. *Please.*" Mrs. Bell handed me the cream-coloured sheet. Closely typed on both sides, it was from an address in Pasadena, California.

Dear Thérèse, I read.

I hope you will excuse this letter from a stranger—although I am not quite a stranger. My name is Lena Sands and I am the daughter of your friend Monique Richelieu . . .

I glanced at Mrs. Bell—her eyes were shining with tears—then returned to the letter.

I know that you and my mother were friends, in Avignon, all those years ago. I know that you knew that she'd been transported, and I know that you searched for her after the war and discovered that she had been in Auschwitz. I also know that you thought she must have died—a fair assumption. The purpose of this letter is to tell you that, as my existence attests, my mother survived.

"You were right," I heard Mrs. Bell murmur. "You were *right*, Phoebe . . ."

Thérèse, I would like you at last to know what happened to my mother. The reason why I am able to write to you like this is because your friend Phoebe Swift contacted my mother's lifelong friend, Miriam Lipietzka, and Miriam called me earlier today.

"But *how* could you have contacted Miriam?" Mrs. Bell asked me. "How could that be *possible*? I don't understand." I told her about the concert programme that I'd found in the ostrich-skin bag. She stared at me. "Phoebe," she whispered, "not long ago I told you that I didn't believe in God. I think, now, that I *do.*"

I turned back to the letter.

My mother rarely talked about her time in Avignon—the associations were too painful—but whenever she did have reason to mention it, Thérèse, your name always came up. She spoke of you with enormous affection. She remembered that you had helped her when she had to hide. She said that you were a wonderful friend to her.

I looked at Mrs. Bell. She was shaking her head, clearly going over the letter in her mind. A tear slid down her cheek.

My mother died in 1987, aged fifty-eight. I once told her that I felt she'd been shortchanged. She said that, on the contrary, she'd had the most marvelous windfall of forty-three years.

Now I read about the incident that Miriam had recounted to me over the phone, when Monique was dragged away by the female guard.

This woman—she was known as "the Beast"—put my mother on the list for the next "selection." But on the appointed day, while my mother was on the back of the truck with the others, waiting to be taken—and I can barely write these words—to the crematorium, she was recognised by the young SS guard who had registered her admission. At that time, hearing that she spoke native German, he had asked her where she came from and she answered, "Mannheim." He had smiled and said that he was from Mannheim too, and on those occasions afterwards when he saw my mother he would always take a moment to chat with her about their home city. When he saw her sitting on the truck that morning, he told the driver that there had been a mistake and ordered my mother to get down. She always said to my father and me that that day— March 1, 1944—was her second birthday.

Lena's letter now described how this SS guard had had Monique moved to work in the camp kitchen, scrubbing floors; this meant that she was working indoors and, more important, was able to eat potato peelings, a little meat even. She began to gain just enough weight to survive. After a few weeks of this, the letter went on, Monique had become a kitchen "assistant," doing some cooking, although she said it was difficult, as the only ingredients were potatoes, cabbage, margarine, and farina—sometimes a little salami—and "coffee" made of ground-up acorns. She did this work for three months.

My mother was then assigned, with two other girls, to cook for some of the female wardens, in their quarters. Because my mother had learned to cook after her twin brothers were born, she did a very good job and the wardens enjoyed her potato pancakes and her sauerkraut and strudel. This success ensured my mother's survival. She used to say that what her mother had taught her had saved her life.

Now I understood Miriam's remark about the true gift that Monique's mother had imparted to her daughter. I turned the letter over.

In the winter of 1944–45, with the Russians closing in from the east, Auschwitz was evacuated. Those inmates who could still stand were forced to march through the snow to other camps farther inside Germany; these were death marches, and any prisoner who collapsed or stopped to rest was immediately shot. After walking for ten days, 20,000 prisoners finally made it to Bergen-Belsen—among them my mother. She said that here was hell on earth too, with virtually no food, and with thousands of the inmates suffering from typhus. The Women's Orchestra had also been sent there, and so my mother was able to see Miriam. But in April, Bergen-Belsen was liberated by the Allies. Miriam was reunited with her mother and sister. Not long afterward, they emigrated to Canada. My mother stayed in a displaced-persons camp for eight months, waiting for news of her parents and her brothers; she was distraught to learn that they had not survived. But through the Red Cross her father's brother made contact with her and offered her a home with his family in California. So in March 1946, my mother came here, to Pasadena.

"You *did* know," Mrs. Bell murmured again. She looked at me. Tears glittered in her eyes. "You *did* know, Phoebe. That strange conviction that you had . . . it was right. It was *right*," she repeated wonderingly.

I turned back to the letter.

Although my mother had a "normal" existence afterwards, in that she worked, married, and had a child, she never recovered from what she'd been through. For years afterwards, apparently, she walked with her eyes cast down. She hated it when someone said "after you" to her, because in the camp an inmate always had to walk in front of the escorting guard. She would become distressed if she saw striped fabric and would not tolerate any in the house. And she was obsessed with food, forever making cakes that she would give away.

Mom started high school but had difficulty applying herself to her studies. One day her teacher told her that she wasn't concentrating. My mother retorted that she knew all about "concentration," and angrily pulled up her sleeve to show the number tattooed on her left forearm. Not long after that she left school, and, although she was clever, she gave up the idea of going to college. She said that all she wanted to do was to feed people. So she got a job with a state-run program for the homeless, and through this she met my father, Stan, a baker, who donated bread to the charity's two shelters here in Pasadena. She and Stan fell in love, marrying in 1952 and working together in his bakery: he made the bread, and my mother made cakes, specializing in cupcakes. Their bakery grew, and in the 1970s it became the Pasadena Cupcake Company. I've been its CEO for the past few years.

"But I don't understand, Phoebe," Mrs. Bell said. "I don't understand how you could *know* this and not have *told* me? How could you *sit* with me, Phoebe, and *talk* to me and not *tell* me what you *knew*?" I glanced at the letter again. Then I read the last paragraph aloud.

When Miriam phoned me today, Thérèse, she said that she had already told Phoebe everything. Phoebe felt that you should hear what had happened not from her, but from me, as I am the nearest thing to Monique herself. So she arranged with me that I would

*write to you, and tell you my mother's story. I am very glad to have
had the opportunity to do so.*

   Yours in friendship,
   Lena Sands

I looked at Mrs. Bell. "I'm sorry you had to wait. But it wasn't my
story to tell—and I knew that Lena would write immediately."

Mrs. Bell's eyes filled with tears again. "I'm so happy," she murmured. "And so *sad.*"

"Why?" I whispered. "Because Monique was alive, but you didn't
hear from her?" She nodded; another tear slid down her cheek.
"But Lena says that Monique didn't like talking about Avignon—it's
understandable, given what happened there; she probably wanted
to draw a veil over that part of her life. Plus she may not have known
if *you* had survived the war—or where you were." Mrs. Bell nodded.
"And then you'd moved to London, and she was in America. Today,
with modern communications, you'd have found each other again.
But in a way you have found each other now."

Mrs. Bell reached for my hand. "You have done so much for me,
Phoebe—more, possibly, than anyone—but I am going to ask you to
do one thing more . . . Perhaps you have guessed what it is."

I nodded. Then I reread Lena's PS:

   *Thérèse, I'm coming to England in late February. I do hope I
   may have the chance to see you then—I know that that would have
   made my mother very happy.*

I handed Mrs. Bell the letter, then I went to the closet and took
out the blue coat in its protective cover. I turned to her.

"Of course I will," I said.

Fifteen

With Christmas around the corner, the shop was very busy, so I had Katie coming in to help on Saturdays. Mum was back at work, feeling happy, and looking forward to seeing Louis again with Dad on Christmas Eve. She decided that she ought to have some sort of party for her birthday on January 10 and joked that she was going to have it on a bus.

I began to plan the fashion show, which was to be held at Blackheath Halls—luckily there'd been a cancellation for the Great Hall on February 3.

I saw Mrs. Bell twice more. The first time she knew I was there, though she was very sleepy from the drugs. The second time, on December 21, she seemed unaware of my presence. By then she was being given morphine twenty-four hours a day. So I sat and held her hand and told her how glad I was that I'd known her and that I would never forget her, and that I even felt a bit stronger now when I thought about Emma. At that, I felt a slight pressure from Mrs. Bell's fingers. Then I kissed her good-bye. Walking home in the gathering dusk, I looked at the cloud-streaked sky and realised that it was the shortest day of the year: the light would soon be returning.

As I stepped inside, my phone rang. It was Sue, Mrs. Bell's nurse. "Phoebe—I'm sorry, but I'm calling to say that Mrs. Bell died at ten to four—a few minutes after you'd left."

I felt my eyes fill.

"She was very peaceful, as you saw," Sue continued. "She obviously felt very close to you. I guess you must have known her for a long time."

"No." I fumbled for the hall chair and reached into my pocket for a tissue. "I knew her for less than four months. But it feels like a lifetime."

After Sue had said good-bye I sat there for a few minutes, the tissue in my hand, as memories of Mrs. Bell filled my mind; then I phoned Annie, who sounded surprised to be hearing from me on a Sunday evening. "Are you all right, Phoebe?" she asked.

"I'm fine." I felt a tear seep into my mouth. "But . . . Do you have a few minutes, Annie? There's a story I want to tell you . . ."

The next couple of days were busy, then on Christmas Eve the shop went quiet. I watched people walking past the windows laden with bags, and I looked across the Heath towards the Paragon and thought about Mrs. Bell and about how glad I was that I'd met her. In helping her perhaps I'd healed some small part of myself.

At five o'clock I was upstairs in the stockroom, sorting things for the sale, putting gloves, hats, and belts in boxes—when I heard the doorbell ring, then footsteps. I went downstairs, expecting to see a frantic customer in search of a last-minute Christmas present; instead, there was Miles, looking suave in a beige winter coat with a brown velvet collar.

"Hello, Phoebe," he said quietly.

I stared at him, my heart banging in my rib cage, then I came down the rest of the stairs. "I was . . . about to close."

"Well...I just...wanted to talk to you." I noticed again the huskiness in Miles's voice that had always tugged at my heartstrings. "It won't take long."

I turned the sign to CLOSED, then went behind the counter, pretending that I needed to do something there.

"Have you been well?" I asked him, for want of anything else to say.

"I've been...fine," he replied soberly. "Quite busy, in fact, but...I just wanted to bring you this." He stepped forward and put a small green box down on the counter. I opened it, then shut my eyes with relief. Inside was the emerald ring that had been my grandmother's, then my mother's, and then mine, and that might one day, it now occurred to me, be my daughter's, if I was lucky enough to have one. I closed my fingers around it for a moment, then slipped it on my right hand. I looked at Miles. "I'm very happy to have this back."

"Of course. You must be." A red stain had crept up his neck. "I brought it as soon as I could."

"So you've only just found it?"

He nodded. "Last night."

"So...where?"

I saw a muscle at the corner of his mouth tighten. "In Roxy's bedside table." He shook his head. "She'd left the drawer open, and I caught a glimpse of it."

I exhaled slowly. "What did you say to her?"

"I was livid, of course—not just because she took it, but because of the lies she told. I said that we were going to get counselling for her about this, because—and this is hard for me to admit—she needs it." He gave a resigned shrug. "I suppose I've known that for some time but didn't want to face up to it. But Roxy seems to have this sense of, of not having...of..."

"Deprivation?"

"Yes. That's it. Deprivation." I resisted the urge to tell him that perhaps he should have counselling, too. "Anyway, I'm sorry,

Phoebe. I'm sorry in every way, actually, because you meant a lot to me."

"Well, thank you for bringing the ring back," I murmured. "It can't have been easy."

"No. I . . . anyway . . ." He heaved a sigh. "There it is. But I hope you have a happy Christmas." He gave me a bleak smile.

"Thanks, Miles. I hope you do too." Now we had nothing left to say to each other; I unlocked the door and Miles left, and I watched him walk down the street until he was out of sight. Then I went back upstairs.

Despite my relief over the ring, the encounter with Miles had upset me. As I was moving some clothes from one rack to another one of the hangers got caught on its neighbour and I was unable to release it; I was tugging at it, trying to unhook it, but I couldn't, so I ended up just pulling the garment, a Dior blouse, off the hanger—so roughly that I ripped the silk. I sank onto the floor and burst into tears. I stayed there for a few minutes, then, as I heard the bells at All Saints' Church strike six o'clock, I pushed myself to my feet. I was heading wearily downstairs when my cell phone rang. It was Dan, which raised my spirits again because, I suddenly realized, the sound of his voice always did. He wanted to know if I'd be interested in going round later for a "private screening" of a "particularly seductive" classic.

"Not *Emmanuelle*?" I said, smiling.

"No, but close. It's *King Kong vs. Godzilla*. I managed to get a sixteen-millimeter copy on eBay last week. But I do have *Emmanuelle*, if you're interested for another time."

"Hm—I might be, actually."

"Come round any time after seven—I'll cook a risotto." I found myself longing to sit with Dan, big and solid and comforting and cheerful, watching a schlocky old classic in his wonderful shed.

Feeling happier now, I got the SALE! banners out of their box, ready to plaster over the windows on Boxing Day to announce the first day of the sale on the twenty-seventh. Annie was going to be

away until early January, as she'd decided to take advantage of this
quiet time of year to write, so I'd gotten Katie to fill in for her, and
then from mid-January onwards Katie was going to work for me
every Saturday. I got my coat and bag and locked up.

As I walked home, the sharp wind stinging my cheeks, I allowed
myself to look forward, if only cautiously, to the new year. There'd be
the sale, then my mother's big birthday, then the fashion show—that
was going to take a lot of organising. Later there'd the anniversary of
Emma's death to get through, but I was trying not to think of that
now.

I turned up Bennett Street, unlocked my front door, and went inside. I picked the mail up off the mat—a few late Christmas cards,
including one from Daphne—then went into the kitchen and poured
myself a glass of wine. From outside I could hear singing, then the
bell rang. I opened the door.

Silent night, Holy night . . .

There were four children, with an adult, collecting for Crisis.

All is calm. All is bright . . .

I put some money in their tin, listened to the end of the carol,
then closed the door and went upstairs to get ready to meet Dan. At
seven I heard the bell again. I ran down and picked up my purse
from the hall table, assuming it to be more carolers.

Once I opened the door, however, I felt as though I'd been
plunged into ice water.

"Hello, Phoebe," said Guy.

"Can I come in?" he asked after a moment.

"Oh. Yes." I thought my legs would give way. "I . . . wasn't expecting you."

"No. Sorry. I just thought I'd drop by, as I'm on my way to Chisle-
hurst."

"To see your parents?"

Guy nodded. He was wearing the white skiing jacket that he'd bought in Val d'Isère; I remembered that he'd chosen it only because I'd liked it. "So you survived the banking crisis?" I said as we went into my kitchen.

"I did." Guy drew in his breath. "Just. But . . . can I sit down for a minute or two, Phoebe?"

"Of course," I said nervously. As he sat at the table I looked at his handsome, open face and his blue eyes. His short dark hair was longer than I remembered him wearing it, and visibly greying now at the temples. "Can I get you anything? A drink? A cup of coffee?"

He shook his head. "No. Nothing, thanks. I can't stay long."

I leaned against the counter, my heart racing. "So . . . what brings you here?"

"Phoebe," he replied patiently, "you *know.*"

I gave him a quizzical look. "I do?"

"Yes. You know that I'm here because for months now I've been trying to talk to you but you've ignored all my letters and e-mails and calls." He began fiddling with some holly I'd put around the base of a big white candle. "Your attitude has been completely . . . implacable." He looked at me. "I didn't know what to do. I knew that if I tried to arrange a meeting with you, you'd refuse to come." That was true, I reflected. I would have refused. "But tonight, knowing that I'd be almost passing your door, I thought I'd just see if you were here . . . because . . . There's this unfinished . . . issue between us, Phoebe."

"It's finished for me."

"But it isn't for *me,*" he countered, "and I'd like to resolve it."

"I'm sorry, Guy, but there's nothing to resolve."

"There *is,*" he insisted wearily. "And I need to start the new year feeling that I've finally laid it to rest."

I folded my arms. "Guy, if you didn't like what I said to you nine months ago, then why can't you just . . . forget about it?"

He stared at me. "Because it's far too serious to *be* forgotten—as you very well know. And as I've tried to live my life decently, I can't bear the idea that I would stand accused of something so . . . terrible." I suddenly realised that I hadn't emptied the dishwasher. "Phoebe," I heard Guy say as I turned away from him, "I need to discuss what happened that night just once—and then never again. That's why I'm here."

I pulled out two plates. "But I don't *want* to discuss it. Plus I'm going out soon."

"Well, would you please hear me out—just for a minute or two?" Guy clasped his hands on the table in front of him. He looked as though he was praying, I reflected as I put the plates in the cupboard. But I did not want to have this conversation. I felt trapped, and angry. "First of all I'd like to say that I'm sorry." I turned and stared at him. "I'm truly sorry if I did or said anything that night that might have contributed, however inadvertently, to what happened to Emma. Please forgive me, Phoebe." I hadn't expected this. "But I need you to acknowledge that the charge *you* levelled at me was completely unfair."

I pulled two glass tumblers out of the dishwasher. "No, I won't—because it was *true.*"

Guy shook his head. "Phoebe, it was *un*true—and you knew that then just as you know it now." I put a tumbler on the shelf. "You were obviously very distressed—"

"Yes. I was distraught." I put the second tumbler on the shelf, so hard that I almost cracked it.

"And when people are in that state they can say terrible things." *If it weren't for you—she'd still be alive!*

"But you blamed *me* for Emma's death, and I've been unable to bear the accusation. It's haunted me, all this time. You said that I'd persuaded you not to go and see Emma."

Now I faced him. "You *did* do that! You said that she was that 'mad milliner,' remember, who 'exaggerated' everything." I took the cutlery basket out of the dishwasher and began flinging the knives into the drawer.

"I *did* say that," I heard Guy say. "I was pretty fed up with Emma by then—I don't deny it—and she did make such a drama out of everything. But I only said that this was something you needed to bear in mind before dashing off to see her."

I threw in the spoons and forks. "Then you said that we should go to the Bluebird, as planned, and have dinner because you'd booked it and didn't want to miss it."

"I admit that I said that too," Guy nodded. "But I *added* that if you really didn't want to come, then I'd cancel the table. I said that it was *your* decision." The blood rushing in my ears now, I thrust the cutlery basket back into the dishwasher and grabbed a milk jug. "Phoebe, *you* said that we *should* go out to dinner. You said that you'd phone Emma again when we got back."

"*No.*" I put the jug down on the counter and turned to him. "That was *your* suggestion—*your* compromise."

Guy was shaking his head. "It was yours." I felt the familiar sliding sensation. "I remember being surprised, but I said that Emma was your friend and that I'd go with your judgement on the matter."

I was filled with sudden dismay. "Okay . . . ," I conceded quietly. "I *did* say that we should have dinner—but only because I didn't want to disappoint you, and because it was Valentine's Day so it was going to be special."

"You said we wouldn't be out for too long."

"Well, that's right," I said. "And we *weren't*. Then when we got back I *did* phone Emma—I phoned her right away; and I *was* going to go round to her house then, right *then*." I stared at Guy. "But you *dissuaded* me. You said that I'd probably had too much to drink to get into the car."

"I *did* say that, yes—because I knew you almost certainly *had*—we both had."

"Well, there you are then!" I slammed shut the dishwasher. "You *stopped* me from going to see Emma."

"No." Guy was shaking his head. "Because *then* I said that you should go round to her house in a taxi and that I'd go outside and hail one for you. And I was about to do that, if you remember—I'd even opened the front door"—I was no longer sliding, but falling, hurtling into a chasm—"when you suddenly said that you weren't going to go after all. You said you'd decided not to." He was staring at me. "You said that Emma would be okay until the morning." At that my legs gave way. I sank onto a chair. "You said that she'd sounded so tired, and that it would be best for her just to have a long sleep. Phoebe," Guy said quietly, "I'm sorry to bring all this up again. But having something *so* terrible flung at me, without any chance to rebut it, has destroyed my peace of mind all these months. I've been unable to let it go. So I just want—no, *need* you to acknowledge that what you said simply wasn't true."

In my mind's eye I could see the forecourt of the Bluebird Café, and Guy's apartment, then the narrow staircase at Emma's house, and finally her bedroom door as I pushed it open. I drew in my breath. "All right then," I croaked. "All right," I reiterated. "Perhaps... Perhaps I..." I looked away.

"Perhaps you didn't remember it quite right," I heard Guy say softly.

"Perhaps I didn't. You see... I was very upset."

"Yes, so it's understandable that you... forgot what really happened."

"No—it was more than that," I said bleakly. I stared at Guy. "I couldn't bear the thought of having to blame only *myself.*"

Guy reached for my hand and enclosed it in both of his. "Phoebe, I don't think you *were* to blame. You couldn't have known how ill Emma was. You were simply doing what seemed to be right for your friend. And the doctor told you that it was very unlikely that she would have survived even if she had come into the hospital the previous night..."

"But it's not knowing for *sure,*" I protested, feeling... broken. "It's the terrible, tantalising possibility that she *might* have survived if I'd only done things differently." I covered my face with my hands. "And how I wish, wish, *wish* that I *had.*"

As the tears came, my head sank to my chest. Then I heard Guy's chair being scraped back and he came and sat next to me. "Phoebe, you and I were in love," he whispered.

I nodded desolately.

"But what happened just . . . smashed everything up. When you phoned me that morning to say that Emma had died, I knew instantly that our relationship wouldn't survive it."

"No." I swallowed. "How could we have been happy after . . . that?"

"I don't think we could," he agreed. "It would always have cast a shadow over our lives. But I couldn't bear to have parted from you on such awful terms. How I wish that it had never happened."

"How I wish that too," I murmured. "I wish it with all my heart." The phone was ringing, forcing me to surface from the fantasy of what might have been. I grabbed a kitchen towel, pressed it to my eyes, then answered.

"Hey, where *are* you?" Dan asked. "The film's about to start, and they get snotty with latecomers here."

"Oh. I will be coming, Dan." I coughed to hide my tears. "But a little later, if that's okay." I sniffed. "No . . . I'm fine, I think I'm just getting a cold. Yes, I'll definitely be there." I glanced at Guy. "But I don't think I can face Godzilla and King Kong."

"We won't watch it then," I heard Dan say. "We don't have to watch anything. We can just listen to music, or play cards. It doesn't matter—just come whenever you can."

I put the phone back in its cradle.

"Are you with someone now?" Guy asked me gently. "I hope you are," he added. "I want you to be happy, Phoebe."

"Well . . ." I wiped my eyes again. "I have this . . . friend. That's all he is for now—just a friend, but I enjoy being with him. He's a good person, Guy. Like you."

Guy inhaled, then nodded. "I'm going to go now, Phoebe. I'm glad I've seen you."

I walked him to the front door. "I wish you a happy Christmas, Phoebe," he told me. "And I hope this year will be a good one."

"For you too," I said quietly as he hugged me. "I'm sorry, Guy," I whispered. "I'm sorry."

Guy held me for another moment, then he left.

I spent Christmas Day with Mum, who had at last, I noticed, taken off her wedding ring. She had the January issue of *Woman & Home* with its "Ring in the Old" fashion spread, featuring my clothes with a prominent credit. A few pages further on I saw a photo of Reese Witherspoon at the Emmy Awards wearing the midnight-blue Balenciaga gown that I'd got at Christie's. So this was the A-lister for whom Cindi had bought the dress. Seeing such a big star in a gown I'd sourced gave me a buzz.

After lunch Dad phoned to say how thrilled Louis was with the Lights'n'Sounds baby walker Mum had given him the day before and with my Thomas the Tank Engine starter set. Dad said he hoped we'd both come and see Louis again soon, and as we watched the *Doctor Who* Christmas special, Mum made more of the blue pram coat she's been knitting Louis and which I'd given her the aeroplane buttons for.

"Thank God they're getting a nanny for Louis," she remarked as she looped the yarn over the needle.

"Yes, and Dad mentioned he's going to do some teaching at the Open University, so that's given him a boost." Mum nodded sympathetically.

On the twenty-seventh our sale began and the shop was jammed. I was able to tell everyone about the vintage fashion show and to ask those customers I had in mind whether they'd be willing to model the clothes. Carla, who'd bought the turquoise cupcake, said she'd love to—she added that it would be the week before her wedding. Katie said she'd happily model her yellow prom dress. Through Dan

I got in touch with Kelly Marks, and she told me she'd be thrilled to wear her "Tinker Bell" dress, as she called it. Then the woman who'd bought the pink prom dress came in. So I explained that I was putting on a vintage fashion show for charity and asked her if she'd model her cupcake dress for it.

Her face lit up. "I'd love to—what fun! When is it?" I told her. She got out her engagement book and wrote it down. "Model... happy... dress," she murmured. "The only thing *is* ... No, it's okay. February first will be fine."

On January 5 I took the morning off to go to Mrs. Bell's funeral at the crematorium on Verdant Lane. It was a very small affair: there were two friends of hers from Blackheath, her home help, Paola, and her nephew, James, and his wife, Yvonne.

"Thérèse was quite ready to go," Yvonne said after the ceremony as we looked at the flowers. She drew her charcoal-colored wrap more closely round her shoulders in the bitter winter wind.

"She did seem contented," said James. "When I saw her the last time she told me that she felt quite calm and ... happy. She used the word *happy*."

Yvonne was examining a spray of irises. "The card on this one says *With love from Lena.*" She turned to James. "I never heard Thérèse mention anyone named Lena—did you, darling?" He shook his head.

"*I* heard her mention that name," I told them. "But I think it was a connection from a long time ago."

"Phoebe, I've got something for you from my aunt." James opened his briefcase, then handed me a small box. "She asked me to give this to you—to remember her by."

"Thank you." I took it. "Not that I'll ever forget her." I couldn't explain why.

When I got home I opened the box. Inside, wrapped in newspaper, I found the silver carriage clock and a letter written in Mrs. Bell's then very shaky hand.

My dear Phoebe,
This clock belonged to my parents. I give it to you not just because it
was one of the things I most treasured, but by way of reminding
you that its hands are going round, and with them all the hours
and days and years of your life. Phoebe, I implore you not to spend
too much of the precious time you have left regretting what you did
or didn't do, or what might or might not have been. And whenever
you do feel sad, I hope you will console yourself by remembering the
inestimable good that you did me, your friend,

   Thérèse

I reset the clock, gently wound it with the little key, then put it on
the centre of my sitting-room mantel. "I will look forward," I
promised as it began to tick. "I will look forward, Mrs. Bell."

And I did—first of all to my mother's birthday.

She held her party—a sit-down supper for twenty people—in an
upstairs room at Chapters wine bar. In her short speech Mum said
she felt that she'd "come of age." All her bridge friends were there,
and her boss, John, and a couple of other people from work. Mum
had also invited a pleasant man named Hamish whom she mentioned she'd met at Betty and Jim's Christmas party.

"He seemed nice," I said to her over the phone the next day.

"He's very nice," Mum agreed. "He's fifty-eight, divorced, with
two grown-up sons. The funny thing is that the party was very
crowded, but Hamish started talking to me because of what I was
wearing. He said he liked the pattern of little palm trees on my outfit. I told him that it was from my daughter's vintage dress shop.
That then led to a longer conversation about fabric because his father worked in the textile industry in Paisley. Then he phoned me
the next day to ask me out. We went to a concert at the Barbican.
We're going to the Coliseum next week," she added happily.

In the meantime Katie, her friend Sarah, Annie, and I were
working nonstop on the fashion show. Dan was going to do the
lights and sound and had assembled a montage of music that would

take us seamlessly from Scott Joplin through to the Sex Pistols. A friend of his was going to build the catwalk.

On Tuesday afternoon we went to the Great Hall to do the run-through, and Dan brought with him a copy of that day's *Black & Green* in which Ellie had written a preview piece about the show.

There are still a few tickets available for the Passion for Vintage Fashion Show, which will take place at Blackheath Halls tonight. Tickets are £10, and will be redeemable against purchases at Village Vintage. All profits will go to Malaria No More, a charity that distributes insecticide-treated nets in sub-Saharan Africa, where, sadly, malaria kills 3,000 children every day. These bed nets, which cost £2.50 each, will protect up to two children and their mother. The show's organiser, Phoebe Swift, is hoping to raise enough money for the charity to buy a thousand of them.

During the rehearsal I went backstage to the dressing room, where the models were getting ready for the fifties sequence and were all in New Look suits, circle skirts, and wiggle dresses. Mum was wearing her coatdress; Katie, Kelly, and Carla were in their cupcakes; but Lucy, the owner of the pink one, was beckoning to me. "I've got a bit of a problem," she whispered. She turned round and I saw that the top of her dress gaped by a good two inches.

"I'll get you a stole," I said. "That's odd," I added as I studied her. "It fitted you perfectly when you bought it."

"I know." Lucy smiled. "But I wasn't pregnant then."

"You're . . . ?"

She nodded. "Four months."

"Oh!" I hugged her. "That is so . . . *brilliant.*"

Lucy's eyes were shining with tears. "I can still hardly believe it myself. I couldn't mention it when you first asked me to be a model because I wasn't at the telling stage; but now that I've had my first scan, I can talk about it."

"So it was the happy dress that did it!" I said delightedly.

Lucy laughed. "I'm not sure, but I'll tell you what I do attribute it to." She lowered her voice. "At the beginning of October my husband went into your shop. He wanted to buy me something to cheer me up, and he saw some lovely lingerie—beautiful slips and teddies from the 1940s."

"I remember him buying those," I said. "But I didn't know who he was. So they were for you?"

Lucy nodded. "And not long afterwards..." She patted her tummy, then giggled.

"Well," I said. "That's... *wonderful.*"

So Aunt Lydia's lingerie had been making up for lost time.

Katie was going to wear the Madame Grès dress that I'd bought at Christie's for the 1930s section; Annie, with her slim, boyish figure, would be modelling clothes from the twenties and sixties. Four of my regular customers would be wearing the 1940s and 1980s garments. Joan was helping backstage with the changing and accessories and was now hanging the clothes on their respective racks.

After the run-through, Annie and Mum put out the glasses for the drinks. As they opened the boxes I overheard Annie telling Mum about her play, which she'd almost finished and which was provisionally entitled *The Blue Coat.*

"I hope it ends happily," I heard Mum say.

"Don't worry," Annie replied. "It does. I'm going to put it on as a lunchtime show at the Age Exchange in May. There's a little fifty-seater theatre there, which will be perfect for it."

"It sounds terrific," Mum told her. "Perhaps after that, you'll be headed for Broadway with it."

"I'll certainly try," Annie told her, laughing. "I'm going to invite some producers and agents to see it. Chloë Sevigny was in the shop again the other day—she said she'd come if she's in London then."

Now Dan and I began to arrange the seating, setting out two hundred red velvet chairs on either side of the catwalk that extended twenty-five feet from the centre of the stage. Finally, satisfied that everything was ready, I went and changed into Mrs. Bell's damson-plum-coloured suit, which looked as though it was made for me. As I put it on I caught the faint scent of Ma Griffe.

At 6:30 P.M. the doors opened, and an hour later every seat was full. A hush descended as Dan dimmed the lights. He gave me the nod. I went up onstage and lifted the mike off its stand, nervously surveying the sea of upturned faces.

"I'm Phoebe Swift," I began. "I'd like to welcome you tonight and to thank you all for coming. We're going to enjoy ourselves, look at some beautiful old clothes, and raise money for a very worthwhile cause. I'd also like to say"—I felt my fingers tighten around the mike—"that this event is dedicated to the memory of my best friend, Emma Kitts." Now the soundtrack swelled, Dan brought up the lights, and the first models walked out . . .

It was a day I'd dreaded for so long. Now here it was. No anniversary would be as hard as this one, I realised as I got into the car and drove to Greenwich Cemetery. Walking down the gravelled path past gravestones recent and gravestones so old that you could barely read the names carved on them, I looked up and saw Daphne and Derek, who appeared calm and composed. Next to them were Emma's uncle and aunt and her two cousins, and Emma's photographer friend Charlie, who was chatting quietly to Emma's former assistant, Sian, who clutched a hanky. Finally, there was Father Bernard, who had conducted Emma's funeral.

I hadn't been to the cemetery since that day—I'd been unable to face it—and so this was the first time that I'd seen Emma's head-stone. The sight of it—the awful, emphatic, irrefutability of it—gave me a shock.

EMMA MANDISA KITTS, 1974–2008
BELOVED DAUGHTER, FOREVER IN OUR HEARTS.

Clumps of snowdrops hung their dainty heads at the foot of the grave, while purple crocus spears pushed through the cold ground. I'd brought a bouquet of tulips, daffodils, and bluebells, and as I laid it down on the black granite it made me think of Mrs. Bell's hatbox. The early-spring sunlight suddenly stung my eyes.

Father Bernard said a few words of welcome, then he asked Derek to speak. Derek said that he and Daphne had called Emma "Mandisa" because that meant "sweet" in Xhosa and she was a sweet person; he spoke of how Emma's fascination with all his hats as a child had led to her becoming a milliner. Daphne talked of how talented Emma was, of how modest she'd always been, and of how much they missed her. I heard Sian stifle a sob and saw Charlie put his arm round her. Then Father Bernard said a prayer, gave a blessing, and it was over. As we all drifted back along the path I wished that the anniversary hadn't fallen on a Sunday—I would have been grateful for the distraction of work. When we reached the cemetery gates, Daphne and Derek invited everyone back to the house.

It had been years since I had been there. In the sitting room I chatted with Sian and Charlie, then with Emma's uncle and aunt; then, excusing myself, I went into the kitchen, through the utility room, and out into the garden. I stood by the plane tree.

I really fooled you there, didn't I?

"Yes, you really did," I murmured.

You thought I was dead!

"No. I thought you were sleeping . . ."

I looked up and saw Daphne at the kitchen window. She lifted her hand in greeting, then disappeared, and now she was walking across the grass towards me. I noticed how grey her hair had become.

"Phoebe," she said softly. She reached for my hand. "I hope you're okay."

"I'm . . . fine, thanks, Daphne. I'm . . . well, I keep myself busy."

She nodded. "You've made such a success of the shop, and I saw in the local paper that your fashion show was a great hit."

"It was. We raised just over three thousand pounds—enough to buy twelve hundred mosquito nets—and so, well . . ." I shrugged. "It's something, isn't it?"

"It is. We're really proud of you, Phoebe," Daphne said. "And Emma would have been, too. But I just wanted to tell you that Derek and I recently went through her things."

I felt my heart freeze. "Then you must have found her diary," I interjected, anxious to get the awful moment over.

"I did find it," Daphne replied. "I knew that I should burn it without even opening it, but I couldn't bear to deprive myself of any part of Emma. So I'm afraid I did read it." I searched her face for the resentment that she must surely have felt. "It made me very sad to think that Emma had been so unhappy in the last months of her life."

"She *was* unhappy," I agreed quietly. "And, as you now know, it was my fault. I fell in love with someone that Emma liked and she was terribly upset about it, and I feel awful at the thought that I caused her any distress whatsoever. I didn't mean to." My confession over, I braced myself for Daphne's censure.

"Phoebe," said Daphne. "In her diary, Emma expressed no anger with you at all; on the contrary, she said you'd done nothing wrong— she said that almost made it worse for her—that she couldn't blame you. She was angry with herself for not being more . . . grown-up, I suppose, about the situation. She admitted that she was unable to conquer her negative feelings, but she acknowledged that she'd get over it in time."

Time she didn't have. I shivered and thrust my hands into my pockets. "I wish none of it had ever happened, Daphne."

She was shaking her head. "But that's like saying you wish life had never happened. This was just life *happening,* Phoebe. Don't reproach yourself. You were such a good friend to Emma."

"No. I wasn't always. You see . . ." But I couldn't torment Daphne with the thought that I might have saved Emma. "I feel I let Emma down," I said instead. "I could have done more. That night. I'm—"

"Phoebe, none of us knew how ill she was," she interrupted,

gently. "Imagine how *I* feel knowing that I was on holiday, and un-reachable..." Tears shone in her eyes. "Emma made an awful... mistake. It cost her her *life,* but we all have to go on. And you must try to be happy now, Phoebe—otherwise two lives will have been spoilt. You'll never forget Emma; she was your best friend and she'll always be a part of who you are, but you must live your life *well.* Now." Daphne hesitated. "I wanted to give you a couple of things of Emma's as keepsakes. Come with me." I followed her back into the kitchen, where she handed me a red velvet box. Inside was the gold Krugerrand. "Emma's grandparents gave this to her when she was born. I'd like you to have it."

"Thank you," I said. "Emma treasured this, and I will too."

"Then there's this." Daphne gave me the ammonite.

I placed it in the palm of my hand. It felt warm. "I was with Emma when she found this on the beach at Lyme Regis. That's a very happy memory. Thank you, Daphne. But..." I gave her a half smile. "I think I'll go now."

"But you will keep in touch with Derek and me, won't you, Phoebe? The door will always be open, so please walk through it sometimes, and let us know how you are."

Daphne put her arms round me, and I whispered, "I will."

A few minutes after I'd got home, Dan phoned. He asked me about my visit to the cemetery—I had told him about Emma. Then he wondered if I'd look at yet another possible site for his cinema—a Victorian warehouse in Lewisham.

"I've just seen it in the property section of the *Observer,*" he explained. "Will you come with me while I check out the exterior? Can I pick you up in twenty minutes?"

"Sure." I welcomed the distraction.

Dan and I had already looked at a biscuit factory in Charlton, a disused library in Kidbrooke, and an old bingo hall in Catford.

"The location's *got* to be right," he said as we drove up Belmont

Hill half an hour later. "I need to find something in an area where there isn't already a cinema within two miles."

"And when do you hope to open?"

He slowed the car and turned left. "Ideally I'd like it to be up and running by this time next year."

"And what will you call it?"

"I was wondering about Cine Qua Non."

"Hmm . . . a bit too highbrow."

"All right, then—the Lewisham Lux."

Dan parked outside a brown brick warehouse and opened the car door. "This is it." As I didn't want to follow him over the locked gate in my silk skirt, I told him I'd go for a stroll. I walked onto Lewisham High Street, passing a bank, a curtain shop, Árgos, and a British Red Cross charity shop. Then I came to Currys, in the window of which were a number of plasma TVs. I suddenly stopped. On the biggest screen was Mags, standing in front of a studio audience, in a scarlet trouser suit and black stilettos. She was holding her fingers to her temples, and now she began to pace. As the audio captioning scrolled across the bottom of the screen, I read, "*I'm getting a military man. A straight-backed sort of fellow. Liked a nice cigar . . .*" She looked up. *Does that mean anything to anyone?* I rolled my eyes, then was suddenly aware of Dan standing next to me.

"That was quick," I said, glancing at his lovely profile. "How was it?"

"Well I liked the look of it, so I'll call the agent first thing. The fabric of the building seems fine, and the size is perfect. Why are you looking at that, sweetheart?" He peered at the screen. "Is she a psychic?"

"That's what she says."

Just think of me as your switchboard operator . . .

I told Dan how I'd met Mags.

"So are you interested in spiritualism?"

"No. Not really," I replied as we walked on.

"By the way, my mum just phoned," Dan added as we strolled

back to the car, hand in hand. "She was wondering if we'd like to come over for tea next Sunday."

"Next Sunday?" I echoed. "I would have loved to, but I can't. There's something I have to do. Something important."

As we drove away I explained what it was.

"Well, that *is* important," Dan agreed.

Epilogue

I am walking down Marylebone High Street, not as I so often do, in my dreams, but for real, to meet a woman I have never met before. In my hand is a shopping bag that I clutch as tightly as if it held the crown jewels.

It was my fantasy that I would one day give Monique the coat...

I pass the ribbon-and-trimming shop.

...and can you believe, it still is?

When Lena phoned me to say that her hotel was in the heart of Marylebone, my heart had lurched. "I've found a nice café close to the bookshop," she'd said. "I thought we might meet there. It's called Amici's. Would that be all right?" And I was about to say that I'd rather go anywhere else because of the painful associations that particular café has for me when I suddenly changed my mind. The last time I'd been there, something sad had happened. Now a positive thing would take place there instead.

As I push open the door, the owner, Carlo, gives me a sympathetic wave, and I see a slim, smartly dressed woman in her early fifties leave her table and come towards me, smiling tentatively.

"Phoebe?"

"Lena," I say warmly. As we shake hands I take in her lively expression, high cheekbones, and dark hair. "You look like your mother."

She seems astonished. "But how do you know?"

"You'll see in a moment," I say. I get the coffees, exchanging a few words with Carlo, then I carry them to the table. In her soft California accent Lena tells me why she's come to London, to attend the wedding of an old friend the next day. She says she's looking forward to it but is very jet-lagged.

Now, with the social pleasantries out of the way, we come to the purpose of our meeting. I open the bag and hand Lena the coat, the story of which she mostly knows.

She fingers the sky-blue cloth, stroking the nap of the wool, the silk lining, and the perfect hand stitching. "It's lovely. So Thérèse's mother made this." She looks at me with a surprised smile. "She was *good.*"

"She *was* good. It's beautifully made."

Lena strokes the collar. "But how amazing to think that Thérèse *never* gave up on the idea of giving it to Mom."

I have kept it for sixty-five years, and I will keep it until I die.

"She just wanted to keep her promise to her," I say. "And now, in a way, she has."

Lena's face fills with sadness. "Poor girl, though, not knowing what happened all these years. Never putting it to rest . . . until the end."

Now as we sip our coffee I tell Lena more about what happened, about how Thérèse had been distracted that fatal night by Jean-Luc, and how she had never forgiven herself for revealing Monique's hiding place.

"My mother might well have been discovered anyway," Lena says. "She used to say that it was so hard staying in that barn, in silence and solitude all day—she would comfort herself by remembering the songs her mother used to sing to her—that it was almost a relief when she was found. Of course she had no idea what awaited her," Lena adds darkly.

"But she survived," I murmur. "And that was . . . a miracle."

"Yes." Lena stares at her coffee, lost in her own thoughts for a few seconds. "My mother's survival *was* a miracle. Which makes my existence one, too. I never forget that. And I often think of that young German officer who saved her that day."

Now I give Lena the padded envelope. She opens it and takes out the necklace. "It's beautiful," she says as she holds it to the light. She fingers the pink and bronze glass beads. "My mother never mentioned this. How does it fit into the story?"

As I explain, I imagine Thérèse desperately searching for the beads among the straw. She must have picked up every one. "I think the clasp is fine," I say as Lena opens it. "Thérèse told me that she had it restrung years ago." Lena puts the necklace on, and the beads glimmer and sparkle against her black sweater. "And this is the last thing." I hand her the envelope.

She slides out the photo and searches the sea of faces, then her finger goes straight to Monique. She looks up at me. "So that's how you knew what my mom looked like."

I nod. "And that's Thérèse, standing next to her, there." Now I point to Jean-Luc and Lena's face clouds.

"Mom was very bitter about that boy," she says. "She could never get over the fact that he'd been her schoolmate and he betrayed her." I tell Lena about the good thing that Jean-Luc did a decade later. She shakes her head in wonderment. "How I wish my mother had known. But she cut off all contact with Rochemare. Though she said she often dreamed about the house. She would dream that she was running through its rooms, looking for her parents and her brothers, and calling out for someone, anyone, to help her."

I feel a tiny shiver run through me.

"Well . . ." Lena hugs the coat, then folds it. "I'll treasure this,

Phoebe, and someday I'll pass it on to my daughter, Monica. She's twenty-six now—so she was only four when my mother died. She remembers her, and she sometimes asks me about her life, so this will help her know the story."

I pick up a paper napkin. It has AMICI's printed on it. "There's something else that'll help her know the story," I say. I tell Lena about Annie and the play.

Lena's face lights up. "But that's wonderful. So the playwright is a good friend of yours?"

"Yes." I think of how much I've come to like Annie in the six months I've known her. "She's a good friend."

"Perhaps I'll come back and see it," Lena says. "With Monica. If we can, we will. But for now..." She slips the photo back into the envelope and puts it carefully in the bag and is about to put in the coat when I stop her.

"Please wait." I lay my hand on a blue sleeve, wanting to connect one last time with this little garment that has touched my life so deeply.

"Okay," I say after a moment.

Lena puts the coat carefully inside the bag, then she smiles. "It's been so good to meet you, Phoebe. Thank you."

"I'm glad I've met you," I say. We stand up.

"So, is there anything else?" Lena asks.

"No," I reply happily. "There's nothing else." Then we say our good-byes and promise to keep in touch.

As I walk away, my phone rings. It's Dan.

ACKNOWLEDGMENTS

I'd like to thank the following people for their help in the planning and writing of this book. For their expertise on vintage clothing, Kerry Taylor of Kerry Taylor Auctions, Sonya Hughes and Deborah Eastlake of Biba Lives, Claire Stansfield and Steven Philip of Rellik, Maryann Holm of Circa Vintage, Dolly Diamond, and Pauline and Guy Thomas of Fashion Era. For information about Provence I'm grateful to Frank Wiseman, and to Georges Fréchet of the Média-thèque Ceccano for making available to me research material about Avignon during the war. For educating me about viticulture I'm indebted to the Boiron family of Bosquet des Papes, and to Nathalie Panissieres of Château des Fines Roches. I'd also like to thank Rich Mead, assistant editor of *Metro* newspaper, Carole Bronsdon, GP, Jonathan and Kim Causer, Peter Crawford, Ellen Stead, Louise Clairmonte for being my "reading friend," yet again, the staff of Blackheath Halls, and of the Age Exchange, and Sophia Wallace-Turner for correcting my French. Any mistakes are my own.

I'd like to thank everyone at Random House, above all my editor, Kate Miciak, both for her deeply touching enthusiasm for the novel and for her superb editing, which has enhanced the text in so many ways. In the U.K. I'm hugely indebted to my wonderful editor, Claire Bord, and to Lynne Drew, Amanda Ridout, Alice Moss, Fiona McIntosh, and all at HarperCollins. Grateful thanks also to Rachel Hore. I owe a huge debt of gratitude to my agent, Clare Conville, and to Jake Smith-Bosanquet, Sue Armstrong, and all at Conville and Walsh. Finally I would like to thank Greg, Alice, and Edmund for all their love, support, and endless patience during the writing of this book.

BIBLIOGRAPHY

The following books provided helpful background during the course of my research:

Houtte, Alison, and Melissa Houtte. *Alligators, Old Mink & New Money: One Woman's Adventures in Vintage Clothing.* Orion Books.

Jackson, Julian. *France: The Dark Years, 1940–1944.* Oxford University Press.

Langbein, Hermann. *People in Auschwitz.* Translated by Harry Zohn. University of North Carolina Press, with the United States Holocaust Memorial Museum.

Marrus, Michael R., and Robert O. Paxton. *Vichy France and the Jews.* Stanford University Press.

Odulate, Funmi. *Shopping for Vintage: The Definitive Guide to Vintage Fashion.* Quadrille.

Rosenberg, Maxine. *Hiding to Survive: Stories of Jewish Children Rescued from the Holocaust.* Topeka Bindery.

Weil, Chrisa. *It's Vintage, Darling! How to Be a Clothes Connoisseur.* Hodder & Stoughton.

A Vintage Affair

ISABEL WOLFF

A Reader's Guide

A LETTER FROM ISABEL WOLFF

Dear Reader,

Thank you for reading *A Vintage Affair*—I hope, naturally, that you enjoyed it. But I also hope that you may carry away from it certain thoughts, not just about the aesthetic, and sentimental, value of lovely old garments, but about the way in which those garments can transform us, not just from without but from within. I had long wanted to write a novel that would have vintage clothing at its heart— because I've always loved and worn vintage myself, and also because I try to imbue my novels with deep feeling, and I recognised the possibilities for poignancy in vintage clothes. For as Phoebe says, when you buy a vintage garment you're not just buying fabric and threads—you're buying a piece of someone's past. I've never been able to look at a vintage dress or suit without wondering what stories it might tell. Who was the woman who first owned it? What kind of life did she have? Was she sad or happy, frustrated or fulfilled? Was she married or single? Did she have children? If the garment is from the 1940s, I find myself wondering if its owner survived the war. I can never look at a pillbox hat from the 1950s without conjuring the face of the person who once wore it; I look at a pair of brocade evening shoes from the 1930s and imagine the woman who once owned them dancing in them. I see a trouser suit with a BIBA label, and in a flash it's the 1960s and the suit is strutting down the King's Road. So powerful are the echoes that vintage clothes exude that at times I've even wondered whether the spirit of a garment's former owner might still reside within it, just as the contours of their body have moulded its shape. I was also very attracted to the idea of restoration inherent in vintage clothing, for these lovely old garments require careful stitching and cleaning before they can regain their former glory. But not everything in life can be restored, as my heroine, I decided, would know only too well. These were the ideas that filled my mind as I began to write the outline for *A Vintage Affair*.

Once I knew that the book would be about vintage clothes, I knew that it would also, inevitably, be a novel about ageing. It would explore whether we cherish an old thing—be it an old dress, an old marriage, an old friendship, or an old face—or care only for the contemporary, the rejuvenated, or the new. Into this I wove the idea of other old things, notably classic movies and vintage wine. I also decided that *A Vintage Affair* would be a book about relationships across the age barrier, so I gave Phoebe a romance with an older man and, crucially, had her befriend an eighty-year-old Frenchwoman, Thérèse Bell.

I knew the research I would need to do would lead me to some of my plotlines, and so it proved. One of the vintage dress store owners to whom I talked showed me some of the gloriously colourful prom dresses that she sold in her North London shop. She told me that these confections of satin and tulle were so glamorous and frothy that she called them "cupcakes"; I adored the name and decided that Phoebe would sell four cupcakes to four very different women, and that each dress would somehow transform the life of its new owner, giving each woman confidence—courage, even—and hope. Another vintage dress shop owner told me that she bought some of her stock in France, where beautifully embroidered antique petticoats can be found at outdoor markets in provincial towns. This opened up the possibility that Phoebe might do so as well, and that the book could therefore be set partly in Provence. Another shop owner talked to me about the things that she had sometimes found in the clothes she'd bought—pens and coins, old photos and postcards. I knew instantly that in my novel something of great significance would be found in a pocket or purse.

I also decided that there would be one garment that would have a particularly touching story attached to it, a story that would enable me to set the novel partly in the past. At first I imagined that this might be about a love letter that Phoebe finds secreted in the hem of a ball gown or a wedding dress, telling of its owner's long-ago broken heart. But when I realised how big a part Thérèse was going to play, I realised that the garment would be hers, and that it would go back to her childhood in Occupied France. So I decided that Thérèse would come from Avignon, and that the garment would be a blue coat, made for her but which she had promised to take to her best friend, Monique, a Jewish girl in hiding from the Nazis. Instead, Thérèse inadvertently betrayed Monique and has spent the years since trying to live with the guilt.

I realised as I conceived this dark part of the story that it came to me from my grandmother. When I was eight, she told me that her best friend, Hélène, with whom she'd studied at the Sorbonne, had been "murdered." I was too shocked and bewildered to ask how or why, and it was to be a few years before I learned that Hélène, having fled Paris, had been arrested in Lyon in February 1944 and was gassed in Auschwitz a month later. My grandmother spoke of Hélène very often, and did so not just with sorrow but with a regret so deep that it seemed to border on guilt, even though she could have done nothing to help her friend and had no idea what had happened to her until after the war. But I believe that this is what led me to the wartime part of the story. I then linked it to the present-day story, not just through the blue coat, which is what connects Phoebe to Thérèse, but by making Phoebe's own back story one of friendship betrayed. This is what binds these two women, born fifty years apart. As Phoebe says to Thérèse at the end of chapter six, "We both had friends who waited for us to come." I realised that Phoebe would not just be sympathetic to Thérèse's story, she would become emotionally engaged with it almost to the point of obsession, as she sets out to uncover what happened to Monique. In real life there would, almost certainly, have been a tragic denouement to Phoebe's search.

But a novel is a special place, in which the extraordinary can happen; and I always give my heroines that longed-for, elusive second chance to put right something that they've got badly wrong. So Phoebe, through her drive to redeem Mrs. Bell—and through the near magic of beautiful old clothes—is able to help Thérèse find peace at last. In doing so, she heals a part of herself. And so *A Vintage Affair* became in my mind a novel about fashion and friendship, regret and redemption. I loved writing it, and felt uplifted when I finished it. I hope that *A Vintage Affair* may have lifted you up, too.

Isabel Wolff, London 2010

ISABEL WOLFF'S GUIDE TO BUYING AND CARING FOR VINTAGE CLOTHING

1. *Be prepared to spend time looking.* Vintage dress shops are like Aladdin's cave—you never know what you're going to find, so make time to browse.
2. *Know what suits you and stick to it.* If you're curvy, then the boxy shapes of the '20s and '60s are *not* going to work, but the fitted silhouettes of the '40s and '50s will probably look great. Equally, the figure-skimming styles of the 1930s are unflattering if you have a round tummy or a full bust.
3. *Be realistic.* Don't go into a vintage dress shop hoping to be turned into, say, Audrey Hepburn in *Breakfast at Tiffany's*. That style may very well not suit you, and you might miss something fabulous that *would*.
4. *Watch the sizing.* Vintage clothing tends to run small, because in years gone by women were smaller. So if the label says that it's a 10, it's more likely to be an 8 or even a 6. The best thing is to ignore the number on the label and hold the garment up to you.
5. *Don't be squeamish!* The garment may have the odd tiny mark or stain, but it's all part of the garment's history and is a small price

to pay for owning something that is beautiful, highly individual, and may even bear an iconic name.

6. *Check the overall condition of the garment.* Look for moth holes by holding it up to the light; check for underarm stains, which are almost impossible to eradicate except with washing, and not always then. If the garment is going to need serious cleaning, then it's probably best avoided, as the cleaning may not work and might even wreck it—for example, glass sequins and Bakelite buckles can melt or crack.

7. *Know how to store the garments.* Put anything moth-prone in a tightly sealed clear plastic cover. Don't hang satin and lace dresses—fold them between tissue paper and lay them carefully in a drawer.

8. *Air the garments outside.* Vintage clothes can have a mustiness; hang them outside for a while to eradicate it. Wherever possible, wash the garment, and always iron it inside-out, or through a clean damp cloth.

9. *If you're buying vintage as an investment, then buy the best you can afford.* This means buying clothes that have a designer or couture label. Anything by Chanel, Givenchy, or Dior will increase in value over time—as long as it's in good condition. So think *very* carefully about whether or not you're going to wear it—that drop of red wine could halve the garment's value.

10. *Learn about vintage* by reading books such as the *Antique Trader Vintage Clothing Price Guide* by Kyle Husfloen and *It's Vintage, Darling!* by Christa Weil. Visit vintage websites such as Zuburbia, Vintage Vixen, ModCloth, Rusty Zipper, and Viva la Vintage.

A Guide to Vintage Clothing Stores
in Eleven Cities

BALTIMORE

Royal Vintage Clothing
2523 Gwynns Falls Parkway
Baltimore, MD 21216
(410) 523-8664

Forever Alice Vintage Fashions
3360 Greenmount Avenue
Baltimore, MD 21218
(443) 449-5670

Vanessa Vintage Treasures
1132 South Charles Street
Baltimore, MD 21230
(410) 752-3224

BOSTON

Bobby from Boston
19 Thayer Street
Boston, MA 02118
(617) 423-9299

Charles River Street Antiques
45 River Street
Boston, MA 02108
(617) 367-3244

Closet Upstairs
223 Newbury Street
Boston, MA 02116
(617) 267-5757

CHICAGO

Silver Moon
1721 West North Avenue
Chicago, IL 60622
(773) 235-5797

Shangri-La Vintage
1952 West Roscoe Street
Chicago, IL 60657
(773) 348-5090

Hubba Hubba
3309 North Clark Street
Chicago, IL 60657
(773) 477-1414

DALLAS

Ahab Bowen
2614 Boll Street
Dallas, TX 75204
(214) 720-1874

Bon Ton Vintage Clothing
Forreston Vintage Market
124 S. Highway 77 (at Main)
Forreston, TX 76041
(972) 483-6222

LOS ANGELES

The Way We Wore
334 South La Brea Avenue
Los Angeles, CA 90036
(323) 937-0878

Come to Mama
3015 Glendale Boulevard
Los Angeles, CA 90039
(310) 625-8167

Decades
8214 Melrose Avenue
Los Angeles, CA 90046
(323) 655-0223

MIAMI

Miami Twice
6562 Bird Road/6562 Southwest 40th Street
Miami, FL 33155
(305) 666-0127

Sasparilla
1630 Pennsylvania Avenue
Miami Beach, FL 33139
(305) 532-6611

Fly Boutique
650 Lincoln Road
Miami Beach, FL 33139
(305) 604-8508

NEW YORK

The Family Jewels
130 West 23rd Street
New York, NY 10011
(212) 633-6020

Hooti Couture
321 Flatbush Avenue
Brooklyn, NY 11217
(718) 857-1977

PHILADELPHIA

Antiquarian's Delight
615 South 6th Street
Philadelphia, PA 19147
(215) 592-0256

SAN FRANCISCO

Aaardvark's Odd Ark
1501 Haight Street
San Francisco, CA 94117
(415) 621-3141

Old Vogue
1412 Grant Avenue
San Francisco, CA 94133
(415) 392-1522

Buffalo Exchange
1555 Haight Street
San Francisco, CA 94117
(415) 431-7733

SEATTLE

Isadora's Antique Clothing
1601 First Avenue
Seattle, WA 98101
(206) 441-7711

Rudy's Vintage Clothing
1424 First Avenue
Seattle, WA 98101
(206) 682-6586

Red Light Vintage Clothing
312 Broadway Avenue East
Seattle, WA 98102
(206) 329-2200

WASHINGTON, D.C.

Deja Blue
3005 M Street, N.W.
Washington, DC 20007
(202) 337-7100

Mood Indigo
1214 U Street, N.W.
Washington, DC 20009
(202) 265-6366

Sylvia's Vintage Shop
2102 18th Street, N.W.
Washington, DC 20009
(202) 328-9882

QUESTIONS AND TOPICS FOR DISCUSSION

1. Phoebe's dream is to quit her job and open a vintage clothing store. Do you have similar dreams? What do you think stops people from realizing dreams like these? In what way does Phoebe overcome such limitations?

2. Many customers come to Phoebe's shop to buy vintage clothing. Did any of these customers particularly stick out to you for why they wanted something secondhand? What does vintage clothing mean to you?

3. Do you have a favorite article of clothing that has special meaning to you?

4. Do you agree with the line "Every dress has a history. And so does every woman"? Do you think the two are interconnected? Why do you think the author makes it specific to a dress?

5. Do you believe clothing has the power to heal? How?

6. What makes Dan both a good and bad match for Phoebe? What about Miles? Who is the more ideal match for Phoebe—Dan or Miles? Or neither?

7. Miles very abruptly defends Roxy from all allegations. Do you think his behavior is reasonable?

8. Phoebe has a comical, strained, but supportive and loving relationship with her mother. How do you think your own mother would react if you did what Phoebe has done?

9. Who achieves a stronger sense of redemption by the end of the novel—Phoebe or Thérèse? How does each woman put her demons to rest?

10. Katie is a wonderfully positive person in this novel—someone who works hard and saves up to buy the prom dress of her dreams. Do you see her as inherently more noble and deserving of the dress than a character like Roxy, who seems to have things handed to her?

11. Is there something that you are as passionate (and knowledgeable) about as Phoebe is about vintage clothing?

12. Do you think everything Phoebe accomplished would have been possible if she weren't single at the start of the novel? Do you think her lack of attachment helps free her of potentially negative outside influences? Contrast her with Keith's girlfriend, who is defeated at the beginning of the novel but, after shedding Keith, is "walking taller" in her new dress.

If you enjoyed *A Vintage Affair*,

read on for an early look at

The Very Picture of You

the beguiling, moving new novel from Isabel Wolff.
Coming from Bantam Books in fall 2011.

Richmond, England, July 23, 1986

"Ella . . . ? *El*-la?" My mother's voice floats up the stairs as I sit hunched over my sketch pad, my hand moving rapidly across the paper. "Where *are* you?" Gripping the pencil, I make the nose a little more defined, then shade in the eyebrows. "Could you *answer* me?" Now for the hair. Bangs? Swept back? I can't remember. "Gabri-*el*-la?" And I know I can't ask. "Are you in your room, darling?"

As I hear my mother's light, ascending tread I stroke soft bangs across the forehead, smudge them to add thickness, then swiftly darken the jaw. Appraising the drawing, I tell myself that it's a good likeness. At least I *think* it is. How can I know? His face is now so indistinct that perhaps I only ever saw it in a dream. I close my eyes, and it *isn't* a dream. I can see him. It's a bright day and I'm walking along and I can feel the heat rising from the pavement and the sun on my face, and his big, warm hand enclosing mine. I can hear the slap of my sandals and the click-clack of my mother's heels and I can see her white skirt with its sprigs of red flowers.

He's smiling down at me. "Ready, Ella?" As his fingers tighten around mine I feel a rush of happiness. "*Here* we go. One, two, three . . . " My tummy turns over as I'm lifted. "Wheeeeeee . . . !" they both sing as I sail through the air. "One, two, three—and *up* she goes! Wheeeeeeeeee . . . !" I hear them laugh as I land.

"More!" I stamp. "More! *More!!*"

"Okay. Let's do a *big* one." He grips my hand again. "Ready, sweetie?"

"I rea-dee!"

"Right then. One, two, three, and . . . *u-u-u-u-u-p!*"

My head goes back and the blue dome of the sky swings above me, like a bell. But as I fall back to earth, I feel his fingers slip away, and when I turn and look for him, he's gone . . .

"*There* you are," Mum is saying from my bedroom doorway. As I glance up at her I slide my hand hastily over the sketch. "Would you go and play with Chloe? She's in the Wendy house."

"I'm . . . doing something."

"Please, Ella."

"I'm too *old* for the Wendy house—I'm eleven."

"I know, darling, but it would help me if you could entertain your little sister for a while, and she loves you to play with her . . . " As my mother tucks a strand of white-blond hair behind one ear, I think how pale and fragile-looking she is, like porcelain. "And I'd rather you were outside on such a warm day." I will her to go back downstairs; instead, to my alarm, she is walking towards me, her eyes on the sketch pad. Quickly, I flip the page over to a fresh sheet. "So you're drawing?" My mother's voice is, as usual, soft and low. "Can I see?" She holds out her hand.

"No . . . not now." I wish I'd torn out the sketch before she came in.

"You *never* show me your pictures. Do let me have a look, Ella." She reaches for the pad.

"It's . . . private. Mum—*don't* . . . "

But she is already turning over the spiral-bound pages. "What a *lovely* foxglove," she murmurs. "And these ivy leaves are perfect—so glossy. And that's an *excellent* one of the church. The stained glass must have been tricky, but you've done it brilliantly." My mother shakes her head in wonderment, then gives me a smile; but as she turns to the next page her face clouds.

Through the open window I can hear a plane, its distant roar like the tearing of paper.

"It's a study," I explain. "For a portrait." My pulse is racing.

"Well . . . " Mum nods. "It's . . . very good." Her hand trembles as she closes the sketchbook. "I had no idea that you could draw so well." She puts it back on the table. "You really . . . capture things," she adds quietly. A muscle at the corner of her mouth flexes, but then she smiles again. "So . . . " She claps her hands. "*I'll* play with Chloe if you're busy, then we'll all watch the royal wedding. I've put the TV on so that we don't miss the start. You could draw Fergie's dress."

I shrug. "Maybe . . . "

"We'll have a sandwich lunch while we watch. Is cheese and ham okay?" I nod. "I *could* make coronation chicken—that would be *very* suitable, wouldn't it!" she adds with sudden gaiety. "I'll call you when it starts." She walks towards the door.

I take a deep breath. "So have I captured *him*?" My mother seems not to have heard me. I try again. "Does it look like him?" She stiffens visibly. The sound of the plane has dissolved now into silence. "Does my drawing look like my *dad*?"

I hear her inhale, then her slim shoulders sag and I suddenly realize how expressive a person's back can be. "Yes, it does," she answers softly.

"Oh. Well . . . ," I say as she turns to face me, "that's good. Especially as I don't really remember him any more. And I don't even have a photo of him, do I?" I can hear sparrows squabbling in the flowerbeds. "*Are* there any photos, Mum?"

"No," she says evenly.

"But . . . " My heart is racing. "Why *not*?"

"Because . . . there just . . . aren't. I'm sorry, Ella. I know it's not easy. But . . . " She shrugs, as if she's as frustrated by this as I am. "I'm afraid that's just . . . how it *is*." She pauses for a moment, as if to satisfy herself that the conversation has ended. "Now, would you like tomato in your sandwich?"

"But you must have *some* photos of him?" I persist.

"Ella . . . " My mother's voice remains low, but then she rarely raises it. "I've already told you—I don't. I'm sorry, darling. Now I really *do* have to—"

"What about when you got married?" I imagine a thick white leather album with my parents smiling in every photo, my father darkly handsome in grey, my mother's veil floating around her china doll face.

She blinks, slowly. "I *did* have some photos, yes—but I don't have them any more."

"But there must be others. I only need *one*." I pick up my heart-shaped eraser and flex it between my thumb and forefinger. "I'd like to put his photo on the sideboard. There's that empty silver frame I could use."

Her large blue eyes widen. "But . . . that simply wouldn't *do*."

"Oh. Then I'll buy a frame of my own: I've got some pocket money. Or I could make one or you could give me one for my birthday—"

"It's not the *frame*, Ella." My mother seems helpless suddenly. "I meant that I wouldn't *want* to have his photo on the sideboard—or anywhere else for that matter."

My heart is thudding. "But why *not*?"

"Because . . . " She throws up her hands. "He's not part of our *lives*, Ella, as you very well know—and he hasn't been for a long time. So it would be confusing, especially for Chloe—he wasn't *her* father—and it wouldn't be very nice for Roy. And Roy's been so good to you," she hurries on. "*He's* been a father to you, hasn't he—a wonderful father."

"Yes—but he isn't my *real* one." My face has gone hot. "I've *got* a real father, Mum, and his name is John, but I don't know where he is, or why I don't see him, and I don't know why you never ever *talk* about him." Her lips have become a thin line but I can't stop. "I haven't seen him since I was . . . I don't even know that. Was I three?"

My mother folds her slim arms and her gold bangle gently clinks against her watch. "You were four and a half," she answers softly. "So that was nearly seven years ago. But you know, Ella, I'd say that the person who *does* the fathering *is* the father, and Roy does every-thing that any father *could* do whereas . . . John . . . well . . . " She lets the sentence drift.

"But I'd still like a photo of him. I could keep it in here, in my room, so that no one else would have to see it—it would only be for me," I add quickly.

"Ella . . . I've already told you, I don't *have* any photos of him."

"Why . . . *not*?"

She heaves a painful sigh. "They got . . . lost . . . " She glances out of the window. "When we moved down here." She returns her gaze to me. "Not everything came with us."

I stare at her. "But those photos *should* have come. It's mean," I add angrily. "It's *mean* that you didn't keep just one of them for me!" I am on my feet now, one hand on my chair, to steady myself against the clamour in my rib cage. "And why don't you *talk* about him? You never, ever talk about him!"

My mother's pale cheeks are suddenly pink—as if I'd brushed a swirl of rose madder onto each one. "It's . . . too . . . *difficult*, Ella."

"*Why*?" I want to swallow, but there's a knife caught in my throat. "All you ever say is that he's out of our lives and that it's better that way and so I don't know what *happened* . . . " Tears of frustration sting my eyes. "Or why he left us . . . " My mother's features have blurred. "Or if I'll ever *see* him again." A tear spills onto my cheek. "So that's why—*that's* why I—" In a flash I'm on the floor, reaching under the bed, and dragging out my box. It has RAVEL printed on it and Mum's best boots came in it. I get to my feet and place it on the bed. My mother looks at it; then, with an anxious glance at me, she sits down next to it and lifts off the lid . . .

The first drawing in the box is a recent one, in pen and ink with white pastel on his nose, hair, and cheekbones. I was pleased with it because I'd only just learned how to highlight properly. Then she takes out three pencil sketches of him that I did in the spring, in which, with careful cross-hatching, I managed to get depth and ex-pressiveness into the eyes. Beneath that are ten or twelve older drawings in which the proportions are all wrong—his mouth too small or his brow too wide or the curve of the ear set too high. Then come five sketches in which there is no hint of any contouring, his face as flat and round as a plate. Now Mum lifts out several felt-tip images of my dad standing with her and me in front of a red brick house with steps up to the dark green front door, and a brown fence that's more like a railway track. Then come some bright poster colour paintings, in each of which he's driving a big blue car. Now Mum lifts out a collage of him, with pipe cleaners for limbs, mauve felt for his shirt, and trousers and tufts of brown woollen hair that are matted with glue. In the final few pictures Dad is barely more than a stick man. Underneath these I have written *dad,* but on one of them the first *d* is the wrong way round, so that it says *bad.*

"So many," my mother murmurs. She returns the pictures carefully to the box, then she reaches for my hand and I sit down next to her. I hear her swallow. "I should have told you," she says quietly. "But I didn't know how . . . "

"But . . . why didn't you?"

"Because . . . it was . . . so awful." Her chin dimples suddenly with distress. "I was hoping to be able to leave it until you were older . . . but today . . . you've forced the issue." She presses her fingertips to her lips, blinks a few times, then exhales with a sad, soughing sound. "All right then," she whispers. Her hands drop to her lap and she takes a shaky breath; and now, as the "Wedding March" thunders up to us from Westminster Abbey, she talks to me, at last, about my father. And as she tells me what he did, I feel my world suddenly lurch, as though something big and heavy has just slammed into it . . . .

We stay there in my room for a while and I ask her some questions, which she answers. Then I ask her the same questions all over again. Then we go downstairs and I fetch Chloe in from the garden and we all sit in front of the TV and exclaim over Sarah Ferguson's billowing dress with its seventeen-foot, bee-embroidered train. And the next day I take my box down to the kitchen and lift out the pictures. Then I thrust them all deep into the garbage pail.

ISABEL WOLFF was born in Warwickshire and studied English at Cambridge. She is the author of seven bestselling novels and is published in twenty-six languages. She lives in London with her family. Bantam Books will publish her next novel in 2011.

Unlocking Your Genetic History

*A Step-by-Step Guide
to Discovering Your Family's
Medical and Genetic Heritage*

Thomas H. Shawker, M.D.

Amy Johnson Crow, CG
Series Editor

RUTLEDGE HILL PRESS
Nashville, Tennessee

A Division of Thomas Nelson Publishers
Since 1798

www.thomasnelson.com

Published by Rutledge Hill Press, a Division of Thomas Nelson, Inc., P.O. Box 141000, Nashville, Tennessee 37214.

The following items mentioned in this book are registered trademarks or service marks: The American Board of Medical Genetics, The American Cancer Society, The American Society of Human Genetics, Board for Certification of Genealogists, Family History Library, Microsoft Visio, Microsoft Word, Microsoft XP, National Genealogical Society, The National Human Genome Research Institute, The National Library of Medicine, National Society of Genetic Counselors, Periodic Source Index, The United States Department of Energy Human Genome Program.

Library of Congress Cataloging-in-Publication Data

Shawker, Thomas H.
   Unlocking your genetic history : a step-by-step guide to discovering your family's medical and genetic heritage / Thomas H. Shawker.
      p. cm. — (National Genealogical Society guides)
   Includes bibliographical references and index.
   ISBN 1-4016-0144-8 (pbk.)
   1. Medical genetics. 2. Genealogy. 3. Medical history taking. 4. Health status indicators. I. Title. II. Series.
RB155.S44 2004
616'.042—dc22   2004006461

Printed in the United States of America

04 05 06 07 08 — 5 4 3 2 1

To Patty

Contents

Acknowledgments

FOREMOST, I THANK MY WIFE, PATRICIA O'BRIEN SHAWKER, CGRS, for her patience and support during the writing of "The Book." For months, it was the center of the family's life.

I also thank the members of the National Genealogical Society's Committee on Family Health and Heredity for allowing me "time off" to do this book, and I especially thank Anita Lustenberger, CG, CGC, and Thomas Roderick, Ph.D., for their review of the manuscript and helpful suggestions. I owe a debt of gratitude to the authors of the series for sharing their experience with me, especially Cyndi Howells and Ann Carter Fleming, CG, CGL, both of whom kept me informed of the progress of their books and thereby helped me to prepare mine.

Finally, a most profound thanks to the patients I have encountered. Over 80 percent of the patients I see daily have a genetic disease, including many of the diseases discussed in this book. Without exception, I have been amazed at the courage these individuals demonstrate, how they have accepted their fate and moved on with their lives. I am reminded every day how a simple change in one molecule, a change in one of three billion DNA bases, can profoundly affect a human life. If nothing else, I hope that this book opens readers' eyes to the reality of genetic disease and convinces them how fortunate they are to have won when the genetic dice were cast.

INTRODUCTION

Who Should Read This Book?

GENETICS, DNA, THE USE OF DNA TO IDENTIFY VICTIMS OF A CRIME, the discovery of new genes, the successful gene sequencing of the virus that causes SARS (severe acute respiratory syndrome)—not a day passes without a news head-line announcing some new genetic advance or discovery. Companies developing new tests or treatments based on genetics have become the darlings of Wall Street. Using the Internet, individuals are reading about the genetic underpinnings of many human diseases. Everyone has heard about DNA. Human genetics is no longer exclusively the province of physicians, scientists, or geneticists, nor is it solely con-fined to obscure medical and genetic journals. With the unraveling of the human genome, the sequence of human DNA, genetic advances are occurring exponentially. We now know that there are genetic roots to many of the common diseases that affect us, including diabetes, mental illness, cancer, and heart disease. We are dis-covering the influence of genes in our life, in the lives of our families, and in the lives of our ancestors.

Few would deny that we are at the beginning of a medical revolution. The 21st century will see a shift to genetic-based medicine. Medical care will improve as we understand the influence of our genes—which diseases we are susceptible to and how we respond to treatment. In this new century, genetic testing to determine an indi-vidual's predisposition to a specific disease will become commonplace. Gene therapy will replace defective genes. Changes in medicine, the rise in DNA databases, and the increasing use of DNA testing will profoundly affect our society. We will address new problems, such as genetic privacy, genetic discrimination, and the misuse of genetic information. You can help resolve these issues by understanding DNA and genetics. The best place to start is with your family's own health history.

The greatest barrier to knowing that someone might have a genetic disease is the lack of an adequate family health history. In today's very busy practice of medicine, few health care providers take the time to record a family health history when they see a patient. A family health history can be useful to make a diagnosis or may show that there is some genetic component to a disease. You can help; the more information you give to your doctor about your family's health, the better care you will receive. Your doctor can look for early clues of disease or for patterns of illness, and recommend an appropriate screening program. By compiling your family's health history, you help both yourself and your family.

To write a book describing the basics of genetics, discussing rare—and in some cases unpronounceable—diseases and making this information useful and relevant, is a difficult and challenging undertaking. Genetics, DNA, and genetic diseases are complicated subjects. This book shows you how to integrate a family health history into your genealogy; it shows you how to get the appropriate medical information and how to record and analyze your family's health by designing a medical pedigree. You will find that certain ethnic or geographic groups are at an increased risk for some genetic diseases, information for which you should search when doing your genealogy. You will also realize how important a role your family's medical history plays in your own risk of developing common diseases. We discuss many genetic diseases, some rare but interesting, some common, and some that need to be better known. Our tour through genetics includes the basics of genetic inheritance, an understanding of the structure of DNA, and how DNA tests can be used to support your genealogy. You will learn genetic terms such as mtDNA, STR, and SNP, terms that may be unfamiliar even to your medical doctor. You will also see how the techniques of DNA analysis have been used for "deep ancestry," to discover our origins. Because the field of genetics changes so rapidly, we direct you toward useful Web sites where you can find more information about this subject and keep up with the latest discoveries.

There is a lot of information in this book; it is not, nor can it be, "DNA Lite." DNA, genetics, and genetic diseases are by their nature complicated, but the knowledge gained can be rewarding and, in fact, can save your life. As you read, some of you will become interested in compiling and understanding your family's health history. Others will want to understand how to use DNA to supplement their genealogy. And there will be those of you who simply want to know more about DNA, how it is used to identify victims and criminals, how it is used to unravel human history, and how defective DNA can result in a genetic disease. To all of you, I say, *read on.*

CHAPTER 1

Ignorance Is Not Bliss: Know Your Family's Health History

GILDA RADNER WAS ILL. ONE OF THE ORIGINAL MEMBERS OF THE TELevision show *Saturday Night Live*, comic genius Radner did not realize that her body contained a ruthless ticking genetic time bomb—and it had just exploded. Somewhere deep in her pelvis, a single gene, a mistake, one that she had unknowingly inherited, was set in motion. A single isolated cell containing this mutated gene began unconstrained relentless growth, multiplying needlessly and destructively. A cancer was forming; a mass of cells unresponsive to the body's normal control had been created. Suffering from abdominal swelling, bloating, fatigue, and vague stomach pains that were initially thought by various doctors to be due to the flu or exhaustion, Radner was finally diagnosed with advanced ovarian cancer. Born in Detroit in 1946, she was then only 40 years old. Radner endured over two years of surgery, chemotherapy, and radiation therapy, only to die in 1989 at the age of 42. She could not know that her family history of ovarian cancer put her at a brutally high risk of developing the disease. Had the genetic and familial link of ovarian cancer been more widely known, had the significance of her family's medical pedigree been understood, and had the relevance of her ethnic heritage been recognized, she would have known that having an aunt, a grandmother, and a cousin who died from ovarian cancer and a mother who had breast cancer was extraordinarily significant to her own health.

Ovarian cancer is a silent cancer; growing slowly but relentlessly, it shows few symptoms until the disease is advanced. Early detection, however, can be curative.

5

While many ovarian cancers appear to arise spontaneously without a positive family history, some are hereditary. In general, a family history of ovarian cancer, especially if two or more close relatives are affected, is an important risk factor. We now know that at least two mutated genes, BRCA1 and BRCA2, predispose a woman to breast and ovarian cancer. These were discovered in 1994 to 1995, less than a decade after Radner's death. If a woman carries a diseased copy of BRCA1, she has a 65 percent chance of developing breast cancer by the age of 70 and a 39 percent chance of developing ovarian cancer. For BRCA2, the risks are 45 and 11 percent, respectively. About one in 50 Ashkenazi Jews, who trace their origin to central and eastern Europe, are known to carry abnormal BRCA1 or BRCA2 genes and are at increased risk for ovarian and breast cancer. Although Radner died before the BRCA gene mutations were discovered, given her family history, her early age when she was diagnosed, and her Jewish and Lithuanian heritage, she probably carried one of these genes.

A **mutation** is a permanent structural alteration in DNA, a change in its sequence or genetic code. It may or may not have any effect on an organism. A mutation can be characterized by the change in the DNA molecule or by its effect on the organism. Mutations may occur spontaneously or be caused by an agent such as radiation. Once the DNA is changed, all subsequent daughter cells will have the same mutation.

Family Health History

Few of us know our family's health history or have taken the time to compile and analyze it. For instance, not until age 60 did U.S. Secretary of State Madeline Albright, who was raised a Roman Catholic, learn that she came from a family of Czechoslovakian Jews. For some of us, our grandparents were born elsewhere, such as in Europe or Asia. How much do we know about their brothers and sisters living outside of the United States? Are you in contact with all of your cousins? Do you know the state of their health? We live in a highly mobile society, with relatives often scattered around the country. Do you know how they are doing? In Gilda Radner's case, while she knew her family's health history, she could not understand its significance to her own health. Back in the early 1980s, far less was known about the relevance of genetics to family cancers. The past two decades have seen a virtual explosion in genetic knowledge, information that may be significant to you and your family.

Breast Cancer Risk

Early onset of breast or ovarian cancer in multiple family members should raise suspicions of the presence of the BRCA1 or BRCA2 genes, especially if the family is part of a high-risk ethnic group such as the Ashkenazi Jews. But there are almost certainly other genes, yet to be discovered, that convey a cancer risk, as well. Environmental factors—such as a shared diet and a particular lifestyle—that affect the family probably also contribute.

As you compile your family's health history, you may be surprised that what seems to be an isolated disease actually affects several members of your family and therefore might put you and other members of your family at increased risk. For instance, if you find several family members with heart attacks, especially if they occur at a young age, you should realize that you might also be at risk. As genealogists have long known, it is important to research the whole family. Just as tracking the migration of a great-great-uncle might show you the location of your great-great-grandfather, so too might finding out the health history of a second cousin apply to your own health. Even if you are health conscious, eating a healthy diet and exercising regularly, you may still fall victim to your genes.

One Friday in 2002, Darryl Kile, one of the most respected pitchers for the St. Louis Cardinals, went to dinner with his brother the night before a baseball game against the Chicago Cubs in Wrigley Field. At approximately ten o'clock, he returned to the Cardinals' team hotel on Michigan Avenue. The following morning, two hours before the game was to start, the team realized that Kile was not present and called the hotel. Hotel workers had to force open the door, locked from the inside, to find the 33-year-old baseball pitcher dead in his bed. The 6 foot 5 inch athlete had appeared to be in perfect health. Kile had passed the team's spring training physical examination, including routine ECG and blood tests. The team doctor said he had no known health problems and was not on medication. Kile's autopsy revealed an 80 to

90 percent blockage of two of his coronary arteries by atherosclerotic plaques, so-called "hardening of the arteries." The coronary arteries are the arteries that supply the heart with blood and oxygen. It was assumed that the plaques in the coronary arteries blocked the blood supply to his heart and caused his death. His heart was approximately 25 percent larger than normal, indicating advanced and probably long-standing heart disease. During the previous spring training, the players, as part of their medical evaluation, had been given an extensive medical questionnaire that included questions about the family's medical history. Kile had made no mention of the fact that his father had died of heart disease in 1993 at the age of 44. Darryl Kile's death from a heart attack at 33 points out the importance of knowing your family's health history, knowing its importance to you, and sharing this information with your doctor. A family history of heart disease at an early age is one of the major risk factors for developing coronary artery disease. With early detection, coronary heart disease can be treated effectively.

Another athlete who also died prematurely and who also had a family history of early death from coronary artery disease was Jim Fixx. During the 1970s, jogging became an American pastime and, for some, an obsession. A completely new industry sprang up to provide supplies to runners and joggers. It was Fixx, the most famous jogger in America, who through his books almost single-handedly brought the sport of jogging to the American public. One day in 1984, while visiting Vermont, he went for a run and never returned. His body was found on the side of the road. At the age of 52, in peak physical condition, running 10 miles a day, Fixx had died on a run. An autopsy found three of his coronary arteries extensively damaged by atherosclerosis. His father had died of heart disease at age 43. With early diagnosis, effective treatment would have been possible.

Many less life-threatening, but nevertheless serious, diseases also have a genetic basis. If you are a woman and approaching menopause and you know that your mother and aunts had signs of significant osteoporosis, you might consider calcium supplements, exercise, and getting a base-line bone density study. A family history of psychiatric disorders could indicate that you are at higher risk for depression or bipolar disorder and that if you begin to show symptoms, you should seek medical attention. Having several close relatives who had heart attacks at an early age suggests that it is time to have your cholesterol checked. Heart disease, cancer, diabetes, Alzheimer disease, and any one of the thousands of specific genetic syndromes matter to you if they have occurred in your family. The more you know about your family's genetic history, the more you know about the health risks you, your children, and your grand-children face. Knowing your family's health history can be invaluable in helping you modify your lifestyle to prevent illness or to arrange for periodic monitoring by screening tests. For instance, if you know that type 2 or adult-onset diabetes is present in your family, you should keep your weight down and be aware of the early warning signs of the illness.

It Runs in the Family

Writing this book made me more aware of how often family health history is part of our everyday news. As I was typing one Sunday, I heard that the actress Katharine Hepburn had died. Listening to her biography on one of the cable news networks that night, I perked up when I heard that depression and suicide run in her family. We now know that the affective disorders, depression and manic-depression, do indeed have a genetic component. I was even more interested when it was reported that Hepburn inherited some strange neurological disorder. Apparently, by the 1970s, it was widely rumored that Hepburn had Parkinson disease. At the time of her last major movie, *On Golden Pond*, her head was seen to shake visibly. She repeatedly denied that she had Parkinson disease, describing it as the "family shakes" that "runs in my family."

Neurological or nervous system genetic diseases are complex. Many of them, such as Huntington disease or chorea, Parkinson disease, and Friedreich ataxia, are named after their describer. Some are well known and their genetics are understood; many others are obscure. I could not help wondering if the "family shakes" that Hepburn described was ever diagnosed. Was it one of the known neurological diseases, or does her family have some unique, unknown malady that has never been described? It "runs in the family" is exactly the description one hears when there is an inherited genetic disease.

Genetics

A hundred years ago in America, the major killers were infectious diseases. Today, while they are still dangerous and even threatening to make a comeback, most infectious diseases can be treated. Many are controlled, especially the crippling childhood infections such as diphtheria, whooping cough, and tetanus that killed so many of our ancestors' children. With the control of infections, with better nutrition and living standards, with good public health and sanitation, the major killers in America have shifted from the 19th and early 20th century infectious diseases to cardiovascular disease, diabetes, and cancer. More and more, we are beginning to understand the role of genetics in these more chronic killers. One in 20 Americans has a disease with a major genetic component. If you consider that cancer, cardiovascular disease, diabetes, and others, while having an environmental component, also have a genetic predisposition, then probably far more than one in 20 Americans are affected by their genetic makeup.

The Genetic Revolution

In addition to changing the practice of medicine, the genetic revolution will change how we relate to society. The privacy of genetic information, how it may be used by insurers and employers, and who has access to it are all issues that need to be resolved. An informed citizenry, comfortable with the basics of genetics, genetic diseases, and DNA, must help make the important decisions about how this genetic information will be incorporated into our society. Genealogists, by using and understanding DNA testing, may be the nucleus of this citizen expertise. Today, when I attend genealogy meetings, I am encouraged to see genealogists, with no scientific training, using such genetic terms as *SNPs* and *STRs*, and discussing the relative merits of a 12- versus a 24-marker test of the Y chromosome.

The end of the 20th century and beginning of the 21st is a turning point, a medical revolution similar to the one that occurred at the end of the 19th and beginning of the 20th century. Until the 1880s, physicians believed that disease was caused by bad air, filth, or some other environmental factor. The last two decades of the 19th century saw an enormous change come over medicine. With the discovery that bacteria caused disease, medicine left the dark ages. The causes of such dreaded killers as typhoid, cholera, malaria, and tuberculosis were discovered. Knowledge that bacteria could cause postoperative infections revolutionized surgery, as antiseptic surgical techniques were adopted. Treatment, however, lagged behind. Early in the 20th century, physicians could only stand by helplessly as they watched their patient die from a staph infection, waste away from tuberculosis, or succumb to malaria. With the discovery of antibiotics in the middle of the 20th century, physicians could finally act on the knowledge they had accumulated and begin to cure patients of their infections. We are now beginning a second understanding, the importance of our genetic makeup to our health. But like the physicians of the early 20th century, while in some cases we understand quite well the genetics of a disorder, we can't intervene to repair the genetic defect. We can only stand by and watch as a 40-year-old man who has tested positive for the gene that causes Huntington disease waits for his inevitable physical and mental deterioration.

DNA is the chemical molecule, inside the nucleus of a cell, that carries the genetic instructions for the growth and maintenance of living organisms. The **genome** is all of the DNA contained in an organism or a cell, which includes both the chromosomes within the nucleus and the DNA in mitochondria. Chromosome 22 was the first human chromosome to have its genetic code sequenced in 1999 by the Human Genome Project.

Human genetics was born at the beginning of the 20th century. Initially, its influence on medicine was minimal. William Osler's *The Principles and Practice of Medicine* had, by the turn of the century, become the most recognized and most frequently consulted textbook of medicine. A review of its 1,079 pages finds a 50-page section devoted to "Constitutional Disease," including some genetic diseases such as diabetes and hemophilia, as well as such nongenetic diseases as rheumatic fever (an infection) and scurvy (a vitamin deficiency). A review of the remainder of the book finds a few additional pages describing what we now know to be genetic diseases. In contrast, 72 pages are devoted to tuberculosis alone. Genetics continued to lag behind other medical advances during the early 20th century. But by the middle of the century, we discovered that the molecule DNA was the unit of heredity. Genetics began to advance rapidly, and 50 years later, the entire human DNA sequence, the human genome, has been decoded. As in the 19th century, the last two decades of the 20th century saw a profound shift in medical thinking. The field of genetics grew, many genetic diseases were defined, and many specific disease genes identified. Prenatal diagnosis and identification of individuals at risk are now possible for many important genetic diseases. The "final draft" of the human genome, our total and complete genetic material, was announced in 2003, on the 50th anniversary of the discovery of DNA by James Watson and Francis Crick. The decoding of the human genome, the DNA sequence of our 30,000 genes, promises to have as profound an effect on the practice of medicine as did the discovery that germs cause disease.

Clearly, there are many advantages to tracing your genetic history. But before you begin, you need to understand the concept of genes, developed long ago in a small monastery garden, and how some genes are recessive and others dominant, resulting in recessive and dominant diseases. These single-gene diseases have played a significant role in our history and remain important today.

CHAPTER 2

Dominant and Recessive Diseases: Our Genetic Inheritance

THE 1990 EDITION OF *STEADMAN'S MEDICAL DICTIONARY* DEFINES *DISease* as an "illness; a sickness; an interruption, cessation, or disorder of body functions, systems, or organs." This does not differ significantly from the definition of *morbus*, the 19th century term for disease given in the first American medical dictionary, the 1808 *Philadelphia Medical Dictionary* by John Redman Coxe, where a disease is defined as "a total or partial affection of the vital or animal functions." Today, we understand far more about the mechanisms of disease than Coxe did in 1808, and one of the things that we now recognize is the impact our genes can have on our health.

Genes and Diseases

Diseases can be categorized in several ways. Acquired disease is generally disease that is not present at birth but occurs during life. It may or may not have a genetic underpinning. Adult-onset diabetes is generally considered an acquired disease, but its predisposition is genetic. In contrast, congenital diseases are present at birth. They may have a genetic basis, but not all congenital birth defects are inherited; some can be acquired in the uterus. For instance, damage to a developing fetus, such as occurs when a mother contracts German measles during pregnancy, results in a congenital disease in that the damage is present at birth, but it is not a genetic disease. A genetic disease is caused by defective genes. It may manifest at birth or later in life. Most, but not all, genetic diseases are inherited. But trisomy 21 (Down syndrome), a genetic disease in which the patient has an abnormal number of chromosomes, is usually not an inherited trait. It is an imbalance in the genetic material of a specific child, usually related to the mother's advanced age.

Acquired diseases are generally not present at birth but occur during life. **Congenital diseases** are present at birth. Either may have a genetic component.

Genes are the basic unit of heredity. The concept that certain characteristics were inherited in discrete units was discovered 140 years ago by a monk named Gregor Mendel. Working alone in the garden of an Augustinian monastery, Mendel discovered the basic principles of genetics. Before his pioneering work, it was assumed that the progeny would be a blend of the parent's characteristics—cross a tall and a dwarf plant, and the offspring's height should be in between. Mendel planted garden peas to see whether that was true. He found that when he crossed a tall and a dwarf plant, all the offspring were tall. When he crossed these tall progeny with each other, he found that three-fourths of their progeny were tall but that one-fourth was dwarf, proving that the dwarfism trait had persisted through the generations. Mendel eventually postulated that some characteristics are inherited as discrete packages and that

The incidence of Down syndrome increases with increasing maternal age. Are there any genetic conditions that increase with an increase in the father's age? Several seem to be. For instance, the sporadic case of achondroplastic dwarfs and Marfan syndrome seem to occur more frequently when the father is older, suggesting that more mutations may occur with age in the father's sperm than in the maternal egg.

some of the packages were dominant over others. In the pea plants, tall was "dominant"; whenever it was present, either alone or with a dwarf package, the plant was tall. The plant would be dwarf only if it had the dwarf package alone and no tall package. Dwarf was "recessive." After 10 years of work in the monastery garden, Mendel presented his discovery in a single paper to the Natural Science Society of Brunn, Moravia (later Brno, Czech Republic), in 1865. Mendel's work was published in an obscure journal in 1866 and then forgotten until it was rediscovered in 1900.

The word *gene* was coined in 1906 to name the discrete units of heredity that Mendel had found. Because of Mendel, who is now considered the father of genetics, scientists understood the function of genes long before they understood their actual structure. Today, we know that genes are discrete sections of the DNA molecule found on chromosomes.

Your body is made up of cells. Each has a specific function—muscle cells contract, red blood cells carry oxygen, and lung cells exchange oxygen and carbon dioxide from the blood. Within most of the cells of your body is a nucleus, and within each nucleus are chromosomes (see Figure 2.1). These threadlike chromosomes can be seen with an ordinary microscope. Each cell in your body with a nucleus has the same identical set of chromosomes. You have 23 pairs of chromosomes in the nucleus of your cells, a total of 46 chromosomes. One chromosome in each pair comes from your mother and one from your father. Each cell in your body, whether a white blood cell or a liver cell, contains a complete copy of your genetic makeup, a complete set of all the chromosomes. One of these 23 pairs of chromosomes is the sex chromosomes, whose makeup determines whether the individual will be male (XY) or female (XX). The remaining 22 pairs are called autosomes. Because chromosomes are paired, you carry two copies of each gene, located on a chromosome at a specific point (the locus). The genes may or may not be identical on the two chromosomes. A gene can exist in many different forms; these different forms are called alleles.

> **Genes** are the functional and physical unit of heredity passed from parent to offspring. Genes are sections of the DNA molecule and contain the information for making a specific protein.

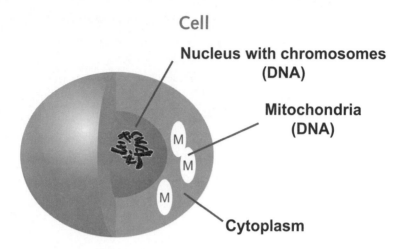

Figure 2.1 Diagram of a typical human cell showing the cell nucleus with threadlike chromosomes containing DNA. Note that there is also DNA in the cytoplasm outside the nucleus in structures called mitochondria.

Chromosomes are the threadlike "packages" of genes consisting of DNA in the nucleus of a cell. Chromosomes were first observed in human cells in the 1880s. By 1916, scientists knew that chromosomes were the physical carriers of genes. It wasn't until 1956, three years after the structure of DNA was described, that researchers found that the correct number of human chromosomes was 46. Up until then, scientists believed that there were 48 chromosomes in humans. The number of chromosomes varies among species. Dogs have 78; cats have 32 chromosomes.

For instance, let's assume there is a single gene for eye color. It can exist as a blue-eye allele or a brown-eye allele. As with Mendel's tall and dwarf genes, the brown-eye gene is dominant over the blue-eye gene. You inherit one allele for each gene from your father and one from your mother. If the two genes or alleles are identical, the person is said to be homozygous for that gene. If the two genes are not identical, then the person is said to be heterozygous. When a gene has two different alleles, the convention is to symbolize the dominant allele with a capital letter and the recessive allele in lower-case. For Mendel's peas, the dominant tall gene is symbolized T and the recessive dwarf gene is t. Plants homozygous for the tall gene are TT, those homozygous for the dwarf gene are tt, and those that are heterozygous are Tt. For our example of eye color, Brown (B) is dominant over blue (b).

Figure 2.2 shows a chromosome pair with the gene for eye color. The single eye-color gene is in one locus on each of a pair of chromosomes. In Figure 2.3, we see that the genes for eye color are both blue; the individual is homozygous for the blue-eye gene and will have blue eyes. In Figure 2.4, the genes for eye color are both brown and the individual, who is homozygous for the brown-eye gene, will have brown eyes. Figure 2.5 shows a pair of chromosomes where there is a brown-eye gene on one chromosome and a blue-eye gene on the other. The individual is heterozygous, but because brown is dominant over blue, that person will be brown eyed. The blue-eye gene is recessive; it may not be expressed in an individual with a brown-eye gene, but it doesn't disappear. It can be passed on to that individual's offspring. This is why two brown-eyed individuals can have a blue-eyed offspring.

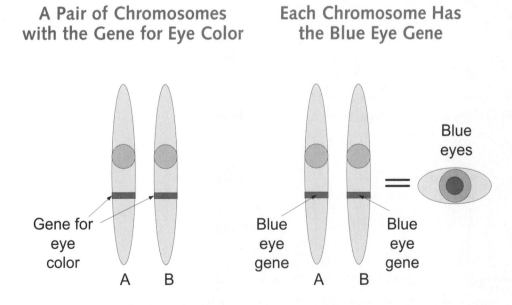

A Pair of Chromosomes with the Gene for Eye Color

Each Chromosome Has the Blue Eye Gene

Gene for eye color

A   B

Blue eye gene

Blue eye gene

A   B

Blue eyes

Figure 2.2 Pair of chromosomes showing the location of a hypothetical eye-color gene.

Figure 2.3 Individual with two blue-eye genes. The individual has blue eyes.

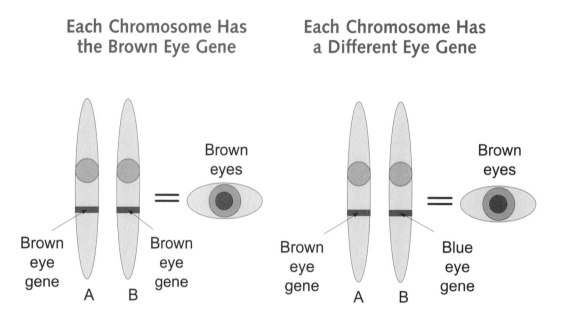

Each Chromosome Has the Brown Eye Gene

Each Chromosome Has a Different Eye Gene

Figure 2.4 Individual with two brown-eye genes. The individual has brown eyes.

Figure 2.5 Individual with a brown-eye gene on one chromosome and a blue-eye gene on the other. Brown is dominant, so the individual has brown eyes.

For the sake of simplicity, in our example we have assumed that eye color is controlled by a single gene; in reality, more than one gene controls human eye color. Eye, skin, and hair coloring occur on a continuum and are controlled by multiple genes. For eye color, the genes for dark are generally dominant over those for light.

Some genes have many types of alleles, some important, some inconsequential. A gene causing disease may be present on only one chromosome of the pair (heterozygous) or on both chromosomes (homozygous). Diseases caused by a single

Early-age baldness, a widow's peak hairline, facial dimples, freckles, and a cleft chin are some of the normal human characteristics that appear to be controlled by a single gene.

gene, for the most part, follow Mendel's laws of heredity. These are the Mendelian diseases.

Single-gene diseases are often expressed as dominant or recessive. Cystic fibrosis is a recessive disease. For an individual to have cystic fibrosis, both parents must have the gene and pass it on to their child. Figure 2.6 shows an individual with two copies of the recessive gene for cystic fibrosis. This individual will have the disease. Figure 2.7 shows the chromosomes of a healthy carrier carrying one copy of the normal gene and one copy of the cystic fibrosis gene. If an individual has only one copy of the cystic fibrosis gene, that person will not show the disease; just as our blue-eye gene is recessive, the cystic fibrosis gene is recessive to the normal gene. Since the cystic fibrosis gene is recessive, its effects are masked by the dominant normal gene and the individual is an unaffected carrier—he can pass the abnormal gene on to his children. This is the pattern seen in unaffected parents who have a child with cystic fibrosis. Both parents, although healthy themselves, have the recessive cystic fibrosis gene.

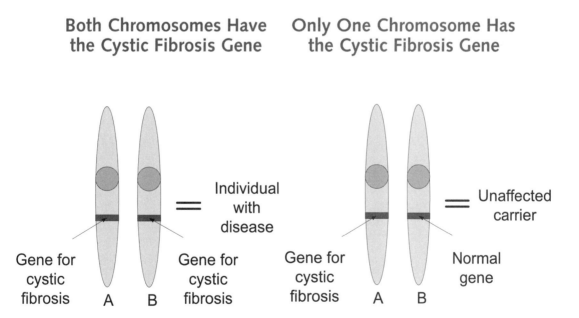

Figure 2.6 Individual with two copies of the recessive cystic fibrosis gene. The individual has the disease.

Figure 2.7 Individual with one copy of the recessive cystic fibrosis gene and one copy of the normal gene. The individual is an unaffected carrier.

Mutating Terminology

The terminology used to describe genes can be confusing. We frequently refer to a gene that causes a specific disease by the name of the disease—for instance, the *Huntington disease gene.* When we say that someone has the Huntington disease gene, we mean he has the mutation, or allele, that causes the disease. Some believe that this terminology is imprecise; since the specific variant gene at the Huntington disease location could be normal, they think the more correct term *Huntington disease gene mutation* should be used to indicate that someone has the mutated gene that causes the disease.

In another instance of tricky terminology, what we consider to be the normal gene is often referred to as a *wild type,* based on the assumption that organisms present "in the wild" do not have mutant genes. Keep in mind that there may be more than one type of "normal," or wild, gene; there may be many different types of normal variants (alleles) for a gene—just as, for some diseases, many different types of mutated alleles may cause the disease.

One Chromosome Has the Gene for Marfan Disease

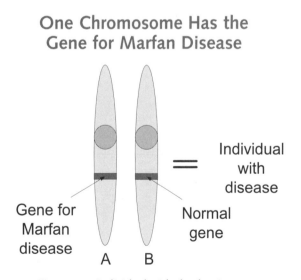

Figure 2.8 Individual with the dominant disease gene for Marfan disease. Only one copy of the Marfan gene needs to be present for the individual to show the disease.

Unlike recessive diseases where two defective genes are necessary to show the disease, in dominant diseases a single copy of the abnormal gene will show the disease. Marfan disease is a dominant disease where affected individuals are very tall, have thin, long fingers, and have chest and spine deformities. Figure 2.8 shows a pair of chromosomes from an individual with Marfan disease. Since the Marfan gene is dominant, only one copy of the gene needs to be present for the individual to be affected.

Recessive Diseases

The December 1848 holiday season was underway in New Orleans. On the dock, men struggled to unload the ship *Swanton* recently arrived from Germany. Disembarking were 280 German immigrants and one additional unwanted passenger, Asiatic cholera, a disease that causes massive diarrhea, leading to dehydration and death. Starting in central Asia and subsequently spreading to Europe, this worldwide plague had finally reached the United States. In New Orleans, 4,000 died in a few short weeks during that mild December. From there, cholera spread rapidly inland and up the Mississippi River on boats that were floating hells. One such boat, the *Peytona*, lost 50 passengers in a single trip between New Orleans and Louisville in 1849. Reaching inland, cholera waited to accompany the '49ers on their way to California to make their fortune. The bacteria, *Vibrio cholera*, quietly waited in contaminated wells, streams, and watering holes for the next group heading for California's gold. Many in search of their fortune drank and died, littering the road to California with wooden crosses or unmarked graves.

The disease spread widely; by the spring of 1849, there were 5,969 deaths in Cincinnati alone. Yet in the middle of this massive epidemic, there were some individuals who carried a recessive gene, making them relatively immune to the plague. There is preliminary evidence that carriers of the cystic fibrosis gene are protected from cholera's diarrhea since the gene blocks the action of the cholera toxin on the small intestines. Asiatic cholera struck the United States in 1832, 1849, 1854, 1866, and 1873, killing millions. It's possible that the relatively high prevalence of cystic fibrosis today is in part a result of evolutionary selection during the 19th century cholera epidemics; cystic fibrosis carriers selectively survived and subsequently reproduced, increasing the proportion of the recessive gene in the population.

Half of the 23 pairs of chromosomes are inherited from the mother; the other half from the father. If only one of the genes is "diseased" and the disease is recessive, the individual is said to be a carrier but shows no symptoms. Carriers of some recessive genes, especially the more common ones, may have an evolutionary advantage. Only when a person receives two defective or diseased genes, one from the mother and one from the father, can he show symptoms of the recessive disease. Carriers with only a single disease gene can lurk in any given medical pedigree, unknown and undetected, until chance partners that individual with another having the same recessive gene and an affected child is produced.

While the disease cystic fibrosis is seen only in those who have a pair of diseased genes, cystic fibrosis carriers seem to have some degree of immunity to diarrhea diseases such as Asiatic cholera. Today, one out of every 25 Caucasians in this country carries a copy of the cystic fibrosis gene; it is one of the most common fatal genetic diseases among Caucasians. Affected individuals with cystic fibrosis, those with two copies of the recessive gene, have abnormally thick mucus in the lungs and bowel, obstructing respiration and digestion. The gene regulates a protein that controls the movement of chloride (as in sodium chloride or salt) out of a cell. In cystic fibrosis, the abnormal lack of movement of chloride out of the cells in the lungs and gut leads to abnormally thick mucus. It also causes excessively salty sweat, one of the tests for cystic fibrosis.

Today, individuals with cystic fibrosis can live to adulthood, but for most of our history, this disease killed in infancy or childhood. If so many died before they could reach adulthood and reproduce, why did this abnormal gene persist? It is postulated that the gene sustained itself and spread because having only one copy conferred an evolutionary advantage. Individuals carrying only one abnormal gene resisted the numerous childhood diarrhea diseases that until the 20th century caused an enormous infant mortality. They also tended to survive the cholera epidemics that swept the U.S. in the 19th century, and they were relatively resistant to typhoid, another common disease of the time. Those who survived would live to reproduce and pass the gene on. The same defect that causes abnormally thick mucus in those with the disease would in its milder form protect those with only one gene from losing large amounts of fluid in the gut when attacked by bacteria such as cholera. Less fluid loss and less diarrhea results in less death by dehydration.

Some of the diseases transmitted by recessive genes seem to have some relationship to race or ethnicity; others are related to specific groups of individuals. An understanding of this relationship can be important to genealogists who are compiling their family health history. For instance, while cystic fibrosis is relatively common in Caucasian Americans, it is less commonly seen in African Americans, in part because the gene arose after humans spread out of Africa about 100,000 years ago. One of the most common recessive diseases in African Americans, however, is sickle cell anemia, a disease that produces malformed (sickle-shaped) red blood cells. Approximately one in 12 African Americans carries a copy of this gene. An individual with only one copy of the recessive gene is said to have "sickle cell trait" and does not show the disease. An individual who has inherited two sickle cell genes will have the disease. The sickle-shaped red blood cells may clog small blood vessels, depriving an organ or part of the body of blood, including vitally needed oxygen. Affected individuals have anemia, jaundice (yellow skin), and episodic pain in any organ or joint.

Although best known as a disease of African Americans, sickle cell disease is also found in those from Mediterranean countries such as Greece, Italy, and Turkey; from some Latin America countries such as Cuba; and from India and Saudi Arabia. All of these areas and Africa have one thing in common: they are all areas that currently have or previously had malaria. The malaria organism, transmitted by the bite of an infected mosquito, multiplies within human red blood cells. Recessive genes such as sickle cell disease change the shape of red blood cells, making them resistant to malarial infection. In malaria-infested areas, children who are carriers of the sickle cell gene and resistant to malaria have an evolutionary advantage; they can survive to reproduce and pass the gene on to their children. The recessive gene thus sustains itself over thousands of years.

Other types of anemia that also affect the hemoglobin molecule—the pigment found in red blood cells that carries oxygen—may show some resistance to malaria. The abnormal hemoglobin C is commonly found in western Africans. Hemoglobin C does protect against malaria to some degree. The chronic anemia, thalassemia, or Mediterranean anemia, first described in 1925, results from a recessive gene; it is seen in populations originating from the Middle East, Greece, Italy, Africa, India, southern China, Taiwan, the Philippines, and southeastern Asia—all tropical or subtropical areas that support malaria. Thalassemia ranges in symptoms from mild to severe. Today, it is estimated that over two million people in the United States carry the thalassemia gene. As with sickle cell disease, individuals with the thalassemia gene who live in malarial areas are relatively immune, especially to the most dangerous form of malaria. Thus, they survive and live to pass the recessive gene on to their children. Yet another anemia that seems to protect against malaria and is found in the same geographic distribution as sickle cell anemia and thalassemia is G6PD (Glucose-6-Phosphate Dehydrogenase deficiency), an X-linked disease that can cause severe anemia under certain specific conditions.

In the 19th century, it was generally understood that Africans were resistant to malaria (and thus made ideal summer field workers in the American South where malaria was present), but were especially susceptible to diarrhea disease. We know why Africans are resistant to malaria, but why does the cystic fibrosis gene have a lower incidence in Africa and Americans of African descent? Surely spoiled food in the tropics caused as much infantile diarrhea as in Europe. Tropical heat, however, also increases sweating. Individuals with the cystic fibrosis gene have increased salt in their sweat. It is postulated that in a hot climate such as Africa, the chronic loss of salt was more of an evolutionary disadvantage than resistance to diarrhea was an advantage.

The Founder Effect

While some of the more common recessive diseases seem to have persisted and become widespread because they conferred some evolutionary advantage, the vast bulk of recessive diseases appear to be detrimental. Every ethnic population has its own set of genetic predispositions—common genes that may lead to certain diseases. This is why it is important to document the ethnic groups to which your ancestors belonged. Recessive diseases can be seen in certain ethnic groups, in groups with a specific religious affiliation, or in groups of individuals living in certain geographic areas. This information can be an important clue in your family's health history. For those recessive genes found clustered in small groups, different mechanisms come into play. Most often, there is a founder effect. The founder effect is seen when small groups of people leave their homes or country to "found" a new land. The genetic makeup of the individuals in the founding colony may not be representative of the population they left and by chance may be carriers of some recessive disease genes. The result is loss of genetic variation since the new colony is formed by a very small number of

The Finnish Connection

Certain populations, such as those in Utah, Iceland, and Finland, have maintained extensive pedigrees and are small enough that they can trace their origins back to the original founders. Records of births, deaths, and marriages have been kept by the Finnish church since the 17th century. Tracking a rare recessive neurological disease called vLINCL, researchers led by Finnish scientist Teppo Varilo used genealogical techniques to show that the ancestry of all Finnish patients with this disease came from a small area in Southern Ostrobothnia, in western Finland, where there was probably a gene mutation that occurred 500 to 750 years ago.

individuals from a larger population and the frequency of these recessive disease genes may be higher than in the original population. A recessive disease present in a "founder" can then be propagated, especially if the group experiences some degree of geographic and cultural isolation.

For example, Tangier disease is a rare recessive disorder of cholesterol (an important type of fat) that was first detected in one single area of the United States, Tangier Island, Virginia. Affected individuals with both recessive genes of Tangier disease can have an enlarged liver and spleen and frequently have premature coronary artery disease. Even carriers of the gene may show abnormal changes in their cholesterol levels. Tangier Island, an approximately three-square-mile island in the Chesapeake Bay, was settled in 1686 by John Crockett and 16 families from Cornwall, England. In 1808, a Methodist preacher, Joshua Thomas, came to the island. Today, Thomas and Crockett are among the most common surnames on the island. The population remained small and geographically isolated; in 1960, there were 876 individuals on the island. While many left the island for a different life, possibly taking their recessive gene with them, few came to the island from the outside. Presumably, one or more of the 17th century founders possessed the recessive gene that was subsequently passed down to their descendants in this small closed community.

Genealogy is integral to your family health history. Imagine the following scenario: You are interviewing your family and filling in your medical pedigree. You find that your paternal great-grandfather was born in Virginia and died an accidental death in his late 30s. If you were only compiling your family health history, you would probably stop there. As a genealogist, however, you feel compelled to verify this fact. A visit to the census records finds your great-grandfather as a child with his parents in Virginia, on Tangier Island. Later census records find him in Richmond. Had you not done your genealogy, you would have missed his origin. You are now alerted to the possibility that your grandfather could have brought the Tangier disease gene from the island with him. This has implications for your family.

Settlement of eastern Canada by the French occurred in two waves. One group settled along the St. Lawrence River in the region that would later become Quebec. The other group, the Acadians, settled more to the east. Acadia was founded in 1604 by the small group of French settlers who settled in Nova Scotia. In 1713, the colony came under English control. Under English rule, these Acadians lived in cultural and geographic isolation. Trouble with the English government, however, led to their end; by 1755, the population of 13,000 French-speaking Acadians was dispersed for refusing to serve England. Their Louisiana descendants, the Cajuns, continued their isolation and today have a higher risk for some recessive genetic diseases, such as the hereditary ataxias, with such symptoms as unsteady gait and impaired coordination (Friedreich ataxia, Charcot-Marie-Tooth disease), infant or childhood deaf-blindness (Usher syndrome), and Tay-Sachs disease, where blindness, dementia, deafness, and seizures occur in the first six months of life.

Further west, the Saint Lawrence Valley was also settled by a relatively small number of individuals, about 14,000, starting early in the 17th century. They gave rise to the six million French Canadians of Quebec living today. Probably fewer than 3,000 of these early settlers account for over two-thirds of the modern gene pool. But the genetic effect of these early settlers is not geographically uniform; the eastern regions of Quebec have a higher frequency of recessive genes, including two rare neuromuscular disorders, than the western part of Quebec. The French Canadians of southwest Quebec, like the Cajuns in Louisiana, show a disproportionately high incidence of Tay-Sachs disease. The founder effect in relatively large groups may show non-uniform geographic distribution, especially, as with the French Canadians, if there is further migration within a small region.

In American Jews, the vast majority of whom trace their origin to eastern and central Europe and are known as Ashkenazi Jews, there are genetic diseases (such as Tay-Sachs disease, Riley-Day syndrome, Gaucher disease, Canavan disease, and Niemann-Pick disease) that are much more prevalent than in the general population. Tay-Sachs is a disease of the nervous system that causes children to die in infancy. Approximately 3 percent of Ashkenazi Jews are Tay-Sachs carriers. In the non-Jewish population, the carrier rate is approximately 0.5 percent. The geographic distribution of two of the Tay-Sachs disease mutations is not uniform. One mutation is more common in central Europe and is probably older than the other mutation, which is found almost exclusively in eastern Europe (for instance, in Lithuania and Russia). Three mutations account for 98 percent of Tay-Sachs disease in Ashkenazi Jews. In the United States, testing has markedly decreased the incidence of this disease.

Riley-Day syndrome occurs primarily in Ashkenazi Jews; it is estimated that about 2 percent are carriers of this gene. The disease causes infantile nervous system problems such as swallowing difficulty, diminished pain sensation, and seizures that generally lead to death in childhood. The relatively high prevalence of these recessive diseases in the Ashkenazi may be due to a type of founder effect. Jews in Poland were massacred in huge numbers in the 17th century. From the small remaining population, their numbers grew back in the following centuries, but the new population had only the genes of those original survivors, the founders.

Strictly speaking, the founder effect occurs when small groups of people leave their home to found a new colony. When there is shrinkage of a population in place, without migration, followed by a great expansion, the effect is called a population bottleneck. Like the founder effect, a population bottleneck can cause a defective gene remaining in the survivors to become more common in the replenished population than it was in the original. This effect, along with the subsequent cultural and in some cases physical isolation of the Jews in Europe, explains the persistence of these recessive genes in today's descendants. In both the founder effect and population bottleneck, the specific gene may convey an advantage; in others, chance alone is at play. Interestingly, there is some evidence that the Tay-Sachs gene also conveys a partial resistance to tuberculosis. Individuals who are carriers of this gene tended to survive the tuberculosis that was prevalent in the European ghettos and especially the tuberculosis that ran rampant in the Jewish ghettos of World War II.

A **founder effect** occurs when a small number of individuals leave to colonize a new area. Subsequent descendants can trace their origin, and their genes, to this small group. A **bottleneck effect** occurs when a population, either by natural disaster or deliberately (for instance, by war), is reduced to a small number of survivors. These survivors subsequently reproduce and multiply so that, as with the founder effect, subsequent descendants can trace their origins to this small group.

In both the founder and bottleneck effects, there is a reduction in genetic variation; if defective genes causing a specific disease are present in the originating small group, it can be disproportionately present in the descendants.

From the beginning, the original colonization of our country showed its genetic imprint. Although the best-known hemophilia carrier is England's Queen Victoria, the hemophilia gene was brought early to this country by those who founded its colonies. In 1803, hemophilia was first described by the Philadelphia physician John Otto as a bleeding disposition that existed in certain families and that only affected males. Today we know that it is an inherited bleeding disorder caused by a deficiency of a protein that causes the blood to clot. Hemophilia is a different type of recessive disease because the recessive gene lies on one of the sex chromosomes. In general, females are disease-free carriers and males have the disease.

Hemophilia in America

William Osler's medical textbook *The Principles and Practice of Medicine* printed in 1892 included hemophilia in the 50-page section devoted to "Constitutional Disease." He recognized the inherited condition of the disease and stated on page 320, "The hereditary transmission in this disease is remarkable. In the Appleton-Swain family, of Reading, Mass., there have been cases for nearly two centuries; and F. F. Brown, of that town, tells me that instances have already occurred in the seventh generation. The usual mode of transmission is through the mother, who is not herself a bleeder, but the daughter of one. Atavism through the female alone is almost the rule, and the daughters of a bleeder, though healthy and free from any tendency, are almost certain to transmit the disposition to the male offspring. The affection is much more common in males than in females."

In his notes of 22 May 1897, a Johns Hopkins medical student records his professor's lecture: "Hemophilia is the form of bleeding due to a general depravity that is constitutional and hereditary. In a bleeding family, the boys bleed but it is transmitted almost exclusively through the girls. In the Appleton's of Reading, Massachusetts, the bleeders can be traced back 200 years." Oliver Appleton of Ipswich, Massachusetts, was born in 1677 and, although a hemophiliac, lived to the age of 82, passing on his hemophilia gene. He was thought to have inherited his hemophilia gene from his mother Mary (Oliver) Appleton, who received the gene from her father, John Oliver. John Oliver, who migrated to Newbury, Massachusetts, from Bristol, England, in 1639, was probably the first hemophiliac in New England. This Appleton family hemophilia gene has been traced to the 20th century, through almost 400 years and 13 generations.

Other known pre–Revolutionary War carriers of hemophilia in New England included Susannah Shepard (1739–1813) in New Hampshire and James Hawley, who died at the age of four in Connecticut from the hemophilia gene passed from his mother Keziah Smith. Also in Connecticut, Sarah Hyde Collins, born in 1729, bore four sons, all of whom had hemophilia. Studies by geneticist and genealogist Thomas Roderick, Ph.D., show that 80 percent of those alive today in Maine with hemophilia B descended from one couple who settled in Cherryfield, Maine, in the late 1700s. This founder effect was passed down through the generations so that today the frequency of hemophilia B is equal to that of hemophilia A in Maine; normally, the B type is only about 25 percent as frequent as type A, the more common form of hemophilia.

One of the earliest newspaper accounts of hemophilia in America was an article in 1791 describing Isaac Zoll, a 19-year-old son of Henry Zoll, who, with others of German extraction, moved from Pennsylvania to Frederick and Shenandoah counties in Virginia around 1777. Five of Isaac's brothers bled to death. Hemophilia was unfortunately well represented in early America, but one peculiar difficulty for tracing X-linked recessive diseases in which the woman is the carrier is that it is easy to lose the carrier-women in history as they marry and drop their maiden surnames.

The Amish take their name from Jakob Ammann, a Swiss Mennonite Bishop who split from the Mennonite movement in 1693. The Amish began moving to America around 1720, with the Old Order Amish now found in Pennsylvania, Ohio, and Indiana. While not geographically isolated, they remain culturally isolated, marrying only within their group. Ellis van Crevald disease, where there are extra fingers on the hands, short stature, and often congenital heart disease, is found in high frequency in the Amish living in Lancaster County, Pennsylvania. This gene was traced back to Samuel King and his wife, whose name is unknown, who immigrated to eastern Pennsylvania in 1744. The Amish in Holmes County, Ohio, have a high frequency of hemophilia. Cases of PK (pyruvate kinase deficiency), a form of hemolytic anemia inherited as a recessive gene and characterized by the premature destruction of the red blood cells, is seen in those Amish living in Mifflin County, Pennsylvania, and Geauga County, Ohio, who descended from a single 18th century couple, Jacob and Ferona Beiler. Culturally isolated intermarrying groups allow a recessive gene to persist once it is introduced by a founder.

Although certain recessive genes may be contributed by the founders, other recessive genes may be notably absent. While multiple sclerosis is not thought to be a simple one-gene recessive disease and is probably controlled by multiple genes, there is some evidence that one or more of these genes may be recessively inherited. The Hutterite Brethren, an Anabaptist movement, consists of a closed religious community, similar to the Amish, who live in the four western Canadian Provinces and in the states of Washington, Montana, Minnesota, and North and South Dakota. From a small group of founders, probably fewer than 100, today there are over 30,000 individuals. The incidence of multiple sclerosis in Hutterites is lower than the surrounding population, suggesting that this recessive gene was not introduced into this closed population by its founders.

These are only a few examples of recessive diseases that occur in specific groups. Other examples abound. For instance, in the small isolated Appalachian communities of the western part of the Carolinas, there is increased incidence of a specific type of rare recessive muscular wasting (Charcot-Marie-Tooth peroneal muscular atrophy). In the Mennonite community in Pennsylvania, we find Maple syrup urine disease; the Amish in the same state show glutaric aciduria. Among the Native Americans, the Hopi show an increased incidence of oculocutaneous albinism II, and there is increased cystic fibrosis among the Pueblo and Zuni.

In other countries, we find a form of congenital blindness in Iranian Kurds who settled on the plains of northeastern Iran. In certain counties in northern Sweden, there is a high frequency of Gaucher disease type III, an inherited disorder with an enlarged liver and spleen, anemia, weakness, and seizures; the gene was introduced into the region by individuals living there in the 16th and 17th centuries. Among Afrikaners of South Africa, we find hereditary hemochromatosis and Fanconi anemia. In the French Canadian population of Yarmouth County, Nova Scotia, there is an unusual form of Niemann-Pick disease, type D, unrelated to the type found in the Ashkenazi Jews and thought to have been introduced to their descendants by Joseph Muise and Marie Amirault in the 17th century. The list goes on and on and is added to daily.

When compiling your family's health history, it is important not only to document the presence of specific diseases, but also to consider race, ethnicity, social groupings and patterns, and areas of habitation, all of which might have a relationship to a specific recessive disease and might suggest a recessive gene in your pedigree. Individuals carrying the recessive disease show no symptoms; the gene can hide in your family's pedigree. Properly done genealogy is essential in compiling a complete and accurate history of your family health.

Dominant Diseases

Unlike recessive diseases, in which two abnormal genes must be present for the disease to be seen, only one abnormal gene needs to be present for a dominant disease to be expressed. The disease is transmitted directly from one generation to the next by either parent, and generally, both sexes are at equal risk. Expression or severity of the disease may vary, and symptoms can be so mild that the disease may appear to "skip" a generation. In general, dominant diseases are milder than recessive diseases and tend to occur later in life. This makes sense if one considers how an abnormal dominant gene persists in the population. If the disease was severe and occurred in childhood, the affected individual would not live long enough to reproduce and the gene would disappear. Unlike recessive diseases, there is no true asymptomatic carrier state for dominant diseases, but some individuals who have the disease show only a few symptoms.

A gene is considered **dominant** if it almost always results in a specific physical characteristic, for example, a disease, even though the individual has only one copy. With a dominant gene, the chance of passing on the gene (and therefore the disease) to children is 50 percent for each pregnancy. In contrast, a gene is considered **recessive** if two copies of the gene, one from each parent, must be present to express the specific characteristic.

Dominantly inherited diseases can also occur in populations as a result of the founder effect. The Afrikaner population, or Boers, of South Africa are all descended from a small group of 17th century settlers, primarily Dutch, and some German and French Huguenots. A settlement was established at the Cape by the Dutch East India Company in 1652, and a small number of settlers arrived in the latter part of the 17th century. One estimate is that currently one to three million white Afrikaners are descendants of about 40 settlers and their wives. There are diseases in Afrikaners that are virtually absent in South Africa's black population.

One of these diseases is FH (familial hypercholesterolemia). This disease occurs worldwide and is one of the more common genetic diseases. In the United States, about one person in 500 carries an FH gene, meaning that as many as 500,000 Americans may be affected. Cholesterol, a type of fat needed for normal cell function, is delivered to the cells of the body by another chemical called LDL (low density lipoprotein). LDL and the accompanying cholesterol are removed by the liver. In FH, there is a defective gene for the liver LDL receptors with the result that cholesterol is not removed and consequently builds up in the body. A high blood level of choles-terol increases the risk of atherosclerosis, the accumulation of fat on the inner lining of arteries. Individuals with FH, therefore, will have abnormally high cholesterol resulting in early onset of atherosclerosis, coronary artery disease, and heart attacks. Because it is a dominant disease, if you have one copy of the gene (heterozygous) you will have elevated cholesterol and a high chance of having a heart attack starting in your 30s and 40s. By age 70, virtually all the men and three-quarters of the women with this gene will have had at least one heart attack. About one person in a million is homozygous, or has two copies of the dominant FH gene. Individuals who have two copies of this dominant gene have extremely high cholesterol levels and heart attacks in childhood and the teenage years.

FH is especially prominent in Afrikaners due to the founder effect. About one in 100 have the gene. The high incidence of FH in Afrikaners is probably due to multiple, not single, founder mutations of the gene. Three mutations are responsible for more than 90 percent of FH in Afrikaners. One of these, V408M, has also been identified in a group of individuals of Dutch origin in western Canada. This group can be traced back to Andijk, a small village in the northwestern Netherlands, the same region where some of the first colonists left in the 17th and 18th centuries to settle South Africa. Almost certainly, the gene originated there and was introduced into both South Africa and western Canada.

Another dominant disease seen in high incidence in the three to four million Afrikaners is VP (variegate porphyria). VP causes darkening of the skin, increased body hair, acute attacks of abdominal pain, constipation, rapid heart rate, and vary-ing degrees of disorientation and mental disturbances. There may be a severe reaction to barbiturate anesthetics. The high incidence of VP seen in white South Africans is a result of the founder effect. According to one estimate, about 8,000 individuals in South Africa have porphyria inherited from either the Dutch settler Gerrit Jansz or his wife, Ariaantje Jacobs, who was sent from an orphanage in Rotterdam as part of a pro-gram to provide wives for the Dutch settlers of the Cape in the late 17th century. VP is also seen with increased frequency in Finland.

Mad King George

Another type of porphyria played a crucial role in the quest for America's independ-ence from Britain. George III became king of Britain in 1760. He was thought to be mad; many believe that he suffered from the dominant disease AIP (acute intermittent porphyria). When George III succeeded his grandfather and ascended the throne in 1760, Britain was a world power with a loyal American colony. Twenty years later, America was winning its freedom and England's politics were in shambles. George's reign also saw problems with France, Ireland, Canada, Australia, and India. For years, George III suffered from periodic attacks of abdominal cramps, irritability, hallucinations, delusions, and unintelligible speech. "Mad George" also passed urine the color of port wine, a characteristic of porphyria. Drinking exacerbates porphyria, but in the 18th century, alcohol was a customary treatment for many diseases and George was "prescribed" brandy. Ultimately, George III lost the most prosperous colony in the empire in a war that many at the time believed should not have happened.

George's porphyria can be traced to his grandmother, six generations removed, Mary, Queen of Scots. James I, Mary's son, was known to pass purple urine but otherwise was not severely affected. The gene passed from James to George I, then to George II, who passed it to his son, Frederick Prince of Wales, the father of George III. Of these affected individuals, only George III showed severe symptoms, a characteristic of the variable expression seen in many dominant diseases, where some individuals show severe disease while others show few or no symptoms. After losing the "colonies," in 1788 George III was forcibly bound in a straitjacket and confined to a mental asylum for a year. He recovered, but by 1810 he was judged insane, and he died 10 years later. His oldest son, the Prince of Wales, who ruled as Prince Regent until ascending to the throne as George IV at his father's death, is shown in a 1792 political cartoon as a corpulent, apparently dissipated, 30-year-old man surrounded by full and empty bottles of pills. Like his father, George IV had porphyria, but as with his grandfather, great-grandfather, and great-great-grandfather, the disease was relatively benign.

The Importance of Location

A particular type of muscular dystrophy, OPMD (oculopharyngeal muscular dystrophy) is inherited as a dominant disease. Beginning in adulthood, there is progressive difficulty in swallowing and the eyelids begin to droop. Although it has a worldwide distribution, OPMD has its highest incidence in French Canadians. Several genetic and genealogical studies have shown that all French Canadian cases of OPMD can be traced to a founder couple whose daughters migrated from western France to Quebec in 1634. The disease is also seen in Cajuns. Due to the historical links between French Canadians and Cajuns, a team of investigators consisting of molecular geneticists, neurologists, and genealogists reporting in the *American Journal of Medical Genetics* in 1999 postulated that the same founder existed for OPMD in French Canadians and Cajuns. Surprisingly, however, they found a different disease gene, or allele, in Cajuns. Cajuns with OPMD, as well as German and English affected individuals, have different disease gene alleles from French Canadians, which suggests that multiple founders have contributed to the disease.

The French Canadian OPMD is especially prevalent in the Saguenay-Lac St. Jean area of Quebec, Canada. Saguenay-Lac St. Jean (SLSJ) is a geographically isolated region 200 kilometers northeast of Quebec City. Settlement began in 1838 almost exclusively by Catholic French Canadians, who settled SLSJ primarily from another isolated region, Charlevoix, located east of Quebec City on the north side of the St. Lawrence River. Settlement started in Charlevoix in 1675, but because of the small amount of cultivable land available there, many moved on to SLSJ. The result was a strong founder population in SLSJ. Besides dominant genetic diseases such as OPMD, at least 13 recessive diseases, rare elsewhere, occur frequently in this small population. Interestingly, two other recessive diseases, Tay-Sachs disease and Friedreich ataxia, were apparently excluded from the founders; though highly prevalent in Quebec, especially southeastern Quebec, these diseases do not appear in SLSJ.

Why is all this information about genetic diseases occurring in certain populations important to genealogists? Just as in the earlier scenario in which we traced an ancestor to the small population of Tangier Island, let's imagine that you are interviewing your family and filling in your medical pedigree. You find that your paternal great-grandfather, at the age of 40, died in 1870 in California from "apoplexy," which generally means a sudden death, as from a stroke or heart attack. You search the census and find him living with his wife in California in 1850; by 1860, four children are listed, one of whom is your grandfather. Your great-grandfather gives his place of birth on the 1850 census as Canada and on the 1860 census as Quebec. He appears to have been born around 1830. Armed with the research, you either search the records of Quebec or hire a professional who is comfortable with the French records of that province. You find that he was born in Charlevoix. Apparently, at the age of 18 or 19, he left Canada for California, drawn as were many other '49ers, by the lure of California gold. If you were only tracing your family's genealogy, you might stop there, but as a genealogist compiling your family's health history, you investigate further.

Through a review of the genetic literature, you learn that Charlevoix and the Saguenay-Lac St. Jean regions are geographically isolated and have a concentration of several genetic diseases, including OPMD. Another dominant disease common to the region is FH (familial hypercholesterolemia). If you have one copy of the gene (heterozygous), you may have a high cholesterol level in your blood and an increased chance of having a heart attack at a young age.

Your ancestor died at age 40 of apoplexy, which could be a stroke or a sudden heart attack. Having researched your family's medical history, along with your genealogy, you are now alerted that there is a possibility your great-grandfather brought the FH disease gene from Quebec with him to California. He had four children. What were their fates? What about your great-grandfather's brothers and sisters? Did any of them die "suddenly" at a young age? Could the FH gene be in your family? Could it have been passed down to you?

Marfan Disease

Abraham Lincoln towered over other men, giving rise to speculation that Lincoln may have had Marfan disease, a rare Mendelian disease, affecting about one in 10,000 persons. Marfan disease is a dominant disease of the connective tissue; affected individuals are very tall and thin, have long thin fingers, and suffer chest and spine deformities. Affected individuals can sometimes show dislocation of the lens of the eye and are at risk for myopia (nearsightedness) and retinal detachment. The most serious feature is that the aorta, the major artery arising from the heart, is abnormal. When the disease is left unrecognized and untreated, death can occur from heart failure or rupture of the aorta, sometimes at a relatively young age. Marfan disease can arise spontaneously; about a fifth of Marfan individuals are thought to be new mutations. Expression of the disease varies, and an individual with the gene may show only a few features of the disease or may be severely affected. Early death from a ruptured aneurysm may be the only clue that this disease lurks in the family tree. Other serious consequences include heart failure from incompetent heart valves and poor vision, even blindness. Besides Lincoln, famous individuals who are thought to have had Marfan disease include the classical piano composer Sergei Rachmaninoff and the virtuoso violinist Nicolo Paginini. Long slender hyperextensible fingers can be an asset to a musician.

Paginini, who lived from 1782 to 1840 in Genoa, has been widely hailed as the greatest violin virtuoso of all time. He was described as tall and thin, with long, sinuous fingers apparently capable of such a wide range and independence of motion on the violin that it was thought he had undergone some surgical procedure to free up his fingers. In a world without electronic mass media, he was nevertheless a superstar celebrity due to his incredible musical talents, dissipated lifestyle, and obvious contempt for the masses. He made his fame and fortune from the violin, with outrageous exhibitions of showmanship and dexterity. But it was over 50 years after Paginini's death in 1896 that a Paris pediatrician first described the clinical features of Marfan disease.

We may never know for sure whether Paginini suffered from Marfan disease, but Lincoln is a different story. Even though he left no living descendants to test, there exist authentic memorabilia from that terrible night of his assassination—items still stained with Lincoln's blood. Many believe that proving one of our greatest presidents had a genetic disease would help to counteract the public's unfavorable attitude toward these diseases. Although it may be technically impossible with current technology, perhaps in the future we can test Lincoln's blood to find out whether he had Marfan disease.

Tall individuals with large hands can be assets in some sports. At 6 feet 9 inches, Chris Patton was the University of Maryland's upcoming basketball star. After he suddenly died while playing an informal game, an autopsy found a ruptured aorta from Marfan disease. The 6 foot 5 inch athlete Flo Hyman was considered the best American woman volleyball player ever. While playing in Japan in 1986, she was sitting on the bench after being taken out of the game for a routine substitution. Without warning, she fell over dead. An autopsy showed that 31-year-old Hyman had died of a ruptured aorta resulting from Marfan disease. Neither Patton nor Hyman knew they had Marfan disease; both were judged to be in superb physical shape.

Huntington Disease

Having written over 1,000 songs, including "This Land Is Your Land" and "So Long It's Been Good to Know You," Woody Guthrie is considered by many to be the father of American folk music. He was inducted into the Rock and Roll Hall of Fame in 1988, and in 1998 the United States Postal Service issued a stamp in his honor. A product of the depression, the dust bowl, and World War II, Guthrie, born in 1912, dropped out of school at the age of 14 and left his home in Oklahoma with his harmonica to become an itinerate musician. Over the ensuing years, his wandering took him to Texas, California, and New York. In the latter half of the 1940s, Guthrie began to behave erratically and had difficulty playing and remembering his music. He was found wandering aimlessly, lurching around with slurred speech. Believed to be an alcoholic, he underwent hospitalization for detoxification. Later, he was diagnosed with schizophrenia. Guthrie was finally correctly diagnosed in 1952 and spent his last years in and out of hospitals until he died in 1967 of Huntington disease, a dominant disease that had also killed his mother.

Huntington Disease

Huntington disease, or Huntington chorea, is named for George Huntington, a physician who described an unusual hereditary disease in 1872. He had treated several patients on Long Island who suffered from progressive mental deterioration and involuntary twitching movements. Some of the patients belonged to families that had been treated by Huntington's father and grandfather, both also physicians. George Huntington believed that the disease was brought to Boston in 1630 from Bures, a small village in Suffolk, England.

As Guthrie was growing up in the town of Okemah, Oklahoma, neighbors noted his mother Nora's occasional strange behavior. There were house fires, one in 1909, and another in 1919 that killed Guthrie's sister Clara. In 1927, Nora tried to set her sleeping husband Charley on fire. He survived, but she was admitted to a mental institution. She was later diagnosed as having Huntington disease and died in 1929 at the age of 40. Guthrie worried that his mother's disease might have been passed on to him. He may or may not have shared her diagnosis with physicians during his numerous hospitalizations.

Huntington disease affects one in 10,000 individuals and is more common in Caucasians than in African Americans or Japanese. Both sexes can be affected. Because the disease is dominant, a child with an affected parent has a 50 percent chance of inheriting the gene; if he has the gene, he will get the disease. The age of onset is highly variable, but the disease generally occurs in the 30s and 40s. Huntington is a progressive motor disability with the gradual development of involuntary movements and mental disturbance progressing to dementia. There is mental impairment, memory loss, personality changes, abnormal involuntary movement of the arms and legs (chorea), difficulty speaking, emotional disturbance, and seizures. The dementia and movement abnormalities are progressive and relentless; eventually, institutionalization is necessary. Death usually occurs about a decade and a half after the first symptoms of the disease appear. In 1967, Guthrie's wife, Marjorie, who cared for him during his deteriorating years, created the Committee to Combat Huntington Disease. It later became the Huntington Disease Society of America.

The Elephant Man, Joseph Merrick

Many of us have seen the 1980 movie *The Elephant Man* starring Anthony Hopkins and John Hurt. The movie depicts the heartbreaking story of the life of Joseph Merrick, a deformed individual who spent most of his years in a circus freak show in Victorian England. Born in 1862, as Joseph Merrick grew, parts of his body began to grow faster than the rest. The right side of his head enlarged, as did his right hand and arm. By the time he was in his teens, his right hand was so deformed as to be useless. The only work he could find was in a freak show. The right side of his head and nose were so overgrown that he was dubbed "the Elephant Man." In 1884, British surgeon Frederick Treves took Merrick to Whitechapel Hospital in London, where he lived for four more years. Merrick's head was so large and deformed that he had to sleep sitting up. One morning he was found lying down in bed, suffocated by the weight of his own head, dead at the age of 27.

The leading medical authorities of the day believed that he had elephantiasis, an infectious disease with which they were familiar from Britain's colonies in the tropics. But early in the 20th century, it was postulated that Merrick suffered from neurofibromatosis. First described in 1882, this dominant disease is not uncommon, appearing in one in 3,500 individuals. It is characterized by skin spots and skin tumors, but can have many other manifestations such as skeletal abnormalities and tumors of various nerves. The neurofibromas are benign growths that develop beneath the skin or in deeper areas of the body. The number of neurofibromas can vary from a few to thousands. Although the disease is transmitted as a dominant disease, it is estimated that about half of new cases arise spontaneously.

In 1988, after further review of Merrick's condition, it was postulated that instead of neurofibromatosis, he actually suffered from a rarer genetic condition, Proteus syndrome, first described in 1979. It is characterized by irregular growth of parts of the body, including the head, and by multiple lesions of the lymph glands. Its inheritance is not known; only isolated cases are seen.

Genes, chromosomes, and dominant and recessive diseases are all important basic concepts in genetics. In the next chapter, we expand our discussion of genetics to include inheritance and the more common diseases, such as diabetes, cancer, and heart disease.

CHAPTER 3

When Genes Go Bad

AN INDIVIDUAL HAS A DIFFERENT SUSCEPTIBILITY TO A GIVEN DISEASE based on his or her genes. Diseases can be arranged on a spectrum ranging from purely genetic diseases such as Huntington disease to diseases that are exclusively the result of the environment, such as those caused by trauma. In between is the vast bulk of human disease. Coronary artery disease, cancers, asthma, and other common diseases are a complex mixture of underlying genetic makeup and environmental factors such as lifestyle, diet, and occupation. Even infections have a genetic component because one's immune system, or how the body fights the infection, is determined genetically.

There are many types of genetic disorders or diseases:

- Chromosome diseases
- Single-gene diseases
  - Dominant inheritance
  - Recessive inheritance
  - X-linked inheritance
- Multifactorial diseases
- Other genetic diseases

Chromosome Diseases

Chromosome diseases occur when there is either a missing or added segment of part or all of a chromosome. This segment includes a large group of genes, and affected individuals usually have multiple problems. Almost every cell in your body has a nucleus, and within the nucleus are chromosomes. These chromosomes are composed primarily of DNA (deoxiribonucleic acid), the coiled spiral molecule that is the basic unit of heredity. When cells reproduce, the chromosomes and DNA are also replicated so that the two daughter cells have the same number of chromosomes (see Figure 3.1). There are 46 chromosomes (diploid) in every cell, arranged in 23 pairs of chromosomes. All of the cells in your body have the same 46 chromosomes with the exception of the cells of reproduction (gametes), the maternal egg and male sperm. By necessity, these have to have one-half the number of chromosomes (see Figures 3.2 and 3.3). Each has 23 chromosomes (haploid) so that when fertilization occurs, the normal number of 46, or 23 pairs, is present in the fertilized embryo.

Of the 46 human chromosomes, two are sex chromosomes, X and Y, which determine the sex of the child (see Figures 3.4 and 3.5). The pair of sex chromosomes for

Chromosomes—Division (Mitosis)

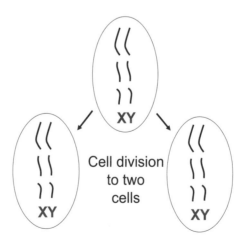

Figure 3.1 Diagram of a simple cell with four pairs of chromosomes. The XY pair indicates that this is a male. After cell division, the two new cells have the same number of chromosomes.

Males—Prior to Fertilization

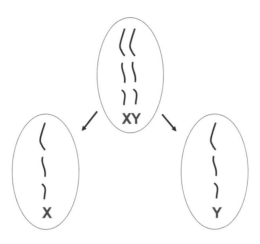

Figure 3.2 The halving of the number of chromosomes in production of the male sperm. In this instance, two sperm cells will be produced; 50 percent of the sperm cells will have an X sex chromosome, and the other 50 percent will have a Y sex chromosome.

Females—Prior to Fertilization

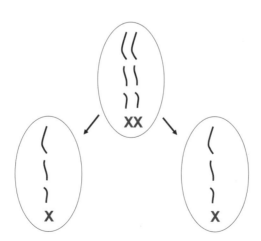

Figure 3.3 The halving of the number of chromosomes in production of the female egg. In this instance, two egg cells will be produced; 50 percent will have one of the original X sex chromosomes, and the other 50 percent will have the other X.

Necessarily, the human egg and sperm are **haploid**; each contains 23 chromosomes, half the normal number, so that the fertilized embryo contains the normal number of 46, the **diploid** number.

men is XY, for women XX. The remaining 44 chromosomes occur as 22 pairs. The 46 chromosomes are distinct and can be classified by their appearance and size, the human karyotype (see Figure 3.6). The process of determining an individual's chromosome pattern is called karyotyping. It is a photographic enlargement of the chromosomes arranged by size. Except for the sex chromosomes X and Y, the 22 pairs of remaining chromosomes, or autosomes, are numbered starting with the largest, number 1, and ending with the smallest, number 22. You have a chromosome number 1 inherited from your father and a chromosome number 1 inherited from your mother. Our closest living relative, the chimpanzees, have very similar chromosomes, but they

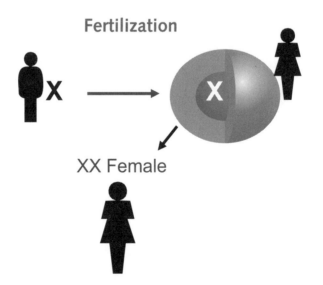

Fertilization

XX Female

Figure 3.4 A sperm containing an X chromosome uniting with the female egg. A daughter is produced.

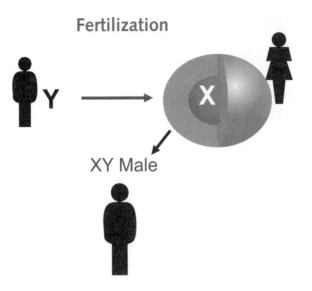

Figure 3.5 A sperm containing a Y chromosome uniting with the female egg. A son is produced.

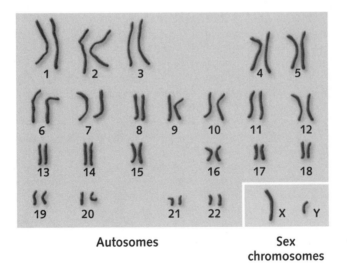

Autosomes

Sex
chromosomes

Figure 3.6 A karyotype of the human chromosomes. The 23 pairs are arranged from largest (pair 1) to smallest (pair 22). The pair of sex chromosomes (XY) is seen in the lower right. The X and Y chromosomes indicate that this individual is a male. (Courtesy of the National Library of Medicine.)

> An **autosome** is any chromosome other than a sex chromosome. Humans have 22 pairs, or 44 autosomes.

have 24 pairs whereas we have 23. It appears that our chromosome number 2 was produced during evolution by a fusion of two chimpanzee chromosomes.

A chromosome looks like a long tube with a single kink or constriction, the centromere (see Figure 3.7). The centromere divides the chromosome into two arms, a short arm designated *p* (for petite) and a longer arm designated *q*. For instance, the hereditary breast cancer gene, BRCA1, is found on the long arm (q) of chromosome 17.

In chromosomal disorders, there is either an excess or a deficiency of the genes contained in whole chromosomes or chromosome segments. During division, parts of a chromosome or an entire chromosome is either lost or abnormally retained. Since each chromosome contains thousands of genes, the loss of, for instance, half of a chromosome would result in the loss of hundreds of genes. Many of these losses or additions are lethal and incompatible with embryonic development. Chromosomal disorders account for nearly half of all miscarriages in the first few months of pregnancy. In general, the effects of a chromosomal disorder are seen in infancy. For live births, about seven out of every 1,000 are affected.

The most common chromosome disorder, and historically the first one to be described, is Down syndrome,

Each Chromosome Has a Short Arm (p) and a Long Arm (q)

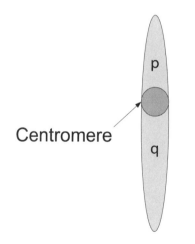

Figure 3.7 Typical chromosome showing a short arm (p) and a long arm (q).

named for John Langdon Down, who in 1866 was the first to characterize it. Superintendent of a home for the mentally retarded, Down noted that many of his patients bore a striking resemblance to each other. All had a flat face, a small nose, and most strikingly, narrow slanting eyelids so that they appeared "mongoloid." Almost a hundred years elapsed between Down's clinical observation and the discovery by a French geneticist, Jerome Lejeune, that individuals with Down syndrome had an extra chromosome. Instead of the normal two chromosomes numbered 21, there is an extra; thus, individuals with Down syndrome have three copies of chromosome 21, or trisomy 21 (see Figure 3.8).

Down syndrome occurs in approximately one in 800 births; its incidence is directly related to the age of the mother, rising as the age of the mother increases. It is thought that in older mothers, during the reduction in the chromosome number to form an egg, two instead of one chromosome 21 end up in the egg. On fertilization, the male contributes another chromosome 21 so that the fetus has three, or trisomy 21. At age 20, a mother's chance of producing a child with Down syndrome is about one in 1,500; by age 45, the mother's chance is about one in 30. In rare instances, a parent's two chromosome 21s become joined and a parent will continue to produce a child

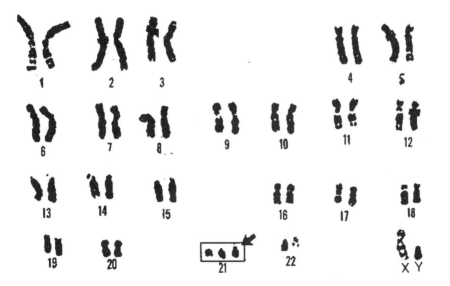

Figure 3.8 A karyotype of an individual with Down syndrome showing an extra chromosome 21 *(arrow).* (Courtesy of the U.S. Department of Energy Human Genome Program, *www.ornl.gov/hgmis.*)

with Down syndrome. A karyotype of the parents of a Down child should be performed if more children are contemplated. To detect a child with Down syndrome, a prenatal test is routinely offered to all pregnant women over the age of 35, an amniocentesis, in which a few tablespoons of the amniotic fluid surrounding the baby are removed and tested. Individuals with Down syndrome can have varying degrees of mental retardation and a distinctive facial appearance. More significantly, they can have major malformations of the heart and bowel. Most have some degree of hearing loss. The incidence of leukemia is increased in Down syndrome, and those with Down syndrome can develop symptoms of Alzheimer disease at an early age.

Though trisomy 21, resulting in Down syndrome, is the most common trisomy, other trisomies include 13, 18, and rarely 8, 9, and 20. Trisomies are generally severe; many such fetuses are stillborn or spontaneously aborted. Trisomy 13 and 18 cause severe, multiple congenital abnormalities in infants. Trisomy 13 children usually die within a month or two of birth; trisomy 18 children die within a year.

Conversely, parts of or even an entire chromosome can be missing. A missing chromosome, resulting in a total chromosome count of 45 rather than 46, is called monosomy. Except for an absent X chromosome, monosomy is so severe that it is rare in live-borns. Normal females have two X chromosomes. If one is missing, so that there is only a single X chromosome, the condition is called Turner syndrome. Women with Turner syndrome are short, have webbing of the skin of the neck, and are infertile.

Loss or addition of a chromosome generally occurs as a mistake in cell division. For example, trisomy 21 (Down syndrome) results when chromosome division fails to form the egg and instead of the normal one copy of chromosome 21 being present, both remain, with a third added from the sperm at fertilization. Other chromosome diseases involve additional or missing parts of chromosomes or rearrangements—deletions and duplication of parts of chromosomes; translocation, where there is transfer of a segment from one chromosome to another; and inversion, where a broken piece of a chromosome is reattached in a reverse direction.

Although they are genetic diseases, many chromosomal disorders are usually not hereditary and do not run in families. Some are hereditary and carry a predictable recurrence risk. If a chromosomal abnormality is found in an offspring, the parents should also be tested. If they are normal, then the abnormality is thought to have occurred in the sperm or egg and the parents do not have an increased risk of producing another child with a chromosomal abnormality. For instance, Turner syndrome is not hereditary and does not run in families.

Suspect a chromosomal abnormality when a child is born with multiple congenital abnormalities. Varying degrees of mental retardation and growth retardation are common. Other signs that there may be a chromosomal disorder include diseases of sexual differentiation, undiagnosed mental retardation, and a child from a mother who has a history of multiple miscarriages.

Single-Gene Diseases

In contrast to chromosomal disorders, single-gene diseases can become evident at any age. Although single-gene diseases are frequently diagnosed in children, some do not become apparent until adulthood. Since these diseases are caused by a change in a single gene, they are transmitted by Mendel's laws of heredity. Thousands of these single-gene diseases or syndromes have been identified.

Such Mendelian diseases are the best understood of genetic diseases. A dominant disease is expressed when only one copy of the diseased gene is present. A recessive disease will be seen or expressed only if both genes on the chromosome pair are diseased. As noted in the following table, the 23 pairs of chromosomes are further divided into those genes found on the single pair of sex chromosomes and those found on the remaining chromosomes, the autosomes.

	Dominant	**Recessive**
Autosome chromosomes	Autosomal dominant	Autosomal recessive
Sex chromosomes	X-linked or sex-linked dominant	X-linked or sex-linked recessive

Dominant Inheritance

For dominant disorders, the one abnormal gene may be contributed from either the mother or the father. The disease is transmitted directly from one generation to the next, and generally, both sexes are at equal risk.

Autosomal dominant diseases such as FH (familial hypercholesterolemia) generally result when one affected parent passes the diseased gene to the child. When one parent has an autosomal dominant disease, each child has a 50 percent risk of inheriting that

disease. A Punnett square is a graphic display of the contributions of each parent combined to show the genetic makeup of the children. By convention, the female gene pair
is listed on the top, the males along the left. In Figure 3.9, a Punnett square displays the
genes of the mother (Bb) and the genes of the father (bb), where B is the autosomal
dominant diseased gene and b is the normal gene. In this instance, the mother with the
Bb gene shows the disease. The boxes show all the possible combinations of how this
gene can be inherited in her children if she mates with a normal male (bb). Each child
has a 50 percent chance of inheriting the disease (Bb) or of being normal (bb). This does
not mean that if she has four children, half would be affected and half would not. The
probability is 50 percent for each child because each birth is an independent event. The
probability of having four children with the disease is the product of each child's probability: (½) × (½) × (½) × (½) = ⅟₁₆ or 6.25 percent.

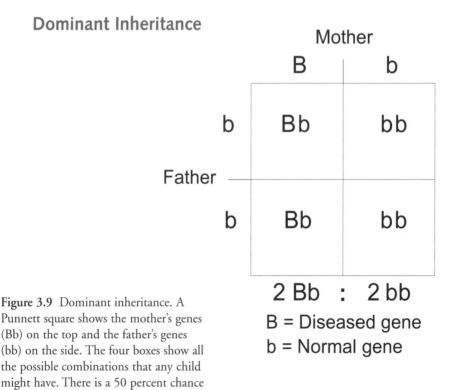

Dominant Inheritance

Figure 3.9 Dominant inheritance. A
Punnett square shows the mother's genes
(Bb) on the top and the father's genes
(bb) on the side. The four boxes show all
the possible combinations that any child
might have. There is a 50 percent chance
that any child will receive the B gene and
show the disease.

Generally, the more lethal autosomal dominant diseases kill early in life and the individual does not live to reproductive age to pass the gene on. An autosomal disease that kills young or is so severe that the individual does not reproduce tends to pass out of the population. Therefore, the appearance of this type of severe disease is due to a new mutation. Common autosomal dominant diseases are generally less severe than autosomal recessive diseases. For most, onset occurs in middle age or later (as in Huntington disease), both sexes are equally affected, and the degree of severity varies—some individuals with the disease are severely affected, others only mildly or, in some cases, not at all. This variability of disease expression is called penetrance. Some dominant disorders may exhibit incomplete penetrance and appear to "skip" a generation or the disease may appear to be an isolated new case of a dominant disorder. In this instance, the careful examination of close relatives may show that the abnormal gene is also present, ruling out a new mutation. Genes don't "skip generations"; they are there but perhaps not expressed so that the individual appears unaffected. Most often, affected individuals have only one dominant diseased gene. On occasion, especially if the gene is common in a given population, an individual can get two copies of the diseased gene. Generally, such individuals are severely affected.

Recessive Inheritance

For an individual to show symptoms of a disease transmitted by recessive inheritance, genes from both the mother and the father must be abnormal. Male and female children are at equal risk. In any given family, the disorder is mainly found in siblings, with the parents being unaffected carriers.

The Punnett square for recessive inheritance is seen in Figure 3.10. In this example, both parents are carriers (Bb), where *B* is the normal gene and *b* is the diseased recessive gene. There are three possibilities for the children: BB—completely normal; Bb—carrier; and bb—diseased. Each child has a 25 percent chance of being completely normal (BB), a 50 percent chance of being a carrier (Bb) like the parents, and a 25 percent chance of expressing the disease.

With some recessive diseases, the heterozygous individual or carrier may appear to be disease free but may actually be affected at a chemical level. In many recessive diseases, the carrier individual has one good gene and can produce only one-half the amount of an important chemical, but that may be enough to keep that person disease free. An affected individual without at least one copy of the normal gene will not be able to produce any of the important chemical and will show the disease.

Recessive Inheritance

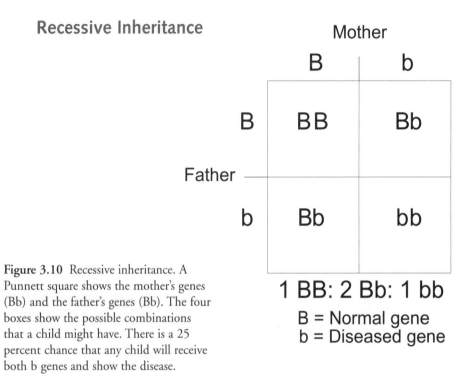

Figure 3.10 Recessive inheritance. A Punnett square shows the mother's genes (Bb) and the father's genes (Bb). The four boxes show the possible combinations that a child might have. There is a 25 percent chance that any child will receive both b genes and show the disease.

Recessive diseases appear at a younger age more often than dominant inherited diseases do; they may appear in infants and young children, tend to be more severe than dominant diseases, can occur more frequently in certain ethnic groups, and like dominant diseases, affect both sexes equally. Individuals who live in isolated groups, either geographically or socially, or two parents who share a recent ancestor (for instance, first cousins who marry) have an increased chance of carrying the same recessive gene and passing the gene to their children.

Recessive inheritance is the main problem with marriage between close relatives. Marriage between first-degree and second-degree relatives, such as siblings, parents, aunts, uncles, nieces, and nephews, is generally considered incest and is illegal. Marriage between third-degree relatives, most commonly first cousins, may or may not be legal depending on the state. First cousins share one-eighth of their genes—the genes they received from their common grandparents. The risk of first-cousin marriages producing a child with a recessive disease is actually minimal; for second-cousin marriages, there is probably no more risk than in the general population. But if there is a known recessive disease in the family or if the first-cousin marriage occurs within the environment of a small interbreeding community, the risk increases. Incestuous marriages—those between first- and second-degree relatives—do carry a relatively high risk of producing an abnormal child.

Conversely, the appearance of a child with a recessive disease to normal parents, especially if it is a rare disease, does suggest something about the parents. It may be just coincidence that two completely unrelated individuals happen to carry the same rare gene. It might also be that the two carrier parents have ancestors who lived in one of those areas where there is a high incidence of the rare disease due to a founder effect. Or the carrier parents may be distantly related to a common ancestor who had the rare disease gene. The appearance of a recessive disease has implications for genealogists. If there is a child with a rare recessive disease in the family, genealogists should search the parents looking for a common ethnicity, a common geographic area, or a common ancestor.

X-linked Inheritance

So far, we have discussed autosomal inheritance, that is, inheritance on the non-sex chromosomes. X-linked inheritance is another type of inheritance. Although Mendel did not recognize X-linked inheritance in his work with pea plants, it is considered Mendelian because it involves a single gene. In X-linked inheritance, the disease gene is found on the X chromosome, one of the sex chromosomes, and is transmitted from mother to son. This is the means of transmission for the X-linked or sex-linked diseases, the best known of which is hemophilia. Since the sex chromosomes, X and Y, also determine the sex of a child, the disease has a different manifestation depending on the sex of the child.

X-linked inheritance implies that the gene is located on the X chromosome. About 150 million base pairs are present on the X chromosome with approximately 3,000 to 5,000 genes. **X-linked diseases** (also called *sex-linked diseases*) are generally seen only in males; unlike females, males have only one X chromosome. If there is an abnormal gene, such as the one that causes hemophilia or Duchenne muscular dystrophy, it will be seen in males.

The Punnett square for X-linked inheritance is seen in Figure 3.11. A normal female has two X chromosomes, or XX. A normal male has an X and a Y chromosome, XY. While there are a few diseases carried on the Y chromosome, for most sex-linked diseases, the abnormal gene is found on the X chromosome. Women have two X chromosomes, so if one of these is abnormal—for instance, carries the hemophilia gene—the woman will not show the disease because the normal gene on the other X chromosome masks the influence of the abnormal gene. If a male, who inherits his single X chromosome from his mother, receives the abnormal gene, he will show the disease.

X-linked diseases are never transmitted from father to son; the mothers are carriers of the disease and can pass their defective gene to their sons. Daughters cannot be affected but stand a 50 percent chance of being carriers. Since males only transmit an X chromosome to a daughter, there is no male-to-male transmission. If an affected

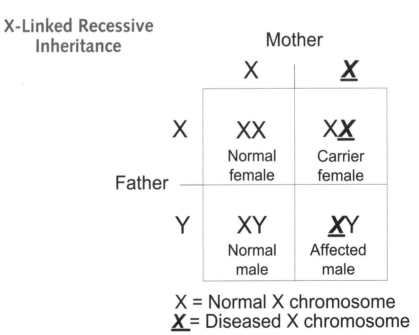

Figure 3.11 X-linked recessive inheritance. A Punnett square shows the mother's sex genes (XX) and the father's sex genes (XY). One of the mother's X chromosomes carries the diseased gene; 50 percent of the daughters will be carriers and 50 percent of the sons will have the disease.

male reproduces, he will transmit his defective X gene to his daughters, all of whom will be carriers; his sons will be normal. This carrier state for X-linked inheritance can give rise to the belief that the disease "skips" a generation. It does not; the gene is there. It is simply not being expressed.

Queen Victoria not only ushered in the Victorian age; her role in history was to introduce the gene for hemophilia to her descendants. Through her, the hemophilia gene spread through many ruling families of Europe. Hemophilia possibly arose as a spontaneous mutation in Queen Victoria, but more likely it arose in one of her parents and was passed to her. Since she was an only child, it is impossible to know. In any case, there is no record of hemophilia in Victoria's ancestors. Queen Victoria passed the hemophilia gene to one of her four sons, Leopold, who had mild symptoms and lived to father a female carrier before succumbing to the disease, and to her two daughters Beatrice and Alice (see Figure 3.12).

Inheritance of the Royal Hemophilia Gene

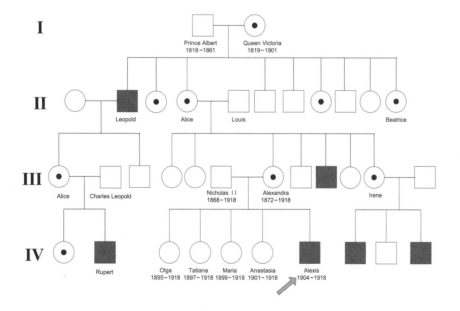

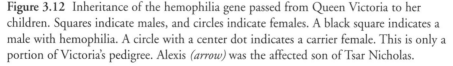

Figure 3.12 Inheritance of the hemophilia gene passed from Queen Victoria to her children. Squares indicate males, and circles indicate females. A black square indicates a male with hemophilia. A circle with a center dot indicates a carrier female. This is only a portion of Victoria's pedigree. Alexis *(arrow)* was the affected son of Tsar Nicholas.

Beatrice passed the hemophilia gene on to the royal family of Spain. Alice, born in 1843, was Victoria's second daughter. She married Louis IV, the Grand Duke of Hesse, and had two sons, one of whom died of hemophilia, and five daughters. One of the daughters, Irene, passed the gene to the royal families of Germany, and another daughter, Alexandra, passed the gene to the royal family of Russia. In Russia, the gene may have hastened the fall of the tsar and the rise of communism. Alexandra married Nicholas II, tsar of Russia, a Romanov. Their first four children were all daughters. In 1904, a son, Alexis (denoted by an arrow in Figure 3.12), was born but began to show bleeding shortly after birth. This was a time of turmoil in Russia. The parents' preoccupation with their afflicted child to the exclusion of the affairs of state and war, along with Russia's losses in World War I, combined to result in the overthrow of the tsar and the establishment of communism, thus shaping the political theater for most of the 20th century. Ironically, while a gene may have contributed to Nicholas's downfall and eventual death, genetics many decades later would help to identify his body and the bodies of his family (see Chapter 11, pages 221–224).

Most X-linked diseases are recessive; female carriers are generally not symptomatic but, on occasion, may have mild symptoms. In the extremely rare instance when the father is affected and the mother is a carrier, a daughter will receive two

Colorblindness

Red or green colorblindness affects approximately 7 percent of males. It is transmitted by X-linked inheritance, with the genes for red or green vision on the X chromosome. An absent red or green gene makes the individual colorblind. The gene for blue vision is found on chromosome 7; it is the rarest form of colorblindness and is not transmitted by X-linked inheritance. Women can also be colorblind, but they need the abnormal gene on both X chromosomes. X-linked inheritance should not be confused with the effects of sexual gender on the expression of a gene. For instance, male pattern baldness can come from either side of the family. It is probably inherited as a dominant trait, but has less penetrance in females, likely because of the difference between male and female hormones.

copies of the affected gene and show the disease. X-linked dominant disorders are rare. When they occur, the woman will show the disease since the disease gene on her X chromosome is dominant over the normal gene on the other X chromosome. Both males and females are affected, and the disease transmits similarly through dominant inheritance.

Single-gene diseases, transmitted by Mendelian inheritance as autosomal dominant, autosomal recessive, and X-linked, are some of the most important genetic diseases to understand. In the next chapter, you will see some typical pedigrees showing this inheritance, patterns that you can look for in your own pedigree. The Web site Online Mendelian Inheritance in Man *(www3.ncbi.nlm.nih.gov/omim/)* lists thousands of single-gene diseases, and more are being found every day.

Multifactorial Diseases

Chromosomal and single-gene diseases are relatively uncommon compared to the multifactorial diseases, which are the genetic basis for many common diseases of adult life. Multifactorial diseases have both a genetic and an environmental component in which there is a complex interaction between one or more genes with the environment. The genetic component is thought to reflect the cumulative effect of many genes; each gene is incapable of causing the disease alone, but together, the genes can form a genetic predisposition. The disease itself is not determined by the genes; they only determine its predisposition. There appears to be no certain set of genes predisposing to one type of specific disease, but rather it appears that many different types of genes can cause predisposition to the same disease. Diseases such as diabetes, high blood pressure (hypertension), coronary artery disease, some psychoses (severe mental illnesses), and many cancers are a complex interaction of many genes with the environment. These diseases

In **multifactoria! diseases,** a complex interplay of multiple genes and environment occurs. These diseases are distinct from **single-gene diseases,** which are transmitted by classical Mendelian rules of inheritance.

tend to occur later in life, are frequently chronic in nature, and may need the proper environmental stimulus to be seen.

Multifactorial diseases are familial but do not show the distinct inheritance patterns of single-gene diseases. The term *familial* basically means that a given condition is present in the family to a greater extent than that in the general population. There are familial diseases that are not genetic; for instance, black lung disease may occur in a family where all the males, father, son, and grandson, work in a coal mine. Some familial diseases—for instance, cystic fibrosis—have a well-understood genetic background. We usually don't call these familial since we understand the genetic inheritance. Familial diseases for the family health historian means that while we understand that there is some genetic component, the inheritance is not well understood. When the genetic inheritance is established, we tend to call it a multifactorial disease. When we are only assuming that there is some genetic component, we tend to call it familial. The distinction between *familial* and *multifactorial* is not precise, however, and there is a tendency to use the terms interchangeably.

In contrast to Mendelian single-gene inheritance with its well-understood rules of heredity and risks, assessing the risk of an individual for a multifactorial disease is much more difficult. You may be at increased risk, but that does not mean you will eventually get the disease. You may have not gotten the set of genes that puts you at risk, or you may not have been exposed to the specific environmental stimulus that would bring on the disease. For instance, type 2 or adult-onset diabetes may run in your family, putting you at increased risk. Knowing this, you may work very hard to keep your weight down and therefore avoid the disease. Alternatively, even though the disease is in your family, you may not have gotten the particular gene or set of genes that would put you at risk.

Normal human appearance can be considered as multifactorial traits. Skin color, height, and fingerprints are examples of complex inheritance. An individual may be genetically programmed to reach a certain height, but if there is poor childhood nutrition, that height may never be reached. The term *environment* when used in the context of multifactorial traits is defined broadly. For instance, the fingerprints of identical twins should be identical as they have exactly the same genes, but they are found to be different. It is thought that the ridge pattern of the fingers is altered by the "environment" of the uterus as the fetus during weeks 6 through 12 of development touches its fingers to the uterus.

Other Genetic Diseases

Other genetic diseases include those rare diseases carried on mitochondrial DNA (mtDNA), and those carried on the Y chromosome. Mitochondria are small ovoid structures in the cytoplasm of the cell that produce energy. There may be a few dozen to several thousand of these structures in a cell. They contain their own DNA, mtDNA. In general, the diseases carried on mitochondrial DNA and the Y chromosome represent a very specialized collection that the family health historian need not know. On the other hand, if you are doing genetic testing to support your genealogy, you will become very familiar with mitochondrial DNA and Y chromosome inheritance.

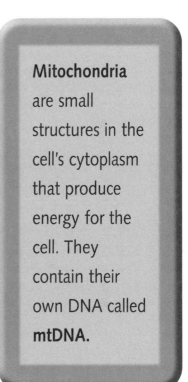

Mitochondria are small structures in the cell's cytoplasm that produce energy for the cell. They contain their own DNA called mtDNA.

The small Y chromosome does contain some functional genes, those largely responsible for "maleness." About 20 rare diseases have been found to be Y-linked, compared to about 250 X-linked diseases. Diseases transmitted by mitochondrial inheritance include some neuropathies (diseases of the nervous system), muscular abnormalities, and eye disorders; all are rare. The children of an affected mother will all have the abnormal mitochondrial gene, but only the daughters can pass it on to their children. This unusual inheritance pattern can be used to establish genealogy by testing normal mitochondrial DNA and tracing the maternal line.

Now that you understand the basics of genetics and inheritance, it is time to document the health history of your family. You begin the same way you began compiling your family's genealogy—by interviewing your relatives.

CHAPTER 4

Compiling Your Family's Health History

FAMILIES, A CONCEPT CENTRAL TO GENEALOGY, ARE ALSO FUNDAMENTAL to the field of genetics. If a disease has a genetic basis, it will occur in family members, it will "run in the family," or be a "family trait." So in addition to following the genealogical principles of naming ancestors in time and place, if you are a genealogist interested in your family's health, you need to add another dimension to your genealogy. You need to know the causes of their deaths and whether they had any serious illnesses.

Begin by doing your genealogy. Genealogists interested in their family's health history should compile a complete and accurate family pedigree first. Every individual must be included; assemble all the names of your relatives—parents, grandparents, uncles, aunts, cousins, and so forth. This requires the use of all the tools available to the genealogist: personal interviews; birth, death, and marriage records; census records; military records; passenger arrival records; and any other records. With each verifying document, the pedigree becomes more accurate. For some, a genealogy computer program may be helpful. You can produce a pedigree chart that you will then use to construct your family's medical pedigree.

As you interview relatives, find out about their health and the health of other family members. Design a medical pedigree, using the standard symbols recognizable to medical professionals (see Chapter 6). Finally, analyze the pedigree, looking for evidence of a family genetic trait. Compiling your family's health history should be done in conjunction with good genealogy. The more accurate your family's pedigree, the

Standards for Sound Genealogical Research
Recommended by the National Genealogical Society

Remembering always that they are engaged in a quest for truth, family-history researchers consistently

- Record the source for each item of information they collect
- Test every hypothesis or theory against credible evidence, and reject those that are not supported by the evidence
- Seek original records, or reproduced images of them when there is reasonable assurance they have not been altered, as the basis for their research conclusions
- Use compilations, communications, and published works, whether paper or electronic, primarily for their value as guides to locating the original records or as contributions to the critical analysis of the evidence discussed in them
- State something as a fact only when it is supported by convincing evidence, and identify the evidence when communicating the fact to others
- Limit with words like "probable" or "possible" any statement that is based on less than convincing evidence, and state the reasons for concluding that it is probable or possible
- Avoid misleading other researchers by either intentionally or carelessly distributing or publishing inaccurate information
- State carefully and honestly the results of their own research, and acknowledge all use of other researchers' work
- Recognize the collegial nature of genealogical research by making their work available to others through publication, or by placing copies in appropriate libraries or repositories, and by welcoming critical comment
- Consider with open minds new evidence or the comments of others on their work and the conclusions they have reached

more accurate your family's health history will be. Information obtained by genealogy—age at death, cause of death, ethnicity, place of living—can all be factored into a medical history of your family.

The Interview

You begin compiling your family's health history the same way that you began your genealogy: You interview your family. As many relatives as possible should be interviewed and preferably face-to-face. It is helpful to record your interviews on audiotape. Something a relative said may not seem important at the time, but as you compile your family's health history, it could take on additional significance. If you can't interview a family member in person, then conduct the interview by phone or, as a last resort, send an explanatory letter and a questionnaire by mail. Today, one's relatives may be scattered across the United States or even around the world. Fortunately, the Internet and e-mails are becoming almost universal and give us a tool to help contact our relatives. There are many Internet search engines that can be used to find mailing or e-mail addresses for "lost" relatives.

If you have physicians or nurses in the family, gravitate toward them. They should quickly understand the value of your project, may know about health-related problems in the family, and may be helpful in convincing other family members to

Ask Great-Aunt Mary

When compiling your family's health history, pay particular attention to the older members of the family. In fact, seek out the oldest members of the family first to interview. Genealogists in the dead of night, after a fruitless day at the archives searching for that long-lost ancestor, dream of just one hour alone with now deceased Great-Aunt Mary. If only they had paid attention when at family reunions, Great-Aunt Mary would ramble on about the old country and her parents. The same holds true for compiling your family's health history. The older members of the family know things about long-dead family members. They may know some family health tradition that has not been passed down to the family's younger members. As each generation passes, important information is lost.

participate. Some family members will not have any information or will want to remain silent about the family's diseases. On the other hand, you may also find that family members who previously expressed no interest in the family's genealogy will realize the benefit of compiling a family health history, and perhaps will realize then that there is some value to genealogy.

One approach is to hold a family reunion; this provides a better excuse for tracking down relatives than trying to obtain a medical history. Family gatherings or reunions are an ideal time to compile more of your family's health history. Planning and conducting a family reunion is outlined in Sandra MacLean Clunies's book in this series, *A Family Affair*. There are several approaches. You might broach the subject of diseases in the family to the group and see what comes up. Any disease themes that appear can be followed up later with individual private interviews with family members. Another approach is to present your case to the group, explaining why the family health history should be recorded and that you, as the family historian and genealogist, would like to compile and store that information. Following this general introduction, which will likely generate discussion and hopefully agreement as to its importance, you can hand out a medical questionnaire similar to the one included in Appendix A of this book, to be completed and returned to you (see Medical History Interview form on pages 270–271 and accompanying explanation).

Do not forget to talk to in-laws and close friends about the family members in whom you are interested. While non-relatives obviously do not fit into your genetic pedigree, they may be able to supply important medical information about your family member.

You are delving into a family member's intimate medical history, so it is imperative that you stress that all information will be kept confidential, even from other family members, unless it is urgent that they be informed. If so, you promise to get that family member's permission before revealing any of the information you have to other family members. Once you have the questionnaire, you can follow up any promising leads with a one-on-one interview with the family member.

Along with compiling your family's health history at a reunion, you might also urge your family to think about participating, as a family, in an organ or bone marrow donor program. The idea that the family can make a genuine contribution to its own health or to others should also increase their understanding about why compiling a family health history is so important.

In general, take a three-phased approach to interviewing your relatives.

First, explain why you want the information and how useful it could be to other family members. Explain the purpose of the interview: that you as the family genealogist would like to chart the medical conditions in the family. Be candid up front, explaining what you intend to do and why compiling the family's health history may eventually be useful and valuable to a grandchild, nephew, or niece. For instance, your grandparents may be reluctant to tell you about the medical history of their brothers and sisters, but when you point out to them that the information may be of value to the health of their future great-grandchildren, they may understand.

Second, ask open-ended questions about the overall health of the family. At least at the beginning of the interview, ask open-ended questions that require an explanation rather than a simple yes or no answer, such as, "What diseases or illnesses seem to occur frequently in our family?" Ask about any infant or childhood deaths, miscarriages, therapeutic abortions, or stillbirths. Be sure to ask about children who may have died in infancy. Infant deaths can be important but are seldom volunteered spontaneously. It is all too easy, for example, for your great-uncle to forget that his brother had a child 10 or 15 years ago who was slow to develop, had frequent seizures, and died at age two. Such family tragedies are frequently considered "best forgotten."

Ask whether there were any marriages into an ethnic group other than that of the family. Find out whether there were any sudden or unexplained deaths in the family. Ask what they know of the health history of deceased family members. Go through the list on the questionnaire one by one (see Medical History Interview on pages 270–271). This can get delicate; one needs to be careful how such questions are phrased. Remember, some individuals still find it distasteful to discuss such things as cancer or birth defects. For each deceased relative, ask about the cause of death, the death date, and age at death, and whether the family member had any major diseases, hospitalizations, or surgical operations. For all answers, get approximate ages when the event occurred.

Third, ask the individual you are interviewing about his or her own health history. Note the relationship of the individual to the remaining members of the family. Determine whether any degree of consanguinity, such as a cousin marriage, is present. Record the individual's age at the time of the interview, the birth date, approximate height and weight, serious diseases, hospitalizations, surgical operations, age of onset of any serious disease, ethnic origin, infertility or choice to not have children, and for women, record the number of successful pregnancies, as well as unsuccessful pregnancies—miscarriages, stillbirths, pregnancy terminations, or ectopic pregnancies.

Consanguinity is a marriage between individuals who are second cousins or closer. In some cultures, such as the Middle East and parts of Africa and South Asia, consanguineous marriages are the custom. Since both partners can have some identical genes inherited from a recent common ancestor, it does increase the chance that both individuals will carry the same recessive gene and pass it on to their children.

A Review of Systems

Go through what physicians call a "review of systems" for each individual, asking specifically whether they have ever had a problem in the following areas:

- General: overall appearance, height, abnormal appearance or number of fingers or toes, mental problems, learning disorders, treatment for mental problems
- Heart and blood vessels: heart attacks, strokes, high blood pressure, congenital heart disease
- Lungs: asthma, chronic lung disease, cystic fibrosis
- Stomach and intestines: peptic ulcer disease, gallstones, liver disease, chronic bowel disease, cancers
- Nervous conditions: epilepsy, senility, seizures, headaches, alcoholism, psychiatric problems, mental retardation

- Muscle, bone, and skin conditions: muscular disorders, osteoporosis, arthritis, skin diseases, Parkinson disease, Tourette syndrome

- Blood: bleeding disorders, sickle cell anemia, hemophilia, porphyria, other anemias, leukemia

- Kidneys, bladder, genitals: kidney disease, prostate cancer, reproductive system problems, and sex chromosome abnormalities

- The sensory system: seeing or hearing problems, facial abnormalities

- Hormone and metabolic conditions: thyroid disease, diabetes, allergies, autoimmune diseases

- Cancer

You can ignore the common childhood diseases such as chicken pox, measles, and mumps. They are of little genetic interest. Take note of serious infectious diseases such as pneumonia, flu, meningitis, or strep throat. While the diseases may have been serious and even life threatening, unless there is some underlying problem with the family's immune system, they have no genetic implications. They should be recorded, however; for instance, rheumatic fever as a young adult might explain a subsequent death from a "heart condition" and show that the heart condition was not due to a genetic disease.

Be Specific

It is important when interviewing and compiling your family's health history to be as specific as possible. For instance, you may be told that a 78-year-old uncle died of "bone cancer" when he actually had prostate cancer, which frequently metastasizes or spreads to bone. Someone described as dying from "brain cancer" might indeed have had primary brain cancer but could also have died from a metastasis to the brain from lung, breast, or kidney cancer. Because many, especially the older generation, feel that it is inappropriate to mention the word *cancer,* you may find a number of euphemisms such as "female trouble" or just that they "wasted away." A report of a woman having a "pelvic tumor" or "female tumor" needs to be investigated further. If the pelvic tumor is cancer of the ovary, this indicates an increased risk to other women in the family. If the pelvic tumor is cancer of the uterus, there is a different risk.

Family Legends

As with preparing your genealogy, beware of family legends. They are frequently wrong and need to be verified. For instance, my father always told me that his grandfather, my great-grandfather, was blinded in the Civil War. On investigating, I found that while he did serve in the Civil War, he was not injured. He became blind from cataracts 30 years later. Not only did he have cataracts, but also his son, my grandfather, had cataracts, and his son, my father, has cataracts. It is safe to say that this condition runs in my paternal line.

An 80-year-old individual dying of a "stroke" or, possibly more specifically, a "cerebral hemorrhage" means one thing; when a "stroke" happens to someone in his early 40s, it has a different significance. The 40-year-old may have bled from a brain aneurysm, from a brain vessel malformation, or from an abnormally high cholesterol level that might have genetic significance.

Some medical words are specific. Generally "dying of a heart attack" for an 80-year-old means essentially that atherosclerotic or calcium buildup in the coronary arteries, those that supply the heart, blocked the blood flow and deprived the heart of oxygen. The result is that part of the heart died, and the heart damage was severe enough to kill the individual. Synonyms that essentially mean the same thing include *myocardial infarction* and, although not strictly correct, *coronary thrombosis*. Other disease names are less specific. *Mental retardation, blindness*, and *epilepsy* are all terms that you may encounter, yet they are not sufficiently specific to use in compiling your family's health history. Mental retardation can have many causes, some genetic, some not. You would need to find out why that person was mentally retarded. Was the individual so affected that he or she had to be institutionalized? If so, where are the records? What was the diagnosis? Was it a chromosomal disease such as Down syndrome? Was it a recessive disorder such as Tay-Sachs or maple syrup urine disease? The appearance of these diseases can have a profound effect on your family's genetic burden. Was it some influence by the mother during the pregnancy such as heavy alcohol consumption resulting in fetal alcohol syndrome in the child or did the mother contract German measles during pregnancy? These have no effect on your family's genetic history. Therefore, it is important that you delve into any disease name and be as specific as possible.

Physicians name diseases in many different ways depending on their understanding of it. *Consumption* became *tuberculosis* once we knew that the tuberculosis germ caused this disease. For some diseases known primarily as a collection of symptoms or signs with no known cause, the name is descriptive, for instance, *essential hypertension.* For some, the name is based on an abnormal laboratory value, for instance, *hypothyroidism,* or a low level of thyroid hormone in the body. Other names, such as *Down syndrome,* reflect the name of the discoverer. Now that we know that Down syndrome is caused by an extra chromosome 21, the name for this condition is shifting to *trisomy 21* because of our understanding of the physical basis of the disease.

Always look for what physicians call the etiology, the cause of the disease. A person may be blind, but what is the etiology? Is it macular degeneration, diabetes, glaucoma, a childhood tumor, or trauma? You should also keep in mind that when discussing the cause of death, there is generally an immediate cause and an underlying cause. For instance, a man might be described as having died of pneumonia, a lung infection, when the information you really care about is that the individual had lifelong severe diabetes. You might hear that a relative died of liver failure or liver cancer when the individual's liver actually failed because of the extensive spread of tumor from cancer of the colon. When interviewing a family relation, ask about all the symptoms you can, including how long an illness lasted and whether the individual was hospitalized. With that information, you may be able to verify and support the cause of death.

As with all genealogy research, it is vital to document your sources. For a personal interview, your citation on the transcript, notes, or audiotape should be specific, as in the following example:

Interview with Henry Jones (Henry Jones, 123 Wall St., Bowie, MD 20715-4015) by Thomas Shawker, 21 June 2003.

Finally, a family health history must be kept up to date. Each year, update the family's health history to find out whether any new diseases have made their appearance or if a diagnosis for an existing condition has changed. New children may be born into the family. How is their health? As your family members get older, they may show a multifactorial genetic disease, such as cancer or diabetes.

As any genealogist knows, interviewing family members is only the beginning; information about family members should be verified. You should also document any statement about diseases or illnesses of family members. To do this, you need to investigate the medical records available to genealogists.

CHAPTER 5

Do You Speak Medicalese?

GENEALOGISTS DOCUMENT BIRTH, DEATH, AND MARRIAGE DATES, BUT genealogists are often not used to documenting significant illnesses or causes of death. Proper genealogical technique starts with the family interview. You do not record the death date of an uncle, as relayed to you by another uncle, as a fact. You verify it with the appropriate documentation. The same holds true for medical information. This is a problem for the family health historian; medical documentation can be difficult to locate and obtain.

In general, compiling a family's health history is 20th century research; while genealogists pride themselves on how far back in time they can take a given line, our goal is different. It is to account for every descendant from at least our four grandparents, and ideally, from our eight great-grandparents. If you can go further back in time, before the 20th century, and obtain accurate medical information, even better. The further back you go, however, the fewer medical records you will find and those that you can find might be less helpful either because the causes of death are inaccurate or simply because so many of our ancestors in the 19th century died of infectious diseases. In general, medical records in the 20th century are more reliable and easier to obtain than 19th century records, but every once in a while, a 19th century record can be of value.

Compiling a family health history by interviewing relatives is one thing; verifying the medical conditions by examining medical records is more difficult. There is no uniform policy for allowing access to medical records across the country or from institute to institute. What records may exist may be incomplete or inaccurate. State laws and hospital policies vary as to how long medical records are retained, and it is becoming more difficult to access such records.

Authorities require permission to release a medical record. This can be given by the individual for his or her own records or, if the individual is deceased, by an immediate family member or the closest living family member. The Health Insurance Portability and Accountability Act (HIPAA) that took effect in April 2003 makes it more difficult for the family health historian to obtain medical records. For instance, under that act, there are two mechanisms for a surviving family member to obtain the protected health information of a deceased relative. The first is when a living family member is under medical care. If a family member is receiving medical treatment, a hospital may release a decedent's protected health information without authorization to the health care provider who is treating the surviving relative. The second mechanism recognizes a deceased individual's legally authorized executor or administrator as the decedent's personal representative with respect to protected health information. That personal representative can get the medical information of the deceased or provide the appropriate authorization for its disclosure.

It is not this book's purpose to review the different types of genealogical records; several other books in the NGS genealogy series cover that subject in detail. The first book in this series, *Genealogy 101* by Barbara Renick, is an excellent introduction to genealogy and genealogical records. However, in the following sections, we discuss the records you should seek out and use when compiling your family's health history. Refer to Appendix A for a Medical History Records form (pages 272–273) that you can use to organize the medical information you find. This form should be used in conjunction with the Medical History Interview form mentioned in the previous chapter; detailed explanations of both forms are included in Appendix A.

Death Certificates

The most readily obtainable and useful medical record available to the family health historian is the death certificate (see Figures 5.1 and 5.2). Death certificates should be obtained on every deceased family member. How to go about obtaining vital records such as a death certificate is covered in other books in this series, but certainly a few comments about death certificates and how to understand them will be useful here.

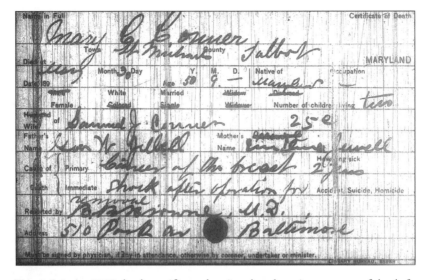

Figure 5.1 An 1890 death certificate showing that the primary cause of death for this 50-year-old woman was "cancer of the breast," and the immediate cause was "shock after operation for." (Courtesy of the Maryland State Archives.)

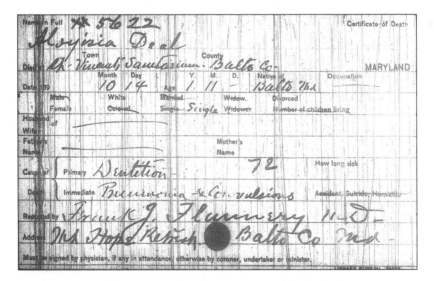

Figure 5.2 An 1893 death certificate for a two-year-old who died in a sanitarium. The primary cause of death was "dentition," and the immediate cause was "pneumonia and convulsions." While the cause of death is not significant, it is important that this two-year-old was so severely impaired that she needed to be institutionalized. Could she have had a severe genetic disease? (Courtesy of the Maryland State Archives.)

A death certificate is kept in the locality where the individual died, not where the burial occurred. The year that death certificates began to be used varies among localities. For most states, death certificates began to be used in the late 1800s to early 1900s. In New York death registration began in 1880, Maryland 1898, Ohio 1908, New Mexico 1919. At times these years may be misleading. For instance, Ohio kept death records, including the cause of death, in the county probate courts beginning in 1867.

Death certificates are not standardized across the country, and the information they contain varies from state to state. No two states use exactly the same death certificate form. Even within a given state, the death certificate itself has changed from an early version to the one currently used. There may be different death certificate forms used within a state. For instance, New York City uses a different form for death certification than the one used throughout the rest of New York State. Regardless of the form, all states require that the death certificate be registered and filed at the state level. You will occasionally find that death certificates are filed at the municipal or county level, as well. You should become familiar with the policies and procedures of the state in which you are interested.

Death certificates should be sought for all individuals in the family tree. If you do not have death certificates for your aunts, uncles, and cousins, get them. Even if you know the cause of death, get the record. To obtain a copy of any death certificate in the United States, you should write to or visit the appropriate office in the state in which the death occurred; generally, this is a state's vital record office. Older death certificates are often stored in a state archive or state library, and it may be necessary for you to search there. The Web can be most useful for this type of research. Vital record information, including where to write for death certificates, can be searched at *www.vitalrec.com*. That site contains information about where to obtain vital records from each state, territory, and county of the United States. It includes guidelines on how to order those records and includes links to Web sites for foreign vital records.

Many states and counties have indexes to recorded deaths. Some local genealogical and historical societies may also have indexed the death certificates for their locality and may publish their index as either a book or their society's periodical. The Family History Library of the Church of Jesus Christ of Latter-day Saints has also microfilmed death indexes for some states. Many are quite complete. For instance, the death indexes for California cover 1905 to 1988. Check the current Family History Library Catalog *(www.familysearch.org/Eng/Library/FHLC/frameset_fhlc.asp)* for the state and year in which you are interested.

Family History Library Catalog

For those who are unfamiliar with the Family History Library Catalog, it may be found online at *www.familysearch.org;* click on the Library tab. The catalog represents the holdings of the largest genealogy library in the world, the Family History Library. The Church of Jesus Christ of Latter-day Saints, also known as the LDS, maintains this repository in Salt Lake City, Utah. It has numerous library branches, the Family History Centers, around the world. Church volunteers have fanned out to every state in the country and many other countries, to courthouses, archives, and libraries, and photographed original material, transferring the documents to microfilm. These microfilms are available at the library in Salt Lake City and can be ordered at your Family History Centers. To find out what is available, access the online catalog, which is also available on CD-ROM.

The recording of a death certificate is begun by a licensed physician in the state in which the death occurred. This may be the family physician or, if the death occurred in a hospital, may also be a partner to the family physician or a house-staff physician, either of whom may be unfamiliar with the case. The attending physician may delegate the filling out of the death certificate to an inexperienced resident or intern who knows nothing about the deceased. The physician certifying the death will record the immediate cause of death and any supporting conditions and then sign the certificate. Most of the other information on the death certificate is filled out by the funeral home at the time arrangements are made for the funeral. It is the funeral director, not the physician, who is responsible for completing and furnishing the information to the appropriate authorities. The funeral home completes the death certificate by interviewing the family's representative, generally the individual who is making the funeral arrangements. Much of the information on a death certificate is best regarded as "hearsay" and is only as accurate as the person who provided it. Names of the deceased's mother and father may be missing or misspelled, the deceased's occupation may be in error, and the birth date can be completely wrong.

Most knowledgeable genealogists know that apart from the time, place, and general cause of death, the information on the death certificate is only hearsay and needs to be verified. Once the death certificate is filled out, in most jurisdictions, the funeral home files the certificate with the appropriate government official or office and provides certified copies of the death certificate to the family.

Generally, the information available on a death certificate includes both the primary cause of death and the contributing factors. For most states, there is a Part 1 on the form where the physician fills in the immediate cause of death and then a Part 2 with one or two lines for the contributing or underlying cause of death. It is frequently the contributing factors that are the most interesting. For instance, pneumonia may be given as the primary cause of death but it is the contributing cause, diabetes, that is of genetic interest. A common mistake is to list the underlying and immediate cause of death out of order. A listing of the duration of the illness is also standard on most death certificates. This can be useful in understanding the medical condition. For statistical purposes, the causes of death are coded using the International Classification of Diseases (ICD). Currently in its tenth revision (ICD-10), this standardized list contains cause-of-death titles and codes used to classify mortality data from death certificates. More information about the ICD can be found at *www.cdc.gov/nchs/about/major/dvs/icd10des.htm.*

The cause of death and the contributing illnesses can be wrong. Most physicians do not receive formal training in how to fill out a death certificate correctly. In fact, they are generally told that the death certificate must be filled out quickly so as to not cause a delay for the family and the funeral arrangements. Funeral arrangements cannot begin until a doctor has signed a death certificate. It has been stated that there is a 30 percent error rate on death certificates even in the 20th century. While that sounds dreadful, and it is, it should also be understood that an "error" might not mean that the cause of death is incorrect. It may merely mean that the death certificate is incomplete or filled out incorrectly. Probably the major error is that the cause of death may be nonspecific or incomplete. Recording that the cause of death was "cardiac arrest" or "respiratory arrest" is incorrect and unhelpful. After all, at the time of death, everyone's heart and breathing stop. Many studies continue to document the inaccuracies found in death certificates. In 1993, one large teaching hospital reviewed the death certificates completed at its institution and rejected 63 percent because either they were incomplete or the cause of death was vague and nonspecific. Another medical institute found that even checking a yes/no box on the certificate, such as noting whether an autopsy was performed, was incorrect a quarter of the time. This is because death certificates may be filled out before permission for an autopsy is requested. The physician who fills out the death certificate may not be the same individual who asks the family for permission to perform an autopsy. Some causes of death or related illnesses or conditions, such as drug abuse, AIDS, and alcoholism, go underreported. Physicians are aware that the family will see the death certificate, first with the funeral director and later when they file copies with the appropriate authorities.

Some causes of death are considered too sensitive to list. For instance, an individual found frozen to death on the street may have the cause of death listed as "exposure" and the contributing cause "chronic alcoholism" ignored. Suicide may also go unreported because of insurance claims. As with all other medical terms, dig into them to find out the etiology. Those who committed suicide may have done so because of depression, learning they had a terminal malignancy, or discovering that they were showing early signs of Huntington disease, which they knew was in the family. All these causes are important for you to know for your family's medical pedigree.

Today, we have sophisticated imaging, biopsies, endoscopies, and laboratory tests to help us with the diagnosis. That is fortunate since fewer and fewer autopsies are being performed, for a variety of reasons. They are expensive and time-consuming, and many physicians have stopped asking for them because they fear malpractice suits.

Although death certificates vary from locality to locality, you can generally expect to find the following information on modern certificates:

- Full name of the deceased
- Place of death
- Sex
- Color or race
- Marital status
- Date of birth
- Age
- Occupation
- Residence
- Birthplace
- Name of father
- Birthplace of father
- Maiden name of mother

- Birthplace of mother

- Name and address of individual providing the information

- Date of death

- Cause of death

- Place of burial

- Name of funeral director

Notice who signed the death certificate. Possibly the physician is still in practice and might have some additional information. If the death certificate indicates that a medical examiner signed or the individual was referred to the coroner, there may be additional records that can be searched.

Coroners and Medical Examiners

In 1194 the coroner system was established in England as a way of protecting the financial interests of the Crown. The Articles of Eyre in England provided for the election in each county of three knights and a clerk to function as keepers of the Crown—"crowners"—to ensure that any money due the Crown was collected at the time of death. By the early 1600s, when the system was brought to this country, *crowner* had been corrupted to *coroner;* the first recorded autopsy in America was performed in Massachusetts in 1647. Generally, coroners are not medically trained. Since the colonial period, they have been citizens elected to the position. They serve as administrators and

A **coroner** is a public official, either elected or appointed, who investigates any sudden or unnatural death. Many coroners are lay individuals and not physicians. They conduct an investigation called a **coroner's inquest** with a coroner's jury called for that purpose. In many states, the medical examiner system has replaced the coroner. An appointed position, a **medical examiner** is a physician. Many, especially in larger jurisdictions, are trained in forensic pathology, a recognized subspecialty of the American Board of Pathology.

conduct inquiries into the manner of death. They do this by examining the circumstances surrounding the death, interviewing witnesses, and examining the state of the body. Any medical function is delegated to a physician.

In response to the numerous epidemics of the 19th century, boards of health were formed, primarily in the cities, to keep death records. The medical examiner system was first established in Boston in 1870 and in Baltimore in 1890; that system required that the coroner be replaced by a physician, the medical examiner. Maryland in 1939 developed the first statewide medical examiner system in the United States. By 1991, 41 out of 50 states had adopted the medical examiner system. The medical examiner's office is headed by a Board Certified Forensic Pathologist, who acts both as an administrator and as a director of the medical and scientific investigation. Unlike the elected coroner, the medical examiner is a public employee, generally hired for his medical qualifications.

Under state laws, a coroner or medical examiner is charged with the investigation of unexpected, sudden, violent, or unexplained deaths. Customarily, private physicians fill out the death certificate for natural deaths and coroners or medical examiners fill out the death certificate for unnatural deaths. Some states use different forms for the medical examiner or coroner than those that are used by private physicians.

Begin your search by finding the location of the coroner's or medical examiner's office in the specific locality where the death occurred. Copies of the coroner's report, which may also be called an inquest report or a postmortem record, are public records and can be obtained either in person or by signing a written request. The Family History Library may have filmed some of these records for your state. Check their catalog under State, County, and Vital or Court Records. Records from the medical examiner's office tend to be more difficult to obtain; they are considered private medical records and generally are released only to the next of kin. In this case, you may need to contact the next of kin to obtain these records for you.

Medical examiner and coroner reports are invoked when the cause of death is "suspicious," possibly indicating a crime, or when the death is unexpected, as when a young, apparently healthy individual is found dead. In some states, a coroner or medical examiner may also be involved if disposal of the body is to be permanent, such as a burial at sea or a cremation. If a body was referred to the coroner or medical examiner for a violent death, such as a murder or suicide, there may have been an article about the death in one of the local newspapers. Check the newspapers in the area around the date of death. Violent deaths might also generate police reports that can be searched.

Just because a case is referred to a medical examiner doesn't mean it will be accepted and a report produced. Most of the time, medical examiners simply review the case and release the body, allowing the physician to sign the death certificate. In my younger days, I worked in a busy inner-city hospital emergency room in Maryland. Policemen, firefighters, and ambulances would arrive with individuals that I had to pronounce dead. I interviewed the family and, if possible, discussed the case with the family's doctor. Since Maryland had a medical examiner system, and since the individual had died before reaching the hospital, by law I had to call the medical examiner's office. After discussing the case over the phone, and perhaps after a few more phone calls, they would make a decision about the disposition of the body. In only a few instances did they accept the case for their own investigation. Most of the time, either I or the family physician would sign the death certificate.

Nor is there automatically an autopsy when a coroner or medical examiner is involved. Although increasingly fewer autopsies are being performed in hospitals, if permission was granted and an autopsy (sometimes called a postmortem or post) was done on a family member, by all means, try to get a copy. An autopsy will have the best medical information that you can obtain. In addition to an autopsy performed by a medical examiner or requested by a coroner, it is still common for physicians to request permission from the family for an autopsy at most hospitals, even if the cause of death appears obvious. This is especially true if the hospital is a "teaching hospital"—one connected with a medical school and one that might have a residency program in pathology. Such institutions use autopsies to help train their residents. Generally, the causes of death and diseases found on the autopsy report are more reliable than those found on the death certificate. You will have to hunt for the report; if it is a teaching hospital, start with the pathology department. One you locate the autopsy report, consult someone with medical training to help you understand it. As noted earlier, don't be surprised if the cause of death given on the death certificate differs from that found by the autopsy. It is rare for a death certificate to be upgraded and changed based on the autopsy results. Although the initial examination of the body is done quickly and the body released, complete autopsy results with microscopic tissue examination and chemical tests can take weeks, and the completed death certificate is needed right away to bury the individual, probate the estate, and file a life insurance claim.

Obituaries

Newspapers have been published in the United States for over 300 years, beginning in colonial times. Obituaries and death notices are just as old. You should look for obituaries. While the older obituaries tend to have more medical information, even modern obituaries sometimes provide a clue as to the cause of death with a statement such as "Send all donations to the American Cancer Society." Keep in mind, though, that the clue may be misleading. The American Cancer Society may have been the deceased's favorite charity because his wife died of cancer; the deceased individual could have had a fatal stroke.

If the date of death is known, search the local newspapers. If you can't get the death date from a death certificate, search for a cemetery to get the death date from its records or from the tombstone. Look at all the newspapers that might have covered that geographical area. If the individual lived near a state boundary, look at the newspapers in the adjacent state. Also, occasionally the hometown of the individual prints an obituary of an individual who dies elsewhere. If the individual belonged to a specific ethnic group and lived in a large city, check the newspapers that catered to that ethnic group for an obituary. Obituaries in ethnic papers may give more details about where the individual originated in the "home country." Many historical societies and libraries maintain a newspaper clipping file of obituaries. You can also use obituary and newspaper indexes that have been compiled and published. For instance, *Prince George's County Maryland, Marriages and Deaths in Nineteenth Century Newspapers* by Shirley and George Baltz (Bowie, Maryland: Heritage Books, 1995) includes the following obituary:

GORDON, CHARLES G.M.—Mrs—widow of Capt GORDON, USA Ret., D at her home, the old rectory of St. Matthew's Parish, in Bladensburg, Tues afternoon. She was on the stairway when death came from a paralytic stroke & had, a few minutes before, been playing with her grandchild. She was abt 65 years of age. Two daus—Mrs. A. D. BAILER & Miss BESSIE GORDON—survive. Prince George's Enquirer, Upper Marlboro, MD, 3/24/1899.

Cemetery and Funeral Records

Cemetery and funeral records occasionally give the cause of death. In my own case, a visit to the cemetery and a review of their records provided the cause of death of a long-estranged uncle. A search on the Internet will frequently give you the address and phone number of a cemetery in another state. Write to the cemetery and explain why you need any medical information they might have on the individual. Enclose a stamped, self-addressed envelope, and offer to pay for any cost to search for or copy the information.

Find the funeral home that made the arrangements for the deceased. If you have a death certificate, the funeral home will be listed there. If not, talk to relatives who might remember the funeral or look for an obituary where the funeral director or funeral home may be listed. A complete listing of the name of every funeral home in the United States including its address, phone, and fax number can be found in *The National Yellow Book of Funeral Directors*, available in many libraries or at *www.yelobk.com/ybfd/main.html*. The funeral home will have their own records and may have kept a copy of the death certificate and obituary. While funeral home records are private and the funeral home is under no obligation to share them with you, in practice, most do. You need to know the date of death since few funeral homes keep a name index and most file their records by date. Most states did not require death certificates until the beginning of the 20th century, so earlier funeral home records will be less informative than those kept as a result of completing the death certificate.

Cemeteries and funeral homes can be found online at *www.funeralnet.com*. A sophisticated search engine allows you to search by state, city, and county. For funeral homes, you will get their address, phone and fax numbers, Web page, and a link to send them an e-mail. For cemeteries, you will get the physical address of the cemetery, complete with a map, and the mailing address. Funeralnet also contains a search engine to retrieve recent obituaries by last name.

Figure 5.3 shows page 355 of the *Gleanings from the Records of the Francis Gasch's Sons Funeral Home, Prince George's County Maryland 1860–1940*. While this publication and others similar to this may not list the cause of death, a review of the entries does show a wealth of genealogical information, including references to newspapers where an obituary may be found and, of course, the date of death, which can help in your search for a death certificate. Although a funeral home may not allow the cause of death to be published, the home may give you more information if you contact it directly.

355

Lemmons, Edith A.

Lemmons, Milan Ray 26 Oct 1929. Died Landover, MD. Transfering body in New York. Husband, Douglas A. **Lemmons**, 321 6th St., SE, Washington, DC. [Note: *Evening Star*, 25 Oct 1929, p. 9, reports died suddenly 21 Oct 1929. Service at St. Peter's Church, 2nd and G Sts., SE, Washington, DC. Burial Utica, NY. Wife and son of Douglas **Lemmons**. Also, picture and story, 22 Oct 1929, pp. 1 & 2.]

Baker, Wallace Bruce, Dr. 29 Oct 1929. Burial Ft. Lincoln Cemetery, Brentwood, MD. John G. **Baker**. Notice in papers. [Note: *Evening Star*, 28 Oct 1929, p. 9, reports died 27 Oct 1929 at the residence of his father, John G. **Baker**, 232 8th St., SE, Washington, DC. Age 34 yrs. Husband of Helen Johnson **Baker**.]

Erhart, Katheryn 3409 Campbell St., Brentwood, MD. 29 Oct 1929. [Note: *Evening Star*, 28 Oct 1929, p. 12, "Deaths Reported", reports died at Sibley Hospital, Washington, DC. Age 5 yrs.]

McDonald, Mildred 3430 Evans St., Brentwood, MD. 29 Oct 1929. [Note: *Evening Star*, 28 Oct 1929, p. 9, "Deaths Reported", reports died at Children's Hospital, Washington, DC. Age 1 month.]

Davis, Frank Daniel 31 Oct 1929. Colored. [Note: *Evening Star*, 30 Oct 1929, p. 9, reports died 28 Oct 1929 at Bladensburg, MD. Age 44 yrs. Service at St. Paul Baptist Church, Bladensburg, MD. Son of the late Thomas and Hattie Belle **Davis**; brother of Howard G., Irving, and Bessie M. **Davis**, and [Mrs.] Beatrice B. **Moon**.]

Edwards, Mary E. 06 Nov 1929. Burial Lorraine Cemetery, Baltimore, MD. Miss Alice **Gray**, 427 N. Carey St., Baltimore, MD. Mrs. **Philips**, Berwyn, MD. Notice in papers. *Evening Star* (2 days). [Note: *Evening Star*, 04 & 05 Nov 1929, p. 9, report died 03 Nov 1929 at Berwyn, MD. Age 73 yrs. Funeral from the residence of her sister, Miss Alice **Gray**. Mass at St. Paul's Catholic Church, Baltimore, MD. Wife of the late J. E. **Edwards**.]

Harper, James William 07 Nov 1929. Burial Loudon Park Cemetery, Baltimore, MD. Mrs. Edna H. **Thompson**, Riverdale, MD.

Harris, Hubbard 705 Minnesota Ave., Washington, DC and Capitol Heights, MD. 08 Nov 1929. Removing remains from Capitol Heights to Hyattsville, MD. [Note: *Evening Star*, 06 & 07 Nov 1929, p. 9, report died 05 Nov 1929 at his residence, Greater Capitol Heights, MD. Age 36 yrs. Burial Cedar Hill Cemetery, Suitland, MD. Husband of Mildred **Harris** (nee **Thompson**).]

McGinnis, Virginia Nerna 10 Nov 1929. Hearse to Martinsburg, WV.

Rideout, Corlena M. 11 Nov 1929. Hearse and service to Herndon, VA. Notice in papers. *Evening Star*; *Washington Post*. [Note: *Evening Star*, 09 Nov 1929, p. 7, reports died 08 Nov 1929 at 7:00 p.m. Funeral from Berwyn Presbyterian Church, Berwyn, MD. Burial Chestnut Grove Cemetery, Herndon, VA. Wife of the late Edward H. **Rideout**.]

Newell, Robert B. 11 Nov 1929. Burial Ft. Lincoln Cemetery, Brentwood, MD. [Wife] Alice C. **Newell**, Mt. Rainier, MD. Notice in papers. *Evening Star*; *Washington Post*. [Note: *Evening Star*, 10 Nov 1929, p. 7, reports died 09 Nov 1929 at Sibley Hospital, Washington, DC. Age 46 yrs. Funeral from St. John's Episcopal Church, Mt. Rainier, MD. Only son of the late Joseph E. and Susie Fellows **Newell**; father of Robert B, Jr., Charles, and Thomas **Newell**; brother of Mrs. Carroll T. **Neale**, West Point, VA and Mrs. J. T. **Robertson**, Richmond, VA.]

Briggs, Douglas Warren 13 Nov 1929. Burial Laurel, MD. Thomas **Douglas**, Branchville, MD.

Figure 5.3 Page 355 of the *Gleanings from the Records of the Francis Gasch's Sons Funeral Home, Prince George's County Maryland 1860–1940*. Compiled by the Records Committee of the Prince George's County Genealogical Society, Inc., Bowie, Maryland, 1996. (Courtesy of the Prince George's County Genealogical Society.)

If a funeral home is no longer in business, write to the other funeral homes in the area, again with a stamped, self-addressed envelope, and ask whether they have the records or know what happened to them. You can also check with the local genealogy or historical society, or the local library, or inquire at the cemetery where your ancestor is buried to see whether they know where the records are. Be sure to check whether the Family History Library has microfilmed any records or if cemeteries or funeral home records have been published.

Hospital and Physician's Records

Hospital records and other medical documentation are becoming increasingly harder to obtain, especially with the recently enacted federal laws regarding patient privacy. In some cases, the hospital may have destroyed its older records, but it may also have microfilmed them. Once you find the hospital that likely treated your family member, contact the medical records department. Generally, only the patient or the attending physician has access to the records. If the individual has died, the next of kin can request the records. You may need to enlist the aid of the medical records department to obtain the proper consent form. This form can be sent to the next of kin, who then signs the release form and returns it to the appropriate medical facility. Some medical records departments require the death certificate before releasing any record; this is another good reason to start your family medical history search by compiling all the death certificates you can.

Records of private physicians can be even more elusive. The death certificate will list the doctor and sometimes the doctor's address, as well as the hospital where the individual died. Again, it never hurts to inquire. Once you do obtain the records, you will need to enlist the aid of someone with medical knowledge; interpreting hospital and physician's medical records, for instance, biopsy, imaging, surgical, or laboratory results, is not a task for a layperson. If while compiling your family's health history, you become suspicious that there is a significant genetic disease in the family, enlist the aid of a medical geneticist or genetic counselor. These professionals are able to obtain and interpret the family's medical records.

The Federal Census

The federal census is one of the major record groups genealogists use for their research. The census can give us clues about the health of our 19th and early 20th century relatives. When genealogists "search the census," they are actually searching what is more accurately known as the population schedules of the federal census. In the second half of the 19th century, an additional schedule was filled out that can contain important health information. These federal mortality schedules were included from 1850 to 1880, with Colorado, Florida, Nebraska, and the territories of Dakota and New Mexico also using mortality schedules in 1885. The 1890 mortality schedules were destroyed, along with the rest of the census, in a fire, and the 1900 schedules were destroyed before World War I, after analysis. These schedules predate the introduction of death certificates.

The mortality schedules are part of what is known as the non-population schedules; the census taker used them to record the deaths in a household for the year preceding the census (see Figure 5.4). Why were they compiled? Medical questions had begun to show up on the federal census before the first mortality schedule in 1850. The very first census of 1790 was a relatively simple enumeration of population so that legislatures could apportion the proper number of seats in Congress. By 1820, a social movement began to grow in this country for building institutions for the benefit of the deaf, mute, and blind. Some educational innovations in Europe had shown

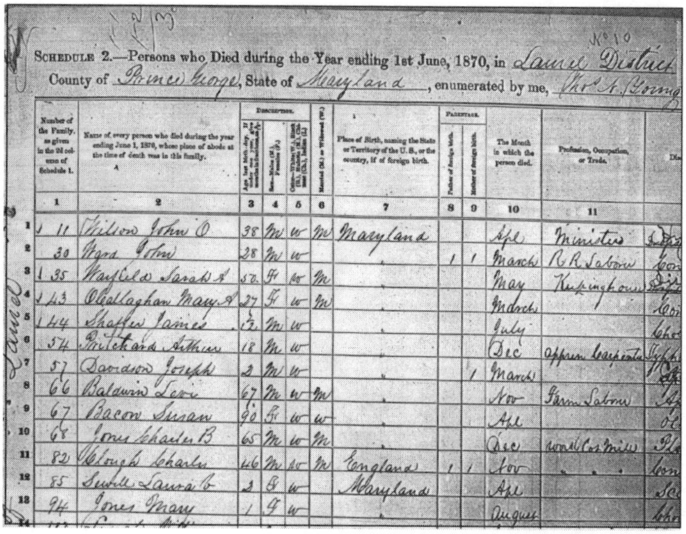

Figure 5.4 Example of a portion of the 1870 mortality schedule for Prince George's County, Maryland. (Courtesy of the Maryland State Archives.)

that it was possible to communicate with and train these individuals. Thomas Gallaudet in Connecticut expressed a great desire to learn more about the deaf and dumb. Another New Englander, Dorothea Dix, expressed a similar interest in the mentally ill. Before building institutions to house and teach these individuals, it was necessary to know how many were affected. The federal census responded to these social movements by putting questions about the deaf, dumb, and blind on the 1830 population schedule; questions about the insane and idiotic appeared in 1840.

The **mortality schedules** of the federal census were initiated in the census of 1850. These are special forms that recorded information about individuals who had died during the year preceding the census. They provide a listing of deaths in the second half of the 19th century, a time before the recording of vital statistics began in most states.

There was also a growing concern for the overall health of the country. Again, this concern was initiated in Europe and spread to the United States. Following the large 1832 Asiatic cholera epidemic and an epidemic of typhus in London in 1838, the British Parliament asked journalist and lawyer Edwin Chadwick to investigate the conditions of the working class. Chadwick presented his report in 1842 on the sanitary conditions—or more correctly, the unsanitary conditions—in London. While no one knew then that germs caused disease, it was generally thought that filth and unsanitary conditions could. Chadwick's report stimulated an already growing public health movement in this country and influenced a Bostonian, Lemuel Shattuck. Shattuck's interest in vital statistics was influenced by his interest in genealogy. His report on a census for the city of Boston in 1845 was an impetus for enlarging the 1850 federal census. Another trend in the early 19th century was the development of the science of statistics, including the use of quantitative approaches to medicine and disease. In one of the first books on statistics published in America, *Principles of Statistical Inquiry* by Archibald Rusell, the author called for broadening the questions on the federal census to obtain more information about the population of the United States.

All these social and scientific trends coalesced to produce the 1850 census. It is generally regarded by genealogists as the first "modern census" because every individual is named on the population schedule. Part of this census was the mortality schedule. There were actually six schedules, including the population and mortality schedules, for the 1850 census. The push to collect information about the American public continued through the remaining half of the 19th century, with the census collecting more and more information on such subjects as health, agriculture, manufacturing, mining, commerce, and industry.

The mortality schedules recorded the name, cause of death, and other information for a family member or occupant of the dwelling for the year immediately preceding the census. For instance, for the 1850 census, deaths were recorded if they occurred from 1 June 1849 to 30 May 1850. All the mortality schedules contain the name of the deceased, race, sex, age at death, whether married or widowed, occupation, and the month the individual died. The status of free or slave was included in the 1850 and 1860 schedules. The place of birth of the father and mother was added to the 1880 schedule.

Some indexes are available. Listing the individuals on the mortality schedule is a favorite topic for county genealogical societies. Some indexes are in printed format; some can be found on the Web. A search of the Family History Library Catalog will also turn up some indexes. The schedules themselves can be difficult to find. Before the establishment of the National Archives, the federal government gave them to the states. Some can be found in state historical societies, state archives, or universities. Some microfilmed copies came back to the National Archives, and some can be obtained from the Family History Library.

While there are many genealogical uses for the mortality schedules, we are primarily concerned with the medical information, which can be obscure and not very useful. For the early mortality schedules, the cause of death is given by whomever the census taker interviewed. On later schedules, the cause of death was verified by local physicians and therefore tended to be more accurate.

The causes of death in the 19th century were largely due to infectious disease; genetic diseases were buried under the complex terminology of the 19th century and hidden by the great infectious killers of that time—tuberculosis, malaria, typhoid, cholera, and for children, diphtheria and dysentery (see Figure 5.5). In the 19th century, many individuals died from infections before a deleterious gene could make its appearance. For instance, a woman living in the 19th century with the abnormal BRCA1 gene may have died of smallpox in her 20s, long before she could develop breast cancer. Nevertheless, an inspection of the 19th century death records can occasionally give you a clue about

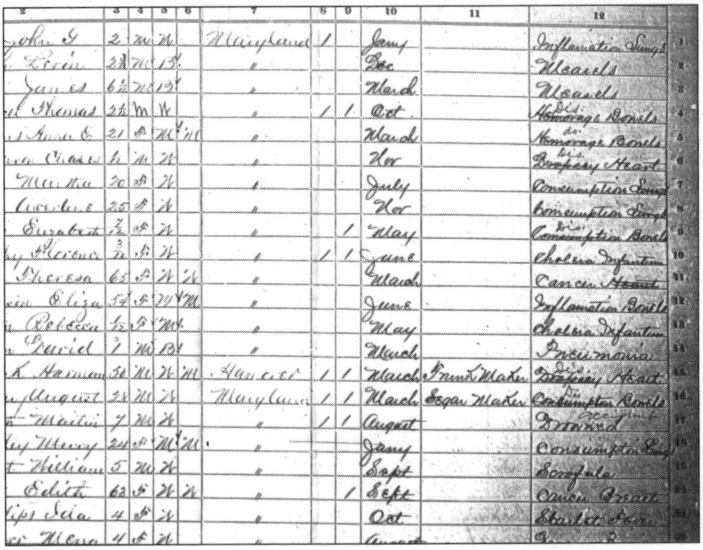

Figure 5.5 Portion of a page from the 1870 mortality schedule for Baltimore showing the causes of death. As is typical for this time period, the vast majority of deaths are from infectious diseases. Individual number 11 died from "cancer," and individual number 20 died from "cancer breast." (Courtesy of the Maryland State Archives.)

some possible underlying genetic disease. For instance, if polycystic kidney disease is known to be in the family and you find a 19th century ancestor dying of "Bright's disease," you should be suspicious that the individual was affected (see Figure 5.6). Hypertension, or high blood pressure, can also occur in polycystic kidney disease, so look for death by "apoplexy" (stroke), especially if in a young person. If you are looking for inherited cardiovascular disease, a 19th century individual dying at a young age of apoplexy might qualify.

The social movements of the early 19th century caused some health questions to be included in the population schedules of the federal census even before the 1850 mortality schedules. As mentioned earlier, beginning in 1830, the census recorded individuals who were deaf, dumb, or blind. The categories insane and idiotic were added for the 1840 through the 1880 census. The 1880 added crippled, as well as sick or disabled. The 1885 census taken for Colorado, the Dakota Territory, Florida, Nebraska, and the New Mexico Territory has the same format as the 1880 census. The 1890 Special Enumeration of Civil War Veterans and Widows, which (unlike the destroyed 1890 population schedules) still

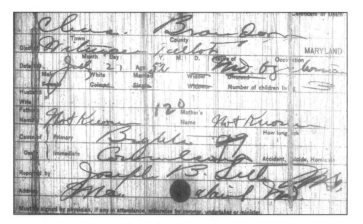

Figure 5.6 Death certificate from 1892 for a 52-year-old man who died of "Brights" and "convulsions." If polycystic kidney disease were present in the family, this death certificate would be compatible with an affected individual. (Courtesy of the Maryland State Archives.)

exists, can lead to pension files with medical information. For the 1900 census, health questions were dropped, only to reappear under the category blind, deaf, and dumb for the 1910 census. Health questions were dropped for 1920 and 1930. While all this census information is interesting and should be included in your family's medical pedigree, it is frequently too nonspecific to be of any use. There are many other causes of deafness or blindness than genetic ones. Other clues that might be helpful on the population schedule include ethnicity. Ethnicity can often be inferred from the birthplace. Since 1880, the census asked for the birthplace of the father and mother of each person, and in 1910, the census asked what language was spoken in the household.

In 1880, special schedules of the census known officially as the Supplemental Schedules, 1–7: Dependent, Delinquent, and Defective Classes were used. These supplemental schedules are commonly known as the "defective schedules" or the "DDD schedules." If an individual living at home was blind, insane, deaf, or an idiot, additional information was filled out on a special form. These forms were also used when the census taker visited an orphanage, poorhouse, prison, asylum, or other similar type of institution. In all cases, the individual was listed first on the standard population form, and then the individual's name, along with population schedule page and number, was copied to these seven schedules. An *idiot* was defined as someone whose mental facilities were arrested in infancy or childhood and certainly would include any of the genetic syndromes that cause mental retardation. *Insanity* was defined broadly and could include those that today we would regard as truly mentally ill, but would also include senility, as in Alzheimer disease, dementia from any cause, and even post-stroke dementia or the late stages of syphilis. Questions about the form of the illness; its cause; whether an individual may have been under treatment in an institution and, if so, where; and whether the individual had seizures are some of the many questions asked. For those listed as deaf or blind, the cause and duration was recorded, including whether the condition was present at birth. Those individuals found in a public institution, such as a poorhouse or asylum, were asked about disabilities and the type was recorded. When using this form, the census taker was urged to discuss the case with the local physician to ensure accuracy.

There is no index for these supplemental schedules, so you will need to find the individual first in the population schedules. These schedules can be even harder to find than the mortality schedules and are scattered in historical societies, state archives, and universities, with only a few at the National Archives. Their location, when known, is listed in Ruth Land Hatten's article, "The 'Forgotten' Census of 1880: Defective, Dependent, and Delinquent Classes" in the *National Genealogical Society Quarterly*.

Other Records

Military service and pension records are well worth finding. In my case, my great-grandfather was hospitalized during the Civil War. When I went to the National Archives and requested his pension file, I was rewarded with his complete hospital records, including his physical examination and laboratory results. The federal government also holds medical records other than those included in the compiled military service records or pension files. A listing of medical holdings in the National Archives appears in the article "Medical Holdings in the National Archives: Patient Records Prior to World War II" in the *National Genealogical Society Quarterly*. Briefly, these include records in the Bureau of Naval Personnel, the U.S. Coast Guard, the Bureau of Medicine and Surgery, the Department of the Treasury, the Bureau of Indian Affairs, the Public Health Service, and the Records of the Adjutant General's Office.

Another source of medical records for the early 20th century is the files of the Eugenics Record Office (ERO). As Thomas H. Roderick describes in his article in the *National Genealogical Society Quarterly*, the ERO, established in 1910, became a repository for genetic and genealogical information. A vast amount of data was accumulated over the course of 34 years. Eventually, it became obvious that much of the genetic data was useless; nevertheless, there is still an enormous amount of genealogical and medical data available. For instance, the Record of Family Traits consists of a 12-page form that, in addition to questions about name, age, education and so on, contains questions about "grave illnesses," lesser diseases, surgical operations, and cause of death. In addition to extensive forms and pedigrees, the ERO also collected obituaries from many of the major newspapers of the country. With the closing of the ERO, 18 tons of records were transferred to the University of Minnesota in 1948. Some of these records may not be available for viewing yet, but many have been filmed by the Family History Library; a search of the Family History Library Catalog for the keyword *eugenics* found the *Indexes to the Files of the Eugenics Record Office, ca. 1900–1940.*

Records of the Hearing Impaired

A specific set of medical records focuses on the hearing impaired. In an article in the *National Genealogical Society Quarterly*, Thomas Jones discusses the availability of deafness-focused records for genealogical research. These include early deaf-school records, Alexander Graham Bell's records on the genealogy of deaf individuals, and E. A. Fay's marriage surveys in the Gallaudet University Archives. Some of these records may be of value should you find a deaf individual in your medical pedigree, such as a relative listed as deaf in the census. Because of the interest in the hereditary aspects of deafness, these records are rich in genealogical information.

Other records, including insurance records, records of institutions such as orphanages and prisons, and immigration records, can be useful, though many are difficult to find. The records of asylums, sanatoriums, and poorhouses may not have survived. If the institution still exists, start there. If not, check with the local historical society. Look for published abstracts. Check the Family History Library Catalog. If you believe that there might be insurance records, find out what insurance companies were in the area at the time your ancestor lived; city directories can be helpful. Find out whether the insurance companies still exist or who might have their records. Contact the current insurance company, ask for the company archives or public relations officer, and inquire about the availability of records.

Search publications of local genealogical societies, which may have compiled and printed hospital records. For instance, the Prince George's County Genealogical Society in Maryland for many years published local hospital records in their bulletin. In the December 1996 issue, three pages of entries appear, including this one:

> June 9, 1898/ Husman, Anna Maria, Balto St./carcinoma of breast—recurrent/WF 66, died 1898 June 15.

Research Aids

How do you find abstracts, such as hospital records, mortality schedule indexes, or coroner's records, that might have been published in genealogical periodicals? The major finding aid is PERSI, the Periodical Source Index prepared by the Allen County Public Library in Fort Wayne, Indiana. Originally published in multiple-book volumes, it is now available on a searchable CD-ROM. PERSI is the largest and most widely used index of genealogy articles in the world. The database is updated annually and contains well over a million entries, all fully indexed and searchable on the CD. For instance, a search for the keyword *coroner* in an article title on the 2000 PERSI CD returned 126 entries, including *Coroner's Inquest Reports 1865–1903* from Pulaski, Arkansas, and *Coroners Reports 1873–1902* from Park, Colorado. A similar search using the word *mortality* returned 2,599 entries, virtually all of which are listings of mortality schedules, indexed, compiled, and published by local genealogical societies. Books and microfilm records can be searched by using the Family History Library Catalog. A search of that catalog for the keyword *coroner* returned 278 matching titles.

Analyzing the Information

As you accumulate medical information about your family, you will need to evaluate it. If possible, attempt to examine the original source. For instance, the 1804 coroner's report seen in Figure 5.7 was originally reviewed on microfilm at the Maryland State Archives and abstracted for publication in the *Prince George's County Genealogical Society Bulletin* as part of a series of Coroner Reports Abstracts. When I decided to publish the report in this book, I returned to the archives and requested the original 1804 manuscript. I then made a transcription from the original. Rather than making a copy from the microfilm, I requested a higher quality digital scan of the original for reproduction here.

The Genealogical Proof Standard was developed by the Board of Certification for Genealogists (BCG) and is found in *The BCG Genealogical Standards Manual* (Washington, D.C.: Board for Certification of Genealogists, 2000). It is used by genealogists to measure the creditability of their research. More information on this standard and other standards developed by the board can be found on its Web site *(www.bcgcertification.org)*.

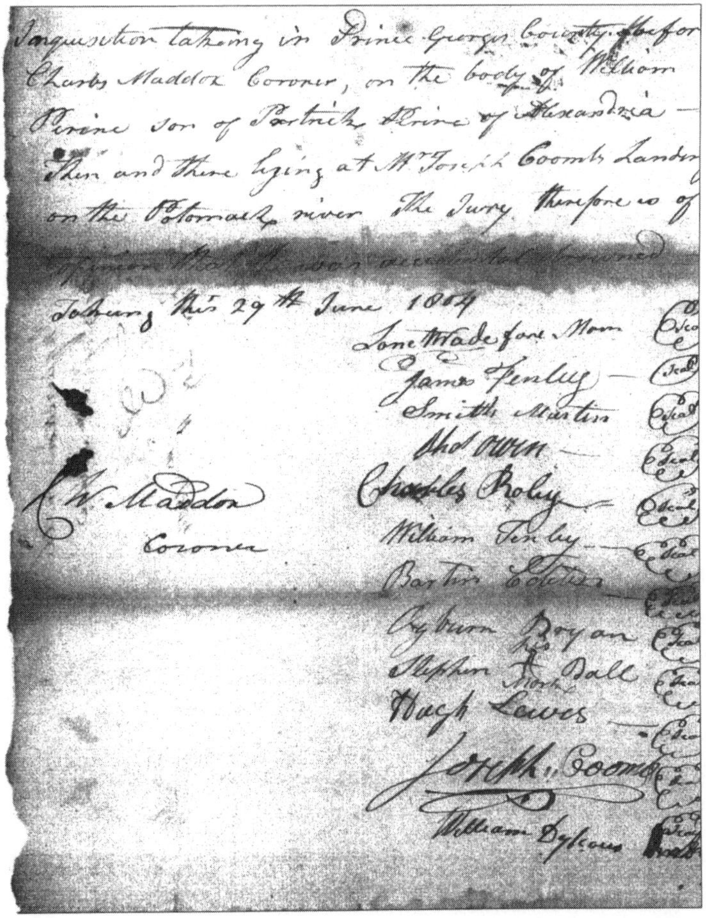

Figure 5.7 An 1804 coroner's report. (Courtesy of the Maryland State Archives.)

Genealogical sources include documents, books, artifacts, records, and even individuals you interview. There are two forms of sources: the original, which is the first or earliest source that contains information, and the derivative, which is any other source derived from the original. An abstract or a transcription prepared from the original source is derivative. A transcription is an exact copy of the entire document. When assembling your documents, it is generally best to make a copy for your records, but you may need to make a transcription if photocopying a microfilm or original document cannot be done. An abstract, in contrast to a transcription, includes only the relevant data in the record; redundant and repetitive words are ignored.

In genealogy, an **original source** of information is the person or record whose information did not come from data already spoken or written. The original source is the most authoritative source. A **derivative source** is any other source of information—a person or record that repeats something already spoken or written.

Once you have the source, you must next analyze the information. Genealogical standards divide that information into primary knowledge and secondary knowledge. Primary information, such as the doctor filling out the death certificate, is provided by someone with knowledge of the event. Secondary information is given by someone who doesn't have personal knowledge. It is important to understand that a source, even an original source such as the death certificate, contains both primary and secondary information. For instance, all the information on the coroner's report is classified as primary knowledge since the individuals were present at the time the report was prepared and attested to it with their signatures. In contrast, only some of the information on a death certificate is considered primary knowledge. The information supplied by the physician, the name of the deceased, the time of death, and the cause of death are considered primary because the physician had primary knowledge of the event. Other information, such as that given by a relative to the funeral home director when completing the death certificate, will vary. The spouse of the deceased will know the decedent's address. That same spouse may or may not know the name of the decedent's parents and where they were born. If the individual giving the information happens to be a niece or nephew, the address of the decedent may not be correct. Perhaps the niece or nephew visited the decedent only occasionally and had a vague idea of the address or may only dimly remember the name of the decedent's parents and place of birth. The genealogical standards for information should always be used when evaluating information from a source.

> **Primary information** is given by an individual who participated in the event that is the subject of the record. **Secondary information** is given by someone who heard of the event from someone else. Sources and types of information, as well as how it is evaluated for genealogical purposes, are detailed in the *Standards Manual* by the Board for Certification of Genealogists (Washington, D.C., 2000).

The final process of analyzing the evidence is to decide whether the evidence is direct or indirect. Direct evidence answers the question specifically. A specific cause of death on a death certificate is direct evidence, although, as has been noted, it is not necessarily correct. A cause of death given in a mortality schedule such as apoplexy, while relevant, is only indirect evidence that the individual may have had high blood pressure.

Before you evaluate evidence, though, keep in mind one other directive: Document your source. Source citations are extraordinarily important. Serious, responsible genealogists are obsessive about citing their sources. They are an essential part of compiling your family health history and genealogy. If you are constructing your medical pedigree and are unsure of a great-grandparent's date of death, you need to turn to your notes. Did you get the date of death from a death certificate? From an obituary? From a relative who had a funeral mass card? Did you copy the mass card? Are you relying on the memory of an 80-year-old relative as to the date of death? Perhaps another source has given a different date of death than you have recorded. Good genealogical practice dictates that you must analyze the evidence. To do so, you must start with the source. If you have not correctly cited your source, you cannot evaluate the evidence. Doing genealogy or your family's health history will generate an enormous amount of information. Always correctly cite your sources.

Documenting Your Medical History

As you research your family's medical history, remember to cite your sources. Here are some examples of correct documentation:

- Robert Radclift, death certificate 72-1234 (1972), Maryland State Archives, Annapolis, Maryland.

- Robert Radclift obituary, *The Baltimore Sun,* Baltimore, Maryland, 9 May 1972, page 12, column 2.

- Robert Radclift tombstone, section 2-41, Immanuel United Methodist Church Cemetery, Prince George's County, Maryland; transcribed by the writer on 14 June 1992.

In general, genealogists use the *Chicago Manual of Style*, modified by the format recommended in *Evidence!* by Elizabeth Shown Mills. The proper genealogical techniques for citing sources have been covered in other volumes in this series. The same principle applies to any medical information that you acquire. The citation should be placed on the front of each document and on every page of a multipage document. This ensures that should the document be photocopied, the document's citation will be included. Putting a citation on the back of a document will almost guarantee that the citation either will not be copied or, if it is copied, will be on a separate page that can become separated from the source. When compiling your family's health history, be sure to practice good genealogical techniques.

Now that you have interviewed your family and documented significant illnesses or causes of death, it is necessary to put all your findings into a form that you can understand. This is done by drawing your family's medical pedigree.

CHAPTER 6

Draw Your Pedigree

MEDICAL PEDIGREES ARE KEY TO UNDERSTANDING YOUR FAMILY'S health history. They are the best way to understand your family's health and the single best way to present the information to your doctor. A medical pedigree is a graphic description of your family showing the relationship between individual members, any significant diseases, and the cause of death. Ethnicity, infertility, birth defects, age of disease onset, stillbirths, and infant deaths are also shown. If there is a genetic disease, a pedigree may reveal the pattern of inheritance; it will show who is affected and who could be affected.

Your pedigree also forces your doctor to pay attention to your family's health history; sadly, in today's hectic health care field, there are medical-care providers who do not pay enough attention to an individual's family health history. Be sure to remove the names of your family members, especially if you want your doctor to keep a copy of your family's health pedigree. Your doctor doesn't care about the names, and you never know where the pedigree might end up. This is good advice in general; the complete pedigree with the names of your family members should not leave you. Never give a copy to anyone, for any reason.

Most genealogists are using genealogy software to keep track of their families. These programs are extremely powerful databases and, in many cases, are indispensable for genealogy. They frequently have fields for cause of death; medical information can be added in the "notes" section for an individual, and some programs have room for putting in a medical history. As far as I know, however, none have the ability to

97

create a medical pedigree report directly from the program. For compiling a medical history, start with the family information contained in your genealogy database and then convert that information into a medical pedigree.

Format

If you are going to take the time and effort to research your family's health history, present it in a format that is recognizable by health professionals. Standard medical pedigree charts use a format familiar to physicians, geneticists, and genetic counselors.

On the Web or in popular books on genetics for genealogists, you will encounter the term *genogram*. Do not use genograms to chart your medical pedigree. Genograms are family tree diagrams that depict the individual's psychosocial role in the family. They are used as a family assessment tool and to depict family relationships. Superficially, genograms may appear to resemble a standard medical pedigree, but they are not. As one Web page explains, "genograms can vary significantly and are only limited by your imagination." When you are trying to communicate your results to a physician or genetic counselor, there is no place for imagination. You should be using symbols that are standard and well understood. A review of genograms on different Web pages shows that they do not agree among themselves as to the various symbols and, worse, some of the symbols used are not used in actual medical pedigrees (see Figures 6.1 and 6.2).

Genograms do have a role. They were developed in the 1980s by a family therapist to depict psychological relationships between family members. A genogram is a behavioral family tree showing emotions, communication, and psychological relationships between family members. They have been used for this purpose by clinical psychologists and family therapists, but are not used by geneticists.

Although those who advocate using genograms frequently state that most medical professionals are familiar with them, I can assure you that they are not. The term appeared in only two of the nine current editions of medical or genetic dictionaries that I reviewed. The book describing genograms, published in 1985, is not in my institution's medical library. More than likely, if you take a genogram to a physician's office, especially if it includes nonstandard symbols, it will probably be dismissed or, worse, misunderstood. If you want to trace your family's psychological interactions and family dynamics, use genograms. Just don't use them to show medical information.

It was in response to the profusion of symbols and inconsistencies in human pedigree symbols that the National Society of Genetic Counselors formed the Pedigree

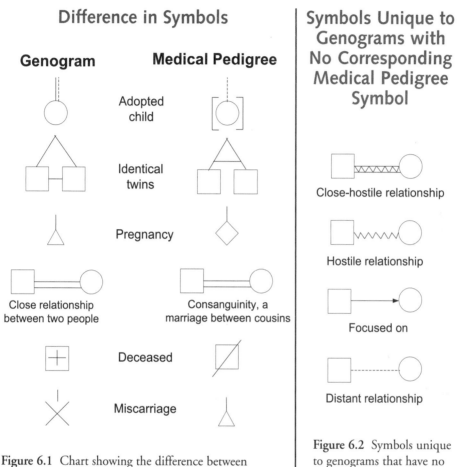

Difference in Symbols

Genogram   **Medical Pedigree**

Adopted child

Identical twins

Pregnancy

Close relationship between two people

Consanguinity, a marriage between cousins

Deceased

Miscarriage

Symbols Unique to Genograms with No Corresponding Medical Pedigree Symbol

Close-hostile relationship

Hostile relationship

Focused on

Distant relationship

Figure 6.1 Chart showing the difference between genogram symbols *(left column)* and standard medical pedigree symbols *(right column)*.

Figure 6.2 Symbols unique to genograms that have no counterpart in standard medical pedigrees.

Standardization Task Force. After several years and multiple reviews at several national meetings and by several national genetic organizations including the American Board of Medical Genetics and the American Society of Human Genetics, a consensus was reached. A standardized human pedigree nomenclature was published in 1995 by Robin Bennett and others in the *American Journal of Human Genetics*. These forms and symbols are used in this book (see Figures 6.3–6.7).

A medical pedigree generally goes back three to four generations. Width is more important than depth. By width, we mean including all of your aunts, uncles, and cousins. While genealogists will frequently pick a single ancestral line and go back in

Basic Individual Shapes

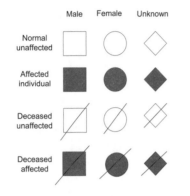

Figure 6.3 Standard pedigree symbols for individuals.

Lines of Biological Relationship

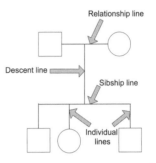

Figure 6.4 Pedigree symbols for biological relationships.

Additional Relationship

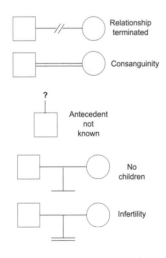

Figure 6.5 Pedigree symbols for additional relationships.

Twins

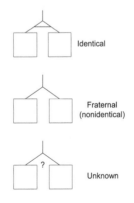

Figure 6.6 Pedigree symbols for twins.

time as far as they can, it is important that a medical pedigree extend horizontally, as well as vertically, so that all the aunts, uncles, great-aunts and great-uncles, and first and second cousins are included. If you have reliable information that is further back in time, include it, but it is more important that the medical information you include be accurate.

Constructing the Pedigree

Few physicians have the training, interest, or time to construct a pedigree for you. Even geneticists or genetic counselors, who work with medical pedigrees, may frequently be interested in one specific disease or symptom complex. They will ask questions related to the client's problem, such as inquiries about advanced maternal age or evidence of a specific genetic disease suspected to be in the family. For genealogists, the search is more general. They are

Adopted Individuals

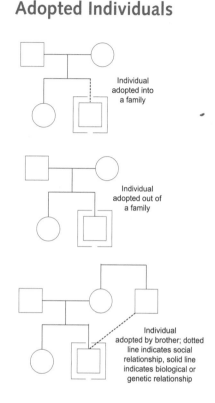

Figure 6.7 Pedigree symbols for adoption.

not looking for a specific disease but are compiling a chart of all the diseases in the family. Their goal is to compile and analyze the complete family health history. Ultimately, no one knows your family better than you and no one will take the time that you will to compile your pedigree.

The very first thing you must do is compile an ancestor chart. Basically, you must do your genealogy. Construct family group sheets with everyone listed, including that cousin or second cousin who died in infancy. It should be as complete as possible. This can be difficult; many of us have lost track of our cousins, who might be scattered around the country or around the world. If we are older, our parents, aunts, and uncles may be dead and the information about the family's diseases that they could have provided is gone with them. Compile the pedigree chart using the standard form and the symbols seen in Figures 6.3–6.7. Put in your relatives' names, birth dates, and where applicable, death dates. While you are interested in finding out the family's diseases, you might get comfortable with the family pedigree by charting some of the family's physical traits—for instance, eye color, height, weight, or baldness.

An **ancestor chart**, also known as a *pedigree chart*, is a graphic representation of your parents, grandparents, and great-grandparents. A **family group sheet** is used to display the information about one family, including major life events such as birth, death, and marriage. Both of these basic genealogical tools are described in two books in the NGS series, *Genealogy 101* by Barbara Renick and *The Organized Family Historian* by Ann Carter Fleming.

Genetic counseling books of only a few years ago recommended that the counselor draw the pedigree chart by hand at the time of the interview with the client. Although some medical geneticists continue to compile pedigrees by hand, genealogists should use computers. You will be doing multiple pedigrees for your family, one for each trait or disease. I suggest a computer drawing program. Construct your medical pedigree using the standard pedigree symbols, filling in all the vital data. Your master pedigree chart with the individuals named is the one you will use as a template to chart medical conditions. It should be kept private. Generally, no more than one or two medical conditions should be charted per pedigree. You can create as many disease charts as you need. Just call up the master pedigree; then fill it out for a specific trait and save it under a different file name. For instance, if your family has both diabetes and cancer, you may want to do a separate pedigree tracking each: one pedigree showing individuals affected with cancer, including the primary site and type, and one pedigree showing individuals with diabetes, including age of onset. You can add text or shade male and female symbols to show an affected individual. If you wish to show the pedigree to someone else, you can easily remove the names.

There are specific programs that can be used to construct a medical pedigree, but they tend to be expensive and complicated. If you plan to do many medical pedigrees, however, you might want to investigate one of them. For simply doing your own family's pedigree, such programs are not necessary. Many simple drawing programs are available

A list of pedigree drawing software is available at *www.sfbr.org/sfbr/public/software/ pedraw/dos_peddrw.html* or *www.kumc.edu/gec/prof/genecomp.html#pedigree*.

that can be used instead. The pedigree chart in Figure 6.8 was created with Visio, a drawing program available with Microsoft Office. Word-processing programs now include the basic symbols of squares, circles, and lines that you need to design a pedigree chart. The pedigree chart seen in Figure 6.9 was done in Microsoft Word XP and is almost identical to the chart in Figure 6.8, which was done with a drawing program.

Pedigree Prepared with Visio

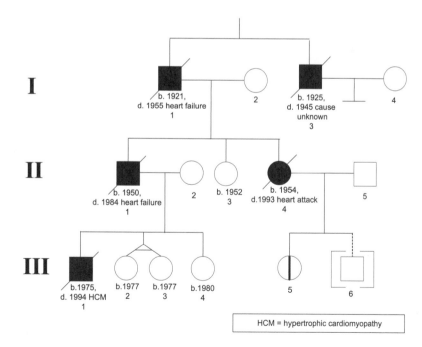

Figure 6.8 Sample pedigree prepared with Visio, a drawing program. While not a program designed specifically for genetic pedigrees, this program, and other drawing programs, can be easily used to produce professional results.

Pedigree Prepared with Microsoft Word

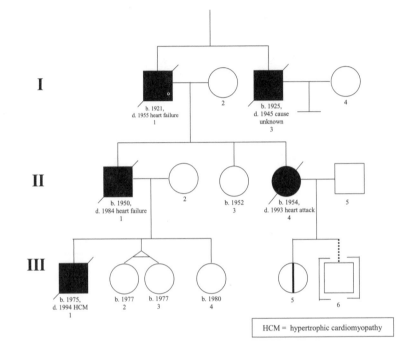

HCM = hypertrophic cardiomyopathy

Figure 6.9 The same pedigree seen in Figure 6.8 prepared using Microsoft Word.

Design

The master pedigree and various working pedigrees that are only for your use should include the name of your family members. If you intend to show the pedigree to a medical professional, remove the names and substitute numbers. Another practice—one that can help further protect your family's privacy and is in a form that is easier for a geneticist to understand—is to remove the spouses from a pedigree. But the master pedigree with names should include the spouses since this will help you keep everyone straight.

For clinical geneticists, the "client" is the individual who either is affected with a genetic disease and is seeking advice, or is a family member who could be affected and is seeking genetic counseling. This individual is called a proband and is identified in

How to Draw a Medical Pedigree Using Microsoft Word XP

To draw a medical pedigree using Microsoft Word XP, follow the steps below. Other word-processing programs have similar features.

1. Open a new document, go to File, Page Setup, Landscape to pick landscape mode for the document.

2. Go to View, Toolbars, Drawing, and check to open drawing toolbar.

3. Click on the rectangle, and draw a box. Click on the box, move the mouse to the drawing area, hold down the left mouse button, and draw the box. Adjust the size. Do the same for the circle. You now have the basic male and female symbols. To ensure uniformity, when you need another male or female symbol, click on the original, and copy and paste. To fill in shape with color to show that the individual is affected, right click on the shape. Click Format AutoShape, Fill, Color, and pick a color.

4. Draw the horizontal and vertical lines for relationship, descent, sibship, and individuals by clicking on the line icon and drawing the line. Pick the line weight from the line style icon, or if you need a dash, pick from the dash style box. Lines, boxes, and circles can be resized or moved by selecting the object and moving it with a mouse, or it can be nudged into place by selecting and holding the control key while moving the drawing component with the keyboard arrow keys.

5. Text can be added by selecting the text box. Adjust the size of the font by highlighting the text and selecting the font and size. If the text box has a box around it, select the text box border (not the text inside), right click, and click Format Text Box, Line, No Color. If the text box intrudes and cuts off part of a square or circle symbol, select the text box border (not the text inside), right click, and click Order, Send to Back.

6. Triangles, diamonds, brackets, arrows, and virtually every shape you need to draw a medical pedigree are available in the AutoShapes section of the drawing toolbar.

a medical pedigree with an arrow. Since this is your family's pedigree, I suggest that you identify yourself as the proband or client.

Start your pedigree with yourself and your immediate family—parents, siblings, and children. For each, put down the birth date and, if applicable, the death date and cause of death. Then move on to second-degree relatives: aunts, uncles, nieces, nephews, grandparents, grandchildren, half-sisters, and half-brothers. Then record third-degree relatives: great-grandparents, great-grandchildren, great-uncles, great-aunts, half-uncles, half-aunts, first cousins and other cousins. Remember, this is a pedigree that records biological, not genealogical, relationships; it is not necessary to record the spouse of a family member if there are no children. Ethnicity and place of birth can be important; remember that some genetic diseases are known to occur in certain ethnic groups and in certain geographic areas. Be sure to include any significant environmental or occupational factors on your master pedigree. Once you have your master pedigree, save it under a new file name, then call up a duplicate and begin to chart serious illnesses or surgical operations. Include the age of onset for any serious medical condition.

Hair Today, Gone Tomorrow

While you are compiling information about the family's diseases, you might get comfortable with the family pedigree by charting some of the family's physical traits, for instance, baldness. Baldness is not really a disease, although judging from the amount of money men spend on "curing" this condition, one would not know that. Baldness can occur from some skin conditions, thyroid disease, or nutritional defects, but by far the most common cause for baldness is male pattern baldness. We have all seen families where the father is almost completely bald and the male children have full heads of hair. We usually say that the boys "got their mother's hair." In many ways, that is true. The genes for baldness can be inherited from either the paternal or the maternal side of the family.

Baldness in men depends on a complex interaction between the genes, age, and levels of the male hormone. In men who carry the baldness genes, normal levels of male hormone affect the hair follicles once a certain age is reached, damaging them so that hair falls out and is not replaced. The distribution of the pattern of baldness depends on the distribution of the baldness genes in the hair follicles. Certain groups are at increased risk while others are relatively immune. Caucasian men are at greatest risk for male pattern baldness; Chinese, Native Americans, and to some extent, African Americans are at less risk. Women can also have thin hair, but their lower level of male hormone protects them from the most severe male pattern baldness. Chart the thin hair or baldness trait in your family for your own interest, but it might be wise not to share that particular pedigree with the other members of your family, especially the men.

Use the standard symbols shown in Figures 6.3–6.7. Males are represented by squares, females by circles, unknown sex by diamonds. For a couple, males are placed to the left of females, if possible. Each generation has its own line, numbered using roman numerals. The horizontal line connecting a man and woman who are partners is known as the relationship line; the vertical line from that couple leading to their children is the line of descent; the horizontal line connecting all the children of the couple is the sibship line, and the vertical line leading to each child is the individual line (see Figure 6.4). Siblings are listed in birth order, with the oldest to the left and the youngest to the right.

For pregnancies that are not carried to term, use *TOP* for termination of pregnancy and *SAB* for spontaneous abortion; in those cases, the individual line is shortened. Twins share one vertical individual line and are symbolized by whether they are identical (monozygotic) or fraternal (dizygotic), or unknown. The symbol for adopted individuals is put in brackets. Geneticists place either an individual's age or date of birth below the symbol. Genealogists should use the date of birth, rather than an age, as they will be using the pedigree chart for years. For deceased individuals, put a slash through the symbol and record the age at death and cause of death. For divorce or separation, the horizontal relationship line should show a slash. A double relationship line in a medical pedigree indicates a consanguineous union.

Geneticists shade the box or circle to show an affected individual with one or more conditions. Genealogists should do the same. When tracking what might be a specific genetic disease or familial condition in the family, genealogists should also shade in the affected individuals and put in the age of onset for the disease. This shading needs to be explained in a legend. The legend should also contain the date the pedigree was constructed, any unusual symbols, and an explanation of any abbreviations. Any abbreviations used should be included in the legend. For instance, *CHD* on a medical pedigree could be coronary heart disease or congenital heart disease; the legend identifies which is which.

Start with a disease in the family that might have a genetic component. Suppose your mother had breast cancer at age 42 and her sister had breast cancer at 49. The early age of onset could indicate a genetic condition or an inherited susceptibility to this common disease. Check the family for all other instances of cancer and note these on your pedigree. Remember, information about unaffected family members is just as important as information about which family members have a specific condition, since full information will enable you to make a more accurate estimation about the presence of a given disease in a family.

Let us look at one example of a completed pedigree to see how it can be used. In the example seen in Figure 6.9, boy III-1 died suddenly during a football game at the age of 19. An autopsy by the medical examiner found that he had died from familial HCM (hypertrophic cardiomyopathy), a genetic disease with a dominant inheritance. The family's pedigree shows that the dead boy's father II-1 had died of an undiagnosed heart condition at an early age, as had his aunt II-4. Testing of the family showed that the dead boy's siblings appeared unaffected, but his cousin III-5 had the condition (the vertical line in the circle is used here to show an affected live individual); III-5's mother II-4 (the same individual as the aunt just mentioned) presumably also had the condition. The cousin III-5, although still healthy, will need careful medical monitoring of her heart. HCM, like other autosomal dominant diseases, does not "skip" generations; if a child has the disease, then at least one parent must also have the gene. As seen in this case, autosomal dominant diseases affect both sexes.

A medical pedigree is not only useful to you, but also of immense value to your sisters or brothers, your children, and your grandchildren. It needs to be periodically updated. All pedigrees should have a date; if you call it up to add new material, change the date. Family health history pedigrees are not static. A family health history is an ongoing project; it changes as the health of the family members does. Once you have compiled your pedigree chart, review it yearly. This requires you to renew your contacts to find out whether new diseases have made their appearance in the family or if a puzzling medical condition has finally been diagnosed. The pedigree also needs to be reevaluated in light of the new findings of genetics. While cancer of the breast and ovary were thought to be familial in the 1980s, the discovery of the BRCA genes in the 1990s significantly established that fact and provided one method of inheritance with important consequences to family members.

Now that you have drawn your master pedigree, and made multiple copies and added any diseases that affect the family, it is time to analyze your results. You need to look for any warning signs that suggest a genetic disease and look for patterns of inheritance for single-gene diseases. You also need to make note of multifactorial diseases, those without a discrete inheritance, that appear in the family. The next chapter discusses those issues.

CHAPTER 7

What Have I Found?

THE ANALYSIS OF YOUR PEDIGREE CAN VARY FROM THE SIMPLE TASK of noting what serious diseases are present and finding out more about those conditions and whether they have a genetic component, to the complex task of actually determining a pattern of inheritance, such as dominant or recessive.

The Warning Signs

What are some of the signs in your pedigree that might suggest a genetic condition or some form of familial disease? Look for the following:

- Early age of onset of a common disease, for instance, cancer of the breast, colon, or prostate, or heart disease before age 50
- Several closely related members of your family with the same disease, especially if it is relatively rare
- Sudden unexplained death in a healthy family member, especially if the individual is relatively young
- Unexplained problems in the offspring of parents who are cousins
- An individual with several medical problems
- Someone with a cancer in paired organs, such as cancer in both the right and left kidneys

109

- Three or more miscarriages or stillbirths in one couple

- An unusual physical feature, especially if there is some health problem in an individual

- Unexplained movement or nervous disorders, or problems with sight or hearing, especially if the onset is at an early age

- A severe mental illness, possibly requiring institutionalization

- Delay in development of an individual, especially if associated with some degree of mental retardation or learning difficulty

- An infant who fails to thrive and who shows multiple recurrent or chronic infections

- A child with a congenital anomaly, such as congenital heart disease, facial abnormalities like cleft lip or cleft palate, or an abnormality of the spinal cord, ear, hands, or feet

- An unexplained surgical death or reaction to surgical anesthesia

These are some of the warning signs that might indicate a genetic disease is present in the pedigree. In evaluating a pedigree, ask how prevalent a disease is in the family. Investigate the disease to see whether it is known to have a genetic component. If so, is it inherited as a single-gene disease, which would show Mendelian inheritance, or is there a complex pattern of inheritance, such as would be seen in a multifactorial disease? Is it a more or less one-time chromosomal disorder such as Down syndrome? Any condition, especially if uncommon, that shows up in the family pedigree more than once should be scrutinized, but be sure that you understand the medical condition and know whether it has a genetic factor. In the next chapter, we describe some of the conditions you should look for, and in Chapter 12, we list Web sites that provide more information. If one family member dies of rheumatic heart disease, an acquired condition that follows a strep infection (streptococcal bacteria), it should not be considered as "heart disease" and compared to another family member who died suddenly of a heart attack at age 34.

Understanding the degree of genetic relationship between family members is important for estimating genetic risk, especially for multifactorial diseases. First-degree relatives are defined as one's children, parents, and siblings; first-degree relatives share one-half of their genes with you. Second-degree relatives include grandparents, grandchildren, aunts, uncles, nieces, and nephews. Second-degree relatives also include any half-sisters or half-brothers. Second-degree relatives share one-fourth of their genes. Third-degree relatives include great-grandparents, great-grandchildren, great-uncles and great-aunts, half-uncles and half-aunts, and first cousins. Third-degree relatives share one-eighth of their genes. The chart shown in Figure 7.1 illustrates the degrees of relationship. The closer the relationship, the more you are at risk for a multifactorial disease. Prostate cancer, for instance, in a first-degree relative would put you at greater risk than prostate cancer in a third-degree relative.

If you or a first-degree relative has what might be a genetic disease, start your analysis with that disease. Look for other instances of the disorder or evidence of the disease. For instance, if you or a close-degree relative has cancer, see whether other family

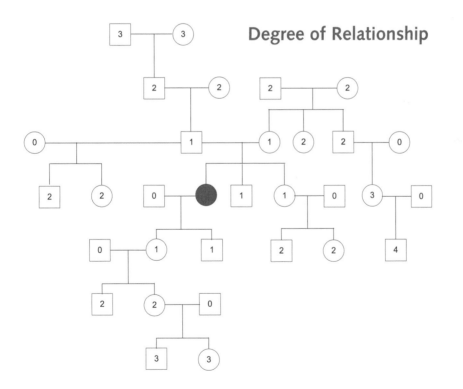

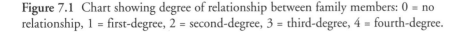

Figure 7.1 Chart showing degree of relationship between family members: 0 = no relationship, 1 = first-degree, 2 = second-degree, 3 = third-degree, 4 = fourth-degree.

members had or have cancer. Find out the type of cancer, the organ of origin, the age of onset, and if applicable, the age of death. Early age of onset of certain cancers may indicate a genetic factor. Examine the racial and ethnic origin of everyone in the family. Where did they live? Where are they from? As we know, certain genetic diseases occur in particular ethnic groups and in certain geographic areas.

Patterns of Inheritance

With multiple instances of the same disease or similar disorders, look for patterns of inheritance. Who is affected, and what is their relationship? Could it be a single-gene disease? Figure 7.2 shows an example of an autosomal dominant disease inheritance. With a dominant disease, each generation is affected—each affected individual has one parent with the disease. Other characteristics of a dominant disease include the following:

- The disease can affect both males and females.
- Transmission can occur from male to male (father to son).
- The degree of severity can vary.
- The disease may appear relatively late in life.

Autosomal Dominant Inheritance

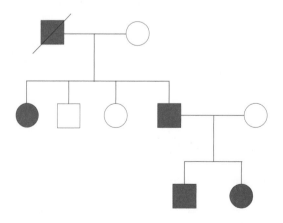

Figure 7.2 Autosomal dominant disease pedigree.

It All Comes Down to a Single Gene

Of the thousands of single-gene diseases transmitted by dominant, recessive, or X-linked inheritance, these are some of the most common:

Dominant	Recessive	X-linked
Adult polycystic kidney disease	Alpha-1-antitrypsin deficiency	Christmas diseases
Familial adenomatous polyposis coli	Cystic fibrosis	Colorblindness, red-green
Familial Alzheimer disease	Friedreich ataxia	Duchenne muscular dystrophy
Familial hypercholesterolemia	Galactosemia	Fragile-X syndrome
Huntington disease	Gaucher disease	Hemophilia
Marfan syndrome	Hemochromatosis	
Neurofibromatosis	Niemann-Pick disease	
Porphyria	Phenylketonuria	
Retinoblastoma	Sickle cell anemia	
Von Hippel-Lindau syndrome	Thalasemia	
	Wilson disease	
	Xeroderma pigmentosum	

In Figure 7.3, we see an example of an autosomal recessive disease inheritance. The most typical pattern is a mating between two individuals who are normal (do not show symptoms of the disease) but are carrying a recessive gene. Affected individuals tend to be limited to a single generation, the progeny of these two individuals. Like autosomal dominant inheritance, both males and females tend to be affected equally. Recessive diseases tend to share certain characteristics:

- The disease may seem to "skip" generations.

- The disease may appear in a brother and a sister.

- Both males and females can be affected.

- The disease may be associated with certain ethnic or geographic groups.
- The disease may be severe.
- Onset at a young age is common; and the disease can appear in a newborn, infant, or child.

Autosomal Recessive Inheritance

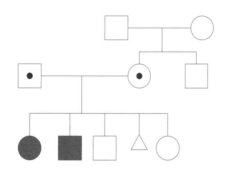

Figure 7.3 Autosomal recessive disease pedigree. The central dot indicates an individual carrying the recessive gene.

Autosomal Recessive Inheritance in Extended Family

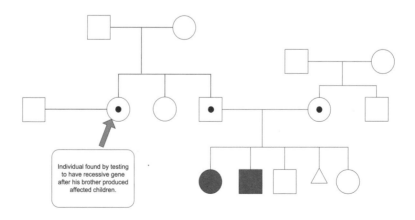

Individual found by testing to have recessive gene after his brother produced affected children.

Figure 7.4 The pedigree seen in figure 7.3 extended to show another involved individual.

With recessive inheritance, the parents are usually unaware that they each carry a recessive gene until the birth and diagnosis of an affected child. Since in many cases, the disease appears only once in the pedigree, it is important that a proper diagnosis be made and the genetic component recognized. Once the child is properly diagnosed with a recessive disease—that is, having two copies of the recessive gene—it becomes clear that both parents carry the gene.

The siblings of these parents should then be notified and tested, especially if they are of childbearing age. Figure 7.4 extends the pedigree shown in Figure 7.3 to show a sibling with the gene. If a sibling with the recessive trait marries another individual with the same recessive gene, they can also produce affected children. The chance that this individual will marry another individual with the recessive gene depends on its frequency in the population. If it is a close intermarrying group, as has been discussed earlier, chances are higher than they would be for a marriage with anyone in the general population. Similarly, if the new mate is a first cousin or even closer, there is an increased chance that this individual will carry the recessive gene that has already been demonstrated to be in the family.

X-linked diseases are caused by diseased genes carried on the X chromosome. Females (XX) do not usually show the disease, but are carriers. The disease appears in males who inherit the abnormal gene on their single X chromosome. In Figure 7.5, the pedigree of an X-linked disease is displayed; the disease descends from the maternal grandmother and affects only males in that line. There is no transmission of an X-linked recessive gene from father to son since the father contributes only the Y chromosome to his son. Figure 7.6 shows a more common format of this same pedigree in which, for the sake of brevity, the normal mate is not included. The following characteristics are associated with X-linked diseases:

- Generally, only males are affected.

- The affected individual has a normal father.

- The pedigree shows normal females.

- There tend to be fewer males in the pedigree or more males dying as children.

X-linked Inheritance

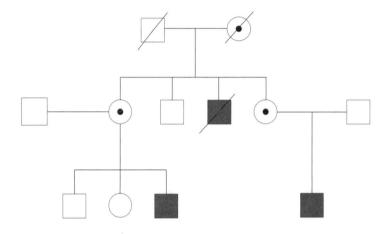

Figure 7.5 X-linked pedigree.

More Common Medical
Pedigree Format

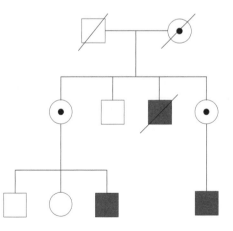

Figure 7.6 The same X-linked pedigree as in Figure 7.5, with spouses removed.

Cousin Marriages

Even if you see only one instance of a disease in your medical pedigree, the disease may still have a genetic basis. A related family member may have the disease gene, but it may not be expressed, it could be so mild that it is never recognized, or the family member may have died at a young age from an acquired condition such as an infection or trauma and never have had the chance to show the genetic disease. Alternatively, there may be only one apparent occurrence of a genetic disease in the family because the disease arose as a mutation in that individual alone.

Look for any marriages between first cousins. First-cousin marriages do increase slightly the chance that both members of the couple will have the same recessive gene and therefore can have an affected child. The risk is only slightly above that for second- or third-cousin marriages; although these should be noted in your pedigree, they are generally not a cause for alarm. If there is a common grandfather who is suspected of having a recessive disease, the risk increases.

We have talked about the importance of small populations and the founder effect for specific genetic diseases, but it is important to realize that this effect can be overestimated. Chances are that if you continue your pedigree far enough back, you will find that some of your ancestors lived and died in small population groups. Many areas of our country were founded by small groups, and in certain areas such as New England, many of these populations retained representatives of their original gene pool and intermarried.

In his article "Interconnecting Bloodlines and Genetic Inbreeding in a Colonial Puritan Community: Eastern Massachusetts, 1630–1885," John Kingsbury analyzed the incredibly interconnecting bloodlines and genetic inbreeding in the colonial Puritan community of eastern Massachusetts. The first European settlers of the small rural Massachusetts Bay Colony, by necessity, had to intermarry extensively. Kingsbury shows that though the couple Frances Joanna Bullard and Willis Albert Kingsbury were fourth cousins at the time of their marriage in 1885, each of them was the product of five or so generations of cousin unions. While many children of the original families had moved on, for the most part these farms were owned and operated by sons and daughters of the original settlers. For more than 200 years, these stable farming communities lived with limited courtship, restricted by the distance one could travel by foot, horse, or buggy. Intermarriage between cousins was inevitable. Yet there is evidence that these individuals were aware of the danger of inbreeding and tried to avoid it. As Kingsbury points out, because the inhabitants made wise choices, both genetically and generationally within that geographic area, the total genetic inbreeding was minor and probably not genetically significant.

Familial Diseases

A genetic component might be present if the disease occurs more than once in the pedigree, especially if the disease or condition is seen in first-degree relatives, such as parents and children, or between siblings. It is incorrect, however, to assume that if several people in the family have the same condition, it must be genetic. Common cancers—for instance, breast cancer—may show more than one occurrence in a pedigree, but that does not necessarily mean there is a genetic underpinning. Common diseases occur commonly. The same disease could occur because the family may be exposed to a similar environmental stress, such as a hazardous occupation, a similar specific diet, a history of smoking, or where the family lives.

Historically, many diseases that were thought to "run in the family" were eventually found not to be genetic but the result of family exposure to a common environment. In the 19th century, tuberculosis, or "consumption," was thought to be inherited. The disease might have been present in several family members and was thought to be "in the blood." The taint was so strong that families often hid the fact that one of their members had consumption since this could hurt the marriage opportunities of a young girl in the family. After all, no one would want to marry into a "consumptive" family. But the appearance of tuberculosis in the family, as we know today, was simply the familial occurrence of an infection; tuberculosis could be acquired from an affected family member by other family members living in close contact. It had nothing to do with genetics.

When analyzing your medical pedigree, take notice when there is a gap in producing children during a woman's childbearing years. Genealogists know that if a woman has two children in two to three years, then has a gap of three to four years when there are no living children, this could indicate a miscarriage or stillbirth, or the father's absence.

This is thought to be especially important during 19th and early 20th century marriages rather than in the second half of the 20th century, when family planning was more reliable and available. But as Sharon DeBartolo Carmack points out in her article "Immigrant Women and Family Planning: Historical Perspectives for Genealogical Research," there was a great deal of planned parenthood undertaken in the 19th century, as well. Some believe that as early as 1850, one out of every six pregnancies was willfully terminated. In lieu of a more effective program, and given the ready availability of willing midwives, abortion was used as contraception. From our standpoint, finding out that there was a stillbirth or miscarriage does not necessarily tell us anything about the health history of the individual since there is always the possibility of human interference with the pregnancy. Not surprisingly, maternal death during an abortion was usually recorded as something else, such as uterine bleeding or hemorrhaging, tetanus, or blood poisoning.

As we have earlier discussed, if during your analysis of disease patterns on your medical pedigree, you see something that may be significant, you should verify the information as much as possible. Obtain any medical records that you can on possibly affected family members, and look for the results of any medical tests, pathology reports, or autopsy reports. Look up the medical condition and related conditions on the Internet. Learn whether the condition has any known genetic component and whether it is known to have a familial occurrence.

Multifactorial diseases such as diabetes, high blood pressure, mental illness, coronary artery disease, and many cancers are familial, but you will not see the distinct inheritance patterns of single-gene diseases. These diseases tend to be more chronic and to occur in adulthood or later in life. Look for these diseases occurring in first-degree relatives. As a rule, if you have one of these multifactorial diseases in a first-degree relative, you are at greater genetic risk.

As important as one's genes are, it is also important to understand that many factors play a role. For some single-genes diseases, expression can be variable. Figure 7.7 shows a dominant inherited condition. The individual indicated by the arrow must have the disease gene because her father and children have the disease, but because of incomplete penetrance, she shows no symptoms. Some individuals with the defective disease gene will show a severe form or expression of the disease; for others, the condition may be mild.

This variability applies even more so to multifactorial diseases, since the relationship between the abnormal genes and the interplay with constitutional factors and environmental factors is complex. For instance, infection is not generally considered a genetic disease, yet the immune response a body can mount to fight an infection is genetically determined. This immune response is balanced with such constitutional factors as age, sex, and nutritional state.

Even the socioeconomic status of the individual can enter into the mix. In the 19th

Autosomal Dominant Inheritance

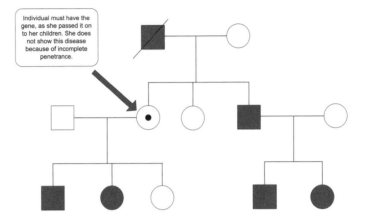

Individual must have the gene, as she passed it on to her children. She does not show this disease because of incomplete penetrance.

Figure 7.7 Autosomal dominant pedigree showing an individual who must have the gene but shows no symptoms.

century, those groups, frequently new immigrants, living in the terrible tenements of our cities—suffering poverty, overcrowding, filth, and poor nutrition—were subject to terrible infectious diseases with many deaths. Had some of these individuals lived in better conditions and with good nutrition, they might have been able to resist these infections. While our immune system has a complicated genetic inheritance, there are discrete diseases of the immune system that are single-gene disorders and inherited by Mendelian rules, including CGD (chronic granulomatous disease) and Wiscott-Aldrich syndrome. In a pedigree, these may show up as a pattern of repeated infections in childhood.

DNA is relatively stable; once removed and stored correctly, it can be tested repeatedly as more is learned about the significance of the genetic code. Genetic tests are now available for many specific diseases, and most likely more will become available in the future, as will comprehensive inventories of an individual's genetic code that will give immediate information about that individual's family—parents, siblings, children, and grandchildren.

If after charting a family pedigree, you believe there is a genetic disease in the family, perhaps one that was completely unknown, seek professional help. In all cases, if you are suspicious that a serious genetic disease is present in your family, make an appointment with a genetics counselor or genetics professional and review the pedigree with that individual. A medical professional can order the appropriate medical records and recommend any biochemical, genetic, or imaging studies to investigate the family more thoroughly.

Undoubtedly, you now have some diseases listed in your pedigree and have some concern that they might play a role in your family's health. The next chapter discusses some of the more common and significant genetic diseases.

CHAPTER **8**

Common and Important Genetic Diseases

WE WILL NOW GO THROUGH THE REVIEW OF SYSTEMS PRESENTED IN Chapter 4 and point out some of the significant genetic diseases that fall into these categories. The classification is artificial; many genetic diseases affect multiple areas of the body. In general, I have picked the most obvious symptom and placed the disease into that category. The first category in the review of systems in Chapter 4, the "general" category, while useful for compiling a medical history, is not useful for categorizing diseases.

These diseases have been selected because they are common or important genetic diseases. Both single-gene and multifactorial diseases are included. There are thousands of single-gene diseases; obviously, a choice had to be made to discuss the most significant ones. For complex diseases, the list includes the most common and significant. It is not a complete overview of genetic diseases; such a list would fill many volumes.

The Heart and Blood Vessels

Heart Attacks and Strokes

Coronary artery disease, which can lead to a heart attack and death, is caused by atherosclerotic obstruction of the coronary arteries, those arteries that supply blood to the heart muscle. The same obstruction can occur in other arteries. When it occurs in one of the carotid arteries in the neck, which supply blood to the brain, it can result in a stroke, or in the new terminology, a brain attack. The development of atherosclerosis is a result of both genetic and environmental factors. High cholesterol, a fatlike substance in the blood, can cause coronary artery disease or stroke by accumulating on the inner walls of blood vessels. This accumulation, or atherosclerosis, narrows the vessels, reducing blood flow. Narrowed coronary arteries can deprive the heart of blood, causing chest pain (angina) on exertion. If one or more of the coronary arteries becomes completely blocked, damage to the heart occurs (a heart attack). Those who find a family history of coronary artery disease occurring at a young age (under age 60) might be at high risk and should have their cholesterol, low-density lipoproteins (LDL), and high-density lipoproteins (HDL) checked. Again, this tends to be a result of many genes interacting with the environment, a multifactorial disease. There are, however, lipid disorders that are single-gene Mendelian diseases.

> **Atherosclerosis** is a disease that causes the inner lining of arteries to thicken, which narrows the lumen of the artery, impeding blood flow. **Plaques,** or **atheromas,** are raised patches that form on the inner wall of arteries; these appear more commonly in individuals with high cholesterol then in those with normal levels. In the coronary arteries, the blood supply to the heart may become blocked by these plaques, causing damage or death to the heart muscle (a heart attack). Atherosclerosis in the carotid arteries in the neck, which supply the brain with blood, is one of the causes of strokes.

The autosomal dominant disorders, FH (familial hypercholesterolemia), FCHL (familial combined hyperlipidemia), and familial hypertriglyceridemia predispose to premature atherosclerosis, and possibly early death from heart attacks and strokes. These cause atherosclerosis, coronary artery disease, and heart attacks, generally at an earlier age than those without the gene, affecting males and females equally. A family history of heart attacks, especially occurring at a young age, should raise suspicion of FH in the family. If FH is found, all first-degree relatives should have their cholesterol tested and, if it is found to be elevated, they should be treated. First-degree relatives also include children, so it is generally recommended that children with this disease be treated as well. Incidentally, don't look for death by a heart attack in 19th century records; it wasn't until 1912 that physicians began to diagnose this disease.

Atherosclerotic heart disease, where there is occlusion of the coronary arteries and a subsequent heart attack, is the single most common cause of death in the United States today.

High Blood Pressure

High blood pressure, or hypertension, can also lead to coronary heart disease, early strokes, and kidney failure. High blood pressure occurs when the blood pressure is above 140/90. This high pressure puts a strain on the heart and blood vessels. Some diseases of other organs, such as the kidneys or adrenal glands, and a few single-gene Mendelian disorders, such as polycystic kidney disease, can also cause hypertension, but for the majority of individuals with hypertension, probably 9 out of 10 , there is no obvious cause. This common type of hypertension, called essential hypertension, is probably a complex multifactorial disease with genetic, environmental (generally dietary), and racial factors. Essential hypertension is more prevalent in African Americans than Caucasians and is generally more severe; it starts at an earlier age and more often causes severe problems such as strokes and kidney damage. Hispanics have a lower incidence of hypertension than African Americans or Caucasians. A history of hypertension in a first-degree relative increases the risk for hypertension.

Blood pressure instrumentation was not standardized until 1920, and even as late as the 1940s, hypertension was not recognized to be a problem. Since older medical records or causes of death do not include hypertension, in those records look for a diagnosis of stroke, heart attack, heart failure, or kidney disease, especially if they occur at an early age, as an indicator of possible hypertension in the family.

Heart Muscle Disorders

Some types of cardiomyopathies can be inherited. Cardiomyopathy is a disease of heart *(cardio)* muscle *(myo)*. The heart muscle becomes weak and its pumping function is affected. Dilated cardiomyopathy is the most common; the heart enlarges (dilates) and loses its ability to pump, causing heart failure. Acquired causes of heart muscle damage include damage from a heart attack, a viral infection, and toxins. In many cases, the cause is not known. Some of these can be familial and have a genetic basis. Once the diagnosis of dilated cardiomyopathy is made, only half of those individuals are alive five years later. It is the main indication for a heart transplant. Studies have shown that dilated cardiomyopathy can be transmitted in all fashions. It may not show well-defined inheritance but be familial. In some cases, it may show single-gene inheritance and be autosomal dominant, autosomal recessive, X-linked, or even possibly transmitted through mitochondria. Autosomal dominant inheritance is the most common, but there may be incomplete penetrance or the disease may vary in its level of expression. A rare genetic condition called Barth syndrome can cause dilated cardiomyopathy in male children during the first year of life or later.

Cardiomyopathy is a disease of the heart muscle that weakens the muscle and therefore the ability of the heart to effectively pump blood. In addition to genetic causes, cardiomyopathies can occur from toxins, from several metabolic diseases, or from viruses. The end result is the same: heart failure with fatigue, shortness of breath, and swollen legs, among other symptoms.

The other form of cardiomyopathy is hypertrophic cardiomyopathy. In this condition (also known as idiopathic hypertrophic subaortic stenosis—IHSS, asymmetrical septal hypertrophy—ASH, or hypertrophic obstructive cardiomyopathy), the heart walls thicken. This thickening reduces the size of the heart's chambers and obstructs blood flow. Most cases are inherited; there are often few symptoms, but it is a cause of sudden death due to a sudden irregularity in the heart's rhythm. One investigator showed that hypertrophic cardiomyopathy was the most frequent cause of sudden death in young athletes during sports. Some believe that familial hypertrophic cardiomyopathy may be more common than is suspected.

Both types of cardiomyopathy may be associated with irregular heart rhythm, which can result in sudden and unexpected death. Normally, the heart contracts or beats in response to an electrical surge that travels from the top of the heart to the bottom. It is this electrical rhythm that is detected with an EKG. If the electrical impulse cannot travel through the heart, it is "blocked," or more specifically, since the impulse travels through a "bundle" of specialized tissue, the individual is said to have a "bundle branch block." Blocks in electrical conduction can be caused by damage to the heart muscle, as could occur from a heart attack and in association with the cardiomyopathies. In many cases, blocks are minor and cause no symptoms. On other occasions, an individual may need a pacemaker to establish a normal heart rhythm. Familial heart block may be inherited as an autosomal dominant condition. Symptoms vary depending on the degree of involvement but can include shortness of breath, fainting, and sudden death due to a complete loss of the normal heart's rhythm.

Congenital Heart Disease

The causes of congenital heart diseases vary. Some are caused by chromosomal diseases when part of a chromosome is absent or there is an abnormal additional amount of chromosome material. Examples include some of the trisomy syndromes, such as trisomy 21 (Down syndrome), trisomy 18, trisomy 13, and Turner syndrome (missing one of two X chromosomes). Congenital heart disease can also be seen as part of a single-gene disease, such as Ellis van Crevald disease where, in addition to dwarfism and extra fingers, affected individuals have an atrial septal defect (ASD), an abnormal opening between the upper two chambers of the heart. A ventricular septal defect (VSD), an abnormal opening between the lower chambers of the heart, is also common; most are isolated events, a few are part of a genetic syndrome. Family inheritance of congenital heart defects alone, without other genetic abnormalities, is also seen. MVP (mitral valve prolapse), a deformity in the valve in the left side of the heart, has an estimated incidence of about 5 percent and may follow a dominant inheritance pattern or occur as part of a single-gene syndrome. Symptoms can range from none to chest pain and shortness of breath. Possible complications as an adult include mitral valve regurgitation, where the valve does not close completely; endocarditis, where there is an infection on the diseased valve; and even, rarely, sudden death.

Congenital heart disease is one of the most common forms of birth defects. While it may be associated with a specific genetic syndrome, most cases are sporadic. Only about 10 to 20 percent are eventually found to be part of a recognized genetic syndrome or are found to have a genetic cause.

The Lungs

Asthma

There is a genetic component to asthma, with an interaction between the genes and exposure to allergens in the air. Asthma does appear to "run in the family" although its exact mechanism of inheritance is not known. Children of parents or even a single parent with asthma show some increased risk of having the disease. This is important information for the pediatrician to know, as it can help the doctor determine the cause of a breathing problem or chronic cough in the child.

Chronic Lung Disease

Among the multifactorial diseases is COPD (chronic obstructive pulmonary disease), or chronic lung disease, consisting of emphysema and chronic bronchitis, characterized by slowly progressive deterioration in breathing. Dust, a smoking history, and air pollution are environmental effects that can exacerbate this condition and, incidentally, affect entire families, simulating a genetic disease. Alpha-1-antitrypsin (AAT) deficiency, however, is a discrete genetic disease that may cause the onset of COPD symptoms before the age of 40. This relatively common genetic condition, occurring in approximately one in 2,500 Caucasians, is rare in African Americans and Asians. Normally, the body's white blood cells are an important defense mechanism to fight infections such as pneumonia. But an enzyme released by white blood cells can also attack the body's tissues, including the lungs. The protein AAT normally functions to protect the body against this enzyme. If AAT is absent, the lungs, and occasionally the liver, are vulnerable to the body's own defensive mechanisms.

AAT deficiency is transmitted as recessive, so only individuals who have two copies

Chronic obstructive pulmonary disease (COPD) is the name given to chronic lung disease that is a combination of chronic bronchitis and emphysema. Both conditions can cause chronic and progressive shortness of breath and heart failure. While some COPD is caused by the inherited condition alpha-1-antitrypsin deficiency, most is caused by cigarette smoking and air pollution.

of the defective gene will show the disease, generally an early onset of COPD, frequently in their 30s and 40s. The disease is caused by a mutation in the SERPINA1 gene found on chromosome 14; over 70 different versions, or alleles, produce different amounts of AAT, from normal levels to very low levels. Carriers, those with only one copy of the diseased gene, while generally normal, depending on what allele they have, can be at increased risk of lung disease, especially if they smoke or are exposed to a high level of air pollution. The disease may also cause liver disease, including cirrhosis and liver cancer. Affected patients with this gene can run the entire gamut of being severely affected to having little problem.

Cystic Fibrosis

Cystic fibrosis (CF) is rare in African Americans and even rarer in Asian Americans. If both members of a couple are carriers and they have children, each child has a 25 percent chance of inheriting both of the abnormal genes and having the disease and a 50 percent chance of inheriting one abnormal gene and becoming a carrier. Individuals with the disease are prone to chronic lung infections and disordered absorption of food. Cystic fibrosis was first identified in the 1930s. The nature of the disease varies; some children become severely ill from birth, while others have little problem until later in life. Even in adults, the severity of the disease can vary.

The Stomach and Intestines

Peptic Ulcer Disease

Peptic ulcer disease is a heterogeneous group of diseases characterized by the presence of an ulcer in the upper gastrointestinal tract: the stomach and duodenum. Approximately 20 percent of first-degree relatives may also have peptic ulcer disease. Like other multifactorial diseases, environmental factors such as infection with the microorganism *Helicobacter pylori*, medications such as aspirin, and possibly stress can predispose one to this condition. Individuals with blood group O have an increased risk, and it may be seen as a result of some rare genetic diseases.

Gallstones

Gallstones are very common. There is evidence of a familial predisposition to this disease. Some Native American populations show a high incidence of it. One estimate is that first-degree relatives stand a fourfold chance of also having the disease. But for many individuals, gallstones have no symptoms, so the true incidence of this disease in certain families is unknown.

Celiac Disease

Celiac disease (CD), also known as celiac sprue, nontropical sprue, and gluten-sensitive enteropathy (GSR), is a multifactorial disease involving genetics and environment. It is an abnormal sensitivity of the small bowel that cannot tolerate a protein called gluten found in wheat, rye, and barley. Ingestion of gluten damages the small intestine and interferes with absorption of nutrients from food. Inheritance is familial. About 10 percent of an affected person's first-degree relatives will also have the disease. Classically, the disease is seen in children who show recurrent diarrhea and a failure to grow and thrive, but the disease may not be diagnosed until adulthood. Celiac disease affects people differently. Some develop symptoms as children, others as adults. Other features of the disease include anemia, loss of bone with subsequent fractures, skin rashes, and nerve damage (peripheral neuropathy). Autoimmune diseases—caused by the individual's own immune system—occur more frequently in patients with celiac disease and include type 1 diabetes, Graves disease of the thyroid,

JFK's Health History

An intriguing theory has recently arisen about the health problems of America's 35th president, John F. Kennedy. Apparently, he was chronically ill for most of his life, beginning with "colitis" at the age of 17. This continued throughout his life, with diarrhea, abdominal discomfort, and problems maintaining weight. His doctors prescribed Lomotil, paregoric, and Metamucil, among others, to control his bowel symptoms. In addition to his bowel problem, President Kennedy suffered from osteoporosis of the spine and Addison disease, an autoimmune disease of the adrenal gland. Given the long history of "colitis," his Irish ancestry, and his Addison disease, it is possible that John F. Kennedy had celiac disease. The osteoporosis of the spine could have been a result of the disease or of the steroids he was prescribed to help control his bowel symptoms.

Addison disease, and lupus. Adults with celiac disease have variable symptoms but can have abdominal bloating and pain, chronic diarrhea, problems maintaining weight, and pale, foul-smelling stools. The discomfort and abdominal bloating may lead to the mistaken diagnosis of irritable bowel disease.

One large study suggested that celiac disease is a much greater problem in the United States than had previously been appreciated, but its true prevalence in this country is difficult to know, as many patients do not have typical symptoms, may have very mild symptoms, or show no symptoms at all. Some believe that the disorder affects one of every 120 to 300 individuals in the United States and Europe. Others believe that it is less common, more in the range of one in 1,000. The disease is rare in Asia but appears throughout Europe, with Ireland, especially the western counties, seeming to have an exceptionally high incidence.

The only treatment for celiac disease is to follow a gluten-free diet. In patients with untreated or severe disease, there is a higher incidence of gastrointestinal cancers or lymphoma, a group of cancers originating in the lymph nodes.

Colon and Pancreatic Cancer

Cancer of the colon, or large intestine, is common in the United States. In most cases, cancer develops in a polyp or growth from the lining of the colon. Colon cancer can be familial and can occur in families with a high incidence of other cancer types. There are two genetic familial forms: FAP (familial adenomatous polyplosis), also known as multiple polyposis of the colon, and HNPCC (hereditary nonpolyposis colon cancer).

In FAP, multiple colon polyps, or growths, appear, in some cases completely covering the colon. While initially benign, these polyps have a high predisposition to turn cancerous. FAP is usually diagnosed in individuals in their 20s, and cancer of the colon or rectum develops when the individuals are in their 30s or 40s. Individuals with FAP can have hundreds or thousands of polyps in their colon, and the chance of developing colon cancer by age 50 is very high. Gardner syndrome is a variant of FAP in which, in addition to pre-malignant polyps, there are also cysts of the skin and bone. Both conditions are due to mutations in the long arm (q) of chromosome 5, and asymptomatic family members can be tested for the mutant gene.

In HNPCC, we see families with an increased incidence of colon cancer but few, if any, predisposing polyps. For some, there is only an increased risk of colon cancer. Others with this disease have a risk not only of colon cancer but also of cancer of the uterus, ovary, kidney, breast, bladder, stomach, and pancreas, and probably others. As with other hereditary cancers, early age of onset and multiple affected family members are common.

Another cancer that can be familial is pancreatic cancer. There are about 30,000 new cases of pancreatic cancer a year in the United States, compared to about 200,000 new cases of breast cancer. Pancreatic cancer is very serious, and successful treatment is difficult. Between 5 and 15 percent of pancreatic cancers may be familial. Considering the older age of onset, the number may be higher—potentially affected family members may die of other causes before they show the disease. Other genetic diseases such as HNPCC and mutations in the BRCA2 gene are also associated with pancreatic cancer.

Probably the most famous pancreatic cancer family is that of former President Jimmy Carter. President Carter's father, James Earl Carter, died of pancreatic cancer at the age of 58. Of James's children, President Carter's brother Billy died at the age of 51, his sister Ruth Carter Stapleton died at 54, and his other sister Gloria Carter Spann died at 63—all from pancreatic cancer.

Liver Disease

Liver disease can occur in association with several well-defined genetic syndromes, many of which are the result of an abnormal buildup of a specific chemical, such as glycogen storage disease (GSD), in which the chemical is glycogen; Wilson disease, a disease where copper accumulates in the liver and brain; and hemochromatosis (HFE), a disease where excessive iron accumulates in the liver and other organs.

Individuals with GSD have an inherited inability to release glycogen to the body. The food we eat contains glucose (sugar), which is necessary for the body to function. Generally, the body stores the excess glucose as a different molecule, glycogen, which is a long chain of glucose molecules. Glycogen is stored in the liver and muscles. When the body needs energy, it breaks up the glycogen into its component glucose to supply the body's needs. It is this break-up mechanism that is missing in those with GSD, generally inherited as an autosomal recessive. There are about 11 types of GSD. Symptoms vary depending on the type—few symptoms may appear, or the disease may be life threatening. Because glycogen is stored in the liver and muscles, these organs tend to be most affected. For most, the disease begins in childhood with low blood sugar and growth retardation; the liver may be enlarged from glycogen accumulation and muscles may be weak. Some may experience permanent liver damage and even liver cancer and heart failure due to weakness in the heart muscle.

Wilson disease is a recessive genetic disease in which excess copper accumulates in the liver, brain, and other organs. About one in 100 individuals carries this abnormal gene. Individuals may have jaundice, abdominal pain, tremors, spasticity, difficulty speaking, and mental changes, including apparent psychosis, in their 20s and 30s. Diagnosis can be difficult. The liver disease in Wilson disease may be misdiagnosed as hepatitis. It is important to diagnose Wilson disease early because liver cirrhosis can occur before there are any symptoms. The gene, ATP7B, is located on chromosome 13. As with other genetic diseases, many different types of mutations or alleles can exist. For Wilson disease, more than 200 mutations of ATP7B have been recorded, making it difficult to design a simple genetic screening test. Treatment is to remove the excess copper; a drug can be given that binds with copper and allows it to be excreted from the body. With proper treatment, the disease progress can be halted. Without treatment, death occurs early. Once the disease has been diagnosed, it is imperative that relatives be evaluated.

HFE (hemochromatosis) is an autosomal recessive disease where excessive amounts of dietary iron are absorbed from the intestines and the amount of iron increases in the body. The excessive iron is deposited in the liver, heart, pancreas, and skin, causing heart failure, cirrhosis of the liver, diabetes, arthritis, and a dark skin coloring. Symptoms begin in men after age 30, and later in women. Although both men and women can have the disease, women show fewer symptoms because they regularly lose iron in their menstrual blood. Since hemochromatosis is recessive, an individual with only one copy of the diseased gene is a carrier, and may have a slight increase in iron absorption, but does not develop the disease. Hemochromatosis is often undiagnosed and, consequently, untreated. The early symptoms of fatigue, arthritis, and loss of sex drive are all too common. The disease is relatively easy to treat once diagnosed and individuals can lead a normal life. Treatment is simply to remove blood periodically by frequent blood donations; because hemoglobin, the red blood cell pigment, contains iron, removing blood removes the excess iron.

Some estimates suggest that about 10 percent of individuals may have a copy of the abnormal gene, making hemochromatosis probably the most common autosomal recessive disease. One study in Utah found one in 333 had two copies of the gene and the disease. Hemochromatosis is seen most often in those who trace their heritage back to northern Europe, especially those of Celtic or Nordic origin. High frequency has been reported in Australia for those individuals of Scottish or Irish descent, in Afrikaners where as many as one in six may be a carrier, in Danes, and in northeastern Quebec. The disease is less common in African Americans, Asian Americans, Hispanic Americans, and Native Americans.

It is fascinating to speculate that hemochromatosis arose because it conveyed an evolutionary advantage. One can imagine an ancient Celtic population living with an iron-poor diet that had a few fortunate individuals who were able to absorb and store more iron than the rest. Possibly this was especially important to menstruating women, keeping them from iron-deficiency anemia and allowing them to have children and pass the gene on.

Glycogen storage disease and Wilson disease can become evident during adolescence; hemochromatosis may not become obvious until middle age. Both hemochromatosis and Wilson disease, characterized by excess deposition of iron and copper in the liver, respectively, increase the risk of liver cancer. Siblings of individuals affected with Wilson disease or hemochromatosis should be evaluated before liver disease occurs.

Gaucher disease results in an accumulation of a certain type of fat in the liver, spleen, and bone marrow. The liver and spleen become enlarged, and changes in the bone marrow cause bone deformities. There is bone pain and anemia. It is one of the most common genetic diseases of Ashkenazi Jews, with one out of 10 a carrier for the type 1 form of this recessive disease. Today, there is a treatment to supply the afflicted individual with the missing enzyme. Type 2 disease is a fatal nervous disease of infancy similar to Tay-Sachs disease. Type 3 Gaucher disease is a slowly progressive nervous disease with survival into adulthood. Neither type 2 nor type 3 is seen with increased frequency in Ashkenazi Jews.

Nervous Conditions

Epilepsy

Based on data from Iceland, where whole population medical information is accessible, about 55 of every 100,000 individuals have epilepsy. Epilepsy is a group of disorders characterized by recurrent seizures. Some epilepsies can be connected to previous head injury, others to alcoholism; some follow a stroke or brain infection. In the majority of cases, the cause for epilepsy is unknown. The risk is high in the first year of life and low in midlife, but rises to its highest incidence in the oldest age group. A genetic cause for epilepsy should be suspected if the onset of seizures occurs at an early age, if there are other members of the family with seizures, or if there is some evidence of congenital abnormalities or mental retardation. Close to 200 genetic syndromes have some degree of seizures.

Migraines

Migraine headaches, where there is intense pain in the temples or forehead that sometimes lasts for days, show strong familial links. They affect women more than men. Migraine headaches in a first-degree relative bring higher risk. It is the most common type of episodic headache. A cluster headache is a variant in which the pain is above the eye or involves the temple. It also is strongly familial.

J. M. S. Pearce, writing in the medical journal *Cephalagia*, notes that Thomas Jefferson (1743–1826) beginning in 1803, describes periodic headaches, occurring daily for two to three weeks and lasting several hours. His description suggests that Jefferson may have suffered from migraine or cluster headaches.

Alcoholism

It is estimated that about 20 million Americans have a serious drinking problem. Results of twin studies suggest that the tendency to abuse alcohol is influenced by genetics. It does run in families; first-degree relatives of alcoholics are generally considered to be at some degree of increased risk. A study of Swedish children adopted at birth showed that children of alcoholic parents were at greater risk of alcohol dependence than children of

Alcohol Consumption in America

From the American Revolution until the early 20th century, alcoholic beverages were consumed in what were, by today's standards, enormous amounts. People had a generally favorable view of alcoholic beverages, with most believing that alcohol improved health and helped ward off fever. Considering the quality of the drinking water supply in those days, they may have been right. Nevertheless, excessive drinking was recognized as a problem. In 1852, a Swede named Magnus Huss coined the term *alcoholism*, which he defined as a chronic disease resulting from dependence on alcohol.

There was some effort in the mid-decades of the 19th century to curb alcohol consumption, but by the 1870s, this temperance movement waned and again the country looked upon drinking favorably. Contributing to the problem were patent medicines, which were widely used in the late 19th century. Their popularity was probably due to their "active ingredient." Most were primarily alcohol, including, for instance, the widely popular Hostetter's Celebrated Stomach Bitters (88 proof) and Parker's Tonic (83 proof). By 1900, temperance again set in, resulting in Prohibition in 1920.

nonalcoholics. Genetics may also play a role in determining whether an alcoholic goes on to develop liver disease.

Psychiatric Conditions

Bipolar affective disorder (manic-depressive illness), unipolar affective disorder (major depression), schizophrenia, and possibly panic and obsessive-compulsive disorders can all have a genetic basis. Inheritance is multifactorial; presumably, there is a genetic predisposition compounded by environmental factors. For instance, severe depression can be triggered by stress, such as a death or serious illness in the family.

Clinical (major) depression is not just feeling "down." There is a profound loss of energy, a general apathy, impaired concentration, and feelings of guilt. Symptoms can interfere with everyday activities such as work, eating, and sleeping. Symptoms persist for weeks to months, and individuals can become suicidal. Depression affects one in every five people. It is estimated that over 50 percent of those who commit suicide

Mental Disease and Creativity

Some believe there is a relationship between affective disorders and creativity. There does seem to be an increased amount of either depression or bipolar disease among the artistically gifted. Edgar Allan Poe, Robert Schumann, Vincent Van Gogh, Lord Byron, Cole Porter, Paul Gauguin, Tennessee Williams, Mark Twain, Ezra Pound, Virginia Woolf, and Ernest Hemingway are some of the artists who suffered from an affective disorder. If the affective disorders do have a genetic component, then they should be seen in close family members. A review of the medical pedigree of the poet Alfred Lord Tennyson, who suffered lifelong bouts of depression, shows that two of his great-grandfathers, one of his grandfathers, his father, and five of his seven brothers suffered from depression and bipolar disorders.

have an affective disorder. First-degree relatives of those with depression are at increased risk of also becoming depressed, and possibly suicidal. In the *Archives of General Psychiatry*, September 2002 issue, it was reported that children of parents who had attemtped suicide have six times the risk of attempting suicide themselves, compared to those whose parents had never attempted suicide.

Individuals with bipolar disorder show wild mood swings, varying from depression to periods of hyperactive (manic) behavior. It is not as common as depression; about 1 percent of the population suffers from this disease. The actor Patty Duke describes her bipolar affective disorder in the book *A Brilliant Madness*. Bipolar affective disorder appears to be a strongly genetic disease. Children with one bipolar parent have a 10 to 30 percent chance of developing the condition; having two affected parents raises the risk to 75 percent.

Schizophrenia is characterized by disturbed emotion, disordered thinking, and erratic behavior; the onset is generally in the late teens or early adulthood. Delusions, withdrawal, and hallucinations occur. First-degree relatives of those with schizophrenia are at increased risk of acquiring the disease, and if one identical twin has the disease, the other twin is at high risk. Schizophrenia does have a significant genetic component, but its mode of inheritance is not clear. As with many relatively common disorders, such as cancer and diabetes, schizophrenia is generally not a single-gene disorder but multifactorial. There are probably multiple genes involved, possibly associated with some environmental factor.

Autism, occurring in childhood, also has a strong genetic component. Affected children are characterized by impaired language and social actions, repetitive behavior, lack of interest, and general incapacitation. Siblings have an increased risk of bearing an autistic child. Autistic behavior can also be seen in the autosomal dominant disease tuberous sclerosis, which is characterized by an acne-like rash on the face and some degree of mental retardation. Autistic behavior, seizures, and epilepsy are seen in the majority of affected individuals. These individuals also develop benign, noncancerous tumors of the kidney, eye, brain, and heart. As with many dominant inherited diseases, expression varies. Autism can also arise spontaneously in an affected child of normal parents. It is estimated to occur in one in 6,000 births and perhaps more, with probably many individuals undiagnosed.

The affective disorders and schizophrenia have a definite inherited component. How much normal behavior is inherited? Studies have shown that identical twins, who have identical DNA but who are separated and raised independently in different environments, show similar personalities and intellectual traits. Identical twins with the same genes are more similar than fraternal twins who share only half their genes. Not only is susceptibility to an affective disorder or schizophrenia inherited, but there also appears to be an inherited component to personality and intelligence. How and how much remain questions to be answered in the future.

Mental Retardation

Severe mental retardation usually has an underlying genetic cause, either a single-gene disease or a chromosomal abnormality. Any child or adult with unexplained mental retardation and some unusual physical feature should raise suspicion of a chromosomal defect. Moderate mental retardation without an obvious cause is seen in the general population, but two important genetic causes are Down syndrome and fragile-X syndrome. Down syndrome is probably the most common genetic form of mental retardation, but since it occurs sporadically and is related to the age of the mother, it is not usually inherited. Fragile-X syndrome is probably the most common inherited cause of mental retardation.

Fragile-X syndrome is believed to affect about one in 1,000 males, causing some degree of mental retardation in most. Its name comes from the unusual appearance of the single X chromosome found in males. A small tip of the chromosome appears to dangle from the rest and is prone to breaking. Males with fragile-X have a normal childhood but, as adults, have a long, narrow face, with protruding ears, a long jaw, large testicles, and hyperextensible finger joints; they may have seizures and mitral valve prolapse, a defect in the heart's valve. The degree of mental retardation, hyperactivity, and learning disabilities varies. Males are primarily affected in this X-linked disease. Carrier females can also be affected but generally show less severe symptoms. Fragile-X syndrome should be suspected in any mentally impaired individual. It was the first human disease to be associated with an increase in the number of repeats of the gene.

In phenylketonuria (PKU), a faulty liver enzyme fails to convert the chemical phenylalanine to another substance; consequently, phenylalanine builds up in the body and results in mental retardation in infancy. Early diagnosis of PKU is important because it is treatable. Treatment is dietary. A low phenylalanine diet throughout life helps prevent mental retardation and the other complications of the disease, such as peculiarities of gait, stance, and epilepsy. All newborns in the United States

The PKU Gene

Carriers of the recessive gene for PKU have a lower chance of miscarriage. It appears that the gene affords some protection against a fungus that grows on grain and produces a toxin. We know that PKU is more common in those of Celtic origin, the Irish and Scots, whose cool wet climate favored the development of moldy grain. Presumably, the gene conveyed some resistance to the toxic effects of eating moldy grain for pregnant women, who were therefore less likely to miscarry and so could pass the gene to their live children. Just as sickle cell anemia conveys a resistance to malaria, PKU may have afforded a survival advantage to those with the gene in their specific environment. PKU has over 30 different disease alleles, and certain types are seen in different populations. PKU is rare in Ashkenazi Jews and in African Americans. The PKU seen in French Canadians and Jews in Yemen is due to a different type of diseased gene than that seen in the Irish or Scots. One investigation of the frequency and distribution of PKU in Norway suggests that the PKU gene found there was probably of Celtic origin, being brought to Norway by the Vikings who brought back wives and slaves from Ireland and Scotland, where there are high frequencies of PKU.

are tested for PKU. The defective gene is found on the long arm (q) of chromosome 12.

Canavan disease, named after Myrtelle Canavan, who first described it in 1931, can cause mental retardation, tremors, and muscular paralysis in early infancy. In infants there can be feeding difficulties, failure to achieve head control, problems swallowing, and even blindness. On average, death occurs before the second birthday, but some children can survive to adolescence. Approximately one in 37 Ashkenazi Jews is a carrier.

Children with Niemann-Pick disease (NPD) show developmental delay, blindness, and an enlarged liver and spleen. This is type A or infantile Niemann-Pick disease, the most frequent type. It begins in the first months of life; with progressive loss of muscle function, death usually occurs in the first few years of life. Type B is less severe and individuals can live into adulthood. Type C usually affects children; type D is probably a rare variant of type C. The symptoms of all forms of Niemann-Pick vary considerably, and the rate of progression is different in each individual. Certain types of NPD seem to affect certain populations. For instance, types A and B are found in the Ashkenazi Jewish population; type B is found in Tunisia, Morocco, and Algeria; type C appears in the Spanish-American population of southern New Mexico and Colorado; and type D is present in the French Canadians of Nova Scotia.

Dementia

At the other end of the age spectrum, dementia in the elderly does not necessarily have a genetic basis but may be the result of infection, toxic changes, or vascular insufficiency to the brain such as from multiple strokes. About 15 percent of people who live to the age of 65 will have some form of dementia; the percentage rises to 35 percent by age 85. Alzheimer disease (AD) is one of the most common causes for dementia; about 4 million Americans are affected. It begins insidiously with some memory loss and seemingly innocent absentmindedness—a "senior moment." Later, memory loss becomes more significant, with loss of judgment, mood swings, and changes in personality. The contribution of genetic factors to those individuals whose Alzheimer disease occurs at an older age is not clear. Examination of the brain at autopsy shows characteristic changes, but diagnosis during life can be difficult. It is generally believed that first-degree relatives of someone with late-onset Alzheimer disease have twice the increased risk compared to the general population. Most

The chance of getting Alzheimer disease increases with age so that as many as half of those over the age of 90 may show some symptoms of the disease. Diagnosis can be difficult, and can be confirmed only at autopsy, but new research suggests that positron-emission tomography (PET) scanning of the brain may be of value in diagnosing Alzheimer disease.

recently, a particular form of the apoE4 gene on chromosome 19 appears to correlate with the onset of this disease.

There is a form of Alzheimer disease that occurs in individuals under the age of 58. It seems to be inherited in a more Mendelian fashion, in some cases as a Mendelian dominant. Children of someone with early-onset Alzheimer disease have a nearly 50 percent risk of inheriting the disease. This was the disease originally described by Alois Alzheimer in 1906, which for a long time was called presenile dementia. Dementia occurring in the elderly was thought to be part of the normal aging process. It is now known that the dementia seen in the elderly is identical to early-onset Alzheimer disease in its symptoms and in the damage done to the brain. The early-onset Alzheimer tends to be inherited as an autosomal dominant, and the late onset is more multifactorial, but definitely familial.

Many prominent figures have suffered from Alzheimer disease. In August 2002, the actor Charlton Heston announced that he had the disease. Cyrus Vance, secretary of state under President Carter, suffered from Alzheimer disease before his death. The most famous Alzheimer sufferer is, of course, former President Ronald Reagan. President Reagan's brother Neil, and probably his mother, both died of Alzheimer disease.

Muscle, Bone, and Skin Conditions

Short Stature

Short stature may of course be a normal variant. One must look at the heights of the parents, siblings, and grandparents. If a child does not seem to be growing, there are many relatively simple tests, such as an X ray of the hand and wrist, to determine whether there is a developmental delay. Detecting a short stature individual in the family pedigree does not mean a genetic condition is present. Because of health and nutrition, most of our ancestors tended to be short. Other causes, especially in the 19th and early 20th centuries, could include chronic childhood diseases, such as kidney diseases, malabsorption of food, multiple infections, and by today's standards, poor prenatal care of the mother. If the short stature is disproportionate—for instance, if the arms and legs are disproportionately short compared to the trunk—there probably is an inherited condition. The classic short stature single-gene disease is achondroplasia, transmitted as a dominant. Affected individuals have short arms and legs compared to the body trunk. Short stature is also seen in chromosomal disorders such as Turner syndrome, where affected females have only one X chromosome rather than the normal two.

Autoimmune Diseases

The major histocompatibility genes, HLA, on chromosome 6 help regulate immune response, the body's ability to fight an infection. The HLA, or human leukocyte antigen system, is a group of closely related alleles that are inherited as a unit (haplotype) and influence susceptibility and resistance to disease. They code for cell surface structures (antigens) that allow the body to recognize its own cells and to reject foreign material. They are also important for organ transplants; doctors do tissue typing, matching certain genes in the HLA complex, to ensure that a potential recipient and the donor organ match.

Certain HLA types apparently cause a faulty immune response and, through a process we don't understand, can predispose a person to certain diseases. In these autoimmune diseases, normal cells of the body are believed by the body to be foreign cells, so the body mounts an inflammatory response against them. In effect, the body attacks a portion of itself. Rheumatoid arthritis, lupus erythematosus, Reiter syndrome, psoriatic arthritis, and ankylosing spondylitis are some of the diseases associated with specific HLA types in humans.

Ankylosing spondylitis (AS) occurs in young individuals, especially men, and is a painful rheumatic disease that primarily affects the spine and pelvis. It begins in young adulthood with symptoms that vary widely but generally include lower back pain and stiffness. The most common result is stiffening of the spine and loss of motion, with difficulty walking or standing.

HLA-B27 is seen in over 90 percent of those with AS, compared to about 6 percent without the disease. Not all who have HLA-B27 get AS, but their risk is higher. Possessing certain HLA genes, therefore, increases the risk for these autoimmune diseases and since HLA genes are inherited, there is a family risk. For instance, first-degree relatives of individuals with AS have a modest increased risk for developing the disease, and if they are found to have HLA-B27, their risk is 85 percent higher than those who do not. Although a parent with AS has a 50 percent chance of passing the HLA-B27 gene to a child, the actual chance that such a child will show AS is less than 50 percent and probably less than 10 percent as everyone with the HLA-B27 does not automatically get AS.

Multiple sclerosis is the most common autoimmune disease involving the nervous system. As with other autoimmune diseases, for some reason the body's own immune system begins to attack parts of the normal body. In multiple sclerosis, the target is the protective covering of nerves in the brain and spinal cord. The disease is probably a multifactorial disease that occurs primarily in those of northern European descent with a genetic susceptibility and some environmental event acting as a trigger, possibly some infection. Relatives of people with multiple sclerosis are at some low risk of developing the disease. Usually beginning in early adult life, the disease is characterized by numbness and tingling in the extremities and can progress to paralysis and incontinence. Symptoms vary widely between individuals.

Arthritis

Rheumatoid arthritis causes joint inflammation and deformity and is another autoimmune disease. The actual name *rheumatoid arthritis* was coined in 1859. It is characterized by painful, swollen, stiff, and deformed joints, primarily involving the joints of the fingers, wrists, and toes.

Familial Mediterranean fever (FMF) is an autosomal recessive disease in which there is pain in the joints, chest, or abdomen with short bouts of fever and a red skin rash. The disease is thought to have left Spain during the Inquisition and settled around the Mediterranean. Today, the disease is seen mainly in Armenians and Sephardic Jews, as well as Arabs, Turks, and others from the Middle East.

Famous individuals who suffered from arthritis include President James Madison. He was treated for what was probably rheumatoid arthritis by the famous Philadelphia physician Robley Dunglison, who reported that Madison's fingers, wrists, and feet were crippled. Historical figures plagued by gout include Charles Darwin, Samuel Johnson, and Benjamin Franklin. The drug colchicine, an effective treatment for gout, was introduced into the United States by Benjamin Franklin, who had successfully used this for his gout while he was serving as ambassador to Paris. Franklin was to remark on his deathbed that "only three incurable diseases have fallen to my share . . . the gout, the stone, and old age."

Another arthritis, gout, can also have a genetic component. The inheritance for gout is generally thought to be autosomal dominant with incomplete penetrance in women; therefore, it is more frequent in men. Each at-risk family member should be evaluated and, if affected, should be treated to prevent gout or kidney problems.

Osteoporosis

Genetic factors are also thought to be involved in the development of osteoporosis. In osteoporosis, the density of the bone diminishes and the bones are weaker, more fragile, and prone to fracture. It is seen in our aging population. While women are more affected than men, men are also affected and whites are affected more than blacks. Osteoporosis causes 1.5 million fractures and costs more than $14 billion annually in the United States. The predisposition to osteoporosis is determined genetically, but it is multifactorial with many genes involved. Studies of identical and fraternal twins have shown that genetic factors have an effect on the amount of calcium in bones. Unquestionably, genetics plays a major role in the development of this disease and, especially if you are a woman, it should be searched for in your family's medical pedigree.

Osterogenesis imperfecta (OI) is characterized by increased weakness of bones, in effect, a severe form of osteoporosis. Involvement ranges from very severe, causing death in infancy (known as type II), to very mild cases. Almost all forms of OI are transmitted by dominant inheritance, but a few types are recessive. Typically, affected individuals show an increased history of bone fractures and some degree of hearing loss. Ehlers-Danlos syndrome (EDS) shows joint hypermobility and skin fragility

Dealing with Osteoporosis

Osteoporosis, where the density of bone diminishes, leading to increased brittleness and fractures, is a major health problem in the United States. Postmenopausal white women are especially susceptible; it is estimated that as many as 9 million have osteoporosis, with many others having some significant loss of bone mass. Although we do not yet know the genes that cause this disease, we do know that there seems to be a strong genetic component.

If it appears that you may have osteoporosis in your family, it is important that you exercise and consume an adequate amount of calcium. For women, a base-line measurement of bone density might be helpful. There is evidence that the amount of bone mineral seen in women in the third and fourth decades of life correlates with the subsequent development of osteoporosis in menopause when estrogen levels drop. Though hormone replacement therapy continues to be used to replace estrogen in postmenopausal women, recent studies indicate that its use may lead to other health complications, such as an increased risk of breast cancer.

and is transmitted as an autosomal dominant. While there are several types of EDS, type 4 is the most serious; in addition to fragile skin and easy bruising, there can be a rupture of one of the main arteries of the body, causing sudden death.

Paget disease of bone (PDB) is a bone disease characterized by excessive bone formation and reabsorption. It usually occurs in individuals over the age of 40 and causes bone deformity, bone pain, and deformities. Like osteoporosis, there is increased fracture risk and, when it affects the skull, it can cause deafness and neurological problems. There is a familial tendency; first-degree relatives of someone with PDB are at increased risk. In some instances, there is a suggestion of an autosomal dominant mode of inheritance.

Skin Conditions

Some skin conditions are inherited or are evidence of a genetic disease. Psoriasis may be related to the HLA genes, but probably is a multifactorial inheritance. First-degree relatives of individuals with psoriasis are at increased risk. Albinism, or lack of skin coloring, consists of a group of diseases, most of which are inherited as recessive traits. The most common sign of neurofibromatosis (NF) are the skin changes. In NF, there are flat, light, tan skin spots ranging in size from less than an inch in diameter in children to several inches in adults. The skin changes are usually present at birth in children or generally make their appearance in a few years. They occur in unusual areas, including the armpits and groin. What appears to be freckling in the armpits, while not seen in everyone with neurofibromatosis, is strong evidence of the disease.

Pigmented skin spots on the face, eyelids, ears, lips, and backs of the hands or soft tumors involving the skin and eyelids may be the only external sign that a patient has Carney complex (CNC1), an autosomal dominant disease. Affected individuals can have an abnormal hormone level from the adrenal glands and thyroid. The most serious complication from this syndrome is a benign heart tumor, known as a cardiac myxoma. While benign and not cancerous, these tumors can kill either from heart failure, by blocking the heart valves, or from a stroke, when bits of tumor break off and travel to the brain.

Skin cancers can be seen in a few defined genetic conditions, such as albinism, where there is lack of skin pigmentation, and xeroderma pigmentosum (XP), a recessive disease characterized by an abnormal sensitivity to sunlight. In addition to fair skin and sun exposure, an important risk factor for the development of melanoma, the most severe type of skin cancer, is a history of a family member with melanoma. In some instances, a dominant-transmitted inheritance is seen in families. In individuals who have a family history of melanoma, there is an earlier onset of disease and an increased frequency of multiple tumors.

Muscle and Nerve Disorders

Many muscle and nerve disorders are hereditary; any individual with an unexplained muscle disease should have a genetic workup. Charcot-Marie-Tooth disease is the most common hereditary disease of the peripheral nerves. Most cases are inherited as dominant, but X-linked and recessive inheritance also occurs. Onset is in childhood or young adulthood, and the characteristic feature is weakness in the muscles of the feet and lower legs, leading to gait disturbance. Other findings include loss of sensation in the extremities, eye problems, and abnormal curvature of the spine. There are varying clinical manifestations, and some individuals carrying the gene may not show symptoms.

Duchenne muscular dystrophy (DMD) is the most common inherited disease of the muscles, affecting one in every 5,000 male children. It is inherited as an X-linked recessive and, like hemophilia, affects males who inherit an abnormal X chromosome. The disease becomes apparent in childhood, generally when a boy around the age of five or six becomes weak and has difficulty walking, and eventually moving.

Muscular dystrophies are inherited muscle disorders where there is progressive loss of muscle fibers. Their classification is confusing; once the genetics are understood, we will be able to better characterize these disorders. Currently, muscular dystrophies are classified by the age of onset, the mode of inheritance, and what particular areas of the body are affected.

The individual becomes almost totally disabled by his teen years and is likely to die in his 20s from difficulty breathing.

Friedreich ataxia (FRDA) begins in late childhood or in the teen years with a lack of coordination, generally affecting gait first, then hands, speech, and eye movements. Over half the affected individuals will also have heart problems. FRDA is inherited as a recessive disease. It has a prevalence of one in 50,000 Caucasians, but is rare in sub-Saharan Africa and in the Far East. There is increased incidence in parts of Quebec and in the Cajun population of Louisiana. One unusual type of early-onset ataxia, inherited as a recessive disease, is spastic ataxia Charlevoix-Saguenay type (SACS), which probably originated from a couple who lived in Quebec City around 1650. An autosomal recessive disease that is common in Japan is Nonaka myopathy (NM), a muscular dystrophy with onset in early adulthood that tends to affect the muscles of the extremities. Other ataxias, for instance, the spinocerebellar ataxias (SCA), are transmitted as a dominant. Machado-Joseph disease (MJD) is a dominantly inherited ataxia that was found to occur in descendants of William Machado, a native of an island in the Portuguese Azores. The disease was found originally in Portuguese immigrants living in New England and later in individuals living in California. The disease begins after age 40, causes gait abnormalities with features similar to Parkinson disease, and causes problems with eye movement.

ALS (amyotrophic lateral sclerosis) is a lethal paralytic disorder of middle and later life in which there is progressive spasticity and muscular weakness. Publicized by the deaths of Lou Gehrig and David Niven, ALS usually causes death in several years from an inability to breathe. About 90 percent of the cases are sporadic and about 10 percent are familial, usually showing autosomal dominant inheritance. A rarer form, juvenile ALS, seen in those from North Africa and the Middle East, has its onset of symptoms before the age of 25 and tends to progress more slowly than the adult form.

Ataxia telangiectasis (AT), an autosomal recessive disorder, can show up as a lack of muscle control in infancy that gets worse at the child begins to walk. Red marks appear on the face and neck. There is increased risk of pneumonia, diabetes, and cancer, especially lymphomas and leukemia, both cancers of the white blood cells.

Extra fingers and toes can be seen in about 200 genetic syndromes, including the autosomal recessive Ellis Van Crevald syndrome (EVC), the autosomal dominant Pallister-Hall syndrome (PHS), and the McKusick-Kaufman syndrome (MKKS) originally described in the Old Order Amish. The Bardet-Biedl syndrome (BBS) is an autosomal recessive inherited disease that causes mental retardation, obesity, and an abnormal pigment of the retina of the eye, as well as a wide variety of other signs and symptoms such as high blood pressure, genital malformations, and diabetes. There is a relatively high frequency of this disease in Arabs.

Familial dysautonomia (FD) is a recessive disease where the most distinctive clinical feature is absence of tears with emotional crying in the affected child. Other signs include difficulty feeding, difficulty maintaining body temperature, vomiting, delayed development, and problems with walking, speech, and coordination. In 1993, the FD gene was localized to the long arm of chromosome 9.

Homocystinuria is a rare autosomal recessive inherited condition in which, because of a missing enzyme, an abnormal amount of the amino acid homocystine appears in the blood and urine. Major clinical manifestations involve the nervous system, eyes, skeleton, and blood vessels. Some degree of mental retardation may be present. There is frequently dislocation of the lens of the eye. The skeletal features may resemble those of Marfan disease, with affected individuals being tall and long limbed, with long thin fingers, and sometime spine deformities. There is a tendency to increased clotting in arteries and veins. The disease occurs five times more frequently in Ireland than in the general population; a national newborn screening program for homocystinuria was started in Ireland in 1971.

The spinal muscular atrophies (SMA) are disorders that cause muscular weakness by affecting the nerves. Cases that appear in childhood are inherited as recessives and generally cause progressive muscular weakness and difficulty moving. Problems with breathing can result in an early death. Spinal muscular atrophies that begin in adulthood are less severe. Inheritance varies.

Most problems with the spinal cord are present at birth. What are known as neural tube defects (the neural tube is an embryonic structure that develops into the brain and spinal cord) occur as isolated events but may occur as part of a genetic syndrome. The most common is spina bifida, where there is a congenital defect in which one or more of the bones of the spinal cord fail to develop completely and part of the spinal cord is exposed on the back. Symptoms vary from minor (leg weakness, cold feet, and urinary incontinence) to severe, in which part of the spinal cord protrudes through the skin in the back, and, even with corrective surgery, the individual may require a wheelchair.

Pope John Paul II, the actor Michael J. Fox, former U.S. Attorney General Janet Reno, and former Heavyweight Boxing Champ Muhammad Ali all suffer from Parkinson disease (PD). Parkinson disease was first formally described in "An Essay on the Shaking Palsy," published in 1817 by a London physician named James Parkinson. Today, over one million Americans suffer from this chronic neurological disease. It occurs most often among the middle-aged and elderly. Symptoms include muscular rigidity, a mask-like facial expression, a typical "pill-rolling" tremor of the fingers, occasionally tremor of the head and neck, slow movement, and poor balance when walking. In PD, recognizable changes are found in an area of the brain known as the substantia nigra, which produces the chemical dopamine; individuals with PD have a shortage of dopamine. Some cases of PD may be drug-induced or the result of an infection. In the vast majority of cases, there is no obvious cause. PD inheritance is probably multifactorial. It is suspected that Parkinson disease usually results from the combination of a genetic predisposition and an as yet unidentified environmental trigger. A positive family history is a risk factor, and some investigators believe that in some instances there may be a form of dominant inheritance.

Anesthesia Deaths

An unexplained surgical death or reaction to surgical anesthesia in a family member can be an important clue that there may be an underlying genetic disease that causes difficulty with surgical anesthesia. Cholinesterase deficiency in an individual may be inherited as a recessive trait. Individuals suffering with this deficiency react badly to a drug commonly used during anesthesia, succinylcholine. Succinylcholine is used to relax the muscles; with cholinesterase deficiency, individuals may not begin breathing on their own at the end of anesthesia. A preoperative test for this condition is available. A dominant inherited disease, malignant hyperthermia, also known as malignant hyperpyrexia, is another condition that can cause a devastating reaction to anesthesia. It is the most common cause of death from general anesthesia, producing a potentially fatal reaction to certain anesthetics agents. With this condition, there is an acute elevation in body temperature occurring either during surgery or shortly thereafter. This high temperature can result in kidney failure, brain damage, breathing problems, and with prolonged high temperatures, death. Overall incidence of malignant hyperthermia is hard to estimate, but is believed to be about one in 10,000 to 15,000. Reactions occur most often in children and adolescents. Certain groups seem to have an especially high incidence, including residents of north-central Wisconsin, valley dwellers in parts of Austria, and descendants of some of the original settlers in Quebec, including, reportedly, the descendants of Michel and Marie Dupuis (also spelled De Puy or De Pue) who emigrated from France to Nova Scotia in 1651.

> Individuals with malignant hyperthermia and cholinesterase deficiency appear perfectly normal; a family history of unexplained surgical or anesthetic death is key to recognizing the risk of having this disease before a surgical tragedy occurs.

Tourette Syndrome

Tourette syndrome is transmitted as a dominant disease. Affected individuals show abnormal movement and abnormal vocal expression, and have involuntary tic-like movements. Onset occurs in late childhood. The disease may be mild or severely disabling and most often affects males. About 10 percent of patients have a family history of Tourette syndrome, and it is more frequent in Ashkenazi Jews and rare in blacks.

Samuel Johnson, born 1709, was described by his biographer James Boswell as having a lifelong history of disordered movements, tics, mannerisms, and ritualistic behavior. J .M. S. Pearce, writing in the *Journal of the Royal Society of Medicine*, believes that Dr. Johnson's symptoms are typical for the syndrome described in 1885 by Gilles de la Tourette. Pearce notes, "It is not without interest that periodic boundless mental energy, imaginative outbursts of inventiveness and creativity are characteristic of certain

Tourette patients. It may be thought that without this illness, Dr. Johnson's remarkable literary achievements, the great dictionary, his philosophical deliberations, and his conversations may never have happened."

The Blood

Anemia

Sickle cell anemia and thalassemia are recessive diseases that affect the blood's hemoglobin. The most common thalassemia is beta thalassemia, or thalassemia major, in which there is severe anemia in infancy. The liver and spleen are large, the bones thin and easily fractured, and if the disease is not treated, death occurs in the first decade of life.

Anemias are characterized by a lowering of the amount of hemoglobin in the blood. **Hemoglobin** is the iron-containing pigment found in red blood cells and is responsible for carrying oxygen from the lungs to the body's tissues. Red blood cells are produced in the bone marrow.

Anemia can be caused by reduced or defective production of red blood cells or by their excessive destruction. In iron-deficiency anemia, there is less hemoglobin due to a deficiency of iron, generally because loss of iron is greater than dietary intake. Due to menstrual blood loss, women tend to have low body stores of iron. Other causes of anemia include some vitamin deficiencies and abnormal hemoglobin molecules, as seen in some genetic diseases, such as sickle cell anemia.

One of the most common inherited enzyme deficiencies is G6PD (glucose-6-phosphate dehydrogenase deficiency), which is transmitted as an X-linked recessive disease and affects males. Individuals with G6PD may appear normal or may show a minimal anemia. Only with certain environmental triggers does G6PD become symptomatic. Certain drugs, infections, and for some individuals, the ingestion of fava beans (called favism) are some of the agents that can cause what is known as a hemolytic crisis. During a hemolytic crisis, the red blood cells burst;

there is jaundice, headache, fatigue, and shortness of breath from too few red blood cells. Hemoglobin from the destroyed red blood cells can darken the urine. During the Korean War when American soldiers were given the antimalarial drug primaquine, approximately 10 percent of African American soldiers and Caucasian soldiers of Mediterranean descent developed an acute anemia in response to this drug. Treatment for G6PD is minimal, and the crisis is over when the instigating agent is removed.

Hemophilia

Hemophilia A is the classic and most common type of hemophilia, accounting for about 80 percent of all cases. In hemophilia, a protein necessary for clotting is either deficient or absent. Affected sons show symptoms in infancy with easy bruising and spontaneous bleeding into joints. Unchecked internal bleeding can be fatal. A similar disease picture is seen in hemophilia B, although a different clotting factor is affected. Both hemophilia A and B are inherited as an X-linked disease. In hemophilia A, the deficiency occurs in clotting factor 8. There are other congenital hemorrhagic disorders that have a deficiency in two clotting factors. A rare inherited anemia of abnormal clotting factors 8 and 5 has been seen in individuals from the Mediterranean region, including Spain, Italy, Yugoslavia, Greece, and Algeria. Asian and Sephardic Jews have also been affected, but not Ashkenazi Jews. Other inherited blood clotting disorders include Von Willebrand disease, transmitted as a dominant, and hemophilia C, a recessive disease seen especially in Ashkenazi Jews.

Another rare bleeding disorder, transmitted as autosomal recessive, is Hermansky-Pudlak syndrome (HPS). HPS was first described in 1959 when two patients with albinism and a bleeding disorder were encountered. Individuals with HPS are frequently legally blind. They have a lifelong bleeding tendency and are light skinned or albino. In the United States, the highest prevalence is in the northwestern quarter of Puerto Rico, where one out of 1,800 individuals has this recessive disease; HPS may be one of the most frequent single-gene or Mendelian disorders in Puerto Rico. This severe disease is caused by a mutation in HPS1; frequently death occurs from lung failure. The origin of the abnormal gene has been traced to an area in southern Spain. A milder form of HPS, the gene HPS3, has been found in central Puerto Rico and in individuals other than those in Puerto Rico, including, in one study, Ashkenazi Jews. Symptoms of HPS may be mild and the disease not recognized.

Porphyria

The porphyrias are actually a group of diseases; most are inherited as dominant traits, some as recessive. The term *porphyria* derives from a Greek word meaning "purple" and refers to the reddish-purple color of an affected individual's urine. The disease is the result of improperly formed heme, a portion of the hemoglobin. The attacks may occur spontaneously or, as in G6PD, be triggered by some environmental stimulus such as certain drugs and alcohol consumption. Porphyria is relatively rare. The episodic attacks that begin in adulthood can be confused with primary psychiatric psychosis, and the abdominal pain can be mistaken for appendicitis, pancreatitis, or some other abdominal condition.

Other Blood Disorders

Leukemia and lymphomas can occur in some recessive genetic diseases. Inherited leukemia is rare; one type, CLL (chronic lymphocytic leukemia), does show some familial tendency. Fanconi anemia (FA) is an autosomal recessive disease that depresses all elements of the blood. Abnormal skin pigmentation, short stature, and malformation of the kidneys, heart, and hands, including thumb and forearm abnormalities, also occur. It affects males and females equally and is found in all ethnic groups. Due to a founder effect, an unusually high frequency of FA occurs in white Afrikaners. The disease can lead to leukemia; individuals are also at risk for other cancers, particularly in the esophagus and digestive tract. In Bloom syndrome, an autosomal recessive disease, there is short stature, a narrow face, and an increased susceptibility to some cancers such as leukemia. Approximately one in 100 Ashkenazi Jews is a carrier for Bloom syndrome.

The Kidneys, Bladder, and Reproductive System

Kidney Diseases

Congenital malformations of the kidneys and other parts of the urinary tract are a frequent component of chromosomal disorders. Multiple kidney cysts in children are present in several genetic syndromes. In adults, multiple cysts may be an indicator of either adult polycystic kidney disease or Von Hippel-Lindau syndrome, both autosomal dominant diseases.

Adult polycystic kidney disease, or autosomal dominant polycystic kidney disease, is one of the most common genetic diseases that causes kidney failure in adults.

Progressive kidney failure and hypertension, or high blood pressure, occur as an adult. Other features of the disease include small aneurysms or focal enlargements in the blood vessels of the brain, cysts in the liver, and abnormalities in the heart valves. Infantile polycystic kidney disease, also known as autosomal recessive polycystic kidney disease, is the most common kidney cystic disease in children. Large kidneys full of cysts are present at birth. Inherited as a recessive, other features include liver scarring, hypertension, and growth retardation.

Occasionally the appearance of an infant's urine may be the first clue that there is a genetic disease. Alkaptonuria, dubbed the "black diaper syndrome," is characterized by urine that turns black and by severe arthritis. It was the first autosomal recessive disease recognized in humans. With maple syrup urine disease, an infant's urine smells like maple syrup. Affected infants show lethargy, mental retardation, irritability, vomiting, and coma. It is another one of the recessive diseases seen in Ashkenazi Jews.

Overall, about 30,000 kidney cancers are diagnosed each year in the United States. Although at the moment, it is thought that about 5 percent of kidney cancers are due to underlying genetic causes, this is one of the most rapidly expanding areas in clinical research, and most researchers believe that this percentage will climb higher. There are recognizable syndromes in which kidney cancer occurs. Unlike nongenetic kidney cancers that occur after age 60, hereditary cancers occur at a younger age. Von Hippel-Lindau disease (VHL) is characterized by benign blood vessel tumors of the eye and spinal cord, and by kidney cysts and tumors. About half the individuals affected by this autosomal dominant disease will get kidney cancer, generally at a young age. The kidney cancers in VHL are frequently bilateral, occurring in both kidneys, and multiple cancers may appear in the same kidney. Kidney cancer occurs in tuberous sclerosis; there are also several other hereditary kidney cancer syndromes.

Kidney stones may be the result of an overactive parathyroid gland, the gland that controls the calcium level in the body and which in a minority of cases may be part of a genetic disease. Kidney stones also appear in gout, which can transmit as an autosomal dominant disease. Kidney malformations have a genetic basis; many, such as kidney duplication, are inherited as autosomal dominants and vary in severity from none to lethal. Couples whose child has a kidney malformation should request a prenatal diagnosis with ultrasound imaging for subsequent pregnancies.

Cystinosis is another rare autosomal recessive disease affecting both children and adults. It is characterized by kidney failure, problems with vision, muscle weakness, diabetes, and low thyroid function. A high frequency of this disease, consistent with a founder effect, is seen in the French Canadian population.

Diseases of the Female Reproductive System

Certain gynecologic diseases, such as endometriosis, some forms of polycystic ovary syndrome, and some forms of premature ovarian failure, appear to have some genetic basis. A growing body of evidence, based on reports of familial clustering and increased prevalence among first-degree relatives, suggests a role for genetic factors in endometriosis. In endometriosis, fragments of the lining of the uterus, the endometrium, are found outside the uterus in other areas of the pelvis. It is a cause of infertility. Having a mother or daughter with endometriosis makes a woman five times more likely to get the disease. The risk of getting endometriosis if a first cousin has the disease is lower than that, but still higher than the general population. Symptoms vary widely from none to severe pain during menstruation.

Polycystic ovary syndrome (PCOS) is a complicated disease that includes large ovaries, frequently with cysts; obesity; excessive hairiness; and irregular or absent menstrual periods. A cause of infertility, PCOS also brings an increased risk of diabetes. The disease is transmitted as autosomal dominant and may be both one of the most common reproductive endocrine disorders of women and one of the major causes for female infertility in the United States. First-degree male relatives of those who are affected have an increased frequency of early baldness or excessive hairiness. Even when conception occurs, women with PCOS have a much higher risk of miscarriage.

Repeated miscarriages showing up in a pedigree should alert you to a possible chromosomal abnormality. Although infertility has many causes, many of which are not genetic, there are a few rare but important genetic diseases primarily involving the number of X chromosomes that result in infertility.

Women with one X chromosome have Turner syndrome. The disease was described in 1938 by Henry Turner when he reported seven young adult women who were dwarfed and had failure of sexual development. Affected women do not have menstrual cycles and are infertile. Turner syndrome occurs in one in 2,000 female births. In addition to short stature, ovarian failure, and infertility, females with Turner syndrome can also have early osteoporosis, high blood pressure, congenital heart disease, kidney malformations, and thyroid abnormalities. There are other disorders in the number of sex chromosomes for women, such as an additional X chromosome.

Women with three X chromosomes generally appear normal, although they may tend to be tall. The XXX syndrome is relatively common in women and may be associated with learning difficulties, menstrual irregularities, and infertility.

Diseases of the Male Reproductive System

Males have as many genetic causes of infertility as women, and we see many different types of chromosomal abnormalities in infertile men. Normal men have an X and a Y chromosome. Men with an extra X chromosome, XXY, have Klinefelter syndrome, the most frequently seen chromosomal abnormality in sterile men. Klinefelter syndrome occurs in about one in 1,000 male births. Affected individuals may have learning or behavior disorders. Men with Klinefelter syndrome show small testes and little pubic or facial hair, are tall with long hands and legs, and may develop breasts. An additional Y chromosome can occur, as well. It is estimated that one in 1,000 men are XYY, but other than being tall, the vast majority of them are normal in appearance and behavior.

The prostate gland is a small gland in men at the base of the bladder. It can become inflamed in younger men, causing prostatitis, or enlarged in older men to the point where it blocks the passage of urine. Prostate cancer is a leading cause of cancer deaths in men. The cause is not yet understood, but there is a genetic contribution. Individuals whose father or brother has prostate cancer are twice as likely to develop the disease as men without an affected father or brother. One recent report suggests that having a brother with prostate cancer is a stronger risk factor than having another affected family member, such as a father. If two first-degree relatives have prostate cancer, the risk increases fivefold. The risk also increases as the number of affected family members increases and with an early age of onset—under the age of 55 for any affected relative. Male carriers of the BRCA2 mutation are at increased risk of prostate cancer, especially at an early age.

Another cancer that can be seen in families is testicular cancer. Affecting about one in 500 men, it is the most common cancer seen in young men. The known risk factors for acquiring this disease are an undescended testis, where the testis fails to drop normally into the scrotum in infancy, and a family history of testicular cancer. Brothers of men with testicular cancer have an 8 to 10 times greater risk of developing the disease, and sons have 4 times the risk of a man in the general population. Men with familial testicular cancer are also at increased risk of having a second cancer in the other testis.

The Sensory System

Problems with sight or hearing are very complex. Many genetic diseases affect sight or hearing, but there are also numerous environmental causes, such as infection and exposure to drugs. Early onset, either childhood or young adult, of a sight or hearing problem should raise suspicion of a genetic cause and suggest the need for a medical evaluation.

Deafness

Congenital deafness can be due to nongenetic causes, but once environmental causes such as rubella infection, other illness, and physical injury are excluded, over half the remaining causes of congenital deafness have a genetic basis. Several hundred genetic syndromes have some degree of hearing impairment. Many different types of inheritance—dominant, recessive, and X-linked— can cause deafness. Some syndromes are expressed at birth, while others occur later in life. In some instances, a specific genetic syndrome cannot be recognized, but inspection of a family's pedigree may show increased incidence of hearing impairment. Isolated childhood deafness, especially if due to damage to the hearing nerve, is most likely inherited as a recessive trait, less often dominant.

Pendred syndrome (PDS) accounts for as much as 10 percent of hereditary deafness. First described by Vaughan Pendred in 1896, this syndrome is transmitted as autosomal recessive; the defective gene is found on chromosome 7q. Deafness may be present at birth or develop in early childhood. PDS is also associated with thyroid enlargement.

Hearing impairment is common with increasing age; over half the elderly have some degree of hearing loss. A conduction defect, that is, impairment of the transmission of sound through the ear, is more often seen in adults. Otosclerosis, or gradual immobilization of the inner ear bones, is one of the more common causes of conduction hearing loss in adults. As with almost all dominant disorders, penetrance—the chance of showing the disease—varies.

Vision Impairment

Glaucoma is frequently seen in families, and first-degree relatives are at increased risk. In glaucoma, the fluid pressure within the eye is increased and results in damage. Glaucoma insidiously causes defects in the visual field. A cataract, the loss of the transparency of the lens of the eye, occurs frequently in older individuals. The development of cataracts at a relatively young age, the badly misnamed presenile cataracts, may also indicate an underlying genetic cause, with all types of inheritance, especially dominant inheritance, contributing to this condition.

Age-related macular degeneration (ARMD) is one of the leading causes of blindness and visual impairment among older adults. The macula is the part of the retina that sees fine detail in the center of the vision. This is the area damaged in ARMD. The cause of ARMD is multifactorial; it is certainly age related but may also be associated with environmental risk factors such as hypertension, cigarette smoking, diet, and cholesterol level. Genetic factors also contribute to this disease, and family aggregation can be seen. Because of the late onset of the disease, it is difficult to compile in pedigrees, but it can appear in successive generations, which suggests a dominant inheritance to be most likely.

> It is estimated that approximately 30 percent of those above the age of 75 have some sign of age-related macular degeneration (ARMD).

Like hearing loss, vision impairment either in childhood or before middle age can also be caused by a large number of genetic syndromes; probably over half of vision impairment before the age of 45 has a genetic cause. For instance, Best disease is an inherited condition transmitted as a Mendelian dominant and is characterized by gradual loss of vision, similar to the macular degeneration seen in the elderly. Six is the average age of onset for Best disease, but the disease may not be detected until much later because visual acuity may remain good for many years. Although the evaluation of visual disorders is very complex, any severe visual loss in a child should be evaluated for a genetic component.

Another condition is retinitis pigmentosa (RP), a degeneration of the retina of the eye. Normally, light enters the eye and is focused by the lens in the front of the eye onto the retina, the inner lining of the eye that converts the light to a nerve signal. RP can cause blindness by damaging these retinal cells. These are a group of inherited disorders transmitted most often as a recessive disease, less often as a dominant or X-linked trait. RP causes progressive decreased peripheral vision and diminished night vision beginning as a young adult.

If the lens of the eye cannot focus correctly on the retina, farsightedness (hyperopia) can occur, producing difficulty in seeing near objects. Poor focus can also result in nearsightedness (myopia), where there is difficulty seeing objects at a distance. It is thought that in both conditions, the eyeball is not round. In farsightedness, the eye is too short from back to front; in nearsightedness it is too long. This tendency to have an abnormally shaped eye is inherited.

Seen in infancy, retinoblastoma is a malignant tumor of the eye. About half the occurrences are hereditary, and those are transmitted as a dominant trait with a type of incomplete penetrance. The tumor may affect one or both eyes and usually occurs before the age of five. The affected gene appears to lie on chromosome 13. These individuals are also at risk for developing other cancers as adults, such as cancer of the bone and melanoma, a malignant skin cancer.

Facial Abnormalities

Facial abnormalities are relatively common. Visible ear malformations may be a clue to a more serious genetic syndrome involving the kidneys, heart, or skeleton. A mentally retarded male with large, protruding ears should suggest fragile-X syndrome. A malformed external ear in an infant could indicate a malformation of the inner ear and the need for an auditory evaluation. Cleft lip or cleft palate is associated with several hundred genetic syndromes, including trisomy 18 and trisomy 13. Either or both may be seen in single-gene diseases or have a multifactorial inheritance. Or they may not be genetic at all, but result from conditions in the uterus or a maternal cause, such as fetal alcohol syndrome or certain drugs taken during pregnancy. Any child with a cleft lip or cleft palate should be medically evaluated for an associated genetic syndrome.

Hormone and Metabolic Conditions

Endocrine Diseases

The endocrine system consists of glands in the body that produce and release into the bloodstream certain chemicals known as hormones. Hormones regulate various bodily functions, like sugar levels in the blood, and regulate growth and sexual development. The MEN syndromes (multiple endocrine neoplasia) include a wide variety of hyperactivity and tumors of multiple hormone (endocrine) glands in the body. The tumors can be benign or cancerous. There are several subtypes; all are transmitted as dominant traits. They are usually detected because of an elevated hormone level and subsequent symptoms related to the elevated hormone level. For instance, MEN type 1 can have a specific type of hormone-producing tumor in the pancreas that results in peptic ulcers, as well as tumors and increased function of the other endocrine glands. In addition to ulcers, symptoms can include low blood sugar, symptoms related to high serum calcium levels such as kidney stones, or symptoms related to problems with the pituitary, a gland in the brain that can cause headaches or visual problems. In MEN type 2, there is a type of thyroid cancer and a tumor of the adrenal gland.

The **endocrine glands** in the body are specialized organs that secrete chemicals directly into the blood and collectively make up the endocrine system. These chemicals are necessary for body function and development. Examples of endocrine glands include the ovaries, which secrete the hormone estrogen, and the specialized cells of the pancreas, which secrete insulin to regulate blood sugar.

Congenital adrenal hyperplasia (CAH) applies to a group of syndromes in which the adrenal gland is prevented from making the normal amounts of several important steroid hormones. The two adrenal glands are small triangular structures that sit on top of each kidney. They are endocrine glands—structures that secrete hormones. With classic CAH, genital ambiguities and salt wasting (loss of salt from the body) may be present at birth or in infancy. CAH can affect the fetus in the womb. In an attempt to produce a normal level of steroids, the adrenal gland becomes overactive and produces elevated levels of other hormones. One of them, androgen, is the hormone that produces "maleness." A female child may be born with masculine-appearing genitals, and boys may have early male sexual development. Other forms have milder late-onset symptoms such as early puberty. The late-onset CAH is the least severe. Boys and girls with this condition will have rapid growth, and girls will also have unwanted hair growth and abnormal menstruation.

It is transmitted as an autosomal recessive trait, and the gene is more frequent in Ashkenazi Jews, Hispanics, Yugoslavs, and Italians.

The thyroid is a gland found in the front of the neck above the collarbone. It is an endocrine gland and produces thyroid hormone. An enlarged gland can cause visible swelling of the front of the neck and is called a goiter. Graves disease, or hyperthyroidism, is a disease characterized by overactivity of the thyroid gland and overproduction of thyroid hormone. An autoimmune disease, Graves disease does occur in families, but its genetics are unknown. Affected individuals experience weight loss, tremors, nervousness, and a rapid heart rate. Occasionally, there is bulging of the eyes. Infants may be born without a thyroid or with a low-functioning thyroid gland. Such children have cretinism, which consists of mental retardation, stunted growth, and coarse facial features. Thyroid cancer may have some genetic component; familial forms have been reported. One particular type of rare thyroid cancer, medullary cancer of the thyroid, can be inherited and can be part of genetic endocrine syndromes.

Diabetes

Diabetes has been recognized since antiquity. The second century Greek physician Aretaeus described it as "a melting down of the flesh and limbs into urine." Tests for sugar in the urine were developed in the 1840s. Nevertheless, this diagnosis was rare and usually confined to what today would be called type 1 diabetes. Typically, a young person begins losing weight, passing large quantities of urine, and having an intense thirst. Until the discovery of insulin in 1922, the disease usually ended in death. Sugar, or glucose, supplies the body with energy and is absorbed from our food. The body's sugar level is controlled by a hormone called insulin that is normally secreted by the pancreas. In diabetics, either too little or no insulin is produced (type 1) or the cells do not respond correctly to the insulin (type 2). As a result, there is an abnormally high level of sugar in the blood.

Today diabetes is one of our most common diseases. There are two types: type 1, also known as insulin-dependent diabetes mellitus (IDDM) or juvenile diabetes, and type 2, also known as noninsulin-dependent diabetes mellitus (NIDDM) or adult-onset diabetes; both have a genetic component. Typically, type 1 occurs in a young individual, who then requires insulin injections to survive. It is generally thought that the body's own immune system, used by the body to fight off infections, is misdirected to destroy the insulin-producing cells in the pancreas. The majority of diabetics have type 2, which begins in middle age and is associated with obesity. The pancreas produces insulin, but the body is unable to use it correctly. Almost 2,000 individuals are diagnosed every day in the United States with type 2 diabetes, which can generally be controlled with drugs and weight loss. Long-term complications of diabetes include eye, kidney, nerve, and blood vessel damage, all of which lead to blindness, kidney failure, neuropathy or nerve damage, and poor circulation.

Both types of diabetes show multifactorial inheritance. Type 1 diabetes has an association with the HLA genes found on chromosome 6 and brings an increased risk for the individual to develop other autoimmune diseases. Other genes, plus environmental factors, have a role in type 1 diabetes. The risk of acquiring type 1 diabetes is 10 times that in the general population if you have a sibling or parent with this disease. Type 2 diabetes also shows a complex multifactorial inheritance.

Mexican Americans, African Americans, Asian Americans, Pacific Islanders, Hispanics, and some Native Americans, such as the Pima Indians in the Southwest, have a higher prevalence of type 2 diabetes than the general population does. The increased risk for family members of diabetics is specific for the type of diabetes; for instance, if one family member has type 2 diabetes, the increased risk for the remaining family members is for type 2 disease, not type 1 diabetes. In addition to occurring as a primary disease, diabetes may be a component of another genetic dis-

Did Beethoven Die of Diabetes?

In October and November 1826, the composer Ludwig van Beethoven was at his brother Johann's country home at Gneixendorf completing the new finale to the String Quartet in F major, Op. 130. In December, he developed chills and fever, began drinking large quantities of fluid, had difficulty breathing, and started coughing up blood. His physician correctly diagnosed him as having a lung infection. His symptoms evolved to abdominal pain, weight loss, and eventually a wound infection from the repeated attempts to tap fluid from his abdomen. In a 1993 article, P. J. Davies makes a good case for Beethoven's having died from an acute onset of diabetes, with complicating pneumonia and kidney disease. Beethoven died in 1827 at the age of 56, before a clinical test for sugar in the urine became available in the 1840s.

order. Over 50 genetic syndromes are associated with diabetes, including cystic fibrosis, hemochromatosis, and some muscular dystrophies.

Immunodeficiencies and Allergies

Single-gene abnormalities in the immune system can result in severe immunodeficiency—an inability of the immune system to function. Most are recognized in infancy. They include severe combined immunodeficiency (SCID), showing both recessive and X-linked recessive transmission; DiGeorge syndrome, a recessive; and chronic granulomatous disease (CGD), generally an X-linked recessive. Milder familial immunodeficiencies may go unrecognized, but the family may be "infection prone."

SCID is a primary immune deficiency that results in serious infections during infancy. It is a group of diseases, but generally it involves defective lymphocytes, the type of white blood cells that help fight off infection. You should suspect SCID when an infant has repeated infections, especially severe infections that may not respond to antibiotics. Other signs include an infant who fails to gain weight and who has a family history of frequent infections, perhaps with other family members dying at a young age from an infection. A founder effect, resulting from a bottleneck of the population, is thought to be the reason for the high frequency of SCID in the Navajo and Jicarilla Apache Indians of the Southwest.

Allergies include asthma, hay fever, some rashes, and food; there are also allergic reactions to medication. When recording allergies, it is not so important to record what causes the allergic reaction as it is to document a family history of allergies. If they "run in the family," you should watch for allergic reactions in yourself and your children.

Cancer

Today, one person in four will develop cancer and one in five will die from it. It is the second leading cause of death in the United States. Cancer has been with us throughout history. The term *carcinoma* was coined by Hippocrates (460–370 B.C.), the father of medicine, and the term *sarcoma* was given by Galen, a Roman surgeon who lived A.D 131–201. In 1838, Johannes Muller, a German scientist, realized that cancer consisted of an abnormal growth of cells, termed a neoplasm ("new growth") or tumor. Tumors are divided into two groups: benign and malignant. Benign tumors are slow growing, have a cellular structure similar to the tissue that they arise from, and most important, do not invade or spread (metastasize) to other organs. Malignant tumors, or cancers, have a more abnormal cellular structure, generally grow rapidly, and most important, infiltrate, invade, and spread throughout the body. This ability to metastasize is generally the lethal event. About 60 to 70 percent of lung cancers and 50 to 60 percent of cancers of the colon have metastasized by the time of discovery.

The Naming of Cancers

A diagnosis of cancer is made by microscopic examination of a tissue sample obtained by a biopsy. Generally, cancers that arise from what is known as connective tissue are termed *sarcomas.* A cancer arising from fat is known as a *liposarcoma,* with *lipo* indicating "fat"; if arising from bone, the cancer is an *osteosarcoma, osteo* meaning "bone." If the cancer arises from what is known as epithelial tissue, it is a carcinoma and given the name of the type of epithelial cell. For instance, cancers arising from epithelial cells such as squamous cells are called *squamous cell carcinomas* whether they arise in the lung, skin, or cervix of the uterus.

Unfortunately, the naming of cancers is not standardized; some tumors retain their original historical names. *Wilms tumor,* named for its discoverer Max Wilms (1867–1918), is the name given to the specific type of malignant kidney tumor that occurs mainly in children. The specific cancer found in lymph nodes is *Hodgkin disease,* named for its discover, Thomas Hodgkin (1798–1866).

Cancer is not a single disease, but all cancers are genetic diseases. For reasons that are not understood, in a given cell in the body, there occur changes or mutations in the DNA within chromosomes in the nucleus, and those mutations make the cell cancerous. The cancer cell's abnormal DNA is transmitted to the cell's daughter cells as the cell divides. In some cases, large changes occur in the chromosomes. For instance, a loss of some of the chromosome 22 has been linked to the development of one form of leukemia. Although a genetic disease, cancers are not hereditary. For most cancers, the change occurs in one of the body's cells, for instance, a change in a lung cell causes lung cancer to develop. The mutation occurs in an adult and is not passed to the next generation. For most cancers, we do not know the specific chromosomal functional or structural changes, or the actual change in the DNA, that results in the disease. Cancer is generally multifactorial. Presumably, there is a genetic predisposition, along with risk factors such as sex, age, and race, to which are added certain environmental factors.

A few human tumors such as retinoblastomas, a childhood cancer of the eye; Wilms tumor; and the cancer that arises in FAP (familial adenomatous polyplosis) of the colon, are hereditary and occur with high frequency in certain families. Cancer may also be part of a well-recognized genetic syndrome such as VHL (Von Hippel-Lindau syndrome), where there are multiple kidney cancers and tumors of the brain, spinal cord, and eyes. Other well-known genetic syndromes where cancer can arise include neurofibromatosis, hemochromatosis, and Down syndrome (trisomy 21).

For cancers that are not part of a well-defined genetic syndrome, the picture is less clear. Certainly there appear to be families with a high incidence of cancer, and most investigators believe that the development of cancer depends on a genetic susceptibility coupled with an environmental stimulus. Many theories attempt to explain this cancer susceptibility in certain families; the most widely accepted is that it takes multiple changes in the DNA to produce a cancerous cell. Individuals in cancer families are born with one or more damaged areas. Having already damaged DNA or a defective gene, those individuals with cancer susceptibility are at a higher risk of acquiring the additional environmental damage that leads to cancer. It is thought that these individuals are born with one copy of a damaged gene inherited from either the mother or father. Cancer occurs when the complementary previously normal gene inherited from the other parent is damaged. When both genes are damaged, cancer occurs. Those who do not have an inherited damaged gene start life with two normal genes and require damage to both genes during life to convert the cell to cancer. Individuals in cancer families, therefore, may have a head start toward developing cancer and may develop their cancer at a relatively younger age.

In contrast, normal individuals require a lifetime of damage to convert a normal cell to cancer; thus most cancers, those that are not part of a well-defined genetic syndrome where the inheritance is understood, are seen in older adults. We do see genetic changes in these individuals. For instance, a mutation in the p53 gene, found on chromosome 17, is seen in many different forms of cancer, such as cancer of the colon, breast, bladder, lung, skin, and liver. The p53 gene is a tumor suppressor gene, the normal function of which is to control cell growth. When these genes stop working, tumors can develop, with unrestrained cell growth. Generally, it is thought that both copies of a specific tumor suppressor gene must be damaged for unrestrained growth to occur.

Another type of gene that regulates cell division is the proto-oncogene. These function normally to promote cell growth. When these genes are mutated to oncogenes, they promote the development of cancer. It is thought that just one abnormal allele is enough to activate an oncogene. In certain cancer-prone families, therefore, it is possible that an increased tendency to mutate either the tumor suppressor genes or the proto-oncogenes is inherited, and with the appropriate environmental stimulant, cancer will occur.

An **oncogene** is a gene capable of causing the transformation of normal cells into cancer cells. A **tumor suppressor gene** is a protective gene that normally limits the growth of tumors. When a tumor suppressor gene is mutated, it may fail to keep a cancer from growing. BRCA1 and p53 are well-known tumor suppressor genes.

Mutations in proto-oncogenes and tumor suppressor genes occur in the body's cells. When they occur in the liver, liver cancer occurs; in the lung, lung cancer. While alterations in the p31 gene are seen in cancers that develop in specific organs in individuals, a mutation in the p31 gene can also occur in the germ line, the egg or sperm DNA, and be a hereditary cancer. Affected individuals have a hereditary family cancer syndrome called Li-Fraumeni. This autosomal dominant syndrome was originally described in four families with breast cancer and other types of cancer. Many other types of cancer were later found in this syndrome in which there is a genetically transmitted abnormal p31 gene; this syndrome includes leukemia, melanoma (skin cancer), and cancers of the brain, lung, prostate, pancreas, bone, and adrenal gland. As with many cancer families, the diverse tumor types in family members characteristically develop at unusually early ages, and multiple primary tumors are frequent. Affected individuals have a 50 percent chance of developing some cancer by the age of 30, and almost all will develop cancer if they live to retirement age.

The concept of tumor suppressor genes and proto-oncogenes as the cause for cancer may be too simplistic. No one doubts that cancer is a genetic disease with alterations to the cell's DNA. While the concept of mutations to these cancer-related genes is one of the most common theories to account for the transformation of a normal cell to a cancer, some researchers have postulated other explanations. For instance, some think that there is a gradual breakdown of DNA with the formation of many random mutations that eventually cause a cancer. Finding the genes associated with cancers and understanding their effect is one of the most researched areas in medicine today.

Almost everyone will have at least one individual in the family pedigree with cancer. The only clues that a given individual may be carrying a familial cancer-predisposing gene are the family health history and the individual cancer characteristic. Cancers with a hereditary predisposition tend to occur at a younger age than nonhereditary cancers. In those families with a high occurrence of cancer, there may be multiple cancers in many different organs. When the incidence of cancer in the family is high, it is thought that the first mutation occurs in the DNA of the egg or sperm and is thus transmitted to the offspring. Many of these familial cancers would be transmitted as dominants. In compiling your family's health history, for each individual with cancer, record the site of origin, the age of onset, how the diagnosis was made, and the stage (extent) of the cancer at the time of diagnosis.

Breast Cancer

Breast cancer is one of the most important and serious malignancies affecting women. About one in 10 American women will develop breast cancer, so it would not be unusual to find this disease in any given family. Approximately 5 percent of breast cancers are hereditary. The recently identified genes BRCA1 (breast cancer gene 1) and BRCA2 (breast cancer gene 2) account for the majority of hereditary breast cancers. Normally, these genes produce a specific protein that limits the growth of cells. An abnormal gene does not produce this tumor-suppressing protein, and a breast cancer with unrestricted growth results.

Individuals with mutated BRCA1 and BRCA2 genes have a substantial lifetime risk of developing cancer of the breast and ovary. Men can also carry the BRCA1 and

The **BRCA1** and **BRCA2** genes were the first breast cancer genes to be identified. Mutated forms of these genes are believed to be responsible for about half the cases of inherited breast cancer, especially those that occur in younger women. Both are tumor suppressor genes.

BRCA2 altered genes. Since these genes are not on the sex chromosomes, men as well as women can pass them on to their daughters and sons. An important point that is often overlooked is that a woman can inherit the BRCA genes from her father, increasing her risk of cancer of the breast or ovary. There is some evidence that men with the BRCA mutated genes appear to be at higher risk for prostate cancer, and possibly other cancers, including male breast cancer.

The altered BRCA1 and BRCA2 genes are dominant; only one abnormal gene needs to be present. Although breast cancer is common, having several individuals with this disease in the family can indicate that an abnormal BRCA gene might be present. More than 100 mutations occur in BRCA1 and BRCA2, but only three mutations, two in the BRCA1 gene and one in the BRCA2 gene, account for the vast majority of mutations in Ashkenazi Jews; genetic tests are available. More recently, it appears that the BRCA1 gene may also affect chemotherapy. One group of investigators in London have found that a functioning BRCA1 gene made the cells extremely sensitive to some chemotherapy drugs such as Taxol, but resistant to the effects of other chemotherapeutic agents such as Cisplatin.

In the more common nonhereditary, or sporadic, forms of breast cancer in those without the BRCA genes, there is still a familial component. Daughters whose mother had breast cancer have three times the risk of developing the disease, compared to women without this familial incidence. Breast cancer in two first-degree relatives, such as a mother and a sister, increase the risk tenfold.

Identifying Cancer Risk

To define a risk for cancer, it is important to examine the family pedigree. Findings that should raise concern include

- Cancers that occur early in life
- Cancers occurring in paired organs, such as a cancer in both the right and left kidneys
- Multiple different types of cancers in a given individual
- Rare types of cancer, especially if it occurs in more than one family member
- Multiple closely related family members with the same type of cancer
- Cancer in first-degree relatives

When compiling your family health history, record all cancers; be especially diligent about finding the age of onset and the specific type of cancer. In the hereditary breast-ovarian cancer syndrome resulting from the BRCA genes, women tend to have premenopausal onset of breast cancer. Similarly, in the hereditary colon cancer syndromes, onset occurs before the age of 50. While age of onset of cancer is important, cancers that occur in later life, the late-onset cancers, can also show a familial clustering. For instance, a family history of bladder cancer is also a risk factor for the disease. A case can be made that there is an inherited basis to cancer at almost all sites and all ages of onset.

Although this chapter has introduced the more common and significant genetic diseases, it really only touches the surface. You should research any medical condition that you find in your family, using the Web sites listed in Chapter 12. Keep in mind that the field of genetics and genetic diseases is rapidly changing and it is important that you get the most up-to-date information available. The Web pages listed in Chapter 12 should provide that information.

While we have discussed chromosomes and genes and how abnormal alleles at a gene can cause genetic disease, we have not yet examined the actual physical structure of a gene. In the next chapter, we explore the structure of the DNA molecule, discuss what a gene actually is, and move on to what DNA tests are available to complement your genealogy research.

CHAPTER 9

Tracking Your Genes: Molecular Genealogy

THE FIELD OF MOLECULAR GENEALOGY REALLY INCLUDES TWO TOPICS: the creation of your family's health pedigree and the use of genetic testing for genealogy. Up to this point, we have discussed chromosomes and genes, described how genes are inherited, and defined genetic disease. We have shown the techniques for compiling your family's health history and designing your family's medical pedigree. In order to understand genetic diseases more completely and to learn how we can use genetic testing in our genealogy, it is necessary that we understand the structure of DNA.

What Is a Gene?

Although we have been using the term *gene*, we have never actually described its physical structure. Although by the 1940s geneticists were using *gene* to refer to the basic unit of heredity, they didn't know its physical form. They knew that genes controlled the production of some chemicals in the body. The phrase "inborn errors of metabolism" was coined in the first part of the 20th century, just after the rediscovery of Gregor Mendel's work, by English physician Archibald Garrod. He recognized that a rare recessive disease named alkaptonuria that produced black urine in newborns was caused by a defect in the body's normal biochemical pathway. He postulated that a defective gene caused the wrong chemical to be produced, resulting in a disruption in a metabolic pathway in the body, an "inborn error of metabolism." Garrod's concept of how a gene functions remains true today.

171

By the middle of the 20th century, most scientists assumed that genes, the agents for the transmission of genetic information, had to be a protein. Proteins are large molecules made up from 20 different smaller molecules called amino acids. The particular sequence of a long chain of amino acids making up a protein could be the genetic code.

The Genetics of Blood Types

Early in the 20th century, human blood groups were found to be inherited. Each individual has two copies, or alleles, of the genes that determine their blood group. Genes for A and B blood groups are dominant over the gene O. An individual with the genes AA or AO will have blood group A; an individual with BB or BO will be type B. To have group AB, an individual would need the codominant genes AB, and for blood group O, the genes OO. An individual with AB blood type can receive any type of blood; an individual with type O blood can donate blood to anyone. The prevalence of blood groups differs in different populations. For western Europeans, approximately 45 percent are type O, 42 percent are type A, 10 percent are type B, and 3 percent are type AB. Type B blood is more common in Asians (23 percent) but surprisingly rare in Native Americans, who are of Asiatic origin. Type B blood was presumably absent in the original founders of the Americas when they migrated from Asia.

There was one problem with this idea. Chromosomes, the small threadlike structures in a cell's nucleus that appeared to be the physical units of heredity, are not composed of proteins. Investigation into their chemical composition found that chromosomes instead consist of a large molecule called DNA (deoxyribonucleic acid). DNA itself consists of only four chemical bases, adenine (A), cytosine (C), guanine (G), and thymine (T). Assuming DNA was the chemical that contained the genetic code, how could these four different bases contain the complex genetic information necessary to produce a human being? The answer was in the structure of the DNA molecule.

In 1953, Francis Crick and James Watson, supported by Rosalind Franklin and Maurice Wilkins, discovered the structure of DNA. X-ray images of the molecule from Franklin and Wilkins suggested that DNA was a helix. Working with models, the group finally came up with the structure, a ladder with the four bases making up

DNA

- Coiled helix molecule
- Alternating sequence of four base pairs: A, G, C, T

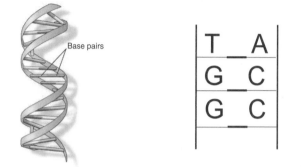

Figure 9.1 The structure of DNA.

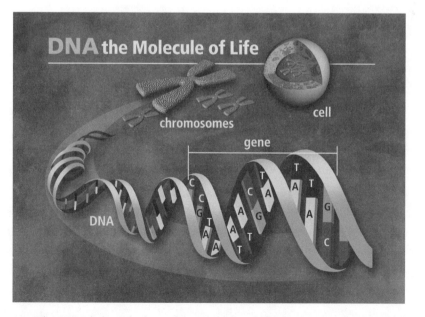

Figure 9.2 The DNA helix. The bases form the rungs of the ladder, and the helix is tightly coiled to form chromosomes. (Courtesy of the U.S. Department of Energy Human Genome Program, *www.ornl.gov/hgmis.*)

its rungs (see Figure 9.1). The ladder was coiled like a spiral staircase so that a very long molecule could be compressed into the tiny microscopic chromosomes (see Figure 9.2). This is the now famous double helix structure of DNA. It is the order of the bases, the rungs of the ladder, that is the genetic code.

Just as Mendel's work had been ignored after publication, the scientific reception was modest for several years after Watson and Crick's paper. Eventually its significance was realized, though, and Watson, Crick, and Wilkins received the Nobel Prize in 1962. Rosalind Franklin had died of ovarian cancer in 1958 at the age of 37. Her early death was ascribed to her exposure to radiation as she produced X-ray images of crystals. That's possible, but since Franklin was Jewish, she could have had an abnormal BRCA gene that resulted in her early death.

By the end of the 1950s, it had become obvious that genes, the base sequence of DNA, provided the specific proteins; this reaffirmed the idea of "inborn errors of metabolism." Proteins are essential. Some are enzymes that regulate the body's chemical reactions; others are structural and form the basis of many of the body's tissues, such as muscles, tendons, cartilage, and skin. Proteins are large molecules that consist of hundreds to thousands of the 20 different smaller amino acid molecules. The order of these amino acids is set by the DNA base sequence of the gene that controls the production of a given protein.

Mathematically, a sequence of at least three bases is required to specify one of the 20 amino acids. The first three-base code, for the amino acid phenylalanine, was discovered in 1961; by 1966 the entire genetic code had been discovered. Our genetic code consists of an alphabet of four letters: A, G, C, and T. These four letters are combined into three-letter "words." That is the dictionary of all living things.

A **base pair** consists of the two bases that form the "rung of the DNA ladder." In DNA, the base adenine is always paired with thymine and the base guanine is always paired with cytosine. The sequences of these bases are the "letters" that spell out the genetic code. In DNA, the code letters are A, T, G, C, which stand for the chemicals adenine, thymine, guanine, and cytosine, respectively. A DNA nucleotide is made of a molecule of sugar, a molecule of phosphoric acid, and a base.

The Structure of DNA

So what are these bases A, C, G, or T, the four letters that form our genes? The answer lies in the DNA model itself. Each "rung" of the ladder is made up of two bases. If we split the ladder down the middle to form two half ladders, a small part of the outer rail of the ladder (a sugar-phosphate molecule) and one of the two bases together form a nucleotide. Reassembling the ladder, we have two nucleotides that together form the rung and complete the ladder—a base pair. The four bases in human DNA (A, C, G, and T) form two types of rungs: the T-A rung and the G-C rung (see Figure 9.3). That is, when a T appears on one side of a single rung, an A will be on the other; when one side of a rung has a G, the other side will have a C. This is the principle of complementary base pairs. This is an important principle because it allows the DNA molecule to replicate and helps ensure the integrity of the base sequences.

Two Types of Rungs in the DNA Ladder

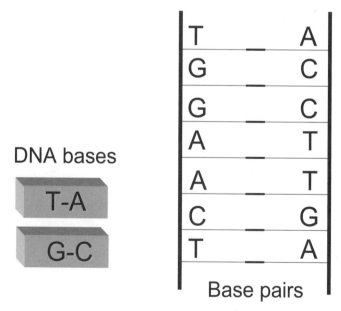

Figure 9.3 The two types of rungs in the DNA ladder: the T-A rung and the G-C rung.

Approximately 3 billion base pairs comprise the human genome, the sequence of human DNA. They are the molecular "letters" that spell out the instructions for constructing and maintaining a completely functional human being. The human DNA base sequence is almost (99 percent) the same in all people.

How Does DNA Function?

How is a protein formed based on the base coding of DNA? In practice, a small part of this ladder splits and the base sequence on one side of the ladder is "read." The nuclear DNA code is read three bases at a time by another molecule that transmits this information out of the nucleus into the cytoplasm, where the small molecules of amino acids are added one at a time to assemble a protein (see Figure 9.4).

Reading the Genetic Code

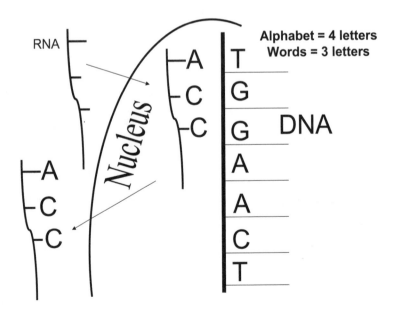

Figure 9.4 Reading the genetic code. A small molecule (RNA) similar to DNA enters the nucleus and "reads" the genetic code three bases at a time. Since whenever there is a T, there must be an A, and whenever there is a G, there must be a C, this small transfer molecule can carry a replica of the genetic code outside of the nucleus, where proteins are formed.

Cells must replicate. If cells replicate, DNA must replicate. The base pairing, or principle of complementary bases, explains how DNA replicates. If an A always requires a T and a C always requires a G, then each strand or half of the ladder is complementary to the other half. If you know the order of bases on one side of the ladder, then you know the base sequence of the other half. If the rungs of the ladder are cut in half, both halves of the ladder can rebuild themselves, creating two ladders with the same base sequence as the original. This is exactly how DNA replicates itself and preserves the genetic code. The double-stranded molecule unzips, and the two halves of the ladder regenerate themselves, producing two perfect daughter DNA molecules identical to the original (see Figure 9.5).

DNA Replication

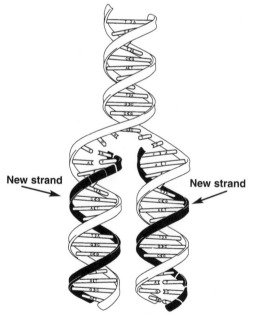

New strand

New strand

Figure 9.5 Replication of DNA. The rungs of the ladder split and form two new DNA molecules, preserving the base sequence. (Courtesy of the National Human Genome Research Institute.)

Each chromosome consists of a single tightly coiled DNA molecule. If the human DNA in these chromosomes were uncoiled and stretched out, it would be 6 feet long. Amazingly, the molecule is so tightly coiled that it fits into the chromosomes of a cell nucleus and is visible only under a microscope. Each gene is found at a specific location on a chromosome and is a specific section of the DNA molecule (see Figure 9.6). Other than for the X and Y chromosomes, because your chromosomes are paired, you have two copies, or alleles, of each gene. Each individual allele has a different order of DNA bases (A, C, G, and T) and therefore can be distinguished by DNA sequencing.

It is estimated that there are about 30,000 genes in the 23 pairs of chromosomes. Genes range in size from a few hundred bases to over a million, with the average gene having about 3,000 bases.

As we have seen, a word, also known as a codon, consists of three base pairs, each specifying one of 20 amino acids. As the

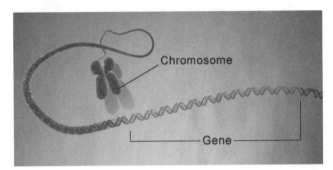

Figure 9.6 A diagram of a gene, which consists of a portion of a DNA molecule. The DNA molecule with its gene sections is tightly coiled to form a chromosome. (Courtesy of the National Library of Medicine.)

A gene is found in a specific location on a chromosome. Genes can have many alternate forms called **alleles.** If there were a single gene for eye color, it could be a blue-eye or brown-eye allele. Everyone inherits two alleles for each gene, one from the mother and the other from the father. Different alleles produce variation in inherited characteristics such as hair color or blood type or can cause disease.

DNA code is read and transmitted to the cytoplasm, the amino acids are linked together and a protein is formed. In practice, when a specific protein is needed by the cell, the portion of the DNA code is read by another molecule called RNA (ribonucleic acid). Each set of three base pairs specifies a particular amino acid. As the RNA molecules read the code from DNA, they compile the type and number of amino acids needed for that protein. The triplet base code for the amino acid methionine is ATG. Some amino acids have more than one triplet code. For instance, the amino acid glutamine is coded by CAG and CAA. Three codons, TAA, TAG, TGA, do not produce amino acids but are stop codons. When these are encountered, amino acid coding stops.

Amazingly, only a small percentage of the 3 billion base pairs in our entire genome is actually functional. The rest, approximately 95 percent, is called "junk DNA" and consists of long stretches of base pairs that seem to have nothing to do, are not genes, and do not code for protein. It is this junk, or non-coding, DNA that is used for genealogical testing.

There are about 30,000 human genes, compared to about 13,000 for fruit flies and 9 for human immunodeficiency virus (HIV). The number of human genes is surprisingly low; before the Human Genome Project deciphered the human genome, most expected the number to be closer to 100,000. Chromosome 1, the largest human chromosome, has the most genes, approximately 3,000; the Y chromosome has the fewest, at 231 genes.

Mutations

A mutation is a change in the usual DNA sequence of a particular gene, a physical change in the genetic material. It can involve a change in a single base (see Figure 9.7), the loss of one or more bases, or the addition of one or more bases. A point mutation is the change of a single base, for instance, the substitution of an A for a C. Some changes are neutral or inconsequential and cause no change in the eventual protein. Other changes can be harmful, inserting the wrong amino acid and causing the wrong protein to be produced (see Figure 9.8). At the chromosome level, mutations can be additions or deletions of large portions of a chromosome, affecting many genes (see Figure 9.9).

Mutations can arise spontaneously or be caused by exposure to some environmental agent, such as radiation. If mutation occurs in the male sperm or female egg, it will be passed down to the child following fertilization. Mutations may occur in the body, for instance, in an adult organ. Such a somatic or body mutation will not be passed on to the children. A mutation in a body cell, for instance, a breast cell or lung cell, causes that cell to reproduce itself relentlessly, which eventually causes cancer of the breast or lung. Though these mutations are not passed down to children, it's possible that the potential for a body cell to mutate to a cancer can be passed down. Mutations that occur in that portion of the DNA that is a gene can cause disease. When

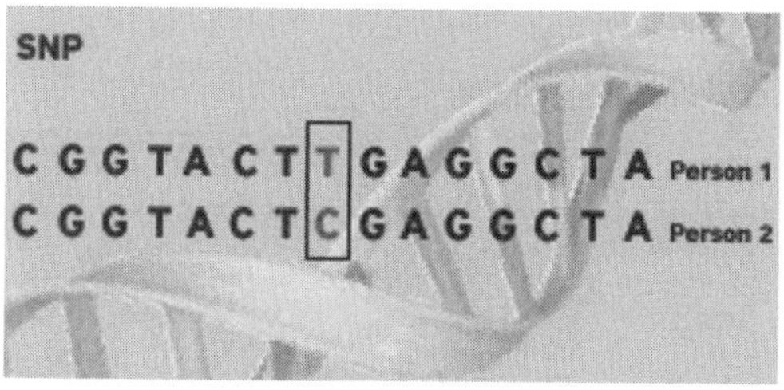

Figure 9.7 Two different individuals whose DNA base sequence differs by one base. A change in one base is called a SNP. (Courtesy of the National Human Genome Research Institute.)

How the Change in a Single Base Can Change the Protein Produced by the Genetic Code

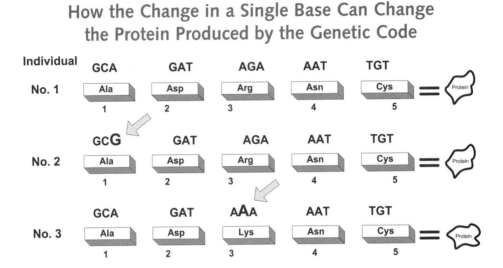

Figure 9.8 A portion of the genetic code of three individuals. Individual number 1 has the correct code. Individuals number 2 and 3 have mutations. In individual number 2, there is a change in one base; a G substituted for an A. This is inconsequential because the same amino acid, Ala, is produced and the resultant protein is the same. A base change in individual number 3, where an A is substituted for a G, causes the wrong amino acid, Lys, to be produced; the resulting protein is changed and wrong.

Hundreds of Alleles

Although any single person can have only two alleles of a gene (one from the mother, the other from the father), there may be many different types in the population. For instance, hundreds of different alleles of the breast cancer genes BRCA1 on chromosome 17 and BRCA2 on chromosome 13 have been found. In the Ashkenazi Jewish population, because of a founder effect, two BRCA1 and one BRCA2 alleles are found most often. For cystic fibrosis, one specific mutation, or allele, accounts for about 70 percent of disease genes, but there are hundreds of others, including some that do not cause the disease. Genetic testing can be complicated by the large number of allelic variants that can cause the same disease. For cystic fibrosis, for example, many laboratories are equipped to test only for the more common alleles causing the disease, those generally having a detection rate of 80 to 90 percent.

Types of Mutation

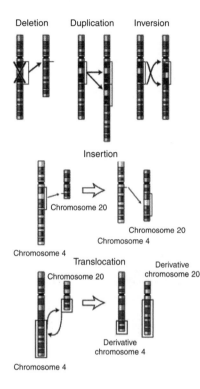

Deletion   Duplication   Inversion

Insertion

Chromosome 20

Chromosome 4

Chromosome 20
Chromosome 4

Chromosome 4

Translocation   Derivative chromosome 20

Chromosome 20

Derivative chromosome 4

Chromosome 4

Figure 9.9 Mutations involving portions of a chromosome. (Courtesy of the National Human Genome Research Institute.)

a mutation occurs in the non-coding DNA, or junk DNA, no disease occurs, but the mutations can be used for genealogy testing.

Different mutations can cause the same disease. For instance, the disease cystic fibrosis results when there is a three-base-pair deletion, CTT, and subsequently the loss of a single amino acid, phenylalanine, in the protein the gene constructs. The cystic fibrosis gene is found on chromosome 7. The CTT deletion is the most common mutation in individuals of northern European ancestry, but there are hundreds of others in the over 6,000 base pairs that make up the CF gene. The CTT deletion is less common in cystic fibrosis seen in African Americans, southern Europeans, and Ashkenazi Jews.

Spontaneous mutations can account for the sudden appearance of a genetic disease in a family. For instance, two normal parents produce a child with neurofibromatosis, a dominant disease known to have a relatively high rate of new mutation. Presumably, the mutation occurred spontaneously in either the father's sperm or the mother's egg. If a mutation occurs in an individual's sperm or egg, it will be passed on to the children, and they in turn may pass it on to their children.

Mutation rates vary with the gene. Neurofibromatosis and polycystic kidney disease have relatively high mutation rates. Marfan and Huntington diseases have low mutation rates. In the lethal osteogenesis imperfecta (OI) type II disease, which causes "brittle bones," numerous fractures are present at birth and death occurs in the first year of life. When this disease occurs, it must arise as a new mutation in each individual because affected individuals almost never live to reproductive age to pass on the abnormal gene.

In the case of Huntington chorea, the age of onset of the disease is late, after the average reproduction age, so the disease gene can be passed on to a new generation before the individual shows signs of the disease or knows that he or she carries the disease gene.

DNA is also found in another region of the cell besides the chromosomes; it is found outside the nucleus in small structures called mitochondria. These structures are important to a cell's function because they supply energy to the cell. We believe that millions of years ago when life began, a small independently living organism, a primitive bacteria, entered a cell and parasitized it. These primitive bacteria lost their independent existence and became part of the cell. They contain their own DNA, and like the DNA in chromosomes, they can also mutate and cause disease, although diseases caused by mitochondria are relatively rare.

So we have two sites of DNA: in the cell's nucleus in chromosomes and outside the nucleus in mitochondria, or mtDNA. Both types of DNA are used in genealogy for testing.

DNA occurs in two sites within cells. The first site is the chromosomes in the cell nucleus. This DNA can be tested to detect medically significant mutations that might cause disease. This site includes the Y chromosome, which can be tested to help verify paternal genealogical relationships. The other location of DNA in the cell is in mitochondria. Mitochondrial DNA, or mtDNA, is found within mitochondria lying outside of the cell's nucleus, in the cell's cytoplasm. Mitochondrial DNA is maternally inherited and can be tested for genealogy to help verify maternal relationships.

Using DNA for Genealogy

The genetic revolution has put an exciting new technology into the hands of genealogists. It is now possible for genealogists to order genetic tests, not for detecting a medical disease, but to help verify their genealogy. Understanding these tests—of the Y chromosome and mtDNA—can be difficult, yet these tests are one of the most exciting topics in genealogy today. There is no doubt that genetic testing has become an area of intense interest for genealogists. You can't open any major genealogy

As DNA testing becomes incorporated into genealogy, we can expect that DNA testing and genetic diseases will become a recognizable subspecialty in the field. Eventually the National Genealogical Society may offer official recognition to those who complete a formal course, or the Board for Certification of Genealogists may offer certification.

journal without seeing an advertisement for some company that wants to test your DNA or an advertisement for a surname group that is recruiting individuals with the same surname who are willing to donate their DNA. Any large genealogical conference invariably has one or more vendors offering DNA testing. The major genealogical societies have also embraced DNA testing. The New England Genealogical and

DNA Testing Services

Many commercial firms cater to genealogists, including these:

Personal Data Testing for Your Family

- Family Tree DNA, Houston, Texas *(www.familytreedna.com)*
- Oxford Ancestors Ltd., Oxfordshire, United Kingdom *(www.oxfordancestors.com)*
- Relative Genetics, Salt Lake City, Utah *(www.relativegenetics.com)*
- Trace Genetics, Davis, California *(www.tracegenetics.com)*
- GeneTree DNA Testing Center, Salt Lake City, Utah *(www.genetree.com)*
- DNA Heritage, United Kingdom *(www.dnaheritage.com)*

Deep Ancestry: Your Ethnic Roots

- African Ancestry, Washington, D.C. *(www.africanancestry.com)*
- AncestrybyDNA, Sarasota, Florida *(www.ancestrybydna.com)*

Historical Society devoted a large part of their Summer 2001 issue of *New England Ancestors* to genetics and genealogy and has since started a permanent column on this topic. The *National Genealogical Society Quarterly* devoted a special issue in September 2001 to the results of the Thomas Jefferson Y chromosome testing.

DNA Storage Services

An article on preserving your DNA can be found on Kevin Duerinck's Genealogy Web page (*www.duerinck.comm/archvdna.html*). Services that provide everything from home storage kits to remote safe storage of your DNA and, in some cases, offer DNA testing include

- DNA Filer (*www.dnafiler.com*)
- Gene Link (*www.bankdna.com*)
- CAT Gee (*www.catgee.com/catgee/control/home*)
- DNA Analysis (*www.storedna.com/html/storage.html*)
- Affiliated Genetics (*www.affiliatedgenetics.com/FSDNAB.htm*)
- Gene Saver (*genesaver.com/index.html*)

Basically, two types of tests are offered to genealogists: tests of the Y chromosome and tests of mitochondrial DNA (mtDNA). The Y chromosome test is used to identify paternal ancestors; the mtDNA test is used for maternal ancestors. There are two reasons for using these specific tests. The first is the method of inheritance; the Y chromosome is inherited strictly through the male line, and mtDNA is inherited through the female line. The second reason is that they are inherited as an intact package; there is no intermixing with other genetic material. Y chromosomes and mtDNA do not recombine. During replication, the other chromosomes, the autosomes, do recombine so that, for instance, the single chromosome 20 that you received from your mother is not exclusively that of your mother's father or mother but a mixture of the two.

Laboratories or commercial vendors who offer these tests to genealogists collect your DNA by sending you a kit with what looks like a couple of small toothbrushes and several small vials with an antibacterial solution. You simply scrape the inside of your cheek, put the material in the vial, and mail it back to the company. A few weeks to a month later, the results of your DNA test will be sent to you. Both the Y chromosome test and the mtDNA test report the results in terms of the structure of DNA. Many companies will also maintain your DNA in a database, notifying you when some other individual is tested and matches your DNA.

Creating the World's Largest Genealogy Database

Based in Utah, the Molecular Genealogy Research Project at Brigham Young University (*molecular-genealogy.byu.edu*) is assembling a database based on genealogical pedigrees and genetic testing. Individuals are invited to donate a blood sample and cheek swab, along with a genealogical pedigree, ideally going back six generations. To provide privacy, individual names are not recorded in the database, but relationships and the date and place of birth are. Individuals are given a genetic identity based on the results of the testing. In addition to Y chromosome and mtDNA testing, the project is also looking for markers on the autosomal chromosomes.

Using Y chromosome and mtDNA alone provides a genetic fingerprint for only two of your great-grandparents. The other six would need to be "fingerprinted" by using other family members and descendants. The compilers plan to fill in these gaps by testing the autosomes, trying to track which chromosomal material came from the mother and which from the father. They will do this by testing for markers on the autosomes, ideally where the chance of crossover is rare. The result should be a genetic database consisting of three separate groups of haplotypes: the Y chromosome, mtDNA, and the autosomes.

The project's goal is to compile the world's most comprehensive genetic and genealogical database. Basically, the compilers hope to locate a specific set of markers at a specific geographic location at a specific point in time. When completed, the database could be used by genealogists to add to their family's pedigree. The extensive database could also be used by geneticists to investigate genetic disease in much the same way that geneticists now use small well-documented groups in Iceland and Finland.

DNA testing can be used in genealogy to

- Determine whether two people descend from a recent common ancestor
- Reconstruct families
- Investigate descent through one name (as for surname societies)
- Sort out individuals with the same surname
- Uncover lost or forgotten relationships
- Add supporting evidence to your genealogy
- Provide some clues about your ethnic origin

Y chromosome and mtDNA testing are tools that can be used to verify family relationships and, along with your documented genealogy, make your family's history even more accurate and reliable. DNA testing can't prove that your genealogy is correct, but it can add supporting evidence to genealogy or disprove it completely.

In addition to offering Y chromosome and mtDNA testing, some laboratories also offer "ethnic" testing. For instance, some will report the possibility of Native American heritage and others will relate your DNA to a specific region in Africa. This is done by comparing the results of a DNA test to specific databases.

The most common DNA test used in genealogy today is the Y chromosome test. To understand why the Y chromosome is so useful, we need to examine how it is inherited and how we test it.

CHAPTER 10

Y Chromosome Testing: Your Father's Father's Father . . .

ANALYSIS OF THE Y CHROMOSOME HAS BECOME ONE OF THE MOST exciting developments in genealogy. More and more individuals are using Y chromosome testing to validate their genealogies. The test is becoming very popular with single-ancestor or surname societies.

Y Chromosome Inheritance

As we now know, there are 23 pairs of chromosomes in any cell's nucleus (see Figure 10.1). One of these pairs is the sex chromosomes. For women, the sex chromosome pair is XX; for men, XY. A woman's egg contains one of her two X chromosomes. The male sperm contains either the man's X chromosome or his Y chromosome. If the sperm containing the male X chromosome fertilizes the egg, the result will be a daughter (XX). If the sperm containing the male Y chromosome fertilizes the egg, the result will be a boy (XY) (see Figure 10.2).

The way in which the Y chromosome is inherited is what makes it useful to genealogists. Since all males are XY, the Y chromosome comes from the father, and his from his father, and so on (see Figures 10.3 and 10.4). The Y chromosome is handed down intact—no crossover or mixing with other chromosomes occurs; it is inherited as an integral unit over thousands of generations.

The inheritance of the Y chromosome establishes the Y line. Notice in Figure 10.5 how the same Y chromosome is inherited from male to male, from great-grandfather

187

Cell

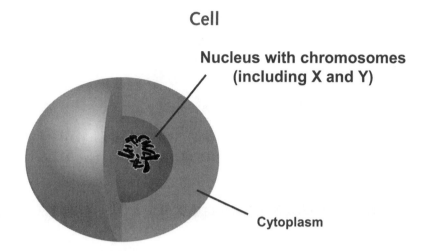

Figure 10.1 Diagram of a typical human cell showing the cell nucleus with chromosomes.

Possible Combinations of X and Y Chromosomes

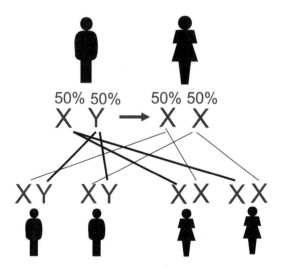

Figure 10.2 Possible combinations of X and Y chromosomes in the children. Half the sperm will have a Y chromosome; half will have an X. The female egg will have one of the mother's two X chromosomes.

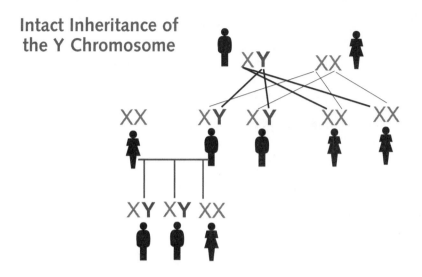

Figure 10.3 Intact inheritance of the Y chromosome. A male gives his Y chromosome to his sons, who then give the exact same Y chromosome to their sons.

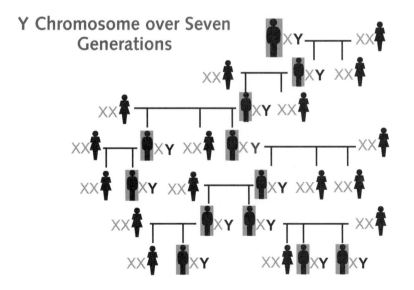

Figure 10.4 The Y chromosome handed down from father to son over seven generations. The Y chromosome of the males at the bottom of the chart should be identical to the Y chromosome of the male at the top of the chart.

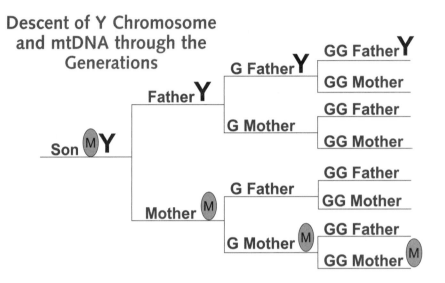

Figure 10.5 The Y line of Y chromosome descent *(top of chart)* and the M line of mtDNA descent *(bottom of chart)*.

to grandfather to father to son. The oval structure with an *M* on the chart represents mitochondrial DNA (mtDNA), to be discussed in the next chapter. Notice that mtDNA is inherited through the mother and her mother and so on, establishing the M line.

So how do we identify a specific Y chromosome? Fortunately for genealogists, in addition to genes, a large amount of non-coding DNA, or junk DNA, is present on the Y chromosome. Testing involves sampling specific segments of the nonfunctioning, or nongene, portion of the Y chromosome.

How to Analyze the Y Chromosome

We analyze the Y chromosome by examining certain specific locations, or markers, on the chromosome. The type of marker that interests us here is known as a short tandem repeat (STR) or microsatellite. STRs consist of short arrays of repeat units ranging from one to six base pairs in length; they can be repeated many times and can be any sequence of bases. It is the number of repeats that are counted and reported at a marker site when you request a Y chromosome test for genealogy. For

The Male's Responsibility

The Y chromosome is much smaller than the X chromosome and has no more than a few dozen genes compared to the 2,000 to 3,000 present on the X. Recent evidence suggests that the Y chromosome may contain some fertility genes that, when faulty, can result in an infertile male. The part of the Y chromosome that confirms maleness is a single gene, SRY (sex-determining region Y chromosome). Nature defaults to females. If this gene is not present or is not working properly, a female child is produced. In other words, it is not the woman who is responsible for producing a male child. It is a functioning SRY gene on the male's Y chromosome—so it is actually the male's responsibility. Such a pity that Henry VIII's wives were unaware of this fact!

instance, the STRs could look like this: CAG CAG CAG CAG (four repeats of the base sequence CAG). The number of repeats at a given DNA locus is different for each person, making it a useful tool to identify individuals, both for forensic purposes and for genealogy.

In practice, particular portions of the Y chromosome non-coding DNA, or junk DNA, are examined, all areas where there are known to be repeats of bases. The markers are identified as DYS (DNA Y chromosome segment) and are depicted in Figure 10.6. The range of the number of alleles varies depending on the DYS. For example, the number of repeats, or the allele range, of DYS392 is generally between 7 and 16. At DYS392, the repeated base sequence is TAT (see Figure 10.7). If we examine the Y chromosome of two individuals and count the repeats at marker DYS392, we might get the following result:

Individual A: TATTATTATTATTATTATTATTAT   = DYS392 = 8

Individual B: TATTATTATTATTATTATTATTATTAT = DYS392 = 9

At the locus DYS392, individual A has eight repeats of TAT and individual B has nine. While these two hypothetical individuals didn't match in their number of

Nonfunctional Portion of the Y Chromosome

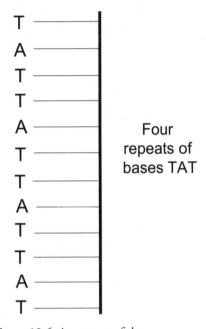

Four repeats of bases TAT

Figure 10.6 A segment of the nonfunctioning portion of the Y chromosome showing the TAT sequence repeated four times.

repeats at DYS392, they could match at another 24 markers, suggesting that they have a recent common male ancestor. Originally, the commercial firms offered a 12-marker test, but most now offer 25 markers or more. The report of the number of repeats at each marker gives the haplotype of that chromosome. A haplotype is a series of DNA sequences, specific alleles, or markers on a chromosome.

When comparing two individuals to see whether they have a common ancestor, as suggested by their genealogies, the more markers tested, the better; 25-marker tests are better than 12-marker tests. If 24 or 25 out of 25 markers match between two individuals, then, at least statistically, there is a 50 percent chance that the most recent common ancestor lived no longer than seven generations ago. If 23 or fewer out of 25 markers match, the individuals are probably not related within the genealogical time period. Some genealogists use the less expensive 12-marker test as a type of screen to see whether there is an approximate relationship. Many firms allow you to use the 12-marker test first and then follow up with the additional markers later. If using 12 markers, a match of 11 or 12 between two individuals suggests a recent common ancestor.

Why are 11/12 or 24/25 also acceptable, rather than a complete match at every marker? We generally allow for a mutation. If a common ancestor had one set of 25 markers and had two lines of male descent down to the present day, then testing the male descendants should show the same 25 markers as the ancestor and all descendants should be exactly the same. If a mutation occurs to one marker, then one individual may match in only 24/25 markers. We know mutations occur. If they didn't, everyone would have the same DNA and the test would be useless. We assume that

**Four Repeats on the
Nonfunctional Portion**

Reported as
"DYS ### location" 4

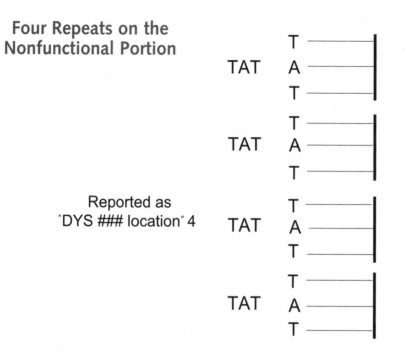

Figure 10.7 The same segment seen in Figure 10.6, showing the four repeats of the sequence TAT. In practice, the number of repeats is reported for this specific location, DYS, on the chromosome.

within the genealogical time period, one mutation can occur and not negate the relationship. A one-marker difference between two individuals who have good genealogical proof that they are in a direct male line from a given ancestor is considered a mutation. This is especially true if there are, for instance, four or five directly descended individuals with identical markers and one directly descended individual with one marker off. When comparing two individuals, a 24/25 or better match with good genealogy should indicate a shared ancestor, but you won't know exactly who or when. This is where good genealogy enters the picture.

Genealogy

At its simplest, Y chromosome testing can be used to see whether two individuals with the same surname are related. Perhaps a connection between different branches of a family with the same surname is suspected but cannot be proven from the genealogical research. Assuming that the individuals have a male line to a common ancestor, descendants can have their Y chromosomes tested to see whether there is a match. The testing can also help determine whether individuals with what appears to be a derived surname are related. For instance, is a certain American of Irish descent with the surname Brian related to the O'Briens of County Clare or the O'Briens of County Tipperary? What results would you get if you simply tested many males in a country with the same surname?

Bryan Sykes accomplished this in 2000. The investigators found 9,885 individuals with the surname Sykes registered to vote in the United Kingdom. The highest concentration of Sykes was in the counties of West Yorkshire, Lancashire, and Cheshire. The DNA from 48 individuals with the surname Sykes was analyzed from these three counties and compared to a control group of 139 English males from all over the country and a group of "non-Sykes"—unrelated male neighbors in the same three counties. The Y chromosome was evaluated at four STR locations.

The haplotype of 15-23-11-14 (for DYS19, DYS390, DYS391, and DYS393, respectively) was seen in approximately 44 percent of Sykes and was not seen in any of the two groups of non-Sykes controls. If four additional Sykes whose haplotype was only one repeat off are included, then 52 percent of Sykes shared the same haplotype. A change of one repeat number from the original Sykes number would not be unlikely, considering the Sykes name is estimated to have originated 700 years ago. Obviously, this type of Y chromosome typing could be useful for investigating the genealogical link between individuals with the same surname for whom a common ancestor is not known.

For the other Sykes who did not have this haplotype, it was postulated that this was due to a series of "non-paternity events" occurring over the centuries. A non-paternity event, also known as a false paternity, occurs when a supposed father and son are found not to be biologically related. There can be many reasons: affairs outside of marriage, a

A **non-paternity event,** also known as false paternity, is a situation in which the presumed father is found not to be the true biological father.

Finding an Ancestor's Y Chromosome

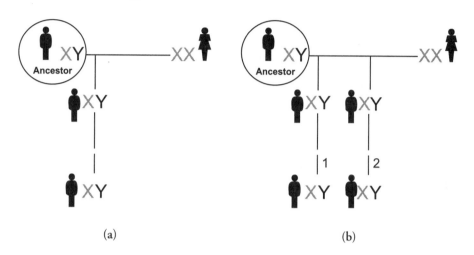

Figure 10.8 Y chromosome testing of living male descendants to determine the probable Y chromosome haplotype of an ancestor.

bridal pregnancy in which the groom is not the father, a son taking his stepfather's name, a birth after the death of the father when the widow has remarried, an unrecorded adoption, and of course, an improper conclusion from genealogical evidence.

How do you determine whether the Y chromosome of a living descendant is that of an ancestor? In Figure 10.8(a), the Y chromosome of a living descendant is tested and it is assumed that since the genealogy shows a direct male descent, the Y chromosome of the living descendant at the bottom is identical to that of the ancestor. But one line is not sufficient; other direct male descendants should be tested. Their Y chromosomes should match each other, as seen in Figure 10.8(b). What if the second line shows a different Y chromosome than the first, as seen in Figure 10.8(c)? Then we don't know which Y chromosome is the ancestor's. We must keep testing. In Figure 10.8(d), we have added the Y chromosome results from another line. Here we see that the two Y chromosomes labeled number 1 match, and the Y chromosome labeled number 2 doesn't match. By testing as many lines as possible and getting identical Y chromosome matches, you can increase your confidence that you have identified an ancestor's haplotype.

Figure 10.9 shows the results of testing the descendants of Jonathan Porter. Males are depicted by squares; each square in a given vertical line represents an ancestor. Jonathan had five sons: Jacob, Thomas, William, Henry, and Peter. Seven male descendants had their Y chromosomes tested. Individuals 1, 2, 3, 4, and 8 had identical Y chromosome markers. Individual 7* differed by one repeat, which was considered a mutation; thus, he was assigned to the Porter haplotype (black squares). Two individuals, 5 and 6, differed from the Porter haplotype in 8 of 12 markers, DYS 390, 393, 19, 385a, 385b, 388, 389-1, and 389-2, but did agree between themselves. Their squares are striped. For individuals 5 and 6, it is thought that a non-paternity event occurred; presumably, these two individuals have the same father in the second generation, but he is not William. Two non-paternity events in the same sibship occurring by the same outside father suggest an unusual family situation. One can only speculate, but possibly, an unrecorded adoption occurred. For instance, if William married a widow, her young sons could have been absorbed into the Porter family and become known as Porters.

If two individuals are an exact match in their Y chromosome, they share a common ancestor. The concept of the "most recent common ancestor" (MRCA) is a statistical construct based on the presumed mutation rate and the number of markers tested. For instance, if two individuals match exactly for a 12-marker test, there is a 50 percent probability that their MRCA will be found within the last 14 generations. A complete match in a 21-marker test has a 50 percent probability that their MRCA will be found within the last 8 generations. To have a 90 percent probability that two individuals have an MRCA no more than one generation ago requires a complete match of more than 500 markers. This is where good genealogy helps. Good genealogical research will

Results of Y Chromosome Test

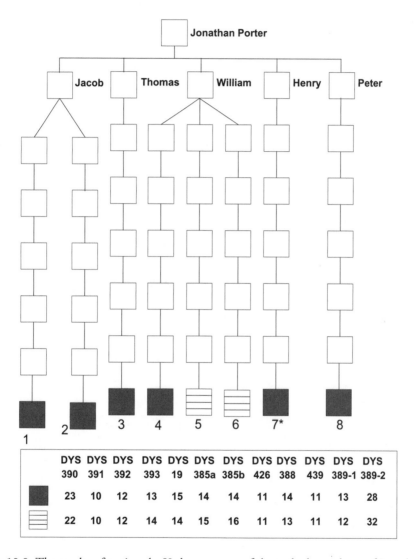

Figure 10.9 The results of testing the Y chromosome of the male descendants of Jonathan Porter. DYS stands for DNA Y chromosome segment. The numbers below each DYS identify the location on the Y chromosome; for instance, DYS 390 is one area on the Y chromosome and DYS 393 is another. The numbers to the right of the black square are the number of repeats found for each DYS or location and are the "Porter haplotype." The numbers to the right of the striped square are the number of repeats found in individuals 5 and 6 and represent the "Non-Porter" haplotype.

indicate the probable common ancestor. In searching for the Y chromosome of a common ancestor, you should test as many Y line descendants as possible. Each exact match increases the probability that the individuals are related to that ancestor.

Thomas Jefferson and Sally Hemings

On New Year's Day 1772, Thomas Jefferson married Martha Wayles Skeleton, a young widow. Less than a year later, Martha's father, John Wayles, died, leaving 135 slaves to his daughter and son-in-law. One of them was Sally Hemings, the daughter of John Wayles and his slave Elizabeth Hemings. Sally Hemings, therefore, was the half-sister of Jefferson's wife, Martha. Elizabeth Hemings, Sally's mother, was herself half-white, sired by an African mother and an English sea captain. Sally, then, was three-quarters white.

In 1782, Martha died at the age of 33 after bearing Jefferson six living children, only two of whom, both daughters, survived to adulthood. Jefferson's only son died at birth. Now a widower, in 1784 Jefferson accepted the post of America's first minister to Paris. It is generally assumed that during his stay in Paris Jefferson became involved with Sally, who apparently resembled her half-sister, the deceased Martha.

Even as Jefferson served as the third president of the United States, rumors spread that he had fathered children with his slave, Sally Hemings. The first accusation came in 1802. A family with the present surname Woodson believed that Sally's first son, their ancestor Thomas Woodson, was sired by Jefferson. Sally's last son was Eston, born in 1808. He reportedly resembled Jefferson. Family tradition among the descendants of Eston Hemings was that Jefferson was his father.

As reported in *Nature* in 1998 by Eugene Foster and others, a Y chromosome analysis was done of the descendants of Jefferson's paternal uncle, Field Jefferson, and compared to the descendants of Thomas Woodson and Eston. No Y chromosome data was available from male-line descendants of Thomas Jefferson because he had no surviving "legitimate" sons. In order to determine the Jefferson Y chromosome, it was necessary to use Jefferson's paternal uncle. Although Figure 10.10 shows only a few lines, the investigators tested the Y chromosomes of five male-line descendants of two sons of Jefferson's paternal uncle Field Jefferson. They also tested five male-line descendants of two sons of Thomas Woodson and one male-line descendant of Eston Hemings.

The investigators found that the Y chromosomes of the descendants of Field

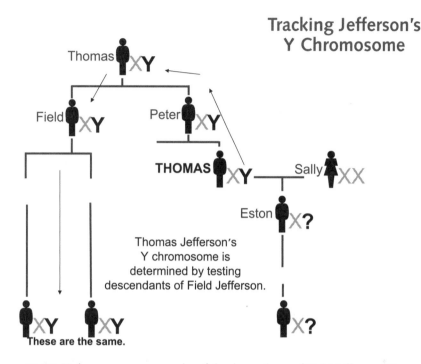

Figure 10.10 Y chromosome test results of the descendants of Field Jefferson, Thomas Jefferson's uncle. By inference, Thomas Jefferson had the same Y chromosome markers as Field's descendants.

Jefferson were the same (see Figure 10.10), suggesting that this was the true Jefferson haplotype. The Y chromosome of the descendants of Eston matched that of Field's descendants (see Figure 10.11), the presumed Jefferson Y chromosome. The descendants of Thomas Woodson should have shown the Jefferson Y chromosome if they were descendants. But theirs was completely different, showing that Thomas Woodson's father was not Thomas Jefferson (see Figure 10.12).

The Y chromosome markers of the descendants of Eston matched those of Field's, suggesting that a Jefferson fathered Eston with Sally Hemings. But was it Thomas or some other Jefferson, such as a nephew? The National Genealogical Society tackled this problem in an issue devoted exclusively to the Jefferson-Hemings controversy. In this issue, Helen Leary applied genealogical proof standards to examine the question. Her findings, along with the Y chromosome analysis, indicate that Thomas Jefferson was almost certainly the father of Eston. Despite this, to this day, the descendants of Eston have not been included in any official Jefferson reunion.

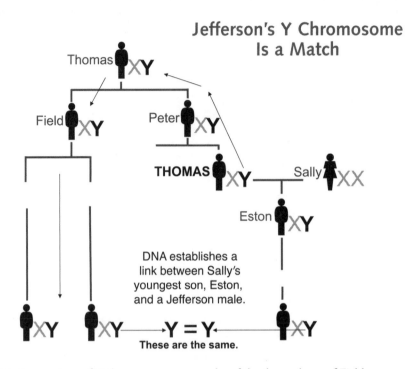

Figure 10.11 Comparison of Y chromosome test results of the descendants of Field Jefferson and the descendants of Eston Hemings. The Y chromosome markers of the descendants of Eston are identical to those of the descendants of Field Jefferson.

The following table from Foster's article in *Nature* shows the Y chromosome haplotypes for Field Jefferson, Eston, and Woodson:

DYS =	19	388	389A	389B	389C	389D	390	391	392	393	156Y
Field Jefferson	15	12	4	11	3	9	11	10	15	13	7
Eston	15	12	4	11	3	9	11	10	15	13	7
Woodson	14	12	5	11	3	10	11	13	13	13	7

The Y chromosomes of the descendants of Field Jefferson and Eston show identical markers. At five locations, DYS 19, 389A, 389D, 391, and 392, the number of base repeats for the Jefferson and Woodson haplotypes are different. They are different Y chromosomes.

Jefferson's Y Chromosome Haplotype

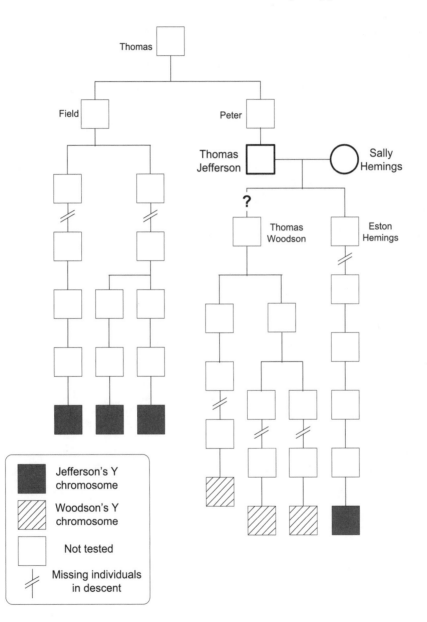

Figure 10.12 Comparison of Y chromosome test results of the descendants of Field Jefferson, Thomas Woodson, and Eston Hemings. Woodson's descendants do not match the Jefferson Y chromosome haplotype.

Actually, the Jefferson and Woodson chromosomes were analyzed further:

Markers	YAP	SRYm8299	sY81	LLY22g	Tat	92R7	SRYm1532	MSY1
Field Jefferson	0	0	0	0	0	0	1	(3)5,(1)14,(3)32,(4)16
Eston	0	0	0	0	0	0	1	(3)5,(1)14,(3)32,(4)16
Woodson	0	0	0	0	0	1	1	(1)16,(3)27,(4)21

As with the STRs, the markers for the descendants of Field Jefferson and Eston are identical. Markers YAP through SRYm1532 are seven additional markers known as biallelic markers and can be either 0 (the natural or wild state) or 1 (the mutated state). Field Jefferson and Woodson differ at one marker, 92R7. The final marker is the minisatellite MSY1; Jefferson and Woodson differ here, as well. A minisatellite is similar to a microsatellite or STR, but the number of base pairs repeated is longer. Although these types of markers are not yet commercially available to genealogists, undoubtedly they will eventually be offered. The descendants of Thomas Woodson show that he could not have been Thomas Jefferson's son. As Foster points out in his article, the Jefferson haplotype is rare in the population and has not been seen outside of the Jefferson family. It has not been seen in 670 European men typed with the microsatellites or 308 European men typed with MSY1.

The analysis of Jefferson's Y chromosome was printed in 1998, and the analysis of the genealogical evidence was published in the special edition of the *National Genealogical Society Quarterly* in 2001, but the controversy has not ended. In the *Northern Virginia Daily*, 3 May 2003, under the heading, "Plot Thickens in Monticello Dispute," the story relates that the descendants of Sally Hemings are charging that their Internet chat group was infiltrated by the head of the Jefferson family association, who pretended to be a 67-year-old black woman. The head of the Jefferson family association admitted that the real spy was his wife, who was trying to help her husband's efforts to keep the slave descendants out of the upcoming annual Jefferson reunion. The story goes on to state that even though the Hemings descendants were formally excluded from membership, some members of the Jefferson family association continue to believe that they should be included—presumably believing the validity of the Y chromosome test.

Jefferson's haplotype is rare. Some Y haplotypes are more common than others. Finding two possibly related individuals with a common haplotype would be less significant than finding two individuals sharing a rare haplotype. This is where genealogy enters the picture. Y chromosome tests cannot be used in isolation. Genealogists do not automatically conclude that two individuals with the same surname in a given town are related. Similarly, one cannot conclude that any two individuals with the same genetic markers are related. The results of the DNA tests must be evaluated in the context of well-documented genealogy. If your genealogy shows that two individuals are probably related and the DNA tests give the same results, this supports your genealogy. It does not tell you they are brothers, or father and son. It tells you they have a common ancestor. On the other hand, if the results show that they are not related, then it has disproved your genealogy.

As we have seen in the analysis of Jefferson's Y chromosome, there are different types of markers on the Y chromosome than the commercially available STRs. The short tandem repeats, STRs, mutate rapidly and are useful to define haplotypes for genealogy. Other markers such as single nucleotide polymorphisms (SNPs—pronounced "snips") represent the change in a single DNA base, for example the substitution of G for T; these markers are more slowly mutating and are useful for anthropology and for defining lineages known as haplogroups. Currently, commercial DNA testing firms are offering 25-STR-marker tests. There may be as many as 150 locations where STRs are located, so more locations could be examined. Alternatively, as was done with Jefferson's chromosome, other markers besides the STRs can be tested.

Terms Used in DNA Testing

Microsatellites (also known as *short tandem repeats* or *STRs*) are repetitive stretches of short sequences of two to six bases of DNA. They can be used as genetic markers to track inheritance in families. The exact pattern of microsatellites, plus other markers, forms a given individual's **haplotype**.

A **haplogroup** is a family of commonly occurring haplotypes; it is usually defined by slowly changing markers such as **SNPs** (single nucleotide polymorphisms, pronounced "snips"), which result from the insertion, deletion, or substitution of a single base in the DNA molecule. **Unique event polymorphisms (UEPs)** are unique events in the history of human DNA that alter the DNA sequence and that are subsequently inherited. Many SNPs are UEPs.

Starting Your Own Y Chromosome Project

You may now want to begin DNA testing for yourself or as part of a surname society. It is probably best to decide on one laboratory or vendor and to send your DNA samples to that establishment. The commercial laboratories can vary in how they report their results; some will test at different DYSs than others. Most laboratories now testing seem to be doing a very professional job and maintain good quality control. But research the vendors carefully. Examine their Web page. Find out what type of services they offer. Find out how many markers they test. Talk to others who have used the vendor and determine their level of satisfaction. If you are starting a major project, inquire about discounts; most commercial firms offer discounts for groups.

If you are going to start a DNA testing program for your surname society, learn all you can about the technology so that you will understand the results. Most of the commercial laboratories are good about helping you. Visit the Web and look at the

Doing Y Chromosome Testing for a Surname Organization

When planning Y chromosome testing for a surname organization, follow these steps:

- Recognize that you will need to be the coordinator.
- Establish a hypothesis—a purpose to begin testing.
- Contact others using family mailing lists, family organizations, and family reunions.
- Establish a Web page where you can post the results.
- Research the vendors carefully to see what services are offered.
- Pick a single vendor.
- Seek group discounts for the cost of the tests.
- Search the Web for other surname organizations to see their approach.
- Organize the study and keep the participants informed.
- Use family newsletters, mailing lists, and Web pages to contact and keep participants informed.

Web pages of some of the other surname societies who are doing DNA testing and examine their results. A listing of the better ones is included in Chapter 12.

Establish a hypothesis—a purpose; you don't want to just start random testing. Probably the best approach is to identify several established lineages for your family surname and, based on their genealogy, hypothesize that the living individuals have descended from one common ancestor. Your hypothesis is that you have identified a group of individuals with a common surname and established lineages. Then test the hypothesis. Does the Y chromosome testing show that there is a common ancestor? Is the hypothesis true?

You will need to contact others and convince them to undergo DNA testing. In addition to e-mail, letters, and phone calls, use a Web page, use any family mailing lists, or contact individuals at a family reunion. If successful, you will get individuals to undergo Y chromosome testing at their expense. Consider sending out a waiver to all participants explaining the purpose of the test and relieving you of any legal liability.

As the results are returned, you will begin collecting the data and compiling the results. Use a family newsletter, mailing list, or Web page to advertise the project and, once the project is underway, to post the results. It is best to assign numbers to participants when posting the results; keep the actual names of the participants private. If you have planned correctly and have good genealogies, you will begin to see the Y chromosome results for that surname and be able to estimate that it represents the documented ancestor. Continue testing other descendants to see whether those results support your initial hypothesis.

Deep Ancestry

Y chromosome testing is actually fairly new. Mitochondrial DNA, or mtDNA, testing has been used in historic and prehistoric investigation since the 1980s. Though the use of Y chromosomes for similar studies is more recent, it has confirmed what mtDNA had already revealed: Modern humans arose about 100,000 years ago out of Africa. That is very recent by evolutionary standards.

Short tandem repeats have a high mutation rate and are therefore ideal for looking at relatively recent relationships such as those examined in genealogy. As we know, STRs consist of short tandem arrays of repeating units ranging from two to six base pairs in length. To go into deeper relationships, it is necessary to use different markers

So many human fossil remains have been found in East Asia that some believe modern humans arose in this region, challenging the "out of Africa" theory that modern humans arose in Africa and spread to the rest of the world. Recent Y chromosome analysis, however, suggests that settlement of Southeast Asia from Africa occurred 18,000 to 60,000 years ago and, with the retreat of the glaciers in the last Ice Age, spread northward to China and Siberia and south and east into Indonesia and the Pacific islands.

on the Y chromosome, markers that change far more slowly and thus stretch our ability to cluster relationships over hundreds to thousands of years. These single nucleotide polymorphisms (SNPs) are the substitution of one DNA base for another. For instance, at a particular base location, a C may be substituted for a T. This is also known as a biallelic marker or a binary. Since SNPs occur very slowly, they are useful in anthropological studies to assess what is known as deep ancestry.

We saw some of these markers in the analysis of Thomas Jefferson's Y chromosome, the biallelic markers that can be either "on" or "off" at a given location. Using these types of markers, geneticists have defined Y chromosome haplogroups—large families of individuals—the equivalent of "races." The term *haplogroup* refers to the categorization of Y chromosomes by the more slowly mutating markers, while the term *haplotype* is used for sublineages or "subfamilies" of haplogroups defined by variation of STRs. These haplotypes add a further measure of diversity within the haplogroups. Y chromosome analysis is beginning to shed light on some of the most fascinating genealogical and historical problems. Mutations on the Y chromosome have become powerful tools for the investigation of human diversity, complementing that information obtained from mtDNA.

Jewish Y Chromosomes

Today's Jews descended from the ancient Israelites who lived in the historic Israel over 2,000 years ago. Since they scattered around the world for the next two millennia, the question can be asked, "Did Jews retain their genetic identity following the Jewish Diaspora?" In one study of Ashkenazi, Roman, North African, Kurdish, Near Eastern,

Yemenite, and Ethiopian Jews, M. F. A. Hammer and fellow researchers found that despite their long-term residence in different countries, most Jewish populations were not significantly different from one another at the genetic level. Most of the Jewish populations clustered with the Middle Eastern non-Jewish populations including Palestinians and Syrians. This supports the hypothesis that the paternal gene pools of Jewish communities from Europe, North Africa, and the Middle East descended from a common Middle Eastern ancestral population. Another study, this one led by Almut Nebel, supports this and shows that even when Jewish groups are living within a larger non-Jewish population, there is little mixing. For instance, Kurdish Jews living in Kurdistan genetically are not closer to Muslim Kurds than the Ashkenazim living in Europe. Conversely, Muslim Kurds resemble other populations living in the same area, such as Turks and Armenians, and these populations are closer to Jews and Arabs than to Europeans.

Analysis of Y chromosome markers was used to trace the origins of Jewish priests. The Jewish priesthood was established about 3,300 years ago with the appointment of the first Israelite high priest. Following the Exodus from Egypt, males of the tribe of Moses were assigned special priestly responsibilities and male descendants of Moses' brother, Aaron, served as priests (Cohanim). This designation of Jewish males to the priesthood has continued through today and follows patrilineal descent. Today, this group may be named Cohen or related names such as Kahn and Kane. An analysis of the Y chromosome markers of current Jewish priests (Cohanim) in a paper in *Nature* in 1997 showed a clear distinction between their markers and their lay counterparts. Interestingly, the same distinction between priests and lay individuals was seen whether the subjects were of Ashkenazic or Sephardic origin. These two Jewish communities developed within the Diaspora during the past thousand years. The results are consistent with an origin for the Jewish priesthood before the division and formation into Ashkenazic and Sephardic communities.

Another study, this one led by M. G. Thomas and published in *Nature* in 1998, specifically characterized the Y chromosome at six microsatellites and six "unique-event polymorphisms" (UEPs) in a sample of 306 male Jews, including the priestly Ashkenazic and Sephardic Cohen, from Israel, Canada, and the United Kingdom. It was found that a single haplotype (the Cohen modal haplotype) was strikingly frequent in both Ashkenazic and Sephardic Cohanim. Using a standard mutation rate, the time at which the Cohen chromosomes were derived from a common ancestral chromosome appears to be between 2,100 and 3,250 years before the present, during or shortly before the Temple period in Jewish history.

Investigation of the Jewish Levites, another male caste by tradition descended from Levi, the third son of Jacob, showed a specific Y chromosome haplogroup, but only in the Ashkenazi Levites, not in the Sephardic Levites or others. This specific haplogroup is rare in other Jewish groups but found in non-Jewish eastern Europeans. It is not Near Eastern in origin. This suggests to Doron M. Behar, who investigated the Y chromosomes of Levites, that there was a non-Jewish European founder whose descendants had Levite status. This presumably occurred after the Ashkenazi separated from the other Jewish populations.

The Jewish priestly Cohen modal haplotype has also been found in South Africa. For years, the Lemba tribe of southern Africa claimed Jewish ancestry as descendants of the Ten Lost Tribes of Israel, which were exiled 2,700 years ago by the Assyrians. The Lemba have kosher-like dietary restrictions, male circumcision rites, and other Semitic traditions. They became commonly referred to as the "black Jews" of southern Africa. An analysis of their Y chromosomes found that there was a high frequency of the Jewish Cohen modal haplotype, known to be characteristic of the paternally inherited Jewish priesthood, which supports the Lemba claim to Jewish origin.

Genghis Khan

Tatiana Zerjal and others, reporting in 2003, found a Y chromosome lineage with several unusual features to be present in 16 populations throughout a large region of Asia, stretching from the Pacific to the Caspian Sea. About 8 percent of the men in this region share these features. The authors suggest that the lineage originated in Mongolia about a thousand years ago. They believe that it is the genetic footprint of Genghis Khan (1162–1227). Genghis Khan, born Temuchin, unified the nomadic tribes, became the ruler of Mongolia, and then swept out of Mongolia to capture Peking, Russia, and Persia. Often slaughtering the conquered people, especially the men, Genghis Khan established the largest land empire in history. He and his men had many children, with some of the male descendants continuing to rule much of this large area for generations. The authors believe that the Y chromosome of a single individual, Genghis Khan, spread rapidly and is now found in 8 percent of the males throughout a large part of Asia.

As the genealogical and scientific communities continue their testing, more information about origins of specific groups will be assembled. Eventually, as the number of individuals being tested increases, we may begin compiling information about our

Charles F. Kerchner Jr. is analyzing the DNA of individuals of Pennsylvania German extraction to test the hypothesis that a significant percentage of people with Pennsylvania German (or Pennsylvania Dutch) heritage have some trace of eastern Asian haplotypes, thought to be brought into southern Germany during the Huns' and Mongols' invasions of Europe. You can find out more about this DNA project by visiting Kerchner's Web site at *www.kerchner.com/pa-gerdna.htm*.

ethnicity and place of origin. Humans throughout history have shown an amazing ability to migrate and marry at will. I suspect it will be hopeless to believe that we can look at a set of DNA information and determine that one of our ancestors came from some one place. Nevertheless, the concept remains intriguing.

The Irish Surname

A study from Trinity College in Dublin, printed in the journal *Nature* in 2000, typed 221 Y chromosomes from Irish males (see Figure 10.13). They divided the Y chromosomes into haplogroups and divided the 221 males based on the origin of their surname into six categories: Scotch, English, or Irish, with the Irish surnames further divided into the four provinces of ancient Ireland—Ulster, Munster, Leinster, and Connaught.

One particular haplotype, type 1 (R1b), was seen in high frequency in Ireland. For those men with Scottish names, 53 percent had the type 1 haplotype; for those with English names, 62 percent. In Ireland, however, in the two eastern provinces, Leinster and Ulster, the percentages of those with type 1 was 73 percent and 81 percent, respectively. In Irish names seen in western Ireland, the percentage increased. For the province Munster in southwest Ireland, the percentage was 94 percent, and in the northwest province of Connaught, an astounding 98.5 percent of men with Irish surnames were type 1. So if you believe that your Irish surname derives from one of the modern counties of Connaught, such as Mayo or Galway, and you find that your Y chromosome is not haplogroup 1, you might be in the 1.5 percent who doesn't have that group, but you might also want to reexamine your genealogy.

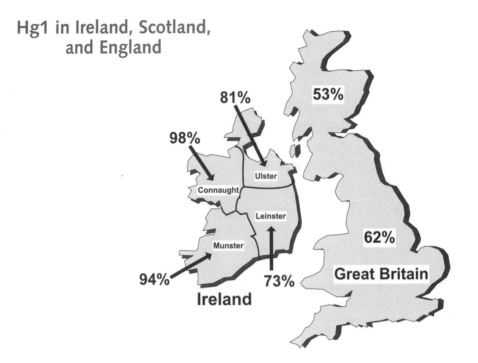

Figure 10.13 Frequency of haplogroup 1 (Hg1) in Great Britain and Ireland.

Identification

Since the O. J. Simpson trial in 1994 for the murders of Nicole Brown Simpson and Ronald Goldman, DNA fingerprinting has been constantly in the news. It is now common for the news media to discuss DNA evidence as a new sensational case comes to trial. Many municipalities are compiling DNA databases of all convicted felons. Recently, there have been several well-publicized cases of convicted felons who, after years in prison, have been released on reexamination of the evidence using the latest DNA fingerprinting techniques.

Although genealogists are using the concept of repeating bases on the Y chromosome, the FBI and police departments around the country use repeating bases on other chromosomes as a form of DNA testing for forensic purposes. Developed in the 1980s, DNA testing today relies on the same principle as Y chromosome testing: the detection of short pieces of DNA in the "junk region" of our chromosomes that repeat over and over again. This DNA fingerprinting is revolutionizing criminal investigation. The STR, or short tandem repeat, test has replaced some of the older methods of DNA testing.

The FBI in 1997 recommended a 13-marker series of STRs for forensic use as a DNA fingerprint; this test evaluates 13 different STR markers on different chromosomes plus a marker that determines the sex of the individual from whom the DNA sample was obtained. This is now the standard used for DNA identification.

In a similar fashion, STRs on specific markers can be used to identify paternity. One-half of a child's chromosomal DNA is inherited from the mother, and the other half is inherited from the father. Unlike the X and Y chromosomes, all other chromosomes are paired. For instance, both the mother and father will have a pair of chromosome 11, each with a marker. The child will also have two chromosomes 11, one inherited from the mother, the other from the father. For paternity testing, we look at the child's chromosomes to see whether the markers present could have come from the alleged father. On chromosome 11, there is a marker called HUMTHO1, which has a four-base repeat. The father and mother will have a marker on each of their pair of chromosomes 11. If the mother has at HUMTHO1 a 6 and 9 repeat and the father has a 7 and 8 repeat, the child of this couple must have either 6, 7; 6, 8; 9, 7; or 9, 8. A paternal contribution of 7 or 8 is compatible with that individual's being the father. If the paternal contribution is not a 7 or 8 repeat, someone else is the father. In practice, multiple markers are used; when two or three markers do not match the alleged father, that is evidence of non-paternity. Other relationships, such as sibship, can be determined using the same techniques of shared markers.

Disease

The concept of repeating base sequences in the nonfunctioning portion of chromosomes can also occur in the functioning portion of chromosomes, where it can occur in genes and cause disease. Repetition of a series of bases is an unusual mutation to cause disease, but we now know of over a dozen diseases that result from the abnormal repetition of base groups. Huntington disease, the same disease that killed Woody Guthrie, is one of those diseases. The gene that causes Huntington disease was found in 1993, and there is now a genetic test for it.

The genetic defect that causes Huntington disease is found on chromosome 4. The huntingtin gene contains one specific triplet of base pairs, CAG, which codes for the amino acid glutamine. In normal individuals, this triplet, CAG, is repeated—it "stutters"—similar to the Y chromosome marker repeats. Unaffected individuals may have the CAG repeated up to 37 times. In Huntington disease, the base triplet CAG is repeated over 37 times, in some cases up to 250 times. Individuals who show a repeat number of 37 to 41 may or may not show the disease. If an individual shows a repeat number above 42, the disease will always occur. This means that an excessive number of the amino acid glutamine is incorporated into the resultant protein, huntingtin, an abnormal protein that appears to be toxic to nerve cells in the brain. The destruction of brain nerve cells causes the symptoms of the disease. The more repeats there are, the earlier the age of onset of the disease. The number of triplet repeats can change with each generation, but if the number of triplet repeats increases, the genetic condition begins earlier with each generation—so a grandchild may show symptoms at an earlier age than did the affected grandfather.

DNA testing is available and can show whether the defective gene is present. But many whose family history shows they are at risk choose not to be tested because there is no effective treatment. It is generally agreed that such a decision is ethically responsible when it comes to children whose family history shows that they are at risk. For adults, though, whether to test becomes a terrible decision.

Individuals with fragile-X syndrome have a narrow face with a prominent forehead, a large jaw and ears, and moderate to severe mental retardation. Fragile-X syndrome is caused by an increased number of repeats in a specific portion of the X chromosome. The higher the number of repeats of the three bases, CGG, the more severe the disease. Normal individuals have up to 50 repeats of CGG. When the number of repeats exceeds 200, fragile-X syndrome is present. The number of repeats tends to change with each generation, and with more repeats, the symptoms become more severe. The fragile-X gene is transmitted as an X-linked recessive. About 8 percent of the males with the abnormal X gene are affected, and about two-thirds of female carriers have some degree of mental deficit when they receive the abnormal X gene from their mother. Mental retardation is rare in carrier females when the abnormal X is received from the father. The diagnosis of fragile-X syndrome should be considered in any child with undiagnosed mental retardation.

Friedreich ataxia (FRDA), transmitted as an autosomal recessive trait, also has a triplet of bases, GAA, that is abnormally repeated. Found on chromosome 9, the normal number of repeats ranges from 5 to 13. When the number of repeats is in the 30 to 60 range, the individual is still normal but is at increased risk of passing an even larger number of repeats on to a child. Those with FRDA have 66 to 1,700 repeats of GAA, with most on the order of 600 to 1,200 repeats. Fewer repeats tend to be associated with a later onset of the disease.

Fragile Grandfathers

It may not be Parkinson disease. Men in their 50s or 60s who have gradually worsening symptoms of tremors; difficulty in initiating movement; problems with walking, balance, and writing; impotence; and memory loss may not have Parkinson disease but may have a newly diagnosed disease related to fragile-X syndrome. This disease, fragile-X-associated tremor/ataxia syndrome (FXTAS), is caused by a mutation on the X chromosome in a gene called FMR1, or fragile-X mental retardation 1 gene. Normal individuals have 6 to 40 CGG repeats. When there are 200 or more repeats of the bases CGG, the individual develops fragile-X syndrome, one of the most common forms of inherited mental retardation. Individuals with 55 to 200 repeats, known as a premutation and once thought to be innocuous, can have FXTAS. This premutation appears to affect approximately one in 700 to 800 men and one in 250 women.

Women do not seem to show the disease, probably because they have an additional X chromosome to compensate for the X chromosome with the disease. About a fifth of women with the premutation may, however, have premature menopause. For affected men, the disease appears in older individuals, especially grandfathers of children with fragile-X syndrome. Although FXTAS appears to occur only in about a third of male carriers, you need to know that having a mentally retarded grandchild with fragile-X syndrome may put you at risk for the disease.

The most common form of adult-onset muscular dystrophy is myotonic dystrophy (DM), transmitted as autosomal dominant. It also is a disease of repeating triple bases; if they increase in number over multiple generations, the severity of the disease also increases. A grandfather may have a mild form of the disease, his son worse, and his grandson could be severely affected as the number of repeated triplets increases. General weakness, weakness of facial muscles, cataracts, difficulty in speaking, and abnormalities of heart rhythm are some of the many varied symptoms of this disorder. Unlike the other muscular dystrophies, DM begins in the hands and feet rather than the body trunk and only later does it progress to the trunk muscles, although there is early involvement of the muscles of the head and neck. Symptoms begin in middle age, but in some of the more severely afflicted, changes may be seen in the 20s.

The gene is found on chromosome 19, and the triplet base is CTG (or GCT).

Normal individuals have fewer than 50 repeats of this triplet; those with the disease have 51 to hundreds of repeats. Mildly affected individuals have from 50 to 80 repeats, while the severely affected may have as many as 2,000 repeats. The larger the number of repeats, the more severe or earlier the onset of the disease.

Due to the founder effect, the prevalence of DM in the Saguenay-Lac St. Jean region of Quebec province is 30 to 60 times higher than in the general world population. Many of the affected individuals were found to have traced their ancestry to a couple who settled in New France in 1657. DM is rare in sub-Saharan Africa, supporting the theory that the disease arose after modern man left Africa over 100,000 years ago.

If the Y chromosome test can be used to help trace our paternal ancestors, what DNA technique is available for our maternal line? The next chapter addresses that question.

CHAPTER 11

Mitochondrial DNA: Tracking Mom's Line

29 OCTOBER 2003: MODESTO, CALIFORNIA. DURING THE PRELIMINARY hearing to determine whether Scott Peterson must stand trial in the slaying of his pregnant wife, Laci Peterson, the prosecution presents an expert FBI witness who testifies about the mitochondrial DNA test used on a strand of hair. The witness goes on to state that the FBI has been using mitochondrial DNA testing since 1996. What is mitochondrial DNA?

mtDNA Inheritance

Just as Y chromosome analysis can help confirm the relationship in a surname or Y line, mitochondrial DNA, or mtDNA, can help confirm the maternal line. This line has been called the umbilical or M line (see Figure 11.1). Mitochondria are structures in the cytoplasm of a cell; like chromosomes in the cell nucleus, they also contain DNA (see Figure 11.2). The number of mitochondria in each cell varies, but there can be as many as a 1,000 mitochondria in every human cell, each with its own DNA. These tiny structures help produce energy for the cell. With 16,569 base pairs and about 37 genes, mitochondrial DNA is far smaller than chromosomal DNA, which consists of slightly more than 3 billion base pairs and about 30,000 genes.

Unlike the long chains of DNA found in chromosomes, mitochondrial DNA exists as a circular double-stranded loop. It is estimated that in the portion of mtDNA that is tested, mutations occur about once every 300 to 600 generations or about once every

215

The Y Chromosome and mtDNA Only Define Two of the Eight Great-Grandparents

Figure 11.1 The M line of mitochondrial DNA descent *(bottom of chart)* and the Y line of Y chromosome descent *(top of chart).*

Cell

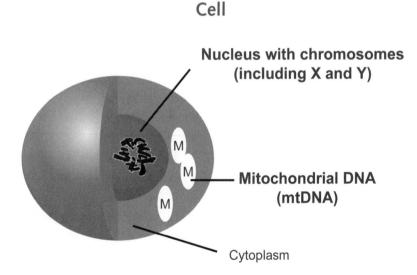

Figure 11.2 Diagram of a typical human cell showing mitochondria with mtDNA outside of the cell nucleus in the cytoplasm.

The Value of mtDNA

We have known since 1963 that mitochondria have their own DNA. The number of mitochondria in a cell varies. In general, every cell in the body contains hundreds of mitochondria, each with several loops of DNA. Body cells that require a high-energy source, such as muscle cells, contain thousands of mitochondria. The human egg contains nearly 100,000, while the human sperm has only approximately 50 mitochondria. In any given cell, there is only a small amount of nuclear or chromosome DNA but thousands of copies of mtDNA. It is this abundance of mitochondrial DNA compared to nuclear, or chromosomal, DNA that makes mitochondrial DNA so useful for anthropology—only mtDNA can be recovered in old or ancient remains.

6,000 to 12,000 years, although some newer evidence suggests that changes may occur more often. In any case, the mutation rate suggests that two individuals descended from a single woman in colonial times should have the same mtDNA sequence.

At the time of fertilization, nuclear chromosomes from a sperm enter the egg and combine with the egg's nuclear DNA. The sperm has 23 chromosomes, as does the egg, so that at fertilization the fetus will have 46, the normal human component of chromosomes. The male also contributes as one of these 23 chromosomes either an X chromosome to produce a daughter or a Y chromosome for a son. Outside of the nucleus, in its cytoplasm, the female egg has its own mitochondria, the mother's mtDNA. The male sperm also has mitochondria with mtDNA, but very little compared to that present in the woman's egg. Although there is debate as to whether the male mitochondria ever enters the egg, most geneticists believe that it does not or that, if it does, it is destroyed so that after fertilization, regardless of the sex of the fertilized egg, only the mother's mtDNA is present. When the fertilized egg divides into two cells, then four, then eight, and so on, it is the mother's mitochondria in the cytoplasm of those cells (see Figure 11.3). That means the mother's children, boys or girls, will have the mother's mtDNA, not the father's (see Figure 11.4). Mitochondrial DNA is passed from a mother to all her children, but only the daughters can pass on their mother's mtDNA (see Figure 11.5).

Division of Fertilized Egg

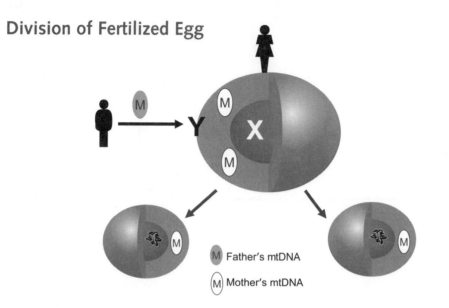

Figure 11.3 Division of the fertilized egg into two cells. It is the mother's mitochondrial DNA, not the father's, that is passed to the new daughter cells.

All the Children Get the Mother's DNA

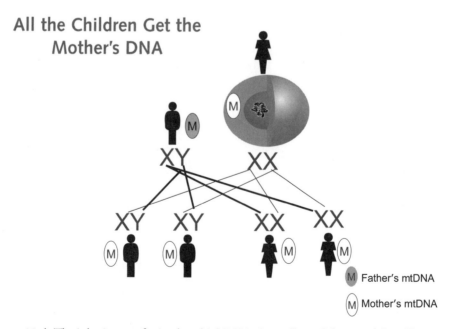

Figure 11.4 The inheritance of mitochondrial DNA. Regardless of the sex of the offspring, all the children have the mother's mtDNA.

The Maternal mtDNA Is Passed through the Maternal Line

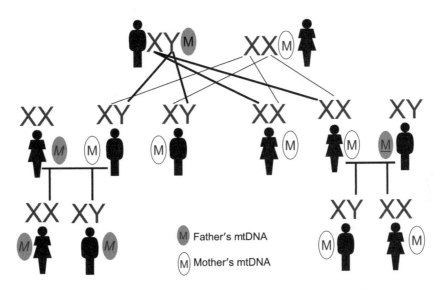

Figure 11.5 The passing on of mitochondrial DNA. All of a mother's children receive her mtDNA, but only the daughters can pass it on to their children.

All the mtDNA in the cells of your body are copies of your mother's mtDNA, and the mtDNA in her body are copies of her mother's, your maternal grandmother. Your mtDNA, then, is identical to that of your maternal grandmother, or her mother, your great-grandmother, or her mother and so on (see Figure 11.6). The DNA in your chromosomes comes from your eight great-grandparents. Your mtDNA comes only from one, your maternal great-grandmother. Therefore, mtDNA is passed down through the M line. By serving as a genetic marker for the maternal line, mtDNA can be very useful for genealogists. But the M line is the hardest to trace genealogically because the woman's surname changes upon each of her marriages. Genealogists know that determining a woman's maiden name can be daunting.

How to Analyze mtDNA

As with the Y chromosome, testing for genealogy is performed on the nonfunctioning portion of the mtDNA molecule. For Y chromosome analysis, the number of repeats is reported; for mtDNA, analysis is simpler. Here the analysis is for SNPs

mtDNA over Seven Generations Descends through the Female Line

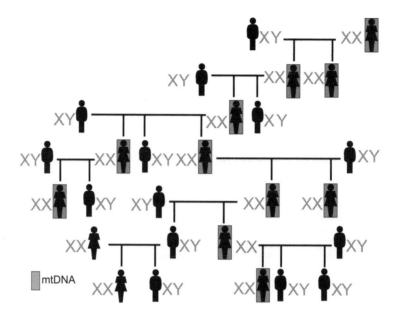

Figure 11.6 The mtDNA handed down from mother to child over seven generations. The mtDNA for the children at the bottom of the chart should be identical to the mtDNA of the female at the top of the chart. The male siblings of each daughter will have the same mtDNA; since they can't pass it on, they are not shown in this chart.

(single nucleotide polymorphisms). SNPs are the substitution of one DNA base for another. For instance, at a particular base location, a T may be substituted for a C.

Most of the variation in mtDNA between individuals, and the areas that are useful to genealogists, are found in two regions of the mitochondrial DNA that are known to accumulate base substitutions at a relatively high rate. These control regions are known as hypervariable regions, HVR1 and HVR2. The standard sites for hypervariable region 1 (HVR1) starts with the base numbered 16024 and goes to the base numbered 16324. For HVR2, the bases in positions 63 to 322 are sequenced. Many laboratories will sequence more than the bases included in the hypervariable regions. For instance, one laboratory sequences HVR1 at 470 positions from base positions numbered 16100 to 16569. Others may sequence fewer bases. These hypervariable regions have no known genetic function.

In keeping with its probable bacterial origin, mitochondrial DNA is a circular molecule, unlike the linear DNA found in human chromosomes. The hypervariable regions (HVR1 and HVR2) are portions of the mtDNA where there is high DNA variability; these regions can be tested for genealogical purposes.

The results of a test of mitochondrial DNA are reported as a change in the base at a particular location in these hypervariable regions. In order to report a change in a base, we need a standard to compare the sample to. The base sequence of mtDNA was discovered in 1981. This original base sequence is known as the CRS (Cambridge reference sequence). A sample is measured against this standard. For instance, after testing your sample and sequencing the bases, you may get back a report such as this: 16093C. This means that your sample has the same base sequence as the CRS except at one position, position 16093, where your sample shows a C, rather than the T seen in the CRS.

Like most of the Y chromosome, mtDNA never gets the opportunity to undergo recombination. The absence of recombination in mtDNA is a major advantage for tracing your maternal line since it means that the mtDNA descends unchanged. As with Y chromosome testing, when comparing the mtDNA results of two individuals, there should be no or little difference in the base sequence. This is taken as evidence of a common ancestor, again with the results backed up by good genealogy. As with Y chromosome results, a match between two individuals indicates a common ancestor, but it is not clear exactly who or when. Once again, this is where good genealogy enters the picture.

Genealogy

Tsar Nicholas II of Russia married Princess Alexandra of Hesse. As we saw in Chapter 3, Alexandra carried the hemophilia gene from her grandmother Queen Victoria.

The tsar and tsarina had five children. The first four were daughters: Olga, Tatiana, Maria, and Anastasia. Their fifth child was a son, the heir Alexis, born in 1904. Alexis had hemophilia. Symptoms of excessive bleeding appeared during Alexis's first year of life. Presumably, Alexandra recognized the condition immediately because she had heard of its effects in her brother, Frederick, who died at the age of three.

In desperation over the fate of the only male heir, the royal family brought in the mad monk Grigory Novykh, nicknamed Rasputin, which is Russian for "debauched one." Siberian mystic, monk, and con artist, Rasputin became an influential favorite of the court for his seeming ability to stop Alexis's bleeding. While Nicholas was preoccupied with his troops in World War I, Alexandra, with Rasputin as her personal advisor, ruled Russia. Rasputin's influence led to the appointing of church officials, cabinet ministers, and the military, appointments that were usually to his advantage and to Russia's detriment. Rasputin was eventually murdered, but by then the damage to the imperial regime was too severe. The people revolted against Nicholas and the monarchy. On 2 March 1917, Nicholas was forced to abdicate his throne. The imperial family was imprisoned and taken to Siberia. One night in July 1918, Nicholas, Alexandra, their children, and a few servants were murdered by the Bolsheviks in the cellar of the house in which they were imprisoned. Their bodies were buried in a shallow grave and forgotten.

In 1991, a burial site in Siberia was uncovered. It contained human remains. Could these bodies be the ill-fated Romanovs? The skeletons were sorted and, although buried for almost 75 years, still yielded good mtDNA samples. Fortunately, the pedigrees of European royalty are well documented. For Empress Alexandra, her grandnephew Prince Philip of England, husband of Queen Elizabeth II, would have her identical mtDNA (see Figure 11.7). The test of Prince Philip's mtDNA against the bodies of the presumed empress and children matched, establishing the identity of the tsarina and her three children.

For Tsar Nicholas, finding a relative was more complicated. Tsar Nicholas II's maternal line was traced by genealogy to two living relatives, Countess Xenia Cheremeteff-Sfiri and the Duke of Fife. Their mtDNA matched perfectly to each other, but when compared with the presumed tsar, there was a discrepancy. At position 16169, the tsar showed a C while that of his relatives had a T. Further tests revealed that the tsar's mtDNA was unusual. He had two types of mitochondrial DNA in his body. In position 16169, some of the tsar's mtDNA contained a C, but other mtDNA had a T, matching his relatives. Eventually, the dead body of the Grand Duke Georgij Romanov, the tsar's younger brother, was analyzed; his mtDNA showed the same mixture as that of Tsar Nicholas, proving conclusively that the body found in the grave was that of the last tsar. The bodies of the youngest daughter, Anastasia, and Crown Prince Alexis were missing.

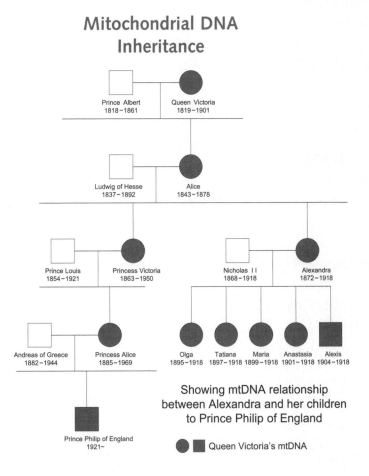

Figure 11.7 Pedigree showing how Prince Philip of England would have the same mtDNA as Empress Alexandra and her children.

A footnote to this story is the role of Anna Anderson. In 1920, a woman attempted suicide by jumping into a canal in Berlin. Rescued by the Germans, she spent the next 18 months in a mental hospital. There, under interrogation, she revealed that she was the long-lost Anastasia, daughter of Tsar Nicholas and Empress Alexandra. Moving to America, she adopted the name Anna Anderson and pressed her claim of royalty in court. Anna Anderson asserted for years to be the missing Anastasia. Her legal claim was rejected, but when she died in 1984, many believed her story. There was even a movie about her life, implying that she was Anastasia. In 1994, a piece of tissue from surgery she had in the 1970s was found and tested. If she were Anastasia, her mtDNA would be an exact match of Empress Alexandra and Prince Philip. Analysis showed conclusively that she was not related to the Romanovs. She was not Anastasia.

Starting Your Own mtDNA Project

Obviously, an mtDNA project is harder to organize than a Y chromosome project. For the Y chromosome, there is the accompanying surname. Males with the same surname can be tested to determine whether there is a relationship. To use mtDNA, you must establish a pedigree and trace the mtDNA, much the same as in the mtDNA pathway seen in Figure 11.7. As with a Y chromosome project, you start with a hypothesis and determine which individuals to test. In this case, the hypothesis may be that the pedigree chart you have designed is correct. If so, then the mtDNA should substantiate your pedigree and show that the relationships are valid.

Alternatively, you can combine mtDNA with Y chromosome analysis to build a

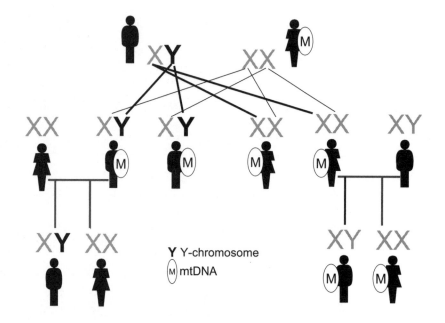

Inheritance of Y Chromosome and mtDNA

Figure 11.8 Inheritance of the Y chromosome and mtDNA.

Characterizing Your Ancestors
Using Y Chromosomes and mtDNA

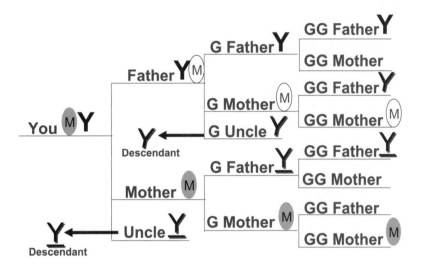

Figure 11.9 How other lines on a genetic pedigree might be completed.

Because the Y chromosome test yields information about only the all-male patrilineal or Y surname line and mtDNA reveals information about only the all-female matrilineal or M line, if
you do genetic testing, you know about only two of your eight great-grandparents. The other
six great-grandparents can be typed, but you will need to test relatives, aunts, uncles, or
cousins who descend in the appropriate line. If an analysis of your mtDNA shows that you
have Native American ancestry, it means only that one of your eight great-grandparents may
have been Native American; it reveals nothing about the remaining seven.

genetic pedigree of your ancestors. Figure 11.8 shows how Y chromosomes and mtDNA
are inherited. Figure 11.9 shows how you can take advantage of this inheritance to build
your family's genetic pedigree. Your uncle may be dead and unavailable for testing, but
he may have a son, your first cousin, who can be tested to identify the Y chromosome.

Deep Ancestry

While any given cell will have only a single Y chromosome with its DNA in the nucleus, the cytoplasm of that cell may contain hundreds of copies of mtDNA. Mitochondrial DNA is therefore far more plentiful than Y chromosome DNA in tissue samples. This greater quantity permits mtDNA to be isolated from old biological material, in some cases ancient biological material, where no nuclear chromosomal DNA can be detected.

Mitochondrial DNA has been used extensively to study human ancestry. A substantial number of mutations have appeared in mtDNA along maternal lineages as human populations colonized different geographical areas of the world. Mitochondrial DNA has been typed into haplogroups or families. These haplogroups seem to be confined to continents and large land areas. For instance, in sub-Saharan Africa, haplogroup L is found in 70 to 100 percent of individuals. It is possible to determine human migration and origin based on the diversity of the mtDNA observed today.

mtDNA appears to have answered the question of where we come from. The answer is, from Africa, somewhere between 100,000 and 200,000 years ago. The most diverse mtDNA sequences are found in Africa. That higher level of diversity is consistent with our belief that the older a population is, the more mutations would have accumulated. mtDNA indicates that modern humans originated in Africa and, from there, populated the rest of the world.

If my mtDNA is the same as my mother's, and her mother's, and her mother's, this line can be continued back through time to one ancestor, the mitochondrial "Eve." This is not the Eve of the Bible, but actually the most recent common ancestor through the matrilineal line of descent of all living humans. It is estimated that this Eve probably lived 120,000 to 150,000 years ago. But just because we are all related to Eve through our mitochondrial DNA does not mean that we all have the same mtDNA. Quite the contrary. Over time, mutations have occurred in the mtDNA. In fact, it was by analyzing the mutations and assuming a certain rate at which they occurred that researchers could date this mitochondrial Eve.

Strange "human" bones were found in 1856 as German workers were digging a quarry in the Neander Valley near Dusseldorf. Given the name *Homo neanderthalensis*, or Neanderthal man, the species appeared to be a relative of modern man. The bones of Neanderthal man were eventually found in many parts of Europe and the Middle East. Neanderthals were about a third larger than modern man, of greater muscular strength, with low foreheads and protruding brows—the classic "cave man" depicted in films. Modern man and the Neanderthal coexisted in Europe for a time. Then abruptly, about 30,000 years ago, the Neanderthals disappeared, leaving only modern man. Did the two coexist peaceably? More important, did Neanderthal mtDNA, and therefore possibly nuclear DNA, become part of our genetic makeup? Do we have Neanderthal man in our genes?

Mitochondrial Eve is the name given to the one woman in prehistory whose mitochondrial DNA has passed down to all humans alive today. She lived probably 150,000 years ago. A similar case can be made for a Y chromosome "Adam."

Investigators extracted mtDNA and identified a 378-base pair sequence of mitochondrial DNA from a 30,000-year-old Neanderthal arm bone. Although Neanderthal DNA is more similar to human DNA than to that of a chimpanzee, researchers found that the Neanderthal mtDNA sequence differed markedly from all modern human mtDNA. Neanderthal's mtDNA is similar enough to that of modern man to indicate that they were on the same evolutionary tree, but the two species probably diverged from each other about 600,000 years ago. Most important, there is no evidence of Neanderthal's mtDNA in our mtDNA. Neanderthals did not contribute to our gene pool during our coexistence for many thousands of years in Europe. On encountering Neanderthal, modern man either couldn't or wouldn't breed with them. Presumably modern man eliminated Neanderthal, either deliberately or inadvertently, possibly by multiplying faster, competing more successfully for food, or replacing them from their ecological niche.

Mitochondrial DNA mutates at a slow rate and is ideal for tracing human evolution. mtDNA testing is the molecule of preference for characterizing prehistoric samples because it is relatively plentiful in older material. Ancient bones, teeth, and even soft tissues have yielded mtDNA for analysis. Using mtDNA, geneticists have determined that modern man separated from the great apes about 5 million years ago, much sooner than anthropologists had believed. This estimate is based on the mutation rate of mtDNA and the amount of difference between our mtDNA and that of the great apes. Today, based on mtDNA evidence, we believe that our genus *Homo* originally left Africa 2 million years ago, populating Europe, and eventually giving rise to Neanderthals. More recently, around 100,000 years ago, modern man arose in Africa, left and populated Europe, and in the process removed Neanderthal and other traces of that original migration.

mtDNA and Anthropology

Anthropology had confirmed that American Indians came originally from Asia, crossing the land bridge at the Bering Strait to populate North America. There is lack of agreement as to when this happened and whether there were one or several migrations. Some mtDNA testing has supported the idea of three separate migrations that occurred around 12,000 years ago, an idea originally suggested by examining linguistic and dental information. Other mtDNA studies have put the migration earlier, about 30,000 years ago. Some Y chromosome testing has also suggested a single and early wave of migration to the Americas, while other studies have suggested two separate waves 13,000 to 16,000 years ago. At the moment, the time and number of migrations to the Americas is not clear.

American Indian mtDNA is descended from Asian mtDNA. Almost all Native American mtDNA belongs to one of five mtDNA haplotypes: A, B, C, D, and X. These haplogroups are almost exclusive to Native Americans. Y chromosome studies have also substantiated an Asian origin for Native Americans and have suggested that some markers, for instance, DYS199T, are seen in increased frequency in Native Americans. This DYS199T is a SNP, a change in one base from a C to a T, and is now known as marker M3. There are other Y chromosome markers for Native American ancestry. An analysis of the prehistoric Anasazi Indians of the southwest United States showed a low to absent frequency of haplogroup A, a moderate to high frequency of haplogroup B, and low frequencies of haplogroups C and D, with a few having haplogroup X. Modern North American Native American mtDNA is equally geographic, with different mixtures of the five haplogroups occurring in different frequencies. Present-day Native American southwestern populations share the same variety and proportion of haplogroups as the ancient Anasazi. Commercial DNA testing firms now offer DNA testing to determine whether you have Native American ancestry through mtDNA or the Y chromosome.

Y chromosomes and mtDNA analysis have been used to investigate migratory populations and historical invasions.

Where Did the Gypsies Come From?

The Roma group of individuals arrived in Europe about a thousand years ago. Early Europeans thought they might be Egyptian, hence the corrupted name *gypsies*. The oral traditions and language suggest that their origin is the subcontinent of India. In an article in the *American Journal of Human Genetics* in 2001, David B. Gresham and others examined the Y chromosome and mtDNA of 275 Romani men from 14 distinct Romani populations. They found Y chromosome and mtDNA haplogroups that were common to Asian populations, but not to Europeans. They postulate that the Romani probably consisted of a small group of founders, splitting from a single ethnic population of India.

An interesting problem has been who settled Polynesia. The Norwegian explorer Thor Heyerdahl, living in Polynesia, became convinced that it had been settled from the east, possibly South America. To prove his theory, he constructed a balsa wood raft, the *Kon-Tiki*, and showed that with this type of vessel, it was possible to reach Polynesia from Peru. Genetic evidence, however, shows that Polynesian DNA resembles Asian DNA, supporting a southeastern Asian origin for the Pacific populations, not a South American one.

Matthew E. Hurles and others have investigated the Y chromosome and mtDNA on the Polynesian island of Rapa. The mtDNA was, as expected, similar to that of the other Pacific populations with a southeastern Asian origin, but the Y chromosome information was unexpected. They found Native American and European haplotypes for the Y chromosome. They postulate that the non-Polynesian Y chromosome haplotypes were contributed by the crew of the slaveship *Cora*, overpowered and captured in 1863, with the crew assimilated into and consequently breeding with the native population.

Identification

It is possible to do DNA analysis of a single hair. For a nuclear DNA analysis, such as a Y chromosome test, you will need the root of a plucked hair. When there is no hair root, it is still possible to test the mtDNA of the human hair shaft alone. Mitochondrial

DNA has been used in forensics to identify human remains. In some cases, chromosomal DNA may be too sparse or degraded and only mtDNA may be available. Mitochondrial DNA can be recovered and analyzed from teeth, bones, and hair shafts. Bodies recovered from mass graves in South America and Kosovo have been identified by comparing their mtDNA with surviving siblings or maternal relatives. The victims of 11 September 2001 were identified in a similar fashion. When suitable relatives can be matched, mitochondrial DNA is useful for identifying victims of accidents and crimes.

Disease

We type an individual's mitochondrial DNA by the difference in base sequence from a reference standard. As we have seen, a change in one base, for instance, a substitution of a thymine (T) for a cytosine (C), is called a SNP (pronounced "snip")—single nucleotide polymorphism. These point mutations occur in our nuclear DNA, as well. It is estimated that the human genome with its 3 billion base pairs, contains about 10 million SNPs. A family of the same types of SNPs form a haplotype. Substitution of a single base is one of the most common types of mutations and can occur in both coding genes and non-coding regions.

Many human diseases are caused by the substitution of a single base in nuclear DNA, a point mutation. In sickle cell anemia, there is a single base substitution of a T for an A in the DNA portion that codes for blood's hemoglobin. The result of this single base substitution causes the amino acid valine to be inserted into the hemoglobin molecule instead of the normal glutamic acid. The result is abnormal hemoglobin and sickle cell disease.

Not until 1988 was the first human disease linked to a defect in mitochondrial genes. In that year, young-adult blindness (Leber hereditary optic neuropathy) was found to be due to a defect in an mtDNA gene.

We have known since 1963 that mitochondria have their own genes on their DNA, but not until 1988 was the first human disease caused by a defect in mitochondrial genes discovered. A form of young-adult-onset blindness, LHON (Leber hereditary optic neuropathy), was traced to the mitochondria. LHON patients, typically in their late 20s or early 30s, have painless, central vision loss leading to blindness in both eyes. Not all LHON is familial, but in familial cases all affected individuals are related through the maternal lineage, consistent with the inheritance of human mtDNA. This mitochondrial disease is passed through the mother. Consistent with mitochondrial inheritance, while a son can be affected by receiving his mtDNA disease gene through his mother, he cannot pass it on to his offspring. For LHON, penetrance varies and, depending on the specific allele, so does the degree of disease severity. Today we know of at least 18 allelic variants associated with the disease, but more than 95 percent of individuals with LHON harbor one of three mtDNA point mutations.

Other mitochondrial diseases have been found, but in general, these diseases are rare. Variability in disease expression is common since human cells contain hundreds of mitochondria, some of which may have a diseased gene while others may be normal. Since mitochondria are involved with the cell's energy production, any genetic defect in mitochondria would affect those types of cells most susceptible to a drop in energy. Mitochondrial diseases therefore tend to affect muscle and nervous tissue, such as the optic nerve, as in LHON.

The newest technology available to genealogists is mtDNA testing, and as yet it is underutilized. Y chromosome testing, with its link to surnames, is far more easy to apply. Yet mtDNA can fill in your genealogy by helping to track those elusive female ancestors, the ones who have the annoying practice of changing their surnames when they marry. Both the field of DNA testing for genealogy and the field of medical genetics are rapidly changing. In the next chapter, we explore how you can use the Internet to stay up-to-date.

CHAPTER 12

More Information on the Internet

ONCE YOU HAVE CONSTRUCTED YOUR FAMILY'S HEALTH PEDIGREE AND found specific diseases, you need to know more about them and whether they have a genetic component. Fortunately, we live in an age when information on medicine and genetics is available with the click of a mouse. There are many good online databases where you can find information on genetics and genetic diseases. Perhaps you are interested in a specific genetic disorder because one of your family members has recently been diagnosed with the condition or you might want to learn what genetic disorders are common in your ethnic group. This chapter points you to Web pages on general genetics, on medicine, and on Y chromosome and mtDNA testing for genealogy.

The National Library of Medicine

The premier source for medical information is the largest medical library in the world, the National Library of Medicine (NLM), located on the campus of the National Institutes of Health (NIH) in Bethesda, Maryland, and on a computer near you at *www.nlm.nih.gov.* The NLM began more than 160 years ago as the library of the U.S. Army Surgeon General. The NLM's databases are free and anonymous; you are never asked to register or divulge any personal information. Nor do they link to sites that require people to register personal information. At its home page, under Health Information, you will be taken to a list of the databases, two of which, MEDLINE and MEDLINEplus, will be especially useful as you look up health-related topics and genetic diseases.

Medical Dictionaries

Medical terminology can be confusing. Fortunately, medical dictionaries are available on the Web. Current medical terms are defined at the following sites:

- *cancerweb.ncl.ac.uk/omd/index.html*
- *www.medterms.com/script/main/hp.asp*
- *www.medic8.com/MedicalDictionary.htm*

For historical medical terms and their approximate current meaning, search these sites:

- *www.paul_smith.doctors.org.uk/ArchaicMedicalTerms.htm*
- *www.rootsweb.com/~njmorris/disease.htm*
- *www3.nb.sympatico.ca/pebbles2/tools.html#disease*
- *www.geocities.com/Heartland/Hills/2840/diseases.html*

MEDLINE

The first database at the NLM is MEDLINE/PubMed, known simply as MEDLINE. This is the world's major medical information database and is used by millions of physicians. These databases are available free over the Internet to everyone at *www.pubmed.gov.*

When you call up MEDLINE, you are presented with a search screen where you can enter words or phrases. The search produces a set of retrievals, including article titles, authors, and journal citations; many articles also have an associated abstract for review. The actual articles can be obtained either through a national network of over 4,000 medical libraries or online through the PubMed Central service where MEDLINE contains links to the full-text version of articles at participating publishers' Web sites. If you live near a medical school, you can obtain the article from the medical library there. Another useful feature is the See Related Articles button appearing below the citation. If you find an article on the topic you want, click this button to bring up additional related articles. MEDLINE is geared to the medical professional, so the abstracts can be difficult to understand. It is, however, the absolute last word on what the medical profession knows about a given topic.

PubMed Central (PMC) at *www.pubmedcentral.nih.gov* is the National Library of Medicine's digital archive of life sciences journal literature. It was developed and is managed by the National Center for Biotechnology Information (NCBI) at the NLM. Participation by publishers is voluntary, but subject to PMC's editorial standards. Access to PMC is free and unrestricted. You can search the entire database of published articles.

MEDLINEplus

The second database available at the NLM is MEDLINEplus *(MEDLINEplus.gov)*. MEDLINEplus offers information specifically aimed at consumers and patients (see

MEDLINE: A Database with a Past

What is now MEDLINE started in 1879 as the *Index Medicus*, a published compilation of the titles of the world's medical literature. By the mid-1950s, each year's output covered several large volumes. By the 1960s, the NLM began to store the information in an electronic database, MEDLINE, and by the early 1970s, it became available for searching by medical librarians and registered users. The original database covered approximately 200 journals and was "capable of supporting up to 25 simultaneous users." I had to take a several-day course in the early 1980s to get a password to use this database. Using my IBMPC XT (complete with a "massive" 10MB hard drive and the original Microsoft operating system, DOS), I could access the database using my computer and modem from my home. With the introduction of the Windows operating system, the database became somewhat easier to use, but still required some degree of training.

In 1996, MEDLINE/PubMed was opened to the general public, at no cost, through the Internet. Today, its database covers the contents of over 4,500 current medical journals, with its older database, OLDMEDLINE, providing content dating back to the mid-1960s. There are over 12 million bibliographic citations, many of which are now abstracted. By 2001, there were more than a quarter of a billion searches a year.

The journal *Nature* maintains a Web page and devotes a section to genetics (*www.nature.com/genomics/*). There you will find links to original research papers from *Nature* and *Nature Genetics*, as well as links to other major publications.

Figure 12.1). Once MEDLINE was open to all through the Internet, use soared. About a third of all MEDLINE searching was being done by nonmedical professionals. MEDLINEplus was introduced in 1998 as a service designed for the general public. It consists of authoritative articles on medical topics written for the nonmedical professional. This site, which gets over 60 million "hits" a year, should be among the first you visit to find information about a particular disease or medical condition. MEDLINEplus lists hundreds of health topics and contains a medical

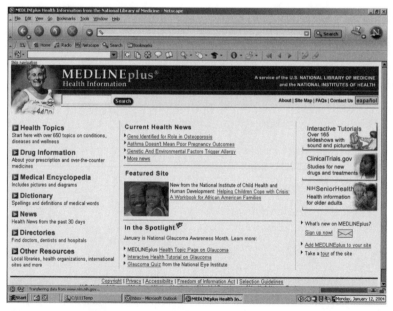

Figure 12.1 MEDLINEplus, the National Library of Medicine's database, which is geared to give information specifically aimed to meet the needs of consumers. (Courtesy of the National Library of Medicine.)

encyclopedia, medical dictionary, detailed information about prescription drugs, directories of health professionals and hospitals, and links to a variety of health organizations and medical libraries in the United States.

You can query MEDLINE/PubMed or MEDLINEplus separately or use the NLM's newest search engine, the NLM Gateway *(gateway.nlm.nih.gov)*. One query will search MEDLINE/PubMed, OLDMEDLINE, MEDLINEplus, LOCATORplus (the NLM's actual library catalog), ClinicalTrials.gov, DIRLINE, Meeting Abstracts, and HSRProj. Type in the word *hemophilia,* and you are presented with a screen that tells you what is available on that subject in the numerous NLM databases. ClinicalTrials.gov is an NLM database of nearly 6,000 clinical trials using a specific treatment for a specific condition. It was developed in response to a 1997 law that required a registry for both federally and privately funded clinical trials. Introduced in 2000, ClinicalTrials.gov lists, for each clinical trial, a statement of purpose, whether the trial is currently recruiting patients, the location of the trial, and contact information.

A separate division of the NLM is the National Center for Biotechnology Information (NCBI). This division can be reached from the NLM Web page *(www.nlm.nih/gov/hinfo.html)* under Molecular Biology/Genetics or directly *(www.ncbi.nlm.nih.gov)*. The NCBI was established in 1988 as a national resource for molecular biology information. While much of the site is technical, such as the GenBank DNA sequence database, there are some useful areas for the consumer. One is an online book, *Genes and Disease*, which includes descriptions of clinical symptoms and brief summaries of the molecular basis for genetic diseases.

Online Mendelian Inheritance in Man

For genetic diseases, the most important database, maintained by the NCBI, is the Online Mendelian Inheritance in Man (OMIM) *(www3.ncbi.nlm.nih.gov/omim/)*. This online database catalogs human genes and genetic disorders and is authored and edited by Victor A. McKusick, M.D., and his colleagues at Johns Hopkins Medical School and elsewhere. It contains textual information, pictures, and reference information about virtually every known inherited or heritable single-gene genetic disease and contains many links to pertinent MEDLINE articles about the topics. It does not contain information on chromosome diseases. As of the summer of 2003, the database was approaching 15,000 entries. You can use OMIM's exceptional search capabilities to search by disease name, text, OMIM number, references, allelic variations, clinical synopsis, and more, and you can search any of these fields alone, or in any combination, or search the entire database. OMIM is a computerized database version of McKusick's monumental book *Mendelian Inheritance in Man*, now in its 12th edition. The online version is the most current and is updated daily. You can search for records that have changed in the past week, the past two weeks, the past month, and so on.

Other genealogy books in this National Genealogical Society series offer extensive listings of Web pages that are useful for doing genealogy and for compiling your family's medical history. Pamela Boyer Porter and Amy Johnson Crow's *Online Roots* and Barbara Renick's *Genealogy 101* are excellent references on basic genealogy and genealogy on the Internet.

Other features of OMIM include a Gene Map, a cytogenetic location of the genes that are described in OMIM, and the OMIM Morbid Map, an alphabetical list of diseases described in OMIM and their corresponding cytogenetic locations. Before using the OMIM, be sure to read the Frequently Asked Questions (FAQs). OMIM is absolutely the last word in single-gene Mendelian genetic diseases.

Genetics Home Reference

Another project of the NLM is the Genetics Home Reference Web site *(ghr.nlm.nih.gov/ghr/page/Home)*. This is one of the NLM's newest Web sites and is designed to give consumers information about genetic conditions and the genes responsible for those conditions (see Figure 12.2). Going to this page opens topics such as "Help Me Understand Genetics" and "Browse Genes and Conditions." Created for the lay public, the explanations are simple and written in an easily understandable fashion. The site is searchable by genetic disease, and there is a tutorial on understanding genetics. Other features on the site include a glossary of genetic terms, links that take you to clinical trials related to the disorder you are searching, and more advanced genetic information.

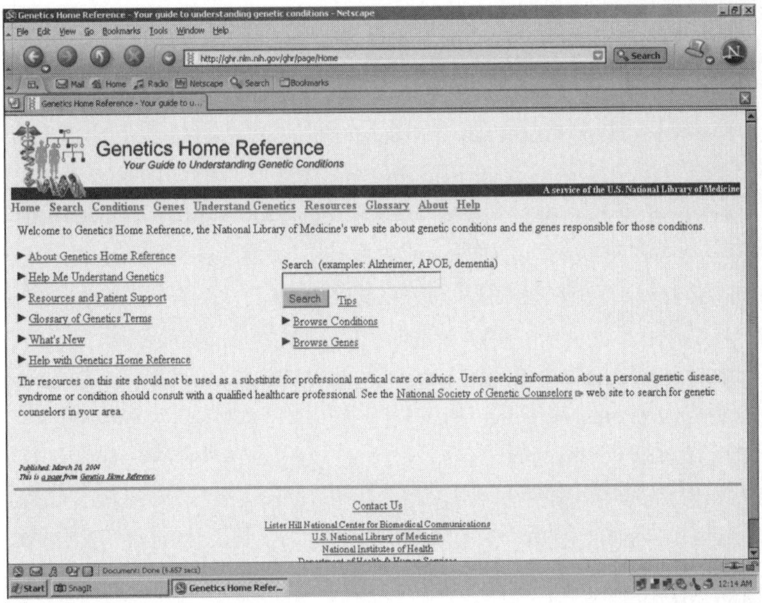

Figure 12.2 Genetics Home Reference, one of the newest of the National Library of Medicine's Web sites. (Courtesy of the National Library of Medicine.)

The National Human Genome Research Institute

Like the National Library of Medicine, the National Human Genome Research Institute (NHGRI) is also part of the National Institutes of Health (NIH). The institute was formed from the Human Genome Project. The Human Genome Project was begun in 1990 to identify all the genes in human DNA and to determine the sequences of the approximately 3 billion chemical bases of this DNA.

The NHGRI home page *(www.genome.gov)* has a Newsroom, featuring the very latest genetic discoveries. Under Health, one can access Genetics FAQ, which includes easy-to-understand answers to such questions as "What are genetic disorders?" "How do I find more information about a specific disorder or learn whether a particular disease has a genetic component?" and "What is genetic testing?" On the Genetics FAQ page, under Health, you will find a link to Specific Genetic Disorders. On that page are links to pages focusing on specific genetic disorders, as well as a link to Online Health Resources, an extensive list of online resources for specific diseases, general health information, and genetics and genetic disorders.

In addition, the Specific Genetic Disorders page includes a link to the Office of Rare Diseases (ORD), which can also be found at *rarediseases.info.nih.gov*. Established in 1993 within the Office of the Director of NIH, ORD contains information on more than 6,000 rare diseases, including clinical features, current research, publications from scientific and medical journals, ongoing studies, and patient support groups. ORD offers links to other sources of information, as well, including a page by the National Cancer Institution on understanding gene testing *(www.gene.com/ae/AE/AEPC/NIH/index.html);* Helix, a directory of laboratories that test for genetic disorders *(healthlinks.washington.edu.helix);* and CORN, the Council of Regional Networks for Genetic Services *(www.cc.emory.edu/PEDIATRICS/corn/corn.htm).*

Cyndi's List

Long recognized as the definitive source for links to genealogy sites, Cyndi Howells also maintains a section on genetics, DNA, and family health at *www.cyndislist.com/dna.htm*. Several hundred links can be found under the following classifications:

General Resource Sites
Ethnic Groups and Localities
Genograms
Mailing Lists, Newsgroups, & Chat
Professional Services & DNA Kits
Publications, Software, & Supplies
Surname Studies
Thomas Jefferson

Other Government Web Pages

The federal government offers much free information online.

Cancer.gov *(www.cancer.gov/cancerinfo)*. The cancer information Web page of the National Cancer Institute (NCI) includes information on the genetics of cancer.

The Center for Disease Control and Prevention *(www.cdc.gov)*. The CDC is, like NIH, another agency of the U.S. Public Health Service. Based in Atlanta, the CDC is most well known for monitoring and tracking infectious diseases, but the agency is interested in all diseases, including genetic ones. On the CDC's Web page, click Genomic Events to go to the CDC's Office of Genomics and Disease Prevention *(www.cdc.gov/genomics/)*. Under Information on that page, you will find books such as Genetic Basics; articles on autosomal dominant and recessive disorders, as well as on numerous genetic diseases; and several glossaries of genetic terms.

Combined Health Information Database *(chid.nih.gov/welcome/welcome.html)*. CHID is a bibliographic database produced by the health-related agencies of the federal government. It provides titles, abstracts, and availability information for health information and health education resources. Online since 1985, CHID is updated quarterly.

GeneReviews *(www.geneclinics.org)*. This publicly funded medical genetics information resource was developed for physicians, other health care providers, and researchers. The site contains *GeneReviews*, an online publication of expert-authored disease reviews; Laboratory Directory, an international directory of genetic testing laboratories; Clinic Directory, an international directory of genetics and prenatal diagnosis; and Educational Materials, which contains a glossary of genetic terms, and articles about genetic services.

Healthfinder *(www.healthfinder.gov)*. An award-winning federal Web site, Healthfinder was developed by the U.S. Department of Health and Human Services, together with other federal agencies. Since 1997, Healthfinder has been recognized as a key resource for finding the best government and nonprofit health and human services. It links to carefully selected information and Web sites from over 1,800 health-related organizations and serves as the official federal Internet gateway to consumer health information, including government, university, nonprofit, and public sector sites.

Virtual Library of Genetics *(www.ornl.gov/TechResources/Human_Genome/genetics.html)*. This site is maintained by the U.S. Department of Energy, Oak Ridge Laboratory.

Universities

Many universities also maintain useful Web pages on genetics.

The Biology Project at the University of Arizona *(www.biology.arizona.edu/human_bio/human_bio.html)*. The Biology Project offers problem sets and tutorials on genetics, DNA forensics, and the genetics of blood types and colorblindness.

The Genetics of Cancer, Northwestern University Medical School and DePaul University in Chicago *(www.cancergenetics.org)*. This resource center will take you to another site, InTouchLive, where there is extensive material on the genetics of cancer, including both clinical and basic information on cancer, heredity, and the roles that genes can play in the development of various cancers.

The Genetic Science Learning Center at the Eccles Institute of Human Genetics of the University of Utah *(gslc.genetics.utah.edu)*. This site includes a page devoted to "helping people understand how genetics affects their lives and society." It discusses chromosomes, genetic disorders, cloning, stem cells, and genetic testing of newborns.

The University of Illinois at Chicago College of Medicine's Department of Molecular Genetics *(www.uic.edu/depts./mcgn/genres.html)*. This site presents genetics resources, including many links to professional societies involved with genetics.

The University of Kansas Medical Center Genetics Education Center *(www.kumc.edu/gec/)*. Geared toward educators interested in human genetics, this site includes a Genetic and Rare Conditions page *(www.kumc.edu/gec/support/)* with a listing of genetic diseases, information on genetic counselors and geneticists, a listing of national and international advocacy organizations, and numerous genetic dictionaries and glossaries.

The University of Pittsburgh Genetics Resource Center *(www.pitt.edu/~edugene/resource/).* The Genetics Resource Center site includes helpful online patient information brochures about many genetic diseases. It also contains an extensive and useful list of links to other genetic sites.

The University of Utah *(gslc.genetics.utah.edu).* This site covers the basics of genetics, including an explanation of DNA, chromosomes, genetic disorders, and genetic testing of newborns.

Organizations

Numerous organizations are involved in genetic diseases, and many maintain useful Web sites.

The Alliance of Genetic Support Groups *(medhlp.netusa.net/www/agsg.htm).* AGSG is dedicated to helping individuals and families with genetic disorders. This Web site provides publications, listings of events, and listings of support groups.

Cold Spring Harbor Laboratories *(www.dnaftb.org/dnaftb/).* Here you will find animations on Classical Genetics, Molecules of Genetics, and Genetic Organization. A companion site *(www.yourgenesyourhealth.org/)* contains listings and discussions of common genetic diseases.

The Federation of American Societies for Experimental Biology *(www.faseb.org/genetics/).* This site provides links to many American genetic societies, links to educational material on genetics, and links related to genetics.

The Genetic Alliance *(www.geneticalliance.org).* This Washington, D.C. coalition represents more than 600 consumer and health professional organizations. Its site allows you to search by disease to find genetic disease support groups. Also included are a glossary of biological and genetic terms, a calendar of events, and an electronic newsletter, *Alert,* which publishes the latest developments in genetics research.

Genetics Society of America *(www.genetics.org).* Here you will find full-text articles from *Genetics*, the official journal of the GSA.

The International Communication Forum in Human Molecular Genetics *(www.hum-molgen.de/).* This site provides Internet sources for the latest in genetics and human molecular biology. With more than 8,000 subscribers, it maintains professional forums discussing the ethical and social implications of genetic advances, maintains forums and reviews of current genetic subjects, and updates a calendar of upcoming events. Although written for the professional, it has a good Genetic News section.

Karolinska Institute *(www.mic.ki.se/Diseases/alphalist.html).* On this Web page, Sweden's largest center for medical training and research lists specific diseases and disorders, including many genetic diseases.

The National Organization for Rare Disorders *(www.rarediseases.org/info/about.html).* One of the best known genetics organizations, NORD is a federation of approximately 140 voluntary health organizations dedicated to helping people with "orphan" diseases. These rare diseases affect fewer than one in 200,000 individuals. There are more than 6,000 orphan diseases, including many genetic disorders, which affect approximately 25 million Americans. You can search NORD's database of over 1,000 diseases with brief descriptions. A longer full-text report can be purchased for a small fee. There are also links to organizations and support groups for each disease. NORD's Web site includes a newsletter, the *Orphan Disease Update*, and searchable databases for organizations and orphan drugs, which are used to treat orphan diseases.

The Saint Barnabas Health Care System *(www.sbhcs.com/genetics/resources/index.html).* This site provides information on Jewish genetic diseases, including discussions of Tay-Sachs, Canavan, Niemann-Pick, and Gaucher diseases, as well as Fanconi anemia, Bloom syndrome, and familial dysautonomia. Links are provided to Jewish disease organizations, and there are articles on genetic testing and counseling.

Pharmaceutical Companies

Pharmaceutical companies also maintain Web pages dealing with genetics.

GlaxoSmithKline *(genetics.gsk.com/overview.htm)*. This site contains a basic introduction to genetics, DNA, mutations, and genes, and offers interactive animations. It includes a timeline of genetic discoveries for those interested in the history of the field.

Merck *(www.merck.com)*. Merck offers online *The Merck Manual of Medical Information, Second Home Edition,* featuring a comprehensive review of diseases.

Johnson & Johnson *(www.jnj.com/product/conditions/index.htm)*. This company offers short, single-paragraph descriptions of various diseases and conditions, with links to information about pharmaceuticals used for treatment.

Mailing Lists

Mailing lists are maintained for a specific topic. They are free; you need only sign up to join. Every e-mail you send is received by every member of the list, and you receive every e-mail sent by a member. There are several useful lists.

Medical-Pedigree. This mailing list is for anyone interested in medical pedigrees, illness and disease, causes of death, hereditary factors, and medical computer software. To join, send an e-mail to *MEDICAL-PEDIGREE-L-request@rootsweb.com* with the single word *subscribe* in the message subject and body.

Genealogy-DNA *(lists.rootsweb.com/index/other/Miscellaneous/GENEALOGY-DNA. html)*. Here, rootsweb offers another excellent list for those interested in discussing

The Internet search engine Google can be used to find a discussion group on a specific genetic topic or disease *(groups.google.com)*.

DNA testing for genealogists. To join, go to the site or send an e-mail to *Genealogy-DNA-L-request@rootsweb*. Your posted questions will be answered by extremely knowledgeable experts. This exceptional site is a "must" for anyone interested in using genetic testing for genealogy.

Y Chromosome Family Projects

Kevin Duerinck maintains a list of surname Y DNA projects at *www.duerinck.com/surname.html*. At the time of this writing, his list included over 600 projects, many with multiple variant spellings of surnames. Another list of DNA projects can be found at *freepages.genealogy.rootsweb.com/~allpoms/genetics1a.html*, a page maintained at Chris Pomery's DNA Portal.

A brief list of surname DNA projects follows. Names were selected based on the size of participation, whether they were an older established project, the strength of accompanying discussions, uniqueness of design, or the quality of the writing. Reviewing these projects will help you learn more about DNA testing and how it relates to genealogical research. This is only a small sample; refer to the Duerinck or Pomery list for a surname of interest to you.

- Beal *(hometown.aol.com/bealsurnamedna/index.html)*
- Bolling *(www.bolling.net/bfa_dna_participants.htm)*
- Devine *(hometown.aol.com/donndevine/myhomepage/heritage.html)*
- Duerinck *(www.duerinck.com/genlinks.html)*
- Graves *(www.gravesfa.org/dna.html)*
- Hill *(www.livingston.net/hilldna/)*
- Kay *(homepages.rootsweb.com/~kayefile/dna.html)*
- Klein *(www.roperld.com/littlegenetics.htm)*
- Lindsay *(clanlindsay.com/dna_project.htm)*
- Mumma *(www.mumma.org/DNA.htm)*
- Pomery *(freepages.genealogy.rootsweb.com/~allpoms/genetics.html)*
- Rice *(www.widomaker.com/~gwk/era/haplotype.htm)*
- Roper *(www.roperld.com/RoperGenetics.htm)*

- Rose *(ourworld-top.cs.com/Christine4Rose/rosedna.html#anchor120164)*

- Savin *(www.savin.org/dna/y-chromosome-project.html)*

- Steadham *(homepages.rootsweb.com/~tstiddem/Pages/dna.html)*

- Stidham *(homepages.rootsweb.com/~tstiddem/Pages/dna.htm)*

- Strickland *(members.aol.com/stricklandquery/dnaproject.htm)*

- Walker *(freepages.genealogy.rootsweb.com/~fabercove/)*

- Wells *(www.rootsweb.com/~wellsfam/dnaproje?dnaproj1.html)*

DNA Databases

There are two databases available on the Internet where you can compare the results of your mtDNA and Y chromosome tests.

The Mitochondrial DNA Concordance *(shelob.bioanth.cam.ac.uk/mtDNA/toc.html)*. Using this repository for the results of mtDNA studies, you can check the results of your mtDNA against the database to see where else in the world your particular mtDNA mutations have been found. It is important to read the directions for its use.

Y STR Database *(ystr.org)*. Using the results of your Y chromosome test, here you can find the geographic areas where your haplotype has been located and get a general idea if you have a rare or common haplotype.

Other databases can be found on some of the surname project Web pages and at some of the commercial vendors' Web pages.

The Internet is a marvelous tool and I urge you to use the Web sites described here to stay abreast of a very rapidly evolving subject. Nevertheless, there are some questions that the Internet can't answer. The new technologies are raising important questions about the ethics, privacy, and future of genetics and genealogy—questions that we address in the next chapter.

CHAPTER 13

Ethics, Privacy, and the Future of Genetics and Genealogy

INVESTIGATING YOUR FAMILY'S HEALTH HISTORY IS SERIOUS. YOU MAY find significant medical conditions that could affect you and other members of your family. What you might learn about a genetic disease in your family has profound implications for your relatives. What do you do with this information?

Investigating Family Health

Your family members may not want to know. For some, finding out that they may have inadvertently harmed other family members may cause guilt or sadness. The diagnosis of a genetic disease in one individual may put other members of the family at risk, especially if you uncover a condition that is a dominant or X-linked disease. In some instances, other family members may be found to be at risk, even though they may know nothing about your investigation into the family's health history. The family health historian should not disclose any possible genetic problem to members of the family but should seek professional help. If a genetic disease is verified, a genetic counselor will discuss the implications of the disease and assist you in judging the risk to other family members.

Generally, when an individual seeks the services of a genetic counselor, it is because there is a concern about the possibility of a genetic disease in the family. Not infrequently, there has been a birth of an affected child or an adult in the family has recently been diagnosed with a genetic disease. The genetic counselor will

Genetic counselors are health care professionals with graduate degrees and training in medical genetics and genetic counseling. They frequently work as members of a health care team to provide information, to interpret the results of genetic tests and medical data, to assess risk of a genetic disorder, to explain possible treatments or preventive measures, and to provide support to individuals or families who have genetic disorders or may be at risk.

compile a family pedigree based on an interview with the subject, perhaps interview other family members, and then verify the medical information by requesting medical records. The counselor will discuss options for medical and genetic testing to confirm or disprove the presumptive diagnosis. The counselor is looking for evidence that your concern about a specific genetic disease is valid. In investigating a possible genetic disease, a genetic counselor will request medical documentation, such as death certificates. You will need to do the same, but as a genealogist, you have probably already done so.

Even if you don't find a significant disease that you need to seek professional help for, you will probably find familial diseases or conditions that seem to run in your family. How much should you share with your family members? Probably little, if any at all. Your family health history might include information on suicides, alcoholism, HIV positive status, pregnancy termination, pregnancy conceived by assisted reproductive technologies, or non-paternity events, all information that may not be generally known by members of the family. Let it be known that you have the family's medical information; if asked by a family member, you may want to give general answers without revealing any specifics. Be sure, however, that the information is available if something happens to you and that it will not be swept away and lost.

Finally, never publish any of the family's health history in any form, even without names. For instance, even though your great-grandparents may have been dead for a hundred years, they and their siblings have descendants, most of whom you have never met. Publishing your grandparents' names and genetic information can reveal genetic information about your distant cousins.

Knowing that one has a genetic disease can be important. Genetic diseases are

Standards for Sharing Information with Others
Recommended by the National Genealogical Society

Conscious of the fact that sharing information or data with others, whether through speech, documents or electronic media, is essential to family history research and that it needs continuing support and encouragement, responsible family historians consistently

- Respect the restrictions on sharing information that arise from the rights of another as an author, originator or compiler; as a living private person; or as a party to a mutual agreement

- Observe meticulously the legal rights of copyright owners, copying or distributing any part of their works only with their permission, or to the limited extent specifically allowed under the law's "fair use" exceptions

- Identify the sources for all ideas, information, and data from others, and the form in which they were received, recognizing that the unattributed use of another's intellectual work is plagiarism

- Respect the authorship rights of senders of letters, electronic mail, and data files, forwarding or disseminating them further only with the sender's permission

- Inform people who provide information about their families as to the ways it may be used, observing any conditions they impose and respecting any reservations they may express regarding the use of particular items

- Require some evidence of consent before assuming that living people are agreeable to further sharing of information about themselves

- Convey personal identifying information about living people—like age, home address, occupation, or activities—only in ways that those concerned have expressly agreed to

- Recognize that legal rights of privacy may limit the extent to which information from publicly available sources may be further used, disseminated, or published

- Communicate no information to others that is known to be false, or without making reasonable efforts to determine its truth, particularly information that may be derogatory

- Are sensitive to the hurt that revelations of criminal, immoral, bizarre, or irresponsible behavior may bring to family members

treated both preventively, through modifying lifestyle and perhaps regular medical testing, and symptomatically when the condition becomes apparent. A genetic disease can be monitored for its occurrence and treated when it appears, but for many inherited diseases, no effective therapy is available. Genetic conditions are also treated through reproductive decisions, such as whether to have children, to have prenatal testing for the disease, or to adopt.

Genetic Tests

In the 1970s, President Nixon, some said in an effort to attract African American voters to the Republican party, instituted a program to offer block grants to states that would institute testing for sickle cell anemia. Several states began testing children as they began to enter the school system. There was a public backlash. If the carrier state for sickle cell anemia caused no health problems, what was the point of testing? Many suggested an ulterior motive, possibly to label individuals for future health or employment discrimination. Eventually, the program was scrapped, a failed experiment in the application of genetic science to society.

Genetic testing can be defined broadly as an analysis of DNA, chromosomes, proteins, and certain metabolites in order to detect heritable diseases. DNA testing is of particular concern since it contains the entire genetic history of an individual and has the greatest potential for misuse.

Testing and Family Information

Routine genetic testing is already in place. Virtually every newborn is screened for PKU (phenylketonuria) and congenital hypothyroidism, and many are also screened for Tay-Sachs disease. Over 2 million pregnant women a year are screened to see whether their fetuses have a spinal cord defect or Down syndrome. We are seeing genetic testing performed on healthy adults who have a known or suspected familial disease. This predictive use of genetic testing replaces the individual's prior risk, based on population or medical history data, with risks based on the information found about his or her particular gene structure. The risk to society is that individuals in good health will be discriminated against because genetic testing will show that they are at increased risk of becoming ill in the future.

Genetic information is not simply medical information about an individual. It is medical information about both the individual and that individual's family. If a genetic test reveals information about the risk to an individual, it also reveals information about the risk to his or her blood relatives. This type of information is very different from that obtained during the routine practice of medicine. Normally, there is a privileged confidence between a single patient and the patient's doctor. Information about medical health is revealed to that patient and that patient alone. But when the information revealed to a patient is the result of a genetic test, it also indirectly reveals information about other family members. Think of genetic testing as family testing, not as a medical test of one individual.

Quality

Genetic testing is in a period of rapid growth. Over 500 commercial, university, and health department laboratories provide tests for inherited disorders in the United States. Most laboratories performing genetic tests voluntarily participate in quality assurance programs sponsored by various governing bodies—but they are not required to do so. Consequently, consumers have no assurance that a given laboratory is performing adequately. With the explosion of medical information on genetic structure, genetic tests may be introduced and used before they have been demonstrated to be effective and useful and before the potential consequences of the test are fully understood. Many laboratories are advertising genetic tests and making them available directly to the public. Consumers using these laboratories may not be informed of the benefits and risks, of the sensitivity and specificity of the test, and of the significance of a positive or negative result. Even nonmedical genetic testing can cause problems. It may, for instance, reveal an unexpected non-paternity.

I do not recommend that you order a medical genetic test on your own. The results can be complicated and hard to understand. You need to know what a specific test can and cannot tell you. Different mutations or alleles can result in the same disease. Genetic testing is usually performed for the most common mutation causing the disease, but there may be others for which it does not test.

Testing should be conducted by the proper medical professional, one trained to understand and explain the results to you and its medical implications, someone prepared to provide pre- and post-test counseling to guide you through the process. The identification of an inherited condition in an otherwise well individual could cause real harm from loss of medical insurability, possible loss of employment, and personal stress.

Privacy Concerns

The increasing availability and use of genetic testing raises additional concerns about privacy. As with all medical records, a loss of privacy can have serious consequences. No individual should be subjected to unfair discrimination based on the results of a genetic test, but an individual might be denied insurance or work throughout their lives because of a gene for a disease they never develop or one that is unlikely to occur until later life, possibly after retirement age. Insurance companies may define a positive genetic test as a preexisting condition, even though the individual may show no symptoms, and so deny coverage.

Because of the unique family implications of genetic testing, once the results are no longer private, blood relatives could be stigmatized, discriminated against, and labeled like the individual who is tested. Not only the individual who has the test but the entire bloodline could be subject to discrimination, such as denial of or additional charges for health or other insurance, employment discrimination in hiring and firing, loss of adoption rights, or loss of educational and military opportunities. Implications can extend down through the generations. Positive results of a genetic test may have implications for future children and their children.

Some physicians are reporting that patients, suspecting an inherited condition, would like to have a genetic test but don't because they fear that the information is going to get in the wrong hands. Others are requesting anonymous testing so that their results will not become part of their medical record. I suspect an entire new industry of anonymous genetic testing will spring up on the Web, bypassing the medical establishment completely.

Until now, genetic discrimination has been confined to individuals who belong to a family with a well-defined genetic disease. Members of Huntington disease families with its onset in later life may find it very difficult to get health or life insurance once the information is disclosed. Patient advocacy groups for polycystic kidney or Von Hippel-Lindau disease, diseases with a late-life risk, are reporting that afflicted individuals are forgoing testing of their children for fear the information will become public and their children will become uninsurable. Genetic counselors agree and do not believe that children should be tested for genetic diseases that will not occur until adulthood. When mature enough, that individual should be informed of the genetic risk and offered the option of genetic testing.

For many genetic diseases, early identification of the individual at risk is desirable so that proper medical treatment and monitoring can be initiated at the earliest age. For other genetic diseases, such as Huntington, where there is no treatment, the desire of an individual at risk to not be tested is understandable. The fear is that the American public will reject genetic testing because of possible discrimination and tragically turn its back on what promises to be a medical revolution.

Our history is not encouraging.

Eugenics

The term *eugenics* literally means "good in birth" and was popular during the first part of the 20th century. It was coined in 1883 by Francis Galton, based on his earlier book, *Hereditary Genius: An Inquiry into Its Laws and Consequences*, published in 1869. With the rediscovery of Mendel's laws of heredity at the beginning of the 20th century, many scientists wondered if these laws of genetics operated in humans. In 1904, the Station for Experimental Evolution was established at Cold Spring Harbor, Long Island, under the direction of geneticist Charles Davenport. It later evolved into the Eugenics Record Office (ERO) in 1910. Its purpose was to investigate the genetics of human behavior. Davenport and his staff compiled large pedigrees of families showing traits such as musical ability, mechanical aptitude, and literary skill. Vague, undefined, and derogatory terms such as *moron* and *feeblemindedness* were used to label individuals.

Eugenics suggested a way to "improve" the human race by encouraging the breeding of the "right" individuals and discouraging breeding by "the wrong sort." Eugenicists of the early part of the 20th century found a lot of "the wrong sort." The latter part of the 19th century and the beginning of the 20th century saw a new type of immigrant to the United States. Between 1900 and 1920, about a million immigrants per year were processed through Ellis Island. But instead of northern Europeans—the "right sort"—immigrants were pouring in from southern and eastern Europe. These new immigrants were considered undesirable, and it was thought they would "dilute" the quality of the American gene pool.

> **Eugenics** was an effort to apply the principles of genetics toward improving the human race.

Eugenicists lobbied to restrict certain immigrations and to prevent interbreeding of the "races," and some extremists lobbied for forced sterilization laws. The Immigration Restriction Act of 1924 drastically limited immigration, established a quota system favoring northern Europeans, and especially limited the number of individuals coming from southern and eastern Europe.

By 1907, Indiana passed the first of the forced sterilization laws, allowing for the compulsive sterilization of criminals, idiots, and imbeciles. California followed in 1909, sterilizing mentally ill individuals living in the state's institutions. Other states followed. In 1927, the U.S. Supreme Court upheld a Virginia law that allowed the state to surreptitiously sterilize women in Virginia institutions for the mentally retarded. By 1940, 30 states had adopted sterilization laws and over 50,000 "unfit" individuals had been sterilized in the various states. This number almost certainly underestimates the actual number since in many cases no records were kept.

By 1935, a scientific review of the material at the ERO concluded that its work was without merit, and the ERO was closed in 1939. But while the eugenics movement with its sponsorship of forced sterilization and improvement of the race was discredited in America, it was admired in another country, Nazi Germany.

Government's Role

What is our government doing to address the issues raised by the increasing use of genetic testing? As the U.S. Human Genome Project was coming into being, it was recognized that the information obtained once the human genome was decoded would have profound implications for society, raising complex medical, legal, social, and ethical issues. The Ethical, Legal, and Social Implications (ELSI) Program was established to address these issues of genetic research. The NIH National Human Genome Research Institute (NHGRI), which grew out of the project, has committed a certain portion of its budget to ELSI issues, as has the other partner in the Human Genome Project, the Department of Energy. ELSI was founded in 1990 and has continued to examine the implications of genetic research.

In 1990, the Americans with Disabilities Act (ADA) was signed into law. By 1995, the U.S. Equal Employment Opportunity Commission modified the definition of *disability* to include individuals subjected to discrimination on the "basis of genetic information relating to illness, disease or other disorders." The Health Insurance Portability and Accountability Act (HIPAA) of 1996 guarantees the "portability" of health insurance for workers who are changing jobs. HIPAA also prohibits the exclusion of an individual from group health insurance based on health status or genetic information. In 2000, President Clinton signed an executive order to prevent genetic discrimination in the federal workplace. While it does not affect the private sector, it does serve as an example of how to try to prevent the misuse of genetic information.

Individual states have also addressed the issue of genetic discrimination. For instance, Maryland in 1999 passed legislation to prohibit health insurers from using a genetic test, the results of a genetic test, genetic information, or a request for genetic services "to reject, deny, limit, cancel, refuse to renew, increase the rates of, affect the terms or conditions of, or otherwise affect a health insurance policy or contract." Almost all other states have also enacted legislation.

In the United Kingdom, the Human Genetics Commission and the National Screening Committee are considering whether newborns should have comprehensive genetic screening including, when the technology becomes available, a comprehensive map of their individual genome. It is thought that this genetic information could be used by the health care system through the life of the individual. Concerns over the storage, privacy, and protection of each individual's genetic information will need to be addressed.

The New Genealogy

Y chromosome testing, mtDNA testing, and other types of DNA tests will become an integral part of genealogy, but this combination of genetics and genealogy can raise problems of its own. Hereditary societies that base their membership on proof of a pedigree will be affected. What will they do with a member who has a properly documented pedigree but who tests negative for the Y chromosome type of that ancestor? Conversely, if an individual presents himself without genealogical documentation, will the organization accept DNA evidence as proof of the correct lineage? Could you claim to be a Native American if DNA testing shows that you have that specific group of markers? At a time when we are trying to eliminate profiling by race, there is the danger that DNA tests, by allowing us to be categorized into different ethnic groups, not by physical appearance but by the science of genetics, will perpetuate racial divisions.

Predictably, commercial firms are now offering to test DNA for ethnic or geographic origins. One commercial firm is offering to examine DNA SNP markers to produce a profile of your ancestry. They compare any individual sample against four separate databases: Indo-European, sub-Saharan African, Native American, and eastern Asian. For instance, an individual's DNA profile could reveal the following proportions: 90 percent African, 6 percent Indo-European, and 4 percent Native American ancestry. Another firm has concentrated on African American ancestry, analyzing mtDNA and Y chromosomes and comparing the results to their database of African tribes and groups. On one Internet site, a commercial testing service will offer customers a detailed breakdown of their genetics to qualify for "race-based college admissions or government entitlements."

Genealogy by genetics may look like an innocent pastime, but if genetic testing as a determinant of identity were to find its way into our social and legal institutions, it could take on a meaning and significance never intended. In all these tests, it is important to remember that the M line (mtDNA) and Y line (Y chromosome) are only a small part of the genes inherited from your ancestors. For instance, you have eight great-grandparents who have given you your DNA, of which the M and Y lines constitute only one-fourth. You have 16 great-great-grandparents, and those Y and M lines contribute only one-eighth of your DNA. So while you may learn your "ethnic origin" using the Y line or M line or both, you are learning about only a small percentage of your actual ancestry.

DNA databases are proliferating. The Department of Defense now has the largest DNA database, with tissue samples of over 3 million individuals. Its DNA Registry has been storing DNA samples from all newly enlisted service personnel. Many states are putting together DNA databases of convicted felons. England has gone further, storing the DNA not only of convicted felons but also of everyone arrested of any crime. It is no stretch of imagination to assume that eventually we will all have our DNA stored in some database.

At the moment, DNA databases are only for identification, the counting of the short tandem repeats on the various chromosomes. It is conceivable that in the future, some doctoral candidate will want to analyze the DNA database for some other characteristic, like how many carry the gene for Huntington disease. What is the prevalence of Huntington disease in the population of young male recruits joining the army? What if the information as to who has the gene "leaks out"? Imagine what medical insurance companies would do with that information. Or even the army? Would the army accept a man for a military career, perhaps promote him to a high rank, knowing that in his 30s and 40s, he will begin to show personality changes, mental impairment, and involuntary movement leading eventually to institutionalization—in other words, that he tests positive for Huntington disease?

Today, police departments around the country are establishing DNA databases, just as they have put together fingerprint databases. But while fingerprint databases reveal only identity, DNA databases, especially if the original DNA sample is retained, have the potential to reveal other information about the individual. If one moves away from counting the STRs used to establish identity and looks for genes that are known to expose the individual to the risk of a genetic disease, then where does it stop?

While many crimes have a statute of limitations, rightly due to the forgotten memory of eyewitnesses and the loss of critical evidence, how does DNA evidence fit? DNA evidence pointing to a particular suspect may become available decades after the crime has been committed and long after the statute of limitations has expired. Do we just ignore the fact that we now know who the rapist of a 13-year-old girl was 32 years after the crime occurred?

What about starting your own personal DNA database? Should you archive your and your family's DNA? I would say yes, provided that the DNA sample is kept secure. Home kits are now available using a cheek swab similar to that used by companies to secure DNA samples for Y chromosome and mitochondrial DNA testing. You can store a DNA sample to be used for future genealogical research, for identity testing, and for medical testing. The simplest technique is to rub the inside of your cheek with a foam-tipped swab and then transfer the material to a card treated with a DNA preservative. Such samples can be stored at room temperature. Although the longevity of such a sample is not accurately known, samples stored for at least a decade have been found satisfactory and presumably will last longer. Another simple technique is to use a finger prick and store dry blood spots on absorbent paper. Alternatively, you can employ the services of a commercial firm and have your or your relative's blood drawn and archived. One firm on the Web even offers to copyright your DNA so that no one can clone you without your permission!

21st Century Medicine

Just as the discovery of bacteria changed the face of medicine at the end of the 19th century, so too will genetic discoveries change how we classify and label disease. Once it became understood that a microorganism caused diphtheria, the other names for the condition—throat distemper, croup, and putrid sore throat—disappeared. Same disease, now labeled correctly.

Today, certain entities that we thought of as one disease have been found to be more than one. For instance, there are the classic and common neurofibromatosis 1 (NF1) and the rarer neurofibromatosis 2 (NF2). They were thought to be one disease with two variations. We now know they are completely different because the abnormal genes for these two conditions are on different chromosomes. The NF1 gene is on chromosome 17, while the gene for NF2 is on chromosome 22.

In other cases, what we thought were separate diseases were found to be the same. Gartner syndrome with premalignant polyps and cysts of the skin and bone was thought to be a distinct disease. Based on its genetics, we now know that it is not a separate disease but a variant of FAP (familial adenomatous polyplosis) since both conditions are the result of mutations in chromosome 5.

Cloning Potential

When one thinks of human cloning, we usually think of "Dolly" the sheep and the first mammal to be successfully cloned from an adult body cell. This type of cloning, producing a new individual, is known as reproductive cloning and, for scientific, moral, safety, and ethical reasons, is not acceptable for humans. Another type of human cloning, however, holds great promise. This is the concept of nonreproductive or therapeutic cloning. It may be possible, as with reproductive cloning, to insert material (the nucleus) from an adult human body cell into a human egg cell where the nucleus has been removed and, after a few days and a brief period of growth to a few hundred cells, isolate certain cells called stem cells. These stem cells have the potential to form many types of human tissues, such as heart muscle and nerves.

Can stem cells be used to treat the adult donor? Yes. Since the nuclear material was cloned from an adult patient, the stem cells could be transplanted back to the same patient with no fear of rejection; the stem cells would be an exact genetic match to the donor. Could this technology be used to produce stem cells that would, for instance, develop into heart muscle cells and be used to treat an individual in heart failure due to a severely damaged heart? Could we replace nerve cells and repair spinal cord injury? Could a genetic defect in the DNA be repaired before the stem cells are returned to the donor so that we could correct such gene defects as hemophilia or sickle cell anemia? Could this technology hold the key to curing now incurable disease or replacing damaged body organs? Only time and future research will reveal the answers to these questions. But first we must address the ethical issues they raise.

Although actual gene therapy, that is, replacing a missing or defective gene, is probably a decade away, genetics will also affect how individuals are treated. For instance, adverse reactions to prescription drugs are common and related to our genetic makeup. In the future, gene profiles developed for an individual may be able to predict who may or may not be able to take a certain drug. Some chemotherapeutic agents used to treat cancer may be effective in some individuals, but cause life-threatening damage in others. Our genetic makeup, with its coding for enzymes to metabolize or not metabolize the drug, may make the difference. Once these genes are identified, patients will have a genetic test to determine their response before such drugs are administered.

By now, you know that genes are the encoding portions of the DNA, and that the remainder of the DNA is called, inelegantly, "junk DNA." This portion is used for genealogy testing. If you are like me, you are probably uncomfortable with the concept that much of our DNA is "junk." From a biological standpoint, it doesn't make sense. Why hide the genes among all of this junk DNA? What evolutionary advantage did that confer? Each time DNA replicates, it must replicate this junk as well. Now, there is new evidence that this junk DNA does function, not in the same way perhaps as genes that code for proteins, but in other ways. These mechanisms are under intense investigation. Some geneticists believe that much of what makes one individual different from another may lie in the junk DNA and that this portion of the DNA may contain the secret of human complexity. We are just beginning.

DNA and genetics are viewed as mysterious, something only scientists and doctors in long white coats are privy to. It need not and should not be that way. Genetics—whether it points to a genetic disease in your family, identifies the victims of 9/11, or convicts a serial rapist—is now an important part of 21st century life. The recent completion of the Human Genome Project signifies an entirely new and exciting era in medicine. Just as the discovery that germs caused disease in the 1880s revolutionized medical diagnosis and the discovery of antibiotics in the 1940s revolutionized medical treatment, the discoveries in genetics at the beginning of the 21st century will revolutionize medical understanding and bring about a transformation in medicine we cannot even imagine.

Epilogue

WE BEGAN THIS BOOK WITH THE TRAGIC TALE OF GILDA RADNER'S DEATH from ovarian cancer. Her story did not end with her death. In 1981, the Roswell Park Cancer Institute in Buffalo, New York, established the Familial Ovarian Cancer Registry. Two years after Radner's death, the registry was renamed in her honor, the Gilda Radner Familial Ovarian Cancer Registry *(www.ovariancancer.com)* (1-800-OVARIAN). By the year 2000, the registry had enrolled over 1,600 affected families, and it continues to sponsor research into the causes, detection, and prevention of familial ovarian cancer. In the 2000 edition of the registry's newsletter appeared a letter that, with permission, I have reproduced in its entirety.

> *When I recently retired from teaching, I was thrilled to be able to become a volunteer at the Gilda Radner Familial Ovarian Cancer Registry. This enriching experience has brought about an unbelievable chain of events for my sisters and me. There is an important message in our story that I would like to share with other women.*
>
> *My volunteering at the Registry was prompted by the lingering memories of my mother's death from ovarian cancer in 1960 when I had just turned 13. This horrible disease took her life at age 47 and caused intense pain for our family. My father was left to raise three teenage daughters. Reserved and stoic by nature, he tried to shield us from his grief and therefore seldom mentioned our mother. We were led to believe that she had no remaining relatives. When our father died from renal cancer in 1983, our link to our mother was gone.*

263

Although we kept the painful images of our mother's final months, we were told by our doctors that because we had only one family member with ovarian cancer we had no greater risk than the average woman for contracting this disease. As adults, the three of us were careful to have annual checkups and I in fact had pelvic ultrasound and CA125 twice a year. In 1995, at age 48, I had a hysterectomy and oophorectomy [surgical removal of the ovaries] due to ovarian cysts. My sisters both had an ovary removed due to endometriosis.

During the past several months as I read the moving letters from family members of ovarian cancer victims as they wrote to give donations to the Registry, I felt a need to answer some nagging questions. My sisters and I believed that our maternal grandmother had died of cancer, but what kind was unclear. Could it be that she too had died from ovarian cancer, placing us at increased risk for the disease? I decided to send for my mother's hospital records. Perhaps there would be mention of her family history. I soon learned the grim details of her illness. At age 44, she had gone to the doctor for abdominal discomfort and swelling. During exploratory surgery, the doctor found advanced bilateral adenocarcinoma of the ovaries. Surprisingly she lived two years after this, although the doctor had given her an extremely poor prognosis.

On the afternoon that I received those medical records, I immediately went to my computer and began to do a family search on two genealogical websites (www.familysearch.org and www.ancestry.com). Starting with my mother's name, I was able to construct within 30 minutes a family tree going back four generations. The amazing news was that my mother's ancestors were Jewish and members of the Church of Latter Day Saints, a fact that neither of my parents had disclosed to us! From my work at the Gilda Radner Registry I knew that my mother's diagnosis at a young age and her Ashkenazi Jewish ancestry are often associated with a genetic tendency for ovarian cancer. My husband and I spent the entire weekend researching both sides of my mother's family. Curious as to who had supplied all of the information to the website, we decided to contact a woman listed as the source, asking her if she might be one of our relatives. Her reply, "I have been looking for Louise's (my mother) daughters for nearly 30 years!" The woman who supplied the information to the website is our cousin's daughter, and we soon learned why she had been trying to find us. Although we were delighted to discover that we have relatives living in Montana and throughout the United States, we were shocked to learn that we have six relatives who have died at an early age from ovarian and/or breast cancer.

My sisters and I have recently undergone genetic testing to determine if we have one of the three gene mutations most commonly seen in Ashkenazi Jewish women with a family history of ovarian/breast cancer. While my older sister and I had negative test results, we were saddened to learn that my twin has a mutation of the BRCA1 gene. She recently had a prophylactic oophorectomy and is seriously considering having a prophylactic mastectomy. Fortunately, she has no daughters to worry about. Her son will have genetic testing at a later time to see if he has inherited the gene mutation as it would place him at a higher risk for breast cancer and possibly prostate cancer.

I cannot begin to tell you how glad I am that I sensed the need to pursue my mother's background and that there are options available for my sister, which unfortunately were not available to my mother, grandmother, aunt, cousin, and two great aunts. My message is that every woman needs to know the medical background of her family. If they do not know the details, they should be persistent in searching for them. The Web has made this kind of research much easier than it ever was before. This search may save a woman's life and the lives of her children.

My sisters and I are grateful to you and to all the people who are dedicated to finding the causes of ovarian cancer. Although we would not have chosen this family history, it is satisfying to know that our family is contributing to the search for better methods for detecting and preventing ovarian cancer.

Forms for Compiling Your Family's Health History

THERE ARE TWO FORMS. THE FIRST, MEDICAL HISTORY INTERVIEW, IS to be used for interviewing family members. The second, Medical History Records, is a review of medical records. The forms are intended to be used together.

The form for interviewing family members, Medical History Interview, includes an area to record the date of the interview, the name of the interviewee, and the place of the interview. Next is the name of the family member whose history you are compiling. It may or may not be the same as the interviewee. Following the name is identifying data so that you can place the individual in the family tree. It includes sex, birth date, birthplace, and names of the individual's mother and father. There are then questions about the reproductive history of the individual, including the name of the spouse and any possible relationship of the spouse to a member of the family, and information on the number of live and dead children, miscarriages, and any health problems with the children. For children, you are interested in any diagnosed genetic disease; any birth deformity, such as cleft lip or palate, clubfoot, or extra digits; and congenital heart disease. Obviously, the children will rate a separate sheet as you compile their health history.

The next part includes personal information about the individual, including height, weight, ethnic and racial background, and religion. If the individual you are interviewing is the same as the individual you are compiling medical information on, it is easy to get reasonably accurate weight and height. If it is another family member, have the interviewee estimate height and weight. Other personal information

267

includes occupation—if there are many, put down the ones that may affect the individual's medical conditions. For instance, a secretary's job would have less impact on health than a coal miner's. Under personal habits, include drug and alcohol use, smoking, bizarre diets, or lifestyles. Under unusual or abnormal physical conditions or appearance, you may want to put your own observations of the individual.

The next section includes serious illness(es) and age of onset, surgical operation(s) and the age the individual had the surgery, and any medications used by the individual, for instance, insulin or high blood pressure medication. The section concludes with a question about what diseases "run in the family." The next section is a "review of systems" similar to the list of genetic diseases found in this book. It serves as a checklist of questions so that you can cover all possible genetic conditions. The very last section includes a space for your comments.

The second form, Medical History Records, is medical history compiled from records. It starts with the same information found on the Medical History Interview form (in case the pages get separated) and includes the name of the individual, sex, birth date, birthplace, and the names of the father and mother. Assuming that this form will be used on deceased family members, it starts with the death date, the age at death, place of death, and the cause or causes of death, including the source (death certificate, interview with family member, and so on). The information about the death includes where the individual is buried; whether cemetery records were obtained and, if so, the information they contain; whether funeral home records were obtained and, if so, what they revealed; and so on. The information sought includes death certificates; any medical examiner or coroner reports; whether an autopsy was performed and, if so, what it revealed; and any obituary or other published notice about the individual's death and what that notice revealed.

You will notice at the very top of the form the statement "copies attached." This is to remind you that if you obtain a death certificate or obituary or any other death record, it is important that you keep a copy with these forms. The form continues with space to record your search of hospital, hospice, or institution records, and military service or pension records. Other records include the federal census, especially useful if the individual lived and died in the 19th century; specialized institutions, such as orphanages and special schools; and finally, any family's private papers or diaries and any special comments by family members that you may have encountered in your interviews. The last section gives you space for your comments on causes of death and diseases—your opportunity to summarize the medical information on this individual.

Although both of these forms have copyright notices, please feel free to duplicate them for your own personal use.

Medical History Interview

Interviewer: _____

Date: _____ Interviewee: _____ Place of interview: _____

Name of Individual: _____

Sex: M F   Birth date: _____   Birthplace: _____

Father's name: _____   Mother's name: _____

Reproductive History

Spouse: _____ Marriage date: _____ Relation of spouse to family: _____

Live children's names and birth dates: _____

_____

Dead children's names and ages at death: _____

_____

Miscarriage: Y N   Age of mother at time: _____ Number of weeks pregnant: _____

Health problems with children: _____

_____

Personal Data

Height: _____ Weight: _____ Ethnic/racial background: _____ Religion: _____

Occupation: _____ Personal habits: _____

_____

Unusual or abnormal physical conditions or appearance: _____

_____

Serious illness(es) and age of onset: _____

_____

Surgical operation(s) and age: _____

_____

Medications used: _____

_____

Opinion about what diseases "run in the family": _____

_____

Review of Systems

1. The heart and blood vessels: heart attacks, strokes, high blood pressure, congenital heart disease:

_____

2. The lungs: asthma, chronic lung disease, cystic fibrosis:

_____

3. The stomach and intestines: peptic ulcer disease, gallstones, liver disease, chronic bowel disease:

_____

4. Nervous conditions: epilepsy, senility, seizures, headaches, alcoholism, psychiatric problems, mental retardation:

_____

5. Muscle, bone, and skin conditions: muscular disorders, osteoporosis, arthritis, skin diseases, Parkinson disease, Tourette syndrome:

_____

6. Blood: bleeding disorders, sickle cell anemia, hemophilia, porphyria, other anemias, leukemia:

_____

7. The kidneys, bladder, genitals: kidney disease, reproductive system and sex chromosome abnormalities:

_____

8. The sensory system: seeing or hearing problems, facial abnormalities:

_____

9. Hormone and metabolic conditions: thyroid disease, diabetes, allergies, autoimmune diseases:

_____

10. Cancer:

_____

Comments

_____

_____

Medical History Records (Copies Attached)

Name of Individual:_____

Sex: M F   Birth date: _____   Birthplace: _____

Father's name: _____   Mother's name: _____

Death date: _____   Age at death: _____   Place of death: _____

Cause(s) of death (and source): _____

_____

Where buried: _____

Cemetery records: Y   N
Record information: _____

_____

Funeral home records: Y   N
Record information: _____

_____

Death certificate obtained: Y   N
Cause(s) of death on certificate: _____

_____

Other information on death certificate: _____

_____

Medical examiner or coroner report: Y   N
Autopsy performed: Y   N
Record information: _____

_____

Obituary/other published notices: Y   N
Record information: _____

_____

Hospital/hospice/institution records: Y   N

Record information: _____

_____

Military service or pension records: Y   N

Record information: _____

_____

Other Information

Censuses

Federal and State population schedules: _____

_____

Federal Mortality schedules: _____

_____

Homes

Orphanage: _____

_____

Special schools: _____

_____

Family

Private papers: _____

_____

Comments by family members: _____

_____

Comments on Cause of Death and Diseases

_____

_____

APPENDIX **B**

National Genealogical Society Standards and Guidelines

THE NATIONAL GENEALOGICAL SOCIETY HAS WRITTEN A SERIES OF genealogical standards and guidelines, designed to help you in your family history research. NGS developed these as a concise way to evaluate resources and skills, and serve as a reminder of the importance of reliable methods of gathering information and sharing it with others.

The NGS Standards and Guidelines appear in this book. They also appear online at *www.ngsgenealogy.org/comstandards.htm.*

Guidelines for Using Records, Repositories, and Libraries
Recommended by the National Genealogical Society

Recognizing that how they use unique original records and fragile publications will affect other users, both current and future, family history researchers habitually

- Are courteous to research facility personnel and other researchers, and respect the staff's other daily tasks, not expecting the records custodian to listen to their family histories nor provide constant or immediate attention
- Dress appropriately, converse with others in a low voice, and supervise children appropriately
- Do their homework in advance, know what is available and what they need, and avoid ever asking for "everything" on their ancestors
- Use only designated workspace areas and equipment, like readers and computers intended for patron use; respect off-limits areas; and ask for assistance if needed
- Treat original records at all times with great respect and work with only a few records at a time, recognizing that they are irreplaceable and that each user must help preserve them for future use
- Treat books with care, never forcing their spines, and handle photographs properly, preferably wearing archival gloves
- Never mark, mutilate, rearrange, relocate, or remove from the repository any original, printed, microform, or electronic document or artifact
- Use only procedures prescribed by the repository for noting corrections to any errors or omissions found in published works, never marking the work itself
- Keep note-taking paper or other objects from covering records or books, and avoid placing any pressure upon them, particularly with a pencil or pen
- Use only the method specifically designated for identifying records for duplication, avoiding use of paper clips, adhesive notes, or other means not approved by the facility
- Return volumes and files only to locations designated for that purpose
- Before departure, thank the records custodians for their courtesy in making the materials available
- Follow the rules of the records repository without protest, even if they have changed since a previous visit or differ from those of another facility

Standards for Use of Technology in Genealogical Research
Recommended by the National Genealogical Society

Mindful that computers are tools, genealogists take full responsibility for their work, and therefore they

- Learn the capabilities and limits of their equipment and software, and use them only when they are the most appropriate tools for a purpose
- Do not accept uncritically the ability of software to format, number, import, modify, check, chart or report their data, and therefore carefully evaluate any resulting product
- Treat compiled information from online sources or digital databases in the same way as other published sources—useful primarily as a guide to locating original records, but not as evidence for a conclusion or assertion
- Accept digital images or enhancements of an original record as a satisfactory substitute for the original only when there is reasonable assurance that the image accurately reproduces the unaltered original
- Cite sources for data obtained online or from digital media with the same care that is appropriate for sources on paper and other traditional media, and enter data into a digital database only when its source can remain associated with it
- Always cite the sources for information or data posted online or sent to others, naming the author of a digital file as its immediate source, while crediting original sources cited within the file
- Preserve the integrity of their own databases by evaluating the reliability of downloaded data before incorporating it into their own files
- Provide, whenever they alter data received in digital form, a description of the change that will accompany the altered data whenever it is shared with others
- Actively oppose the proliferation of error, rumor, and fraud by personally verifying or correcting information, or noting it as unverified, before passing it on to others
- Treat people online as courteously and civilly as they would treat them face-to-face, not separated by networks and anonymity
- Accept that technology has not changed the principles of genealogical research, only some of the procedures

Guidelines for Publishing Web Pages on the Internet
Recommended by the National Genealogical Society

Appreciating that publishing information through Internet Web sites and Web pages shares many similarities with print publishing, considerate family historians

- Apply a title identifying both the entire Web site and the particular group of related pages, similar to a book-and-chapter designation, placing it both at the top of each Web browser window using the <TITLE> HTML tag, and in the body of the document, on the opening home or title page, and on any index pages
- Explain the purposes and objectives of their Web sites, placing the explanation near the top of the title page or including a link from that page to a special page about the reason for the site
- Display a footer at the bottom of each Web page that contains the Web site title, page title, author's name, author's contact information, date of last revision, and a copyright statement
- Provide complete contact information, including at a minimum a name and e-mail address, and preferably some means for long-term contact, like a postal address
- Assist visitors by providing on each page navigational links that lead visitors to other important pages on the Web site, or return them to the home page
- Adhere to the NGS "Standards for Sharing Information with Others" (see page 251) regarding copyright, attribution, privacy, and the sharing of sensitive information
- Include unambiguous source citations for the research data provided on the site, and if not complete descriptions, offering full citations upon request
- Label photographic and scanned images within the graphic itself, with fuller explanation if required in text adjacent to the graphic
- Identify transcribed, extracted, or abstracted data as such, and provide appropriate source citations
- Include identifying dates and locations when providing information about specific surnames or individuals
- Respect the rights of others who do not wish information about themselves to be published, referenced, or linked on a Web site
- Provide Web site access to all potential visitors by avoiding enhanced technical capabilities that may not be available to all users, remembering that not all computers are created equal
- Avoid using features that distract from the productive use of the Web site, like ones that reduce legibility, strain the eyes, dazzle the vision, or otherwise detract from the visitor's ability to easily read, study, comprehend, or print the online publication
- Maintain their online publications at frequent intervals, changing the content to keep the information current, the links valid, and the Web site in good working order
- Preserve and archive for future researchers their online publications and communications that have lasting value, using both electronic and paper duplication

Guidelines for Genealogical Self-Improvement and Growth
Recommended by the National Genealogical Society

Faced with ever-growing expectations for genealogical accuracy and reliability, family historians concerned with improving their abilities will on a regular basis

- Study comprehensive texts and narrower-focus articles and recordings covering genealogical methods in general and the historical background and sources available for areas of particular research interest, or to which their research findings have led them

- Interact with other genealogists and historians in person or electronically, mentoring or learning as appropriate to their relative experience levels, and through the shared experience contributing to the genealogical growth of all concerned

- Subscribe to and read regularly at least two genealogical journals that list a number of contributing or consulting editors, or editorial board or committee members, and that require their authors to respond to a critical review of each article before it is published

- Participate in workshops, discussion groups, institutes, conferences and other structured learning opportunities whenever possible

- Recognize their limitations, undertaking research in new areas or using new technology only after they master any additional knowledge and skill needed and understand how to apply it to the new subject matter or technology

- Analyze critically at least quarterly the reported research findings of another family historian, for whatever lessons may be gleaned through the process

- Join and participate actively in genealogical societies covering countries, localities, and topics where they have research interests, as well as the localities where they reside, increasing the resources available both to themselves and to future researchers

- Review recently published basic texts to renew their understanding of genealogical fundamentals as currently expressed and applied

- Examine and revise their own earlier research in the light of what they have learned through self-improvement activities, as a means for applying their new-found knowledge and for improving the quality of their work-product

Glossary

Adenine (A): One of four base pairs of DNA.

Allele: The specific form of a gene occupying a specific location on a chromosome; an alternative form of a gene. Also a particular structure or sequence of DNA.

Alu: A sequence of approximately 300 bases which has inserted itself into a specific region of the DNA.

Amino acid: One of 20 types of small molecules that form proteins. Three DNA bases encode for each of the amino acids.

Autoimmune disease: A disease characterized by the action of the body's own immune system against itself.

Autosomal disease: A genetic disease carried on one of the 22 pairs of autosomes or non-sex chromosomes.

Autosome: All of the chromosomes other than the two sex chromosomes; humans have 22 pairs of autosomes.

Base: The building blocks of DNA that are the genetic code. They are A (adenine), T (thymine), G (guanine), and C (cystosine).

Base pairs: Complementary pairs of DNA that bind together; adenine to thymine, and guanine to cytosine.

Biallelic marker: See **UEP.**

Binary: See **SNP.**

Bp: Base pair.

Cambridge reference sequence (CRS): The sequence of bases found in the hypervariable regions of the mtDNA that is used as the standard for interpreting mtDNA genealogy tests. Individual mtDNA testing reports a difference in the base sequence between the tested sample and this reference sample. On a larger scale, it is used to type mtDNA for studies of human evolution and population genetics. The original CRS was published in 1981 and revised in 1999.

Carrier: An individual who has one diseased gene and one normal copy and does not show any symptoms. In recessive diseases, such carriers will remain symptom free; in some dominant diseases, the carrier is presymptomatic and does not yet have symptoms, but should eventually show the disease. The term is also used for X-linked recessive diseases in which the carrier is female and the affected individual is a male.

Cell: The basic unit of life; generally has a nucleus with chromosomes and cytoplasm with mitochondria containing mtDNA.

Centromere: A constriction seen in each chromosome.

Chromosomal diseases: Disorders caused by the addition or deletion of parts or complete chromosomes.

Chromosome: Small threadlike structures that reside in the cell's nucleus and are composed of DNA. Each human has 23 pairs of chromosomes, with one of each pair derived from the mother and the other derived from the father.

Codon: Three DNA bases that specify a single amino acid used to construct proteins.

Complex traits: Inherited characteristics that are controlled by more than one gene.

Congenital: Any condition that is present at birth. It can be either genetic or "acquired" while the fetus is in the womb, or a combination of both.

Consanguinity: A sexual relationship between blood relatives; varies in degree.

CR: Control region, also called *hypervariable region (HVR)* because the majority of mtDNA mutations occur in that segment.

Crossing-over: The physical process of the exchange of genetic material between chromosomes so that genes lying on one chromosome are not always passed on together to the descendants.

Cytoplasm: The material within the cell but outside the nucleus.

Cytosine (C): One of four base pairs of DNA.

Daughtered out: The extinction of a line due to loss of a breedable male.

Deletion: A missing portion of DNA or a missing portion of a chromosome.

Dementia: Loss of mental capacity.

Diploid: Having the number of chromosomes in most human cells; humans have 46 chromosomes (23 pairs). For the egg and sperm prior to fertilization, there are one-half the number or 23 chromosomes (the *haploid* number).

Dizygotic twins: Fraternal twins; twins produced by two separate eggs, fertilized separately.

DNA: Deoxyribonucleic acid; the molecule whose sequence of bases forms the genetic code. A coiled double-stranded molecule resembling a ladder where the "rungs" consist of four different paired bases, A to T, and G to C. (A = adenine; T = thymine; G = guanine; C = cytosine.)

Dominant inheritance: A single dominant gene that is always expressed in male and female children. If a trait is dominant, one copy of the gene on either chromosome is sufficient; if recessive, both copies must be present for expression, one on each chromosome.

Double helix: The structure of DNA that looks like a coiled ladder or spiral staircase.

Duplication: A repeat of a gene or DNA sequence; presence of an extra piece of a chromosome.

DYS: DNA Y chromosome segment; used to name a specific location or "marker" on the Y chromosome. DYS numbers are assigned in the order in which they are discovered. Markers on other chromosomes—for instance, chromosome 3—would be labeled D3S. The DYS numbering scheme standards are set by HUGO, the Human Gene Nomenclature Committee, London.

Etiology: The cause of a disease.

Exon: The base sequence of DNA that codes for amino acids.

Expression: The degree to which a genetic disease shows in the affected individual. A variable expression is characteristic of autosomal dominant diseases, in which the individual with the disease gene may show a spectrum ranging from no sign of the disease to severely affected.

F1: Children; the first generation in a pedigree.

F2: Grandchildren; the second generation in a pedigree.

Familial: A medical condition that is common in the family; some familial conditions may be genetic, others may be environmental.

First-degree relatives: One's children, parents, and siblings; first-degree relatives share one-half their genes.

Founder effect: The effect seen when small groups of people leave their homes or country to "found" a new land. The genetic makeup of the small number of individuals in the founding colony may contain disease genes, which result in a high frequency of this disease gene in the subsequent population that expands from these individuals.

Gamete: The mature germ cell, egg or sperm, which has a haploid set of chromosomes.

Gene: A specific portion of the DNA sequence that is the basic unit of heredity. A sequence of DNA bases that code for a specific protein. Alternate forms of a gene are called *alleles*.

Gene frequency: The percentage of specific gene alleles occurring in a population.

Genetics: The study of the patterns of inheritance.

Genetic code: The sequence of DNA bases.

Genetic load: The number of recessive gene alleles in a population.

Genome: The total and complete genetic material of an organism; the complete DNA sequence, including all the DNA found within the chromosomes and mitochondria.

Genotype: The combination of genes present in an organism; the specific allele present at a given gene locus.

Guanine (G): One of four base pairs of DNA.

Haplogroup: A specific set of Y chromosomes or set of mtDNA that is characterized by slowly mutating markers and that is characteristic of a specific population.

Haploid: Having one-half the diploid number; containing only one of each pair of chromosomes. In humans, the haploid number is 23 chromosomes. A haploid number of chromosomes is found in the egg and sperm.

Haplotype: A series of known DNA sequences, specific alleles, or markers on a chromosome. It can be a DNA sequence inherited unchanged from father to son in the Y chromosome, defined by microsatellites, or the pattern inherited from mother to child in the mitochondrial DNA.

Hereditary: Determined by genetics and capable of being transmitted to the next generation.

Heterozygous: Having two different alleles of a specific gene on each chromosome pair; see **homozygous**.

Homozygous: Having two identical alleles of a specific gene on each of a pair of chromosomes; see **heterozygous**.

HLA: Human leukocyte antigen. The HLA haplotype is a group of closely related alleles found on chromosome 6 and inherited as a unit. It codes for cell surface antigens that are involved in self-recognition and are important for organ transplants and some autoimmune diseases, such as rheumatoid arthritis, lupus erythematosus, and ankylosing spondylitis.

HVR1: Hypervariable region 1, the most widely used segment on mtMDA for testing, covering 16024 to 16365. There are also HVR2 (73–340) and HVR3 (438–574) regions.

Inborn errors of metabolism: A specific group of genetic diseases in which a specific enzyme is defective and prevents a normal biochemical function.

Indels: Insertions or deletions of the DNA at specific locations. YAP is one such insertion into DNA. Considered a unique event polymorphism (UEP).

Junk DNA: Those portions of DNA that have no functioning genes. Changes or mutations in these areas are passed unchanged in succeeding generations. Genealogical studies concentrate on analyzing the junk DNA regions; medical genetics studies only the functioning portions of DNA where there are genes.

Karyotype: A chart of chromosomes arranged by size.

Kb: Kilobase; 1,000 base pairs of DNA.

Loci: Plural of *locus*.

Locus: A specific location on a chromosome.

LTR: Long tandem repeats; minisatellites.

Marker: A specific portion of a chromosome.

Meiosis: A cell division that produces one-half the number of chromosomes in the sex cells, converting a diploid number to a haploid, so that when fertilization occurs, the new individual will have the normal number of chromosomes. See also **Mitosis.**

Mendelian inheritance: After Gregor Mendel, the transmission of single-gene traits and diseases according to specific rules.

Metastasis: The spread of a cancer from its original site to some remote location in the body.

Microsatellite: A short DNA sequence, that repeats, also known as a *short tandem repeat (STR).*

Minisatellite: A DNA sequence, longer than a microsatellite (STR), that is generally repeated more than 5 times and as many as 30 to 40. While microsatellites consist of 2 to 5 bases, minisatellites may be 10 to 60 base pairs in length. Minisatellites mutate much more quickly than microsatellites. Minisatellites are typed by MVR-PCR (minisatellite variant repeat PCR). The only minisatellite known on the Y chromosome is MSY1 (DYF1555S1), composed of 48 to 114 copies of a 25-base unit with 5 sequence variant repeat types.

Mitochondria: Small ovoid structures in the cytoplasm of the cell that produce energy and contain their own DNA, known as mtDNA.

Mitochondrial DNA: See **mtDNA.**

Mitosis: Cell division to produce two daughter cells, each containing the same number of original chromosomes.

Mitotype: The sequence of bases on mitochondrial DNA.

MLE: Most likely estimate. Generally, an estimate of the most recent common ancestor (MRCA) between two matched individuals and commonly presented in the number of generations.

M line: The line of descent from mother to daughter of mitochondrial DNA (mtDNA); also known as the *umbilical line*.

Monosomy: Presence of only one of a pair of chromosomes. For instance, normal females have two X chromosomes; if there is only one present (XO), this is a monosomy and is called Turner syndrome.

Most recent common ancestor (MRCA): An analysis of the different mutations in Y chromosomes and mtDNA among individuals using an estimated mutation rate to determine when individuals had a common ancestor.

MSY1: See **Minisatellite.**

mtDNA: Mitochondrial DNA. mtDNA is inherited from the mother by both her sons and daughters, but only the daughters can pass it on to the next generation. See also **mitochondria.**

Monozygotic twins: Twins that are identical, having originated from a single fertilized egg.

Multifactorial: Determined by multiple genes and the environment. A trait or disease can be multifactorial.

Mutation: A physical change in the genetic material; a change in the base sequence of DNA. It can involve a change in a single base (a point mutation), the loss of bases (deletion), or the addition of bases. The mutation rate is the frequency of mutations occurring at a given locus per generation.

Non-paternity event: A situation where the presumed father is found not to be the true biological father; also known as *false paternity*. It can occur, for instance, with a bridal pregnancy where the groom is not the father, an affair outside of marriage, illegitimacy, a son taking his stepfather's name, a birth after the father's death and the mother's remarriage, an unrecorded adoption, or an improper conclusion from genealogical evidence.

Nucleotide: One of the four bases (A, T, C, G) of DNA, along with a phosphate and sugar molecule.

Nucleus: A structure within a cell that contains chromosomes.

Organelle: A structure within a cell.

PCR: Polymerase chain reaction; a chemical reaction that allows the replication of a specific portion of the DNA chain, producing many copies.

Pedigree: A chart consisting of symbols of individuals showing their relationship, medical history, and health status.

Penetrance: The percentage of individuals who carry a disease gene and show symptoms of the disease. A trait, although fully penetrant, can vary in its level of expression (expressivity) or severity.

PERSI: Periodical Source Index; an index of genealogical periodical articles created and updated yearly by the Allen County Public Library in Fort Wayne, Indiana. It is available on CD-ROM.

Phenotype: The expression of the genotype in an organism.

Point mutation: A change in one base in the DNA chain.

Polymorphic locus: A specific portion of a chromosome that can have two or more DNA sequences or alleles.

Population bottleneck: The reduction in the variety of genes in a population when that population is suddenly reduced in size, leaving only a relatively few individuals.

Protein: A large molecule consisting of chains of small molecules, the amino acids. The sequence of amino acids is determined by the genetic code.

Pseudoautosomal region: Area on the Y chromosome that may swap genetic information with its partner X chromosome. This area is not used for testing.

Recessive: An allele whose expression is masked by another dominant allele. Recessive diseases are expressed only if there are two copies of the recessive genes.

Recessive inheritance: The presence of two recessive gene alleles that are then expressed; affects both male and female children.

RNA: Ribonucleic acid. RNA is similar to DNA but contains ribose rather than deoxyribose. It is used by the cell to read the DNA code and to synthesize proteins.

Second-degree relatives: One's grandparents, grandchildren, aunts, uncles, nieces, and nephews. Also includes half-sisters and half-brothers. Second-degree relatives share one-fourth of their genes.

Sex chromosome: A chromosome that determines sex. Human males have two: an X and a Y gene; human females have two X genes. The remaining 22 pairs of chromosomes are non-sex chromosomes (autosomes).

Sex-limited: A trait not located on the X chromosome that affects individuals of one sex only.

SNP: Single nucleotide polymorphism (pronounced "snip"); a change in one base, for instance, a thymine (T) changing to a cytosine (C); a point mutation. A SNP changes (mutates) more slowly than a microsatellite (STR); it is also known as a *biallelic marker* or a *binary*.

SRY gene: The single portion of a Y chromosome that determines the sex of a child. If expressed, the child will be male; if not expressed, the child will be female.

STR: Short tandem repeat; also known as a *microsatellite*. This repeated sequence of two to five base pairs can be repeated many times. Changes (mutations) occur more often than UEPs, and the number of repeats found at an allele may increase or decrease.

Syndrome: A recognized collection of symptoms or findings that form a distinct clinical entity.

Tandem duplication: A duplicated segment of DNA located adjacent to the original sequence on a chromosome.

Third-degree relatives: One's great-grandparents, great-grandchildren, great-uncles, great-aunts, half-uncles, half-aunts, and first cousins. Third-degree relatives share one-eighth of their genes.

Thymine (T): One of four base pairs of DNA.

Trinucleotide repeat: A repeated sequence of three bases. It is used in Y chromosome testing for genealogy. It also occurs in functional genes and can cause disease (triplet repeat disorders).

Trisomy: An abnormal state in which there is an additional chromosome; having three chromosomes instead of the normal two.

UEP: Unique event polymorphism; generally consists of indels and SNPs that only occur once in human history.

Umbilical line: The line of descent characterized by mother to daughter of mitochondrial DNA (mtDNA); also known as the *M line*.

VNTR: Variable number of tandem repeats. Minisatellites with repeats of 9 to 80 base pairs, compared to STRs, which have 2 to 5 base pair repeats.

X-linked gene: A gene that is located on the X chromosome.

YAP element: A benign insertion of material (indel) into the Y chromosome from another chromosome; also known as the *Y Alu polymorphism*.

Y line: Genetic and genealogical descent through the Y chromosome.

Bibliography

Chapter 1. Ignorance Is Not Bliss: Know Your Family's Health History

Mitchell, Joan Kirchman. "A Genetics Resource Guide for the Family Health Historian." *National Genealogical Society Quarterly* 82 (1994): 131–143.

Chapter 2. Dominant and Recessive Diseases: Our Genetic Inheritance

De Braekeleer, Marc. "Hereditary Disorders in Saguenay-Lac-St-Jean (Quebec, Canada)." *Human Hereditary* 41 (1991): 141–146.

Gabriel S. E., K. N. Brigman, B. H. Koller, et al. "Cystic Fibrosis Heterozygote Resistance to Cholera Toxin in the Cystic Fibrosis Mouse Model." *Science* 266 (7 October 1994): 107–109.

Reilly, Philip R. *Abraham Lincoln's DNA and Other Adventures in Genetics.* New York: Cold Spring Harbor Laboratory Press, 2000.

Scacheri, Peter C., Carlos Garcia, Richard Hebert, et al. "Unique PABP2 Mutations in 'Cajuns' Suggest Multiple Founders of Oculopharyngeal Muscular Dystrophy in Populations with French Ancestry." *American Journal of Medical Genetics* 86 (1999): 477–481.

Chapter 3. When Genes Go Bad

Gelehrter, Thomas D., Francis S. Collins, David Ginsburg. *Principles of Medical Genetics.* Baltimore: Williams & Wilkins, 1998.

Chapter 4. Compiling Your Family's Health History

Clunies, Sandra MacLean. *A Family Affair: How to Plan and Direct the Best Family Reunion Ever.* Nashville, Tennessee: Rutledge Hill Press, 2003.

Lustenberger, Anita A. "How to be a Family Health Historian." *National Genealogical Society Quarterly* 82 (1994): 85–96.

Roderick, Thomas H., and Darlene G. McNaughton. "Concerns for the Family Health Historian." *National Genealogical Society Quarterly* 85 (1997): 120–125.

Saxbe, William B., Jr. "Heredity and Health: Basic Issues for the Genealogist." *National Genealogical Society Quarterly* 84 (1996): 127–133.

Chapter 5. Do You Speak Medicalese?

Carter, James Byars. "Disease and Death in the Nineteenth Century: A Genealogical Perspective." *National Genealogical Society Quarterly* 76 (1988): 290–300.

Hatten, Ruth Land. "The 'Forgotten' Census of 1880: Defective, Dependent, and Delinquent Classes." *National Genealogical Society Quarterly* 80 (1992): 57–70.

Jones, Thomas W. "Deafness-Focused Records for Genealogical Research." *National Genealogical Society Quarterly* 81 (1993): 5–18.

Mills, Elizabeth Shown. *Evidence! Citation & Analysis for the Family Historian.* Baltimore: Genealogical Publishing Co, 1997.

Renick, Barbara. *Genealogy 101: How to Trace Your Family's History and Heritage.* Nashville, Tennessee: Rutledge Hill Press, 2003.

Roderick, Thomas H., V. Elving Anderson, Robert Charles Anderson, et al. "Files of the Eugenics Record Office: A Resource for Genealogists." *National Genealogical Society Quarterly* 82 (1994): 97–113.

Saxbe, William B., Jr. "Nineteenth-Century Death Records: How Dependable Are They?" *National Genealogical Society Quarterly* 87 (1999): 42–54.

Scott, Craig Roberts. "Medical Holdings in the National Archives: Patient Records Prior to World War II." *National Genealogical Society Quarterly* 82 (1994): 114–130.

Chapter 6. Draw Your Pedigree

Bennett Robin L., Kathryn A. Steinhaus, Stefanie B. Uhrich, et al. "Recommendations for Standardized Human Pedigree Nomenclature." *American Journal of Human Genetics* 56 (1995): 745–752.

Chapter 7. What Have I Found?

Carmack, Sharon DeBartolo. "Immigrant Women and Family Planning: Historical Perspectives for Genealogical Research." *National Genealogical Society Quarterly* 84 (1996): 102–114.

Kingsbury, John M. "Interconnecting Bloodlines and Genetic Inbreeding in a Colonial Puritan Community: Eastern Massachusetts, 1630–1885." *National Genealogical Society Quarterly* 84 (1996): 85–101.

Chapter 8. Common and Important Genetic Diseases

Brent, David A., Maria Oquendo, Boris Birmaher, et al. "Familial Pathways to Early-Onset Suicide Attempt." *Archives General Psychiatry* 59 (2002): 801–807.

Davies, P. J. "Beethoven's Nephropathy and Death: Discussion Paper." *Journal of the Royal Society of Medicine* 86 (1993): 159–161.

Lustenberger, Anita A. "A New Use for Your Genealogy: Cancer Risk Counseling." *National Genealogy Society Newsmagazine* 25 (2000): 46–47.

Pearce, J. M. S. "The Headaches of Thomas Jefferson." *Cephalagia* 23 (2003): 472–473.

Pearce, J. M. S. "Doctor Samuel Johnson: 'The Great Convulsionary' a Victim of Gilles de la Tourette's Syndrome." *Journal of the Royal Society of Medicine* 87 (1994): 396–399.

Chapter 9. Tracking Your Genes: Molecular Genealogy

Gonick, Larry, and Mark Wheelis. *The Cartoon Guide to Genetics.* New York: Harper Collins Publishers, 1991.

Chapter 10. Y Chromosome Testing: Your Father's Father's Father . . .

Behar, Doron M., M. G. Thomas, K. Skorecki, et al. "Multiple Origins of Ashkenazi Levites: Y Chromosome Evidence for Both Near Eastern and European Ancestors." *American Journal of Human Genetics* 73 (2003): 768–779.

Bortolini, Maria-Catira, F. M. Salzano, M. G. Thomas, et al. "Y-Chromosome Evidence for Differing Ancient Demographic Histories in the Americas." *American Journal of Human Genetics* 73 (2003): 524–539.

Devine, Donn. "DNA Testing Can Pick Up Where the Paper Trail Ends." *National Genealogical Society Newsmagazine* 28 (2002): 326–328.

Foster, Eugene, M. A. Jobling, P. G. Taylor, et al. "Jefferson Fathered Slave's Last Child." *Nature* 396 (1998): 27–28.

Hammer, M. F. A., J. Redd, E. T. Wood, et al. "Jewish and Middle Eastern Non-Jewish Populations Share a Common Pool of Y Chromosome Biallelic Haplotypes." *Proceedings of the National Academy of Sciences* 97 (2000): 6769–6774.

Hill, E. W., M A. Jobling, and D. G. Bradley. "Y Chromosomes and Irish Origins." *Nature* 404 (2000): 351–352.

Jobling, Mark A. "In the Name of the Father: Surnames and Genetics." *Trends in Genetics* 17 (2001): 353–357.

Jones, Thomas W. "The 'Scholars Commission' Report on the Jefferson-Hemings Matter: An Evaluation by Genealogical Proof Standards." *National Genealogical Society Quarterly* 89 (2001): 208–218.

Lander, Eric S., and Joseph J. Ellis. "Founding Father." *Nature* 396 (1998): 13–14.

Leary, Helen. "Sally Hemings's Children: A Genealogical Analysis of the Evidence." *National Genealogical Society Quarterly* 89 (2001): 165–207.

Nebel, Almut, Dvora Filon, Bernd Brinkmann, et al. "The Y Chromosome Pool of Jews as Part of the Genetic Landscape of the Middle East." *American Journal of Human Genetics* 69 (2001): 1095–1112.

Rice, Robert V., and J. F. Chandler. "DNA Analyses of Y Chromosomes Show Only One of Three Sons of Gershom Rice to be a Descendant of Edmund Rice." *New England Ancestors* 3 (2002): 50–51.

Roderick, Thomas H. "The Y Chromosome in Genealogical Research: From Their Y's a Father Knows His Own Son." *National Genealogical Society Quarterly* 88 (2000): 122–143.

Skorecki, K., S. Selig, S. Blazer, et al. "Y Chromosome of Jewish Priests." *Nature* 385 (1997): 32.

Sykes, Bryan, and Catherine Irven. "Surnames and the Y Chromosome." *American Journal of Human Genetics* 66 (2000): 1417–1419.

Thomas, M. G., K. Skorecki, H. Ben-Ami, et al. "Origins of Old Testament Priests." *Nature* 394 (1998): 138–139.

Thomas, M. G., T. Parfitt, D. A. Weiss, et al. "Y Chromosomes Traveling South: The Cohen Modal Haplotype and the Origins of the Lemba—the 'Black Jews of Southern Africa.'" *American Journal of Human Genetics* 66 (2000): 674–686.

Travis, J. "The Priests' Chromosome? DNA Analysis Supports the Biblical Story of the Jewish Priesthood." *Science News* 154 (1998): 218–219.

Zerjal, Tatiana, Y. Xue, G. Bertorelle, et al. "The Genetic Legacy of the Mongols." *American Journal of Human Genetics* 72 (2003): 717–721.

Chapter 11. Mitochondrial DNA: Tracking Mom's Line

Gresham, David B., B. Morar, P. A. Underhill, et al. "Origins and Divergence of the Roma (Gypsies)." *American Journal of Human Genetics* 69 (2001): 1314–1331.

Hurles, Matthew E., E. Maund, J. Nicholson, et al. "Native American Y Chromosomes in Polynesia: The Genetic Impact of the Polynesian Slave Trade." *American Journal Human Genetics* 72 (2003): 1282–1287.

Ivanov, Pavel L., Mark J. Wadhams, Rhonda K. Roby, et al. "Mitochondrial DNA Sequence Heteroplasmy in the Grand Duke of Russia Georgij Romanov Establishes the Authenticity of the Remains of Tsar Nicholas II." *Nature Genetics* 12 (1996): 417–420.

Lindahl, Tomas. "Facts and Artifacts of Ancient DNA." *Cell* 90 (1997): 1–3.

Malhi, Ripan S., Jason A. Eshleman, Jonathan A. Greenberg, et al. "The Structure of Diversity within New World Mitochondrial DNA Haplogroups: Implications for the Prehistory of North America." *American Journal of Human Genetics* 70 (2002): 905–919.

Roderick, Thomas H. "Umbilical Lines and the mtDNA Project." *National Genealogical Society Quarterly* 82 (1994): 144–145.

Sykes, Bryan. *The Seven Daughters of Eve.* New York: W. W. Norton & Co., 2001.

Chapter 12. More Information on the Internet

Perego, Ugo, and Scott Woodward. "Genetics and Genealogy: The Molecular Genealogy Research Group." *National Genealogical Society Newsmagazine* 27 (2001): 86–87.

Porter, Pamela Boyer, and Amy Johnson Crow. *Online Roots: How to Discover Your Family's History and Heritage with the Power of the Internet.* Nashville, Tennessee: Rutledge Hill Press, 2003.

Chapter 13. Ethics, Privacy, and the Future of Genetics and Genealogy

Devine, Donn. "There's a Genetic Disease in the Family: Should We Be Tested?" *National Genealogical Society Newsmagazine* 26 (2000): 278–279.

Elliot, Carl. "Adventures in the Gene Pool." *Wilson Quarterly* (Winter 2003): 12–21.

Reilly, Philip R. "Public Concern about Genetics." *Annual Review of Genomics, Human Genetics* 1 (2000): 485–506.

Index

295

National Genealogical Society

. . . . the national society for generations past, present, and future

What Is the National Genealogical Society?

FOUNDED IN 1903, THE NATIONAL GENEALOGICAL SOCIETY IS A dynamic and growing association of individuals and other groups from all over the country—and the world—that share a love of genealogy. Whether you're a beginner, a professional, or somewhere in between, NGS can assist you in your research into the past.

The United States is a rich melting pot of ethnic diversity that includes countless personal histories just waiting to be discovered. NGS can be your portal to this pursuit with its premier annual conference and its ever-growing selection of how-to materials, books and publications, educational offerings, and member services.

NGS has something for everyone—we invite you to join us. Your membership in NGS will help you gain more enjoyment from your hobby or professional pursuits, and will place you within a long-established group of genealogists that came together a hundred years ago to promote excellence in genealogy.

To learn more about the society, visit us online at *www.ngsgenealogy.org.*

Other Books in the NGS Series

Genealogy 101
How to Trace Your Family's History and Heritage
Barbara Renick

A guide to basic principles of family research, this is a book the uninitiated can understand and the experienced will appreciate.

$19.99
ISBN 1-4016-0019-0

Online Roots
How to Discover Your Family's History and Heritage with the Power of the Internet
Pamela Boyer Porter, CGRS, CGL
Amy Johnson Crow, CG

A practical guide to making your online search more effective and creative. Includes how to know if what you find is accurate and the best way to make full use of the Internet.

$19.99
ISBN 1-4016-0021-2

A Family Affair
How to Plan and Direct the Best Family Reunion Ever
Sandra MacLean Clunies, CG

Family reunions can create memories and celebrate a common heritage. Here's how to do it with a minimum of fuss and maximum of good times.

$19.99
ISBN 1-4016-0020-4

Planting Your Family Tree Online
How to Create Your Own Family History Web Site
Cyndi Howells, creator of Cyndi's List

A guide to creating your own family history Web site, sharing information, and meeting others who are part of your family's history and heritage.

$19.99
ISBN 1-4016-0022-0

The Organized Family Historian
How to File, Manage, and Protect Your Genealogical Research and Heirlooms
Ann Carter Fleming, CG, CGL

A guide to the best way to file, label, and catalog the wide variety of material and information related to a family history.

$19.99
ISBN 1-4016-0129-4